Ravenshade

A Tale of Alterra: The World that Is

For Chris

BY

Thank you for riding with me!

C.S. MARKS

PARTHIAN
PRESS

Ravenshade

BY **C.S. MARKS**

Cover Art by John Connell
Interior Design and Maps by Carie Nixon
Illustrations by C.S. Marks
Edited by Leslie Wainger

ParthianPress.com
ISBN: 978-0-9912351-2-4

The Author's Website: CSMarks.com

For Thaylon and Mom

Home is a place where my heart can sing freely
Where fear and doubt fade, and the spirit find rest
I dare not return until duty release me
When all is made whole, and I meet the last test.

Home is a word that to him has small meaning
A dark place of shelter from love and from light
In her stony embrace he can hide from redeeming
'Til fate drives him forth again into the night.

I will go home, home to the Greatwood
Stars burn bright above, shine on all souls the same
In this life or the next, I will see my fair country
When my people are free, and forgotten his name.

Black as a raven's wing, cold as the stone
Old as the mountain's heart, ever alone
The stars, they are bright tonight, shining above
How can they reach a soul who has never known love?

—Gaelen Taldin

Table of Contents

Foreword

"Write what you know" is a well-established maxim among writers. This might prove difficult when it comes to fantasy, as I would suspect very few of us have Elves living in our back yards, or have recently engaged in an epic battle against the Powers of Darkness. Yet even fantasies (at least the good ones) deal with very real, human issues. We can draw on our experiences in this world to enhance the telling of the tale in our imaginary world. Sometimes, if we do our jobs well, the characters inhabiting those fantasies seem as real as their flesh-and-blood counterparts. We cheer them on, weep with them, curse them, suffer with them, and mourn them when they're gone. They become our friends.

Writing what you know makes the story come to life—personal experiences breathe life into it. For example, readers have often commented on the depth and realism of the horses in these books. That's because I have spent most of my life in the company of horses. I know what it's like to ride at speed for a hundred miles in a day over rough terrain, and can empathize with Fima when I am barely able to move the next day. Several of the horse characters (Toran, Finan, Eros, Réalta, Angael, and Siva) are modeled after my own animals. I did not mention my horses in any acknowledgments, but I probably should have.

I can relate to the trials of the long road, having spent years as a field biologist tramping all over various parts of North America and Australia, and I know what it's like to cope with rain, cold, and heat. I have kept watch on many a dark night, taking in the sights, scents, and sounds of my surroundings. Like some members of the Company, I have occasionally wished for civilization…yet I, too, was awed by my first sight of a starlit desert night.

I have been surprised and elated at the number of young readers who have taken up these books and loved them. I hope these works may serve as an example to them—that they will identify with and admire some of the upstanding characters within these pages. Emulating the behavior of a man like Rogond is not a bad thing.

Even with the slightly darker nature of *Ravenshade*, I am pleased to state that I can look the parents of a ten-year-old in the eye and assure them that the books are suitable for most young readers.

I hope also that my readers will be inspired to produce writings of their own. Some have done so already, to my delight. My advice to any would-be authors is this—don't let anyone tell you that you can't do it. If a story is asking to be told, then tell it.

I would encourage those readers who wish to learn more of Alterra to contact me. You can find the information on the copyright page—we'd love to have you join us on Facebook, as well. I would enjoy hearing from you and answering whatever questions you may have. Watch for new features, such as the Alterran languages lexicon, on the site.

This has been a long journey for the characters and for me, yet it has only begun. I finished the last chapter with mixed emotions, because I was not ready to bid farewell to these hardy souls with whom I had spent so many enjoyable years. I have seen this part of the story through its development, bringing it to a climax and then to an end. I've already started a new Alterran series, the *Undiscovered Realms*, as I have come to know this world, and the characters in it, very well indeed. Writers, as we have been told, should write what they know.

—C.S. Marks

R. Eros
Mona
Tuathas
Monadh-ainnas
Agean Calad
Dominglas
Elvenhold
Brùnner Ia
Barrens
Tal-ailean
Darkm
Laban
Twilight
Shores
Monadh-ailan
Tùr
Dorcha
R. Dominglas
Gwyr Farsing
Srath
R. Ambros

Lands and Realms of
Alterra
(in part)
R. Brocca
Monadh-hin
High Pass
Monadh-talam
(mountain home)
Iolari Pass
East Gate
Cos-domhain
West Gate
R. Artan
Lon Artan
Brunner Aigred
nnefíonn
Tal-sithian
Falad Capell
T
S
A
D
100 miles

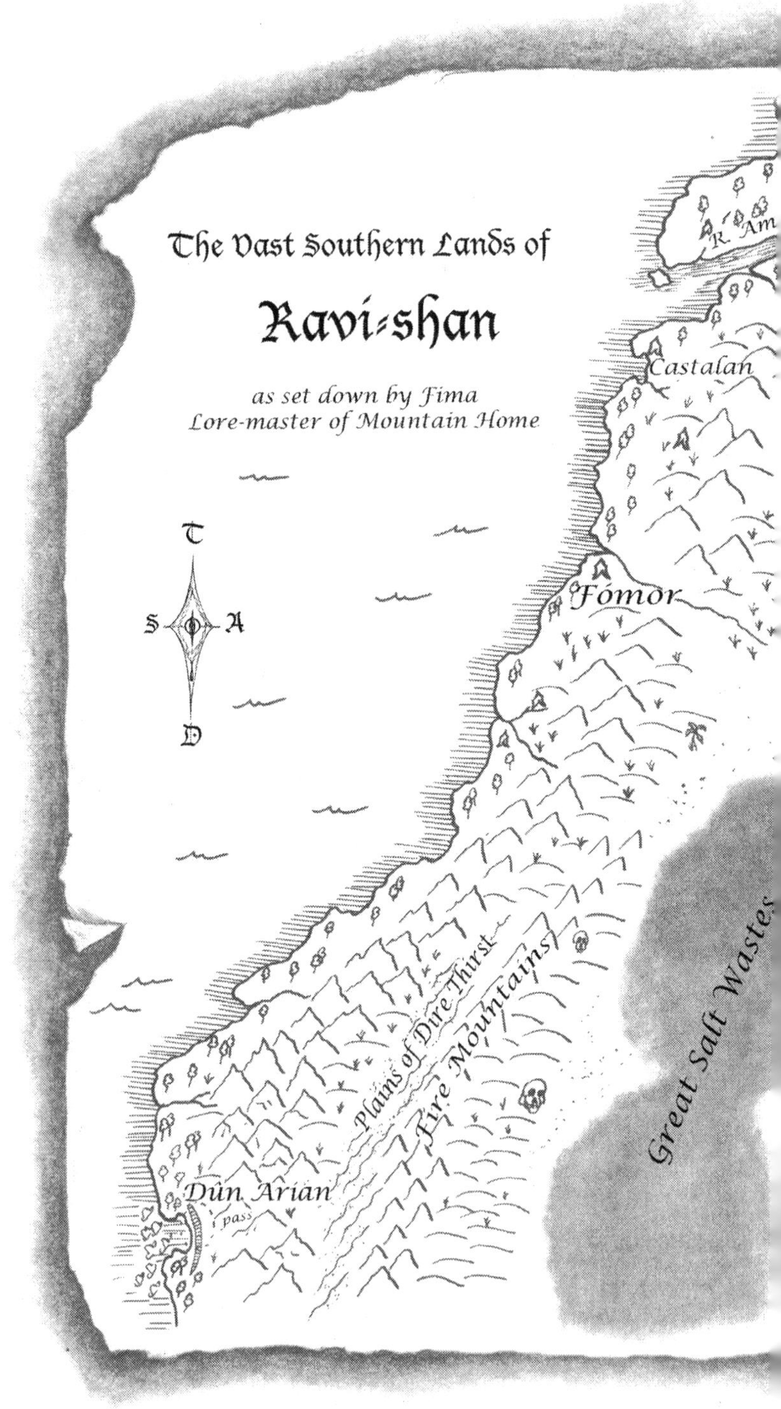
The Vast Southern Lands of
Ravi-shan
as set down by Fima
Lore-master of Mountain Home
T
S
A
D
R. Am
Castalan
Fómor
Plains of Dire Thirst
Fire Mountains
Great Salt Wastes
Dûn Arian
pass

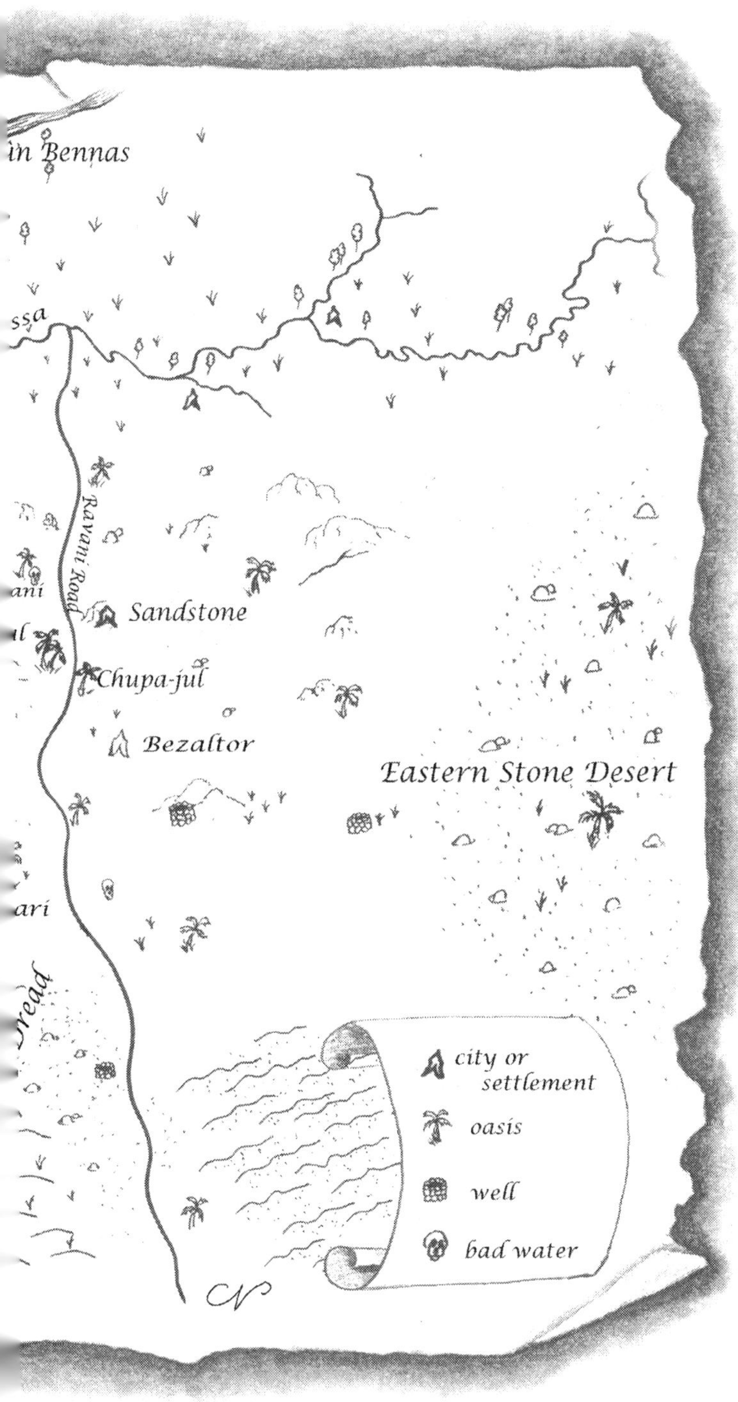
Bennas
Ravani Road
Sandstone
Chupa-jul
Bezaltor
Eastern Stone Desert
city or settlement
oasis
well
bad water

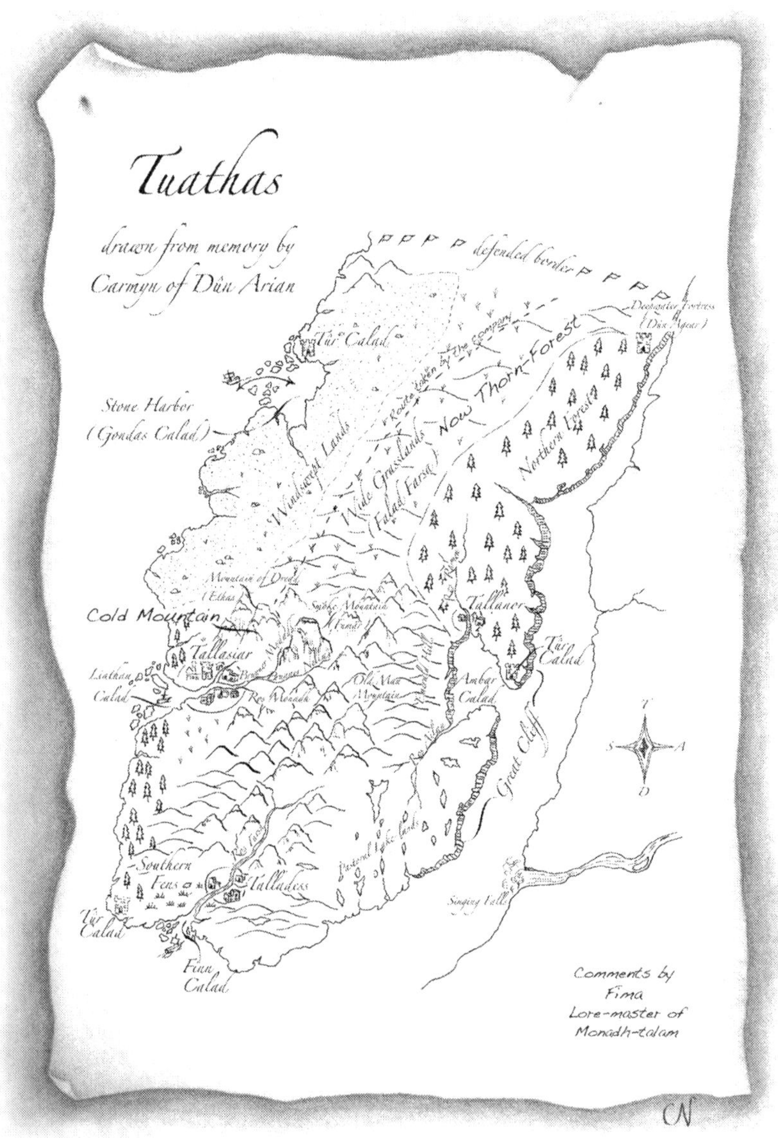
Tuathas
drawn from memory by
Carmyn of Dûn Arian
defended border
Tûr Calad
Stone Harbor
(Gondas Calad)
Route taken by the company
Now Thorn-Forest
Windswept Lands
Wide Grasslands
(Falad Farsa)
Northern Forest
Mountain of Dread
(Ethas)
Cold Mountain
Smoke Mountain
Tallasiar
Tallanor
Tûr Calad
Liathan Calad
Ros Monadh
Old Man Mountain
Ambar Calad
Great Cliff
T
S
A
D
Pastoral Lake-lands
Southern Fens
Talladess
Tûr Calad
Finn Calad
Singing Falls
Comments by
Fima
Lore-master of
Monadh-talam
CN

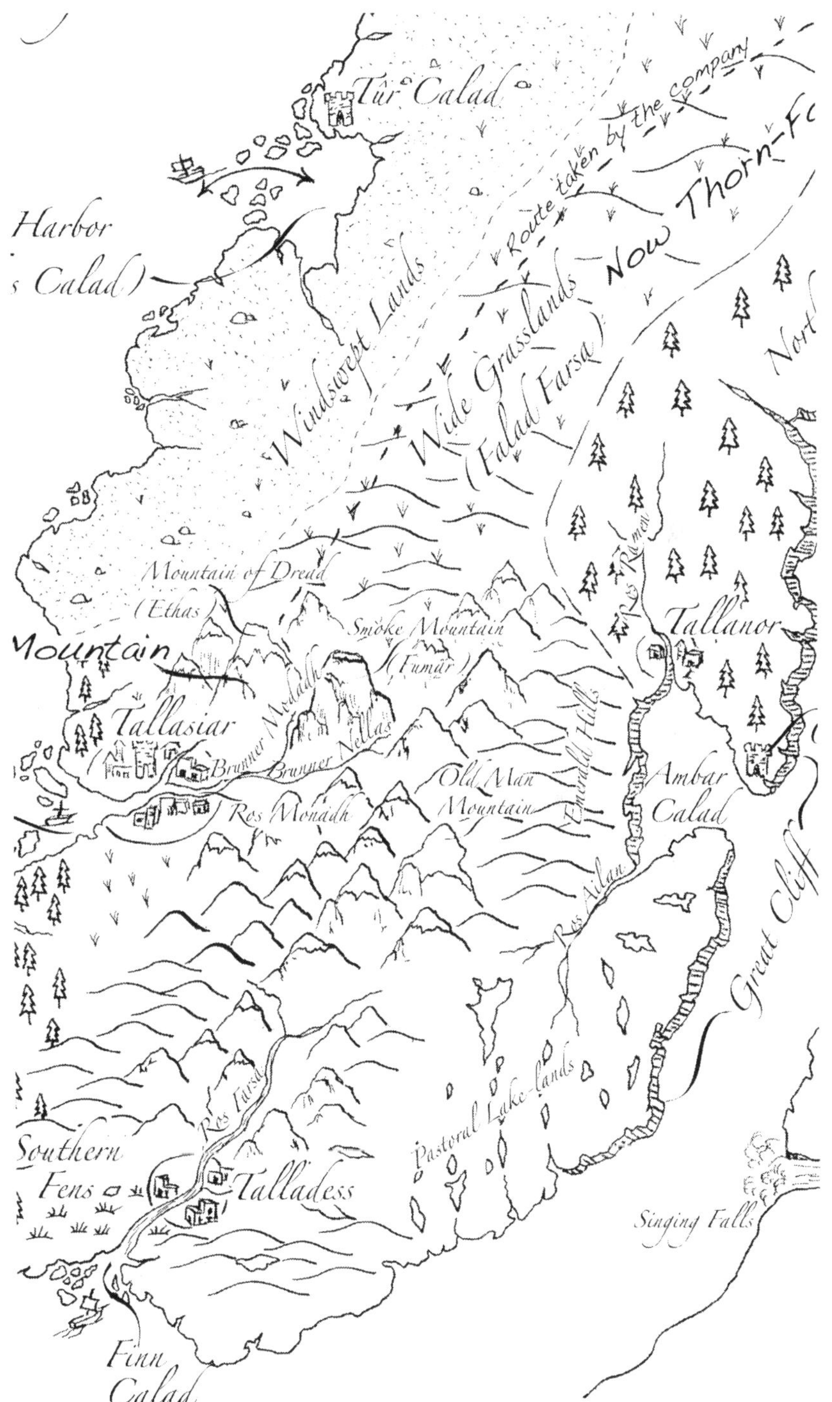

Tür Calad
Harbor
s Calad)
Route taken by the company
Now Thorn-F
Windswept Lands
Wide Grasslands
(Falad Farsa)
North
Mountain of Dread
(Ethas)
Mountain
Smoke Mountain
(Fumar)
Ros Ramen
Tallanor
Tallasiar
Brunner Medadh
Brunner Nellas
Brunner Nellas
Old Man
Mountain
Emerald Hills
Ambar
Calad
Ros Monadh
Ros Ailan
Great Cliff
Ros Farsa
Pastoral Lake-lands
Southern
Fens
Talladess
Singing Falls
Finn
Calad

Prologue

I'm cold.

So cold…I cannot stop shaking. Everything hurts. The cold is terrible, but the sounds I hear are worse.

I've been hearing them for a while now. They drown out the comforting, steady beat of the drum—that sound that tells me the world is safe…that I am safe. The drum-beat has risen to a frightening crescendo, as it has done many times before, but these sounds are new. Sounds have pierced my dark haven before, but not like these. I do not know how to describe them—only that they terrify me. The walls of my sanctuary are closing around me, no longer in safe embrace. I feel their agony. Something hurts me. It cuts my face, and I taste blood. I've tasted it before…and I like it.

Whatever made the blood…hard, cold, and sharp, has withdrawn, but everything hurts. The Something has gripped me! It rips me from my warm place, though I struggle against it. Light burns my eyes. Still, I must try to open them. The world is no longer safe. What are these things that would grab my limbs and hurt me so? They shake me, they slap me…but I cannot cry out, though I would wish to. The world spins—a horrible dance of shadow and shapes, and I know nothing of them. Will they kill me? I'm afraid.

Why is everything red?

My own drum-beat is strong, but it races with my terror. I try to breathe through the blood and ooze covering my face. Something wipes it away, and I shudder as it touches me, screwing my eyes shut, trying to make the Light stop burning them. I would give anything to be warm again.

Something tugs at my belly. The thing that hurt my face…I can see it now. Thin and cold—the only thing here that is not red—moving savagely back and forth, pulling at my flesh. Then it stops, and I am free. Now it is red, too.

The Light brings awareness, awakening my thoughts. I must live. I must breathe. I want to cry. I want to be warm. I want to feed. I want to be safe. I want to be loved. I breathe, tasting the air and filling my lungs for the first time, and then I cry. At first, I can only hiccup. I am still shaking so hard…but then I draw in another deep breath, and I wail. Perhaps, if I make enough sound, someone will hear me. Perhaps someone will save me. The sound of my own voice frightens me, and I am screaming now. *Please…I am so cold! Won't anyone help me?*

I hear sounds—I think they must be voices—but I do not know what they mean. Something wraps me up, and the cold fades a little, but I am still shaking. I don't understand anything that is happening. And then, I see her. *This is my mother! She will love me…feed me…keep me warm and safe.* Something rips at her, exposing more of her flesh, and lays me down beside her.

She brings everything I need—warmth, food, comfort—and I drink. The hot milk runs down my throat, filling my belly. I am voracious, pulling at her frantically, desperate for the things she will give me. But I can feel her life-force, and it is not strong. Worse than that—I can feel her emotions. Something makes me look into her face.

Even I am aware that she is beautiful. Her eyes are blue—the first blue I have beheld—and her hair is golden. But her face and hair are smeared with red, even as I am. There is a Light within her, and that Light does not hurt me…not yet. It radiates from her, and it is familiar. I long for her to embrace me, to keep me safe. Our eyes meet for the first time.

Will you love me?

Her face twists into a grimace as her eyes fill with loathing. Her thoughts reach me—I can perceive them. *Monstrous…hideous…evil…*

But I am innocent! Please love me. I start to cry again, terrified and forlorn. She cringes back at the sound of my voice.

It bellows like a beast. I would rather die than look upon it again!

She shoves me away, her life-force ebbing further. She will not love me. Her loathing burns my soul. I am not evil! How can I make her understand? I reach for her. *Please, hold me. Do not push me away! I need you! I love you! I am innocent!*

Her eyes soften for a moment, and then grow hard, cold, and dead. Her sorrow is overcome by revulsion, disgust. I see my own hands—desperate, grasping—they are not like hers. I have not yet seen my own face. Her only thought: *I cannot love you.* She shoves me away, and I know she would kill me if she had the strength.

Something…someone…presses my face into her flesh again, even as she tries to push me from it. Then her body stiffens, and her life-force drains from her. I can feel it. I look into her eyes for the last time, and see only hatred. *I am innocent! Will you not care for me? I am your son!* I long for her love, but will never receive it. This time, when I drink, the milk has already grown cold.

1
At the Edge of Darkness

It is said that one of the greatest gifts we are given lies in the ability to make choices. Often we are told that we are at the mercy of Fate, and sometimes it may seem to be so, yet such claims do not survive close scrutiny. Feet may be set upon a path, but the way they travel on that path is directed by choice. One may even turn from the path altogether, if the strength is there.

Gaelen Taldin, a Wood-elf of the Greatwood Realm, had summoned her bitterest and most deadly foe, Gorgon Elfhunter, to stand before her that he might pay for his dark and terrible crimes. Gorgon, cruel beyond all reason, had tortured and killed Gaelen's friend, the gentle and steadfast Thorndil, only to announce his return in a manner that she could not ignore. Gaelen was a being of Light, and yet her choice to face her enemy had come from the darkest of emotions: hatred, rage, guilt, grief. Her hatred of Gorgon and her grief for those he had slain had drawn them both to the very edge of Darkness. Her rage and guilt had unbalanced her, and had fueled the reckless courage that had allowed her to summon him to this reckoning. She chose the battlefield.

Gorgon Elfhunter, on the other hand, had been taken unaware. He was normally so highly attuned to the dark emotions of his mortal enemy that he would live out the rest of his days wondering how she could ever have concealed her plan from him, yet she had done so. This pathetic, undersized She-elf, unsophisticated and unenlightened, had dared to gaze into Gorgon's mirror. She had drawn him from his hiding place to stand before her, though he did not yet know the nature of the realm in which they stood. He was unprepared, confused, and not a little fearful—his body felt strange, almost as though he walked in a dream. There was very little sensation in his strong limbs, but there was weariness. A mist surrounded his enemy such that he could not see her clearly, yet as he looked into her eyes he knew that, although she shared his weariness, she did not share his confusion. Gaelen had walked in this realm before.

She had taken a desperate chance in using the mirror. It was bound to Gorgon, meant to be used by him alone. The Shadowmancer had given it to him, and it was his until he breathed his last. Gaelen was the vessel, the servant of the mirror and therefore of Gorgon. She was never meant to control it. She did not know what would befall—perhaps she would die, or turn to ashes, or simply lose her mind. Yet she would not allow fear to dissuade her, for she would confront Gorgon and make him pay for his dark deeds…it was the only way to be free of him.

When their eyes met for the first time, there was an immediate exchange of astonishment from Gorgon and profound fury from Gaelen. He took a step back from her bright gaze—she would have withered him into ashes had she been capable—but her strength had been drawn away by the mirror and by the journey into this shadowed place, and for a few moments they stared at one another in fascination as she slowly mastered herself. Then, Gorgon smiled.

Ah, little Vixen! Well met at last! I summoned you, and you have come out to face me. Even I must admire your original choice of battlegrounds. What place is this? He looked around at the swirling, multicolored mists that surrounded them, taking note of the darkness at his back. Something told him that he must avoid stepping beyond the mists into that blackness, for he would never return from it.

We meet on the edge of Eternity, said Gaelen. *Here your evil will end, for I intend to see you thrown into darkness. You will wish you had never drawn breath before I have finished with you!*

Gorgon laughed. *Do you not know that I wish that already? Yet I must fulfill my life's purpose of preying upon the Elàni, and I shall begin with you. Approach me if you dare!*

Gaelen was smiling now. *Oh, have no fear, Dark Horror,* she said. *I will meet your challenge. But first, I must correct you. You did not do the summoning here…it was I who commanded you. You would never have had courage enough to face me had you known.*

At these words the smile faded from Gorgon's face, for there was truth in them. He had thought to lure Gaelen and her companions into harm's way and take them down one by one, striking them from the shadows until only Gaelen remained. Then he would meet her upon some battleground where he would surely prevail, for he was many times her size and strength, and he was highly skilled in such things. He would pay her back for the hurts she had caused him.

He snarled and took a step toward her, as the mists lifted so that he could finally see her clearly. Gaelen appeared to be wreathed in a fiery golden-orange glow, her tousled hair fanned by unseen winds, an inner heat emanating from her. Otherwise she appeared much as she did in the physical realm, save for her eyes, which were even brighter.

Such was not the case with Gorgon, whose spiritual essence had never before been seen. His aura, disunited and confused, was like his spirit—the result of the blending of beings so dissimilar that there was no hope of unity. The colors surrounding him, discordant and ever-changing, swirled from muddy yellow to deep indigo. There was blood-red and gold, a sickly green and malevolent purple, but there was also an occasional flash of bright blue-white. Gaelen was both horrified and revolted as she imagined being encumbered with such a spirit.

She looked into Gorgon's pale eyes and saw death and suffering, yet she saw also the bright stars reflected. She perceived his longing for their beauty, and knew that she had given him this gift—it was surely one of the reasons that he so hated her. *You are powerful, Elfhunter, but there is no harmony in your soul…*

He drew himself up before her and, to her astonishment, his features seemed to melt and re-form. Even his eyes changed until a strong Elven face looked back at her, golden hair waving like silk in the odd breeze. The beautiful Elf threw his head back and laughed. *You have no idea how powerful, little fire-spirit…and harmony is over-rated. I have strengths given me by many progenitors, including the Dark Power itself. You have no notion of what you are toying with.* This was true, and Gaelen knew it, yet she simply stared in revulsion at the handsome, strong face with eyes grey and cold and filled with malice. In this form Gorgon was stronger than she, and could well prevail over her.

A pity you could not embrace this part of yourself, for your life would have been much different, she whispered.

Gorgon overheard, and his fury showed immediately upon his face. *I take many forms, and this is the only one of which I am ashamed! Look you now upon me and be afraid!*

His features melted and changed again and again, from the tall, strong Elf into a massive, hideous Ulca, to something resembling a dead, decomposing version of a long-vanquished Elf named Gelmyr, and even to a huge, dark presence with fire in its eyes. This manifestation alone filled Gaelen with fear. Luckily, it was fleeting. Then she watched as he became much smaller and nearly frail, a child without love or hope. She shook her head slowly. *I despise you, Dark Horror, but I hold as much pity for you now as hatred. You truly are the most miserable of souls.*

As she said these words she braced herself, knowing that he would most likely become further enraged, and she would soon do battle. She summoned thoughts of Thorndil hanging from a spike, flayed alive and dripping blood onto the floor. A kind soul and a worthy companion, his only crime in Gorgon's eyes had been his friendship with her. *I have to stop you…here and now!*

She had been right about the effect of her words upon Gorgon; he had settled back into his normal appearance, his face as dark as a thundercloud. *You need not feel pity for me. Feel it instead for yourself! You cannot stand against me, and your very presence is intolerable. Keep your pity, for I will not brook it. Give only your hate!* With those words he rushed at her, and the battle was joined.

Rogond had been frantically searching for Gaelen, but he had not found her in any of her usual haunts. He went to Lord Salastor for aid, and soon the City was united in the search for her. At last she was found in the shadowed alcove by none other than Bint Raed, who despaired at the sight of her, for she was still and cold and would not awaken. Bint Raed covered Gaelen with her own cloak and went to fetch Rogond, leaving two of the citizens to watch over her.

In the meantime, Rogond and Fima had gone to the library, for Rogond held a feeling of foreboding with respect to Gorgon's mirror, and he wanted to make certain that it was still safely hidden.

Fima led Rogond to his private study chamber, expecting to find his leather jerkin with the mirror secured in the secret inner pocket, but neither the jerkin nor the mirror could be found. When the scholars informed him that Gaelen had taken the jerkin, presumably at Fima's request, both he and Rogond guessed the truth.

"It is as I feared," said Rogond. "She intends to use the mirror somehow, to what end I cannot say. Fima...what will it do to her?"

"I don't know," said Fima, trying to subdue his own panic. "But I expect it won't be good. Nothing is written of such matters—even Dardis, who made the mirror, did not speculate upon them. We must find her before she does something truly rash. With luck, she has come to her senses, and has not looked into the mirror herself. Surely she can feel its dark power! She must understand the folly of such an act."

"If she thinks that by such an act she may bring about the downfall of Gorgon Elfhunter, she is gazing into the mirror even now," said Rogond. "Do you have any doubt of it?"

"Yet she must realize that Gorgon commands the mirror, and that she may well give herself up to him if she tries to look into it," said Fima. "That certainly would occur to me."

"You voice a confidence you do not feel, my friend," said Rogond. "Let's waste no more time—we must find her at once! She is no doubt enraged on behalf of Thorndil. I would not expect good sense from her."

Rogond asked the scholars whether they at least knew which direction Gaelen had taken, but they had not watched her go.

"Don't worry...she will be found quickly now that the entire City is searching for her," said Fima. As it turned out, he was right.

As Rogond looked upon Gaelen's lifeless form, the mirror clutched in her cold hand, he knew the truth. She was out of the Realm of Reckoning. Where she had gone none could say, and there was nothing he could do now but wait, and love her, and try to hold hope in the midst of his despair.

Gaelen grappled with Gorgon as he flew at her, and the initial contact between her spirit and his had nearly taken the courage from both their hearts. Gaelen had never before felt the full force of such an evil presence, and Gorgon had underestimated the power with which his small adversary was endowed. Though they had each entertained some of the thoughts and feelings of the other, never had they been exposed so completely to the uncloaked essence of their enemy. They were alike in some ways—willful and headstrong, answering to no one—but otherwise they were very, very different.

Gaelen's wrath was grounded in righteousness. She would prevent Gorgon from doing further harm, and she would avenge those already slain. Thorndil's agonizing death still roiled in her mind, leaving no room for mercy.

Gorgon's strength came from his own misguided sense of justice. In his mind, evil was the true power, and he had no desire to turn from it, for he had known no other. Those who had scorned him were weak, and they deserved their fate at his hands. He had been trained well from the beginning to believe that it was his destiny to bring about their ending. No Elf would walk among the living when that destiny was achieved.

Their diverse energies sparked and crackled and roared like great fires as they wrestled, and the light of them was frightening to see. Yet Gorgon realized, quickly and with some dismay, that here, in this place, size did not matter.

Gaelen in the physical realm would be easy prey—although Gelmyr would have pointed out that Gorgon had not managed to kill her despite several encounters—but Gaelen in *this* place… perhaps she was as strong as he! It was fortunate for Gorgon that, although he had lost his left hand in battle with Gaelen, his spirit still retained it. He needed both hands to contend with his enemy, for they grappled as if on the edge of a precipice, each trying to wrestle the other from the circle of light.

All at once they both grew exhausted and broke contact. Gorgon's last thoughts before they broke apart had been speculations that Gaelen's power might match his own, and he was filled with doubt.

Gaelen watched, fascinated, as the long-dead face and voice of Gelmyr appeared, changed back into Gorgon, and then back again, all the while talking to itself.

She has drawn you to a place where she can defeat you. You were taken unaware! See the fire around her? This is the fire that will consume you, O Misguided Disaster. If you don't believe me, wait and see!

You know nothing of such matters, Èolo! You were taken easily enough. I have prevailed over her until now, and I am delighted that I shall finish her at last. You are wrong again, even as you have always been.

Then why do you allow me to appear, O Wavering, Woeful Warrior? At this, Gelmyr smiled. *I like the sound of that.*

Wavering, am I? Did I waver before those fools attacking the City? I cut them down like wheat! Did I waver when I inflicted pain upon that pathetic old man? I think not.

Yet they were not Elves, Elfhunter! Now there is one before you...why don't you just swat her as you would a fly? You have sworn to do so many times. Go on then...it's just one small Wood-elf...she is surely no match for you. Let's see the power of evil unleashed! I'm waiting...Ha!

Gorgon knew that as long as he doubted his own ability to prevail, Gelmyr would torment him. He could not afford to allow himself to be distracted from his task, and he called upon the strongest part of his spirit, his features transforming into the mask of cold beauty that sprang from his mother's kin, and met his enemy once again.

This time Gaelen was hard-pressed to defend herself, for the spirits of the Èolar were the most powerful among all the free peoples. She resolved that, should Gelmyr appear again, she would not stand in fascination, but would cast the vile creature into the dark void, even as he debated with himself.

Gaelen had been taken to the Halls of Healing and laid in the very same chamber where her friend Fima had fought for his life not so long before. The people of the Citadel were greatly dismayed and confused, for they did not know of Gorgon, and Gaelen was now counted among their most respected and beloved heroines. Eventually they would carve a likeness of her, together with Rogond and Eros, that would stand in the Courtyard of Scholars. But it was unknown at present whether she would live to see it, for she was as cold and lifeless as the stone from which it would be made. There was no aid that anyone could give her, though the healers tried, until at last Fima grew unhappy with their ineffectual poking and prodding.

"Forgive an aged Dwarf," he growled, "but it's obvious that your efforts, though well-intentioned, are not having any effect. Leave her in peace and let her friends aid her if they can. Her trouble is not of the body…there is nothing you can do."

Gaelen still held the mirror, despite Rogond's contention that they should take it from her hand. Fima was afraid that if they did so, she might not be able to return from whatever dark place she had gone, and he was reluctant.

"We don't know enough to act with surety, Rogond. I must think on it awhile." He sighed and shook his head. "I do wish she hadn't taken such a drastic measure. She is definitely in uncharted lands now."

"Here, there be monsters," said Rogond softly. He had seen those words once on a map of an imaginary place where terrible creatures were said to live. Rogond had read and enjoyed the story as a young child. It had occurred to him even then that men feared and imagined monsters because they represented things that were not known or understood. "Now I know this is justified, for Gaelen has gone to a place I do not know, and she faces an enemy not truly understood by anyone."

"Eh…? What's that?" asked Fima, for he had not heard Rogond clearly.

"Nothing…I was just thinking that there is at least one monster in the place where she has gone." Rogond took Gaelen's hand and encased it with his own.

"Such was undoubtedly her intent," said Fima, "but we cannot know whether the creature was drawn to her. She may be wandering alone and lost, trapped in some dark place. The mirror was not hers to command. It may be that Gorgon has taken his vengeance already."

Rogond did not think so. "Gaelen possesses unique insights, and she has gone into this realm before. She is not lost…not yet."

He looked up to see Nelwyn entering the chamber with Galador. Evidently he had returned, and his grim, sad face told the tale—

Gorgon had not been found. *A pity*, thought Rogond. *If we had come upon the creature, I expect he would have been taken easily. It's likely that his malformed and misbegotten soul stands upon the same distant battleground.*

Upon that battleground, Gorgon and Gaelen were locked in desperate conflict. Gorgon had called upon the strongest part of his spirit, striving now as a tall Elf-lord who would have been beautiful were it not for the cold malice in his eyes.

Gaelen's strength was waning. Her confidence had been shaken with the appearance of this powerful manifestation, and she knew that she must divert Gorgon from it lest she lose the struggle. She had thought to cast his soul into the Void, but now it appeared that such would be *her* fate, and she could not imagine a worse fate than that. She would never see her beloved Rain again; she would never see anyone or anything at all, drifting in the endless blackness until it took away her reason and her courage. She would scream then into the dark, but no one would hear and no one would aid her. She knew these things, and her enemy knew them, too.

Soon I will be rid of you once and for all, said Gorgon in a deep, menacing, purring voice quite unlike his usual oily growl. *I must say that you have undone yourself this time. Earlier, I simply would have killed you, but now you will be doomed to darkness, even as I promised long ago. You were a bit too clever for your own good, Vixen. You should not have meddled in affairs too great for you.* His handsome face curled into a sneering smile, though it was taking all the effort he had to remain focused. If she distracted him, his form would change.

Where is Gelmyr? I thought you had vanquished him...did I not see him earlier?

Gaelen had indeed seen Gelmyr, appearing much as he had when they had found his ruined body near the Great River. It seemed a lifetime away. She felt Gorgon hesitate as she spoke of Gelmyr, drawing back just slightly, his smile fading. She twisted from his grasp, backing away as fast as she could, as he charged after her, trying to regain his hold.

Gaelen leaped aside, trying not to let her enemy know of her vulnerability. She managed even to laugh at him as he turned back toward her. *You may appear Elven, but it is plain that your abilities are lacking. Where is Gelmyr? Perhaps he can give you some lessons, and aid you in conducting yourself more gracefully. You may wear a fair face, but you move like an Ulca! And no Elf ever wore such evil in his eyes…you are deluding yourself. I have seen what you truly are.*

You are trying to divert me, but it will not work, said Gorgon, with a confidence he did not feel. He could sense his resolve weakening already…his features were beginning to change. *Yet you are right in that your people are unworthy of the powers of Darkness. Your feeble spirits cannot bear the weight of evil…you are too weak! Even Aincor Fire-heart, who thought himself so mighty as to be invincible, and who brought about great misery because of it, crawled back to the Vault of Eternity upon his death, where he no doubt now cringes and whines in some corner, plagued with regrets over his misdeeds. How pathetic!*

You speak of things you do not know, nor will you ever know them, said Gaelen. She could see that her enemy wavered, and her confidence grew. *I expect Aincor never cringed from anything in life or in death. He was the cause of great suffering, but he had courage. That is something you cannot understand, as you have none yourself.*

You are trying to buy time—you have no more strength, said Gorgon, his face literally darkening as it broadened and flattened back toward its typical configuration. This process still fascinated Gaelen, who found the shift from evil Elf-lord to misshapen monster particularly disturbing. *I have only been toying with you. In a few moments I will rip you from the world as I would a tick from my scalp…you have been no less annoying. Then I will crush you and fling you from me. You are undone!*

Idle threats, said Gaelen. *Will you miss the sight of the stars, Dark Horror? There are none in the Void. And when I have vanquished you, I will destroy the mirror. You will never behold beauty again. When I go at last to the Far Shores of Elysia, I will seek out your poor mother and speak words of comfort, though I know she will weep for you and your dark fate. Our people will forget that you ever existed, save for those whose lives you ended. They will rest better knowing of your doom.*

She meant to enrage him, for then he would be unbalanced and she hoped that she could best him. She would try to lure Gelmyr back out. *It truly is not your fault that you are evil, for you have known nothing else. I'm not surprised that you actually believe the power of Darkness is stronger than that of Light, for you have never truly felt light upon your face… you cannot even bear the sight of it. I shall tell this to your mother in the hope that it will help her understand.*

My mother was as evil a creature as ever drew breath, growled Gorgon, his voice returning to its usual character.

Why? said Gaelen, who honestly wanted to know. *Because she could not love you?*

Gorgon laughed as his chaotic, multicolored aura flared and swirled about him. *Love, Elf-whelp? Love? I have never been tainted by love. That's why my power grows with each passing year. I have never been confused or distracted by love—never torn by it. You cannot say the same, can you? Guard your own fragile heart, She-elf. Love is a weakness I do not suffer, and I am glad of it! I'm weary of words. Let us rejoin our dance, and see whether love prevails. For my part, I will place my wager on a much different emotion.*

If I could love you, I would, said Gaelen, *for it is a grievous wrong that any creature should live by hatred alone. Love is the true power, but of course, you cannot know it. Alas that I must now muster my own hatred of you, and meet you on your terms. You will receive no love from me.*

As if I would wish it, said Gorgon, laughing. *Muster your hatred, then!* Without another word he leaped upon her, and the battle resumed. Gaelen's words belied her thoughts. She knew that only the powers of Light would allow her to prevail. If she held only rancor as a weapon she would surely be lost, for she could not hope to overcome one whose entire life had been devoted to hatred.

When his energy met with hers, the experience was most unpleasant for both of them. Gorgon felt as though he held on to a blazing firebrand, his hands and arms thrust into flame, the heat coursing through him as if to wither him away. The pain was intense, but he called upon his long experience and pushed it aside. If he could bear it long enough, the fire would die.

Gaelen's experience was vastly different. When she grappled with Gorgon, she felt an oppressive, rotting darkness that seemed to pervade her with cold hopelessness, drawing her energy and smothering her light. The pain she felt was that of terrible grief, of devastating and crippling loss. She had experienced such pain only once before…when her beloved Rain had called to her as he died in flames. She had felt that kind of loss then, but she had also felt the presence of the great Evil that had claimed her beloved. She felt it now, too, in the soul of her enemy. Gaelen had spent much of her life subduing the pain of that loss, but she could not vie long with Gorgon, for he had lived much longer and with far greater pain than she.

Gorgon's touch was revolting. Gaelen longed to cry out for aid, but she knew that she must not lose her focus or he would defeat her. They glared into each other's eyes. Gorgon wore his usual semblance, his pale gaze surrounded by dark, scarred flesh. Gaelen summoned up the images of Thorndil as she had known him—a brave but gentle man, much like an older version of Rogond. Then she remembered his unspeakable ending, and the terror and pain she had seen in his dead eyes. She searched back for the memory of her friends in the Greatwood, and of Gelmyr, Belegund, and Gorgon's other victims. Oddly, the memory of Tibo, the harmless little dwarf who so loved the Elves, enraged her the most in that moment.

Her rage fueled a burst of flame from her being that nearly engulfed her enemy, and he tried to release her, for the pain was too great for him to bear. She held on, screaming with effort, but he twisted away from her, becoming like smoke in her flaming hands. Gaelen's fire died back almost at once. She had spent much of her energy in the assault and now appeared to glow only faintly. Her head swam for a moment, and she sagged onto the dark plain.

Gorgon had taken great hurt in that last encounter, panting hard as he crawled backwards from her. He wished more than anything to escape this conflict and return to the physical realm, a realm where he held the mastery. But he knew that so long as Gaelen held the mirror, he was trapped with her. He took hold of his resolve and slowly emerged as the tall Elf, knowing that this form most disturbed her. The Elf smiled a sinister smile, for his enemy was weak. He could feel it. She had spent herself, and now he would have her.

Many hours passed in the Silver City, though it had seemed only moments to Gorgon and Gaelen. Rogond sat with Hallagond,

Estle, Nelwyn, and Galador in the Healing Halls, trying to recall the counsel of Lady Ordath when they had last faced such a trial in Mountain-home. "Do you think she will hear me if I call to her?" he asked Nelwyn.

"I cannot say, Rogond. It's my belief that there are many shores on the edge of Eternity, and I sense that she has gone to one quite different from the one we walked together. The mirror is evil now, for it has been made so, and it has drawn them to their battleground. This thing that has happened is most unnatural."

Galador agreed with Nelwyn. "I expect that any speculation we make will be just that. Fima works now with the scholars to discover what he can, but Gaelen has strayed into unknown lands. I know that you long to aid her, but it may be that any diversion of her mind from the battle will finish her. We dare not risk it."

Hallagond tried to comfort Rogond with a brotherly hand on his shoulder, as Estle scowled. Her tone belied her concern for Gaelen, of whom she had become very fond. "Trust Elves to take such a course, wait and see, sit back and do nothing," she said. "Can you not see that Rogond suffers? Can you not suggest something he might do? Doing nothing is the most painful course of all."

"Hush, Estle," said Hallagond. "This time they're right—there's too much at stake here to act without surety. Rogond may receive insight as to a course of action, or Gaelen may call to him and ask for aid. But until that happens, we dare not interfere."

"She will need aid," said Rogond. "Of that I am certain."

"You are right, North-man," said a strange voice from the doorway. Rogond had heard that voice before, but he never expected to hear it now. He turned and beheld Aryiah, the Seer, slowly entering the chamber, guided by Maji, the Minister of Omens. Rogond bowed in respect as the others stared in confusion at this strange, dark woman with eyes like clouded moons in her scarred face.

"Hail, Aryiah, Seer of Renown," said Rogond. "I pray that your gifts will enlighten us, and I praise the powers of heaven that you have come." His voice betrayed his desperate hope.

"North-man, treasure-stone, steadfast friend and defender of the Elven-fire, the stars have spoken of your plight," said Aryiah. "Know that I have not ventured forth from my chambers in many,

many years, but a terrible battle rages upon a dark and unknown field, and the Darkness strives against the Light. Your beloved cannot prevail against this evil—in its heart lies the power of the Shadowmancer. Her light is strong and bright, but it will wane…it has waned already."

"Can you save her, Spirit-mother?" asked Nelwyn, whose love for Gaelen was as deep as Rogond's.

"I will call to her," said Aryiah. "Gaelen would have aid, but does not know how to summon it, for she is accustomed to facing such battles alone. There is aid from the Light, but she does not know or understand this. Her light will not be enough."

Aryiah had been guided to sit beside Rogond, whereupon she held her hands out before her and began to chant, swaying in rhythm, her eyes closed. The chanting was strange to the ears of all in hearing, and even the Elves found themselves drawn away into a peaceful place, largely unaware of their surroundings. Estle and Hallagond appeared almost to fall asleep, but Rogond resisted, remaining alert in case Aryiah needed him.

Your eyes betray you, said the tall Elf with a sneering smile. *You have exhausted yourself, and now you fear me. Rightly so, little Vixen. Quite rightly so.*

Gaelen tried to muster her strength before the advancing enemy. *"You are no Elf—you're a misbegotten, pathetic, foul creation that should never have been spawned. You cannot deceive me, and I am not afraid of you."*

"Well, then, if I am so pathetic, you will take me easily. Come, then, for our dance is unfinished. The Black Void awaits you, my lady. He mocked her then, smiling and bowing, never taking his pale eyes from her. She was his prey, and he would toy with her. As he engaged her, he called upon the mirror, knowing that it was not within her power to resist. *Come to me, Dark Spirit—the One who gave me power…and life.*

The battle resumed, though neither warrior was at full strength, and it looked for a time that they were evenly matched. Their energies swirled together, the Light and the Dark, but neither prevailed over the other. Yet Gorgon slowly gained advantage, and Gaelen's light began dimming as he pressed her harder. He was still in Elven form, and his power was growing. Gaelen was on the verge of being overcome, as grief and hopelessness overwhelmed her and she cried out in despair. She looked into the depths of Gorgon's evil grey eyes to behold a sight that froze her blood and stole her courage, for she realized that her enemy did not fight alone.

A horrific, dark visage glared back at her, eyes glowing with malice, formless and terrifying, surrounded by eerie black flames. She quailed then, knowing that this was a power far beyond her. A surge of dark energy flowed through Gorgon and he laughed in triumph. He had turned back into his own form, for the Shadowmancer would never look through the eyes of an Elf, evil or not. Gorgon began to slowly wrestle Gaelen toward the endless darkness at his back, and she knew that he meant to cast her there, and that she would be unable to stop him.

She had to prevail now, or face the worst possible fate. Why had Lord Wrothgar come to Gorgon's aid? Was it because he had corrupted the mirror, or was there truly a part of him that had gone into Gorgon's creation? Gaelen did not know.

Gorgon knew that his enemy was outmatched, and he threw his ugly head back and laughed. This was the best outcome he could have hoped for, because now he would torment her before casting her into the Dark. He would not send her to those who loved her, not even in death, for death would never truly come unto her. He would think of her torment whenever he looked at the stars, and it would cheer him. It was no less than she deserved.

These were moments to be savored, for Gorgon knew that Gaelen was aware of what lay before her. Her light had dimmed when she looked into his eyes—she must have seen her own fate. He did not realize that she had seen the Shadowmancer, but it would have made no difference.

Where are your friends, Wood-elf? Where is that pathetic Tuathan? Where is your mighty Elven-king? A pity they will not be here to comfort you as you sail forever into nothingness. It would seem that love has deserted you.

Gaelen tried to muster an answer, but the face of Wrath that glared back at her from Gorgon's eyes had taken her resolve. She understood the last thoughts of a mouse that is taken and toyed with by a cat. Gritting her teeth, she spoke directly to the Shadowmancer.

You killed my beloved…you took him from me. Now we'll see how easy it is to defeat my resolve! Your servant is more vulnerable than you know.

She turned her attention back to Gorgon. *Do you have any message that I should give your mother? Anything I should tell Gelmyr when I see him? For you will not cast me into the Void…my strength is growing, and soon I shall vanquish you. If not, I will at least take you with me into the Dark. Then we shall have Eternity for debate.*

Gaelen had thought to distract Gorgon, and she had succeeded. His aura flared menacingly around him, particularly when he thought of Gelmyr. Yet Gorgon sensed that when Gaelen was truly gone, Gelmyr would be gone with her. *I am done playing with you, Elf, and now our dance will end. Think on your own questions as you turn endlessly in torment. I will spend no more time in debate with you.* He dragged her closer to the blackness as the struggle resumed.

Gaelen heard the strange, rhythmic chanting before Gorgon did, and she wondered as to the nature of it. It was a lifeline—a voice inside her soul that spoke gentle words of guidance.

Gaelen…Gaelen Taldin. Hear my words and be free. You can prevail, but you must summon the souls of the vanquished to aid you. There are those among them who can help in defeating your foe. Call upon them now!

Gaelen gathered her strength for a great effort. She had expected to fight this battle alone; it had not occurred to her that any help would come. She was still uncertain, but she would try. *Spirits of those vanquished by the Elfhunter, tormented and unjustly taken, come to my aid! I call upon you…help me!*

Gorgon looked puzzled. Was it possible that Gaelen could do such things? If so, why had she not earlier? *You are desperate, Elf-whelp. None will come to aid you, and you know it. I hear your hesitation. I suppose it was worth trying, yet I see no spirits of the vanquished. Save your energy for the Void.*

The strange, gentle voice came again. *You cannot have any doubt. Muster your faith, and summon them. They will come if you truly will it.*

This time, when Gaelen called out to the spirits of the dead, there was no doubt in her mind. She closed her eyes, took three deep breaths, and flared brilliant golden-orange as she called to them.

At first there was nothing. Then both she and Gorgon heard

the voices, uncounted numbers of them gathering and approaching the Edge of Darkness. Gorgon had lived a long, long time, and he had killed many Elves. Now they swarmed around the struggling souls as they fought, their beautiful but forlorn faces swirling like mist, for they had little power here. They did succeed in distracting Gorgon for the moment, and he actually let go of Gaelen, for he was dismayed until he realized that they would not touch him. Then he laughed.

Thank you for reminding me of the vast harm I have done to my enemies. Do you now see my power? These multitudes were taken by the Elfhunter alone, and none knew of it save the fallen. When I have finished with you, I shall return to my old life, killing as I will.

I think not, said a voice that rose above the others. Gelmyr, the real Gelmyr, appeared in the forefront, glowing and beautiful as he had been in life. *Your crimes are known to us now, Gorgon. You will fall before the hands of those you have sworn to destroy. You can never return to Elven lands, for you are known!*

The sight of Gelmyr, not dead and rotting, but beautiful and whole, took Gorgon's nerve for a moment. And the words he spoke were true—the warning had spread, such that his intended prey would be more watchful for a time. Yet surely they would relax eventually, and had Gorgon not killed several already as he passed near to the Verdant Mountains on his way southward?

Do your worst, though I expect it is little enough, said Gorgon. *I need not fear. You can do no harm to me in this realm, and precious little anywhere else. I am not afraid of any of you.*

Then a new voice came—wise and deep. *Ah, Gorgon. You are still as proud as ever, and I must say that your ability to speak the Elven tongues has not declined. Yet I sorrow for you, my friend, for so I still hold you. Do you not remember me?*

One of the Shades stepped forward as the others drew back. This one appeared to be of great age. It appeared bent, scarred, and wizened. It was most certainly the soul of an Elf, but this spirit had been forever diminished by torment and cruelty in the depths of Lord Wrothgar's fortress. Not even death could restore him, or so it seemed. Yet he still held his pride and his dignity as he approached the one who had taken his life so long ago.

Old One? Gorgon whispered in disbelief, staring at the gently glowing spirit.

Yes, it is I. I am pleased that you remember me after such a long age...and you have not forgotten your lessons. Yet your deeds have indeed been dark over your long life, and you have never had the comfort or the love that could have turned you back from them. Not since you took my life have you known a friend.

Why look you now so sorrowful, Old One? Can you not see how my power has grown? Look now on all these vanquished ones and know that it was I who slew them. Are you not proud of your apprentice?

The old Elf shook his head. *We should all be sorrowful in the presence of a wasted life. You were given great strength and a ready mind, yet you have ever been turned to the service of evil. It is not your fault. You never had the chance to be anything other than what you are.*

I serve none but myself, said Gorgon. *No one commands me, and my purposes are my own. I hunt and slay the Elàni because I wish it! You speak of good and evil, but all things must be weighed by each soul's measure. To me, a thousand dead Elves is not an evil thing…it is a very good thing.*

You did not slay me at your own behest, my poor, misguided pupil. You and I were friends…deny it if you will! It was no less difficult for you than for me. Yet you took my life at the Black Flame's command. You were his servant then, and his servant you remain—you're just too deluded to know it.

Gaelen had renewed herself in those few moments, for she knew that she did not stand alone. She looked with curiosity upon the old Elf, who so obviously viewed Gorgon differently than did anyone else. *Who are you, Old One?* she said in a soft voice.

The Old One turned to her with a sad smile. *I was once called Halladin, though I had forgotten my own name for years uncounted until the time of my death. I was known only as the Old One, for I had been captive in the Dark Fortress for a long age. My body declined, even as you see me now, and my spirit was all but broken. Yet the Shadowmancer charged me with a task, and so long as I performed it, he would suspend my torment. It was I who taught his Dark Child the speech of the Elàni, and I also taught him some of Elven ways. But my student began to be my friend, and that must not be allowed to happen, for to know love is to turn from hate. Lord Wrothgar ordered Gorgon to slay me with his own hands, and he did so, as much out of fear as anything.* He turned to Gorgon. *He will deny it, but it was so.*

Gaelen was incredulous. *Are you saying that you…that you loved Gorgon? That you called him friend?*

I am, said Halladin.

I don't understand. How can you love a thing that has killed so many of our people, and wishes now only to do further harm?

Ah. But we are his people, too. Perhaps if we had not shunned him so utterly he would have realized it. His spirit is quite strong, as I am sure you are aware.

ENOUGH OF THIS! roared Gorgon, who had been staring at Halladin in disbelief. *Stop speaking of me as if I'm not here! I never called you friend, I have never cared for anyone, and I will never care to be loved. You may have loved me, but it made you weak, and I took your life. And do you know what I did after? Absolutely nothing of consequence. Your death did not even disrupt my daily activities, Old One. It was of no consequence.*

Are you trying to convince me, or yourself? asked Halladin gently.

Suddenly, Gorgon's face twisted helplessly into that of Gelmyr. The long-dead apparition looked over at the real Gelmyr, smiled, and gave him a friendly wave. Then he laughed. *You are in such denial, Elfhunter! I know the truth of it…you ran into a dark corner and hid from the Shadowmancer, and when you were certain he would neither see nor hear you, you wept! I remember it well…I believe it was the last time in your entire, miserable life that you shed a tear of grief.* He looked over at Gaelen and winked.

Gorgon's dark face reappeared almost at once, and his fury was graven upon it. *I will hear no more of this!* he bellowed, as Halladin looked sadly back at Gaelen.

He is truly evil, little one, but he is vulnerable. Yet I am afraid his fury has made him irrational, and he is now very, very dangerous. Guard yourself well! With these words, Halladin bowed and retreated into the mass of souls until he could no longer be seen.

Gaelen squared her shoulders. Had there ever been a moment when Gorgon had *not* been dangerous? Yet now, as he rushed at her, she knew that there would be no respite. She made a silent vow that if Gorgon would cast her into the Void, she would at least take him with her.

They grappled for the last time, their energies swirling wildly around them. They cried out with pain and effort as they strove at the very edge of the black void that seemed to suffocate all light. Gorgon's strength was actually waning now; the encounter with Halladin had unnerved him, and he wavered. Gaelen knew it and pressed her advantage, backing him to within inches of the edge of the Light. But Gorgon reached down within his black soul and summoned the Shadowmancer.

Gaelen heard the hated voice inside her head. *Thou art vanquished, even as thy beloved was long ago. He could not triumph over Me, and so cannot thou.* The face of Lord Wrothgar could not truly be seen, but she felt him smile and it sickened her. All was lost! She could not prevail over the very essence of Evil, and she would receive little aid from the Shades of the dead, save one...if he would hear her.

Rain…Rain! Come to me now, or I will never see you again. If I am heard, let my cry be answered!

Both Gorgon and the Shadowmancer laughed at this, for they knew how afraid she was. Her fears were Gorgon's greatest weapon, and he would use them. He wrested her back toward the abyss; they could both be lost at any moment.

Fool of an Elf! said Gorgon in a voice that came from the heart of Evil itself. *Do you not understand that your Lost King cannot save you? It was he who fled before the Dark Powers, taking a part of you away with him long ago, and hence your spirit has never been whole. You are vanquished because of him. Call upon him and you will surely fail.*

But Gaelen knew that this was not so. Her beloved had taken a part of her spirit when he had been ripped so cruelly from the world, yet he would strengthen her beyond measure if he stood beside her. *Rain…come now to me, and aid me in my task,* she whispered.

She felt him first, powerful and loving, surrounding her with warm, soft light. When the light faded they were as one, and Gaelen knew her soul was whole again—she had joined with her beloved. She heard his voice from within her, but she did not see him, for he looked out at her enemy through her eyes.

Do not be afraid, my love, for I am with thee, he said. Then he looked through Gaelen's eyes into the face of the Enemy, his grey eyes meeting those of the Black Flame. *You cannot withstand the power of the High King!* he said in a deep, thundering voice, causing Gorgon to reel back from him. *There is but a vestige of the Dark One within you, but you face the full wrath and strength of the most ancient Lightbearers! You cannot stand against me, Dark Horror.*

Gorgon knew in his heart that it was so, as the image of Lord Wrothgar flickered and faded. Ri-Elathan's voice was heard once more from the depths of Gaelen's bright eyes. *Your Master has abandoned you, Gorgon One-hand. Taste now fully of the Darkness, or face the Light!*

And so, said Gaelen, *you have your ally, Gorgon, and I have mine. It would seem that yours has deserted you.* Her fire redoubled, and she concentrated not upon the heat of it, but upon the light. She flared so brilliant in that moment that Gorgon turned his head away, roaring with pain, trying to escape her grasp as he had done before, but he could not. He took another step back, faltering upon the edge as Gaelen used the last of her strength to force him over. Every other Shade recoiled from the dark void; none would draw near.

I will take thee with me, Gorgon cried in desperation. *There will be no victory this day for either of us!* He tightened his grip on her as he said this, but Gaelen did not relent. Gorgon was now truly at bay. She had him, and she would finish him. She looked now with fascinated revulsion at his dark face. His features convulsed, changing from one manifestation to the next, but none of them could stand before the Light.

She could feel his terror, but she could also sense the fear growing in the heart of her beloved. If Gorgon made good on his threat, then she would be taken with him, and none would be able to save her from it.

Rain's urgent voice came to her. *Let him go, Gaelen. Do not doubt him...he will not fall without you. You must let him go for both our sakes. If he takes you into the abyss, I cannot follow. You will face him again upon another field, and he will ever doubt himself because of this battle. You have shown him that Evil cannot prevail over you. Let him go...or strive with him forever!*

Gaelen's light dimmed as she heard these words, the last she had expected to hear from her beloved Rain. *You said it was my destiny to rid the world of his foul presence, and now you tell me I must release him? I will not let him take me...I cannot let him escape again! I will not!*

I cannot let you face such a fate, Gaelen, not for this end. He is but one enemy. There will be another time. Let go. His voice and words were gentle, but his tone was commanding. Gaelen did not seem to hear him. She pressed ever closer to an irrecoverable fate, as Gorgon clutched at her as though to the last lifeline of a drowning man.

Aryiah had stopped chanting, and her pale eyes flew open in alarm. "Oh, no…Gaelen, do not let him take you. You will be forever lost! Such a fate you cannot even imagine! No…oh, *no*!" She wrung her hands helplessly and turned toward Rogond, who clutched at her arm.

"Spirit-mother, what must I do?" he asked in desperation.

Aryiah shook her head. "If we do not bring Gaelen back from where she has gone, she is lost to you forever," she said.

"And…and how do I do this?" he asked, frantic.

"I do not know," said Aryiah. "Follow your instincts, Northman. Do what you must!"

Rogond knew what he had to do, and for once in his life he did not pause to consider. He reached out to his beloved and, praying that his instincts were true, he reached for the accursed mirror and tried to pry it from her hand. Her fingers tightened hard upon it—she would not let go. *She thinks her job is unfinished…she's being stubborn. Lord of Light help me!* He tried again, but her grip was strong and he did not wish to hurt her.

*Let go, Gaelen…*he thought, praying that she would hear. *Come back…come back to me! Don't force me to mourn your fate for the rest of my life…come back to one who loves you!*

A tiny moan escaped her lips, and her fingers relaxed enough that he could wrest the mirror from her. Apparently, he had been heard. As he took the thing in his hand, he felt the power surge up his right arm and his head swam. The world wavered in and out of focus—light and utter darkness flashed before his astonished eyes. He felt sickened, nearly overwhelmed by despair. He was not welcome in whatever realm she walked in now. Mustering his strength and choking back the bile rising in his throat, he flung the mirror into the far corner of the room.

All at once, everything around Gaelen vanished in a flash of white light: Gorgon, the Void, and the Shades of the dead, along with her beloved. She heard his voice one last time. *Farewell, my tenacious Gaelen. You will face your enemy again. Your spirit has been restored to you, for I am with you always. Another Shore awaits upon another time, and our reunion will be complete. It will seem as only a brief time of waiting to me…farewell.*

Gaelen shuddered in Rogond's arms, and she grew warmer again, but much of her strength had been taken. She lay, inert and barely breathing, as her companions despaired, for they did not yet know whether she would be whole again.

Aryiah could not assure Rogond that Gaelen would be restored, but she did not question the wisdom of his action in taking the mirror from her.

"You had to do what was done, North-man. If she is lost, it is not on your account. She has looked into the face of horror and faltered on the edge of the darkest of fates. Without your aid she might have gone over. No ill fate that she might face now will compare. You have saved her very soul this day."

Fima, on the other hand, was incredulous. "*What?* How could you have done such a thing without knowing what it would do to her? She has not awakened; it may be that her spirit still wanders and now cannot find its way back. Not even the most learned minds and works could provide enlightenment. How could you have been so… impulsive? It's so unlike you.'

Nelwyn looked into Gaelen's eyes and took both of her hands. "She is with us now, Rogond. She is not lost. She is weak and drained, and in need of rest, but she is with us."

"Is she whole?" asked Rogond, sensing that Nelwyn would know.

"She is whole. In fact, I sense she will be stronger than before, though I cannot explain why. Yet she faced a terrible trial."

Rogond brushed aside a lock of Gaelen's hair, and was shocked to see several strands of silver mingled amid the copper, brown, and gold. Gaelen would be marked forever by her struggle.

"She is so pale…could we still lose her?"

"We may," said Nelwyn, "but I don't think so. She has ever been strong, and I have seen her in worse shape than this. Now she is simply weary. She will take strength from you and others who love her." She sat down beside Rogond, placed a gentle hand on his shoulder, and waited.

Rogond stayed at Gaelen's side for days, leaving her only to tend to his own few needs. Fima, Nelwyn, Hallagond, and Estle took their turns in the watch, speaking quietly to her of whatever they would, but Rogond was always there. When Gaelen finally did awaken, it was his careworn face that she first beheld, and she managed a wan but heartfelt smile.

"It was you...you drew me back from the Void," she said, as he began to weep. "It's curious...I thought I would be angry, for my enemy was vanquished and I had but to finish him, but in doing so I might have been doomed to the worst possible fate. Gorgon would have made certain of it. You saved me, Thaylon. Even the High King was having difficulty swaying my actions." She smiled again despite her exhaustion. "I really must try to be a bit less obstinate in the future."

Gaelen was alive and apparently whole, though she would sleep for many more days. She allowed Rogond to hold her, taking his hand as his tears dampened her hair. She knew that wherever Gorgon was, he was at least as weary as she, for he had faced the Void without hope of recovery. Oddly enough, it was love that had saved them both. *I told him that love was the true power, and when I next face him I will remind him of it...if given the chance.*

Gaelen had been right about the state of her enemy. Gorgon had gone to ground after arranging his terrible display of Thorndil. He had traveled back many miles, using all his skills to confound any would-be pursuers, leaving no tracks or traces behind him. He had been so pleased with his own performance that his mind and soul had been unguarded—in fact, they were quite open, for he would relish Gaelen's grief and outrage. She, on the other hand, had kept her plans concealed, so that when she had gazed into the mirror at last, Gorgon had been unaware until it was too late to guard himself.

Now he was lying on the dusty floor of his sanctuary, the one in which he had imprisoned Thorndil and tortured him. He lay for many days, unmoving and unseeing, slack-jawed, his blank, grey eyes unfocused. He appeared to be quite lifeless even after his spirit returned, and if anyone had found him in such a state, they could have killed him with no effort. Flies buzzed around him, settling on his flesh, but they soon left him, knowing the truth. Gorgon still lived.

The flies had already been drawn to the blood and flesh of Thorndil that remained in this place of torment. Gorgon's one hand was still stained with it. It was fortunate for him that he was underground, for the sun would have finished him had he been unlucky enough to lie alone in the open for so many days without water. He was also fortunate that no night-hunting beasts had been drawn to the blood-stench, for they might have feasted on Gorgon's tough, thick flesh. He had no loving friends to tend him. Gaelen awoke long before he did, and when he finally did awaken, he would recall their conflict with dismay. She had called upon the Light, and it had vanquished him. The fact that he would have taken her with him was of little consolation.

The Elfhunter had been dealt a bitter blow, but as always he would regain his resolve given time. He was shaken, but far from broken, and he would never again allow Gaelen to engage him in the spirit realm. From then on it would be flesh against flesh. In that arena, he would be confident of victory over her.

As he came to himself at last, weakened and barely alive, he began the long process of recovery. Though he had gone many miles from the Citadel already, he would retreat farther for a while and make plans, forsaking this sanctuary for a newer, deeper one. He had learned a few things about himself recently, and not all had dismayed him. The Dark Power was a part of him, even as it had looked through his eyes and robbed his enemy of her courage. If he called upon that power, he would never again fight alone.

Gorgon was highly intelligent, and he had come to realize that it was Rogond, the fool who loved Gaelen, who had taken the mirror and saved him from the Void. *Soon I will be strong again, and then perhaps I'll trap the Vixen and that fool of a Ranger in some hellish place. Then I'll summon that part of myself that has come from the very heart of Darkness, smile down upon the man's dying face, and try to find the words to thank him.*

The evil energies of Lord Wrothgar swirled in the depths of Tûr Dorcha, and he was pleased. His anger toward Gorgon had cooled, and he was aware of his wayward child once more. So much had been gained from Gorgon's possession of the mirror that Wrothgar could not spend too much time in regretting the loss of it. After all, Gorgon had learned many things from it, and now Wrothgar knew of them, as well. The knowledge of Dûn Arian was of considerable interest, yet it was not the most important of Gorgon's revelations. Wrothgar had long suspected that the Stone of Léir had been taken to Tal-sithian, and now he was certain of it.

A great plume of fire and foul vapor burst from the Tower as Wrothgar came to his next plan. He would not summon Gorgon to the Darkmere, for he would not risk such a valuable creature wandering back northward in such weakened condition. Instead, he would send aid—powerful aid.

Wrothgar wanted to tear into Gorgon's mind, willingly or no, and lay it naked before his dark scrutiny. He hoped that the Elfhunter would survive this invasion...Gorgon had only begun to be truly useful, and so many future plans would benefit from his service. Wrothgar sent forth a northward call to the vast wasteland that the Elves once called Tal-elathas, and summoned forth the darkest spirit that had yet been known in Alterra, save for his own.

2
Of Plans and Wise Counsel

Gaelen's battle with Gorgon had seemed to take only a brief time in the ethereal world, but in the physical realm it lasted for days. It had ended abruptly when Rogond wrested the mirror from her hand. He gave it back to Fima, who re-secured it inside the inner pocket of his jerkin for the time being.

Gaelen had awakened four days after her return, but would not regain full strength for some time, as her spirit had been sorely tested. The strands of snowy silver in her hair would testify to the severity of this ordeal for the remainder of her days—a rather prominent lock of it fell across her eyes in the front. During the conflict, Gorgon had touched her there.

Despite her trial, she had gained several things of incalculable worth, emerging both wiser and stronger, with a much deeper and more complete understanding of her enemy.

She sat atop the wall overlooking the sea, as was her habit, lost in her own thoughts. She also knew that she would not ever wish to encounter him in such a place again, where the risks to her very soul were so terrible and final. She sensed that Gorgon feared this fate as much as she did.

Rain came to me when I called upon him, and we were as one—it was almost as if we both still lived. He looked through my eyes, and I through his... our souls merged utterly in those moments. Gorgon could not withstand our combined power, even with his most fearsome ally.

She smiled to herself. *When I lost Rain long ago, my heart was torn... my spirit has never been whole since that day. I didn't realize how deeply wounded I was, and I tried to heal myself, but I have been incomplete. Our reunion upon that dark frontier has mended what was broken, for he has left a part of himself behind. I will always carry him with me now, not just in memory, but as a true part of my being. I have sung songs of abject longing and loneliness, calling out to him beneath the bright stars, but I will not need to do so again. I am free to love Rogond for as long as we both live, without grieving for Rain.*

Had Gorgon known this, it would have dismayed him, for his small adversary was now much wiser and more formidable. She had changed—that much was plain. She seemed less impulsive, calmer, and more at peace with herself. Though the fire of her spirit burned as brightly as ever, it had been tempered by an ancient grace.

Rogond did not understand the nature of this change, but he would not have resented this intrusion upon her heart, because he truly loved her. Gaelen, mindful of his feelings, did not discuss such matters with him, but he knew that her love for him was undiminished. Her heart belonged to him for as long as he lived, and there was now no grief to fetter it.

Gaelen told her friends as much as she cared to about the battle on the Edge of Darkness, and they listened with wonder. Fima seemed especially moved, and for once he did not record her words on parchment, as it did not seem fitting.

Rogond told the tale before Salastor and the Council, for Gaelen was not comfortable doing so. After he had finished, Salastor spoke gently to Gaelen.

"Do you have a sense of this enemy now? Was he weakened, as you were? If so, then perhaps we should muster all our efforts to find him and bring him to bay while he is vulnerable. Does that not seem wise?"

Gaelen considered. "No doubt he has been weakened, for he has no one to tend him. But he has survived for long ages alone, and he is very adept at concealing himself. You and your folk are more than welcome to search for him, but I suspect he has gone too deep to be found. You will need insight to find him—insight given only to me. Gorgon is a more terrible enemy than any you have yet faced. I would rather deal with five of Lokai than with him, yet such is my task and my destiny. Search if you will, and good hunting, but use great care!"

Thorndil was laid to rest beside the other brave souls who had given their lives in the conflict. The Company sorrowed as they said their farewells, Fima and Rogond in particular. They placed a pouch of highly prized and especially fine pipe-leaf beside him. "Someday, my friend, I will see you again, and we will have a fine time sharing our pipes and tales," said Rogond. "Enjoy the leaf until that day."

With the death of Ali, the City had no Minister of Defense, and therefore no commander of its army. Not unexpectedly, the Council suggested that Hallagond be appointed to the post, an honor that he respectfully declined.

"I can accept no permanent duty here," he said, "because I do not know when or where the Company will be called. I must remain with my brother and his friends, for they have need of me. I'm sorry."

"Will you not take charge of our forces in the meantime?" asked Salastor. "Until the Company departs from the City, we will have need of you. Will you not help until then, or until another suitable person may be found?"

"What about Visili?" asked Hallagond. "He has shown his worth many times over. His skills both in battle and as a leader of men are at least as great as my own, and he is willing to serve the City in payment for his past crimes. I will serve as his second until I am called away."

"We have pardoned him of his crimes," said Salastor. "And you're right—he is quite skilled. I shall consider your advice, Hallagond Worm-slayer." They both chuckled at this somewhat lofty title. It was no less true.

Gaelen stood upon the Great Wall, looking out to the east at the gigantic remains of the dragon, giving thanks for the wind, which blew from the west. Much of Lokai's usefulness had been claimed already, including his scales, which would make excellent shields against weapons or flame, his teeth and tail-spines, his venom, and his blood. When the flesh had rotted from his bones they, too, would be useful. One of the Citadel's most eccentric and brilliant architects had been eyeing the great ribs with longing. The scavengers had fared very well, stripping much of the flesh away, but enough remained, rotting in the warm sun, to put a very unpleasant stench in the air.

Gifts gleaned from the dragon were bestowed upon the Company in honor of their very prominent and vital role in his defeat. Hallagond was given a shield made of beautifully carved dragon-scale, together with a blade made from one of the smaller fangs. Rogond and Galador each received a similar blade, for they had stood against the dragon. Fima gained an interesting addition to his arsenal—a tool fashioned rather like an axe, with a handle made of the long, hollow keel of dragon-scale. The blade was made of the very tip of one of Lokai's great claws, which would dig through nearly anything without chipping or splitting. Fima remarked that it would be interesting to test it against his normal weapons of oak and steel, yet he did not favor it, as the balance seemed faulty for some reason.

Gaelen, Nelwyn, and Estle received perhaps the most intriguing gifts. They were each given a phial containing a healthy quantity of a most rare and precious substance. Known as ainya, or dread-fire, it was the essence from which dragons kindled their flames. Collected from the back of Lokai's throat, a single drop of it would start a fire under nearly any conditions. Regrettably, much of it had been spent; the dragon's fire had been greatly diminished ere he had fallen. Gaelen, who was usually appointed the fire-builder when traveling with the Company, was thankful for the gift.

"Now, be careful with this," said Lord Salastor as he handed her the phial. "It will burn anything except dragon-scale. It will stick to flesh, consuming it without mercy, and is very difficult to extinguish."

Gaelen had also requested a large piece of the dragon's hide, which would be stripped of the scales, split, softened, and tanned into leather. Such leather was highly prized, for it was soft, yet the strongest to be had. It would even turn flames aside for a time, though it would burn eventually. A dark chestnut-red in color, it held no dragon-scent by the time it had been seasoned and oiled. Gaelen would make boots, gauntlets, and a jerkin from it that would probably last longer than she would live. She also crafted a pair of boots and a set of gauntlets for Hallagond. "In case you must ever face the fire again," she said with a small flourish. "My fire-cloak may not be available. Consider this part of your wedding gift."

"Estle and I have decided to forego the ceremony for a time," said Hallagond, to Gaelen's surprise and dismay. "We do not wish to marry while there is still a pall of fear and grief over the City, and while our future course remains uncertain."

"Understandable," said Gaelen. "But if you are waiting for certainty, Brother of my Beloved, then you may never marry. There are very few things of which I have been certain. If you are certain of your love for Estle, then you should pledge your heart. Do not wait for tomorrow."

"Ah. But I said only that we have decided to forego the ceremony," said Hallagond. "We pledged our hearts in secret, even as you and Rogond have done."

This was overheard by Fima, who always seemed to be in the right place at the right time. "That is very happy news! Now I shall have a use for that extremely fine bottle of brandy that I purchased to give you on your wedding night. Since that has apparently occurred already, perhaps we might all share it."

"Fima, you are nearly as prone to make unexpected appearances as Gaelen," said Hallagond, shaking his head. "I would rather not call attention to our union, as folk here would do exactly what you are doing and make a fuss about it. Estle does not wish that, and neither do I."

"Well then, perhaps you and I can enjoy one quiet toast together?" said Fima. Hallagond scowled at him.

"Don't worry," said Gaelen. "Fima will not tell anyone. And if I were you, I would take him up on his toast. He has an exceptional talent for judging fine brandy. If you do not join him, then he will be forced to partake of it alone. Surely you would not deny him!"

She approached Hallagond and placed a hand upon his shoulder. "You are so like your brother…in many ways. I'm happy for you."

Hallagond returned the gesture. "My brother is fortunate to have one such as you, although at first I did not know it. May you have a long life together in joy, even as Estle and I would hope for."

Fima rubbed his hands together. "We should definitely drink to that sentiment, Hallagond. Will you join me?"

Hallagond smiled, knowing the fine brandy would not long remain in its beautifully-crafted bottle.

The following morning, Lord Salastor summoned the Company to the Council. "My advisors and I are concerned about this threat to our people," he said, his face grim and somber. "We must decide the fate of the mirror. As long as it exists, Gorgon will be drawn to it, and Gaelen risks being held by its influence. Perhaps it is better that it be destroyed, for then the connection will be broken. Fima, what is your view?"

Fima, who had appeared rather bleary-eyed and disheveled at first, became deadly serious. "Long have I considered this, and I see little benefit to keeping this vile token intact. While it exists there is the chance that the creature might recover it, which would be an unmitigated disaster! It is made only of gold and glass—a hammer and a well-heated forge is all I need to render it harmless."

"Is there any risk to Gaelen?" asked Nelwyn. "I am concerned that somehow her life-force might be caught up within the mirror."

"I cannot say for certain, but I do not believe so," said Fima. "There are scholars here in the City with whom I have conferred, for their knowledge of such things may be greater than mine. All are in agreement that Gaelen is in far greater peril in a world where the mirror exists."

"Then it would seem to be a simple choice," said Rogond. "We should destroy it with no further delay."

"Will you hear what I have to say in this matter, or will you all debate my fate and decide it for me?" asked Gaelen, who had not yet spoken. "It may surprise you to learn that I will fight the notion of destroying the mirror…I do not wish it to be destroyed."

"Why not, in the name of heaven?" asked Fima.

"Because the mirror is my closest connection with our enemy. I do not know whether I will keep my sense of him if it is unmade, and, as much as it pains me, I must keep that sense. He cannot come upon me unaware if I remain vigilant, and he cannot hide from me so long as I possess the…bond…that the mirror has forged. If we destroy it, I don't know what will happen. We may be helpless to evade him, with little hope of finding him. I have sworn not to rest until he is dead at my feet, and to gain that goal I must continue the dance." Her voice, though bitter, was full of resolve. "If I have to, I will look into the mirror again, though I doubt I'll surprise him a second time."

"I'd rather you not do that," said Rogond. "We barely got you back alive the first time."

"You're right, Gaelen, much as I hate to say it," said Fima. "But I would caution that, should Gorgon retrieve his token, we are all in peril—you most of all."

Gaelen looked hard at him. "Should that happen, I will remain alive for not more than a few moments, for I will never be his vessel again." Fima looked downcast, for he knew what she meant. She would take her own life by whatever means available.

"Therefore, you must be certain to guard it well. He will never find it so long as you hold it," she said. She held such faith in him that his eyes grew moist as he looked at her. When Gaelen gave her trust, it was deep and nearly unshakable.

"I have no reply to that, Gaelen," said Salastor. "I know that your faith in Fima is well placed. What, then, shall we do to aid you in finding and defeating this dreadful menace? What can the people of Dûn Arian provide?"

"They can guard themselves," said Gaelen. "This enemy takes any in his path. But I do not believe he will return to Dûn Arian, as we are too well protected here. He is a coward at heart, and he will try to lure the Company to some place where he will hold the advantage. He already knows that he will need aid, and he will seek it from among the ranks of evil as he did before. There is little of real courage in him. He will not strike until he is either certain to prevail, or has no other choice."

"All the more reason to pursue him now," said Estle. "If you are aware of him, perhaps you can do what the searchers could not."

"He is guarding himself," said Gaelen. "He was defeated and he knows it. He will not open himself to me until he is ready, or until he relaxes his vigilance. I would not count on that happening any time soon. He's more wary than ever now…I doubt I could summon him as I did before, and I'd really rather not look into the mirror again!"

"If he can prevent you from sensing him, then what's the use?" asked Estle. "This entire situation is quite unnatural and mysterious, and I don't like it."

"I don't care much for it either," said Gaelen. "But know this—though he is lying low at present, I'll know it if he rouses himself. My vigilance will not waver again until he is dead." She dropped her gaze for a moment. "I could curse myself for my lack of awareness. In a way, Thorndil's death is my fault."

"Nonsense!" said Fima. "If people are going to go around blaming themselves, then we might as well give up. You were distracted by the rather important matter of a battle to the death, with a dragon thrown in just to make things interesting. So stop talking so foolishly."

"All right, Fima," said Rogond. "Let's get back to the matter at hand. What shall we do with the mirror?"

Everyone looked at Gaelen as though expecting her to know. Her ears reddened as she spoke to Salastor. "My lord, I don't know. But I do know that the Light will face the Darkness again. He will call me out, and then we shall see. Until I am further enlightened, I can only wait."

"That is indeed a foolish notion!" said Estle. "You intend to give him the time he needs to prepare and muster an army before you pursue him? You will be defeated!"

"You don't understand," said Rogond. "I know Gorgon is a coward, but he is proud. I expect he is not very effective at mustering an army—he has been alone for far too long, and he is afraid of his Dark Master. I wouldn't expect any army…he will try to lure us as soon as he is able, while he knows that our hearts are still burning with indignation at the fate of our friend Thorndil. We must stand ready."

"I am ready *now*," said Gaelen simply. "It is my greatest wish to see Gorgon dead, for the mirror will have no more power, and I will be free of him at last." She drew herself up, and hope shone in her bright eyes as she thought of that day. "But if we pursue him now, it will be in vain. He is cloaking himself…I have no sense of his presence. He knows that we are on our guard. A coward fears to strike a wary foe."

"Then why wait until he actually summons you?" asked Estle, who still did not understand. "I had expected you to want to pursue Gorgon at once. As soon as you become aware of him, why not move to defeat him?"

Gaelen turned toward her, and Estle beheld for the first time the calm, wise assurance in her eyes. "You do not realize the depth of the connection between us," she said. "He is every bit as aware of me as I am of him. If I pursue him before he is ready, he will go to ground, and he is much more adept at hiding from me than I am at guarding myself. He has been in hiding for much of his miserable life, after all." She looked into the eyes of her friend. "Can you not accept this course? Would you go after him and waste your efforts?"

Estle looked down at her feet for a moment. "Well, of course I trust your counsel I suppose…it's just that I would have expected you to want to raze the desert for miles until you turned him out. Your friend was tortured and killed, and yet you are calm as you stand here and tell us that we should do nothing. It is not what I expected, is all." She looked up into Gaelen's eyes. "There is something different about you…this trial has changed you."

Gaelen's face was grim. "I have changed much less than you think, Estle. The desire to avenge Thorndil burns my heart, yet wisdom tells me that now is not the time for it. I am not descended of the Fire-heart, in spite of all jesting to the contrary. We must make ready to pursue Gorgon and strike him as soon as he reveals himself, but he will not do so until he is certain. He will wait until we relax our vigilance, and then he will call to us. He wants the Company dead, particularly me—his loathing is now so great that I can still feel it in my heart. The very thought of it wearies me. I would not wish such black hatred upon anyone."

She turned back to Salastor. "Gorgon's pride has taken a blow, and he will not come after me again without aid. Now we have an army and he does not, but he will not find what he will need here in the Tal-fásath. He will find aid in a place you or I dare not go." So saying, she took her leave, bowing first to Salastor and then to the Council, as they puzzled over the meaning of her words and what they might imply.

Lord Wrothgar brooded in the depths of Tûr Dorcha, for there was much to be considered. He knew Gorgon's plight, for he had stood with him on the Edge of Darkness. Wrothgar's black soul still burned from the Light sent forth by his enemy, the High King Ri-Elathan. Yet now a plan had come, and as he plotted and worked through it, Wrothgar grew stronger. Should this plan work, his power would increase a hundredfold, and it would not be long ere the Light would fail.

Wrothgar was pleased that Gorgon Elfhunter had not been cast into the Void. Gorgon had been defeated—there was no question of that—but it was only in defeat that Wrothgar could assert any control over him at all. He preferred to think of Gorgon's defeat as a trial by fire, tempering the steel that is forged into a blade. Now the metal was ready to accept the maker's hand.

Wrothgar knew that Gorgon's pride had suffered a near-fatal blow in the conflict with Gaelen, the Wood-elf who somehow managed always to defeat him despite all expectation to the contrary. The Elfhunter needed aid—now more than ever—and Wrothgar could provide it.

There was a spirit whose evil nature was second only to Wrothgar's own, and that spirit moved always at his bidding. It dwelled in the lands known now as Aeglainor, the Realm of Grief, to the Elves, D'hanar to the dwarves, and the Fell-ruin among men. This was the ruin of Tal-elathas, and it was a place of evil and despair. Long had Wrothgar kept his stronghold there, until he had been driven forth by Ri-Elathan's army in the Third Battle. That conflict had cost Ri-Elathan his life.

Wrothgar would not return to the Fell-ruins, for the memory of his defeat sapped his strength and took his confidence. Yet the dark spirit of Lord Kotos, one of the most powerful of the Asari, embraced those lands. He had seen his greatest triumph there, almost single-handedly bringing about the downfall of the Èolar. The ruins served to remind him of the terrible powers of deception and guile that were his to command.

Kotos had not been present during the Third Battle, instead directing Wrothgar's northern army to march on Tuathas, where it was defeated. But Kotos felt no shame or trepidation amid the twisted ruins of Tal-elathas. He had fled there after his defeat, and dwelt there ever after, growing stronger as he spread his evil magic upon the land. No creature of good will would ever dwell there again, and no Elf would even enter it without falling into an overwhelming heartsickness and despair.

The only thing that would ever cause Kotos to leave the Fell-ruin was the call of Wrothgar, his master. That call went forth now from Tûr Dorcha, as Kotos the Great Deceiver would be central to Wrothgar's plan.

Kotos would make his way there, although travel was difficult as he had no physical form. He could place his spirit within an object, such as a weapon, or he could inhabit the bodies of unwary folk. Once there, he asserted control over their will, guiding their actions to achieve his desires. When he reached his destination, he would leave them drained and with no memory of the experience. Sometimes they died, usually as the result of Kotos' failure to encourage them to eat and drink. As he had no such need himself, it was often neglected or forgotten. He would drive his victims forth often without rest for many days, for he cared not for their well-being.

Kotos could even inhabit the bodies of animals, but some were easier to control than others. He had been trapped once in the body of an owl for several weeks before a more suitable host came along. Ravens, on the other hand, could and did house Kotos' dark spirit, flying rapidly to wherever they were bidden. Kotos could even speak through them, for ravens may use human speech. Although they are usually neither good nor evil, the ravens that dwelt in the Fell-ruin were larger and more cunning than most, and they seemed to delight in mischief. They were prone to attack the weak and kill them for sport, not out of need.

The head of the largest clan of ravens in the Fell-ruin was a large, strong male named Kro-aark. It was a relatively common name, yet Kro-aark bore it with pride, for he was the favorite of the Dark Spirit, and sat always at his right hand.

Lord Kotos had told him that there was an important journey to be undertaken, and that he would need to make all speed in accomplishing it. The bird was instructed to don a heavy, golden amulet, placing it about his neck and grasping the bejeweled medallion in the talons of his right foot. He was given a good meal and a long drink, and then he shuddered and fluffed his feathers as the spirit of Kotos entered. He was then made aware of his path and his purpose, and he wasted no time in taking wing, lifting his heavy body with slow, deliberate strokes of his immense black wings, sailing into the choked, grey mist of morning.

Kotos did not take the most direct path to Tûr Dorcha, for he needed to make certain that he skirted the Elven-realms of Mountain-home and the Greatwood Forest. Elves have uncanny senses regarding messengers of darkness, and they would most likely shoot Kro-aark as he passed above them. He was a large target, nearly the size of a small eagle, and the amulet would be easily seen by their sharp eyes.

Thus, Kro-aark flew to the east of the Monadh-hin, crossing them to the north of Tal-sithian, flying into the south of the Darkmere. He had little difficulty until he drew near to the pale mists of the Tower, for a dim-witted Ulcan sentry could not resist practicing with his bow, and Kro-aark fell. Kotos could not move farther without a new host, but as Kro-aark lay upon the ground, the Ulcas approached, drawn to the amulet.

"Get back, you rabble! I'm the one shot the bird, and I'll be the one claiming the prize!" said the sentry. As he bent over to examine the amulet, he was taken with a nearly uncontrollable desire to put it around his own neck, though he did not understand why he should want to place such an object, so obviously Elven-made, anywhere on his person. The others shrank back, expecting their companion to wail in pain, for Ulcas do not bear the touch of Elf-wrought metal very well at all.

Do not be afraid, said a soothing voice inside the Ulca's mind. *This amulet will not pain you, but will comfort you. Do you not feel most wonderfully well at this moment? All your fears have passed from you. Go, now, and take it to the Shadowmancer. He will reward you for your faithful service.*

The Ulca paid no further attention to his fellows. He turned and moved to the Tower as though in a trance, his footsteps slow but deliberate, a faint smile on his twisted face. Once there, he was admitted without incident. Wrothgar knew why he had come.

Soon he stood inside the same polished, black chamber wherein Gorgon Elfhunter had first received his mirror, and the same fires burned gently in the center of it. Wrothgar was here, though the Ulca could not see him. The voice of Kotos came then through his lips unbidden. "Great Lord, I have come to serve. What is Thy Will?"

And the voice of Wrothgar answered. *Yea, Kotos, old friend and most faithful servant, the time has come for a great journey. At the end of it lies power unimaginable, but all thy strength will be needed. Dost thou still have thy powers of beguiling?*

The Ulca threw his head back and laughed then, even as he approached the fire. He first removed the precious amulet from around his neck and cast it aside. Then he strode to the lip of the fiery center and threw himself in without hesitation. As the spirit of Kotos left him, the Ulca screamed in pain and confusion, not having the slightest notion of why he was now falling to his death in a nearly bottomless chasm of fire. He could hear the roaring flames and his own wailing, but he could also hear the laughter of the two most evil beings in Alterra, their energies combining and swirling together in the dark chamber above him, reveling in their dark and wonderful plan.

Gaelen Taldin, Elf of the Greatwood Realm, stood alone beneath the desert stars, appearing small and slight before the great stone that had been set to mark what she had termed the "Grave of the Faithful." It was a monument to the fallen horses on both sides of the battle, who had given their lives in the service of others, for they had not been given the choice of whether to fight. The carcasses had been burned in this place, piled high and set aflame, the smoke billowing all the way to heaven. Finan's had been among them. Gaelen reached out to the stone, which had been inscribed with words she had written.

Here lie the ashes of the faithful.
They served without question, and died therefore with honor.
Green grass and sweet water be theirs for all days.

Artisans had carved a likeness of a beautiful horse's head, but it did not cheer Gaelen as she gazed now into the dead stone eye. She traced the carved words with her slender fingers, and then laid her palm flat against the cool, grey surface. Then she began to sing:

Mahogany and ebony
Dark flag raised to the wind,
Mane of spun smoke shades my eyes
Why did you have to end?

Wind-drinker, spurner of the earth
Ever-loyal friend,
Through lands of fire we moved as one
Why did you have to end?

My faith in you was steadfast
Your worth was plain to see
My love for you was strong and deep
As was your faith in me.

Our time together dwindled
Like the fire in your eye
When the dragon-fire was kindled
Why did you have to die?

Now my wings have left me
And I can no longer fly
Though I may ride, my heart is dark
Why did you have to die?

You were always there to hear me
When my troubles I would share,
When I travel to the Far Shores
I hope to find you there.

Upon that day my heart will soar
And I shall fly again
As we ride together, you and I
Beyond the World's End.

When the song ended, she blinked back tears, though she knew she did not need to hide her feelings from Finan. "My friend, I trust you are resting and enjoying your reward. I miss you terribly, every day." She swallowed hard. "I suppose I shall now need to find another mount, for Siva is in foal. I don't know whether the offspring she carries is yours, but I pray each day that it is so. I will come and tell you when I am certain."

She backed away from the stone for a moment, unsure of how to say what was in her heart. At last, she closed her eyes and whispered, as much to herself as to Finan. "There will never be another to replace you. I shall be forever diminished without you. I will not truly give my heart to another mount. I shall come back and speak to you upon another time."

She turned then and left the stone, pausing only once to look back in the hopes that she would see a vision of her beloved Finan or hear his voice again, but she was denied, hearing only the wind upon the sand.

Lady Ordath, daughter of Shandor the Asarla and Liathwyn of the Èolar, had sensed disquiet in the air for some time now. A feeling had taken hold...something stirring in the hard lands to the north. She had heard the wind lamenting and the rain clouds sighing, as if they would warn of some threatening darkness. They had borne silent witness to the emergence and flight of Kotos, and they spoke to Ordath, for the winds and waters were a part of her dominion. Was this feeling true? If so, what was the meaning of it?

She found herself longing to gaze into the Stone of Léir, to commune with her beloved father, Shandor, and gain enlightenment from him. Taken with a great melancholy, she sought refuge below the bright gardens of Mountain-home, making her way to a deep, cool chamber of stone. Within it, Shandor's body lay un-withered in a tomb of clear, crystal glass. An Èolarin lamp blazed bright blue as the torchlight reached it, but though the light that it gave was welcome, it was cold and without life.

Ordath approached the body of her father, which lay as he had left it, serene and peaceful upon first glance. Only when one looked into the frozen, crystal-blue eyes could the torment be clearly seen.

Tall and well-made, Shandor had lost none of his condition through these long, long years. His hair was of silver, as with many of the Asari, and it lay like a gleaming river, long and silken, about his finely-chiseled face and powerful shoulders. There was strength in every aspect of his physical being, but it was bereft of spirit, useless and unmoving. Tears came to Ordath, as they always did when she beheld him, for she loved him dearly and would have seen him restored. She also knew this would not be, for he had chosen to inhabit the Stone of Léir that he might live forever in his memories.

"Tell me the meaning of this foreboding," she whispered, knowing that no response would be forthcoming. "Please, father…I need counsel. I need the aid of those who see what I cannot. If darkness is stirring, if the Deceiver is abroad again, our people must be ready. Are my fears real, or no? Tell me what I must do."

Shandor, of course, did not answer, for he was not there. His spirit was far away on the Isle of Tal-sithian under the watchful eye of Lady Arialde, his kin. The mantle had fallen onto Lady Ordath, and there would be none to lift the burden from her, no matter how fervently she wished for it.

3
The Challenge of Lord Kotos

Wrothgar appointed his finest Ulcan guardsman to serve as host for Lord Kotos' journey. Fairly tall, straight-legged and strong, he held more courage than most. The strength would be needed, but courage would not matter, as Kotos ruled the actions and the spirit of his host, who would, if so commanded, throw himself into fire as the last had done.

Ulcas made excellent hosts, as they were not afflicted with the tendency to act independently, and were easily led. This one stood with the amulet in his hand as Kotos entered him, encountering no resistance.

Once there, Kotos commanded the Ulca to place the amulet around his neck, whereupon a most wondrous thing happened. The guardsman transformed, his shape shifting into that of a tall, strong man. He appeared to have hair on his head and face, something which no Ulca has, and his gaze was no longer threatening or malicious. Kotos, who directed the transformation, did not wish for his host to attract attention, and so the "man" appeared dressed in plain clothing, as a wayfarer of no great significance.

The amulet had served well for years uncounted. Originally crafted by Léiras for the purpose of allowing the High King's chosen emissary to infiltrate enemy lands of without suspicion, the amulet was later improved by Dardis of the Èolar, who, as with all his folk, could not resist endowing it with greater power simply because it was within his ability to do so. Dardis eventually learned to restrain his desires, and he gained enough wisdom to know that his talents should not be toyed with, but by then it was too late.

In the absence of a living host, Kotos would place his own spirit within the amulet, which had been completely corrupted by him. At first the amulet would serve only those loyal to the High King, but over time Kotos had beguiled it, as he did all things that possessed any spirit of their own. It was his great gift.

The amulet was beautiful, at first glance rather plain until one looked closely, whereupon the intricacy of the golden medallion surrounding the central stone could be seen. The stone, a deep golden topaz, faceted and brilliant, was nearly as hard as adamant. The golden setting was not marred despite its age, and the golden chain would not break. It had traveled the western and northern regions of Alterra for ages now.

Kotos had worn it always. It had allowed him to alter his appearance as he desired, which was of great benefit, for he could not assume a fair semblance without it. In reality he had been frightful to behold.

Since the Third Battle, Kotos could no longer take physical form. He had thought to destroy the northern realm of Tuathas, but the northmen had overcome his dark legions, trapping Kotos and rending his body into small pieces. But his immortal spirit, though defeated, could not be overcome. It fled with the remnants of his army, carried within the great golden jewel in the heart of the amulet.

One of his captains bore the amulet, but he soon fell to the cold and lack of food, and the amulet had been lost, covered with snow and ice for many years. The spirit of Kotos remained within, for he would not be separated from his most precious possession.

At last Kotos had sensed the approach of a suitable carrier. A mountain-troll drew near, and Kotos revealed the amulet, using his power to melt away the covering of snow and ice. It is well known that trolls cannot resist the lure of golden things, and this one was no different. It picked up the amulet as intended, and Kotos then directed it to the ruins of Tal-elathas, for it was there that the forces of Darkness were strongest. In that forlorn place Kotos made his home, directing the evil creatures that dwelled there to build his new fortress, willing them into his service. Any that resisted were tormented and then slain as an example to those that remained, and soon Kotos had surrounded himself with a company of submissive, if not truly loyal, followers. As Kotos' strength increased, the larger and more formidable this company became, as nothing attracts evil as surely as the promise of power.

Now Kotos had important work to do. Lord Wrothgar had charged him with the task of locating Gorgon Elfhunter, and of convincing him to become the physical instrument by which a carefully orchestrated plan would be achieved. This plan, if successful, would ultimately result in the downfall of the servants of the Light in Alterra, but it was a complex plan, with many twists and turns that could so easily come undone. Kotos would need all of his powers of persuasion—even the first task, that of convincing Gorgon Elfhunter to serve, would be daunting enough.

Then there was the matter of Gaelen Taldin, the Wood-elf who had faced Gorgon at the edge of the Void. Kotos would try to avoid her, for she would surely see through a mere physical disguise. It was his belief that if he controlled Gorgon, Gaelen would not know him. If not, if she knew Gorgon despite all efforts, Kotos would slay her at once. After all, he had slain many Elves in his very long life. Gentle Dardis, the greatest creative light of the Èolar, had been taken easily, his wide eyes filled with astonishment and disbelief that his friend Kotos would ever betray him so. It had been easy to throttle the life from him, and this She-elf was surely much smaller and weaker.

Had Gorgon borne witness to these thoughts, he would surely have seen the folly in them, for though it was true that Gaelen was both smaller and weaker, Dardis had not her wary nature, nor her insight, nor her accursed determination.

Kotos had been directed to complete the southward journey as soon as possible, for Lord Wrothgar knew that Gorgon would be most easily taken into the plan before he truly found his feet again. There was always a risk that his enemies might find the Elfhunter and slay him before he could be of service, though that risk was small. Therefore, the hosts that bore Kotos' dark spirit would be driven with little rest, and there could be no mistakes. It was not beyond possibility that the trail would be lost, the host dying in some forsaken area of the Ravi-shan, and Kotos might then be adrift for years without a suitable host. Wrothgar would not be at all pleased should that happen. Even Kotos feared Lord Wrothgar.

As the Man-Ulca went forth from the Tower, Kotos soothed his fears at venturing alone into the wild. *You will be known as Aleck, the blacksmith. You'll be most convincing, for I am a fine worker of metals, oh, yes indeed! We will have no trouble.*

In the person of Aleck, Kotos made his way to Dûn Bennas, traveling by night, there to place himself briefly in the service of the King and pick up a new host, preferably a man, who would be much better suited to the southern journey.

The next host was a good man, Vartan by name, who was possessed of an unfortunate gambling problem and, therefore, a great deal of debt. Kotos, in the person of "Aleck," waited for Vartan as he returned home late at night, and spoke to him as he passed by.

"Vartan, man of the King's guard, would you absolve your debt this night?"

Vartan was suspicious, and a little alarmed. "How know you of any debt? Show yourself, that you may explain this bold question."

Kotos stepped into the torchlight. "I am Aleck, master metal-smith, temporarily in the King's service. I ask you the question once more...will you absolve your debt? It matters not how I know of it, but I bear a gift that will lift this burden from you if you will only accept it. Behold! Here is a trinket worth a Queen's dowry." He stepped closer, so that Vartan could see the amulet around his neck.

It was obviously of great value, and Vartan desired it more than anything. Yet he was still unwilling to trust Aleck.

"Are you saying you would give that golden thing that I might be released from debt? Why, in the name of heaven, should you do so?"

"Because I was once as you are now. I could not keep from wagering, and I nearly lost all happiness as a result. The kindness of a stranger saved me, and I save you now, to pay my debt to him." As Kotos sent forth these words, they nearly sickened him. The thought of sacrificing for the sake of another was a repugnant notion, but he knew that it made for a most convincing lie.

Vartan hesitated for a moment longer, and then extended his hand. It would be such a relief to be free of his burden. "Prove yourself, then, and give me the trinket. I will accept your aid, and will promise to free another man from the same burden, should I ever encounter one." The golden light of the stone flickered in the darkness of Vartan's eyes as he reached for it. Aleck did not move, but bowed his head as though inviting Vartan to remove the amulet.

The moment it left the Aleck's neck, two things came to pass. The spirit of Kotos flooded into Vartan, overpowering him, and Aleck plunged a blade deep into his own vitals, obeying Kotos' final command. Vartan then found himself in a near-swoon, staring in confusion at a hideous, dying Ulca that had suddenly appeared before him. The Ulca's frightened eyes darted this way and that, and a moan of pain and utter bewilderment came forth as his life left him. He sagged down onto the cobbled walkway, his dark blood mingling with the rain that had begun to fall, as Kotos, now in the person of Vartan, smiled in the dark.

After dragging the Ulca into the shadows, concealing the body in a place that would not be discovered for several days, Vartan went back to his own dwelling and gathered provisions. Thankfully, he had no family to come searching for him. Vartan would be leaving at dawn's first light, and by the time anyone missed Aleck, Kotos was well on his way again. The dead Ulca that was eventually found in the City both puzzled and dismayed the people, but it was a mystery that would remain unsolved.

The sun had not yet risen and the pale moon still held sway over the desert lands when the harness-bells of the trader's caravan first were heard. The edges of the sands were pale, like the moon, with a sort of weird, bluish light. The ever-present moan of the wind served as a mournful counterpart to the tinkling bells; some were high and silvery, like water flowing from a spring, while others held deeper, coppery tones more reminiscent of the sound of stones being cast into a deep well.

Kotos had driven Vartan deep into the desert, and they had run out of water nearly two days ago. Now water was all Vartan could think of, for he was dying of thirst. Still, Kotos reassured him, and he shivered in the chill night air, drew his cloak about him, and waited patiently. Soon he was rewarded with the sight of many horses and several dromadin moving steadily on a course to the southeast. *There is our salvation,* said Kotos. *Call to them, and make certain they see you.*

Vartan struggled to his feet and hailed them with what was nearly his last strength, calling out in a voice cracked by thirst, waving both hands in the air. To his relief, the leader of the caravan turned toward him—he had been seen.

The horses were tied head-to-tail; apparently the trader was a horse-merchant. He rode slowly and deliberately forward to stand before Vartan, looking down upon him with disdain.

"*Another* helpless northman? What forces keep driving your folk out here, into the southlands? You should curse them, my friend!" He laughed in an ill-natured way, rubbing his cold hands together. "The name is Radeef, humble purveyor of fine horse-flesh. How may I serve you?"

Kotos sized him up in an instant, and smiled to himself. That smile was visible for just a moment on the face of Vartan, and it did not match the tormented look in his eyes.

It made Radeef wonder whether this man had lost his reason. "How might I assist you, O obviously-lost-and-forlorn northman? Is it water you desire? If so, then take some now, before you pass from the world before my eyes."

Radeef, a superstitious man, would not refuse water to a dying man in the desert, for to do so would no doubt curse him forever, along with his equally disreputable family. "Drink your fill, northman," he said. "Saving your life will keep the Wheel turning in my favor. One never knows what spirits lurk in these lands, lying in wait to trap unwary souls."

What spirits, indeed, thought Kotos.

The northman accepted the water-skin and drank thankfully, taking slow, deliberate swallows of water, feeling some vitality flow back into his dried, sunburned flesh. "I…I need a horse," he said at last to Radeef. "I will not survive without one. Please, might I trade for one of yours?"

"Of course!" laughed Radeef, as he continued to rub his hands together. "But these animals were dearly bought, and have journeyed long. I will not part with them for nothing. What have you to trade?" He smiled as he remembered the result of his last trading encounter with northern folk. It had ended with ten gold pieces to the good, for an animal of no value. It had been one of the best trades he had ever made.

"I have my sword, and it is of very fine make," said the northman. He handed the blade hilt-first to Radeef, but first he made certain that the golden amulet was now visible from beneath his sweat-stained shirt. Radeef caught sight of it, and he lost his breath for a moment. He quickly hid this error through a small fit of coughing.

"Gnats," he said, waving his hand before his eyes. "Those accursed gnats. Sometimes they fly where they shouldn't, eh?" He examined the sword, but then handed it back. "Sorry, I am not interested. I have enough weapons already. What else have you to trade?"

"I have nothing else. Please…I am desperate. Would you truly condemn me to death for want of your most wretched animal? Please, if you are a good man, help me." At this point suppressed laughter was heard from Radeef's men, who had gathered nearby.

"If you are truly desperate, Northman, then you do have something else. That golden thing around your neck, for example… might I see it? It will be of little value to your poor, dead self. If it pleases me, I will trade for it."

"You may see it," was the reply, "but I will not give it into another man's hand. You must stand before me and examine it, if you would take it."

Radeef commanded his dromadan to kneel before the northman, knowing that he would not be harmed. His men knew of no such thing—they clucked and shook their heads at their master's foolishness, keeping weapons at the ready.

"It's bcautiful," said Radeef, "but of questionable worth. The stone is actually rather ordinary. I will trade for a horse of my own selection. What say you?"

Tears actually welled in Vartan's eyes, though they had been difficult for Kotos to muster. "This has been in my family for generations, and it is of Elven-make. It was passed to me by my father upon his death, and I had hoped to pass it to my sons," he said.

"Yet you will pass it only to the desert if you have passed yourself," said Radeef. He had already decided that the amulet would be his, one way or another. It was the most beautiful object he had ever beheld.

"You wound me to the heart," said Vartan in a broken voice. "Yet you have already saved my life with the gift of water, and you are right. Beautiful things are of no use to a dead man. Take the amulet, then, and much joy may it bring you." He bowed his head so that Radeef could take his prize.

Kotos remained with Vartan long enough to receive Radeef's selection, a raw-boned but relatively sound grey gelding, together with a full water-skin. "It's not much water," said Radeef. "You will need to make your way to an oasis quickly. Follow the Ravani Road to the Sandstone settlement. It is not too far away…you will soon see it on the horizon. Make for the great red rock! Farewell, and safe journey to you."

Radeef's men laughed again, for they knew the truth. The Sandstone was still nearly a hundred difficult miles away. This hapless northman would never make it with only one skin of water, yet he seemed not to know, or care.

"In my country, a man shakes hands when a bargain is made," he said, "or there is no bargain. Men must trust one another that much. Will you shake my hand?"

"If I must," said a wary Radeef, spitting first into his own hand before extending it. Vartan did the same. When the two men clasped hands, Kotos occupied Radeef easily, as the dark spirit with which the merchant was endowed offered no resistance to the evil that now flowed into him; it seemed to fit his nature. At first, he was hardly even aware of it.

Vartan, on the other hand, went pale as his strength left him. He sank down onto the sand and moaned, looking around as though he had just awakened from a nightmare.

Radeef took notice, but he did not spend much time in wondering. He was unaccustomed to caring for the troubles of others. *A good thing*, thought Kotos, *for otherwise my new host might have become suspicious.* As it was, Radeef merely laughed.

"Farewell, my hapless northern friend. You have served me well, but now I must leave you. Good luck with the desert, and remember, the Sandstone is very close now. You'll make it!"

He rode forth laughing, as did his fellows, for they had many miles to cover ere they reached water themselves. One of the men lingered, handing Vartan another water-skin in a manner that would not be seen by his fellows, for he was a good man, and he knew Radeef had condemned both man and horse to death otherwise.

It would be several hours and quite a few miles before Radeef would realize that Vartan had gotten the best of the trade. It would seem that honest men were not the only ones who could easily be led astray.

In the fair city of Dûn Arian, the recovery continued. Nelwyn ran her fingers through her long, silken hair as she stood beside Estle, who had become a close friend during this time of trial. Estle fluffed her own hair with the heels of both hands. She would not be able to run her fingers through it as Nelwyn had done, for it was almost wooly in texture and it tended to tangle severely in the damp coastal air. *Never mind…Hallagond seems to like it, and that's all that matters.* Estle tied a bright silk scarf of green and blue around her head, squared her shoulders, and turned to Nelwyn.

"Are you certain of this?" she asked.

"No, I am not certain," said Nelwyn. "I only know that Gaelen is desperately unhappy at the loss of Finan, and now she will not ride Siva. She is unmounted, and that cannot stand, for if she must journey forth she will need a reliable partner. She has convinced herself that there will be no replacing Finan, and she has not ridden since he left her. We must get her back on a horse, and soon."

They stood before the stables, awaiting the arrival of the Master of Horse, a short, barrel-chested man named Khandor. The product of a northern father and a mother descended of Khazi-folk, he had broad, rather eastern features, and his lively brown eyes sparkled with good humor. He reminded Estle of a tall, dark version of Fima, save that Khandor had only a thin, wispy beard and mustache. He was an exceptional rider, as were nearly all Khazi-folk, and he had ridden out with various members of the Company on occasion. He had fought beside them against the Scourge, riding with Ali, who had been his close friend. Now he favored Nelwyn and Estle with a broad smile, for he knew why they had come.

"Well, my fine friends, shall we get to it? We haven't much time before you will both be missed at breakfast. Let me show you what I have available."

He led Nelwyn and Estle to his holding yards, where many new animals were gathered. These were the survivors of the battle; the Scourge's horses had been collected and were now thriving in their new home. Still, the hardship of the desert crossing had marked them, and most were still healing from battle wounds.

"Do you see any here that please you?"

Nelwyn shook her head. "None that truly stand out. And I must say that Gaelen is very difficult to impress when it comes to the matter of horse-flesh. She would not choose any of them, alas." She turned to Khandor. "If we are to convince her, this new mount must be fine indeed. And under no circumstances should it look anything like Finan."

Khandor nodded, his normally lighthearted demeanor now solemn. He knew the tale of Finan and his valiant final stand against the dragon. He had rarely known of a horse so loyal, or a rider so devoted. This would be a difficult bond to reestablish.

"Let me show you something special," he said at once, his face brightening. "We shall need the most special animal for your Gaelen."

He conducted his hopeful visitors round the back of the yards, past the cobbled courtyard and the neatly white-washed stone stables to a small enclosure with its own attached shed. Khandor whistled softly, and a most impressive young horse appeared in the doorway. Silver-grey in color, he had a proud, handsome head and a lovely soft eye. His legs were very correct and strong; he looked as though he could carry Rogond and Hallagond together. He resembled Eros in size and strength, but his coat was fine and silky like the Ravani-bred animals. He was magnificent.

"Where have you been hiding this animal?" asked Nelwyn. "I surely would have noticed him…he is beautiful! Yet I cannot determine his breeding. He is much too large for a desert-bred. What is he?"

"I honestly do not know," Khandor replied. "He is branded on the left hip, but no one here seems to know the design. He came in from the desert one day, his teeth said that he was only two years old then, and he is now five. At least, his body is five…he seems to have the mind of a much younger animal. That's why we don't yet ride him in battle, though he can be ridden. He trained easily, but he cannot resist playing about, hence he is not yet suitable as a war-horse. I had planned to put him over a few mares this season, but there should be plenty of time for that. Do you think Gaelen would accept him?"

"Gaelen?" said Estle with a slow shake of her head. "*Our* Gaelen, ride that huge animal? I very much doubt it."

"Is he swift?" asked Nelwyn. "There is no doubting his strength, but he will need to be both handy and swift for Gaelen to accept him. He must move very, very well."

"We don't know how swift he is, for he is untested," said Khandor, "but he moves like a dancer and he is incredibly light-footed. Watch him now and see."

He took a long whip and cracked it several times. The grey was not impressed at first, looking a little puzzled, but then he began to move about the enclosure in a very fluid, graceful manner that belied the power beneath. He seemed to float above the ground rather than tread upon it. He never took his eyes from Khandor, and as soon as the whip was lowered, he trotted right up to the Master of Horse and jostled him with his large head, nearly bowling him over. "You see how he moves, and you also see that he's a friendly sort," said Khandor, waving the animal off so that he would not be knocked down. "What do you think of him?"

"Most impressive," said Nelwyn. "I have rarely seen a better mover. I don't know whether Gaelen will like him, but she will not deny his quality." The grey now followed behind Khandor, grabbing playfully at his collar and snatching at his hair. Nelwyn smiled. "He seems personable enough, and he is certainly different from Finan. I say, what is the harm in asking her?"

"I will place a wager right now," said Estle. "Gaelen will want nothing whatever to do with this huge, silly animal, and the suggestion will no doubt make her angry. That is my prediction."

"Quite the optimistic view, may I say," said Khandor. He had climbed out of the enclosure to escape the unwanted attentions of the grey, who was now nodding his long head up and down, beseeching Khandor to return and continue the game. "All she need do is say no. No one will force her to take him. He is a fine animal, and very special. He is young, and admittedly foolish, but is as good-hearted as they come. I do not give him up easily, but to Gaelen—and only to Gaelen—I will give him willingly."

"Fair enough, but might I suggest a different approach?" said Estle.

They listened to her suggestion, and all agreed it was a good one. Nelwyn would bring Gaelen by later that morning, after breakfast.

Khandor bowed before Gaelen, welcoming her. "I truly need your assistance," he said. "I would have your view concerning the worth of this animal as a future herd sire. He is untested, and none of my riders can convince him to perform at his best. I believe he has speed as yet untapped, and I require an educated and perceptive opinion. Will you aid me?"

Gaelen both liked and respected Khandor, and she would not refuse him. Yet she thought his request curious. "Why ask my opinion?" she said. "You are most perceptive and educated yourself. Why involve me?"

Khandor spread his hands. "Because, to be honest, my assistant and I do not agree, and I was hoping you could settle our dispute. You see, my First Rider believes that the grey is simply lazy, and that he should be taken out and ridden to within an inch of exhaustion to teach him a good lesson. I, on the other hand, believe in a more conservative approach. My difficulty is that I do not have the time to ride him, and my First Rider obviously does not have the patience. We need to get this animal fit and tested before the next breeding season, and I fear he may break down if I allow my First Rider to take him over."

Khandor sighed dramatically, looking sidelong at Gaelen, who was now focused upon the grey. "If only you would ride him, and oversee his training, I would be most grateful. I would pay you handsomely, as well. Lord Salastor has authorized this himself, as he recognizes the value of the animal."

Gaelen could not deny the young stallion's quality, even as Nelwyn had predicted. Yet a look of great sadness came over her, and she turned away. "I…I don't know, Khandor. I'm flattered by your trust in me, and yet I don't know whether I can do what you require. Ask Nelwyn. She is a wonderful rider with a gentle hand."

"I have asked her already," Khandor replied, his voice both solemn and kind. "She tells me that you have the skills to bring the fire out of the animal, and she does not. He needs the Fire-heart to bring out the strength I know he possesses. Nelwyn will not do."

He moved to stand beside Gaelen, speaking so that only she would hear. "I know your heart and your spirit are diminished, and that you do not wish to ride again. Yet I need your help, and you must ride sooner or later. No one is trying to replace what you have lost, for we know that we cannot. Take my request for what it is."

Gaelen turned away from Khandor for a moment, and then turned back to face him. "I need some time to consider this," she said. "When I have considered, I will find you." She bowed and turned to leave, but he called after her.

"Both this horse and I need your aid. Consider well, and return as you wish. Take him and try him. He is yours until you say he isn't."

Gaelen did not reply, but walked slowly through the gate. Just before she moved from sight, however, she turned back for a last look at the beautiful grey, and Khandor smiled to himself. He had done a good job.

Radeef had stolen away from his fellows as they slept, mounting his puzzled dromadan and urging it to its feet as the moon rose high above him. He would never have chosen this course—it had been chosen for him. He had provided well for himself, taking much of the remaining water, and had at first thought to ride the swiftest of the horses, for something told him that he needed to make for the Sandstone settlement with all speed. Yet none of the horses would suffer him.

Kotos knew it, for he was no friend of horses. Maddeningly perceptive beasts, they would not allow such an evil spirit to approach them. Dromadin, on the other hand, were not so particular, and neither man nor beast had any notion of the dark force that now drove them.

Radeef's men would awaken to find that their master had gone, taking much of their water, having bludgeoned the one keeping watch. They could not follow, for they did not have enough water; they would need to make their way to the nearest oasis. Radeef had taken only his own valuables, and this confused his men even more, as they would have expected him to rob them as they slept. Yet Radeef now had only one possession that he truly cared about—the golden amulet that now hung about his neck.

He urged his laboring dromadan toward the south, a part of him wondering why in the world he should make for the Sandstone, while the rest of him knew, beyond a certainty, that he must.

"*Ehhya!*"

Gaelen had just about lost her patience with the grey, and that did not happen often. *He is so unlike other horses...even the young ones have outgrown such irrepressible playfulness by the time they're three, let alone five. This one reminds me more of a puppy than a horse.*

She had limited experience with dogs, although Ri-Aruin kept several kennels hunting-hounds. They were huge, leggy, shaggy creatures with little humor about them, but their pups were playful and winsome, as with all dogs. Wellyn had once taken Gaelen to visit the kennels so that she could play with a litter of ten half-grown pups. They had swarmed all over her and knocked her down, surrounding her with a forest of lolling pink tongues and frantic, whiplike tails, licking and pawing at her until she nearly panicked. They had pinned her to the ground with their large, hairy feet, and she struggled to escape, though she knew they meant no harm. She burst into nervous laughter as Wellyn waded in to rescue her. He was still very young, yet he was much taller than she, and had little difficulty. When the pups stood on their hind legs, they were taller than Gaelen, who was by then covered with hair, slobber, and lord-knew-what-else. She did not remember the experience as a pleasant one.

This young animal was much the same. Unlike her beloved Finan and gentle, worthy Siva, the grey had little dignity about him. He would not stop nuzzling and nibbling and snatching at her with his teeth, rubbing at her with his large, boney head, following her everywhere and grabbing at her things. He had stolen a comb from her pack and was now walking around the enclosure as though he had taken a great prize. *Well, fine,* thought Gaelen. *Let your mane remain tangled, then!*

She called to him and he turned toward her, still carrying the comb in his mouth. She smiled in spite of herself, but quickly regained her serious attitude and called him to her again. *Might as well get this over with…*

The grey still carried his prized comb, flipping his head up and down while chewing on the handle, as Gaelen grasped his unkempt mane and swung onto his back. She gave a small grunt of effort—this horse was much taller than she was accustomed to.

Typically, as with most of her kin, she experienced an immediate bonding between rider and horse. Yet this one felt large and strange beneath her, and she did not feel a part of him. He did not respond in the way she expected; he was still fixed on playing with the comb and paid her little heed. He began to wander around the paddock, though she asked him to stand. And now, here were Nelwyn and Khandor at the rail to witness the humiliation.

Gaelen muttered under her breath. "You huge, ridiculous puppy, attend me at once, or we shall have harsh words!" *How dare he take me so lightly? How dare he be so beautiful, yet so…wrong? How dare he try to replace Finan!*

Her frustration welled over and she did a most unusual thing, digging her heels into the grey, startling him. He reacted by leaping forward, unseating Gaelen, who did not have her seat and was not expecting the speed and power of his response. She did not even land on her feet, but hit the ground spraddle-legged, raising a sizeable cloud of dust. Both Nelwyn and Khandor gasped in surprise, and then winced. That landing hurt—no question about it.

"I have rarely seen Gaelen unseated in all the years I've known her," Nelwyn muttered. "This is far worse than I thought."

"Give her time. She'll come around," whispered Khandor. "That rascal has a way of getting to you. It's almost as if he annoys you into surrendering." He called out to Gaelen. "Are you all right?"

Gaelen was already on her feet, and her face and ears flushed. She had treated her friends to a sight they had thought never to see. The grey stood facing her, waving his tail gently, regarding her with large, soft eyes. He lowered his head and chortled at her, his message clear. *I'm sorry...I did not mean to unseat you, but something startled me. Will you not ride again?*

He walked up to her and offered his head to be scratched.

Gaelen obliged him, rubbing his ears with her long, clever fingers. "I know better than to startle you. I don't know what came over me...this is not your fault. And now, though I would just as soon never mount you again, I must do so, for my friends are watching and I know they expect it of me. I promise not to startle you again." She sighed and patted his smooth, shiny neck, then walked around beside him and swung aboard. He stepped off immediately, striding forward with grace and power, as she stroked his neck and spoke encouraging words.

"Open the paddock gate," she called to Khandor. "I cannot try him properly in such a small space."

"Are you certain of this?" asked Nelwyn, who worried that her cousin might end up on the ground again.

"No, I'm not certain, but I need to try this animal, and I cannot do it in a small space. Besides, as a friend once said, one must die of something!"

She quirked a half-smile at Nelwyn and urged the grey forward. He responded well, engaging his hindquarters and moving off at about half speed. Gaelen headed for the harbor; there was a long stretch of flat going where the ground was not too sandy, yet it was soft. It would be an excellent place to try him.

Neither Nelwyn nor Khandor would see Gaelen for many hours. She returned as evening approached, flushed and in good spirits. The grey had been playing in the surf for over an hour. Gaelen had given him a good run and then thought to soak his legs, but he insisted on trying to leap into the approaching foam, chasing it as it retreated. This game had worn him out, and he had actually unseated Gaelen once more as he leaped sideways in the churning water...she was still wet. She handed the lead-line over to Khandor. "You have a swift horse, and he will be a worthy mount...*if* he ever settles down."

Khandor bowed before Gaelen and closed the paddock gate. "My thanks, but your task is not ended. Please train him and make him fit, so that he can prove his worth. It's my belief that he will make the perfect mount for Lord Salastor, but not without a rider that has the skill to educate him. Please, will you be his teacher?"

Gaelen thought for a moment. "I will see what I can arrange," she said. Before she left she turned to the grey, who was standing quietly by. "Thank you for lifting my spirits, young one. You have given me some happiness this day, against all expectation. Perhaps tomorrow I will return and we shall continue our lessons. Remember, not so foolish the next time!" She patted him once more, shaking her head as he tried to grab her sleeve.

Nelwyn and Rogond both noticed the change in Gaelen when she returned to their chambers and took supper with them. She was lighthearted, with more energy than they had seen in a long while. Nelwyn smiled to herself. There was one thing that would put Gaelen right quicker than any other, and that was a good ride on a fine horse.

Radeef stayed in the Sandstone only as long as required. He sold his dromadan, acquiring enough silver to provide for himself until he could gain news of the Company's path. In response to his inquiries he was advised to seek out Hari, the horse-provider, for some of the strangers had been in his employ. Radeef and Hari knew one another by reputation, for they shared the same trade, though they were on very different sides of it.

As soon as Radeef entered his yards, Hari disliked him. The horses stood disquieted with tails raised; a few snorted and struck at the ground, alerting the others. This man was not welcome.

Undaunted, Radeef introduced himself, bowing before Hari, who called to his horse-breaker, for he didn't want to be alone with Radeef for some reason.

Though the horse-breaker was a stout, strong man, Radeef was not the least bit intimidated. "I understand you might have news of some friends of mine," he said. "They passed this way some months ago, and I have been following after them, for I would bring news of the man they are seeking."

"What strangers? What were their names?" asked Hari.

"I do not know their names," Radeef admitted, for neither he nor Kotos knew them. "But they were seeking a man named Hallagond. They will want the information I have to give. Will you not aid me?"

"I know of you, Radeef," said Hari in a cold voice. "I cannot imagine that you would go to any great lengths to help anyone other than yourself. I do not trust your intentions regarding my friends, and since you do not even know their names, I doubt they are friends of yours. There are those here who would pay to harm them. I'm sorry, but I can tell you nothing."

"Ah, well, at least I made an effort," said Radeef. "Perhaps you will be convinced when I show you this amulet, which once belonged to the man they seek. Look upon it...is it not of great worth?" Radeef took the amulet from around his neck and extended it toward Hari, who marveled at its beauty.

"Go on, take it," said Radeef. "I trust you will give it back. A thing of such beauty comes not often to one's eye. Take it and look with care."

Hari could not stop himself...he wanted to look closely at the amulet. He wanted to hold it and feel the cool smoothness of it. He wanted to see the beautiful, intricate engraving. He wanted to *possess* it.

The moment Hari touched the golden thing, Kotos could see into his mind. He flowed from Radeef into Hari, who had not expected such things and was taken aback, clutching at the amulet and gasping.

"What devilry is this!" said Hari's horse-breaker, thinking that his employer had been bewitched. Hari stared blankly ahead, then swallowed hard, blinking as tears started in his dark eyes. Kotos left him, flowing back into the amulet, commanding Radeef to place it once more about his neck.

"What devilry?" Radeef replied, composing himself as he once again shared consciousness with Lord Kotos. "Your master was obviously overcome by the beauty of the amulet, nothing more. It can affect some folk that way. You see? He has recovered his wits already. Since you will not provide me with the information I seek, I will take my leave of you. But if the Company returns to this place, and they still have not found Hallagond, tell them of the amulet, won't you?" Radeef smiled and bowed, and then he left them.

Hari would remember nothing of the amulet other than its beauty, and when he returned home that evening he said nothing of the encounter with Radeef to his wife. He insisted on washing not only his feet, hands, and face, as was customary, but his entire body. Despite this effort, he still went to his bed feeling as though he would never truly be clean again.

Kotos had learned what he needed to know in his brief encounter with Hari. Honest men did not guard their thoughts, though this one had been wary. Although he had not known of the Company's path when they departed in haste from the Sandstone, Hari had since learned from those traveling to and from the Chupa oasis that the Company had gone there, and so Radeef would leave at once. He stole a dromadan, earning himself a death sentence should he ever encounter its rightful owner, and headed out into the starlit night.

It took longer than expected to reach the Chupa oasis, and by the time he did, Radeef was in a bad way. Both he and his animal were exhausted and nearly mad with thirst, for they had pressed hard day and night, and had taken little rest. Radeef had underestimated the amount of water he would need, and to make matters worse, one of the water-skins had leaked. He had hoped never to feel such thirst…it was as if his guts had shriveled inside skin that now hung on him like a wrinkled parchment. His throat was nearly glued shut, and his eyes felt as though they would be rasped away inside their sockets.

His dromadan had fared no better, for it had been laboring hard. Now its steps were halting and its breath whistled in the dusty air. It had acquired a deep, dry cough that told the tale…without water the beast would die within a day.

Kotos still urged Radeef forward, for to rest now would probably mean the death of his host. He was disgusted with the weakness of this man, supposedly so wise to desert ways. *How could the fool have attempted this crossing without sufficient water? Now water must be obtained, to the exclusion of all else. I must get him within sight of the oasis, so that if he drops in his tracks he will be seen by a new host. He must not die alone, to lie with the amulet until discovered by chance.*

The dromadan lifted its head, thick white froth coating its half-open mouth, eyes glazed with thirst. It gave a sort of half-hearted bellow, scenting the air, and all at once its expression grew brighter. There was water nearby, and the clean, white dwellings of the Chupa oasis could now be seen. Radeef smiled, then a cracked, hysterical laugh came forth. In truth, it was Kotos who laughed, not Radeef, for the possession of a new host was now assured. Both Radeef and the dromadan would make for the oasis, and there they would remain.

Kotos knew he would need a stronger host for the next step in the journey. That was well, for he had grown weary of Radeef's small mind. Though it was easily controlled, it was tedious. He preferred a host that would occasionally challenge his abilities, and he had learned that such a host, one that kept at least the vestige of an independent mind, took far better care of itself. Lord Wrothgar had warned him that the ultimate challenge would soon be faced.

Gorgon Elfhunter had never allowed his thoughts to be controlled, had never knowingly permitted the invasion of his senses nor interference with his own desires. Kotos hoped that his next host would present more stimulation, for he would need all his skills to achieve a rapport with Gorgon. It would not do to have his wits dulled inhabiting a simple-minded scoundrel like Radeef.

The next host chosen would be a man both fit and capable, with a ready but innocent mind. Such men were not wary of Kotos until it was too late, but once inhabited they presented challenges, for they would try to reassert their own wills. For brief and rare moments they would succeed. In those moments they would make intelligent decisions regarding their own welfare, and Kotos would thus allow them to regain their wits from time to time. He intended to stay in the Chupa until he found the right host.

Radeef made his way into the settlement, staggering into the nearest sanctuary, a tavern with the proprietor's name, "Haifa," engraved on a wooden plank over the front door. There he collapsed in a dry, dusty heap. The patrons regarded him with mild disinterest until one of them actually recognized him. He was given water and revived, but when it was discovered that he had no coin, he was laughed out of the tavern. "Come back when you can pay, Radeef!" said Haifa. "Water you may have, but no wine this day."

No matter, wine was the last thing Radeef needed. What he needed was a cool, quiet place to rest, some food and water, and a hospitable host. Radeef had been to the Chupa before, and he knew of the inn known as the Golden Fig Tree.

The proprietor, a man named El-morah, was known to offer aid to wayfarers in need. He fed and clothed Radeef, allowing him to wash the desert from his body, and in exchange he was given Radeef's half-dead dromadan and the promise that he would work to pay his debt. El-morah would have little use for the dromadan, but laborers were always appreciated.

El-morah's wife, Mohani, was not pleased with this arrangement. She did not trust Radeef from the moment she beheld him, and she knew him by reputation. El-morah, however, had not seen the same man his wife had seen, for he had looked into the bewitching eyes of Lord Kotos the Persuader, and all of Mohani's admonitions would be in vain.

Gaelen, Nelwyn, and Estle sat atop the Great Wall, looking out to the east over the moonlit land. The stark, white bones of the dragon glinted in the pale light, casting dark stripes and curves of shadow that made an eerie, dark counterpart upon the stony ground. One could still smell the decay, though it was no longer so stifling that the men on the east watch required cloths covering their faces to blunt the stench—a little aromatic oil on one's mustache would suffice.

Estle passed a skein of liquid to Nelwyn, who sat beside her. "Take this, both of you, and try it! It's a wine made from honey. I expect you'll both find it delectable."

"Wine made from honey? What an appalling notion!" said Gaelen, whose courtesy had abandoned her for the moment. "You mean to say that someone actually took honey, which is the most perfect and precious foodstuff to be had, and…and *fermented* it? That would destroy all of its uplifting qualities, at least it does so to other sweet things that are fermented. But perhaps I am wrong. I will try some to be sure." She and Nelwyn each took a hefty swallow of the honey-wine, and turned their faces aside so that Estle could not see the grimaces they made.

Estle chuckled at them. "That good, is it?"

Nelwyn had a difficult time regaining control of her facial expression. When she finally did, she turned to Estle. "That does *not* taste like honey. What it does taste like, I will not say, although I'm not ungrateful to you for sharing it. It was a thoughtful gesture."

Gaelen said nothing, but made a small sound that might have been a suppressed snort of laughter.

"Well, I like it, and therefore I'll drink it," said Estle as Nelwyn handed the wine back to her. "You must both go thirsty, alas."

"Don't be concerned," said Gaelen. "We are not dismayed. Nelwyn and I have brought our own provisions and they are quite satisfactory, if I do say it." She drew forth a small clay vessel filled with wild forest honey, the kind that is nearly black, and a skein of clear wine. She carefully added the honey to the wine, and mixed it well. The result was a deep amber fluid that would bring cheer to any Wood-elf.

"Do you remember when you asked me whether I could feel the effects of wine, and I replied that it depended on the wine? Well, both Nelwyn and I will feel this!" She passed some to Nelwyn and they both drank heartily. They shared with Estle, who agreed that the mixture was appealing, though it was very sweet.

Something in the combination of honey and spirits will affect a Wood-elf much more than honey alone. Estle had never seen Elven folk quite so tipsy. In fact, Nelwyn, who was usually beyond graceful, attempted to dance atop the battlement and nearly fell from it. She was grabbed by Estle, who hung on to her right arm as she dangled precipitously, laughing so hard that she could do nothing to aid herself.

Estle panicked, calling to Gaelen for assistance, but the little menace was so bent over with mirth that she was not even remotely helpful. Fortunately, Nelwyn recovered her wits enough to struggle to safety, laughing all the while. Estle shook her head. "All right, Gaelen, I take your point. It does, indeed, depend on the wine!"

The two Elves stopped laughing and stared at Estle in silence as though she had just said something frightfully important. Then they both fairly roared with laughter again, falling together in a heap. The stars distracted them, and they lay on their backs, their wide eyes filled with a thousand tiny jewels of light, chuckling and snickering every so often until they finally calmed.

"You two are not nearly as formidable as you would have us all believe, you know," said Estle. "I could have taken you both with no effort at all…so much for the invincible Wood-elves!"

"But, Estle, you are our friend," said Nelwyn. "We do not need to be invincible before you...is that not so?"

"Too right," Gaelen put in, her speech indicating that she was still quite tipsy. "We need not fear with such a capable guardian as you. You would let no harm come to us, is that not true?"

"Nelwyn nearly fell to her death, no thanks to you that she didn't," growled Estle. "You're both lucky I was here to pull her back. It's not really a thing to joke about. When you sober up, you'll be in quite a different mind, I expect."

"Ah, no doubt we will," said Gaelen. "But until then I intend to enjoy the mind I'm in right now." At this she sent forth another quiet rill of laughter, and then appeared to have fallen asleep. Nelwyn had done the same. Estle called to them and prodded them, to no avail.

"So now I must sit alone with my thoughts and watch over two drunken Elves…whoever would have thought such a thing?" said Estle. She smiled and settled back, enjoying the remainder of the honey-wine, and was soon sound asleep beside her immortal friends.

Galador stood, shadowed and silent, in the lee of the northern battlements, a slight smile on his face. He had borne witness to all of the evening's events, and though he had not cared much for the sight of Nelwyn dangling from the edge of the wall, he had not interfered. He trusted Estle, but of much greater importance, he trusted Nelwyn. He had seen her performance during the battle, when she had been beleaguered almost without hope, and she had stood strong before the enemy. His heart had swelled with pride in her, and though it pained him to release her from his protection, he now knew that he could relax his vigilance a little. Nelwyn, like her cousin Gaelen, could take care of herself.

The original seven Asari in the West of Alterra were named Baelta the Bright, Léiras the Far-sighted, Cuimir the Beautiful, Duinar the Guide, Arialde the Pure of Heart, Shandor the Guardian, and Kotos the Perceptive. Their gifts were many, but the greatest gifts were given to Shandor and to Kotos, who were said to be the mightiest of the seven. For many long ages they were as brothers, dwelling together in the realm of the Èolar, the most learned and enlightened of the Elves. There they would debate the nature of evil and how it should be dealt with.

Kotos maintained that it was necessary to go out into the lands where evil held sway, therefore to learn more of the Enemy. He believed that the understanding of one's foe is necessary to recognize and overcome it. Shandor did not agree, and he cautioned Kotos, saying that going into such places would expose the heart to corruption—one could not encounter terrible, all-consuming darkness and not be altered by it. Kotos would not listen, for he was proud and he knew when he was right, and so he would often leave Tal-elathas, venturing forth into lands under the sway of Wrothgar, and there Wrothgar ensnared him.

Kotos held many powerful gifts, but his greatest fascination was with the inner workings of the mind. He became a great healer of those touched with afflictions of the mind, and he could overcome guilt, grief, or madness. He was also incomparable in his ability to read the hearts of others, and to see into their inmost thoughts. This he at first turned into persuasion, but later, as darkness took hold of him, he became not just a persuader but a beguiler, and then a deceiver. Wrothgar had secured a very powerful ally, for Kotos still presented a fair and beneficent face to the world. Even Shandor did not see the darkness shading his soul.

Kotos had been infected by Wrothgar with the lust for power, and he greatly desired the dominion of Tal-elathas. This did not come to pass, for although Tal-elathas was laid in ruin, Shandor drove both Wrothgar and Kotos forth from it. Much time passed ere Wrothgar returned to make his new stronghold amid the dark ruins, bringing Kotos with him. Yet the Third Battle had vanquished them both. Wrothgar had since moved to the Darkmere, where he would remain hidden until his strength was renewed. Kotos' disembodied spirit had found its way back to Tal-elathas, now known as the Fell-ruin. Wrothgar had promised that, should their plans succeed, Kotos would rule it forever.

Wrothgar would send Kotos, his most persuasive and powerful minion, to unite with Gorgon Elfhunter. That alliance would result in a being that would wield not merely strength of arms, but the power to influence the minds and hearts of others. These skills would be necessary for Wrothgar to achieve his heart's desire. Gorgon need not even know the details of the plan at first, because Wrothgar would assure him that, should it succeed, the Elfhunter would also attain his heart's desire. Elves and Men would fall before the Darkness—no Asarla would be able to stop it. But Wrothgar was not a fool, and neither was Lord Kotos. It would take all of their combined powers of deceit to bring about not only the domination of Gorgon Elfhunter, but the unwitting cooperation of Gaelen Taldin.

Wrothgar knew enough of Gaelen to realize how challenging that would be.

4
The Bad Fate of a Good Man

The innkeeper at the Mumari settlement spoke gently to his new guest. The man's journey had obviously been quite difficult. "My friend, you're all in. You need a long rest and a clean bed, and to be made clean yourself. Then I would say you need a meal and a stiff drink! Tell me it is not so."

The traveler looked into the eyes of the innkeeper, swallowed in a dry throat full of dust, and nodded. "It is so," he muttered, casting his deep brown eyes downward.

"Tell me, worthy guest, what is your name?"

The traveler looked puzzled for a moment, as if searching for his name.

It's as if the halls of his mind are empty, thought the innkeeper. *He's had a hard journey, that's for certain.* Then a light seemed to kindle in the traveler's eyes, as though someone had whispered his name in his ear, reminding him.

"My name is Araman…of…of the Sandstone. Yes, that is who I am. Araman." His gaze met the innkeeper's for the first time, and life sparked in his dark eyes as he drew himself up taller. "I have coins, and I can pay for my lodgings. You will please conduct me to my chamber now?"

This last sounded more like a command than a question. The innkeeper, as with most men in his profession, was good-natured and took no offense. He smiled back at Araman. "Of course, my friend. There appears to be some life in you, and that is well. Please follow me." He led his guest to a clean, well-appointed chamber with a basin of cloudy mineral water for washing and a carafe of clear, filtered water for drinking. There was bread and meat and even some figs. Araman pressed some coins into the man's hand and then bade him leave.

"Please do not disturb me," he said. "I do not care for comradeship, and I doubt you will see much of me ere I leave you, but rest assured I will pay for all goods and services rendered. You have my word." He extended his hand to the innkeeper.

The innkeeper took the hand in a firm grip. *There's something about this man that's unsettling. He seems ill-at-ease, though his manner of dress and speech indicate that he was born of the desert. His name is strange—it seemed he had to struggle to remember it—I don't think it's genuine. He doesn't appear to be well-versed in local custom, either. He's ill kept, as if he has not been taking proper care of himself, yet his words come from one obviously well-bred and educated. It's a puzzle. Perhaps a little more inquiry would be helpful.*

"Tell me of yourself, stranger," said the innkeeper in a warm, congenial tone. True to his profession, he had developed a way of making casual inquiries without seeming off-putting, yet now he received an unusual response.

The stranger's eyes went cold and hard, and they glittered with a sort of menacing humor. "Ask me no more questions, for I need not answer them," he said. "And please do not meddle in the affairs of your betters. I shall not be speaking to you again without need. Now leave me in peace."

The puzzle was now even more unclear. The stranger had transformed from a ragged traveler into some sort of imperious lord before the innkeeper's eyes. Everything about him was different. No more the worn, weary traveler in need, there was a fire burning inside this man now. The innkeeper was not certain he liked it.

"Of course, of course I will not disturb you. Only let me know if you require anything, won't you?"

"My apologies," said Araman. "I mean no discourtesy, but I would prefer to remain mysterious. I find it prevents a host of problems in life." He smiled then, looking hard at the innkeeper, who could not hold his gaze.

It was by far the most disturbing smile the innkeeper had ever beheld. He bowed and left the room, closing the door behind him, and he would not speak of his encounter with the stranger to anyone, not even his wife, for something had told him that he must not.

After the innkeeper had gone, Araman washed his face and hands, took a long, refreshing drink of water, and felt life and strength flow back into him. He ate every crumb of food in the room and settled back on his clean, soft bed. He did not sleep at first, for sleep eluded him, and now he rose and crossed to the wash-basin, catching sight of his reflection in the glass. Araman, whose name had once been El-morah, looked back at him, but there was little of El-morah to be seen. The eyes that looked out from the glass were lifeless and cold—the eyes of Lord Kotos. He had secured the perfect host, and now this good man was lost, wandering in search of the memories Kotos had taken from him.

Never before had Mohani so wished for a sister to confide in. It was difficult enough evading the queries of curious customers, as most of them knew El-morah and were accustomed to seeing him behind the counter.

He was one of the most liked and respected men of the settlement, and he had disappeared without warning, without so much as a farewell to his family. At first, Mohani had remained calm, for she trusted her husband and knew that he would not leave without cause, nor would he fail to return to her.

Unless the past has finally caught up with him…

He had gone in the night, arising from their bed as she slept, and had taken nearly all of their gold with him. He had also taken her jewelry. She cursed her lack of perception. Her husband had been putting away provisions for several days, but when asked about it, he shrugged.

"Just in case we should need them, my love." Then he had smiled at her.

Why had that smile filled her with foreboding? Why had she not seen that something was wrong? This had to do with Radeef, that was certain, but he had gone from the settlement as well. El-morah had always believed in being prepared for any disaster…putting aside provisions was not all that unusual. Where under heaven could he have gone, and why?

As the days turned into weeks, Mohani's fears grew deeper and colder. She knew that El-morah had once been involved in pursuits that were neither peaceful nor pleasant. He had a shadowed past that he had kept from her, save for those few details that he knew would not bring harm to her. "You must not inquire, my love, for I cannot tell you…I fear the knowledge might bring woe to our household. Please, let's live our lives from this day forward and not concern ourselves with times past. My life is different now, and I will never forsake it, nor will I ever leave you or the children. This I pledge with all the courage of my heart."

Mohani knew that these words had not been spoken lightly, and she did not take them so. Now, after weeks with no word of him, she began to fear the worst. Perhaps the past had found him and had called him forth to some dire peril. The children missed him terribly and she was having difficulty concealing her ever-mounting fears from them. The loss of their money had presented a hardship, one El-morah would never have inflicted upon his family. She wept now almost every night, and had to work twice as hard each day. Yet despite her frustration and growing resentment, she would have given nearly anything in the world to behold El-morah's warm, brown eyes and ready smile, and to hear his gentle voice again.

Elfhunter…Proud Elfhunter…Awaken to My call. To thee I pledge My aid, for a trial awaits you, with glory at the end of it. Awake now, and receive My thoughts.

The voice of Lord Wrothgar filled Gorgon's anxious mind as he lay in the darkness, lost in a fitful dream. He did not truly awaken, but remained within the dream, though he could see and feel his surroundings. He could hear the voice inside his head. That voice brought both fear and hope to his troubled spirit, for Gorgon had always known that Wrothgar was the true power in the world.

"Yet He is also vengeful," Gorgon muttered to himself. "He might not have forgotten my disastrous defeat in the Barrens of the Darkmere…though it wasn't my fault. I suspected a trap, but He insisted on attacking in spite of my doubts. I dare not point out His role in our defeat…one does not say 'I told you so' to Lord Wrothgar. Oh, no indeed! Still, He came to my aid when I faced the Vixen at the Edge of Darkness. Surely that would not have been so had Wrothgar desired vengeance upon me, would it?"

Gorgon growled despite his fear, and he smiled slightly, recalling Gaelen's terror as she beheld the Dark Face of the Shadowmancer. But then he remembered what had come next. "Wrothgar deserted me just when my need was greatest. Ri-Elathan came, and lent his strength of spirit to Gaelen's. The Lord of Black Flame is surely more powerful than any mere Elf, High King or no...it must have been my own weakness, then, that failed us." He shuddered, wondering whether that realization had occurred to Lord Wrothgar, when the voice came again.

I say again, Elfhunter, awaken to My thoughts. I bring thee aid in the midst of thy despair. Thou hast suffered a mighty blow to the spirit, but I will make certain that it is healed. I will make thee whole again, and set before thee a task that will bring great satisfaction. Join in this task, and return to My service. Refuse it, and I will abandon thee to a lowly fate.

Even as I was abandoned at the edge of the Void? thought Gorgon, but kept this thought to himself.

He could sense the Dark One probing into his memories, questing for knowledge. "Lord, what knowledge do you seek?" he asked, intrigued despite his fears.

The mirror that I gave to thee was lost, said Wrothgar, *and that is unfortunate. Yet it may be recovered and restored to thee upon a time.*

"And much good may it then do me," Gorgon growled in reply. "What else would you ask of me? I am just as glad for the loss of the mirror, as it allowed me to see and feel things that are best not revealed. My life has become more complicated, and my purpose less clear...thoughts turn now in my mind that I cannot vanquish. I'm happy to see the last of the mirror. Though it was a mighty gift, it has brought naught but conflict to my soul."

Gorgon waited in silence, for he did not know how Wrothgar would react to this sentiment, unaccustomed as He was to the lack of proper gratitude. To Gorgon's relief, Wrothgar laughed.

Ah, yes...I had forgotten thy nature. A child is never comfortable learning of disquieting matters, yet they must be learned, Elfhunter. It will please thee, then, that I am sending thee aid. There is one who will teach and guide thee. After thy defeat I sense thou art ready. Return to My service, and visit grief and woe upon My enemies. Now, tell Me of thy journey.

Gorgon told of the desert crossing and of the perils he had faced. He told what he knew of the City of Dûn Arian. He also told of the murder of Thorndil, which had precipitated the near-disastrous confrontation with Gaelen.

It is regrettable that thy presence is known to them, Elfhunter. It would have made matters so much easier were it not. Yet there is no remedy and we must go forward. At the end, if all goes as planned, dominion will be Mine, and the doom of the Elves will be thine. Thou wilt know My messenger by the presence of a golden amulet. Pay careful heed, Elfhunter, and do not disappoint Me. I leave thee now to rest and make ready. The night of glory will come soon.

The voice faded as Gorgon awoke from his dream. He rose to his feet and shook himself, his thick skin rustling and creaking like old leather, walked a few small circles in the darkness, and then sat back down upon the flat stone he used as a bed. He stretched his limbs, noting the weakness in them as they protested their way back into life. Wrothgar had been right about one thing—Gorgon was ready to accept help for the second time, as he truly feared Gaelen. He would not face her again without certainty of victory, which would never come as long as he was alone.

He decided to venture out into the desert night, for he was hungry and growing weaker. Tonight, and each night thereafter, he would feed. He would need his strength in the time to come.

Kotos, in the person of El-morah, had sold off most of Mohani's jewelry, adding to his reserve so that he could purchase additional provisions for the long, hard journey ahead. He had remained at Mumari long enough to gain news of the Company, and he held a sense that they had gone to the southwest, but truly good maps were scarce, and none would point the way to Dûn Arian.

Wrothgar had gained knowledge of it through Gorgon Elfhunter, and had relayed to Kotos an accounting of Gorgon's journey, such that some of the features on Araman's new map now had meaning. The Mountains of Dread, the Great Salt, and the Plains of Dire Thirst, for example, had all been named in the account. Now Lord Kotos would press his host—a good, hard man in his prime—toward the southwest, knowing that the closer he drew to Gorgon, the clearer his path would become.

El-morah had acquired five dromadin, one for riding and four that carried water and other provisions. He would be allowed to come to his senses only at need, for he was desert-wise and possessed valuable survival skills. He was much more adept than Radeef, as well as younger and stronger. El-morah would succeed where Radeef would not, yet Kotos worried that his fine, new host would die alone in the waste, and thereby delay the encounter with Gorgon Elfhunter. That would not be the best way to remain in the good graces of the Shadowmancer. Kotos feared Wrothgar, but he was proud, and knew that he would succeed. After all, was he not also very powerful? Kotos held gifts that Wrothgar did not possess. Because those gifts were absolutely essential to the plan, Kotos knew he had little to fear. Still, his dark spirit was unsettled as he left the comfort of Mumari and headed out across the open desert, looking out through El-morah's eyes at the vast expanse of sand and dust.

Never before had Lord Kotos undertaken such a difficult journey. This vast wasteland was new in his experience, though he was certainly familiar with the great northern expanses of ice and bitter wind. This was different, and although Kotos no longer suffered physical discomfort, his host would suffer greatly before all was ended. If El-morah failed to reach Gorgon Elfhunter, the plan would be delayed. That would not please Wrothgar, who expected Kotos to put things into motion at once, and was not known for patience.

It was fortunate for Kotos that he no longer felt empathy for his hosts, or he would have been compelled to release them as their pain and trial became too much to bear. El-morah could be driven far beyond that point, for he was a much stronger man than most. He possessed the heart of a true warrior, and such men know what it is to serve a higher calling at the expense of their own needs. He was also utterly devoted to family, and Kotos knew that this could be turned to his advantage. Kotos had, at first, completely suppressed his host's thoughts and feelings, and had taken total possession of him. But this was wearisome, for such strong men are not easily overtaken.

After many days and a journey of many miles, Kotos allowed his host to come to himself for brief periods, now calling him by his true name—El-morah. First, he employed a talent that he had developed over thousands of years of manipulating the minds and hearts of others. He implanted in El-morah a false memory, fostering in him the notion that his family had been taken, and that only by reaching his destination could they be saved. El-morah did not know what that destination was, but Kotos did, and so it did not matter.

When El-morah doubted or questioned their course, Kotos would speak to him, appearing as a voice inside his head. The voice could soothe, encourage, or command as needed. El-morah wondered about his sanity, but he could do little to stop the voice, and it was so compelling that he could not resist. After all, it came from within himself, along with the ever-present "memory" of Mohani and the children being cruelly taken to an equally cruel fate if he did not intervene.

Kotos had amused himself by searching El-morah's real memories. It seemed he had once lived in the lands to the south and east of the Stone Desert, where he had become one of only a few hand-picked men—an assassin, or shadow-man. Kotos learned that he had run afoul of his lord, and had been forced from the realm just ahead of another assassin's blade.

El-morah had crossed the Stone Desert, vowing to make a new life for himself elsewhere. When he met Mohani, his choice became clear—she was his reward for showing strength of heart and turning from his violent life. For many years now, he had devoted his entire being to her and to their children, and planned to live out his days in the peaceful role of a merchant, serving his guests and reveling in the relative simplicity of his life. But he always kept one eye open, afraid that his past would catch up with him. Kotos had exploited that fear with ease. *This is a man both true-hearted and valiant; he will serve well, for his devotion to his family makes him gullible. A good thing, for the journey will tax us both.*

El-morah and Kotos had been fortunate with respect to certain parts of the journey. The Mountains of Dread, for example, had not shown their fury, but only rumbled a little. The sands had trembled, disquieting the dromadin, but little else.

Kotos was not dismayed, for he actually understood fire-mountains. In fact, he had made a study of them. He had learned to read the signs surrounding them and to predict their various eruptions. This talent had once served him well; he had turned an entire tribe of men to the service of Wrothgar by promising to quell their imminent demise. Only Kotos had known that the plumes of steam and ash belching forth from the mountain would not lead to an eruption of fire, and the men thus believed they owed him their lives.

The Salt was another matter, for it was long, hard, and unfamiliar. The heat and lack of water took their toll; one of the dromadin went blind with thirst and wandered off. Kotos did not notice until it was nearly out of sight, and he had to send El-morah to retrieve the provisions it carried. It had died by the time they reached it, lying forlorn on the hard-packed crust with its neck outstretched, eyes glazed and desperate. Both El-morah and Kotos were dismayed, for they could ill afford any extra effort. Kotos instructed El-morah to kill any beast henceforth that showed signs of weakness, so long as its burden could be carried by those remaining.

Their next real trial had come when crossing the plain between the Salt and the western Fire-mountains. The wind picked up to a killing speed, and the travelers almost did not reach the shelter of rocks in time. The driven sands were frightening to hear, sounding like a sinister, lethal version of rushing water, overlaid by the howl of the wind. The dromadin were well-protected, flattening themselves with their tails to the wind, eyes and nostrils closed. They required only one or two large stones each. El-morah sheltered between them, trembling with fear until the storm abated.

When they crossed the Fire-mountains, the ever-present storms came. El-morah had never seen their like before. What in the name of heaven had set the sky on fire? What terrible place was this? Ominous forks of lightning snaked in brilliant nets across the red sky, raking the summits of the tall hills as the rumbling thunder filled his ears. By now he was utterly weary, and in the grip of terrible thirst, yet he could not deny the terrifying beauty of the flashing, flickering lights. It was as if there were cracks in the fabric of heaven, and he could see through them into hell.

He stood mesmerized until he heard the urging of his inner voice. *Take shelter until the storm passes, or hell is where we both will be. You must look to your safety. Remember that the fate of your loved ones depends on you. You must take shelter at once!*

El-morah could not deny such a command, for he had not the will, and he knew nothing of survival in the Fire-mountains. He had lost another dromadan, and he led the remaining three to shelter beneath an overhang of rock, falling once more into the realm where no thought was his own. There was still a long and difficult road before him.

Weeks later, the last of the dromadin lay down upon the sand and released its final breath. Kotos had not been mindful of them for some time. He was so close to his quarry now that he could sense Gorgon Elfhunter; he was less than a day's journey away. The Plains of Thirst had nearly put an end to El-morah and, despite all entreaties from Kotos, he fell now, not far from the body of his animal. The water had run out two days ago.

Get up…you have nearly completed your task. You cannot give up now. Get up and struggle on, for your loved ones are lost without you to save them. El-morah stirred and moaned, but his strength had run out. Kotos' voice abruptly changed to a thundering command. *I will not be denied! Get up, you pathetic weakling! You cannot stop now, not when you are so close. It is your purpose in life to carry me hence. Now, get up and fulfill that purpose!* But one cannot summon strength that is not there, and El-morah had passed from the realm of awareness. He would not live long now.

For a moment, Lord Kotos was unsure of what to do. He knew that the Elfhunter was very near; he could sense it. Yet his vessel could not take him there. His terrible cry of frustration could be heard only in the mind of El-morah, who was beyond caring. With a final snarl of distaste at the mortal weakness of his host, Kotos left him, flowing back into the golden amulet, there to await his next stroke of good fortune. Once inside the comfortable and familiar environs of the amulet, his confidence returned. *The ravens will come—they always came to the dying—and then I will persuade one to carry the amulet to the dark lair where Gorgon awaits. It's only a matter of time.*

Enough time had passed since Gorgon's invasion that the City had calmed, though the people had not relaxed their vigilance. Lord Salastor had decreed that the increased watchfulness of the City Guard would continue until it was certain that the Elfhunter no longer presented a threat. When Gaelen heard this, she smiled, knowing that no guard would confront Gorgon if he did not wish it. Her vigilance was far more important, and everyone in the Company knew it. She spent time each day atop the Great Wall, casting her thoughts like a net into the vast lands beyond, questing for her enemy.

Gorgon heard her thoughts, and he drew deeper into himself, for he would not reveal his whereabouts to her. He was not yet ready to face her, and in truth, his greatest dread was that he might not ever be ready, even with Wrothgar's aid. Gaelen had stolen what little courage he had on the edge of the Void. Now he emitted a low, throaty growl that seemed to fill the silent darkness of his lair as he caught a glimpse of movement out of the corner of one eye. He dreaded what would surely come: the sight of his long-vanquished foe, Gelmyr High-elven, his blue, glowing flesh rotting from his bones. No doubt the wretched dead Èolo would be wearing the same insufferable smile he always wore.

Gorgon closed his eyes, waiting for Gelmyr's hated voice, but instead he heard the harsh croak of a raven. He turned his fearsome face toward the dim light filtering into his sanctuary and observed a large, black bird fluffing its feathers and bobbing its head. In its sharp beak there was a heavy golden chain bearing some sort of golden ornament. Even in the dim light, its brilliance shone forth.

Gorgon rejoiced. Here was the golden amulet, by which he would know that his anticipated benefactor had arrived. As if in response to some inaudible command, the raven abruptly hurled the golden thing toward Gorgon, who deflected it with the stump of his left hand in a blur of motion. It fell at his feet, raising a large puff of dust. The raven looked now at Gorgon as if for the first time, gave a croaking call of alarm, and fled.

Gorgon stared at the golden thing in the dust. He was wary, yet intrigued, and he knew that his fortunes were about to change for the better. Gelmyr had not come to torment him since Wrothgar's promise had been made. *Has the wretch somehow been banished?*

Then he remembered that Gelmyr only appeared only during times of self-doubt. With the Shadowmancer's promise, there would be no need to doubt himself…none at all.

Gaelen lifted her head into the wind and scented the air blowing in from the east. An east wind did not bode well, at least not in the Greatwood. East winds brought bad storms…they were unnatural. *There is something afoot…I can feel it.* She shook her hair from her eyes, peered out into the gathering twilight, and opened her thoughts.

Many miles away, Lord Kotos was making his first long-awaited contact with Gorgon Elfhunter, and he sensed Gaelen's quest. *She means to gain knowledge of Gorgon so that she can defeat him—that must not be allowed to happen!* Kotos sent forth a cloud of bewilderment, foiling her efforts and concealing Gorgon from her. But though she gained no direct knowledge, Gaelen knew that her instincts were true. She did not receive such feelings from any other source, and one day she would sense him before he could guard himself. "Then we shall see, Dark Horror. Then we shall see," she muttered, knowing there was no use in questing further, for he had closed his thoughts to her.

5
The Seduction of Gorgon Elfhunter

Rogond lay on his back in the dusty courtyard, sweat stinging his eyes, and struggled for breath. His friend Azori chuckled in a way that suggested more mischief than mirth, his black eyes gleaming, his crooked smile partly hidden by his mustache. "When are you going to learn that sweat is never your friend?" he said, extending his hand to pull Rogond to his feet. "It blinds you, and makes your weapon difficult to hold and control. You need to re-work the grip of your sword, and wear a band of linen around your forehead, like this." He pulled his dark turban aside to show his own sweat-soaked headband. "Remember, my friend, you are not an Elf! You actually sweat like the rest of us."

Rogond smiled back at him. It was difficult to dislike Azori, even if one had just been humiliated in a combat exercise. Besides, he at least appeared to be making an effort to be helpful. "Of course, you're right. You must show me how to improve my blade. How is it lacking?"

"It got slippery. I saw you trying to control it, and you could not hold it steady. You need to re-cover it with sharkskin, like mine. See?" Azori held his blade out so that Rogond could examine it. The grip was of pebbly, dark leather with a grainy texture. It almost felt like hardened sand in his hand. "The skin of sharks and rays is especially suited to this application. Every Corsair's child knows it. That oiled leather you have chosen will not do at all!"

Rogond swung Azori's blade, noting the control afforded by the grip. "This will take some getting used to, for there are times when I want the blade to slip freely, yet it does feel marvelous. I will look to my own weapons right away, and Galador's as well."

"Galador actually *sweats?*" said Azori in a disbelieving tone. "Surely you are mistaken!"

"Oh, he does indeed. He was in a fair lather by the time Hallagond had finished off the dragon, as were we all."

"Lathered, was I?" Galador was approaching and had overheard. "Are you certain it wasn't cast-off from the many surrounding unwashed, uncouth men? That was my recollection of it. I almost felt I needed to shield my eyes from the sweat flying off of Azori alone!"

"Of course, my friend, whatever makes you feel better," said Rogond. He turned to Azori. "I know a sweating Elf when I see one."

Galador drew himself up tall, fixing them both with his most imperious look. "Elves," he said slowly, "do not *lather!*"

"Of course they don't," said Rogond. "Is there any urgency to your errand, or are you just meaning to be sociable this morning?"

"Just being sociable. I arrived just in time, it seems." Galador examined the fingers of his right hand as though they were undeniably fascinating.

"All right," said Azori. "It's obvious that you want someone to ask this question, so I will oblige. In time for what?"

"In time to avenge the humiliation of my closest friend, if you are willing," said Galador. "I need exercise, and you are in need of a challenge. Defend yourself, if you will!"

He drew his own blade, smiled at Azori, and raised both eyebrows, goading him just a little.

Azori's face drew into a broad grin. "A challenge, eh! If you have any to suggest, let me know!" He raised his own blade, crossing it over Galador's, and bowed slightly. But when Galador returned the bow, which was meant to show respect for one's opponent, Azori took full advantage, striking before Galador was prepared, temporarily unbalancing him. Azori was weary from his prior conflict, but he was still in good form and he knew how to press his advantage.

It is conventional in a non-lethal sword fight for the combatants to test one another for a few moments, assessing abilities and weaknesses before flying into a full-scale conflict. This gives them time to flex and warm their limbs, and to gradually bring heart, blood, and breath to their peak. This convention, it seemed, was lost on Azori. Galador was hard put to recover, and he was quickly winded, for he had expected a more gradual escalation of effort.

Regrettably, at least from Azori's point of view, Fima arrived and interrupted the conflict before the outcome could be known.

"Stop this, both of you, and listen!" he said. "Lord Salastor wants to see Rogond and Galador. We shouldn't keep him waiting. You can play your games another day."

Galador did not trust Azori after his previous breach of etiquette, and they continued sparring for a few moments. "Aren't you going to quit?" asked Azori, who was weary and glad the conflict would end. Galador, even winded, was a formidable opponent. "Lord Salastor has called you to stand before him. I'm sure Fima is right in that you should not delay."

"May I trust you to not strike me unaware?" said Galador, who had lost some of his good humor at the start of the fight.

"This fight ends when I say it does," replied Azori with a wicked smile. "And I will say so if you wish it! Just give the word." The conflict had slowed, but it had not ended, and blades were still clashing.

"Fine," replied Galador between breaths. "The word is given, but only because I am called away. We shall continue the challenge upon another time, and things may go differently now that I am wise to your tricks." He lowered his blade, and Azori did the same.

"My fine friend," said Azori, who managed to chuckle even though he was weary and out of breath, "you'll find that I still have many, many tricks of which you are unaware. And I notice that you're sweating now. Try to deny it!"

Galador did not acknowledge this last, his expression indicating that it was obviously untrue, and therefore beneath his dignity to respond. He bowed once more to Azori, but this time kept his gaze firmly fixed on him. "Until another day," he said.

Galador followed Rogond and Fima out of the courtyard. Hc had not sensed anxiety in the people of the City. He was attuned to such things, and he had felt no foreboding. Why, then, had Salastor called this council? He asked Rogond about it.

That question was answered as they reached the massive doorway to Salastor's private council-chambers. "Actually, I asked Salastor if he would counsel with us," said Rogond. "I expected he would summon me sometime today. Let's see if he's ready to receive us." He struck the heavy cast iron bell hanging beside the doorway, and it rang with a very deep, resonant tone.

A door-warden appeared almost immediately, bowing before his distinguished visitors. "Welcome, honored guests," he said. "Lord Salastor is expecting you, Rogond. Are your friends here to accompany you, or do they have separate business this day?"

"No, they're coming with me," said Rogond, and the three of them were ushered in. Lord Salastor of Dûn Arian stood and bowed, directed them to comfortable chairs at the council table, and waited to hear what Rogond had to say.

Gorgon's curiosity had definitely gotten the better of him. He knelt on the dusty floor of his lair, staring at the beautiful golden amulet. *This must be the token announcing the Messenger of Wrothgar. But, who is the Messenger? Is it the raven?*

He began speaking to himself in a low, purring voice. "What Messenger has come? Did the raven steal this golden thing from him? I see no Messenger. Perhaps if I take this golden thing and look more closely, all will be made clear." He could sense a power emanating from the amulet and, though he was wary, he was also eager to receive Wrothgar's promised aid. He reached for the amulet with an uncertain hand, hesitating for just a moment and closing his eyes.

"For whatever fate befall, may Evil come to all, as the Darkness rules the Light, Death take the Elves this night."

He hesitated for only a moment longer before grasping the amulet in his massive right hand. A sudden feeling of comfort came over him; not merely well-being, but genuine comfort. He let out a long breath, held the amulet before his pale eyes, and looked into the depths of the golden stone. There he saw an image forming. It was…a face. Yes, it was the face of a man—old and very wise—with fathomless dark eyes and flowing grey hair and beard. When he smiled, Gorgon knew that this was the Messenger Wrothgar had promised him. That smile would have beguiled nearly anyone except Gorgon Elfhunter, who had seen the face of Evil enough to know it when it appeared. "Very well,

Messenger of Wrothgar. I see your face and I behold your smile. What message do you bring?"

"How courteous of you to speak Aridani to an old man," Kotos replied. For his part, he had been satisfying his own curiosity regarding Gorgon. *It has been a long while since I have seen him…he has matured nicely.* "Hail, Gorgon Elfhunter, and well-met at last. My journey has been long and hard, and I am most pleased to find you. I am the guardian promised by your Master. With my aid, you shall become a force so terrible that no enemy can prevail against us. Yet you must allow me to take certain liberties, and we must work together always. Are you ready to abandon your solitary life, and learn the true nature of your task?"

"I'm certain you did not travel all this way to hear me say 'no,'" replied Gorgon. "Tell me now, if you will."

"I will indeed," said Kotos. "But first, you must tell me of yourself. I have heard something of your history from Lord Wrothgar. He described you as a fearsome, powerful creature. Now that I behold you, I see that it is so. In fact, words fail to convey how formidable you are. He has also said that you are highly intelligent, but in need of experience and guidance. It is your fondest wish to see the last of the Elves, is that not so?"

"That is absolute, undeniable, and irrefutable," said Gorgon with a growl.

"If such a thing came to pass, it would not dismay either of us," said Kotos with a curl of his lip. "Elves have inhabited these lands for far too long. They have kept dominion despite all effort to remove them, yet now our Master believes that their time may be at hand. He has devised a plan that will result in the downfall of not only the Elàni, but of all who refuse to serve the Dark Powers. This plan will only succeed with your assistance. There is no other with your strength—no other with your purpose."

"Tell me, then, what it is you wish of me, and I will decide if it serves my purpose," said Gorgon. He was not naïve enough to believe the flattery Kotos had given, yet he could not help but be intrigued.

Kotos knew that his task was delicate. Gorgon would not be overtaken; he would need to be enlisted as a willing participant in the plan. He was very strong-willed and of independent mind, such that cooperation did not come naturally. Yet he had shown some ability when placed in command of his army in the Darkmere. Kotos was more than up to the task of convincing him. He had beguiled some of the most intelligent and strong-willed beings in all of Alterra, Elves and men alike.

"This may take a while. Are you quite comfortable?"

"I am always comfortable with discussions involving the killing of Elves," growled Gorgon in reply. "Get on with it!"

To Gorgon's surprise, Kotos' face wavered and disappeared. In its place there was a view of a very tall, golden-haired Elf clad in fine armor. He was probably the largest and most magnificent Elf Gorgon had seen, and the sight both angered and frightened him. The Elf appeared to be standing in some form of council-chamber with many onlookers, and he was speaking of the massing of Wrothgar's forces in the ruin of Tal-elathas. Then Gorgon beheld Wrothgar's armies as they swept down upon the Elven-realms, killing every last Elf...save one. The tall, golden Elf was spared and, in fact, he threw his beautiful head back and laughed as the last of his people fell. Gorgon was confused. Why should an Elf rejoice at such a calamity?

The vision faded, along with the tall Elf's laughter, and Gorgon once again beheld the face of the old man. "So, Wrothgar has a plan that will somehow allow His armies to overcome the Elven-realms? He has tried this many times before, and has each time been defeated. Why, now, should the Elves allow Him such advantage?"

"Because they will be beguiled," said Kotos. "They will be deceived by one of their own. Look now, and see."

Another vision appeared then, this time either horrific or delightful depending on the viewer. Elves in all parts of Alterra were dying by the hundreds, being attacked from all sides when they were most vulnerable. There was blood, and filth, and pain in the vision. There were desperate cries of grief and agony, and the wailing of many Elven voices, until all were silenced. Gorgon had never beheld anything so satisfying.

His eyes glittered with ravenous expectation as he looked into the eyes of Lord Kotos, the Deceiver. "*How* may I see this wonderful vision come to pass?" he asked. "Whatever it is, I will do it. Please enlighten me, for the hunger to see this fate visited on the Elves has nearly consumed me."

"We shall see how willing you are when your role in the deception becomes clear, said Kotos. Are you not curious as to the identity of the tall, golden Elf?"

"I am," said Gorgon. "If he were not an Elf, I would call him friend. Who is he?"

"Why my irrepressible Elfhunter," said Kotos with a smile that was almost fatherly, "he is *you*."

"Welcome, Rogond Thaylon," said Lord Salastor with an encouraging smile. "It has been too long since we sat down together. I trust your wounds are healing well?"

Rogond returned the smile and bowed before replying. "My wounds are healed, though I have yet to regain full strength of my right arm," he said. "My thanks to the excellent care of your healers and, of course, to Gaelen, who looks after my shoulder each day. It will be strong again before long, I should think. In the meantime, I'm becoming more adept at left-handed combat, despite the unfortunate outcome of my sparring with Azori earlier." He shook his head and grinned.

Salastor smiled again. "Ah! Well, if Gaelen is tending you, then you will be stronger than ever if she has anything to say about it. It is said that Elves have a kind of magic about them when it comes to healing and touch. I will not pry into your personal affairs by asking if that is so. Please come and sit with me, and let us counsel together. I will always hear your concerns."

"I hope you will not think me foolish, but my thoughts have been troubling, and I would share them," said Rogond. "My friends would also join in the counsel, if it does not displease you."

They sat down together as Salastor offered good brown bread, wine, and sugared figs. "Tell me of your thoughts," he said, "for I see disquiet in you. Does this concern Gorgon Elfhunter?"

"That's a matter for another day," said Rogond. "Today my thoughts concern the continued security of the Silver Fortress and the safety of her people. I have traveled many of the northern lands, venturing now into the distant south. From what I have seen, the strength of men is rebuilding. This both gladdens my heart and troubles it, for I fear your City may not long remain undiscovered. Dûn Arian has maintained her isolation in part because she is surrounded by nearly impassable terrain, but also because she is hidden, and there have been so few men in the world to discover her. There were many Scourge warriors who survived the battle, and they now know of her. Does it not seem likely that others will follow? The scholars say that the only possible way the Scourge could have made the desert crossing was with the dragon's aid; they believe Lokai delved deep into the bedrock to find water that the army could share. If so, then there will be many new water-holes scattered along the Scourge's course. That will make the crossing easier, and some might attempt it who will not have your best interests in mind. What if they bring an army?"

"Well, what if they do?" said Fima. "Then the City will repel them, as they did the Scourge. We still have the Wall in place, after all."

"Yes, we have the Wall," put in Galador, "but our enemies will most likely know about it. The Scourge was not expecting such a thing. Now, it will be known far and wide, if I am any judge of men and their gossiping tongues." He looked over at Rogond and Salastor. "No offense intended."

"None taken," said Rogond, "for you are right. And though I understand your view, Fima, I do not share your optimism. The City's armies have been greatly reduced in number. We have lost many weapons and most of our seasoned fighters. The Scourge has left its mark on us."

Salastor had been listening to the exchange, his chin resting on one hand, his expression thoughtful. "Rogond, do you really believe the City is in danger of invasion?" he said. "We have realized that we will now be more widely known, and that some will try to come here, but the crossing will still be difficult."

"You must be ready for any possibility, in my humble opinion," said Rogond.

Salastor leaned forward. "Then please advise me, all of you. How can we make ready?"

"You must see to the making and re-fitting of weapons, and train a standing army," said Rogond.

"That is something we have not done at any time in our history," said Salastor. "Our people have preferred reason to violence. We have always discouraged aggression here and, in fact, we have insisted that our citizens settle their disputes with consideration. It has served us for five hundred years, and I would not see it changed."

"Just because you have an army doesn't mean you should start fighting amongst yourselves," said Fima. "Rogond is right...you will need a defense force. Alas, so many of your trained fighters have been lost."

"Alas, indeed," said Rogond, remembering Ali. "But now we must make do with what remains. Lord Salastor, I would like to convene a council with your new Minister of Defense and see whether a plan can be made to train more of your citizens in the arts of battle. Fima, I would also appreciate your aid in seeking knowledge in the library. Perhaps the scholars can direct us to helpful manuscripts...instructions in the making and use of weapons. We should no doubt put out a call to all citizens to come forward if they have any training or knowledge of battle skills." He turned to Salastor. "What do you think of this plan, my lord?"

"It's a good plan, Rogond," said Salastor. "But I do not know how willing our citizens will be. The avoidance of violence is very deeply ingrained in them. I hope you are not disappointed, but you will have a task before you."

"They must be convinced while the memory of the Scourge still haunts their thoughts," said Galador. "Your people are peaceful, but they are also practical. Their blood was aroused when their home was threatened. I have every confidence that they will agree."

"Who is the new Minister of Defense?" asked Fima. "I know you asked Hallagond, but he declined. Has anyone accepted the post?"

Salastor shook his head. "They have not, though Visili was my next choice. He has more than paid his debt, yet he is still not trusted by some in the City. I have not as yet asked him." He looked over at Rogond. "I know that you have refused the Ministry, but as the architect of the plan, will you not take leadership of it?"

Rogond smiled at Salastor and shook his head. "Is this how you treat those who try to make helpful plans to aid you?" he said. "You thrust additional responsibilities upon them?"

For once, Salastor did not return the smile. "If I see a job that needs doing, I will see it done myself," he said. "Those who have the skills must stand ready to use them for the sake of the Light, for it is by the Light that they were given. So says Salasin, the Wise."

Fima then stepped in. "Yet one of the most valued qualities of a leader lies in knowing how to assign duties to those most capable. Rogond is a thinker, and he has given you his thoughts. You should not expect to divert him from his primary task."

"And what is your primary task, Rogond?" Salastor inquired. "If it is the tracking and slaying of Gorgon Elfhunter, then I have sworn the services of all in the City to assist you. Will you not now aid us in preparing our defense?"

"I will aid, but I will not lead," said Rogond. "I will not commit to such an important position, for I don't know how long I will be in the City. If the quest against Gorgon takes me hence, I will be gone. Ask Visili, my lord. I will aid him as I can, and Hallagond has offered his services, as have all in our Company. There will be those with talents as yet undiscovered who will show themselves as training proceeds. But now you must convene the Council and enlist the aid of your citizens. I'm sure they will agree. If not, take them to the Memorial of the Fallen and remind them."

He rose and bowed before Lord Salastor. "I must now take leave of you, my lord. Other tasks call me this day. Please let me know at once if I am needed here again."

"You *are* needed here, Rogond," said Salastor. "That cannot be denied. But now see to your other tasks and I will see to mine." He smiled and inclined his head to Rogond, Galador, and Fima, who then turned and left the chamber.

Once outside, Fima declared his intention to go down to luncheon. Rogond declined to go with him, as he had promised to meet with Gaelen by the sea; it was her opinion that soaking in the gentle waters of the harbor was good for his shoulder. She had promised to bring food, and he would not keep her waiting.

Galador decided to accompany Fima to the Courtyard of the Scholars, which was his favorite place to eat and think on a fine day such as this one. Fima was something of a celebrity, particularly to the apprentice scholars, who almost revered him. He would have any food and drink they could provide.

Neither he nor Galador was disappointed, as the table was laden with all sorts of temptations. "The fare is very nearly as fine as in Mountain-home," said Fima, "and that is no small statement."

"Indeed not," said Galador. Though less enamored of food and drink than Fima, he still appreciated a fine meal. As he helped himself to soft bread with butter and honey, he noticed two of the apprentice scholars looking rather pointedly at him, speaking in hushed tones to one another.

"Pray tell what your business is with me," said Galador. "I would prefer that you not discuss my concerns outside my hearing." His tone was friendly enough, but commanding.

The scholars' faces reddened. "We mean no offense," said one. "We just do not understand how it is that you and Lore-master Fima are being so cordial, when it is said that your races have been bitter enemies for many an age…" The scholar's voice trailed off at once, and he dropped his eyes. "Forgive me," he said, "I did not mean any implication."

Just then, Azori appeared from out of nowhere to sit heavily beside Galador.

"Well, obviously these two are friends," he said with a wicked grin."If you need proof, you only need examine the events of this morning, when I had nearly bested you, and your friend Fima came to your rescue with that little, harmless lie about your being summoned to Salastor. He saw that you were about to be humiliated, and he stepped in. Quite a natural thing for a friend to do, I would expect. You had not, in fact, been summoned, had you?"

"No, I hadn't been summoned," said Galador. "But what has any of this to do with my sitting down cordially to luncheon with Fima?"

"Well, I might have taken insult," said Azori. "I need no dwarves to fight my battles for me. I would expect my friends to allow me to finish what I started. Now we shall have to wait until another day to test our skills. Everyone knows the dwarf was simply trying to save you from your inevitable humiliation. You were losing!"

Galador smiled a cold smile and his eyes glittered at Azori. "At least I would have lost honestly, had I lost at all."

Azori shrugged. "Honesty is overrated. Admit it, Galador. You were losing the fight. Are you not angry at Fima's deception? I would feel foolish were I in your place."

Galador was unfazed. "Were you in my place, Azori, you would have seen untold centuries of strife, grief, and pride, and such a small thing, so well-intentioned, would bother you not at all. I don't share your insecurities concerning my own prowess. All is well between Fima and me. He knows I am quite capable of dealing with you, provided you follow at least a few of the rules of civilized combat."

Azori laughed heartily then, clapping Galador on the back, which was a gesture the Elf did not like. "There are no such rules, despite opinions to the contrary," he said.

"Fine," replied Galador. "Then the next time I see a bandit such as yourself, I will simply have Nelwyn shoot him from behind. How fortunate for you that we did not do so earlier!" He smiled as he said this, but his jaw was set and his gaze was still cold.

"My friend," said Azori choosing to ignore the last comment, "you remind me of a cat whose fur has been rubbed backward. In fact, Elves always seem to be miffed about things, much as cats are. I sense you do not like to be touched."

"It depends upon who is doing the touching, and in what manner," said Fima in an attempt to be helpful. This elicited more laughter from Azori, and even a chuckle from Galador, who had to admit to the truth of it.

When all had finished eating, the young scholars turned back to Fima. "Please, Lore-master, will you not enlighten us as to the history of the enmity between Elves and dwarves? It is a tale of which we have only the barest accounting, and there are few here who know anything of it. The elder scholars speak of a terrible conflict in which the great realms of Eádros and Rûmm were lost. Do you know of it?"

Fima shook his head. "Alas, I know much of it. It is one of the most sorrowful tales in all the history of Alterra—a tale of pride, vanity, mistrust, and, unfortunately, love. Love may be the strongest force under heaven, but if it is denied, there follows only grief and darkness. I have read the records set down by Lady Ordath, taken from the reports of those on both sides of the conflict. She has pieced together the most even-handed and accurate of accounts."

"Please, will you favor us?" asked the young scholars, for they were eager to learn and record this accounting of a dark time in their world.

"I will, though it pains me to do so. Any who wish to hear may attend. It is a tragic story, and I will not wish to repeat it. Come to the courtyard at sunset and I will enlighten you."

The scholars rejoiced, for they had not been offered such a treasure ever before in their lives. The War of Betrayal had remained mysterious, and there were details known only to Fima and the scholars of Mountain-home. At sunset, there would be no free space in the courtyard.

"Tell me why I should believe any of this, and I just might refrain from burying you and your precious golden thing deep below the rock, never to be found! I sense that your spirit is locked within. You had better have a most convincing excuse for insulting me in such a way!"

Gorgon's pale eyes were afire, his mouth twisted into a furious snarl as he roared at the face of the old man in the amulet. And for the first time, Lord Kotos—powerful, dark spirit, born of the Light and later consumed by evil—was truly afraid of him. Kotos had not encountered such a strong-willed spirit in a very long time… not since the fall of Tal-elathas. Since he had lost his physical form, he had stayed away from contact with the Elves, for he feared they would know him. And Gorgon was right. Without a suitable host, Kotos would be helpless, unable to do Wrothgar's bidding, and that frightened him even more. He had underestimated Gorgon, as had nearly everyone else.

Kotos had not expected such a violent reaction, but he rejoiced despite his fear. Gorgon's hatred would be the yoke with which to harness him. "Please, Elfhunter, you must calm yourself. I am your friend…never doubt that! We have been charged with a task that will bring you nothing but pleasure, if you will only master yourself and hear of it. Will you now listen?"

"Speak quickly, then, and convince me," Gorgon replied. "That should present little difficulty for one so skilled." His contempt was palpable, and Kotos smiled. Gorgon's immeasurable pride would serve well in the deception.

"You have lived for many long years in this world, but I do not know the extent of your experience in it, and so I will ask this question. Are you aware of creatures that are deadly, but so alluring that their prey cannot resist them?"

Gorgon, who paid little attention to such things, growled and shook his head. Kotos appeared to draw a deep breath before continuing. "They seem beautiful, even feigning the appearance and mating-scent of the victim, who naturally cannot resist them. When the prey has drawn near enough, they strike. There are several forms in Alterra that employ this gift, including myself. My host can appear as I will have him appear, and none can see through the deception unless I will it, often to their undoing. If you are disguised as the tall, golden Elf in the vision, who will suspect that you are Gorgon Elfhunter? You will be able to plan their doom, even as they take you among them. I assure you…they will."

"I know of one who will suspect," rumbled Gorgon. "And what did you mean by 'my *host?*' Are you suggesting that I should allow you to overtake me? I will not be controlled! Know this before you speak further, and put all such thoughts from your mind."

"I speak not of controlling, but of an alliance," Kotos replied. "Would it not be worth suffering the Elves' company to bring about their end? Will you not walk among them to defeat them? It is the only way you will ever prevail. And the one of whom you speak, Gaelen Taldin…she will not know you. That is a promise I can give right now."

"She has beheld my very soul," said Gorgon. "You will not deceive her. She will know me no matter my semblance."

"Not if your spirit is blended with mine. She will be confounded. I have beguiled some of the strongest spirits in Alterra…even the

Lord of Tal-elathas was turned to my purpose. Surely I can confuse a Wood-elf."

To the puzzlement of Kotos, Gorgon laughed. "A *Wood-elf!* Oh, yes, surely she is that. And you should have no trouble deceiving her, oh, *no!*" His eyes narrowed and his face grew dark. "She is the soul I fear the most, for there is an unbreakable bond between us, and she will know me! You do not understand. I cannot stand before her…I will be found out!"

"You must trust me," said Kotos. "What other choice have you? To hide in darkness until you run out of strength and water? You cannot return to your old life, Elfhunter. Lord Magra has seen to that. He has traveled the northern lands to warn the Elàni of you. They will never be taken so easily again. They will hunt you down should you return to the North, unless they are deceived. I am your last hope of victory. I will give courage to you, if you will only allow it. Try, now, and see my power! First, I will make this promise—If you allow the alliance to be formed, and it does not please you, then I will leave you as I found you. I cannot succeed without your willing participation, Elfhunter. Your spirit is strong, and you must agree to the plan or it will fail. I promise you that I will leave you in peace. But think on this…I cannot protect either of us from Wrothgar should you refuse. Therefore, I am understandably anxious to earn your cooperation. What is your will?"

"A promise from Lord Kotos! Well, I can act with surety now, can't I?" said Gorgon.

Kotos was not angry, for he was a creature of nearly limitless patience when he wished to be. He knew how to convince Gorgon.

"I see I might have overestimated you, Elfhunter. I had thought you strong enough that you would not allow me to dominate your actions, yet now you are reluctant to allow my influence? Such reluctance, especially in the face of a solemn promise, can come only from fear and doubt." Kotos searched Gorgon's thoughts for a moment, for he had not yet learned to guard them.

"Would you not wish to banish Gelmyr forever from your awareness? It will be difficult for him to torment you through our combined strength. You will not doubt yourself once that strength is proven. Again, Elfhunter, what is your will? Will the hunter become the hunted, or will he be the destroyer? The choice is yours. I leave you to your thoughts. If you agree, merely place the amulet around your neck. Choose wisely, and do not dwell too long, as our first task must be completed soon. I await your decision." With those words, the amulet went dark as the face of the old man vanished.

Gorgon paced slowly back and forth before the amulet, which he had set upon a stone. He growled and rumbled and purred deep in his broad chest, muttering and debating. He was still afraid, for true courage was a thing he had not experienced, but he was irresistibly drawn to the promise, and to the reward. And then there was the matter of Lord Wrothgar—the outcome of that conflict was certain. What would be the harm? He would prove his strength of spirit to Kotos, trusting him to keep his promise. It bothered Gorgon that Kotos doubted him.

"All right then, let us dance, you and I," he said, as he picked up the amulet and gazed into the depths of the golden stone. There was no response from Lord Kotos, and so Gorgon filled his enormous chest with air, hesitated for just a moment longer, and placed the amulet around his thick, well-muscled neck, having to struggle for a moment to get it over his very large head. Then he sat down upon the stone, waiting.

"Well? Is anything going to happen?" he said to the surrounding darkness. "I feel no different."

The voice of Kotos came to him then, warming him like the voice of an old friend. *It has already happened, Gorgon. Look upon yourself and you will see.*

Gorgon looked down at his arms, legs, and remaining hand. They were scarred and dark, and exactly as they had been when he had seen them last. "I see nothing different," he growled.

You must see yourself as others would see you, said Kotos. *Draw your blade and behold!*

Gorgon drew his bright sword, holding it before his eyes. At first the vision was blurred, and he gave the blade a quick polish, the better to behold a sight that, at first, startled him nearly into dropping it. The beautiful golden-haired Elf looked back at him, his helmet polished to a mirror finish, his armor golden and glorious. His eyes were grey, clear, and bright. He was both hateful and magnificent—Gorgon despised the sight of him at once.

Look once more at your own body, said Kotos, *and you will understand. Only others will see you in this way, as your blade sees you.*

Gorgon took comfort in the sight of his familiar form as he beheld it.

So long as you wear the amulet, you will appear in Elven form. Do you really think your enemies will know you? I can assure you they won't—I won't let them! You can walk freely in their world if you allow me to guide and advise you. Alas, I cannot restore your left hand, but I can give the illusion that it is there. You will tell your enemies that you had been wounded in battle such that you could not heal, and there is no strength in your left hand. That should satisfy them.

Gorgon held his left arm before his sword-blade, turning it this way and that, taking notice of the perfect hand reflected in the blade. Then he tossed his now-beautiful head and laughed. This could succeed! He might truly have the chance to accomplish his life's purpose, for now he could manipulate his enemies openly, and lure them to their doom. What a marvelous turn of fortune!

Inside Gorgon's thoughts, Kotos smiled, for they had gone from conflicted to jubilant, and Kotos knew that he had succeeded in enlisting the aid of the Elfhunter. Now they had a task to perform, and quickly. Kotos whispered to Gorgon, urging him to leave the dark cavern for the open desert. Kotos only hoped that he would arrive in time to save El-morah from death, for the rest of his part in the plan was yet un-played.

6
The Tears of Aontar

By the time they reached El-morah, it was nearly too late. Kotos had directed Gorgon across several miles of open desert to find a man clad in black robes, face down in the sand, breathing what was surely one of his last breaths. Gorgon turned El-morah over, taking note of his cracked lips, his sagging, wrinkled skin, and his limp, nearly lifeless limbs. He shook his head, muttering. "This one is all but gone. He is as dried up as an empty sack. I fear we have found him only to witness his death."

Kotos was undaunted. *Do not give up so easily. Only see what shade and water will do for him. And you had better find something for him to eat as soon as he is able.*

"You drove him too hard," said Gorgon. "He is beyond it now. You will have to make another plan."

El-morah drew a painful breath, his face twisting into a mindless grimace of pain and effort, his back arching.

"You see? He is dying as we speak!"

I drove him as I needed to drive him! You delayed our return with your questions and doubts. Now we must act, and act quickly! Do as I instruct, Elfhunter, and stop this debate. If you do not allow me to direct you, we both will be undone. I don't care about this man, but I need him, and that means you need him! He has an important role to play in our plan.

Gorgon's brow furrowed. Kotos, like Wrothgar, would not admit to being wrong about anything. "As you wish," he whispered, lifting El-morah and carrying him to the shade of stones. Setting the dying man down, he took a vessel of water from his belt and poured a very small amount between El-morah's lips, shaking his head. "He cannot even swallow it. See? It's trickling back out even now. There's no use in this."

Keep trying. He will come around.

Gorgon poured another small sip of water into El-morah's mouth, and then shook him. "Come on, come on and swallow it, or you're dead."

I'm afraid I must intervene for a moment, said Kotos. *I shall be leaving you, but your appearance will not change so long as you wear the amulet. Do not fear.* At these words, he flowed forth from Gorgon and once again dwelled within El-morah, whose lifeless form immediately became more animated. Despite terrible, agonizing thirst El-morah heard the words of Kotos, and knew that if he did not rally he would never see his beloved family again.

You cannot aid them if you are dead. Drink the water that is given to you. Your loved ones need you, and you must drink. Find your strength that you may return to them.

El-morah would have wept, had he been capable. There was so much darkness and doubt in his mind…so much confusion. But he knew that the voice in his head was right, and he swallowed painfully. *That's right. Drink…drink of the water.* El-morah found his strength, and, despite all prediction from Gorgon, he would live.

Gorgon realized two things during this exchange. The first was that he should not underestimate Kotos, whose knowledge was so much greater than his own. The second was far more disturbing. Kotos' presence was comforting, and Gorgon had been disquieted when the dark spirit left him. He almost yearned for the return of his powerful ally, for when Kotos was with him his own strength was supported in a way that it had never been before. Gorgon, who had always dwelt alone in both body and spirit, had now allowed two beings to intrude upon him. The first, Gaelen Taldin, was a bitter enemy to be guarded against. But the second, Lord Kotos the Beguiler, was a guide.

Gorgon looked at his own reflection again, and smiled. *Indeed, I am beautiful and impressive. They will never suspect me…Kotos will see to that. Would this be worth giving in to the will of another?* It was the first time Gorgon had even asked this question of himself, and the answer was clear. Of course it would. He had no other choice. As the spirit of Kotos once again shared his consciousness, Gorgon put all debate from his mind. Kotos thought to use him, but, in fact, Gorgon now viewed Kotos as a weapon to be wielded. *I will be the user, and Kotos will be my instrument.* Denial of reality was a wondrous tonic, and Gorgon would partake of it often, for it would sustain him in the time to come.

Kotos made certain that El-morah would remember nothing of the desert crossing. He would not be able to recall any event, or know what part he had played in it. It would not do for him to regain his senses until the time was right. Gorgon bore him back to the dark underground sanctuary, there to ensure his survival until they were ready to leave for the city. All the while, Kotos instructed him. There were some preparations to make. By the time Gorgon had heard all that Kotos would tell, there was a faint smile upon his beautiful, cold face as well as in the depths of his equally cold heart.

Olan Estelar was the apprentice of one of the most learned star-masters in Dûn Arian. As such, he had measured and mapped the movements of the stars and the moon for several years now. He liked to occupy a position high on the top of one of the hills near the City, where no light would disrupt his view of the heavens. At only twenty years of age, he showed great promise, though his true passion lay in the forces that shaped winds and weather. The stars did not affect the people at all in his opinion, though they were useful as navigational tools.

This night he was recording and mapping movements of the stars since the previous reading—a tricky business requiring all of his attention. At last he set down his precious star maps, rolling them up for storage and transport in weather-tight containers before preparing to rest until dawn. Olan would wait until sunrise to begin his return journey, for he did not like traveling in darkness.

He built a small fire against the chilly night air, warming himself, as his eyelids grew heavy and he dozed for a while. An uneasy feeling began to take hold in the back of his mind…there was something amiss on the plateau. He came to himself, realizing that there was no sound other than the wind. No crickets chirped, no small creatures stirred and rustled as they went about their nightly affairs. In the eerie silence, he first saw the glow of the golden amulet by the light of his dying fire. Despite the undeniable feeling that he should not do so, Olan moved toward it, mesmerized, for he was too young and inexperienced to do otherwise.

Kotos ensnared him as neatly as a crippled fish in a net, flowing into his astonished and relatively innocent mind with ease. *I need you to secure the things I need.*

In a few moments, Olan was heading back toward the city with all speed, despite the fact that he would never travel by night if he could help it. Somehow he knew he had nothing to fear, though he would know very little else until Kotos had finished with him. After that, it would not matter if he ever knew anything again. The amulet was left behind for Gorgon to reclaim; after all, it would not do for El-morah to see him in his true form. No, that would not do at all.

The Courtyard of the Scholars was filled with people by the time the sun had given way to early evening. Those present included all in the Company, as well as about fifty of the City's most learned lore-masters, including Lord Salastor himself. The remaining spaces were filled by curious citizens, for they had learned that Lore-master Fima would be giving an accounting of the War of Betrayal, and that such a thing was not to be missed. Several vendors appeared, intending to sell breads and fruits along with sweet water and wine, but Fima scowled at them as he took his position on the raised stone dais at the northern end of the courtyard.

"This is an accounting of a woeful time so dark and shameful that Elves and Dwarves alike must hang their heads and grieve for what was lost," he said. "It is not fitting that pleasures of eating and drinking should mix with such an event." He turned to the now silent crowd as the vendors bowed and retreated into the shadows. Fima drew himself up tall, and began his tale.

"I'm sure you have all heard of the great realms of Elves and Dwarves. If so then you will have known of the Realm of Light, Eádros, said to be the most beautiful Elven-realm in all of Alterra. Likewise you would know of the Great City of Rûmm, the finest Dwarf-city ever carved from living rock. These two centers of beauty and knowledge were made through the efforts of both races working together, and they stood forth as examples of the magnificence that may be achieved through the blending of innumerable talents. Many skilled hands, quick minds, and fair hearts had a part in their making, for in those times the Dwarves of Rûmm and the Elves of Eádros were friends, and each appreciated the skills and gifts of the others. There was nothing they could not have achieved, given time and desire.

"Both realms had long and colorful histories, but I will give only those facts necessary to the present tale, as my task tonight is a darker one. I must tell you of how they came to ruin, and why." Here, Fima paused and drew a deep breath. "There are dark sentiments buried in each of us that have the ability, in the right circumstance, to turn us from reason, from love, and from light. This is how wars often begin…with feelings of pride, envy, and self-doubt. Not even the most revered of teachers could instruct the people well enough to prevent it.

"Eádros had, in her service, the Asarla Cuimir the Beautiful. He served the Elves of Eádros for thousands of years, instructing and enlightening them, resulting in some of the greatest works of beauty ever seen. His gift was in the appreciation and creation of beauty. Because of his influence, the Elves of Eádros were the finest poets, singers, and artisans in all the world. Majestic, perfect sculptures towered above their Great Halls, interwoven with living trees and plants shaped by loving hands. Their fountains were as sparkling diamonds, their gardens a living paradise. They displayed the incredible beauty of natural light by arranging crystals and stones and water…my heart aches that I have never seen it." Fima looked over at Galador, who had seen the glory of Eádros, and bowed his head in respect. Galador returned the gesture, his eyes misted with the memory of what he had once beheld.

"The City of Rûmm was only a few days' march away, and if it was perhaps not as beautiful, it was no less grand. The Elves enhanced it, once the alliance was formed between the two peoples, and the caverns and halls there were vast and deep, with crystals and carvings and massive pillars of stone. All manner of precious metals could be found there, and the Dwarves wasted no time in fashioning the finest armor and weapons, beautiful vessels, and settings for the rare gems gleaned from within the rock. Elves are best with trees and living things, but no one bests a Dwarf when it comes to the art of the forge. Even Lady Ordath will admit it." Fima raised his eyebrows and looked around the courtyard as though inviting anyone to disagree with him. Naturally, no one did.

"At any rate, both peoples assisted in the enhancement of both dwelling-places, and soon there were underground tunnels and secret pathways connecting Eádros and Rûmm, for each had vowed to come to the defense of the other should need arise. There grew a great friendship— perhaps the first time that Elves and Dwarves at least gave the appearance of real trust—which lasted until the present tale, when it was torn apart and underlying feelings were laid bare. For even though the friendship seemed real enough, there lay beneath it pride, arrogance, suspicion, and doubt. Cuimir tried to teach his people what real beauty is, but he could not warn them of the ugliness of their own emotions. Nor could all the patient study of the most learned of Dwarves guard against the fury that arises from a heart that believes it has been betrayed.

"At the time of this tale, the Lord of Rûmm was named Ivar, the Wise. His eldest son and heir was also named Ivar, for it is Dwarvish custom that heirs be named for their sires, but they are not known by that name until they assume leadership. Therefore, the son was called 'Varni.' Varni was born with a deformity that robbed him of strength and use of his right arm, but his left was clever and skilled. In such an enlightened realm, he endured no open scorn, yet he could see the fleeting looks of pity, and within his heart he doubted his own worth. A very kind and sensitive soul, he delighted in learning and in the making of poems and songs. He had a fine singing voice and he could paint marvelous pictures. He soon attracted the attention of Cuimir the Asarla, who took special delight in instructing him.

"It was decided that a great mural would be painted in the Hall of Council of each realm depicting the friendship between them. Each would be done by a chosen artisan from the other, and, naturally, Varni was asked to paint the great mural in the Hall of Eádros. He agreed, because he loved the lights and waters of that realm, and he loved also the fair voices and faces of the tall, beautiful Elves…perhaps a bit too much in his father's opinion.

"In fact, Lord Ivar was troubled, because he had seen the looks of veiled disdain on the faces of some of the Elves, and even upon some of his own people. He carried some mistrust in his heart even then. Yet because Cuimir himself had made the request that Varni be chosen, Ivar did not oppose his son's wishes, though it meant that he would see very little of Varni for many months to come.

"Varni designed a beautiful piece that would cover not only the enormous wall of the Elves' Great Hall, but also a large expanse of ceiling, for he wanted to depict the coming of Cuimir, who was said to have descended from the heavens. He went to work straightaway, assisted by the Elves, who brought him any and all material that he desired. The affairs of the Council were held in another place while the work was being done so that Varni could paint whenever he wished, hence he rarely left the magnificent Hall with its wonderful, vaulted roof. It was open to the outside world, yet it was so cunningly planned that tall, stately trees sheltered it from all but the hardest rains, and when these fell they were collected in suspended vessels of marble that directed them into fountains and pools below. It was a wondrous realm."

Fima paused again, as he truly loved works of beauty and clever design. He looked around at his audience, waiting for the mental picture his words had described to be painted in their imaginations before he continued.

"One of those who assisted Varni, a maiden named Miradyth, was the sister-daughter of King Doniol of Eádros. She had shown some promise as an artisan, and because her skills paled before those of Varni, she desired to work beside him that she might learn from him. When she saw how truly gifted he was, Miradyth spent untold hours in his presence. She discovered that he was well worth knowing, even aside from his talent, for he was kind and gentle, with a ready sense of humor and something of a knack for story-telling."

Gaelen, who sat quietly between Rogond and Nelwyn, now formed a picture of Varni that resembled Fima, who shared these qualities. For the remainder of the tale, Varni *was* Fima in her mind.

"One day, Miradyth noticed that Varni's left hand was bleeding, for he had cut himself while trimming one of his paintbrushes. She offered to tend him, binding the wound with a beautiful square of silk that she had taken from around her neck. She never imagined the depth of sorrow that would be unleashed by this simple act of friendship and respect, for Varni mistook her intention, and in his heart he desired her. Long had he admired her from his perch upon the scaffolding, and long had he thrilled at the sound of her voice as she greeted him each day. But now a deeper desire swelled within him, for he thought she loved him as more than friend. Had she not given her lovely scarf to bind his wounded hand? Varni knew the scarf was valuable, yet Miradyth had ruined it with blood and paint only to comfort him. Therefore, she must love him.

"In truth, she did love Varni's talent, and his funny ways that were so unlike the other Dwarves she had known, but she did not desire him. One could not blame her, as she was simply incapable. Varni had been enamored of the Elves' beauty and, as his father had feared, he desired always to be more like them. But although they respected his talent and allowed him to dwell among them, he would never attain equal status in their eyes. It seemed that, as with many folk, they confused physical beauty with true worth." Fima saw several heads shaking slowly among the listeners, and he smiled. Despite their denial, they would probably have shared Miradyth's feelings had they shared her place. There were very few statues or paintings of stunted, unlovely folk in Dûn Arian.

"Varni kept his feelings hidden for a time, and he poured his troubled heart into his work. The paintings of the maidens done during this time were hauntingly beautiful, and they all bore resemblance to Miradyth. She could not help but notice, and she was ill-at-ease. She stopped spending so much time with him, turning back to other pursuits, much to the relief of certain of the Elves, particularly her elder brother, Arad. He had long questioned Varni's motives, as well as the wisdom of his sister's 'unhealthy' attachment. Varni, of course, did not understand Miradyth's actions, and he was dismayed, going at last in search of her. He wanted to reveal his heart's desire."

If Fima had attempted at this point to interrupt the tale, he would have been thrown down and sat upon until he finished it. Hundreds of eager eyes were upon him, and a throng of expectant hearts awaited his next words. One unfortunate man was taken with a small bout of coughing, and he received an elbow in the ribs from his neighbor. There was hardly a sound to be heard.

"Varni was very well-spoken, but he was, as I'm sure you can imagine, reluctant and bashful as he confronted his beloved. He stammered out his love for her in a way that, had she loved him, would have been most endearing. Yet to Miradyth it was cause for grief, for she knew that her fears were real and that she must now break his heart. So, to save herself the pain of revealing her true feelings, she told him that he would need to seek permission to court her from King Doniol, knowing full well that it would never be given. She did not possess the courage to trample his feelings by telling him the truth—instead she filled him with false hope. He vowed to go at once to Doniol that he might receive his blessing.

"First he went home to the court at Rûmm, there to confer with his father, Lord Ivar, and tell him of his plan. Ivar was dismayed, believing his son's request ill-advised. He did not approve of intermarriage between Elves and Dwarves. Such a thing had not been seen before, and has not been since, at least not to my knowledge. When Ivar saw the depths of the devotion to Miradyth in his son's eyes, he relented, but he told Varni that he could never assume the Lordship of Rûmm should he marry her. 'The line of the Lords of Rûmm must remain pure,' he said. 'No Elf may influence it. Such was the decree of Fior, the Maker, and such it must be.'

"Varni agreed—he had never truly desired the Lordship of Rûmm—and Ivar was grieved, though his line would not fail, for he had many sons. He had hoped to prevent Varni from a course that would most likely result in a broken heart, and yet in the back of his mind he wondered, for if Doniol actually granted permission for Varni and Miradyth to marry, it would greatly increase the Dwarves' influence in the Elven-realm. In addition, she would no doubt bring a fabulous dowry. Perhaps it would be better to wait and see whether some good could come of it. Ivar had forgotten that nothing good ever comes from greed.

"Varni went before the King and asked for a private council. Doniol was not without foreknowledge of Varni's intention, for Arad, Miradyth's brother, had been in council with him already. As Varni stammered out his request, the expression on the face of the King was kindly, but stern. No blessing would be given—not now nor ever in the future. Surely, Varni must have known this. But then,

Varni posed a question that would ultimately result in the strife to follow. He asked the King 'Why?'

"At first, Doniol did not know how to respond. He considered for a moment, and then directed Varni to stand before the tall glass that stood in one corner of his private chamber. He bade Varni look upon himself. Did he truly believe he was worthy to wed one such as Miradyth? Surely, he must now realize that such a thing could never be. Miradyth could not possibly love him, in fact she did not love him. He should now go back to his own people and be content to live among them without vain aspirations. The sooner he realized that the Elves were above and beyond his affections, the happier he would be."

At this, Gaelen clenched both of her fists in indignation, for she loved Fima and could not imagine ever saying such a thing to him, even if he was short, bearded, and mortal.

"Varni was a gentle soul, but he was also the son of a Lord of Dwarves, and his heart burned fierce in that moment. He had never considered his people to be of lesser worth, and it was now apparent that the Elves did so. He wanted to tell the King of his indignation, to remind him that without the skill of Dwarves, Eádros would not have attained such greatness, but he was silent. Doniol tried to exact the promise that Varni would henceforth keep his distance from Miradyth, and he offered Varni a great reward of riches should he do so. Varni simply stood before the King in shock and anger…did Doniol truly believe that his heart could be turned from true love with jewels and gold? He did not make any promise, but turned and fled from the chamber before Doniol could stay him. He ran from the Elven-realm, tears of shame, indignation, and betrayal burning in his eyes, for he had truly loved the Elves, and had not yet seen their nature. I suppose one cannot blame them entirely, for although they had concealed their disdain out of courtesy, they had not actually denied it.

"Word reached Lord Ivar that his son's request, as expected, had been denied, and that he had fled from Eádros. His whereabouts were unknown, and though the Dwarves searched for him, they did not find him. Doniol aided them, though his response was half-hearted in Ivar's opinion. He sent only a few Elves, and called them back quickly. Ivar himself went to stand before Doniol, requesting an accounting of recent events.

"Doniol responded predictably, at first trying to veil the truth, but Ivar would not be deceived. He demanded to know what had been said to his son that had so dismayed him that he would run and hide from his own people.

"When he heard the words from Doniol, and saw the contempt in his eyes, Ivar was angered. If *this* was the real nature of a friendship with Elves, he would spend no more time in maintaining it. His people were not inferior; they were in many ways more worthy than the Elves, who should certainly be aware of the fact. All of his doubts concerning lack of respect of the Elves for him—for his race—were confirmed. He told Doniol that he had been against the union of Varni and Miradyth from the beginning, but that he had held these feelings back because he knew that he would wound the Elves' feelings otherwise. Well, no longer!"

Fima shook his head as he looked at the dismayed faces in the crowd. "The bad feeling on both sides of the argument spread like fire upon oil, and by the time it reached the high places of Eádros and the deeps of Rûmm it had been altered, augmented, and enhanced. Mistrust and doubt ruled the hearts of the people for the first time in many an Age. Yet the situation might have been saved…had Varni not chosen that moment to try one last time to win Miradyth's heart. He knew the secret ways of Eádros better than many of the Elves, and he also knew where Miradyth would likely be found.

"She was grieved at what her words had wrought, and she sat in despair as she looked upon Varni's unfinished work, wondering whether one capable of creating such beauty should ever feel scorn—hers or anyone else's. She had a good heart, but she simply could not look beyond Varni's appearance, and therefore when he found her and declared once more the depth of his love, she turned away.

"He begged her to come away with him, for he would spend no more time living in a world where he was apart from her. She told him that she could not leave her family, or her beautiful home, and that he must forget his love for her. Varni did not hear her, thinking that she was only afraid to leave the realm, telling her that all would be well, that he would protect her. She stared at him—this stunted, one-armed, unlovely being whose heart was so guileless—and finally spoke the words that she had been afraid to speak. She told Varni that he was incapable of protecting her, that she did not love him, and that he was a fool. She did not mean this last, but she wanted to so dismay him that he would turn from her.

"In Varni's mind, Miradyth had been poisoned by the words of her uncle the King, and by her brother Arad. He decided to try to take Miradyth away with him against her will, knowing that if he could only talk with her and convince her, her love for him would return. Surely, he had seen it! Why would she have sent him to stand before Doniol, if it were not so? Now her heart had been turned, and he must try to turn it back, for he believed that he could not live without her. He reached out with his one good hand, grasped her arm, and would not release her. Varni's left hand and arm were very strong, stronger than Miradyth, and she could not pull free of him. It frightened her, and she struggled, crying out in dismay.

"At that moment, Arad heard his sister's cries and ran into the Hall. He saw Miradyth struggling to break free of Varni and, thinking she was being attacked, he leaped in to aid her, wresting Varni from her and throwing him to the ground.

"Varni was enraged and attacked Arad, for he had nothing further to risk, and they fought fiercely for a few moments. When all was ended, both were wounded, but Arad had prevailed—he was larger, had two good hands, and he despised this Dwarf who had dared lay hands upon his sister.

"Varni's wounds were not mortal and, had his people tended him, he would have lived, but his mind and heart were broken. He struggled up the tall scaffolding, took red paint, and covered the images of Miradyth. 'Here is my blood, which I give at last to you. Take it, my love, and be content!' he cried. Then he turned a blade upon himself, falling down upon the heads of the Elves who had by this time flooded into the Hall.

"There were tears in the eyes of many who witnessed Varni's fall, for most Elves are not cruel people. Yet they were horrified by his loss of reason, and they could not imagine what they would say to Lord Ivar. King Doniol was told of what had happened by Arad, who naturally put forth only his own viewpoint—Varni obviously intended to harm Miradyth and take her by force. He deserved all that he received, and Doniol was owed an apology for the insult upon his family. Miradyth was shamed and grieved, but she said nothing in defense of Varni…nothing to mollify the King. She might keep the respect of her people if they believed she was being attacked without reason.

When Lord Ivar heard of the incident, he wasted no time in doubting the King's explanation. It was obvious to him what had happened—Varni had gone back to say farewell to Miradyth, the King's guard had found him, and he had been slain. His son, a good-natured, happy soul, would never have harmed anyone, much less taken his own life. Ivar sent emissaries to Eádros, demanding that the King hand over those responsible for his son's death at once. Doniol, of course, refused."

Fima's brow furrowed as the depths of his eyes filled with profound sorrow. He told his horrified listeners of the escalation of untruths, bad feelings, and prideful indignation that resulted in the conflict known as the War of Betrayal. This conflict lasted for only a few months' time, but it was so heated, and the two forces were so well-matched and knew all paths of invasion so well, that both realms were threatened.

Cuimir, the Asarla, tried to make peace, but the hearts of both Lords were hardened and darkened. He could not shine light upon them. Arad was killed in the first battle as he attempted to lead the charge upon the Dwarves of Rûmm. Finally, when it appeared that the Dwarves were on the verge of overtaking the Realm of Eádros, and when it seemed that, at the same time, the Elves would break down thc last defenses of the City of Rûmm, Doniol and Ivar decided to destroy all the beauty they had made, rather than allow it to fall into the hands of their former friends. No Dwarf would freely roam the Halls of Light; no Elf would enjoy the beauty of the Deep-delving.

"Cuimir tried desperately to stay the hand and sway the mind of Doniol, but he could not," said Fima. "The halls and caverns were brought down, and as many of the people as could be saved were thrown from their homes into the wild and hostile world." Fima shook his head. "They were not many.

"Cuimir, it is said, would not leave Eádros, for he was so mired in despair that he fell with it. He had tried to teach his people the nature of true beauty, and yet it had eluded them despite his efforts. He had unwittingly led them astray, for true beauty lies not in things, in graceful form, in comely image, or even in spoken word. It lies instead deep within the souls of those who love. Varni's heart was really the only beautiful thing in all of this, and it turned to ugliness in the end. Neither Doniol, nor Ivar, nor Cuimir survived."

There were tears in the eyes of many who listened to Fima's tale. The idea of an Asarla so disheartened, and two such fabulous realms and so many people being lost because of pride, greed, and misunderstanding was inconceivable to many of them.

Fima was not yet finished. After collecting himself for a moment, he looked over at Galador. "The evil that began in that time still lives within many of the Elves and Dwarves of Alterra, even uncounted generations later. Enmity is slow to die in the hearts of both races. I have learned to love the Elves, and most of them have come to hold respect for me, but even I mistrusted them in the beginning. Sometimes I wonder whether we can ever regain what was lost."

Galador rose to his feet and bowed. "I would submit, Loremaster, that what was lost was never truly held. If our peoples had truly been friends, they would not have allowed these events to turn them to such a terrible course. Real friendship can only be made between individuals, and not between peoples. Know that I apologize to you for any part that my people played, for you are my friend, and I will trust you unto my death."

He bowed again, and Fima returned the gesture, saying, "If more of the Elves of Eádros had been of your mind, Galador, then the glory of both realms might yet remain. You would have given heart to Cuimir. Alas, it can never be."

Fima took his leave, but the crowd seemed reluctant to disperse, for their hearts had been torn by the tale. These matters would be thought of and debated for a long time to come. Slowly, the courtyard emptied until only the Company remained. There was still one question in Gaelen's mind—what had become of Miradyth? She supposed that question would forever remain unanswered. At last she sighed, rose to her feet, and took her leave, pausing for a moment and inclining her head respectfully toward the place where Fima had been.

It was a good thing that Kotos possessed such unrivaled powers of persuasion; otherwise, the Forces of Darkness might have met their defeat right then and there. In the person of Olan, he had gone back to the Citadel to procure some important items, including a very strong soap, scented oil, a stiff-bristled brush, and a wooden pail. He also took food and drinking water, a warm blanket, and a flagon of wine. He made one more stop at the apothecary to purchase herbs that would reduce fever. Then he made his way with all due haste back to Gorgon's lair, having been gone for nearly three days. Kotos smiled when he beheld the expression of relief on Gorgon's face.

"About time you got back here," growled the Elfhunter. "The man is not faring so well. I have kept him alive, but not by much." He indicated El-morah, who had taken a fever and now lay shivering in a dark corner, clinging as hard as he could to life. Kotos examined him with concern, shaking his head and clucking softly with Olan's tongue.

El-morah still shivered in misery, wandering from one feverish vision to the next, moaning and biting his lip to keep from crying out. It was fortunate that Gorgon had been ladling water down his throat for several days now, or the chills and hard sweats would have finished him. As it was, he could only ride through the bouts of fever and try to hold on to his strength. When the voice of Lord Kotos camc to him, and Olan's hands placed herbs under his tongue, he did not resist. The herbs took effect almost at once, calming him and easing the fever, sending him into a realm where he would feel no pain. Kotos sent forth the vision of a handsome, golden-haired figure, telling El-morah not to despair—that everything would turn out all right in the end.

Kotos surveyed his charge with satisfaction. "He'll live, I think." He turned back to Gorgon and looked him hard in the eye. "You and I must agree to a task now, one that you will most certainly not enjoy. Yet you must submit to it, Elfhunter, for your disguise is not yet complete. Come with me." Olan did not possess the commanding tone of voice that would motivate Gorgon, who just stood staring at him for a moment. "No arguments!" said Kotos as Gorgon glowered down at him. "Do as I bid, and do not waste time in debate, or we will both be undone. Your transformation is nearly complete, yet this task remains. Come with me now!"

Gorgon made a deep thrumming sound in his broad chest, as he sometimes did when he was thinking things over. At last he sniffed and tossed his long, golden hair back before following Olan to the underground water-source. Olan filled his wooden pail with water, took the bristle brush in one hand, and approached Gorgon, who did not understand what he was about.

"Exactly what do you intend to do with that?" he asked, actually taking a small step back from Olan before he could stop himself. There was a sort of wicked, bemused determination in Olan's eyes that he did not care for at all.

"You must be cleansed, Elfhunter," came the reply. "Nay, you must be scrubbed to within an inch of your life. I can alter your appearance, but your scent I cannot change except through diligence and a lot of soapy water. Do you want that She-elf to catch a whiff of you? From what you have told me, she uses scent like a hound and she will know you at once. That is one risk I am not willing to take. Now be silent, and endure what must be done."

Gorgon stared at Olan in disbelief. His flesh had never truly been clean in his life. "Take off the amulet, and do not fear," said Kotos. "My host will see only what I want him to see, and will remember none of it. Take off the amulet, and then take off whatever else you are wearing and stand before me as the Lord of Darkness made you."

The next hour was memorable for both Gorgon and Kotos. Mercifully, Olan would remember nothing of it afterward. Gorgon was scrubbed until his thick, leathery hide actually pained him, and the smell that arose from the deep crevices of his flesh was indescribable. He lost count of the number of times he felt the urge to throttle the life from Olan, as he stood with his teeth bared and his pale eyes narrowed into an expression of venomous fury. He snarled and growled and fretted and fumed, yet Kotos took no notice—the water in the pail turned blackish-brown, was refilled, and turned black again eight times before all was ended. At last Gorgon's dark, corded limbs gleamed as Olan rubbed them with oil that had been scented with sage and orange peels.

Kotos admired his handiwork with approval, but he cautioned Gorgon that he would need to wait until Olan's senses recovered to know whether all traces of foulness had been extinguished. "Tomorrow we'll see," he said. "Now take your amulet, and accept my congratulations. I know this has not been easy for you, yet it is only the first of many new experiences in store." Kotos sighed. "I still must teach you how to behave. No Elf ever snarled like that. And you will need to learn to use a knife and fork, I fear."

"I bloody well know how to use a knife," growled Gorgon, eyeing Olan's slender frame. "In fact, I'm thinking about using one right now."

"Don't be ridiculous," Kotos muttered, shaking Olan's head. Considering the enormity of what still lay before him, Kotos told himself that he should not dwell on such matters. Neither he nor Gorgon could afford to be discouraged.

In the morning, Olan approached Gorgon and, to his displeasure, inspected him up and down. "Well," Kotos said at last, "I must say that your scent has improved beyond measure since yesterday." He wrinkled Olan's nose a bit. "Yet it seems I have forgotten one very important task. Sit down— my host is not as tall as I would wish."

Gorgon shook his head, looking sidelong at Olan. This could not mean anything good. There followed a very short but heated argument ending in threats, followed by a grudging cooperation. Kotos was not in a patient mood. Olan stood before Gorgon, who was now seated on a stone, and drew forth a dull-bladed knife. "Open your mouth," he commanded, and then set to work. Soon Gorgon's clean, scented body would no longer be betrayed by his foul breath.

The next few hours were spent scrubbing Gorgon's dark armor, using the same stiff-bristled brush, together with sand and water. Gorgon actually aided in this, as he was far stronger than Olan, and it was necessary to remove all trace of scent. Tomorrow they would leave for the City, taking El-morah with them. They would keep their captive in a state of helpless confusion and delirium, for it was essential to the plan. As they packed up and prepared to depart, Olan paused. "I have forgotten…one more task!"

This elicited a look of dismay from Gorgon. "What now?" he snarled, baring gleaming teeth the color of old ivory. "Will you now seek to remove all foulness from my droppings? Surely the Elves would expect nothing less." This last comment apparently amused him and he chuckled to himself.

Kotos was not amused in the least. "Any sort of crude, sarcastic remark like that will mar your respectable illusion. I had best never hear any such words from you once we are in the presence of the City-folk. The task that remains is to give you a name…you cannot exactly introduce yourself as Gorgon Elfhunter, can you?"

Gorgon was chastened. "I understand," he said. "You're right…I must have a name, and learn it so that it will become familiar enough that I will answer to it. What name will you give me?"

"Let me think on it, for it is important. You never know what high-and-mighty folk you will be introduced to before all is ended. Let me think on it."

Four souls left the sanctuary that day, and three approached the City two days later, though only the tall Elf and the man that he carried in his strong arms could be seen. The third presence lurked within the mind of the Elf, who had been named Orrion, after his long, golden hair.

7
The Healing of El-Morah

As Gorgon Elfhunter, now known as Orrion, made his way toward Dûn Arian, he received a thorough introduction to his new life history by Lord Kotos, who dwelled within him. Kotos found Gorgon's real history interesting enough—in fact, Gorgon was possibly the most unique and complex being he had yet inhabited.

Although he had lived for ages in Alterra, Gorgon's mind was still uncluttered, surprisingly so in Kotos' opinion. Yet since the day he had been released from Wrothgar's keeping, Gorgon had led a solitary life. He would go belowground for years at a time, nursing his hatred of the Elves, lapsing into an almost deathlike state. If he had not, his very active mind would have tormented him. Gorgon could be very patient when called for. He would emerge only when the desire to bring suffering to the Elves became too great for him to ignore.

Orrion appeared to be one of the most impressive-looking beings Kotos had seen in a long time. He was enormous, both tall and strong, and very well made. So long as Gorgon wore the amulet, he would appear as a finely-chiseled yet massive Elf, most likely Èolarin, with long, golden hair and beautiful grey eyes. Even his armor was transformed—under the influence of the amulet it, too, was golden—yet the dents and scrapes were still there. The armor had to appear to have seen battle, and it did, but it was also beautiful, with engravings and wrought images that might have been fashioned by Dardis himself

Kotos gave Orrion the illusion of a left hand, but he would not be able to grasp anything with it. *Should anyone wonder about it, you can explain that you lost the use of it in battle long ago. You defended the realm of Tal-elathas beside Ri-Aldamar, but were been taken from the fight, bewildered by dragon-fire and wounded many times before you finally slipped into a deathlike trance. They left you for dead, thrown on the pile of bodies that had been left to rot.*

"Why did they not take my armor?" asked Gorgon.

Ulcas do not care for beautiful things, and they do not like Elven-made objects, recoiling at the very touch of them. You know that! Elves cannot help but place some of their own abilities in the objects that they take great care to make...Ulcas cannot bear it.

When he looked directly at himself, Gorgon saw the familiar dull black, pock-marked armor covering his scarred flesh. Yet his reflected image was so different, and he smiled every time he beheld it. This pleased Kotos, for Elves often smiled at their own reflections...how vain they were!

Kotos knew all about transformations. When he was young, and still a being of Light, he had appeared Elven himself. He had been tall and strong, like Shandor, his closest friend. Yet where Shandor was all silver and blue, Kotos was dark, with glossy blue-black hair and eyes the color of dark grey storm clouds. His limbs had been tawny, like polished maple. He had been beautiful upon a time. Now he had no form, although he could appear in the amulet as a vision of a wise old man, or a noble Elf, or a black, terrible demon if he wished. It was this last that came closest to his nature.

With Kotos as his ally, Gorgon was the most powerful dark agent in Alterra save for Lord Wrothgar. The Elves would never guess his identity, for he neither looked nor sounded nor smelled as he had before. And when they looked into his eyes, they would behold the gaze of the Deceiver, and would never see into the heart of the Elfhunter. Kotos reassured Gorgon over and over, as they traveled the long miles, that even Gaelen Taldin would not know him. Yet Gorgon was uncertain. "She has looked into my soul... she has seen me with no cloak of flesh upon my spirit. How can she not know me?"

You must rely on my judgment. She will see my spirit, not yours, and I will deceive her. She is only a Sylvan Elf, unenlightened and undoubtedly ignorant of worldly affairs. From what you have told me, she will never have beheld one such as myself. She will have no defense against me. Have no fear!

"She is a vixen, and she is wary," said Gorgon. "It worries me that you discount her so. Make no mistake—this Sylvan Elf is the most formidable of our enemies. Do not discount her!"

Perhaps, if she is so formidable, we should arrange to eliminate her. I'm certain the opportunity will arise. Then you can lay your fears to rest.

"I will eliminate her," growled Gorgon, "but it must be at a time of my choosing, and in a manner of my design. She will not go quietly to an easy death! I would rather risk discovery than deny myself the pleasure of tormenting her. Do you understand?"

At this, Kotos laughed. *I do, my friend Gorgon, or, should I say, Orrion! Obviously your desire for vengeance outweighs your fear. Do remember that when she looks into your eyes, won't you? If you cringe back from her, even a little, she will never trust you. Such is the case with any of them! Remember, you have nothing to hide. You are a being of Light.* This statement amused both Kotos and Orrion, who laughed in a malicious way that belied his apparent beauty.

"All right," said Gorgon. "What of the rest of my history? I had been left for dead…"

Yes, that's right, said Kotos. *When you emerged from your deathlike trance, you lost all memory of your past. You wandered northward, into the frozen lands beyond Tal-elathas, traveling by day, huddling against the cold by night. At last you fell victim to a storm of ice, and lay frozen for many, many years. The great Third Battle came and passed, and still you slept in your prison of ice, until an upheaval of a distant fire-mountain released you.*

Your memory began to return, but only in part, and you wandered into the lands around the Fell-ruin, where you saw many terrible things. You have since traveled over the Northern Mountains, and south through the Darkmere, bearing disturbing news. Wrothgar was acquiring forces the like of which Alterra has not seen since the last Uprising, and they were massing in the Fell-ruins to the north.

This news was particularly disturbing to the Elves, who have not rebuilt their numbers since the Third Uprising. The same could be said of men, who had been devastated by pestilence. Alterra is not prepared to repel a full-scale assault by the forces of Darkness—you have been trying to warn everyone.

"What am I doing all the way down here, if the threat is in the Fell-ruin?" asked Gorgon.

You don't really know—you have been driven south on an inexplicable impulse. You don't know why Wrothgar's forces are amassing in the Fell-ruins, either, but so they are. You're a lost being, not truly aware of yourself or of your surroundings. It's a miracle you weren't discovered and taken as you passed through the Darkmere.

Gorgon seemed reasonably impressed with this history. "Being frozen for such a long time would explain why I know so little of recent world affairs, and why I am hesitant when confronting strangers."

Kotos smiled to himself. Orrion would prove to be an odd mix of impressive physical presence and social awkwardness. The story that he had been damaged in battle, and had faced such terrible trials, added to his credibility. He would appear confused much of the time, would not like being surrounded by strange folk, and would not participate in songs or in tale-telling. Kotos would ensure that the right words were ready in Gorgon's mind, and that Orrion would say them.

They stopped only to tend to El-morah, to give him water and make certain he was still breathing. *It is important that this man be alive when we arrive at the Citadel,* said Kotos. *I need to establish you, Orrion, as a person of very special and unique talents, and I need this man to demonstrate them. I have been preparing this deception for a while.*

"Well, you won't need to worry about it much longer," said Gorgon. "There is the gap in the hills that leads to the Citadel. We're nearly there now."

When the sentinels first beheld the golden figure striding toward the Great Gates, they were surprised and awed. Here was a figure straight out of legend standing before them, speaking High-elven in a deep and resounding voice, asking to be admitted. He carried a man in his arms, and that man appeared to be on the verge of death. Because of their recent trials, the City was no longer quite as welcoming as it had once been, and an armed guard met the strange Elf at the gate, but this did not appear to dismay him.

Orrion delivered El-morah into the arms of a tall, grey-eyed man named Visili, who bore him to the Healing Halls at once. There he would be tended and his body restored, but he could not be truly healed. Not yet.

Rogond, Hallagond, and Galador were the first among the Company to learn of Orrion. The news of an Elf arriving in the

City had excited all who heard, and it spread quickly. Soon there were many curious folk gathered outside the Hall of Council, where it was said that Lord Salastor and his councilors were meeting with the newcomer, no doubt to learn of his intentions. As the tale spread, it grew. The people, though they had become accustomed to the sight of Elves in the City, would never have seen anyone quite like Orrion. Not even Galador could match him in size, beauty, or power. The Èolar were larger and stronger in general than the Eádram, who, though tall enough, were inclined to be more lithe and lissome. Orrion looked like a vision from an ancient manuscript come to life.

Despite Orrion's tall stature and prideful demeanor, Gorgon Elfhunter was terrified. He was now surrounded by curious folk, any one of whom would most likely try to kill him were his true nature revealed. Gorgon did not like crowds of people except on a battlefield, and he was now in a frightful state of discomfort. He felt like a trapped animal. Despite all reassurance from Kotos, he wanted to bolt from the chamber where he now stood before the High Council. To Kotos' displeasure and alarm, he began to sweat.

Stop that at once! You must not allow them to see the sweat that runs from your brow...Elves do not sweat like that unless they are laboring hard in extreme heat! Cease your trembling! Look...look around you. These people are nothing compared with you. Can you not see how small and how weak they are? They are in absolute awe of you. Do not cringe before them—you are the mightiest being they have ever beheld. Stand tall and unafraid, for I am with you. You wield more power than all of them put together, so start acting like it!

To his relief, Kotos convinced Gorgon to quell his fears for the moment. Orrion took a deep breath, lifted his head, and stopped sweating. He drew his right arm across his forehead, removing all trace of his fear, and looked into the eyes of Lord Salastor.

Orrion told the Council all that he would tell them, speaking in High-elven. Gorgon had learned the tongue of the Èolar when he was very young, and now it served him well, for the words came forth with practiced ease. They came at the prompting of Kotos, for this first meeting must go according to plan, and they could not afford mistakes. At last he bowed before the Council, asking that he be allowed to rest. "My journey has been long and hard, and I am weary," he said. "Please, might these questions be delayed until I have refreshed myself? I will enlighten thee when I am better able."

It was not like the people of Dûn Arian to be inconsiderate, and they were chagrined. Of course, Orrion would be well cared for—the inquiries of the Council could wait. Lord Salastor himself apologized to Orrion for taxing him. "Take thy rest, Worthy Guest, and partake of our hospitality. Thou art welcome. Forgive us our curiosity at the expense of thy comfort. I humbly ask thy pardon… we shall continue our talks at a later time." He bowed then to Orrion, as did all the Council of Nine.

A warden stepped forward to conduct Orrion to his guest quarters. As Gorgon turned to leave, Kotos spoke to him. *Be aware that some of those you know are present here, and do not be dismayed. Take no notice!* Orrion scanned the crowd, his eyes lighting only for a moment on Rogond and Galador before moving on. They did not appear to know him. *You see? I told you they would not. If you do exactly as I instruct, they never will.* As he left the hall, one event stood out in Gorgon's mind with more clarity than any other. It was the first time in his entire misbegotten existence that anyone had apologized to him for anything.

Orrion soon found himself in a clean, white chamber with a soft bed, a tray of food, clear, cold water, and some sweet, red wine. Kotos advised him to leave the wine alone, as Gorgon would need his wits about him, and Kotos did not know how the wine would affect him.

Orrion was hungry, and he started wolfing down the food until Kotos stayed him. *Stop that! You need to begin to learn manners when it comes to eating and drinking. I would suggest that we begin at once. If anyone sees you gorging like a half-starved dog, there will be questions. Now, take the fork in your hand. Yes, that's right…no, not like that! You appear to be ready to stab someone with it.*

Kotos sighed inwardly as Gorgon gripped the fork in his huge fist as though it were a weapon. How could he convey the lesson? *One moment…step over to the mirror and look within.* Kotos flowed into the glass, allowing the image of the old man to appear there. The old man held up a fork so that Gorgon could see.

"Now," said the old man, "you try." Orrion held the fork in the same manner. "Well done. Now watch me and learn." They practiced together, first with the fork, and then with the knife, until Kotos was satisfied.

Gorgon, by now, had become impatient. "Get on with it, you old fool! I am famished from my journey, and I am weary of this," he snarled.

Kotos' face grew dark and for a moment Gorgon was very nearly afraid of him. "If I hear any sort of discourtesy from you while you are here, you will regret it! I know it doesn't come easily, but if you cannot think of a polite way to say something, don't speak at all until I have enlightened you! Is that now very clear?"

The image of the old man transformed into a sort of malevolent, swirling cloud of inky black and dark purple. Kotos left the mirror and flowed back into Orrion without another word, causing him to take a sharp breath. Being invaded by an angry Kotos was jarring to the system. Kotos calmed almost at once and sent forth soothing thoughts. *There, now...of course you are hungry, my large friend. Let us practice eating in an appropriate manner, shall we?* For the next hour, Orrion demonstrated passable, if inexpert, table manners.

Afterward, he was weary and in need of rest. *You should not sleep*, said Kotos. *You are an Elf, remember? They do not sleep except in very special circumstances. Yet you may rest, and I shall keep the watch, for I require no rest at all. I will alert you if anyone comes.* With these words Kotos flowed back into his amulet, leaving Gorgon's exhausted mind in peace.

In all his long years, the Elfhunter had never encountered anything quite so taxing as standing before that Council with very little idea of how to behave, surrounded by strange men, praying that they would not see through his disguise. He drew the heavy drapes across the windows, darkening the chamber, and then tried to rest on the soft bed. But he was unused to such things, and felt as if he was being suffocated, so at last he lay on the hard, polished floor with his knees drawn up before him. Though this would appear strange, Kotos was not concerned. The people of the Citadel were courteous, and would never enter Orrion's chamber without his permission.

Rogond and Galador had gone to the Healing Halls to look upon the man Orrion had found in the desert. At first, they did not know him. Though he had been made clean and the fever had left him, El-morah looked like someone else. His beard was untrimmed, his hair unkempt, and he was painfully thin, his skin burned by the sun. His eyes, cold and vacant, held none of their former warmth or good humor.

In fact, he seemed to be in a constant state of bewilderment, muttering words that made no sense as though he had lost his reason. Kotos had damaged him, and now he wandered the empty halls of his memory in search of anything he could grab on to. He did not recognize Rogond or Galador.

When Gaelen and Nelwyn appeared, the mystery was solved. When Gaelen had been poisoned by Sajid the Spider, El-morah had aided her. She had been aware of very few sights or sounds on that terrible night, but she had taken note of any and all unfamiliar scents, El-morah's among them. They were forever etched in her memory. She knew him almost at once, crying out in dismay. He had been a staunch friend of the Company, and now he was far from home, without his family, apparently suffering some terrible form of madness. Whatever could have happened to drive him here?

The healers spread their hands, saying there was nothing more they could do. El-morah's condition was not of the body, and his madness was not a thing they could heal. Afflictions of the mind were still a great mystery for the most part.

Gaelen sorrowed for El-morah. He had aided them all, he had been their friend, and he was lost. Now there was nothing to do but wait and hope that he could find healing within himself, but the healers were not encouraging. El-morah was not caring for himself, he would not eat without considerable coaxing and he drank very little water. Estle and Hallagond had both known El-morah, and they, too, were dismayed.

"El-morah is not the only recent arrival with an affliction of the mind," said Galador. "Orrion seemed very odd to me…backward… almost fearful. What would he have to fear here in Dûn Arian?"

"I understand your feeling," said Rogond. "I saw fear in him, too. Yet the citizens did not seem disquieted."

"They are not familiar with the nature of Elves," said Galador. "It is not in the manner of High-elves, particularly Èolar, to show such trepidation. Yet perhaps when we learn more of his history we will understand."

"And when will we learn of it?" asked Gaelen, who had not as yet seen Orrion. Her curiosity was high.

"Soon," said Galador. "Orrion's discomfort in large groups was not lost on Lord Salastor. He has arranged for him to meet with the Council in private within the next few days. Rogond has suggested that perhaps some members of the Company might be present at the meeting, to which Salastor has agreed."

"Well, if only a few of us will be chosen, Galador should be among them," said Gaelen. "After all, he will know one of his own. He should be able to discern whether the history given is plausible."

"It seems you do not trust Orrion already," said Rogond. "You have never even laid eyes on him. Why do you already not trust him? Is it because Galador considers him odd?"

Gaelen thought for a moment, wondering about the answer to Rogond's question herself, but in the end she simply shook her head. *I cannot say...because I don't know.* One thing was certain—her curiosity would not allow her any peace until she had satisfied it.

"I will go to Lord Salastor and suggest that all three of the Elves be invited to attend the next council with Orrion. After all, he will no doubt be much more comfortable in the presence of his own kind," said Rogond.

"We still have the question of what to do about our friend El-morah," said Gaelen. "Fima, are there any helpful writings to be found in the City's vast library?"

"Perhaps if you surround him with things that are familiar, his memory may return," said Fima, who had already been looking into the matter. "Hallagond, Galador, why don't you set about finding some brewed kaffa? Perhaps the taste and aroma will remind El-morah of home."

Finding all the ingredients for a pot of kaffa proved to be more difficult than expected. Estle, who was something of a connoisseur, wrinkled her nose when she tasted it. "This is nothing like the kaffa he is accustomed to," she said. "He will never accept it…it is appalling by comparison!"

"It is *all* appalling in my opinion," said Nelwyn, who had never acquired a taste for kaffa.

"Still, I see no harm in trying," said Galador. "He will be none the worse for it."

Estle took one look at the multicolored film of oil swirling on the surface of the dark brown liquid, and shook her head. "He will think you are trying to poison him if he tastes this."

"Is it really *that* bad?" asked Gaelen, sniffing at the pot. "Smells like kaffa to me…though it is quite different from that of the oasis. Let us see what will happen. Just to be safe, let me add some honey to help conceal the difference. He will surely like it then!"

"Honey? Not in kaffa, you don't," said Estle. "We prefer cane sugar if anything at all. El-morah doesn't take either. We'll just have to offer it as it is. Ugh!"

"All right," said Galador, frowning. "I will take it to him. I surely don't want Estle's attitude to influence him."

"Why not? The objective is to surround him with things that are familiar," said Gaelen. "Surly Estle with her nose in the air is no doubt very familiar." She smiled and raised both eyebrows at Estle, awaiting the reply that would surely come.

"Alas that El-morah has not known you longer, Gaelen, or your lame attempts at insult would also be familiar," said Estle. "I fear he is unaccustomed to those of such little wit."

"Then perhaps you should not be present after all," said Gaelen. "Ah, but your familiar attitude will most likely make up for lack of wit. You can come, then." She bowed and extended her arm in mock invitation, earning her a scowl from Estle, as well as one from Rogond. This was no time for games.

As predicted, El-morah did not react well to the offer of kaffa, throwing it at Galador and claiming that he was being poisoned. Estle sniffed and looked over at Gaelen. "I told you so."

"We did accomplish one thing at least," said Galador as he wiped his face with a cloth. "That's the most life I've seen in him since he came. At least he was not in a stupor when he threw the pot at my head."

"No," said Nelwyn sadly. "But he still does not know his friends. What else can we do to awaken him?"

"I don't know," said Estle. "But don't despair. He was aware that the kaffa you tried to tempt him with was bad…at least he was aware of something. It's a beginning."

Kotos roused Gorgon as the moon was just about to set over the quiet waters of the harbor. *Awake, Orrion High-elven, for the darkness of night is peaking, and it is time for you to go abroad into the City. There are no guards at your door. Awake, for we have another errand. The City is sleeping. Awake!*

Gorgon stretched and shook himself, his dusty black armor shifting with a dull, muffled "clunk."

We should find a way to conceal your armor, for you must remove it. There is a large trunk in the corner of the room…is there a key? Does it lock?

Gorgon moved to open the trunk, which was empty. A brass key lay in a small wooden tray beneath the lid.

When you take your armor off, it will appear black as it does in reality, said Kotos. *No one must be allowed to view it. Take it off and stow it in the trunk under lock and key.*

Gorgon now stood naked in the waning moonlight that filtered through a gap in the heavy drapes. His clean, polished skin was a deep blue-grey. Ulcas are not truly black or brown unless they are dirty, which they always seem to be. Gorgon's clean body was the color of fine slate. Were it not so scarred it would have held a sort of savage, powerful beauty. Under the influence of the amulet, it was spectacular.

Orrion was taller even than Rogond, with immense, broad shoulders, a deep chest, lean, well-muscled midsection, and long, powerful legs. He was sinewy, smooth-skinned, masculine perfection. His long, golden hair flowed like liquid silk, framing a face that was chiseled of marble by a master's hand. His eyes—grey, brooding storm clouds—were fathomless.

They very considerately provided you with a robe, said Kotos. *Now cover yourself, and let us go forth.*

Kotos directed Orrion to the public bath house, a beautiful structure of salmon-pink marble with a lovely pool of warm water within. The scent of flowers and citrus fruits hung in the air.

Bathe yourself in the water. You must do so each night, for otherwise your own scent will return. You must rub your flesh with the oil scented with sage and oranges each time you emerge…your own scent will mingle with the myriad others that steeped in the bath water. Do this, and you will remain hidden.

Gorgon was not pleased about this, but he had come to accept the wisdom of it. He knew that, should Gaelen catch a whiff of him as he truly was, he would be undone.

The people of Dûn Arian were most obliging in providing fine new clothing for Orrion, though the garments had to be specially made. Artisans were hard at work, altering and fashioning a tunic, breeches, and cloak that would be worthy of their noble guest. Gorgon stayed in his chambers until they were ready, venturing forth only by night, stalking through the clean, paved streets like a huge mountain-cat on the prowl. Each day he would eat and rest, and each night he would bathe. Yet he spent very little time interacting with anyone, and so his confidence had not improved.

He was anxious about the impending council, but Kotos reassured him. *You need not fear so long as you allow me to direct you. I have spoken before assemblies far mightier than this! If I could beguile the Kings of Tuathas and Tal-elathas, if I could deceive my brothers Baelta and Shandor, do you not think me up to the task of dealing with a worm like Salastor? He is not even worthy of notice, much less concern. Be not dismayed.*

"It's not Salastor I'm worried about," whispered Gorgon, but Kotos ignored him.

Orrion was magnificent in his new clothing, and even Gorgon had to admit that the feel of the soft velvet against his skin was… enticing. He had shuddered with pleasure as he first slipped on the rich, slate grey tunic and the dark grey velvet breeches. There was a sleeveless jerkin made of soft grey leather that went over the tunic, and a fine belt of black leather.

Gorgon had a bit of difficulty with the fit of both the tunic and the belt at first, because the dimensions of Orrion were more slender than those of Gorgon, whose actual physical form had not changed. It was an interesting illusion, for the Citadel's tailors had measured Gorgon ere they began their task, but when they read the numbers they made no sense. Assuming that they had erred in the measuring, they cut the garments down accordingly, resulting in a rather tight fit. Gorgon drove new holes into the belt to almost the very tip; it was conventional to leave a long tail that was knotted and looped over. Belts most often wore out near the buckle, and this long tail could then be used as the belt was repaired. Items in Alterra were made to last. Fortunately, the tunic was put together with lacing and could be let out. The sleeves were made very loose for freedom of movement. So long as Gorgon wore the leather jerkin, his secret was safe.

He grumbled at the thought of trying to wield a weapon in such restrictive gear, until Lord Kotos pointed out that should he find himself doing battle, it would not matter what happened to his clothing.

You will no doubt tear these fine things to shreds moving in them, but you will not care and neither will anyone else. Let them think they have made mistakes in tailoring. It is of no consequence.

Orrion stood before the High Council on the following day. The nine ministers were present, as were Rogond, Galador, Nelwyn, Gaelen, and Fima. They were seated in the gallery where they could hear the proceedings, but Orrion would not actually stand before them. Orrion stood in the doorway, his eyes sweeping the chamber, and the sight of Gaelen both aroused his wrath and took his courage. His lip curled into a snarl before he could stop himself.

Kotos took hold in less than a heartbeat. *Master yourself at once! Let your face be impassive, and let us hope that no one took notice of that snarl. This is only your first test, Elfhunter. Remember the creature that lures its prey? You are luring her now…luring them all to death. Let that gladden and strengthen your heart. Now master yourself, and stand before them. Remember that you are Orrion of the* Èolar, and they are beneath you—*all of them!* Gorgon took a deep breath, and his face relaxed. *Remember,* said Kotos, *she will not know you. You neither look, nor sound, nor smell as you did before. You can face her unafraid.*

When Orrion bowed before the Council, he was introduced to everyone present, including the Company. Kotos met the eyes of each person as each name was given, and he did not allow any trace of Gorgon to appear in his gaze.

Gaelen looked into his eyes, and was mesmerized. When she first beheld him she felt every hair on the back of her neck stand erect, and a cold vapor creep into her heart. Such feelings in the past had been associated with Gorgon, yet these were not the eyes of the Elfhunter. The longer she looked into them, the warmer and more peaceful she became. Orrion's eyes were beautiful, and deep, and very, very comforting. Gaelen was reminded of a dark grey evening sky that is heavy with rain…rain that would soon fall in her beloved forest, where all was familiar. She could almost smell the rain and the trees. Her mind strayed now, strayed homeward to the Greatwood. The tension left her body, and she sighed. Kotos was satisfied, and moved on to Nelwyn.

Gorgon was relieved and very impressed at Kotos' handling of Gaelen. If he could beguile the Vixen, he could do anything. Gorgon drew taller as confidence swelled within him, even as Kotos spoke words of warning.

The ones to fear are the Wood-elf and the dwarf. They will be the most difficult to deceive. I see, now, why you feared her. She has fallen to my suggestions this time, but I would advise you to stay as far from her as you may. She has insight that the others do not possess. Beware, also, of the Minister of Omens, for the same reason. Now turn your attention to your task, and do not relax your vigilance.

Gorgon stood before the Council of Nine and proceeded, with the aid of Lord Kotos, to enlighten them as to the history of Orrion High-elven. He conducted himself well under Kotos' direction, answering any and all questions with the readiness of a person who desires to be completely open and honest. He admitted that there was still much that had befallen since the Second Uprising that remained unclear in his mind, and that he still could not remember the lay of things in the North. Yet the sight of the Elves had aided him already, and he welcomed Gaelen, Nelwyn, and Galador, for surely now his memories would return. He described the massing of dark forces in the Fell-ruin, showing just the right amount of dread to be convincing. Yet he seemed to grow weary again, and Salastor called a halt to the proceedings.

"We will adjourn until tomorrow, if all will agree," he said. "Our guest should be allowed to rest and refresh himself." He turned to Orrion. "Please avail yourself of whatever comforts you desire. Our City is yours." He and Orrion bowed to each other, and Orrion took his leave.

There was very little discussion among the Council-members, for they did not exactly know what to make of Orrion and what he had revealed. The thought of Wrothgar amassing an army was disquieting, but most on the Council felt that Dûn Arian was too far away to be threatened by affairs in the North. After all, there was nothing to suggest that Wrothgar even knew of the Silver Fortress. But Salastor had heard Rogond's words earlier, and he knew that if the survivors of the Scourge ranged through the southlands, word would spread quickly northward, and he could no longer be certain that the Shadowmancer had not set his black gaze on Dûn Arian. Maji, the Minister of Omens, would no doubt hold some insight. Salastor resolved that he would go and consult with her privately in the very near future.

It was Nelwyn who first thought of asking Orrion if there was anything he could do for El-morah. It would do no harm to ask him, as he had mentioned that he had some talent for healing afflictions of the mind. Elves, who do not suffer pestilence, still may fall victim to forces that unbalance them, such as grief, rage, and despair. Even the Asari may suffer such affliction—Shandor was so consumed by grief that he was driven to place his spirit within the Stone of Léir. He had since become so embittered and withdrawn that it was no longer safe to look within.

Kotos smiled to himself, as he had planted this seed and it had taken root as expected. "Of course, I will aid you if I can," said Orrion. "Take me to your friend and I will minister as I am able." Nelwyn then conducted him to the Healing Halls.

El-morah sat in a chair by the window, gazing with empty eyes into the sun-washed courtyard, and took little notice of his visitors.

Orrion knelt before him, grasped his jaw with a strong right hand, and turned it so that their eyes would meet.

Kotos flowed forth again into El-morah's unguarded mind, for it was Kotos who had taken those defenses away, and it was he who had bewildered El-morah so completely as to close the doors of his memory and his reason. Now Kotos roamed those empty halls, calling out to his host with soothing words. What Kotos had done, he could undo.

Gaelen sat atop the western battlement overlooking the sea, a pensive expression on her face and trouble on her mind. She did not notice Rogond, as she was inclined to be less perceptive when she was brooding about something, and he startled her. She tried to conceal her surprise with a warm smile. "What is your desire, my love? Is there something you need?"

Rogond smiled back at her. "I just wanted to sit with you awhile. I sense you are conflicted about Orrion, and I wanted to hear your concerns."

"I am conflicted," said Gaelen with a sigh. "When Orrion entered the room today, and I first beheld him, all the hair on my neck stood straight up. I felt cold, as though in the presence of evil. Yet when he looked at me, all my fears seemed to…melt away. I don't understand. I have learned to trust the hairs on my neck over the eyes of a stranger, High-elven or not."

She was shivering, and Rogond placed his arm about her. Had the mere memory of Orrion brought this chill upon her?

"My love," he said, "I would sooner trust the hairs on your neck as well. There is little doubt that this Orrion is strange. Why is he here? Why would he undertake such a hard journey without cause?"

"Why, indeed?" said Gaelen. "How does he even know of Dûn Arian? I know Salastor asked him, and he answered, but his explanation seemed…well…odd! Do you take my meaning?"

"I do, and I agree. He said that he did not know that the City existed, but was simply drawn here by forces he did not understand. Now that he is here he seems happy about it, and what evil could he possibly do? He is only one soul now among many."

"There is something else," said Gaelen, who was still shivering a little. "I have not told anyone, because I have not been certain, but I believe that Gorgon has roused himself. A number of days ago I felt it...he dropped his guard for awhile, and then the veil was drawn back over him. I have sensed him but little ever since. A moment here, a moment there...nothing definite, and nothing that will tell me what he is up to. And now, this Elf appears."

Rogond did not comprehend how Orrion and Gorgon could possibly have anything to do with one another. "I admit, Orrion is mysterious and not entirely convincing, but whatever could a High-elf have to do with Gorgon Elfhunter? Surely, if he had even been near Gorgon you would sense it, would you not?"

Gaelen was rapidly becoming frustrated. "I have no idea whatsoever! I have only vague feelings and misgivings. Why the sight of a handsome Èolarin Elf—speaking lovely, courteous words in a tongue that would choke an Ulca—should fill me with mistrust, I cannot imagine. But remember, beloved, Gorgon speaks High-elven...he speaks it well. And, there is something else. I spoke with Bint Raed yesterday, and she told me a most baffling tale."

Gaelen then related the incident involving the measurements taken by the City's tailors, which would indicate that Orrion was much stouter than he appeared. "His tunic appeared to be a little snug to me. Bint Raed can't explain it, either. It's as though...as though Orrion is a different being when you actually put your hands on him."

Rogond looked wide-eyed at her. "What are you saying? If you're suggesting what I think you are, we had better see that you are examined by the healers at once. Your imagination is running away with you. I would suggest putting any such thoughts from your mind."

He was now becoming quite concerned for her, as Gaelen was not prone to such wild flights of fancy. If she voiced these opinions to anyone else in the City, they would think she had lost her reason. He reached up to try to stroke her hair, but she pulled away.

"Just keep both eyes open, that's all I ask," she said. "I will be watching our high-and-mighty visitor very, very closely. I had better start seeing some indication that all is as he claims it to be." She rose to her feet. "I'm going to the horse-yards to clear my head. I will find you later."

Rogond watched her go, knowing he had offended her. *Her instincts are the best predictor of trouble that I have ever known, yet I discounted them. I will, indeed, keep both of my eyes open.*

The healing of El-morah was one of the strangest events Nelwyn had ever witnessed. Orrion never let go of him, as El-morah's expression turned from vacant, to wondering, to pained, to agonized, and finally to awareness, just before his eyes rolled back in his head and he collapsed onto the floor.

Kotos had roamed through his mind, opening doors as he did so. El-morah's memories came back in a rush, from his childhood, when he had escaped the Plague, and then to young manhood, when he was trained as an assassin. His many exploits played through his awareness, and many of those memories were painful, causing him to cry out and struggle as Orrion, with the aid of Nelwyn, held him fast.

Then there were images of happier times with Mohani, and his two sons and two daughters. The return of those memories filled his eyes with tears of longing. Finally, Kotos implanted a false memory that would explain why El-morah had fled the oasis. It would seem that his past had caught up with him, and that assassins had been sent to silence him, for El-morah knew things that could never be revealed. This was El-morah's greatest fear—Kotos was certain of it.

The assassins had killed your entire family, and set the oasis aflame in a fruitless search for you. Your wounded heart had not allowed these images to remain, and instead you believed that, if you could only get far enough away, your family would be saved. You have obviously been deluding yourself, mad with grief, guilt, and despair…

El-morah was a strong-willed man, but he was no match for Kotos in his weakened state. After all, the damage had been done by Kotos in the first place, and only he could undo it. By placing the false memories, Kotos believed that he had concealed his tracks and explained El-morah's presence. Yet he had not taken into account

El-morah's perceptive nature, nor the depth of his devotion to his family.

The false memory might not outlast either of those qualities, but it seemed to have taken hold for the time being, and Kotos returned to Orrion, satisfied that he had done what was necessary.

Orrion lifted El-morah and carried him to his bed, instructing Nelwyn to bring water and to summon the healers. At first they wondered whether El-morah would die, for his strength had been almost completely spent in his encounter with Kotos, but after a few hours they managed to revive him. To the delight of Nelwyn and the satisfaction of Kotos, he sat up and looked around as though he had just awakened from a dream. Nelwyn was the only person in the room that he recognized, but he knew her at once.

"Nelwyn? What is this place, and how did you come to be here?"

"You crossed the desert to the southern realm of Dûn Arian. I do not know why, but you are very far from home, I fear. Yet I am overjoyed that you know me! You have not been yourself, not at all. Orrion has healed you."

She indicated Orrion, whose face assumed a warm expression of genuine concern.

El-morah's face went pale. "Oh…Nelwyn, they are all dead! Everyone I loved is gone. My home no longer exists, and I am still alive. I do not know if I can bear it!"

His eyes were wild, and Nelwyn grew alarmed. The healers made him drink an elixir to aid him, and it soon took effect. El-morah would sleep for a while, but the healers warned that he should never, ever be left alone. Men had taken their lives with far less cause.

Nelwyn turned then to Orrion. "What you did was extraordinary," she said. "Yet I wonder whether he was better off without his memories. I fear they have only begun to torment him. Is there nothing you can do to aid him?" Tears came to her eyes at the thought of the terrible fate that had befallen Mohani and the children, and she could not imagine El-morah's despair.

"I will see what may be done to aid him," said Orrion. "But now I am very weary and I must take rest. I will try to aid your friend as I can."

"Of course," said Nelwyn. "Forgive me. You have a precious gift. Battles such as the one you just fought must be very taxing to the spirit. Please take rest, but take also my gratitude. He is a good man, and you have restored him."

"No thanks are needed," said Orrion. "Soon I may be able not just to restore his memory, but to truly heal his heart. That, I fear, will be a much harder task. His friends, yourself included, are perhaps better suited." He smiled a gentle—almost angelic—smile.

Nelwyn had not often beheld such warmth and sincerity, and her heart was won for the moment. Yet after Orrion had left her, and she kept watch over El-morah, there was a nagging concern that would not abate. Something about the exchange between Orrion and her friend had disturbed her. While El-morah had been very expressive, Orrion's face had remained the same throughout the entire ordeal. It was impassive, yet a little incredulous, as if he did not really comprehend what was going on. It puzzled Nelwyn, also, that despite the intensity of the struggle, she had not seen Orrion once grasp anything with his left hand.

Word of the healing spread throughout the City, and the healers, anxious to give due credit, had proclaimed Orrion to be something of a miracle worker. Orrion seemed uncomfortable with the praise and gratitude heaped upon him, standing with his eyes downcast and his back to the wall so that he could not be surrounded. This was genuine, for Gorgon had received very little encouragement in his life, and despite instruction from Kotos, he had difficulty accepting it. His awkwardness was mistaken for humility, further endearing him to the people of the Citadel.

When the Company heard of the incident, they came at once to see the result for themselves. They stood in El-morah's chamber and looked into the eyes of their friend, who had shaved and dressed. Except for the profound guilt and grief in his eyes, he appeared as a careworn version of the man they had known.

Nelwyn had told everyone of the fate of his family, and Estle had been most grieved by this news, for she had known Mohani well. They had spent time together as friends, and Estle had cared for the children on occasion. Therefore, when she beheld El-morah she had gone to him, at first placing a tentative hand upon his arm, tears welling in her eyes, and then taking him in her embrace as they both wept.

El-morah's tears were silent ones, for he had called upon his long years of training and discipline, and now bore his pain in stony silence. Everyone in the Company shed tears for those good people, even Galador. Finally, after they had paid their respects, they left El-morah to rest. Yet Gaelen lingered for a few moments, as she wanted to speak with him alone.

She approached him and looked into his eyes. "Orrion healed you. What, exactly, did he do?"

El-morah shook his head. "I cannot say, for I do not truly know…I only know that I was lost and bewildered, and did not even remember my own name. Orrion drew me from darkness, and now I am here, among friends, and I am whole. He saved my life in the desert… that much I do remember. He gave me water, and tended me when I was ill."

"You sensed no darkness in him?" said Gaelen, her brow furrowed as she concentrated on her friend's expression.

"The only darkness I know of at this moment is the darkness I left behind me," he said, his eyes misting over again.

Gaelen regretted taxing him, but she pressed on. "Why did you come here? How did you even *know* to come here?" she asked, her voice taking on an insistent tone.

At that moment, one of the healers bustled into the room, distracting El-morah and taking Gaelen by the arm. Her entire body galvanized, and she glared at the healer with fire in her eyes—one did not touch Gaelen without leave. She turned back to El-morah, her eyes gentle again. "Until another time," she said, and left him.

Outside the chamber, Orrion stood with his arms folded, glaring down at her.

She glared right back at him. "You sent that man in to interrupt us, didn't you? Why should you care if I speak with my friend?"

"You were upsetting him—tearing into the fabric of his emotions like a fox tearing at its prey. You show no consideration. He needs time for scars to form…he has not had time yet to even grasp the enormity of his loss. Leave him in peace!"

"What would he have said that might possibly have threatened you?" said Gaelen under her breath.

"Why must you doubt me? I should think I might have earned at least some consideration from you for healing your friend." Orrion's face assumed an expression of genuine injury, as if wounded by her lack of faith.

Gaelen was chastened as she looked into his eyes, for when she did so she truly wanted to trust him. How could she have doubted him? Why was she being so difficult? Could she not simply accept him, as everyone else appeared to have done? "I…I'm sorry. Of course, you're right. I owe you a great debt of thanks, and I have failed to show proper respect. Please forgive me." She dropped her gaze then.

Orrion smiled at her, though the next words that came were very difficult for Gorgon to say. "There is nothing to forgive. I know that I would be wary of strangers were I in your place. I have been told that you are a hunter-scout, and they are trained to be mistrustful and vigilant. But you need not fear me. I do appreciate your respect…I trust I have now earned it?"

Gaelen nodded. Then she thought for a moment. *Let's see how trustworthy you are…*

She extended her right hand as though in friendship. Orrion did not return the gesture, for Gorgon would not allow Gaelen to touch him despite Kotos' screaming at him to do so. Instead he bowed, and then took his leave, to the surprise of several folk who stood in witness.

Later, Gaelen sat once again upon the western wall. Her thoughts, and her course, were now clear. She knew that she had been beguiled again, and she was disgruntled with herself, as she could not imagine how she had allowed Orrion to do so a second time.

From now on, she would play this game by his rules, and give the appearance that she had fallen into line with everyone else. She would share her suspicions only with the Company, and she would continue to keep a close watch on Orrion. There were too many odd occurrences, and too many things that did not make sense from Gaelen's logical viewpoint. The hair on her neck stood erect again as she recalled the wounded, solicitous look in Orrion's eyes. She would never trust anyone who would not take her hand.

Well, Elfhunter, now you've done it. Why could you not simply take her hand when she offered it? You had the chance to reinforce a delicate, developing trust, and you threw it away. You had better not go against my advice again! Kotos was still fuming at Gorgon, and rightly so. That She-elf was trouble; she would waste no time in reporting everything she noticed to her friends, and she would notice a great deal.

"Then you had better not ask me to do things I cannot," Gorgon growled in reply. "I will never touch her again without a weapon in my hand! Since you are so wise, I would have thought you would know that there is a connection of some kind between the Vixen and me. If she touches me, she might just know me. Would that please you, O Great Lord?"

Kotos thought for a moment before he replied. *Very well, perhaps your fear is understandable, but it's obvious that you still don't realize the extent of my power. I would not have allowed her to know you! Now her suspicions are confirmed. If you had done as I asked, they would have been quelled. If there was any thought in her mind that you are Gorgon, those thoughts would have vanished. After all, Gorgon would never take her hand. You are mighty, and even intelligent, but you are very short-sighted at times.*

If Kotos could have done so, he would now have patted Gorgon's head. *It's always better to not argue with me. I know what is best in every case. Remember it, or forget the sight of a thousand dead and dying Elves beneath your feet!*

That was a sight Gorgon very much wanted to see, and he spoke not another word of disagreement.

8
Orrion's Gifts

When the healers examined El-morah, they were amazed. Orrion had done in a few moments what they might not have done in a lifetime, and they greatly desired to question him and learn from him. Naturally, Kotos was not afraid of their examination. Orrion was conducted to a fascinating chamber full of glass vessels, paintings, and charts, where the senior healers were already seated around a long, dark table.

Gorgon was mesmerized. *Try not to stare so…as long as Orrion has dwelled in Alterra, he will have seen these things before,* said Kotos.

When Orrion entered the room, everyone stood and bowed as a gesture of respect. They waited until he was seated before taking their seats again, and Gorgon wondered about it.

You have done a thing that is beyond them, despite all their learning and study. You have within you a power that they cannot comprehend. If they ever did learn the true nature of your abilities, it would terrify them, but as it is they hold you in the highest regard. Accept their admiration with grace. Revel in it! We are beginning to win them over. Feel free to accept any task that you are given.

The senior healer, a kind, grey-haired woman named Zora, asked Orrion about the method employed with El-morah, and whether such method could be learned. Orrion shook his head, baffled for a moment. *Speak my words,* said Kotos. *Always let me answer for you, and all will be well.*

Orrion appeared to consider for a moment longer. "I would not know how to teach such a thing, as it is a gift I have possessed always," he said. "Afflictions of the mind have ever been my fascination…and my challenge. I was blessed with the ability to bring those afflictions to light, and then to banish them. I don't know how I could impart that ability to another."

"Can you heal anyone with such an affliction?" asked Zora. "There are others who are suffering and have been beyond our aid. Will you try your hand?"

"Of course, I will do what I can," said Orrion in a tone of great concern. "Please, I am grateful for your hospitality. Allow me to repay you in my small way."

The quiet humility that Zora saw in the depths of his eyes touched her heart, and Kotos smiled, for he had placed it there.

They led Orrion to a room with a heavy, locked door.

"The soul locked within these walls is desperately ill," said Zora. "He has not spoken a word to anyone other than himself in many years. He does not know his family, and he hears voices in his head that tell him to do terrible things. He has already caused great injury to several people, and was nearly thrown into prison until we realized he was ill. Nothing we have tried can reach him."

"Bring his family here," said Orrion. "I must know everything of him that I can learn."

Zora brought the man's mother, and also his wife, to speak with Orrion. Kotos learned that the man, whose name was Tamar, had been a stone-carver—a gentle family man who had lived in relative contentment until the voices came.

Kotos asked many questions. Tamar had suffered terrible, blinding headaches with no apparent cause. He seemed to change in the wink of an eye from a kindly man to a savage brute and then back again. He would not remember what he had done—only the pain and the voices. They locked him up when he had attempted to bash his infant son against one of the stone blocks he had been carving.

I think I know what afflicts him...I have seen it before. Tell them you're ready to aid him.

"I am ready," said Orrion to Zora. "But first, you must bind him. This will be unpleasant, and he may turn violent, for these demons will be tricky to vanquish and they will not give in easily. Bind him fast, so that I may work on him without risk of injury to either of us."

"That will not be so difficult, for when he is not listening to the voices he is cooperative, though he will not speak," said Zora. The healers put Tamar in strong restraints, sitting him down upon the stone bench along the wall. There was no wooden furniture in the room that could be broken apart and used as a weapon—Orrion would have to kneel before his patient.

Before he began, Kotos instructed Gorgon. *I shall be leaving you again. Say nothing until I return. Place both arms upon his shoulders, and take his head in your right hand as you did with the last one. And try to at least appear as though you understand what you're doing this time, won't you?*

Kotos knew that his task would be both delicate and difficult as he gently flowed forth into the mind of Tamar. Here was a man who had been isolated by walls of madness for years, and those walls would not come down easily. Yet Kotos knew that Tamar was still there, as he had once been, trapped within them. He called out, receiving no answer at first, and then the voices came.

Tamar is not here, said one in an ugly, simpering, high-pitched whine.

He is, and I would speak with him. I will brook no interference from you, said Kotos.

Tamar is our friend, and we keep him from harm, said another, deeper voice.

You have taken him from his life, his home, and his family, replied Kotos. *Now your time has come, and you must leave him. I am here to banish you.* There was demented, ill-natured laughter then, but Kotos was not fazed by it. *Laugh if you will, I will banish you*, he said. *You have no chance against me, for my power is great and you are no match for it.*

Many voices joined in the laughter—Kotos counted at least six different ones. *We will never leave Tamar*, said the deep voice. *And you cannot force us. We will kill him if you try!* At these words, Tamar's eyes grew wide and fearful, as if aware of what was being said. He struggled in his restraints, but Orrion held him fast.

To kill Tamar is to kill yourselves, for you are all a part of him, said Kotos. *Now return to the depths, and trouble him no more! I see the diseased part of him, the part that gave rise to all of you, and I can heal his pain. Begone, and trouble him no more!*

Tamar struggled violently, attempting to lash his head back and forth, growling and gnashing his teeth, Kotos perceived the dark, ominous grey mass in Tamar's brain, and he turned his power on it, shriveling it into nothing. As he did so, the voices shrieked in agony, as did Tamar, who sent forth a high-pitched wail that fairly deafened Orrion. Tamar's face was now dead white; his eyes went vacant and rolled back in his head as he went limp in Orrion's grasp. Gorgon did not know what to do, so he kept his hold on Tamar as the healers rushed in to aid him.

"Do not interfere!" he said in a voice that was not like any the healers had heard before.

Kotos was not yet finished. He still had more walls to bring down. He could hear Tamar weeping, yet despite calling out repeatedly, he received no coherent answer. The voices had all gone silent. Kotos followed the sound of Tamar's weeping, until at last he found what looked like a young man of perhaps thirty years, unmarked and undamaged save for the terror in his eyes. When he saw Kotos, he stopped weeping. *Come no closer*, he said in a trembling voice. *Come no closer, or we are both dead.*

No, my friend, you are wrong, said Kotos. *You will be dead, or might as well be, if you remain in this prison. The voices are gone, and they can neither help you nor hurt you again. It is safe now to come back into the light. The voices are gone…I have vanquished them.*

Not quite all of them, said the young Tamar as his face assumed an evil grin. *I am the strongest of them all, and I am stronger than you. I will kill Tamar if you do not leave us in peace. He would rather die than live without me. Do you understand?* This one was new to Kotos' ears, a malevolent, hissing voice that was most unpleasant.

I understand only that you cannot exist without Tamar, therefore you will not kill him, for you love yourself. Look into my eyes and tell me it is not so. Leave this man in peace, and go back to the darkness. You may return only if Tamar summons you. I assure you that he will not.

No! I will not be ordered! said the voice, as Kotos drew nearer. There it was—the last remnant of disease. Kotos smiled, for he knew he could make short work of it.

I grow weary of you, he said, reaching out with vaporous fingers toward the young man's wavering image.

As Orrion watched in fascination, Tamar began to take hitching, agonal breaths. Was he dying? That surely would not be a good thing, as the healers were expecting a happier result. Gorgon was becoming quite anxious as Tamar's skin was now going bluish, and it seemed that he had little chance. Orrion had not been sent to kill Tamar, but it appeared as though that was exactly what he had done. Yet now, a shuddering breath came forth, and then another, and another. Tamar did not awaken, but his color was coming back.

Orrion breathed a sigh of relief as the spirit of Kotos returned. Gorgon had not been at all comfortable through any of this. He wondered, looking at Tamar's unconscious form, whether the errand had been successful.

It has, said Kotos, *though I do not as yet know what sort of state he will be in when he awakens. That will not happen for a while; he is completely drained of strength. I must say, I am weary as well. Tell the healers to care for him, and to summon you when he awakens.*

When a messenger came to fetch Orrion back to the Healing Halls, there was very good news. Soon the word that Tamar had been restored to sanity had spread throughout the City. Both Tamar's mother and his wife had embraced Orrion, for their ordeal had been terrible and Orrion had ended it. And when Tamar first beheld the eyes of Kotos again, he wept, for he knew that this was the spirit that had come to him in a dream and driven forth the voices of his madness—the source of his unspeakable pain.

Even as Orrion's esteem grew in the hearts of the people of Dûn Arian, mistrust grew in the heart and mind of Gaelen Taldin. She knew that there was something sinister about Orrion, though she could not explain it, even to herself. *Bint Raed was certain her measurements had been correct, and if they were, Orrion is not as he appears. The healings he is performing are…miraculous. Unprecedentedly so! How has such a miraculous healer remained unknown?*

Many questions turned in her mind now…too many questions. And of whom could she ask them? Rogond had already indicated that her thoughts might be considered irrational. Nelwyn, who had witnessed the healing of El-morah, had been so impressed and overjoyed at the result that she would hear no ill spoken of Orrion. Galador? Well…Galador was Galador.

"Perhaps Fima will hear me. At least he has an imagination," she muttered.

She did some of her best thinking while on the back of a horse, and she went to fetch the grey horse she had been working with. "Come, Young One, let's go out under the moon and the stars, and clear our thoughts for a while."

The grey had shown some encouraging signs lately, as if settling down a little. Now, for example, he seemed to sense her disquiet, and for once he did not jostle her or attempt to snatch at her gear. He stood quietly as she swung onto his back, and he walked calmly through the empty streets of the City, the sound of his unshod feet muffled and regular.

Once outside the walls there were hills and stones—and freedom. The grey horse fairly flew over the stones, and his powerful quarters were more than a match for the hills. Gaelen could not help but appreciate his strength and agility. If she could ever love him, they would be all but invincible.

Finally she drew to a halt upon one of the highest hilltops surrounding the City. There she could see Dûn Arian glowing quietly like a dying ember in the light of a thousand torches. She could still hear the sea and smell the salt air, but out here the stars were brighter. The brightness of the stars was the only thing that she truly loved about the desert. She slid down, shaking her head in disapproval at the long drop to the ground from her too-tall mount. Then she settled herself among the stones, turning the grey horse loose to pick at the sparse grasses growing there.

I don't blame Rogond for his doubts...in fact I might have felt the same way myself were I in his position. I know how odd it must sound to draw any comparison between Orrion and Gorgon. Gorgon could never disguise himself so completely...Orrion does not resemble him physically in any way. Yet, I cannot shake off the feeling that we are being deceived. Why do my doubts vanish whenever he looks me in the eye? I saw the faces of the citizens as they spoke with him...as though he were the answer to some heartfelt prayer. Do I have that same look in my eyes? The healing of El-morah was miraculous, and no doubt of it. But Orrion had rescued El-morah and brought him to the City—why not heal him to begin with?

Gaelen shook her head. They would all think her mad if she put forth that opinion. Now Orrion was showing great worth as a healer of those gone mad…perhaps they would ask him to heal her! A bitter smile came over her at the thought. "At least then I might learn his true nature."

She had wrestled with her doubts for days, trying to lay them aside…the fact that Orrion's left hand was dysfunctional, the fact that all measurements taken of him had indicated a much more massive being, and the undeniable fact that her awareness of Gorgon had resurfaced only a few days before the appearance of Orrion. The first and the last could be explained as coincidence, but what about the measurements?

Bint Raed is a sane, sensible person, and I trust her. She has certainly taken more than one set of measurements in her life. If she cannot explain the discrepancy, then it cannot be explained by anything normal.

Gaelen resolved that she would go to Fima and tell him of her concerns. She would put his ready mind to work, and perhaps between the two of them the mystery would be solved. Fima would not doubt her, surely!

She rose and summoned her grey horse, who stood before her with a long tussock of grass dangling from his mouth. He nodded his head up and down, sending sand and soil flying from the roots as Gaelen turned her head aside and closed her eyes. *What a huge, ridiculous puppy you are!* She reached out and grabbed the clump of roots and dirt, holding them fast. "All right, then, have your grass," she said. The grey horse tugged and the stems tore free. He chewed them thankfully, his eyes never leaving hers as he reached out with his silken muzzle and touched her cheek with it. "You're welcome," she said, sighing at the thought of mounting his tall, broad back again. It was always a bit of a struggle for her. Even high tree limbs were easier, as they did not move and were not as round and slick.

The grey horse lowered his head and moved over to stand beside a great, flat stone that was about as high as his knees.

Gaelen smiled. "So! Is this an invitation? For once, I will not object to this concession to my slight stature. How clever you are!" She mounted him with ease, settling onto his strong back, which was becoming comfortably well-muscled, and made her way back to the City. As she rode, she resolved that he would be given a name before she reached the Great Gates. His hoof-beats—soft, yet powerful—echoed from the stony ground. "You are gentle thunder," said Gaelen. "Your name is Toran."

Gorgon had been resting in his chamber, his thoughts quiet for the moment, when he suddenly sat bolt upright as Kotos came to life within him. There was alarm in the voice that Gorgon heard inside his head. *Awake! Guard yourself, for there is someone seeking you. Guard yourself, Elfhunter! Your thoughts have been too easily gained. Guard yourself!*

"Who dares to invade my thoughts?" said Gorgon. "I have no sense of Gaelen Taldin…not at this moment."

It is not the Wood-elf, it is…someone else. There is someone of power in the City. I had not been aware of it earlier…either it is newly arrived or it has been lying dormant…but now I feel it. There is a formidable being here. You must discover who it is, and then we must deal with it. This person can unmask you!

Kotos went silent for a moment, sending forth a web of thought to snare the seeker. *This is a strong and perceptive spirit…and it knows and fears us,* he said at last. *Why have I not felt it before?*

"I would have no idea," Gorgon growled. "But you had better figure it out. I cannot roam through the City inquiring as to the whereabouts of powerful beings. After all, I am a representative of the Èolar…am I not supposed to know everything already?"

Take this not lightly! And the Èolar were not renowned for their conceit. They sought to know all things, and they were well aware that they did not. They were never content with the knowledge they did possess. It was their undoing, in a way.

"I thought *you* were their undoing," said Gorgon with a sneering smile.

So I was, Elfhunter. Yet I could not have taken them so easily had it not been for their irrepressible curiosity. I knew things that they wished to learn, and that is why they trusted me. One is more easily beguiled with the promise of great reward. Even the wise will fall to the right incentive.

Gorgon did not reply because in his dark heart he loathed and feared Kotos. Gorgon, like his fair ancestors, was also irrepressibly curious. Would Kotos use that curiosity to ensnare him as he had the Èolar? Gorgon had chosen to share his inmost soul with this most ancient of dark powers. He had enmeshed his fate with that of the Shadowmancer's right hand, and it overwhelmed and terrified him for a moment.

Have no fear. I will discover the identity of the one who seeks us, and then we will take care of the matter, you and I. We are partners—nay, Elfhunter, we are brothers—united in the task of destroying the Elves. Remember what I promised you? All shall come to pass. Do not fear.

But there was mistrust in Gorgon's heart, though he did not reveal it. Kotos had said that even the wise would fall to the right incentive. Was he using the incentive of destroying the Elàni to gain dominion, so that despite his wisdom Gorgon, too, would fall one day?

Gaelen found Fima, having searched the halls and chambers of the Library until she discovered him. He was immersed in a manuscript detailing the founding of Tal-elathas, for he liked to explore the beginnings of things. The foundation of the Great Realms of Alterra had always fascinated him. He brightened when he saw Gaelen and bade her sit with him.

"Here, Gaelen…look at these renderings of the lost realm of Tal-elathas! Are they not the most beautiful structures? See how clever the design is…they look as though they would stand until the end of time."

Gaelen admitted that the drawings were most impressive, though they were a bit too solid, in her opinion, to be called beautiful. She preferred structures that blended in more with their surroundings. The cities of men seemed to rise out of the landscape and to be separate from it. Elven-realms, particularly those of the Sylvan folk, were made to recede into their surroundings as though they were a part of nature. It would seem that the Èolar had wanted their edifices to be more imposing. Dwarves, who were more like men in their love of large, stone-carved dwellings, would have admired Tal-elathas.

"I'm sorry to interrupt your studies," said Gaelen, "but there are matters I would share with you, and they are important. Please, may we speak for a while?" She took a furtive look around. It would never do for this discussion to be overheard, and though she did not see anyone else nearby, she was uncomfortable. "Please, might we go to your private study?"

Fima wondered what she was on about. He knew Gaelen well enough to recognize that she would never bother him over nothing. "We will go wherever you like. But might I remain for just a while longer? I really would like to finish what I have begun. Is this matter truly urgent?"

Gaelen frowned. "Well, no, not all that urgent. It won't hurt to delay for a few hours, I suppose. But I would hope to speak with you today, at least. This will be difficult enough, and I would not lose my resolve."

Fima raised an eyebrow at her. To hear Gaelen speak of any loss of resolve was most uncharacteristic. "All right, Gaelen. Let's have luncheon together in my chamber at noon. I will have a repast sent in. What would you like?"

"I doubt I will be much in the mood for eating," she said, "but I will join you then. In the meantime, enjoy your manuscript."

"Oh, I will! Our visitor has been enlightening me. In fact, he is returning now. I have so many questions to ask…did you know that he was actually there, at the founding of Tal-elathas? He remembers so much of history, and he is willing to spend time sharing it! It is a great gift to me and to the City."

"What visitor?" said Gaelen, her eyes narrowing beneath furrowed brows. Just as she asked the question, Orrion appeared carrying several additional parchments, which he placed with some ceremony on the table in front of Fima. Gaelen drew back in spite of herself as he looked down upon her with a passive expression.

"Ah! I see Fima has a visitor," he said in his beautiful, deep, purring voice. "Gaelen, I have been told that you have something of an interest in Tal-elathas. Is that so?"

"No, it is not so," Gaelen replied. "Whoever told you was mistaken."

Fima was taken aback by such unwarranted bluntness in Gaelen. She had stopped just short of being rude. Orrion looked puzzled. "That's strange. I would have thought that, since you have such a deep and abiding interest in Ri-Elathan, you would appreciate knowing more of his family. I knew his father, Ri-Aldamar, very well on a time."

"So you did, I'm sure," said Gaelen, trying to unclench her teeth. The pain of losing her beloved Rain was always with her, and she resented the reminder, especially coming from Orrion. "Right now I am more interested in knowing how you came by such personal information. I most assuredly would not have revealed it to you, and there are very few persons who know of it. From where did you gain this knowledge?"

Orrion seemed to not hear her. "Yes, Ri-Aldamar shared many of his gifts with his sons. They were tall and strong, courageous, wise…how fortunate that Ri-Aldamar had the foresight to separate them ere Tal-elathas fell."

Kotos looked hard at Gaelen then. "Ri-Aldamar gave his deep, grey eyes only to Farahin. Iomar's eyes were blue. But Rain's beautiful dark hair came from his mother. Ri-Aldamar's was lighter." Gaelen's thoughts drifted as she heard those words, and a vision of her beloved formed within them, but it was not the vision Kotos would have wanted. A single word came to her mind…*Beware.*

Gaelen shook off the mesmerizing effect of Orrion's eyes and glanced over at Fima. His expression was rapt—a lore-master looking forward to first-hand information from an ancient and noble source. Orrion had won Fima's heart already, and this did not bode well for the future discussion of her concerns.

I'm the only one who ever refers to Farahin as 'Rain' and yet now Orrion has done so. He's deliberately trying to unsettle me!

When Orrion had appeared, every hair on her neck had stood straight up; he needn't have expended any additional effort in unsettling her. But then, when he looked into her eyes…

He is beguiling me. I dare not fall into the trap again. She thought about calling off her rendezvous with Fima, but thought better of it. She knew that at least he would keep her confidence, and perhaps when he was no longer in the presence of Orrion, his mind would clear and he would hear her.

"Are you certain you will not join us?" asked Orrion in an earnest tone, as though he would be truly disappointed should she refuse. She simply shook her head, bowed to Fima, and took her leave.

Have you gone mad? said Kotos. *Why, in the name of heaven, did you call him Rain!"*

"Did you see the look on her face…the hurt in her eyes?" whispered Gorgon. "I just couldn't help myself."

Orrion chuckled and shook his head, and for a fleeting moment Fima both saw and heard the malice there, though it vanished when Orrion turned his deep, wise eyes back upon him.

Gaelen met Fima in his private study at noon. As promised, there was plenty of food available. She knew that Fima disliked eating alone, so she took a piece of dark bread with butter and honey before settling upon an overstuffed chair covered in worn, dark red velvet. Fima looked up from his own plate long enough to raise an eyebrow at her. "You are obviously disquieted. You appear to be perching on that chair rather than sitting in it, as though preparing to take flight at any moment. What has unsettled you?"

Gaelen drew a deep breath. She loved Fima, and in her heart she trusted him, yet she was still reluctant. "Did you finish your work with Orrion?"

"For the moment," said Fima, his eyes growing brighter. "Did you know that Orrion is one of the few souls left alive who actually witnessed the building of the Great Hall of Tal-elathas? He tells me that Dwarves had a fair hand in it, for they got on well with the Èolar. He said he worked side-by-side with many of them over time, and he even remembered their names. All records of them were lost when the City fell, and their contributions to that Great Realm have not been acknowledged since." He rubbed his hands together. "Wait until I tell Lady Ordath! Wouldn't it be wonderful to conduct Orrion back to Mountain-home? I just hope I'm there to record the tales he tells!"

"Does it not seem strange that he remembers so much of times long past, but can neither remember nor locate Mountain-home?" said Gaelen. "I still don't understand why he is in Dûn Arian. It seems a very unnatural journey for an Elf to make."

"He explained that already," said Fima with a very slight wave of his hand. "While he was frozen, his memory was affected. It's often the case that recent events are lost, while very distant ones are retained. I recall when one of my brothers was felled by a boulder, and he could not remember anything beyond early childhood for several weeks."

"But *why* is he here? Why did he not stay in the northlands where he would be more at home? Whatever would motivate him to cross that desert? Would you have done so had you not seen a great need?"

"Perhaps he wanted to warn everyone of the amassing of Dark Forces near the Fell-ruin. He said he heard a call to go south. How many High-elves have you actually met, Gaelen? Are they not given to foresight and insight?"

"Some are," she replied. "But if Orrion was given insight, if his destiny was to warn the Elves against Wrothgar, would he not have been directed to Mountain-home, or Tal-sithian, or even Dûn Bennas? We have no hope of getting a message back to the northern realms with any speed. Wrothgar might have mounted his offensive by now, for all we know. It just doesn't make sense." She sighed and shook her head. "You, of all people I know, are among the most sensible and clear-headed. Yet it would seem that Orrion has won you over, such that you cannot see just how... *odd* he is!"

Fima had stopped eating and was now focused on her. "You might seem odd, too, Gaelen, if you had been frozen in a block of ice for a thousand years. What has he done to make you so wary of him? Since he arrived he has healed our friend El-morah, after first saving his life in the desert, he has since healed many other lost souls here, and he has provided us with a wealth of lore that we had thought forever lost. What harm, or evil, has he caused?"

Gaelen thought for a moment. *I know Fima won't be able to make the connection with Gorgon Elfhunter... I don't blame him. It seems absurd even to me, but... I can't shake it, no matter how many times I try.* "I'm sorry," she said after a long pause. "Now that I think on it, perhaps this is not the time to speak of this matter. I do have concerns about Orrion, but I cannot as yet explain them and I would prefer to watch and wait for a while. But I say this to you now...be wary of him! Do you not think it strange that he promises the very things you most desire? Something about him is...*wrong.* Take nothing he offers without guarding yourself."

She rose from the chair and turned to leave. "Thank you for the luncheon. Perhaps I will reveal more of my concerns upon another time." She was gone then, and Fima was left to wonder what concerns she could possibly have about someone so venerable, so helpful, so beautiful, and of her own kind.

Orrion went out into a dark, rainy night, having bathed and scented his body. He moved in total silence through the deserted streets, avoiding the sentinels as he approached the tall tower that was the home of Aryiah, the Seer. It was her spirit that had drawn the attention of Lord Kotos, for he could sense her power. Aryiah was dangerous, for she was a true seer, and it was possible that she would pierce his disguise. If that happened, both he and Gorgon would be undone. Well, no matter. He would take care of the problem tonight.

He took advantage of Gorgon's uncanny stealth, making his way to the base of the tower. Once there, he summoned Karatsu, the tame crow that had followed his master Okami to the City. Karatsu was highly susceptible to suggestion, and he flew at the bidding of Kotos, who now dwelled within him. Kotos had left Gorgon with instructions, and now he flew forth, spiraling upward on the damp and heavy air to the eight-sided window in the roof of the chamber where Aryiah slept.

Aryiah awakened with a deep and very primal fear gnawing at her heart. She was alert and waiting when Karatsu appeared, fluffing his glossy feathers, lifting his clawed, dark feet slowly and carefully as he stepped onto the window-ledge. He looked down at her with a baleful black eye, shook himself, and gave out one harsh, loud cry. Aryiah, of course, could not see him, and the sound startled her.

Then, to her horror, Karatsu began to laugh, not as a crow does, for they possess a highly developed sense of humor among birds, but as an evil, ill-natured person might laugh. The sound of it froze Aryiah's heart and turned her stomach at the same time.

She heard the voice of Lord Kotos within her mind, for he could speak from afar to people of insight. *Hail, Aryiah, Seer of Dûn Arian! We meet at last. I have felt your presence for many days now, and I believe it's time you and I became acquainted.*

Aryiah said no word as yet, for she was still trying to fathom what sort of being had invaded her thoughts, though she had realized already that it was an evil presence. Kotos would never beguile her, and he knew it. *You have sensed my presence also, have you not? That is why I am here, for I must tell you, to my great regret, that you are a liability, and I cannot allow you to draw breath any longer.*

Kotos braced himself then for the battle to come as Aryiah took flight, running toward the heavy door to her private chamber.

You think to summon your friend Maji? You think she can protect you? Go on and call her! I will simply eliminate her as well. You know I can do it. Go on then, and condemn your friend to share your fate!

Aryiah stopped running and turned back toward Karatsu, who chose that moment to take wing, flying round the chamber and cawing in his harsh crow's voice: "Call her! Call her!"

At last, Aryiah broke her silence. "Who invades my home and my thoughts, and threatens me with death? This is not the first time I have sensed your presence—I cast my thoughts out to you days ago. Give me your name, and let us do battle. It may not be Aryiah who draws her last breath." She crouched down and drew her lips back over her teeth in a sort of desperate snarl, trying to follow the flight of the evil bird with cloudy, useless eyes.

Karatsu, as with all birds of his kind, was mischievous by nature. Yet he was not aggressive or violent, and Kotos needed to exert considerable strength of will to force him to attack. He dropped down hard upon Aryiah, using claws and dagger-like beak to mar her face. She snatched at him, but he was too quick, and she only succeeded in pulling out a few of his feathers. Kotos breathed a proverbial sigh of relief as he directed the bird back to the ledge, for if his host became disabled it would affect the course of the plan.

Orrion, who waited below, was even now setting fire to the tower as he had been instructed. Though fire would not kill Kotos, he did not wish to burn within the tower. He needed to be back on the ground, directing the "heroic" Orrion in a valiant but vain attempt to rescue poor Aryiah, whom he would never have met.

Aryiah would not be taken easily. She began chanting in her strange voice, swaying to and fro, like a mongoose menacing a serpent. She sent her spirit forth, and Kotos met her in the eerie half-light of her seer's vision, where nothing was as it appeared. There he engaged her, and they battled for several minutes, just long enough for the first sign of smoke to curl under the gap in the chamber door.

Aryiah and Kotos strove with one another, the light of her spirit attempting to overcome his suffocating darkness, as moment by moment her chance of escaping her fate ebbed away. At last her strength flagged, for she was old, and she was mortal. She broke apart from Kotos, trying for one final time to force him from her. "Get back, Serpent of Evil! I see you for who you are, and you cannot prevail. Leave me and my people in peace!"

You see only what I have allowed you to see. You think you can defeat me only because I have kept much of my power hidden. It grows every time the soul of a man is turned to Darkness, and that has happened so many, many times! Look you now upon the evil that men have done!

He sent an incredible, horrifying stream of visions through her, detailing the most terrible, perverse aberrations he had witnessed. The greed, hatred, cowardice, ignorance, and ill will of a thousand generations of men hit Aryiah with full force, and her spirit was overcome. She gave one terrible, wailing cry, and was forever silent. Kotos vanquished her, leaving her to stare ahead with her sightless eyes, unmoving and unfeeling, her inner sight destroyed. She could not hear the alarm bells ringing.

Just before Karatsu left the tower, Kotos bowed before Aryiah, reflecting that in the end he had shown mercy by leaving her in such a mindless state, for she would feel nothing of smoke or flame. Though no match for him, she had been a respectable adversary, and it was no less than she deserved.

Maji had been the first to discover the fire, for she had sensed ill fortune and had been roused from her bed. She rang the nearest alarm bell and tried to open the large, wooden door at the bottom of the stairwell, but it would not move. Gorgon had blocked it from the inside after setting the fire, and had climbed out through one of the windows.

The people tried, but no man of the City was large or powerful enough to break down the oaken door without a battering-ram. Several of the men went in search of one as Maji ran outside, wailing and wringing her hands, calling out to her friend.

"Aryiah! Aryiah! Climb up to your window, and jump down. We will catch you!"

Hallagond, Estle, El-morah, and Azori had made their way to Aryiah's doorway, for they were quartered nearby. Thick smoke billowed from the top of the tower, but the fire brigade had not as yet arrived.

Kotos had already left Karatsu. The crow flew over the heads of the people outside, screaming and cawing in alarm as a heavy rain began to fall.

Orrion emerged from out of the rain like a tall tower of muscle and sinew. Though he did not appear to be as massive as Gorgon Elfhunter, he was still easily the largest two-legged being in the City. Hope surged in the hearts of many as he pushed his way forward past the others in the corridor. He leaped toward the heavy door, set his shoulder, and smashed all of his considerable weight against it again and again. The door was beginning to give way after four or five attempts, and everyone wondered whether Orrion would be broken, for his face was drawn into an agony of effort as he threw himself forward, jarring his entire body with enough force to surely damage it.

He stepped back and composed himself, sweating heavily and breathing hard, preparing for one last attempt, when El-morah noticed an ominous red glow visible from the gap under the door, stepped forward, and placed his hand upon it. It was hot enough that he pulled back at once, turning to Orrion and shaking his head, shouting over the din.

"We must not open the door, or it will mean the deaths of everyone standing here. The heat inside is too great, and the space is too narrow. We will all be killed if you open the door— you most certainly." He turned to Maji, who was now weeping, knowing that her friend was lost. "I'm sorry."

The heart-wrenching look of despair that formed on Orrion's face convinced everyone present that he would have died trying to save Aryiah, and their admiration for him grew deeper, as Kotos had intended.

A huge plume of flame and smoke erupted from the tower at that moment, and there was nothing for Maji to do but watch, and wait for the coming of dawn.

It took some time for the last of the smoldering embers to die down so that the ruins of Aryiah's tower could be entered. Members of the fire brigade stood with El-morah and Azori, discussing how best to proceed. The mortar holding the stones had been damaged and weakened by the intense heat. Such a structure would be unsafe to enter, and climbing the staircase would be out of the question.

The heavy oaken door was still standing, though on the inside it had been reduced to charcoal; the flames had been directed upward by the flow of air, for the tower was really nothing more than an enormous chimney.

El-morah wondered whether any part of the structure would now be safe. "If the tower falls, the weight of it may crush the roof of the corridor, and Maji's quarters," he said. "She should be kept elsewhere until we are certain."

The men opened the door with ease now, for the lock had melted and burned away. Azori and El-morah stepped through it with great caution, for they understood the danger. They had knowledge of fires, which were common in desert realms. The very dry air and cold nights made people shelter around poorly-shielded grates in what were essentially tinder boxes. Though there was always a bucket of sand nearby to smother a small fire, water was scarce. Once a fire truly started, it almost always grew out of control.

El-morah had often been pressed into service fighting fires in the Chupa. His tasks had been twofold—to save any persons trapped within, and to prevent the spread of the fire to neighboring structures. Saving any burning structure was known to be impossible.

Azori's experience with fire was more sinister, for one or two of his men held knowledge of how to set fires with intent, but make them appear to have started by accident. They were sometimes well paid for this service, usually performed to eliminate an enemy or to cover up evidence of a crime. While Azori had never set such a fire himself, he had witnessed several that had been intentionally set, and his men had imparted some knowledge of their craft. He stepped carefully through the embers, curious as to what had burned so fiercely in a structure made up predominantly of stone. In fact, there had been heavy draperies hung about the walls of the stairwell for warmth, and the railings had been of wood, with carpeted stairs. Stone stairs were slippery otherwise, and it was felt that the carpeted ones were safer. Yet it still did not seem to be enough to set the entire tower ablaze.

In fact, Gorgon had doused the entire base of the staircase, as well as the draperies, with oil. The oil had provided plenty of fuel, particularly when combined with the air flowing through the windows that were set in three rows up the tower's length. Gorgon had actually set the blaze with an oil lamp that was supposed to be secured upon the wall just inside the doorway; he knocked the bracket from the wall to make it appear that the lamp had fallen on its own. Such a tragic accident!

Azori shook his head slowly as he examined the scene. Hallagond approached him from behind, startling him by tapping him on the shoulder. "You're lucky I didn't have a weapon in my hands," Azori grumbled, fixing Hallagond with a look that might have set the embers on fire again.

"Sorry. I didn't realize you were so deep in thought," said Hallagond, who was disinclined to joke with Azori on such a somber occasion. "Can you make anything out of this?"

"It appears that the lamp fell from the wall, broke into pieces and set the draperies on fire," said Azori. "Either that, or someone has gone to some lengths to make it appear that way."

"Well, which is it?" asked Hallagond.

"I cannot say for certain," replied Azori. "And not being certain, I would prefer to reserve opinion. No sense in looking for demons that don't exist. Besides, we wouldn't want to alert any villains that we are wise to them, would we? Not that there are any to alert… but just in case there are."

He moved to stand with the chief of the fire brigade and held a short conversation with him. Later that day, it was announced to the citizens that one of their number had been taken from them in a tragic accident. Everyone was advised to make certain that all metal lamp-brackets were firm and secure.

Azori did not know Aryiah, but he did know the culture of the City, and it did not seem likely that a peaceable society could spawn such a cruel act. Yet he also knew much of the evil that can sometimes infect the hearts of men, and as such he would reserve judgment. There were things he had seen in the stairwell that would not allow him to do otherwise.

As a result of his unsuccessful attempt to break down Aryiah's heavy door, Orrion's left shoulder was now badly bruised. He lay in the public bath at midnight, soaking in the warm waters, massaging the shoulder gingerly with his right hand. The scent of Gorgon was slowly diluted and removed from his body in the soothing waters, and he was comforted, yet he muttered concern to Kotos.

"I do hope that no one took notice…I must confess that I have finally become aware of my own stench. I sweated hard in the corridor."

Be grateful that you were surrounded by men. Many of them were sweating as well. Their stench is not all that much better than your own. Do not fear.

"They say they're going to pull down the tower. Apparently, it is unsafe. There will be nothing for them to discover that will arouse suspicion, will there?"

Nothing whatever, said Kotos. *You needn't worry about them. They now believe you to be heroic as well as impressive. You did an excellent job of appearing to be heartbroken when you were forced to abandon the rescue. Well done.*

"That was mostly *your* doing," growled Gorgon. "I have never expressed such regrets in my life."

True, but you have proven to be a most receptive and willing vessel for my direction. You have learned to allow me to guide you in all things, despite your strength of will. That is how we both will prevail. But there is something that still troubles my heart, Elfhunter. There is one who will be putting some pieces together…she has already done so. I have seen it in her eyes.

"You refer to the Wood-elf," Gorgon rumbled. "Well, I agree. She knew of the Seer, and she has already noticed far too much."

We could take care of that problem, you and I. She is only one small Wood-elf. She could easily meet with a tragic accident, and then we will not need to be so wary. She is the only one who still holds the likelihood of discovering who you really are.

"That may be, but I must take her alone, and in my own time, and in my own way," Gorgon muttered in a voice that was deadly quiet. "Someday it will be my greatest pleasure to eliminate her, but I will not share that pleasure with anyone, including you. Do not suggest it again."

Very well, have it your way. If you will not eliminate her, we should plant the seeds we need to plant, and then leave them to grow and take root. We should do it soon, before your identity becomes suspect. Now I shall think on how best to proceed. Do not disturb me. With those words, Kotos flowed once more into the amulet, leaving Gorgon alone with his thoughts. Neither being was entirely comfortable in the presence of the other, and Kotos needed time to make careful plans. He wondered which of the Company would be the most trustworthy. Who among them was most innocent, such that it would be difficult to doubt their words? He needed to make a wise choice, for the entire remainder of his plan depended on it. Though he had spent relatively little time interacting with the Company, the choice finally came to him.

As Gorgon lay in the bath, he wondered about many things. Always he had prided himself on his fearsome appearance, striving to look threatening and terrible. And he had been generally pleased with the result—there were not many with the strength of heart to stand before him, not even the Elves. One look at him and their strength left them. Of course, because he stalked them and came on them unaware, it was small wonder that they lost their nerve, as they were usually wounded unto death by the time they even got a look at him. He had always considered his ugliness to be an asset. Yet now, he wondered.

Orrion was beautiful and impressive. People looked on him with admiration, and they even asked him for his opinion. They made him fine clothes and brought him gifts. They respected Orrion where they would never have respected Gorgon. Yet were Orrion and Gorgon not the same being?

Well, there is the small matter of Lord Kotos, yet Orrion is the Elfhunter, too. Beauty, it seems, is really the beguiling influence. Gorgon smiled. He would almost regret returning to his former appearance because he was ever so much more dangerous in this form. *I could influence people, incite them, break their hearts, unite them, or tear them apart. I wonder...will I ever again be content to simply terrify them?*

Yet he could not let himself fall into the trap. Beauty required the amulet, and the amulet came with Lord Kotos attached. Gorgon was both weary and wary of Kotos, and in his heart he longed for the time when all thoughts were his own.

9
The Seed is Planted

Gaelen was shocked and saddened upon learning of the death of Aryiah. She had been away from the City, having wandered for miles to the south under the tall forest canopy, alone with her thoughts.

When I am near Orrion I cannot think clearly, and apparently neither can anyone else. I don't want to air my concerns—I know how ridiculous they sound. Rogond is right...it's absurd to think that Orrion and Gorgon share any connection whatsoever...yet I have seen Gorgon's very soul. His most powerful manifestation looked very much like Orrion...perhaps the connection is not as absurd as it sounds.

She had been alerted, as had every other Elf in the City, by Aryiah's final cry of despair. The Elves had felt this rather than heard it, Gaelen in particular, because she had shared spiritual communion with Aryiah on a time. Then she heard the alarm bells, the sound carried on the north wind. By the time she drew near enough to see the tower, there was nothing to be done.

Everyone praised the heroic actions of El-morah, Azori, and especially Orrion, whose esteem had risen even higher, if possible. There were tears in the eyes of many who witnessed his heart-wrenching failure; the hearts of the people went out to him in his despondency. But when Gaelen heard that Orrion had been present at all, immediate suspicion flared within her. *Aryiah would have been no friend of Gorgon Elfhunter, and if he was managing some illusion to disguise himself, Aryiah might have unmasked him.*

The next morning, when El-morah and Azori returned from examining the ruins of the tower, they found Gaelen waiting for them. She was deadly serious as she questioned them about the night's events. She wanted to know exactly when Orrion had appeared and what all of his actions were, in detail.

El-morah described Orrion's thwarted attempt to break down the door. "He was heartbroken when we told him he would have to give it up. I thought for a moment he was going to weep. I don't believe I have ever seen deeper disappointment." He turned to Azori. "Perhaps we should look in on him…I would imagine his shoulder is causing him great discomfort today."

Azori nodded in agreement, but his eyes were fixed on Gaelen. "Yes, we should look in on him if he will allow it. He is very reclusive during daylight, I've noticed." Gaelen brightened at this. Perhaps Azori was seeing some of what she was seeing.

"Can you blame him?" said El-morah. "He has curious admirers following him around always. No doubt he enjoys his solitude."

"Let's go and look in on him then," said Azori, as El-morah turned and left the chamber. Azori remained behind just long enough to speak to Gaelen.

"There were things about that fire that will not allow me to call it an accident, even though I have done so, for I don't have any real proof—more of intuition than physical evidence. But I have seen the doubt when you look at Orrion, and I want you to know that I share some of it. I can say no more."

Gaelen nodded, her large eyes full of somber gratitude, as Azori turned and left her alone with her thoughts once more.

Kotos was not infallible, but he was very perceptive, and he sensed that his deception was beginning to show too many imperfections. He had seen doubt in the eyes of the woman who had measured Orrion for his new garments. He had heard rumors about suspicions held by some members of the fire brigade. And, of course, there was Gaelen. She was getting closer, sniffing him out like a mangy hound.

It would be best to leave the City while the image of the mighty, beautiful, benevolent Orrion was still intact. It was time to plant the seed that would move the rest of the plan forward, and then take his leave. Kotos smiled, knowing that the citizens would mourn the departure of Orrion. The illusion was too delicate to last, but he couldn't resist a bit of self-congratulation. *I've turned this ugly brute into a beauty—a respectable one at that—and he has fooled them all.*

Well…almost all. Kotos wasn't concerned. Once Orrion had left Dûn Arian, he would never need bother with Gaelen again.

Orrion made his way down to the harbor, to a quiet glade in the nearby forest where Nelwyn was sure to find him.

It was her habit to go to the glade each day as the sun rose high and the light filtering down through the tall canopy was most bright, glimmering green and silver upon a spring of clear water and many stones thick with moss. A great tree, hollow with age but still mighty, served as Nelwyn's new favorite sanctuary. Sometimes she climbed up the enormous trunk and settled in the tallest branches, savoring the salty tang of the wind blowing across the harbor. Orrion had been observing her for several days, and knew where she could be found. He also knew that she would most likely be alone.

This time, when she arrived, he was already there, apparently bent with weeping, sitting upon one of the stones with his face buried in his arms. He did not appear to notice her.

He knew she would try to comfort him, and she drew nearer, obviously disarmed by the awkwardness of his weeping. In fact, Gorgon's own lack of experience with genuine emotion added depth to the illusion, and Kotos was pleased. Nelwyn would not be able to resist him.

He lifted his tear-stained face, and then his eyes grew wide. He flushed and turned aside, attempting to wipe away the tears.

"What do you want?" he asked in a shaky voice. "Please, leave me in peace. I came here to be alone."

"There is no shame in weeping," said Nelwyn as she drew nigh him. "Yet I sense you have not wept in a long while. Your grief is deep, and you have had no one to comfort you. I owe you a debt of gratitude for the healing of my friend. Will you not allow me to pay it, and bring you aid? I will listen to your pain, and I will tell no one. Let me help you if I can."

She moved closer, and he showed no objection even when she sat beside him, placing a gentle hand on his shoulder. Kotos looked into her wide, green eyes and smiled, even as Orrion's face assumed an expression of profound sadness mingled with confusion.

"I appreciate your concern," he said. "But I do not think you can comfort me…no one can. My life and my situation are like no other. You cannot understand."

"Sometimes, understanding is not needed. It is enough only to be heard. Know that you may tell me all of what troubles you, that I will listen, and that I will say nothing of it outside this place."

"You still do not perceive…I cannot share with another what I do not even understand myself," said Orrion. "I know I have concealed it, but I have been fearful ever since I arrived here. People keep asking me to explain myself, but I cannot explain what I do not know. So much is missing…a thousand years of my life have been wiped away. I still have moments when I can barely remember my name—can you imagine it? I was once possessed of great wisdom. I knew things known by few others in this world. Now, I'm helpless. I don't know why I came here, or how, and still some folk do not trust me. Do you know how that makes me feel? I have tried to do good, and yet I am not trusted. But…I don't even know if I'm trustworthy. I'm just so weary of uncertainty!" He rubbed his eyes with the back of his right hand, as a child does.

"When I heard the Seer's cry, I ran to the tower. I have but one good hand...I lost the use of the left one long ago, but I thought I could at least break down the door. I tried to save her, but I failed. Now the weight of her death hangs over me, and it has brought back some of my past. I have failed so many times in my life. I could not save the High King, nor his son Iomar, nor the realm of Tal-elathas. I fell with the rest of them. Why am I not dead? How did I come to be here? I know I must leave soon…there is a destiny that is guiding me. To what end?" He began to weep again. "I'm so confused, and so weary," he said, burying his face in his arms once more.

Nelwyn patted him gently until he calmed. "How did you lose the use of your hand? They say you lost it in battle. You must have been very brave…"

He looked Nelwyn in the eye. "Some things are unforgettable," he said. "I tried to save the High King, and I failed. The loss of my hand reminds me of it every single day."

Nelwyn dropped her gaze. "I'm sorry. I didn't mean to pry."

"It's all right, but I would rather not recount the story, if it's all the same to you." *Actually, I would prefer not to have to make one up at a moment's notice,* thought Kotos. Orrion drew several deep breaths, as if so weary that he might fall asleep at any moment, and

Nelwyn stayed by him. At last he raised his head and looked into her eyes. "You have brought comfort…against all expectations," he said, his grey eyes full of gratitude. "Will you not remain with me for a while longer? I take comfort just in having someone…someone I need not fear, who cares for me despite uncertainty. Will you not stay?"

"Of course, I will remain for as long as you need me," said Nelwyn, obviously relieved and happy to have been of comfort.

She looked into his earnest grey eyes.

That's right, said Kotos. *Look deeply, Nelwyn—my eyes are fathomless, the most beautiful eyes you've ever seen. Your thoughts…they wander…they stray into the realm of waking dreams.*

Nelwyn was not afraid, and Kotos took her easily, for she was willing. He seduced and beguiled her as he had all the others, for she was relatively innocent and her heart was pure. She was not so wary as her cousin Gaelen, who had seen far more ugliness and despair. Kotos planted the seed in Nelwyn's mind, expending all of his power to ensure that it would take root as intended. Then, before he brought her back to herself, he instructed her.

The vision will not come unto you until I am long gone. The moon will wax and wane twice, and then, upon the rising of the third full moon, you will remember.

When Nelwyn truly came to herself, Orrion was gone. He had left a gift for her, a small figure of ebony, hand carved and polished. It was a crow, or a raven, and it delighted Nelwyn, for it was so cunningly rendered that nearly every feather could be seen and touched. With it there was a small scrap of parchment inscribed in High-elven.

Thou hast brought comfort to one in need.
Now he rewards thy kind heart with a gift.
Take the bird, and remember me,
as I will think of thee whenever I behold
the beauty of flight.

My thanks,
~Orrion

Something told Nelwyn that she must destroy the parchment, and she did so, concealing the beautiful carving among her other possessions. Later, when Nelwyn returned to the City, Gaelen wondered why she would not reveal where she had been all afternoon. Even more than that, Gaelen wondered why her cousin would smell of oranges. The only person she knew of in Dûn Arian who regularly smelled of oranges was Orrion High-elven, but Gaelen trusted her cousin, as did everyone in the Company, and she thought no more of it for the moment.

Gorgon Elfhunter stood alone before the looking-glass in his chamber, glaring once more at the beautiful image of Orrion. Kotos was not with him, having retreated into the amulet to plot and plan and weave his webs. Gorgon was exhausted. Not only was the effort of bearing Kotos physically draining, but the effort of mustering so much false emotion had nearly killed him. What distressed him even more was the fact that some of the emotion had been genuine.

Here was the legendary Elfhunter, weeping like a child, awash in self-pity, and the golden-haired Wood-elf had been utterly taken in. But Gorgon would never allow Kotos to expect such a thing of him again. He looked into his own grey eyes with complete, all-consuming disgust and loathing. He longed to return to his simple life where no one ever saw him or spoke to him, wishing for the time when the only Elves he beheld were dead or dying, tormented and crying in pain and terror. Now he was *one of them!* He didn't think he could bear it much longer. He had been wrong to even believe that he could do so. The power he wielded as a result of his beauty was not worth the loss of his identity.

He brandished his long blade and drew it slowly across his left forearm, feeling the cold steel bite deep into his flesh. As he did so, he locked eyes with his reflection, delighting in the pain he saw in Orrion's face. He cut himself again, this time allowing his face to twist into an expression of agony, and the sight of it brought him comfort. Soon he would never need to look at Orrion again.

Lord Kotos had been more than pleased with Gorgon's performance. Wrothgar's dark child was both intelligent and artful when properly directed. Yet he knew that the days of Gorgon's willing cooperation were nearing their end. It was Kotos' plan to separate from Gorgon, leaving the amulet with him so that he could, if necessary, still appear as Orrion. But Kotos intended to remain with the Company for a short while, to make certain that all went as planned. He needed a vessel for this, not to be controlled or influenced, but simply to carry Kotos with the Company.

There was only one such member who could serve as his vessel, and that was Fima, the dwarf. Kotos had attempted to influence the Children of Fior, but had realized that their minds and hearts were made of different material from men or Elves. Kotos could not control them, but he could be carried by them. Fima would never know Kotos was there at all. In fact, Kotos would impart some of his vigor to the aging Fima, lending stamina and strength so long as they were together. Kotos would lie back and wait, and watch his plans unfold.

I must leave you, he told Gorgon, who was in the process of putting on a new, black velvet tunic that had been made for him. *Do not fear. Only stay out of sight of the Company, and follow behind. You will find them. They will travel north this time, avoiding the worst of the desert perils. Gaelen will be with them, and you will follow after her. I will be with them, also. When the time is right, I will rejoin you. For now, we must take separate paths.*

"I'm glad. This place is weighing on my spirit," said Gorgon. "I will take my leave tonight, then?"

You cannot leave without saying farewell to Lord Salastor, and then you must go and see to Lore-master Fima. After that you will be on your own, and I cannot aid you. You must steal away without anyone taking notice. Do you understand?

Gorgon laughed deep in his broad chest. "You have no idea how easily that can be done," he said. "I am among the most adept persons you will have ever known—make no mistake about it." He paused, as though considering a question. "Where are you directing them?"

If all goes well, they will travel to Tal-sithian. Once I am certain their feet are set on the right path, I will rejoin you. As long as my sister, Arialde, rules the Lake-realm, neither you nor I can venture there. But the Company will conduct their business, and then, hopefully, they will emerge. When they do, we will be waiting.

"And the Vixen? If I should have the opportunity to take her during the journey northward…?"

Don't even think of it…it's too late for that now. There will be time later to play with your little Wood-elf. Keep your attention focused on your task, and do not risk discovery. The Company will need their hunter-scouts to aid them in reaching the Lake-realm. This they must do—at all cost—and they must not be distracted. Do you understand?

"I suppose so," growled Gorgon. "Though I still don't know what your ultimate plan is, since you will not share it. Such reluctance makes it harder for me to comprehend the need to follow your instructions, if you take my meaning." He looked into the amulet that hung around his neck, knowing that Kotos could see him.

Very well, if you would be privy to the plan, then I suppose there is no harm in sharing it, said Kotos. *You have passed every test I have set for you.* He then divulged the scheme, as ordered by Lord Wrothgar, and Gorgon was impressed, though he did not understand it in its entirety. He started to ask questions, but Kotos stayed him. *Do not concern yourself with all intricacies of the plan, but only with your own part in it. Know that it cannot succeed without your aid, and that your Master has already promised you great reward. He has told me that you will be permitted to see to the deaths of both Lady Ordath and Lord Magra. You may deal with them as you see fit.*

"To me, they are all the same," growled Gorgon. "The death of Magra will bring no more satisfaction than the death of his lowliest Elven subject. Better Lord Wrothgar should promise that I will oversee the death of the last Elf in the world. Now, *that* would be a reward!" Orrion's face twisted into a smile so full of malice that it would have stolen away the courage from anyone who beheld it.

Kotos looked upon that smile and shook his figurative head. *Now, you see…that is precisely why we need to get you away from here! No Elf ever wore a smile like that. One look at your face right now and Orrion would be unmasked. Finish your preparations, and then make ready to say your farewells to Lord Salastor.*

But Gorgon barely heard him, as he was still imagining the death of the last Elf in the world. The wicked smile remained, even as he finished dressing himself. He paused for one more task, that of cleaning the drops of his dark blood from the floor. His blood was like no other, and it would give him away.

Orrion made his way to the House of Lord Salastor as the sun was setting. He asked the door-warden if he might please be admitted, for he had come concerning a matter of some importance that could not wait until tomorrow.

"If you will make yourself comfortable for a few moments, I will take your message to Lord Salastor," said the door-warden. "I will then conduct you to him, if he agrees."

Orrion bowed and then sat carefully in one of the carved, wooden chairs inside the doorway. The moment the warden left him, he rose to his feet and began pacing.

Stop that, please. You have no reason to be so restive. Sit you back down in the chair, and wait as though you had all the time in the world to do it, said Kotos.

Orrion did so, yet the chair was too small for him, and he fidgeted like a large dog in a small cage. Kotos sighed. *You are hopeless! You had best take several deep breaths, calm yourself, and concentrate on the task before you. Remember, soon you will be free of the City, and you can truly be yourself again.*

Orrion barely had time for one more deep breath before the door-warden returned. "I have been asked to conduct you to Lord Salastor's private dining chamber, if you will please follow me."

When he saw Orrion, Salastor smiled and rose to his feet. "Will you join me in a meal? I was just sitting down to a lonely supper and I would appreciate some company. Will you join me?"

The food on the table was enticing, and Gorgon's mouth began to water. "I don't know…is such a thing permitted?"

Salastor looked puzzled. "Of course! Why ever would it not be? You are an honored guest in our City. Please, do me the honor of dining with me."

Go on, then, said Kotos, to whom the question had really been directed. *Sit down and eat, but remember your manners! It will be good to start your journey on a full stomach. Remember to curb your enthusiasm and eat slowly.*

Orrion did so, making very few mistakes of etiquette. Salastor did not appear to notice any blunders, but finished his own meal. "I hope you are finding the fare in Dûn Arian to your liking," he said. "Now, what was it that you wanted to see me about?"

Do not answer him with your mouth full of food! said Kotos.

Orrion swallowed the mouthful of spice-cake he had been savoring. "I intend to leave the City within the next few days," he said.

"How regrettable! We were just beginning to know you well," said Salastor. "You have performed many wonderful services in the brief time you have been with us. Your healing power has restored several of our citizens, and I have been made aware of your valor in the attempted rescue of poor, ill-fated Aryiah. We were going to have a memorial for her tomorrow, and I was so hoping you would attend. I'm sure she would have wanted you there, for according to the captain of our fire brigade, your efforts were nothing short of heroic. I know many people in the City who will mourn your departure, especially our scholars." He drew a deep breath. "I hope you do not find the question impertinent, but why must you leave us? You would be welcome for the rest of your days."

Orrion paused, as though considering. "I must leave because there are those here who do not trust me, though I have done nothing to earn mistrust. There are other reasons, and they will remain my own, begging your pardon. I can only state that I am being driven forth even as I was driven here, by forces I do not understand. My task here is done—I have warned you of the ever-increasing threat that grows in the North. You cannot be complacent any longer, for the Shadowmancer may find your realm one day. At least now you can make ready."

"Will you require aid?" asked Salastor. "I can send men to aid you. Only say the word, and you need not venture forth alone."

"My thanks, but I prefer traveling alone," said Orrion, with a very faint smile. "I beg you, do not disclose my intentions to anyone else in the City. I would prefer to simply steal away without any great fanfare."

"Will you attend the service for Aryiah tomorrow?" asked Salastor. "I would be honored by your presence, and I will not reveal your intention to leave."

Gorgon would not be at all comfortable at such an event, but Kotos stayed him before he could refuse. *I know it is not in your nature, but you must attend. If you do not, it will seem 'wrong.' There is already enough suspicion surrounding you…tell him you will be there.*

"I will be there," said Orrion. "I dislike large crowds of people, therefore I will not call attention to myself, but rest assured that I will be there. Thank you for safeguarding my intentions. If you will excuse me, I have preparations to make."

Orrion and Salastor rose and bowed to each other, and then Orrion took his leave. After he had gone, Salastor reflected that he had never before seen eyes as deep or expressive, nor felt concern so genuine as he had in Orrion. Dûn Arian would be lessened without him.

Later that night, a most unusual thing happened to Gaelen Taldin. She was riding Toran, flying fast over the stony terrain, bent low over his arched, powerful neck. He did not fear the dark, for his eyesight was keen enough and his bold rider gave him courage. Yet Gaelen's thoughts wandered back to Orrion, and she was not concentrating on her task. Therefore, when Toran abruptly drove his forelegs into the ground and slammed to a halt, she was unseated.

Toran was alarmed, his head and tail raised high in the air as Gaelen, who had not expected this, was thrown forward onto the hard ground to lie flat on her back with the wind knocked out of her. Toran stood frozen in place, like a marble statue, as though afraid to move. Then he gave a mighty snort and ran backward, nearly falling over his hind feet in the effort to escape whatever it was that had frightened him.

Gaelen had recovered her wits and leaped to her feet, drawing her blade. She looked in the direction of whatever had frightened her horse and, at first, saw nothing. Then she heard Toran approach from behind and felt his breath against her back. Apparently, he knew enough to not abandon her. She calmed him, taking hold of the neck rope that had come loose and now dangled from his head-collar.

When Toran snorted again, Gaelen looked out into the night, and this time she beheld the tall figure of Orrion standing silent in the dark, just staring at her. When he realized that she had seen him, he took a few steps toward her and called out.

"Are you all right? That was a hard fall."

Gaelen did not wish to answer him, for she was suddenly very ill-at-ease, but she could not be discourteous. "I am unhurt, thank you. Something startled my horse. He's young, and sometimes unpredictable."

"Perhaps he saw a shadow," said Orrion in a helpful tone.

"Yes, perhaps," Gaelen replied, suspecting that the only shadow Toran had seen was about seven feet tall and looked very much like Orrion. "What are you doing all the way out here, if you don't mind my asking?"

"I was merely enjoying the sight of the stars. They are brighter when one is farther from the City," was the slow and deliberate reply.

Even as he took another step forward, Gorgon was engaged in a raging conflict with Lord Kotos.

She is alone, and she is hurt despite her claim. I can see it. She would be taken now so easily…I could spirit her away never to be found. We would have such a nice, long time together! Oh, my heart aches at the thought of it! Her pain would be my jubilation. So close now…so very, very close!

You cannot, you dare not! Earlier we had the chance, but if you take her now you might as well kill us both! If you take her, the others will be distracted from the plan. They will go in pursuit of you, and then you might as well just let them take you, for if they don't, the Shadowmancer will. Your purpose will be unfulfilled, and the Elves will all breathe a sigh of relief that you are gone.

So…close…I can almost feel her neck in my hand…her blood would be oh, so warm. So warm, so delightfully comforting. No one need know about it. No other suspects me as she does.

You dare not take her now until our plan succeeds, so you can just stop your wishing and whining and salivating. Unclench your right hand and come to yourself. You are called to a higher purpose than the death of one Wood-elf. Use whatever small part of your brain that has not been consumed with the desire for revenge, and THINK!

Orrion took another tentative step toward Gaelen, and for the first time she could actually see his eyes in the darkness. For a moment, she saw both a deep hunger and profound sadness in them. Then, suddenly, all emotions were veiled.

Toran pulled back, snorting again, as Gaelen stroked his neck to calm him. His ears were laid back flat, his nose was wrinkled slightly. It was the first time Gaelen had ever seen a threatening expression in her friendly, playful horse. Gaelen knew that Toran was threatening Orrion out of fear, and she was beginning to be afraid herself.

"Please don't come any closer," she called. "You have unsettled my horse. I do not mean any discourtesy, but I cannot linger and exchange pleasantries. I leave you to your star-gazing."

She kept her eyes locked on Orrion, as though she half expected him to attack her at any moment, swung aboard Toran, and turned him back toward the gates.

Soon Orrion had only a lingering cloud of dust to mark her passing, and Kotos breathed a proverbial sigh of relief. Gorgon, however, was not relieved. He lifted his grey eyes to the stars, clenched his right hand hard enough to bloody it, and opened his mouth in a silent scream.

Aryiah's remains had been collected and placed in a small bronze casket that now sat upon a pillar of marble in the courtyard of the Hall of Omens. The smell of incense mingled with marwani-weed hung in the late morning air, as it often did in this place.

The crowd that gathered now was not large. Few in the City had known Aryiah, and she had seemed fearsome to many. Most of the members of the fire brigade were there, as well as the entire Company, Lord Salastor, and the High Council. There were others present as well, about two hundred in all.

Orrion stood in one of the recessed alcoves that flanked the courtyard, as far to the rear as possible. A few in the crowd had noticed him, inclining their heads in respect, and as he waited for Maji to arrive and begin the service, he took the opportunity to reflect on his recent experiences.

Tonight he would leave the Silver City. Although many aspects would not dismay him, he had come to appreciate some things in this civilized world. He had learned that having a clean body and a clean bed is not such a bad thing. His palate had experienced flavors he had never known before, having lived mostly on unseasoned flesh and whatever lowly fare he could steal. Here he had been encouraged and even expected to partake of any and all things offered to him. The spices, wonderful greens, meats, soft cakes, and savory sauces had both excited and comforted him.

Gorgon had discovered that, in fact, he loved to eat. He especially enjoyed sweets, and he had acquired a taste for wine. After tonight, it was back to eating cold flesh and hard bread when he could find it.

The thing that both amazed and frightened him the most was the reaction of the people to his new persona. They were not afraid of him, not exactly…but they were awed by him. In time, they would come to revere him. On the rare occasion that he voiced an opinion, everyone respected it. No one dared to disagree. He knew that, if he wanted to, he could command them and they would do whatever he asked. Why was that so? It must have been the influence of Lord Kotos; surely the opinions of Gorgon Elfhunter would not be so compelling. Yet some of them *were* his opinions. If Gorgon could have done so without being observed, he would have slapped himself with his one good hand.

Kotos, who had been privy to his thoughts, spoke to him then. *Now do you see why we must leave? I am surprised at how easily you have been lulled by your soft bed and your fine feasts. This place, and the power you are acquiring in it, will seduce you. It will divert you from the task of destroying the Elàni. Surely you would not wish to trade one path for the other? I will make a promise to you, Elfhunter—when Lord Wrothgar's plans are fulfilled and your life's purpose is achieved, I will give you the amulet. You may then return to Dûn Arian, if it pleases you, and rule it as your own realm. You know I have it in my power to see this done. Let that promise satisfy you until that day.*

"Do not try to beguile me," Orrion muttered under his breath. "I know what a promise from you is worth."

Do you, now? I very much doubt that. What you definitely do not know is the extent of the power I can wield. That power can either be your friend, or your enemy. I can be a very good friend, but you do not wish to find out what kind of enemy I can be. Now, don't ever voice doubt in me again. Come, and let us work together!

"Oh, yes…I feel so much more confidence in you now… you are quite the persuasive one," whispered Orrion. Much to the surprise of those standing near to him, he smiled.

Do not trifle with me, Elfhunter! If you do, I will take your sanity and leave you witless! You will not live for one day outside my good graces. Now, here is some persuasion: you had best reestablish the proper respect, or face my wrath!

He sent a bolt of pain through Gorgon's brain that nearly blinded him. Gelmyr's laughter rang with thunderous clarity in his ears. He could neither see nor breathe for a moment, as white light filled his vision. He gasped in pain and tears started in his beautiful grey eyes. Those standing near mistook them for tears of grief. Orrion appeared to be nearly overcome with it.

Kotos had calmed, and now took Gorgon's pain away as easily as he had caused it. *All right, now master yourself. I regret causing you pain. But this is too important to risk losing just because you are too short-sighted to stay on task. Calm yourself, Elfhunter, and let us be partners again. I believe I have made my point.*

Gorgon did not answer him, but Kotos knew that his point had been taken. The Elfhunter had made a bargain with Darkness, and now he was bound by it. There was no turning back.

Maji had arrived, and the service began. As Aryiah had opened her heart to the lights in the heavens, so now the people were invited to open their hearts and think whatever thoughts came to them.

"Be silent and thoughtful," said Maji. "Come and approach Aryiah's remains if you wish, and pay your respects to her, for she was our friend. If our prayers are heard, she will send a sign." All those present bowed their heads and kept their own thoughts.

At first, the only sound to be heard was the deep, clear tone of a bell that Maji struck with a tiny hammer. The sound swelled and rippled, helping to clear the mind and focus the heart. But then, everyone heard the harsh cry of a crow. Karatsu sailed into the courtyard, calling in his strident, discordant voice, circling over their heads. To the surprise and dismay of all, he settled upon the casket, shaking himself and ruffling all of his black feathers.

"He has been summoned," Maji whispered, pausing in her striking of the bell. There was now no sound to be heard. Karatsu scanned the crowd with his black, glittering eyes. He gave a sort of croaking cough, stretched his neck, and shook his head again.

All at once he drew himself up and rose into the air. "Call her! Call her!" he screamed, flying fast over the assembly. "Call her! Call her!" He appeared to be searching the crowd, and Orrion drew back into the shadows, his heart filled with fear.

Do not let the bird see you! said Kotos in alarm. But there was no escape for Orrion, no way out of the alcove except through the crowd.

"Deceiver! Deceiver!" cried Karatsu. "Call her! Deceiver! Call her!"

"*Do* something," whispered Gorgon. "If you are so powerful, do something, or we are undone!"

Kotos did. *Look at the bird, Elfhunter. Look hard at it, and do not let your gaze wander.* He summoned all his strength of will and sent forth a cloud of bewilderment out amidst the crowd. It took nearly every scrap of power he possessed. Karatsu was caught by it and fell from the air to strike Maji's upturned face. The bird scrambled, raking her with his long, black claws quite unintentionally, but it was enough to frighten her such that she fell sideways, knocking the bronze casket to the ground, sending Aryiah's ashes billowing into the air. Everyone in the courtyard felt Kotos' malevolence, and they were overcome with confusion. Maji was weeping, horrified at what she had done. Karatsu screamed, in a normal crow's voice this time. Whatever spirit had occupied him had vanished. He fled as fast as he could from the courtyard, cawing in panic.

Now Lord Salastor and Hallagond were at Maji's side, calming her and helping her to her feet. "It's all right, my people," said Salastor, turning to the crowd. "This was an unfortunate accident, but everything is all right now. Please, let us bring order and dignity back to these proceedings."

Everyone in the crowd was white-faced and shaken, and some were on the verge of weeping. Yet they heard the strong, clear voice of Salastor, and it summoned them to order. Whatever message

Aryiah had intended had been effectively disrupted and obscured.

Lord Kotos was exhausted. Gorgon had never known him to be so weakened, and it alarmed him for a moment. *Do…do not be dismayed. I have spent my powers, but they will return. Sending bewilderment over such a distance, affecting so many, has drained me. The Seer had a strong spirit. It was…it was not an easy thing that was done. Now I must rest. You will see to your preparations, until the evening comes. Then we will go to the lore-master. Do not disturb me until then.*

Gorgon heard no more from Kotos, and when the crowd dispersed, he was left alone to deal with them as they passed by. Many would remark later upon how weary and grieved Orrion had appeared. Of course, that was to be expected. Elves were known for the sincerity and depth of their passions, and Orrion would surely be no exception.

Salastor had offered Orrion a horse, but he had declined. "It is better that I go on my own feet. Besides, those of my race are tireless, and we can travel through terrain where horses cannot go. My thanks for the food and other provisions. I'm sure they will see me well on my way."

Now the sun was setting, and Gorgon roused Lord Kotos from his rest. "Awake, O Great Deceiver, for the twilight is falling. It is time we went to see the lore-master."

Is that a disrespectful tone I hear? I thought I had made myself clear about that, said Kotos.

"Not at all," Gorgon replied. "You are obviously a great deceiver, to have confounded so many in the courtyard. I was impressed."

Do not try to beguile me, Elfhunter. It will not work, growled Kotos. *Yet you should be impressed, and so I will trust you for the moment. Is all prepared as I advised?*

"Yes, all is prepared. I was just saying farewell to my soft bed and to my fine chambers. I sense a change in the weather; the rains will come just in time to make our journey miserable."

You did not mind the rain before you came here, said Kotos. *In fact, you welcomed it. The mighty Elfhunter feared no discomfort, for he had been called to a higher purpose! But do not fear…the journey will get very dry again all too soon. For now, you must go out into the lands north of the City and wait there for me. The Company will head north, and you must follow behind until you can steal in and reunite with me. Then we will work together once more. You will need to be self-reliant again for at least three turnings of the moon, but surely that will not dismay you, knowing that your purpose will be achieved in the end. Be advised: if you do not do as I instruct, if you have any thoughts of abandoning me and stealing my amulet, do not keep them any longer! I will find you in the dark, and you will regret ever drawing breath. Are we clear on that point?*

"So much for friendly cooperation," muttered Gorgon. "Do you think me as stupid as that? Remember that I have allied with you because I want the same result. If I abandon you, the plan will fail and the Elves will not come to grief. That is reason enough, and far more compelling than any threat you can make."

I only wish to be certain of your motives, said Kotos. *Now that you have enlightened me, I will not doubt you again. Now, let us proceed. Fima is most likely taking a late supper in his private study…let us seek him there first.*

Fima was just where Kotos had expected him to be, for he was a creature of habit when he was not traveling. Orrion could hear his dry, rasping cough as he approached. "It would seem that the dwarf is not well…are you certain that he will go with the Company? I will have a long wait for nothing if he remains behind, and as a result I will have a considerable distance to make up to catch them. Are you certain of your choice?"

A fair question. Do not fear—I have made a study of our friend the dwarf, and I cannot imagine his being left behind. When I am with him, he will feel some of my strength. Yet that is the only thing he will feel, as I cannot influence him in any way. My manipulation of him has been based on plain intuition, as for some reason his folk are immune to my suggestions…I have given up trying. I could choose another member of the Company to travel with, but the dwarf is best if I wish to remain undetected. Choose anyone else and we take the risk that the others might see my spirit reflected in the eyes of my host. Remember that I will not require the dwarf's services for long. That is why you should come to me as quickly as you can arrange it. It will take only a moment for our reunion.

Orrion paused outside the doorway to Fima's private study. He could see the old dwarf seated at his study-table, reading manuscripts as he always did, with a plate of cakes at one elbow and a flagon of ale at the other. There were many stout candles glowing gently about the chamber, sending a warm, golden light to aid him. There were several pieces of old, well-used furniture, including a brown leather sofa and three red velvet chairs. It was the picture of comfort, and Gorgon felt drawn to it, yet he knew that he could not remain.

Be careful now, and do not startle him. Remember...all you need do is touch him and it will be done.

Fima heard the soft knock, and looked up to behold Orrion standing in the doorway. Kotos was dismayed to see the mix of emotions play across Fima's face, though they were there for only an instant. It was the first time he had ever seen mistrust in the old dwarf's eyes.

"Forgive my intrusion, but I would speak with you," said Orrion in his most gentle voice. "May I come in and sit with you for a while?"

Fima covered his thoughts with a veil of hospitality. "Of course, you are welcome. Come in and join me." He indicated the sofa, and Orrion obliged, as the table and chairs were set too low for his tall frame. "Would you care for some cakes? They are excellent," said Fima nudging the plate toward Orrion.

"None for me, thank you. I have come to share my intentions, if you would know of them."

"Please do," said Fima, putting his manuscripts aside and turning in his chair so that Orrion had his absolute attention. Kotos studied Fima's eyes with care. The doubt still lingered within them, but it had been overcome now by curiosity.

"I intend to leave the Citadel tonight and continue to wherever I am called," said Orrion. "I do not yet know where that will be, but my purpose here has been fulfilled. The people have been warned of Lord Wrothgar." He paused to allow Fima the chance to react—to speak if he would—yet the dwarf was silent. "I do wish fate would reveal a clear path, but alas, it seems I must walk in uncertainty. I regret leaving this place, and these people, who have made me so welcome. Most of all, I regret leaving the library. There is so much that I would learn."

This was a sentiment Fima could well understand. "Why must you leave now?" he asked. "I understand that you have accomplished your purpose here, but we were just beginning to know you."

Exactly the problem, thought Gorgon. "I cannot say," he replied, his expression veiled. "Please do not press me about it. I could so easily be talked into staying, yet I have felt the call of my destiny, which should not be denied. Say nothing of our meeting to the others, I beg you. I came here only as a courtesy, for I had begun to relish your company and our lively talks of history and lore. I shall miss you."

Orrion extended his hand, Fima took it, and Gorgon was alone in the person of Orrion.

"Farewell, and safe journey," said Fima, unaware that anything had happened. "I shall miss our conversations. One day we must be reunited, for you never finished recounting your recollections of the First Uprising and the building of Tal-elathas. Until that day, then."

Fima released Orrion's very large hand and bowed before him. Orrion returned the gesture, and left the chamber. He stalked through the dark streets, returning to his own chamber for his provisions and armor.

In truth, he was glad to leave the City. How could he have ever thought of remaining here? Lord Kotos was right…it had seduced him and drawn him away from his purpose. In fact, the reason Gorgon wanted to leave was that he was now filled with fear. He could never be comfortable in such surroundings without his dreadful guardian. The sooner he resumed his solitary life, the sooner he could breathe easily again. It would be mid-day ere the citizens would discover that Orrion had donned his golden armor and left them, for they would neither see him nor hear him, and he would leave no trace of his passing.

Kotos settled into the person of Fima Lore-master with some difficulty, as the mind of a dwarf was unfamiliar territory. Once he remembered that he could not take charge, things became easier, yet Kotos was not comfortable with simply being carried about—he was far more accustomed to being in control. Ah, well, no matter… he would not be required to endure this indignity for long. He only needed to remain long enough to ensure that the seed he had planted took root as anticipated. He wondered about the origin of the mistrust he had seen in the old dwarf's eyes, but even as he could not control Fima, neither could he gain access to his thoughts. The halls of a dwarf's mind were closed to him.

Fima viewed Orrion's departure with mixed feelings. He would certainly miss the insights and recollections the Elf had favored him with—Orrion had been a great gift and Fima had written down every word—but he held doubts. These small, nagging doubts, had grown into genuine misgivings after Aryiah's memorial service. Dwarves, of all the races of Alterra, held the closest bond with ravens, and though Karatsu was not a raven, he was a close cousin. The tongue of ravens and crows is not all that different, and Fima had been one of very few at the service who actually understood what the bird had been trying to say.

The early morning sun found Gaelen at the horse-yards, as usual. Because she had taken on the responsibility of training Toran, she assumed some of his care. Now she shook her head as she beheld the untidy state of his shed and paddock. It was not typical of stallions to be so careless. They usually took great care in placing their droppings, as they used them to mark territory. Finan, for example, would leave a single large pile, one pile only, and the remainder of his environs would stay clean and dry.

Toran behaved more as a spoiled child, strewing his hay about when it did not meet his expectations, not caring how filthy his paddock became. Gaelen was exasperated.

She lugged the heavy wooden cart into the enclosure with a sigh. Cleaning up after Toran was always a struggle, for he viewed it as a game and would not leave her in peace. He had even managed to turn over the full cart on one occasion, making her so angry that she threw a stone at him. He had not done such a thing since, but he still would follow her about the paddock, pestering her for attention.

Today, however, things were different. He stood in the doorway to his shed, watching her but not bothering her. His mood was somber for the first time since she had known him. At first, she was worried that he might be ill, and stopped her labors long enough to check on him. His heart and lungs were fine, and he was not fevered. She could hear the normal rumblings of a healthy gut. He had been eating and drinking, and she had plenty of normal droppings to contend with. Toran was troubled, but he was not ill.

What is it? What melancholy has taken you? Are you fearful?

She remembered his reaction to Orrion when she had encountered him only two nights ago. She had not seen Toran since; other matters had required her attention. *You threatened Orrion because you feared him, didn't you?* She stroked his long face as he dipped it down before her and closed his eyes. *There is something not right about him. I don't know why, and I know it makes no sense, but I was afraid for my life. I don't blame you for being fearful.* She patted him again.

"Now, cheer up! I will protect you from the terrible High-elf, have no fear!" But Toran's dread ran deep, and not even Gaelen could take it from him.

"He has not been himself since yesterday," said Khandor, who had appeared at the paddock gate. "I was hoping you could enlighten me. Did something happen that I should know about?"

"Before I answer, please allow me to ask a question of you," said Gaelen. "Has Toran ever threatened anyone? I mean, really threatened them, not in a playful way?"

Khandor's surprise showed immediately on his guileless face. "That horse has never had a threatening thought in his life that I'm aware of. When did you observe him threatening anyone?"

For a moment Gaelen wondered whether she should confide in him, but she knew he was trustworthy. "The night before last, I was riding out over the foothills, when something frightened Toran such that he stopped hard enough to unseat me. I might have broken my neck. When I recovered, I saw Orrion just standing in the shadows, and when I looked over at Toran, he was standing with his ears back and his nose wrinkled—everything short of baring his teeth. I had never seen such an expression in him before."

Khandor considered. "Orrion, you say? That makes no sense. I can understand why Toran was startled... Orrion probably appeared out of nowhere. Horses have better senses than we do."

"Not better than *I* do," said Gaelen. "But I will admit, my thoughts were wandering and I was not paying attention to my surroundings. Toran probably saw Orrion out of the corner of his eye, and it no doubt startled him. But then, why did he threaten?"

Khandor paused again before answering. "What is *your* opinion of Orrion?"

"Ahhh…I am uncertain of him," said Gaelen after a moment.

"You mean you don't trust him?" asked Khandor.

"If I may speak plainly, and know that you will repeat nothing you hear, then I will state that I do not *remotely* trust him," said Gaelen with conviction. It felt so good to finally say it.

"Then might I offer an explanation for Toran's behavior?" said Khandor. "He has obviously bonded with you, and has picked up on your mistrust. He threatens Orrion because you find Orrion to be threatening. Toran has given himself over to his new partner."

Gaelen shook her head. "To be my partner, we both must agree to the partnership. I have not allowed such a bond with Toran… you have set me to the task of training him for Lord Salastor."

"Did I not tell you?" said Khandor.

"Tell me what?"

"My apologies. I thought I had told you…Salastor has chosen another mount. You are free to take Toran for your own, Gaelen. No one else wants him."

How convenient, thought Gaelen, though for just a moment she bristled at the thought of anyone's not finding Toran acceptable. Then she remembered how exasperating he was.

"It doesn't matter," she said. "I could not have made such a bond, even if I had been free to do so. I don't know whether I ever will. There must be another explanation." Her eyes smoldered through unshed tears. Khandor took notice at once.

"I understand that you feel both sorrow and anger," he said. "You still grieve for Finan, and you are angry because you believe that you have betrayed his memory by opening your heart to Toran, even a little bit. Gaelen, Finan is gone. He is gone, and Toran stands here knowing that he is not Finan, but still wanting to be your friend and worthy mount. Can you not just allow him to be Toran, and accept him for what he is?"

"You mean accept him for the untidy, annoying, juvenile, inconvenient, untested creature that he is?"

"Yes. And also accept him for the swift, strong, handsome, tireless, graceful future battle-mount that he is. If Finan were here, he would grieve to see you without a horse."

"If Finan were here, I would not *be* without a horse!" cried Gaelen, who could no longer quell her tears. She threw her pitchfork to the ground in frustration, vaulted over the paddock fence, and disappeared before Khandor could stop her.

After she had gone, Toran emerged from the shed, looking and calling after her. "It's no use, my friend," said Khandor. "You will not convince her today. She will need to consider things for a while longer. Never mind—none of this is your fault. Come and have some breakfast."

Gaelen had stopped running, and now her face burned with tears of shame. She had been rude to Khandor, and she was not being fair to Toran. Why was this situation so difficult? She knew why Toran had threatened Orrion. It was not because he had bonded with her, for she knew that such a close connection had not yet been made. There was only one other explanation that made any sense, and that was that Orrion was evil. Not just odd, but actually *evil.* And although she would keep this insight to herself for the moment, it did not dismay her when Nelwyn finally found her in the afternoon and informed her that Orrion had left the City without a trace.

10
The Rising of Three Moons

The news of Orrion's departure disappointed many of the people, for they admired and respected him. He had, in fact, been the subject of various flights of imagination and had visited the dreams of many. When the citizens asked why Orrion had gone, the Council told them only that he had felt the need to see to his affairs elsewhere. They shook their heads in regret, hoping that he had approved of their hospitality and that his going had not stemmed from any failure to please him.

Though not surprised, Gaelen was amazed at the extent of their devotion. Orrion had not been in the City long, and yet the people almost grieved at his going. *If all it takes is impressive stature and a handsome face, I should rethink my position concerning the respect I hold for the people of Dûn Arian…*

Yet she knew that their admiration involved more than Orrion's seven-foot height or his golden hair…she had been lulled by him more than once. She had seen many things in Orrion's gaze, including the promise of peace and happiness, and the attaining of one's desire. He had drawn her back to the Greatwood, for it was her heart's desire to return there and never leave again. Orrion's eyes had promised that it would be so.

Because Gaelen's suspicions had begun even before Orrion had the chance to beguile her, she had overcome his efforts. And, once it is seen and recognized, a snake is easily avoided. She had since been accumulating evidence in support of her suspicions—this last incident with Toran had confirmed them.

What she did not understand was the exact nature of the tie between Orrion and Gorgon Elfhunter. Now that Orrion had gone she was not likely to, which was a pity in her mind. It was also a pity that she could not express her doubts to the people of the City, for they would not have been well received. She decided to keep her thoughts to herself for the time being.

Gaelen believed that she was alone in those thoughts, but a few of her friends also held doubts. Rogond, Fima, Galador, and Azori each had noticed incidents, coincidences, and peculiarities that did not sit easily upon their minds. Yet because none would share them, the doubts would not be confirmed. Now that Orrion had gone, there was no need to worry about his influence any longer. The suspicions faded with each day that passed.

No one, not even Gaelen, would know that the greater evil was still among them. Lord Kotos dwelled alone with his thoughts in the person of Lore-master Fima. From there he could take notice of whatever goings-on Fima was privy to without being detected by anyone, but he could not exert any influence over Fima, other than to impart some strength and vigor to his body.

Rogond, who spent more time with Fima than many, noticed the change. His friend was not as quickly winded, and the persistent coughing had left him. His face plumped out, and the normal ruddy coloring returned. Rogond thought he even noticed a few strands of dark red hair in Fima's snowy beard. Before it had gone silver, Fima's hair had been dark auburn as with many folk of his line.

Rogond remarked on it as they took supper together. "Whatever you have been eating, my friend, keep on eating it. I have not seen you look so well in a long while."

Fima laughed. "It might not be the eating, but the drinking that is making me feel so vigorous. I have only recently discovered this wonderful, fine ale. Pray, have some!" He filled two clay tankards and offered one to Rogond, who had to agree that it was excellent. He doubted that the ale, while excellent, was the source of whatever miracle had befallen Fima, but he was so pleased to see his friend in good health that he didn't care.

Gaelen made her apologies to Toran, spending extra time currying him and riding him every day. Khandor took notice, smiling as he watched them together. It would not be long now.

Siva was nearing her foaling time, and so Gaelen spent part of each day with her, though the mare was moody and uncomfortable. "Never mind," said Gaelen, stroking Siva with a soothing hand. "Soon your discomfort will end, and you will have a lovely new foal at your side. I wish you could tell me who sired your little one. Well, I suppose we'll just have to wait and see."

Siva nuzzled Gaelen, as though entreating her to bring the whole uncomfortable business to an end. She circled her deep bed of straw several times before lying heavily on her side. She groaned as though in pain, but Gaelen knew that it was simply from the effort to breathe. Lying down beside the mare, Gaelen began to sing to her and to her foal, and soon Siva felt much better. In her womb, the foal heard the song of the Elves for the first time in his life, and his small, soft hooves began to move gently, as though striding in rhythm.

The first full moon since the departure of Orrion rose like a beautiful golden orb over the City, casting light that was at first warm, but would later turn blue and cold as the rich gold gave way to hard, white silver. Gaelen preferred starlight to moonlight, yet she would ride out over the desert lands this night as she did every night. The rains had come, and a clear sky was welcome, yet she had seen distant lightning flickering in the tall clouds gathering over the sea. Gaelen put her nose into the wind. *The storm will come within the next few hours…this will be a short ride, then.*

Toran moved easily over the uneven ground. They had already made the distance to the pass through the brown hills and looked now upon the sands beyond. The desert smelled wonderful, as it was in flower, and the rains had brought forth life in places one would never expect. Most wonderful of all was the broad, flat expanse of water that once had been a lake; it was filled again for the first time in a hundred years. It was nearly four miles across and only about three feet deep at its deepest point. The water was warm and full of rejuvenating minerals. This was Gaelen's destination, and she took Toran into the waters, exercising his limbs and soothing his tendons at the same time. He was breathing hard, and so she halted, allowing him to merely soak his legs and recover his wind.

Both she and Toran heard El-morah before they saw him. He was singing a sort of mournful, plaintive prayer-chant, standing alone on a pile of stones, looking back toward the northeast. Gaelen did not understand the tongue he used—in fact, she did not believe she had ever heard it before—but the pain within was clear.

Toran called to El-morah, knowing a friend, and Gaelen rode slowly and carefully through the waters to the shore, vaulting off and leading Toran to the pile of stones. El-morah had stopped singing, for he had seen her, and now he climbed down to sit upon one of the larger boulders. "Come, Gaelen, if you would join me."

She sat beside him, looking upon his genuine, friendly face and warm, brown eyes. "It is not your habit to be this far from the gates alone, is it?" she asked. "What purpose has brought you here?"

"I have come to be alone, even as you have," said El-morah. "I have called out to my home, and my family, but they do not answer. They cannot hear me, wherever they have gone."

"My apologies for disturbing your solitude," said Gaelen, blushing and turning her face from his. "I would share your pain, if you will allow it."

El-morah shook his head. "I'm glad of your company, and I would hear what you have to say."

"I had not noticed the grey in your hair before," said Gaelen, who was not known for her subtle approach. "It was dark when I saw you in the Chupa. Do you think it was the desert crossing that has marked you, or was it…something else?"

"I do not know," he replied. "But you're right. My hair had barely a hint of grey when I last remembered. Now it appears as though I have aged a great deal. What do you think it means? I have endured physical hardship before, as great as that given by any desert crossing. I have seen war and profound deprivation…I don't believe the silver in my hair is rooted in discomfort."

"Do you see the streak of silver that has come to me?" asked Gaelen, lifting her hair to show him. "That came from a trial of spirit, not of the body—from a presence so evil that its mere touch has marked me. I wonder whether you have also been marked. If so, then you cannot trust your memories. The evil that can mark you thus can also deceive your thoughts."

She drew a deep breath. "You've been searching outward for your loved ones because, in your heart, you know that they are still there to hear you. Tell me I am wrong."

El-morah turned his eyes away. "You are not wrong. There are things that don't seem right, all the more so with time passing. I remember…I remember the oasis burning, and the men sent to find me. I can see their faces. I can hear Mohani screaming, and…the cries of my children. Yet how is it that I am still here? I would have died trying to save them…I would never have abandoned them. Yet, I'm here, and they do not answer to my call. How did I come to be here? The memory of their undoing is so terribly clear that I can hardly bear to recall it, yet I can remember little of the crossing and, in truth, I have no idea where I am. The stars tell me that I have gone south, but I do not know how far. Neither my head nor my heart knows where to turn."

Gaelen knelt down upon the sandy soil. She pointed to a small stone. "Here is the Chupa oasis. And here…over here is the Sandstone settlement. Are you with me?" She looked up at El-morah, who nodded slowly in the moonlight. "Now, here…here is where we are now!" She placed another stone a considerable distance from the first two. "Is it any wonder they cannot hear you?"

El-morah took in a sharp breath. "That's not possible," he said. "Such a journey could never be made by one man alone. Why, in the name of heaven, should I have made it?"

Gaelen knew she had an ally in El-morah, but she struggled with the desire to reveal her fears to him. *Yet he saved my life once…and he is in turmoil. I can take some of his confusion away. He is a man who can keep secrets—I just know it. Besides, if I don't tell someone, and soon, I'll go mad.* She decided to trust her instincts, as they had rarely failed her.

"El-morah, what I say to you now must be kept to yourself. Will you agree?"

He rocked back on his heels, as though surprised for a moment. Then his eyes filled with resolve. "I will."

"Then hear me. Orrion is evil. No one else will believe it, but I know it. He is evil, and now that he has gone, you are beginning to realize that your memories are not beyond questioning."

El-morah went still and silent for a moment, and Gaelen wondered whether he would now suggest that she had lost her own mind. Finally, he spoke to her.

"Orrion? But…he saved my life, Gaelen. He saved my life and restored my awareness. How can he be evil? If he is evil, then why has he not taken control of the City? Why did he leave it? It is my experience that evil folk desire things…power, influence, wealth… what did Orrion gain here? He came, after saving my life, he healed those who were not sane, and he nearly killed himself while trying to save Aryiah's life. He warned us of some great threat to the north, and then he left us without once having asked for anything. How can he be evil?"

"I don't know…but I have come to know him as a deceiver and a beguiler. You made this journey because somehow it suited his purpose. He has manipulated us all! Think on it for a moment… would he be able to heal those who are not sane without influencing their minds? I saw what he did to you. He's been one big contradiction after another ever since he arrived."

She saw the doubt in El-morah's eyes, and sighed. "I don't know how I know it, since you're bound to ask. Just…little things here and there. Little things that add up. And I know one thing that doesn't add up, and that's your presence here."

"He saved my life," said El-morah, but Gaelen saw doubt flickering in his dark eyes.

"Because he needed you. You loved your wife and children above all else. Would you really still be alive had someone murdered them? Would you not have died defending them? You know the answer to that. I'm just saying…your awareness and your memories may be false, my friend. You must trust your heart."

El-morah just sat in silence, considering what she had said.

"Do not confound yourself with too many questions," said Gaelen. "Your heart speaks to you…what does it say?"

El-morah sighed. "I am conflicted at this moment. If you are right, then I will thank you. If you are wrong, and you have filled me with false hope, then I will curse you. But either way, I must now be sure. I will be returning home as soon as my strength is fully regained."

"Well, you cannot go alone," said Gaelen with finality. "We would not allow you to risk your life, now that you have been restored to us."

El-morah lifted an eyebrow at her. "I was not aware that my decisions were yours to make," he said.

"Someone must prevent you from undertaking a foolish course of action," said Gaelen, her ears reddening in the dark.

"Don't worry…I am among the least foolish men you will ever meet," said El-morah. "And you have cheered me, my small but insistent friend. It's good to know that a man has so many fierce hearts looking out for his welfare. I will not undertake the journey without considerable planning."

"And I suppose a man who is not foolish rushes into a corridor outside a burning tower without even a cloth over his face," said Gaelen. "I heard you coughing for weeks! You may not be foolish, but you *are* heroic. Sometimes, heroes do not think clearly."

"From what I've heard, you could stand to take some of that admonition upon yourself," said El-morah with a smile.

Gaelen ignored him. "We must be sure to keep this to ourselves for the time being," she said in a quiet voice, "at least until Orrion has been gone for a while. We must allow memory of him to fade before we reveal our thoughts. Be certain of one thing—he may be gone, but he is not yet finished with Dûn Arian. The evil that brought down Aryiah will revisit the City, if I am any judge. And he has not finished with our Company. You and I must keep our vigilance."

El-morah nodded in the moonlight. "You believe Orrion brought down Aryiah? You should know that you are not the only one that believes her tower was set aflame with intent. When we examined the ruins, I saw doubt in Azori's eyes."

At that moment, Toran looked westward and gave a soft whinny. The approaching thunder could now be heard; it was time to return to the City. "We must leave, or risk being caught in the storm," said Gaelen. "Can you ride?"

"I ride well, thank you," said El-morah. "I'm grateful for the sharing of your horse, but more so for the sharing of your concerns."

Gaelen vaulted onto Toran as he stood beside one of the stones, and El-morah followed her example. They made their way back toward the City as the moonlight disappeared, to be replaced by flashes of lightning. By the time they reached the gates, they were soaked with rain driven by fierce winds. El-morah was indeed an excellent rider; he vaulted off as Toran entered the courtyard, then waved farewell as Gaelen rode through the driving rain back to the horse-yards.

When she got there, Khandor was waiting for her. "The stress of the storm has disquieted Siva, and the foal she carries is coming into the world early—tonight! This is an ill happening. It would not be the first time I had seen a foal arrive before its time because the mare was stressed."

"Yet a simple storm would not distress her so," said Gaelen. "In the Greatwood I learned that it is the foal, and not the mare, that decides when the time is right. It would seem that this foal has made his decision. We do not know when he was conceived, and though the signs would tell otherwise, we do not know for certain that he is not ready. Let us proceed as though there is no difficulty, and perhaps there will be none."

Gaelen found Siva already lying in the straw, looking in confusion at her belly as though she did not understand what was happening.

"Is this her first?" asked Khandor, for if so, it was important to know.

"Alas, I do not know her history, but she is at least ten years old. I cannot believe that such a fine mare has never been bred before." She knelt beside Siva and took stock of her condition.

The birth proceeded without incident, though the foal was indeed early and he was smaller than normal. Both Gaelen and Khandor were dismayed when they beheld him. He did not stand quickly, and his ears were soft, indicating that he might be too young and too weak to survive. His coat was wavy and very, very silky.

"He is too small," said Khandor. "I doubt he will thrive, but we will make every effort. Let's try to get him to stand and nurse."

Gaelen lifted the foal and gently placed him on his feet. Siva licked and nuzzled him, but her efforts were half-hearted, as though she knew that he was not strong. He showed no interest in suckling, but stood shivering in Gaelen's arms, pulling his head away when Gaelen tried to guide him.

"Let's dry him off and get him warm, then we will see if he will take some milk," said Khandor. "Perhaps he is simply too cold now." Gaelen wrapped the foal in a warm woolen blanket as Siva circled the stall, lay down upon her side, and saw to the business of passing the afterbirth.

The next several hours were difficult for everyone. Khandor drew Siva's milk from her, and Gaelen finally managed to tempt the foal into taking some of it, but he was still too weak to stand by himself. At last Khandor left for his chambers, for he was weary and in need of sleep, but Gaelen remained, lying beside Siva in the straw with the foal in her arms, singing a quiet lullaby.

Gaelen enlisted Nelwyn's aid in fostering Siva's foal, for she was a good hand. Still, there were several anxious days. It was nearly a week before the foal could stand on his own for any length of time, and he had needed to be fed by hand, for he did not show enough enthusiasm otherwise. Gaelen and Nelwyn took turns watching him and feeding him. Siva had been worried at first, but they reassured her and she trusted them.

"So, do you have a sense of whose foal this is?" asked Nelwyn.

"Not yet, though I sense he is strong-hearted," said Gaelen. "He is colored like Finan, but that does not mean much. Bay is a common color—even Eros could produce it, and so could Réalta. I won't know for certain until he tells me."

"Look, Gaelen…he is on his feet. Look! He is finally feeding on his own!" whispered Nelwyn in a voice charged with excitement. The foal was, indeed, on his feet, and appeared to have only just discovered his mother's milk. He was now suckling with gusto, his little black tail wagging with enthusiasm. He appeared normal in every respect. Siva jostled and chortled at him, as if to say "It's about time."

When Siva nudged him again, he lifted a hind leg and swatted at her. There was no need to be impatient with him, thank you! Nelwyn smiled. "I believe," she said, looking over at Gaelen, "that he has just told you who his sire is."

By the time the next full moon had risen, the foal was healthy and vigorous. Though he was small, Gaelen knew that he would soon grow into himself. Every day she could see improvement. She was glad to see this wonderful new life frisking and playing, snorting and trotting about. Sometimes, when he stopped in just a certain way, and lifted his head in just the right manner, he was the very image of his sire. Finan would have been proud of his son, despite his difficult beginnings. The little one had already overcome more adversity than most.

True to her word, Gaelen had gone to the Grave of the Faithful to tell Finan all about his fine offspring. "He is very much as I imagine you were when you were little, though he will turn grey, like his mother. He is very gentle and loving, but he has a strong and determined heart. He will grow into a wonderful horse, just like his sire." She had promised herself that she would not weep, and she did not, though the next words were difficult. "Thank you for leaving behind a part of yourself." At this, she turned and made her way back to the City where her friends awaited her.

Nelwyn had gone to the harbor to watch the moon over the water, the third full moon since the departure of Orrion. As she settled herself upon a stony ledge overlooking the deep, quiet waters, she began to drift out of the realm of awareness. An evil seed had taken root in the light of that moon, exactly as Kotos had planned, but Nelwyn did not know it. Now her innocence would serve as fertile soil in which it could grow, as the most terrible dream she had ever beheld began to unfold.

She gasped, falling to the ground, unaware of anything around her except the moon—the terrible, bright, unrelenting moon. She dreamed of Wrothgar, and the Stone of Léir, and Gorgon Elfhunter. He had been placed in command of his own dark army, and the trees of the Greatwood were burning…

Galador and Gaelen had sensed Nelwyn's distress, for this vision had terrified her more utterly than anything in her life. When they found her, she was lying on the shores of the harbor, bathed in moonlight, staring up at the night sky. Galador would have rushed to her side, but Gaelen stayed him.

"Careful! She is not walking in this world. Do not startle her… we must tread lightly!" Galador, who was familiar with Nelwyn's rare and profound foresight, knew that visions must not be interrupted and, though it was difficult, he sat beside his beloved, but did not disturb her. Gaelen sat upon Nelwyn's other side, her senses alerted, ready to respond to any threat that might come.

Nelwyn was obviously in very deep distress; she began to moan and her breath hitched in her chest. She raised her arm and flung it across her eyes, as though trying to fend off an enemy against which she had no defense. Her cries grew louder, and at last she screamed and wailed, sitting bolt upright, her eyes nearly starting from her head, white-faced and unable to breathe for a moment. Galador was alarmed.

"Nelwyn…*Nelwyn!*" he cried, "Breathe, beloved! Come back to me. You are safe…all is well! Come back!"

He surrounded her with the gentle power of his embrace, as all strength drained from her and she began to weep. Gaelen dropped her eyes and released a long sigh of relief, for one must breathe in order to weep.

Then Gaelen's gaze was drawn to movement in the waters of the harbor, and her eyes grew wide. "Galador! Look at the *water!*"

There, in the moonlight, an amazing sight—thousands upon thousands of fish circling slowly, their dark masses occasionally broken by a flash of blue-white belly. Even Gaelen, a Wood-elf whose home was nowhere near any ocean harbor, knew that this occurrence could not be explained. The fish seemed dazed, as though even they could not explain what had drawn them there. There were the great and the tiny, the swift and the streamlined, the odd and the beautiful, all represented in that enormous, circling mass. They did not keep each to their own, but mingled indiscriminately, the predator gliding beside its prey. Gaelen had never seen anything like it. Something had happened here—something only Nelwyn could reveal.

Galador lifted Nelwyn and carried her back to the safety of the City walls. By the time Gaelen had told anyone of the mysterious gathering of the fishes, and folk had gone down to see this incredible sight for themselves, the great mass had dispersed and all was as before.

Nelwyn would not speak of her vision to anyone at first, insisting that only those she knew that she could trust be allowed to hear of it. At last, the Company gathered in her chamber, together with Lord Salastor and Maji, and they listened with horrified fascination to her tale. She told of everything she had seen; her voice sometimes strong and charged with outrage, sometimes plaintive and full of dread. She spared no detail.

"I remember a dying scout, brought before Lady Ordath, whispering dreadful words about Wrothgar. He was advancing on Mountain-home…and another large force had moved up from the Darkmere. He warned Ordath that she must summon aid from the Woodland, and from the Lake-realm, for the strength of Mountain-home would not stand against such a mighty army. Ordath did call for aid, and I remember seeing Magra with her. She told him to have the body of Lord Shandor moved to a safe place. It must not fall into the hands of Wrothgar, or…or the consequences would be disastrous." Nelwyn shuddered. "I felt Lady Ordath's fear, and it was terrible."

"No doubt," said Galador gently. "But Shandor's body is only an empty shell."

"But…his soul is bound in the Stone of Léir. And I saw Lady Arialde—she keeps the Stone—she called to Shandor, and he showed her the future. I remember it…it was as though I stood there with her. The mists within the stone turned dark, like smoke from a battlefield, and we saw the downfall of Mountain-home. Wrothgar led his Dark Armies there from the Fell-ruin and from the Darkmere, and the Elves were vanquished in a storm of fire. Shandor told Arialde to send aid…as many warriors as could be gathered, that very night! Then the Stone went dark, and Arialde went forth—there was no time to waste! But after she had gone, the Stone flickered into life again.

"I heard Shandor's voice, crying out—'Sister? Sister…there is… something more! I cannot see clearly, but there is something more. Arialde! Arialde! You must move the Stone from here at once! It is too late…too late! Oh, sister, what have I done?'" Nelwyn's voice quavered as she recalled Shandor's plaintive cry.

"What did it mean? I felt…desperation. Shandor had seen something more, but I didn't know what it was at first. Then, I knew! Arialde had left the Stone before Shandor could reveal the threat that came not from the north, but from the west. It came not to Mountain-home, but to the *Lake*. Everyone had been deceived. Wrothgar had not been quartered in the Fell-ruin, as all had thought. He had arisen from Tûr Dorcha, and he was making his way to the Lake-realm, which now had only the barest number of defenders remaining within it. He stole into Tal-sithian like an evil vapor, and took the Stone of Léir!"

A collective gasp went up from all who listened to Nelwyn's recounting. "But that would make him invincible!" cried Galador. "He would know when and where to attack, know all his enemies' weaknesses, he would know the outcome of battles before they were fought…it would be the worst thing that could happen!"

"I know you're right," said Nelwyn, "because I saw it! Wrothgar forced Shandor into his service, thereby gaining the foresight to send his armies always to the right place at the right time. They overcame Mountain-home, sweeping down from the north before Magra or anyone else could stop them. I…I even saw Orrion there."

"Orrion was in Mountain-home?" asked Fima.

"Yes, he was there—in the thick of the battle, fighting to the last." She shuddered, recalling Orrion's last moments. "He grew weary, and fell to a troll. It crushed the life out of him…I'll never forget the sound of his ribs breaking."

Tears came to Nelwyn's eyes then, as the worst of the vision bloomed once more in her mind's eye. "Magra died a very bad death, writhing in the clutches of Wrothgar's fire-demons, all his valor gone. Ordath fled deep into the catacombs beneath the mountain, only to be taken like a doe brought to bay by a pack of hounds. Her power flared around her, but it was not enough."

"And what of Gorgon Elfhunter?" said Gaelen in a small, quiet voice.

"He was placed in command of his own army. Oh, Gaelen… they burned the Greatwood. They burned the *trees*…"

Galador embraced her gently. "Was there anything more?"

She shook her head, whispering "Was that not enough?"

"She is drained, and in need of rest," said Galador. "I will take her to our chambers now. Obviously, you all have things to discuss."

"No...*wait!*" cried Nelwyn, pulling away from him. "I have things to say!" The haunted look in her eyes chilled them all. She turned to Maji. "There is something more. The evil that killed Aryiah is still among us."

"Are you sure?" said Gaelen.

"As sure as I can ever be of anything," said Nelwyn. "One thing is certain—I must leave the City with very little delay. The evil that took Aryiah still walks here, and I am in fear for my life. Aryiah was killed to keep these insights from being known, for she might also have received them. Now that I have received them, I cannot stay."

"But you have told us all of your insights, Nelwyn," said Lord Salastor. "Whatever evil took Aryiah did so, in your mind, to prevent such knowledge from reaching the people. There are now ten who know of it...surely the villain will not attempt to kill us all. I believe you are safe for the moment."

"Yet I will not be at ease here, not ever again. I felt the presence of Aryiah's killer, and...I *still* feel it, begging your pardon."

Salastor looked around at Nelwyn's most trusted friends. "Surely you do not believe that the killer is here, in this room?" he said.

"Of course not," said Nelwyn, her ears turning red at the very suggestion. "Still, I know that he is somewhere in the City. So long as I am here, I will not wish to be alone." She did not realize that the killer *was* in the room, looking through the eyes of Lore-master Fima. Kotos had done his job well. It would not be long now, and his waiting would end.

"We must speak now of Nelwyn's vision and what course should be taken," said Rogond. "Why have we, in Dûn Arian, been gifted with such insight? Perhaps Ordath and Arialde have also been enlightened and, if so, then there is not as much to fear."

"And if they haven't, are you willing to take the chance?" said Fima. "We should proceed as though we are the only persons who possess this foresight. We risk far more by making assumptions to the contrary."

"Our course is clear," said Nelwyn. "We must return with all speed to the northlands, to Tal-sithian, and warn the Lady that the Stone must be moved. Then we must travel to Mountain-home, to warn the Elves before Wrothgar has time to strike. I pray that we are not too late."

Fima shook his head. "I don't believe such an offensive is possible," he said. "According to all beliefs of the Wise, the Shadowmancer is not yet strong enough. Perhaps they are wrong, but perhaps Nelwyn's vision is warning us of a more distant future. If so, then we have time to avert it."

"Yet we cannot be sure, and when we are not sure we must act quickly," said Hallagond.

"What you're planning is no small matter," said Azori. "It will take some time to gain the northern lands. And it will be a hard journey, no matter what path is chosen."

"Say nothing of any of this to anyone," said Galador. "We do not want Aryiah's killer to know of Nelwyn's insight, and we must never leave her alone. Let us keep to our own thoughts for the moment and meet again tomorrow. One more day will make little difference."

Everyone agreed to this plan. They dispersed to ponder all they had learned, all save Gaelen and Galador, who remained with Nelwyn. Gaelen's thoughts had been moving in a different direction from the others in the Company, and now she turned to Nelwyn. "You said you had seen Orrion defending Mountain-home. Are you absolutely sure of it?"

Nelwyn nodded. "Yes. He was there, during the last battle. He fought like a cornered dragon, but a troll crushed him." She closed her eyes, trying not to recall the image again. To be crushed beneath the feet of a nine-hundred-pound troll was a gruesome death. She sighed, trying to ward off tears. "He had a kind heart. It would be a pity to lose him."

Gaelen had not seen any evidence of Orrion's kind heart—she saw something quite different in him. Yet Nelwyn had seen him defending Mountain-home, fighting to the death. It made no sense. And Gaelen had suspected Orrion in the death of Aryiah, yet Orrion was long gone, and Nelwyn had said that Aryiah's killer still walked among them. Gaelen was confused, until she remembered that Orrion had it in his power to manipulate the minds of others. Perhaps Nelwyn was being manipulated?

No, that is most unlikely, thought Gaelen. *She is highly attuned to the presence of evil. It would be most difficult to deceive her.* She left Nelwyn to rest with Galador, knowing that she would receive no further guidance. Then she went to find the two people whose thoughts she would share.

Rogond and Fima had gone to Fima's study and were engaged in a lively discussion. When they saw Gaelen, they welcomed her.

Kotos smiled, knowing that Gaelen would never detect his presence. She had only been suspicious when he had shared consciousness with Gorgon Elfhunter. Kotos had deceived the mightiest and most worthy beings in all of Alterra upon a time—neither Dardis, nor Ri-Aldamar, nor Baelta, nor Léiras, nor even Shandor had suspected him. He had little to fear from the likes of Nelwyn or Gaelen.

Nelwyn, in fact, had proved to be the most fertile soil in which to plant his foul seed—the soil of an open, unassuming mind. Now the evil, poisonous vine that sprang from it would take the Company exactly on the path Kotos had intended. Once Wrothgar achieved His desire, the vine would turn on the innocents and strangle them as they slept.

Gaelen, Rogond, and Fima debated far into the night. Fima and Rogond sat on opposite sides of Fima's long, low table, and Gaelen curled up in one of the red velvet chairs like a cat, watching and listening. When dawn came, Fima and Rogond were fast asleep, but Gaelen was still alert, pondering all she had heard, as the scholars stirred and went about their morning duties. There was no question that the Company needed to return north, but Gaelen's purpose in doing so would be quite different from any she professed to have.

The debate had ended in her mind. In the end, she had elected to trust the instincts of Toran over all else.

11
The Long Road North

Because of Nelwyn's contention that there was still an evil presence lurking in Dûn Arian, the Company would leave in secret. Preparations were made in quiet haste. Salastor and Fima met in the underground level of the library, considering various paths to the north in order to decide the best way to be taken. With them was a map-maker, Carmyn by name, who had already spent quite a lot of time studying with Fima. It was his opinion that she could be trusted.

"The ways to the north are three, discounting the way you came," she said. "I would not suggest returning by that path, though Bint Raed was right in leading you, for otherwise the journey would have taken too long. None of these ways are swift, and all have perils. The dangers to our north have protected us from outsiders, but they are inconvenient to those wishing to explore them or cross them." She smiled at Fima. "Map-makers sometimes face difficult tasks, and we are not always accurate. I have found some inconsistencies in the maps you have brought with you, Master."

"That will not do at all!" said Fima. "You must aid me in correcting them, then. You know that my maps were originally set down by others, Elves and men most likely. I have only added to their work. Dwarvish maps of underground realms are very accurate."

Salastor smiled at both of them. It was interesting to note that true scholars, whatever their interest, shared a reverence for learning that made them both methodical and patient. Salastor was a scholar as well, yet he knew that there was some urgency to the Company's departure.

"Regrettably, we won't have time to make corrections now," said Carmyn, who shook very dark brown hair from eyes that were filled with regret. She did not wish to lose the gift of having Lore-master Fima in the Silver City, but she had to help him find his way. She pointed to her own large map. "You may choose the forest path, the mountain path, or the desert path. There are advantages to each. The forest path is the shortest way over land because you will reach the Ambros—you can follow the river north to Dûn Bennas. Those are the King's lands and you will be welcome.

"The mountain path is the most difficult and taxing, and it is also the longest, as you cannot go in a direct line. The desert will skirt the plains of thirst to the west, yet there are long stretches with no water. It will take the least amount of time, if all goes well. If all does not go well, thirst may take you."

"I thought you said the forest path was the shortest," said Fima, who did not like the prospect of another desert crossing.

"So it is, in terms of distance, but in terms of time, the forest can block you. There are places where it is very thick and wild—you will need to make your way around them. The path I will show you will avoid most of the deep ravines and gorges, but the going will not be swift. And then, there is the matter of Fómor."

No one needed any explanation of why Fómor, the fabled city of the Corsairs, had to be avoided. Fomorians were notorious for attacking travelers and not caring whether the travelers lived to tell about it.

"They must not go near there," said Salastor. "They will be set upon."

"They will skirt around the city by many miles, yet there is still the risk of running into the inhabitants," said Carmyn. She turned to Fima. "You must make your way by night, and be as swift as you may. And even the desert path brings you to water-sources used by the people of Fómor. It is this river, here...see this one that seems to spring forth from the sand?" She pointed to the map. "If you take the desert way, you will indeed be happy to see it, yet there are always Fómorians marauding up and down its banks. All three paths cross it—no way is safe."

"Two matters must now be debated," said Salastor. "Who will travel, and what path will they take? When the first is answered, all must agree upon the second. Fima, please come to my private council-chamber in one hour."

He rose and left them, intending to gather the Company. Fima and Carmyn looked at one another for a moment. Then they each took a piece of charcoal in hand and set to work in an attempt to repair as many inconsistencies in Fima's map as they could in the hour remaining to them.

In the end, the two matters Salastor referred to had not taken so long to debate. The membership of the Company would be eight, including the three Elves, Rogond and Hallagond, Fima, Estle, and Azori. Galador, in particular, was not certain of the wisdom of including Azori, but Azori would not leave Estle to face such a dangerous journey without him. "Besides," he said with a wicked grin, "you will be very glad of me if we run into any of the inhabitants of Fómor. I know how best to deal with them. An honest person, such as Galador, would no doubt be thought of as an easy mark."

"That explains why you are confident in your own ability to deal with them," grumbled Galador, who was not looking forward to a thousand miles of watching his back.

"That will do, both of you," said Fima. "Azori is right...Fómor is one of the greatest hazards we face. It certainly will not hurt to have him with us."

Galador's expression indicated that he was not convinced, but he kept his thoughts to himself.

The matter of the road took longer. None were in favor of the arduous way through the hills, but they were divided as to the choice of forest or desert. Estle, Hallagond, and Azori favored the desert, but the Elves, Rogond, and Fima preferred the forest.

"I don't like the sound of deep gorges and ravines," said Azori. "These forests are not like your northern ones—they are not even like the forests near Dûn Arian. From what I have heard, they are thick and treacherous. The threat of pestilence is always there, and strange beasts lurk in the shadows. There are far too many hiding places for comfort! At least in the desert you can see your enemies coming."

"Carmyn has drawn a path that will not require traversing deep gorges, but she did say the forest would make for slow going," said

Fima. "Yet there is always water. And I cannot imagine, with three Elves among our number, that we will ever want for food, either."

"They will not know what is safe to eat in this forest," said Estle, who was loath to admit that she was afraid of the unknown. "Things live in the water—things that will sicken a man. And while the Elves may not suffer pestilence, we of mortal race surely will. There are fevers lurking in those dark, wet places. I fear them more than any lack of water…we survived a desert crossing far worse than this one will be."

"Yet some of us almost died," said Fima, his face drawn at the memory.

"We dare not imperil those of mortal race," said Gaelen. "I will now amend my choice in favor of the desert."

She remembered the terrible fever Rogond had been suffering when she had first met him. He had nearly died, trembling and crying out in torment. She would never see him so miserable again if she could help it. The vote was now even.

"One of us must decide," said Fima. "Who shall be declared the leader of our Company?"

For a long moment, no word was spoken as everyone considered this very difficult and awkward question. Fima had been right in asking it—someone would have to take leadership. He looked hard with his bright blue eyes at each in the assembly. "Are there any volunteers?"

"I would follow anyone except Azori," muttered Galador.

"And I would follow anyone except Galador," Azori replied with a sinister smile.

"As if either of you would be suitable," said Estle. "For this task we need someone sane, sensible, and neither prideful nor reckless. That implies a feminine hand, but disqualifies Gaelen. I submit that, since it was Nelwyn's insight that has set us upon the quest, it should be Nelwyn who leads it."

She looked at the various wide-eyed expressions around her. "Just because a person keeps her thoughts to herself, and is not inclined to be forceful in her opinions, does not mean she cannot lead well. None of you even considered Nelwyn, and yet she is the obvious choice."

"That is the first truly sensible thing I have yet heard from you, Estle," said Gaelen. "And I concur."

"And what if I prefer to not have this choice made for me?" said Nelwyn. "I have not the experience or wisdom in these lands that others have. I am not suitable!"

"You seek the advice of others in making your decisions, is all," said Gaelen. "No one expects you to know everything. Remember…Rogond led us in the search for Hallagond, even though he knew little of the desert. We managed to not only find Hallagond, but we survived the desert because Rogond knew to seek help from those with greater experience."

"We survived in spite of my leadership, not because of it," said Rogond with a shake of his head. "Yet I will follow Nelwyn willingly and with no regret. Is there anyone among you who will not?"

Hallagond nodded. "That's good enough for me. I believe you have just been appointed to the post, Nelwyn. Now, you must decide which road to take. Will it be the desert, or the forest?"

"I will defer to those of greater experience in this matter, as in all others," said Nelwyn. "I cannot take a course that is known to put some at risk of pestilence. Much as I regret saying it, I must now choose the desert."

There was immediate relief on the faces of Estle, Hallagond, and Azori. The dangers of the desert were familiar, at least. Fima, however, was in dread of it and it showed—The desert had nearly killed him the last time. Yet the decision had been made, and he would not challenge it.

"At least now we can properly provision ourselves," said Azori, approaching Nelwyn as though to embrace her or to clap her on the back.

Galador stepped in front of him, and both his eyes and his smile were chilly. "I realize that sutherling customs are different, Azori, but as you have pointed out, we Elves do not like to be touched. I would appreciate it if you would follow our ways with respect to Nelwyn, at least."

Azori was amused. "My apologies. I had forgotten. But am I at least free to abuse Gaelen as I like? May I subject her to the fondling and embracing characteristic of sutherling custom? May I slobber over *her*, then?" His jesting was obvious, and Gaelen smiled. She had liked Azori ever since her first encounter with the Scourge.

"Oh, most assuredly—particularly when she has a weapon in her hand," said Galador, his expression utterly impassive. Nelwyn laughed, and the tension was broken. Galador did indeed possess a sense of humor.

The Company would depart in a few days. This would allow time to repair any questionable gear, trim the feet of the horses, and arrange for additional provisions without arousing suspicion. A few of the citizens would need to be told—Khandor and Bint Raed, for example. But most would awaken on the first day of the Company's absence to find that their respected and beloved new friends had left them. Many would mourn their departure, and few would understand it.

Fima was uneasy as he made his preparations. Rogond had spoken with him about it several times; Fima had long known that his tall friend was attuned to the anxieties of those he cared about. Fima would rather not have admitted it, but he did not know whether he was physically capable of withstanding the challenge of another long desert journey. Rogond understood well how that could be so.

"I don't blame you for worrying, Fima," he said. "I have noticed that your condition has improved of late, in fact you seem to be your old self again, but you alone must decide whether you can face the stresses that will surely find us. Rest assured that we will do everything possible on your behalf, but know also that we will be traveling with all speed. You will need to ride, and ride hard."

"I know," said Fima. "I do wish they had not selected the desert course. However bad the forest is, it surely cannot be as bad as the choking dust and thirst."

"Yet lift your heart, for we will have several experienced guides with us," said Rogond. "And they have assured me that the way we are taking is very easy compared with the way we came to the City. There should be water sources nearly all the way, and two dromadin should carry all the water we need to sustain us in between. I sense that the desert will not burden us unduly."

"You don't need to spend time in reassuring me," said Fima with a thin veneer of confidence drawn over his face. He lowered his voice to a whisper. "The fact is…I'm *old*, Rogond. I have been denying it for many years now, but I have lately come to realize it. I wish that I could stay here, where so much is still unknown to me, but…as it is not my destiny to learn everything there is in the world to know, I will go with my friends. It's just that…when I came here, I was dying. I remained alive because of this place and the things that may be found here. I hope I live long enough to return one day."

Rogond nodded his understanding. "One day, you will return here. If we both survive the upcoming trial, and I am free to do so, I will see you safely back to the Silver Fortress."

"Only if you can talk Gaelen into coming as well," said Fima, who was blustering to hide the fact that he was touched by Rogond's devotion. "And who knows? Perhaps in the meantime I will see Lady Ordath and tell her of my great discovery. Her scholars will turn green with envy!" He paused, smiling. "So it's settled, then! I must leave now, if only to arrange to see Elves turning green. I would pay dearly to see that."

Throughout this discussion, Lord Kotos the Deceiver had been in a state of near-panic. He had never even considered the possibility that Fima would decide to remain behind. If that had happened, things would have been most difficult. There was no other suitable host to bear him. He could not dwell in an inanimate object, for it might be left behind, lost, or cast aside. And he most certainly could not inhabit anyone else in the Company. Only Fima could bear him without detection. Because Kotos could not influence Fima's thinking, he was at the mercy of whatever course the dwarf would choose.

When Fima decided at last that he would accompany his friends, Kotos relaxed, but he was weary and drained. He was glad that the journey would begin soon, as he did not like being a mere passenger—he much preferred being in control. The sooner he rejoined Gorgon Elfhunter, the better.

Had Gorgon been privy to Kotos' thoughts, he would have agreed with them, but only in part. He had hunkered down in the lands north of the City. Gaelen would no doubt alert him once she was on the move. He had removed the amulet, and now faced the world as his true self, crouching in the driving rain, reveling in the feel of freedom. He would not dare disobey Lord Kotos, but it felt so good to know that his thoughts were known only to himself. He could once again decide his own actions. It was true that he had grown accustomed to some of the amenities of Dûn Arian, but he had just as quickly reverted back to his old habits of eating raw flesh and resting in hard, shadowed places. He was only now recognizing the terrible drain sharing consciousness with Kotos had been. Since he had been on his own again, he needed far less rest.

Perhaps it was not entirely Kotos that had drained him. For one such as Gorgon, it was difficult even trying to feign domestication, let alone civilization. He was most content in solitude. Yet he would welcome his dreadful partner when the time came, for only through Kotos could he achieve his heart's desire.

He sighed, gazing into the beautiful golden stone of the amulet, where now only his own dark visage glared back at him. It was regrettable, but Gorgon knew that he would need to travel in the guise of Orrion so that, if perchance someone saw him, they would not try to slay him. Gorgon was tired of Orrion, for he prided himself on his ferocity, which was difficult to convey when cursed with such beauty. There was nothing to do now but linger and lurk, and hope that the Company would soon be on the move.

Gaelen had asked her friends if El-morah might be invited to accompany them. It would make sense, as he would have plenty of company. He could go with them as far north as he desired, making his way eastward at a time of his choosing. Carmyn had indicated that the lands directly between the Chupa oasis and the brown hills were not safe to cross—there were sand-pits scattered all about, and only a very lucky traveler would circumvent all of them. Therefore, El-morah would need to make his way almost as far north as the River Dessa before going east again. Naturally, there was no objection to El-morah's joining the Company. One more desert-wise comrade would not hurt their chances at all. Gaelen proposed this notion to El-morah and he agreed to make ready at once.

Eleven horses and two dromadin stood ready in the small courtyard that led to the hidden northern entrance to the City. The Company had spent much of the afternoon quietly saying farewell to their friends. It had been especially difficult for Nelwyn to leave Bint Raed, and both Gaelen and Khandor had shed silent tears as Gaelen embraced Siva and her beautiful little foal.

"You must give him a name before you depart," said Khandor in a voice that was gruffer than usual. "One day I expect you to come back and claim him. I will care for him until you do."

"I will think on it," said Gaelen. "I will fear no mishap befalling him if you are in charge of his care. I am honored to have known you." She bowed in respect and turned to leave.

"Just take care of our young master Toran," he called after her. "He will impress you one day…I just know it."

"He has already done so," laughed Gaelen, "in ways you cannot imagine. I thank you for him. Now let's hope I survive until he matures!"

Khandor laughed along with her. Then he looked away for a moment, and she was gone.

Visili had arranged to guard the northern entrance this night, for he would see his friends safely on their way. He was accompanied by a very grim Lord Salastor, and Maji, who had been weeping for some time by the look of things. She had become fond of all in the Company.

Eros, Réalta, Gryffa, and Faladinn stood together as Toran ambled over. *Where are we going? Is there to be an adventure? I do hope we will return in time for another feeding…it has been hours and hours since the last one.*

Réalta snorted and threw his head in the air, his ears laid flat back in annoyance. *Foolish creature! Do you not know that such an early feeding means a long journey? You will get another feeding, but it will not be here. Why do you think we are all carrying so much gear? Don't waste our time with such ignorance.*

Faladinn snorted and shook his plain, brown head. *Aren't we the snooty one this morning, Réalta? I wouldn't complain about having to carry so much gear if I were you. What's the matter…is the prospect of a journey taking your good humor? Will you miss your soft bedding and clean feed? Ha! You should come to my lands. Then again, you wouldn't last long, not with as much feed as you require!* He nodded his head up and down, which was his way of laughing, as Réalta pretended to ignore him.

Eros chortled at Toran, moving to scratch the base of the younger horse's neck. *Never mind. Réalta is right; we are going on a long journey. I suppose it will be your first. But be of good cheer. After all, your burden is both light and capable. If I could not bear my Warrior, I would next choose the Singer. She will provide well for you.*

That's right, said Gryffa. *It's a fine thing to bear an Elf. They are very good at keeping us from harm, and they ride light. You need not be afraid.*

Now it was Toran's turn to raise his head. *Afraid? Me? I see you have mistaken me for another animal. Most certainly, I am not afraid. I can hardly wait to go on a long journey. Yes indeed, the prospect frightens me not at all. Where…where are we going?* He began to sidle and fret, betraying false confidence. Toran had not been away from the City for more than a day in a very long time. Yet this was not his first long journey.

I don't know the answer to that, said Eros. *I never know where the Warrior intends to go, but I do know the difference between the gear I carry for a short foray and that needed for a long haul. This will be long. Now, don't disturb me, as I am resting until we depart. I would suggest that you do the same.* He dropped his head again and rested one of his scarred hind legs.

Toran blew through wide nostrils. He would not be able to rest, not now. The whole matter was far too exciting.

Salastor stood before the Company and made his farewells. "I have small gifts for each of you," he said. I would have given more, but I know that I must not burden you, so these gifts are small and practical, to aid you in your journey. The City of Dûn Arian would see your triumphant return one day." He gave a very well made compass to Rogond, and another to Hallagond. He gave Gaelen and Nelwyn each a fine leather pouch, fitted to carry the small phials of dragon-fire at their belts. He also bestowed a container of dark, wild honey, to their delight.

Fima and Azori each received a pouch of excellent pipe-leaf, which they would enjoy, although Azori would probably have preferred marwani-weed. El-morah and Galador each were given a fine, sharp knife in a leather sheath. Estle actually did receive marwani-weed, which pleased her to no end. It always improved her outlook on things.

Rogond bowed before Lord Salastor. "I speak for the Company in expressing thanks for all you have done for us, though no thanks can be adequate. You preside over a wondrous realm, and you have earned your place among the Wise. Our good will and thanks are yours forever."

Salastor returned the gesture. "Your Company saved our City. No thanks are needed from you, for we are ever in your debt. I look forward to the day that you return to us, if the fates are willing. Now speed well on your journey, and our people will pray for your success. May the Lord of Light watch over you."

The Company bowed and bade him farewell, mounting their horses and securing the pack animals. Then they moved with quiet determination through the small, hidden portal into a night that was heavy with the promise of rain. It was a somber beginning, and each soul kept to its own thoughts as the Company put its back to one of the fairest realms of men ever to grace the shores of the World that Is.

Almost everyone's thoughts were focused on the journey ahead, except Gaelen's. *Where is Gorgon? When will I learn what has become of him?* She rode with her mind and heart wide open, trying to catch any sign of him, for in recent days she had become convinced that he was still close by. If anyone had asked her about it she would not have been able to explain, but in fact, she had caught something in the wind.

The journey back northward was quite different from the long and uncertain path the Company had taken since leaving the Greatwood so long ago. They were now certain of their course, they had a fairly accurate map, and they were returning to familiar lands. They knew that they could not tarry, for if Nelwyn's insights were correct, there was some urgency in reaching Tal-sithian. For all they knew, Wrothgar had already achieved his foul victory. Estle asked Hallagond this very question as she rode beside him. "Is it possible that we are returning to a world overwhelmed by Darkness?"

Hallagond shrugged. "I won't say that anything is impossible. Perhaps you should ask Rogond. He knows more of Elves and their foresight than I will ever know."

Rogond thought for a moment before he replied. "I do not believe Wrothgar has taken the northern lands—if he had, the Elves would know it. A shift in the balance so far toward the side of evil would have surely upset them, and I sense no such disquiet in them. We have time, but we must not delay." He set his jaw as he said these words, his grey eyes glinting in the early morning light. At the same time Fima, who rode behind, tightened his hold on Rogond's midsection just a little. This would not be an easy journey for either of them.

Eros swiveled his ears around backward in an expression of momentary annoyance. Whenever Fima became tense, he stiffened up and came down harder on Eros' loins. A tense rider is a weary rider, and a weary rider is a burden.

Eros wrinkled his black and gold muzzle and shook his head. *I do so wish he would relax. I am going to be quite vexed with him if he doesn't…I'm traveling as smoothly as I can.*

Beside him, Réalta was striding along easily with his head and tail in the air. *I am sorry for you, my friend. It's such a shame that you have such a heavy burden, while I bear a Prince of Elves. If I could aid you, I would, but alas, it would seem that the dwarf trusts only you to bear him. Such a pity.*

I could carry him if you want, said Toran. *He doesn't look like so much, and my rider is the lightest of all of them. I'll bear him, Eros, if you get tired.*

Réalta snorted, but Eros put his ears forward again. *You have a good heart, but I fear this rider needs an experienced animal to bear him. He's heavier than he looks.*

Yes, said Réalta. *That's the other reason they will not choose me to bear him. I am not as strong as Eros. No…it's my task to be the swiftest, and so I am. Swifter than all of you!* Réalta was proud of his ability to outrun any other horse in the Company.

How do you know? You have never tested yourself against me, said Toran, increasing his pace just a little as he did so.

You think you can best me? said Réalta, increasing his own pace to match Toran, and then to exceed him. *You're even more foolish than I thought.*

The two silver-grey horses were rapidly working their way to the front of the line. They drew away from Eros and the ever-practical Faladinn, passing Hallagond, Estle, and El-morah. Now only Nelwyn and Azori remained between them and wide open lands.

"Easy, Réalta, no racing today," said Galador. He turned to Gaelen. "It would seem they are urging one another into a challenge."

"No doubt they are," said Gaelen. "Yet we cannot afford such a waste of energy. A pity…I have yet to see Toran's top end of speed. I expect it's something to see."

Galador was unimpressed. "No one bests Réalta." It was true that no one ever had.

"We will see one of these days," said Gaelen, as she drew Toran back. He wanted to defy her, but knew better.

You certainly gave in easily, said Réalta. *Could it be that you know you cannot win?*

I cannot go against the wishes of the Singer, said Toran. He was a good-natured animal, and refused to be baited. Regrettably, he was distracted, and did not notice the stone over which he now stumbled, breaking his rhythm and pitching Gaelen forward onto his withers. She steadied and patted him, but Réalta lifted his nose in contempt.

I don't see the point in challenging you when you cannot even move forward without stumbling. Foolish young animal!

The truth was that although Réalta was still vigorous, the long miles had taken their toll on him. For example, he noticed that on some mornings his legs ached, and he seemed to require more rest than he used to. Toran, whose legs were all springs and steel, and who had no old battle-wounds to contend with, annoyed Réalta. He was unproven and uncouth, and yet he dared think himself worthy to challenge the swiftest horse ever to bear an Elf? Not likely!

Satisfied that his point had been taken, Réalta dropped back beside Eros at the request of Galador.

You're not fooling anyone, you know, said Eros. *Stop worrying so about being the swiftest, and settle instead for being the most wise. Oh…no, I forgot—you can't, because I am!* Eros snorted and chuckled at Réalta, who took a swipe at him with a hind leg. *Ow! I hope that made you feel better*, said Eros. *Toran is young, and he is well made and long-strided. One of these days the years will catch you, my dear friend. That is the way of things. Better to not fret over it.*

Spoken like one with no reputation to lose, said Réalta. *You have never won a race in all your life.*

No, I haven't ever cared to, said Eros. *My talents lie elsewhere.*

"Quit fussing, you two!" said Rogond.

You may believe that Toran is swifter than I am, yet I believe he is stronger than you are, said Réalta, determined to pick a fight with someone.

So what if he is? I have my Warrior. All is right with the world, said Eros, and that was that.

The Company made rapid progress, traveling mostly by night and resting by day. They encountered no one, and with so many desert-wise folk among them their confidence was high. They kept near the boundary of the hills to the west, making between twenty and thirty miles a day, depending on the heat and the footing. After so much time in the moderate, rainy climate of the Citadel they were no longer accustomed to the heat of the deep desert, so when they prepared to rest they would make their way into the foothills where there was shade aplenty. The soil was either sandy or rocky, and both were taxing to the horses. It was fortunate that there were many knowledgeable pairs of eyes and hands to aid them in staying sound.

As the Company prepared to rest on one bright late morning, Galador first spotted a lone rider coming up from behind. "Be alert, everyone. A rider follows us. I cannot determine much as yet…we should conceal ourselves until we can learn more."

Rogond nodded in agreement. "Send the hunter-scouts aloft and see what they can determine," he said. Gaelen and Nelwyn bowed and made their way quickly to the closest vantage point, flattening their bodies upon the rock, concealed in their grey cloaks.

As soon as the mounted figure drew near enough for a good look, they returned to their friends.

"The rider is a woman, though her garb makes this harder to determine, as her hair and face are covered. I believe she has followed us here from the City," said Gaelen.

"And why do you believe that?" asked Azori.

"Because both Nelwyn and I recognize the horse she is riding," said Gaelen.

"We still must be cautious," said Estle. "We don't know who might be following us."

"I know one thing," said Gaelen. "The horse belongs to a woman named Carmyn. Of course, the horse might have been stolen. There is no guarantee that Carmyn is the rider."

"I know Carmyn, and she is a friend," said Fima. "She is one of the most respected map-makers in the City."

"What would a map-maker be doing all the way out here, following us?" asked Gaelen.

"I don't know, but some are very adventurous, even going out and taking their own readings in uncharted lands. I have tried my hand at map-making, and it is no easy task."

Gaelen nodded. "Yes, I noticed that, as I look at your map of the northern lands. The Linnefionn appears much larger than I believe it is."

"Well, Arialde doesn't allow strangers to measure or assess the borders of her realm, and those who try are bewildered into the illusion that the Lake is much larger. I would love the chance to see it drawn accurately one day."

"Why should a map-maker seek to track the Company?" asked Estle, who was still suspicious of the rider.

"We'll soon find out," said El-morah. "We should remain in concealment until she arrives. If she is tracking us, she will come straight here."

"Let's set up camp so that she will not realize we are aware of her," said Azori. He began the task of picketing the horses and tossing their belongings into the shade. Then everyone except Fima, El-morah, and Azori hid among the rocks. When the rider eventually gained the encampment, she removed her head-covering to reveal dark brown hair and a broad, friendly face with intelligent blue-grey eyes. It was indeed Carmyn, the map-maker.

"Hail, Lore-master Fima," she said, looking around for the others. "Where are your companions? Surely they're not afraid of me. I mean no harm."

"Why have you come?" asked Fima. "Is there some urgent matter that drives you here?"

"Might I please dismount and rest from my travels first? I am weary. Keeping up with you has been no easy task."

"Tell me about it," Fima muttered under his breath.

"You should know that we are watching you quite closely until we are certain your intentions are not hostile," said Azori.

"Fair enough," said Carmyn, bowing to Azori, Fima, and Elmorah. She dismounted and led her weary horse, a sturdy roan gelding, to the picket line. After watering him and securing him with the others, she returned to sit beside Fima. "Where are the rest of them?" she asked.

"Look around you!" said Fima with a smile, and Carmyn was shocked to see the three Elves, Rogond, Hallagond, and Estle emerge as though from nowhere. They had been well concealed. The Company allowed their guest to eat and drink before questioning her again.

She turned to Fima. "Well, Master, you left before I could get everything ready to accompany you. I didn't even have the chance to ask permission, but I'm asking now—I want to travel with you, to see the northern lands and record them. Most of all, I don't wish to leave you…I want to learn more, if you will allow it." Fima was touched by this apparent devotion, and he patted her on the shoulder as she sat blushing with her eyes downcast.

"I promise that I will not be a burden, for I ride well and I will not complain. I will apprentice myself to you, and will swear to serve you if only you will teach me." The Company could not help but be impressed with the honesty of her admiration.

Rogond turned to Gaelen, whispering, "What does the hair on the back of your neck say now?"

"It is quite flat and unconcerned. I trust her, and so, I believe, may we all. Everything is as it seems this time. Besides…she got herself here with one horse and no pack animals. She's obviously adept at surviving. I would welcome her."

That was a good enough argument for the rest of the Company, and Fima was delighted to have acquired an apprentice. When it came to the sharing of learning and lore, he was a very giving sort of fellow, especially when he received admiration and devotion in return. Even Lord Kotos would listen on occasion, for there were matters of recorded history which a dark being such as Kotos had almost certainly never been afforded the chance to know.

The Company now numbered ten, and they discovered that Carmyn was a resourceful traveling companion. She had spent some time in the area surrounding Dûn Arian, either alone or with a single apprentice, and she knew how to be sensible in wild lands. She stayed mostly with Fima, and in fact her horse, whose name was Haji, was occasionally allowed to bear two riders. Fima enjoyed traveling with Carmyn, who did not weigh as much as Rogond, hence Haji had little difficulty carrying Fima along with her.

"I had nearly reached the point where I would have needed to turn back," said Carmyn. "I could only carry so much water, and I did not entirely trust the maps of this region, as I did not make them. I'm so glad I found you when I did."

Fima smiled. "Well, I understand your reluctance to rely on others, yet sometimes we must all do so. Rogond! It would seem that we are blessed with another independent female mind!"

"Blessed, or saddled?" said Azori as he rode past.

"That would be yours to determine," said Estle. "Come on, Carmyn…let's gather these independent female minds together and see what mischief they can arrange, shall we?"

"All that would come out of such a gathering is a whole lot of gossip," said Azori, shaking his head in good-natured disgust.

"I have never gossiped in my life," said Gaelen. "Men, on the other hand, seem to spend hours speaking of other people's affairs when they are not present. Do not deny it! I have spent enough time around all of you to know it."

"And when did you hear men gossiping, Gaelen?" asked Rogond, who honestly wanted to know.

"You worked with me on that wall! You heard it yourself," she replied. "Nothing but talk, talk, talk about who was drinking too much, who was married but looking too quickly upon another, who was taking advantage of his relations, and so on, and so on…center of enlightenment, indeed! You are all the same. You would much rather talk than work."

Azori snorted. "Oh, and I know for a fact that my sister, for one, loves to gather with her friends and discuss female issues. Mostly I think they are disparaging one another behind their backs."

"Commiserating is more like it!" said Estle with a toss of her head. "In my lands we have much to commiserate over, such as who is being beaten by whom, whose children are being threatened, who is being forced to marry someone she doesn't like, who is trapped by tradition and is powerless to change her fortunes because of fear for her life, and so on."

Estle was bitter about such things, for she knew that they were true for many women of the Ravi. The mood of the Company had now changed, and there was no more jesting. They rode along in silence until Estle spoke again. "For my part, I have avoided any such trials because my older brother convinces any suitor who would think of abusing me to think again. How fortunate I have been! Mind you… it has put a damper on my love life."

"How does he convince them?" asked El-morah, who thought he knew the answer already.

Estle sighed. "Usually he takes them out in the desert, and they never come back."

Azori shot a wicked look at El-morah, and grinned. "What else can I do? She's my sister."

The Company soon learned that merely looking at a map does not tell the story of how long a journey will take. Drawing a more-or-less straight line between water stops was all well and good, but in practice their course was slower than predicted due to long stretches of bad footing. The horses could not make time under such conditions, as deep sand is probably the worst footing there is, twisting their limbs as it shifted beneath their feet. It held them, and they were weary. It was decided that perhaps the rocky terrain of the foothills would be preferable, until one day Galador pulled up short and declared, to everyone's dismay, that Réalta had gone lame. He stood on three legs with a large, jagged stone lodged in the heel of his left forefoot. Though Galador pried it loose, the damage had been done.

"He is badly bruised," said Gaelen, shaking her head. "He will be lame for a long time…several weeks by my estimation. We must get off these rocks. Like it or not, the deep sand is our only alternative now. At least it will not aggravate this injury too much. But he must rest that foot for a few days...we can go no farther until he can walk, at least." She patted Galador's shoulder. "Never mind. I have a few tricks that might aid him."

The Company was forced to set up camp, and no one was happy about it. They were not certain of the distance to the next available water, and their own rations were running low. "If the animal has not recovered sufficiently in three days, we will need to leave him behind," said Azori. "Otherwise we risk everyone, for to delay further will mean running out of water. If anything else happens to delay us, we will need to sacrifice more than just one horse to survive. We have an extra horse for Galador to ride."

"Let's not speak of such things until we must," said Rogond. "Galador loves Réalta…they have been together for years. Let Gaelen and Nelwyn work on him. It will be Nelwyn's decision in the end, anyway."

Galador, Gaelen, and Nelwyn used all the skills they had to heal Réalta. They poulticed his foot with a paste made from the abundant minerals of the region, and they padded it so that it would not pain him as much. Gaelen made new wraps for both front legs to prevent strains and swelling, especially of the sound limb, which now bore most of Réalta's weight. He submitted to their attentions with no complaint.

During that time there was much debate as to how the Company would avoid disaster as they passed through the lands east of Fómor. The Corsairs were dangerous folk, and they generally liked to murder and rob travelers without asking any questions. Yet they were also known to be inquisitive, and they held a sort of primitive honor and loyalty with respect to one another. Hence,

Azori, who was as near to a Corsair as could be without actually being one, might delay them from violence. "We cannot be certain of that," said Azori. "Although I have been to Fómor, and in fact I have fit in quite well there, it might not be enough to turn them. It is better to avoid any encounters."

"A pity that such inconvenient people have to exist," said Fima, who was not looking forward to any confrontation.

"Ah, but they have been very convenient to Dûn Arian," said Carmyn. "They are the primary reason our City has not been discovered from the north. They guard all the lands near Fómor with jealousy, and most northerners will not take roads that pass through them, preferring instead to send their trade routes far to the east. Hence, they are diverted from the path we are taking now."

"Why have the Corsairs not taken that path, and invaded Dûn Arian themselves?" asked Nelwyn. "If I am not mistaken, they love to plunder...how can they resist?"

Carmyn smiled. "Because they *detest* going overland. They are mariners, and Dûn Arian cannot be gained from the sea. Corsairs are never far from the water, although they will patrol their own realm and guard it. The River Dessa will be especially hazardous. With luck, we will be able to cross it without incident." She laughed and shook her head. "A good thing Corsairs adore their comforts and will not undertake difficult journeys overland. Yet even if they should wish it, I doubt they would find Dûn Arian, and even if they did, there would not be enough of them to storm the walls. Yet they have prevented others from doing so, and in my mind they are therefore quite convenient."

Fima nodded. This made a great deal of sense to him.

On the third evening of their encampment, Rogond noticed Gaelen standing alone atop a nearby prominence of stone, her face turned southward, her frame tense as though she sensed an approaching threat. He moved to stand beside her, climbing the steep way with some difficulty. "What troubles you, Gaelen? You have not been disquieted since we left the Silver Fortress. Why, now, have you become wary?"

Her eyes narrowed. "Because the wind is in the south tonight," she replied. "Gorgon is coming."

"Are you certain?" asked Rogond, who knew better than to ask such a question of her. Of course she was certain.

"He has been following us for some time, yet only now have I been made certain," she said. "He has been tracking us, guarding his thoughts and remaining out of the range of my ability to scent him. It makes sense, I suppose. Now what shall I do? I have vowed never to lead him into Elven lands again, yet that is exactly where we're going."

"If Nelwyn's insight is true, then Gorgon will be the least of our concerns," said Rogond. "And not even Gorgon could gain entry into Tal-sithian, remember?"

"Small comfort for the dozens of Elves he killed near to it," Gaelen replied, her voice bitter and full of guilt.

"Gaelen, he had an army to aid him. Now he is alone, and we are still a long way from any Elven lands. It's possible that he won't even survive to reach them. The only Elf I fear for in all of this is you."

"Not without justification, for it is his great desire to kill me. Yet I sense that he will not do so until another time. I don't know why…he wants to track us, but not to encounter us. Do you take my meaning?"

Rogond nodded. "Then your reassurances will have to suffice, but I shall watch over you, just in case," he said. Then he sat beside her as she crouched down upon the stone like a cat ready to pounce, never taking her eyes from the lands to the south, where even now Gorgon Elfhunter was drawing near to the Company at last.

Réalta's injury had delayed the Company long enough to allow Gorgon to close the gap between himself and the mounted Company. Now Réalta had had one more day to heal, for the Company would break camp at sunset, ready or not. Galador stroked his legs and spoke encouraging yet desperate words. "You must put all your efforts into healing yourself. I cannot stop the Company from leaving, and I would not, for I must choose Nelwyn and my friends over you. Please do not force that choice upon me. There, now, are you not much improved?"

In truth, Réalta *was* much improved, but he had not taken more steps than absolutely necessary in the past two days. "You must at least be able to keep up with us. Otherwise I shall be forced to…to make certain that pain and thirst do not find you."

Galador had difficulty even thinking such thoughts, yet he knew that, should Réalta be too lame to stay with the Company, there would be no choice but to see that his friend was laid to rest. He remembered Gaelen and her insistence upon doing the same for Finan, knowing that he would share in her anguish. Réalta would never survive alone.

"Take heart, beloved," said Nelwyn approaching Galador from behind. She caressed his shoulders, feeling the tension in them. "Réalta has responded well to our healing efforts…do not think such black thoughts until you must."

"Rogond said that the decision would be yours to make, as leader of the Company," said Galador. "Could you leave Réalta behind?"

"I will not need to make that decision, for I overheard my beloved just now, and he knows what must be done," said Nelwyn. "I also believe that his sacrifice will not be required. Take heart!" She embraced Galador, allowing her hopeful energy to recharge his spirits. Réalta would be all right—he had to be.

12
Friends and Shadows

The first day was encouraging. Réalta moved with less pain in the sandy soil, though he was still lame, nodding his head a little with each step. Galador's spirits lifted, as it seemed that Réalta would be able to keep up with the Company so long as they did not set too fast a pace.

Azori clucked and shook his head, for the sand was taxing and risked all the animals. "The going was much easier on the rocks," he said. "Now our animals are weary, and they consume more water than they would otherwise. We have one more horse and one more person to provide for. This course is not a sensible one. I know Galador cares for Réalta, but he is only a horse, after all. There are other horses. Besides, he is lame even now, and he will only get worse. A bruised foot will not improve with treading upon it, even in sand. If he steps hard on one stone, he's finished."

"Perhaps Azori is right," said Galador. "I do not wish to imperil the Company. If you will permit me, I will lag behind with Réalta, and catch you at the next oasis. I need less water than Azori. That way, you can make better time."

"That is unwise," said El-morah. "Although you might need less water, your animals do not. If they should perish, and you are left to struggle on foot, you will not survive to aid the Company. Only Azori, Estle, and I are equipped with the knowledge to withstand the desert alone. These lands may be gentler than others you have seen, but do not underestimate them."

"How far is it to the next oasis?" said Nelwyn.

"If we could maintain the pace we set before, on stony ground, it's only about six or seven days away by my reckoning," said Azori. "Yet if we continue as we have been, it is more like a fortnight!"

"And how many days' water supply remains?" asked Rogond, who was torn between an inherent practical nature and empathy for his friend Galador.

"Seven days will present little difficulty," said Azori. "We might even make ten. But a fortnight is out of the question! We'll be completely out of water in seven or eight days, and more than two days without water will be the death of us all."

"You're exaggerating," said Gaelen. "We have not been as frugal as we might with our water supply. If we start now, we'll survive."

Azori and El-morah were not convinced. Azori, in fact, was incredulous. "You would risk our lives for the life of an animal? It would seem that the desert has not taught her lessons with sufficient severity. Fine, then, I know I'm out-voted. I suppose I'll just continue on, and hope that Gaelen is right, and that I don't end up as a pile of…of dried up dust with a few strips of cloth clinging to it."

"Ah, Azori…do you not know that Gaelen is *always* right?" said Estle with a sardonic smile. "If you didn't, you could always ask her."

"Enough of this debate!" said Nelwyn in the most commanding tone she could manage. "While we sit here we stir up ill feelings and get no closer to our goal. If you truly want me to lead you, then I will. Here is my decision—I will not ask Galador to sacrifice Réalta until there is no other choice. Nor will I ask all in the Company to imperil themselves. All save the Elves will return to the easier path, taking enough water with them to ensure that they reach the oasis. Gaelen, Galador, and I will remain together with enough water for our horses and ourselves, which will be much less than the amount required by the rest of you. Then we will rejoin you at the oasis."

"But you do not know the way," said Carmyn, who was already fond of Nelwyn.

"No, but we will keep the map," said Nelwyn. "Surely Azori, who has traveled these lands, will be able to find the oasis without it."

"Don't put such a burden on me," growled Azori. "I have traveled the lands between Fómor and the north of Mumari, but have never approached this oasis directly from the south, as we are doing. I would prefer to not separate from the map, if it's the same to you."

"Nelwyn is leader of our Company, and I believe her plan to be quite sensible," said Gaelen. "Yet now you would defy her. All along you have been stating that you knew these lands, and yet now you say you don't? Which is it?" She shook her head. "Don't worry…you will not need to separate from your map. Take Fima with you, and when you reach the oasis, he should draw forth Gorgon's mirror. I will be able to find you."

She looked over at Rogond, whose eyes were full of concern and doubt. "Have no fear. Gorgon will follow me, but he will not attempt to take me. Don't ask me how I know it, but I do."

"You know…I could solve this dilemma right now," said Azori. "One well-placed arrow is all it would take."

"Yes, one well-placed arrow," replied Galador, glowering at Azori.

"We are talking about the *horse*, aren't we?" said Hallagond.

"This is not about a horse," said Gaelen. "It's about friendship and loyalty."

"So it is," said Nelwyn. "And now, although I lead you, I do not command you. We should vote on it. Who is in favor of destroying Réalta and returning to our prior course?"

The only hand that went up was Azori's.

"Elves," he muttered. "No wonder they do not thrive in the southlands. Have it your own way, then."

"What are you grumbling about? You still have your map," said Gaelen. "And I, for one, appreciate your efforts in safeguarding the Company. I know you have been looking out for our interests."

"I look out for my own interests. If not for my sister I would never have started on this path, but would be back in the Silver City right now, lounging about in the fine weather, eating and drinking as much as I liked. Don't talk to me about best interests."

Lord Kotos, who dwelled within the person of Fima Loremaster, listened to this exchange with interest. When it ended, his thoughts were conflicted. On the one hand, certain notions concerning the vulnerability of the Company had been reinforced. It would be very simple to influence them—one would need only to appeal to their foolish, unshakable fidelity. On the other hand, he was now concerned about the wisdom of separating himself from Gorgon, who would undoubtedly follow Gaelen and not Fima.

Kotos hoped that he had put enough dread into Gorgon's heart to prevent his straying from the appointed path. Yet it was a relief that Fima would be gaining the oasis sooner rather than later, for it would not do at all for the Company to risk death. They were willing to place the entire quest in jeopardy for the sake of a horse. A *horse!*

Kotos disliked horses, for they were highly sensitive to the presence of evil—in fact, they would not suffer his presence. Toran's reaction to Orrion outside the Citadel was not just in response to Gorgon.

Wrothgar's forces had more fearsome and sinister steeds at their service. Ulcan commanders might rally their forces perched upon the broad, muscular backs of huge, stiff-bristled boars, specially bred for the purpose. These intelligent and ferocious creatures were formidable dark warriors themselves, and they loved to feast upon the flesh of the vanquished. Their independence had not been entirely bred out of them, and it sometimes asserted itself at inconvenient moments. Sometimes battles were begun before the commanders were ready, merely because their animals were impatient. Usually the Ulcas survived their mounts' impertinence, but sometimes they did not. The idea of partnership with and affection for one's riding-animal was as alien to Kotos as it was to Gorgon.

Once Fima reached the oasis, Kotos had already resolved to leave him. There were always birds at water sources, including ravens and crows. Kotos would use one of them to rejoin Gorgon as soon as could be managed. Being carried about helplessly was taxing to his nature, and he looked forward to reestablishing his rather one-sided partnership with the Elfhunter. He was not concerned for the well-being of the Elves; they would find their way to the oasis. Kotos held a great deal of faith in them, for although their foolish affection for Réalta was ill-advised, they were aware of their capabilities, and they were not stupid. Kotos was also quite pleased to have discovered the whereabouts of Gorgon's mirror. Apparently, the Wood-elf could follow it like a beacon. Perhaps one day he would put that to good use.

Gorgon first became aware of the Company's course when he caught their sign in the wind. Like Gaelen, he was acutely aware of the stories that scent could tell, questing with his wide, flat, mutilated remnant of a nose. The scent of men and Elves no longer intermingled— he caught either one or the other depending upon the wind, and it puzzled him. *So, they have separated, then? To what end?*

If Gorgon followed Lord Kotos, as he had been instructed, he would need to divert from Gaelen's path. Fima was not with her...the dwarf-scent still mingled with that of men. Yet Gorgon would not lose the trail of the Vixen. He would keep close behind her like a vile, malignant shadow. He hunkered down in the shade, considering his alternatives. *Is this a test? Has Kotos conjured up this situation so that I can prove my reliability? If so, it is both diabolical and unfair. How can he ask me to divert from the trail of the one soul in Alterra whose demise I most desire?*

Without warning, Gelmyr's much-despised image appeared in Gorgon's mind, laughing and taunting as usual. Gorgon blinked, rubbing his eyes in a vain effort to dispel it.

Well, Dark Disaster! We ARE in quite a state, said Gelmyr, his ill-natured, perfect smile gleaming forth from rotting blue lips. Then he appeared to ponder for a moment. *Yes-s-s-s...it would seem that Master Kotos has placed a choice before you. If I were you, I would remember his words to you concerning the Shadowmancer. You'd better leave the trail of Gaelen Taldin, and do as you have been told, you sniveling, indecisive lap-dog!*

Gorgon tried to contain his rage, for it would please Gelmyr to goad him into fury. "Be quiet, you hideous Elven nightmare! I decide my course as I see fit...do you not know it? I always have done."

Oh, most certainly! said Gelmyr. *Let us recount recent events, then, shall we? Which of your recent actions have been decided by Lord Kotos? Hmmm... let's consider that carefully...could it be all of them? Face the truth! You haven't held an independent thought or made an unaided decision in months. Every step you have taken has been pre-ordained by Lord Kotos the Deceiver! I would laugh at you...if you were not so utterly pathetic. Even I cannot find humor in that. Well, not much humor, anyway. Ha!*

Gorgon's face grew darker as he replied. "You had better just be quiet, or you will succeed in goading me into disobedience—then

I will not be the only one facing the Black Flame! You have no life of your own; your sole purpose seems to be in tormenting me. If I fall to Wrothgar, you will fall with me…try to deny it!"

Alas, I cannot, said Gelmyr. *For you are right. But I care not for you or for your life…I am only the voice of your fears and doubts. Did you not know it? When you die, I will die with you, but with any luck we will remain together for Eternity. You will most certainly have enough fear and doubt to sustain me in the hereafter, rest assured of that! Prove me wrong, Elfhunter. Ha!*

These words were well chosen, as Gorgon truly was afraid of what awaited him upon his death. His fate was most uncertain, and would be known to no one, save perhaps for Lord Wrothgar. Yet the Shadowmancer had never shared such insight with Gorgon, preferring instead to infuse him with the notion that he would live forever, or at least until the last of the Elves had fallen. Recent events had convinced Gorgon that this might not be so. Now he grew sullen and silent, as Gelmyr's accursed laughter filled his mind with images so terrible that he could not continue to harbor them lest he go mad. He would have to follow Lord Kotos, or take the risk of having those images become his future. Yet he could not release Gaelen again…he could *not!*

Listen to me, Elfhunter, said Gelmyr. *I will now say the only words I ever intend to say that will be of benefit to you. You found her before, and you will find her again. She cannot escape you, and you both know it.* He shook his head, his long, matted hair waving in a nonexistent breeze. *I cannot believe I am actually giving you counsel. It would seem that even I am uncertain as to whether I will be allowed to torment you after your death, and I would miss that pleasure very much indeed. Therefore, I will aid you now.* He reached up and scratched his head as if confused by his own action, dislodging a chunk of his scalp as he did so. *Ah, well…and so it goes,* he said. *Now, shall we pick up the trail of the dwarf, you and I? The Elves will not long remain separated from their friends. You know it…take heart!* As he said these words, he faded from Gorgon's vision. Gorgon would rest for a while longer, and then he would rise as darkness fell.

Several days had passed since the Company had divided. Azori and Hallagond led their mortal companions well, leaving the deep sand for firmer ground on which they could make better time. The dromadin had also been divided, and the one that traveled now with Azori's group was bellowing in disgust. Dromadin prefer deep sand to rocky footing; their large, flat feet are well suited to it. The pace was not unduly swift, but it was brisk enough to ensure that the dromadan extended its stride. It was not a real hardship, as dromadin are swifter than horses when there is need. Yet Fima was grateful to be astride Eros, and not rocking to and fro on a long-striding dromadan. It was the intention to make at least twenty miles between one sunrise and the next; hence all the animals would need to trot for much of the time.

The Elves made their way with slow and deliberate steps toward the oasis, keeping a course as near to the north as they could determine. In addition to the dromadan, their horses numbered four. Nelwyn rode as ever upon Gryffa, but Toran was now ridden by Galador. Gaelen actually rode Faladinn, the little brown pack horse, for he required less water and was more efficient than the others. Though Faladinn did not usually care to be ridden, he bore Gaelen willingly, as he had done so before.

Though he was still lame, Réalta resented Toran more than ever. He was even upset with Galador..

He should not choose to ride that upstart! Were there no other horses available? Why did He choose to ride the one other horse in the Company that was tall, silver-grey, and swift? Perhaps he will even consider Toran to be a replacement! What if I am never sound again? What if I can no longer bear him or, even worse, what if he decides that...that the young one is swifter, stronger, and more beautiful?

Réalta's tail switched from side to side in agitation as he considered that unpleasant prospect. He limped along, trying to ignore the ever-increasing pain in his foot, wishing that he had Eros' good humor to lift his spirits.

Toran sensed Réalta's discomfort and ambled over one bright morning as the Elves made ready to rest during the heat of the day. This proved to be an error in judgment, as Réalta took a substantial piece of Toran's hide with his teeth.

Get away from me, you worthless upstart! It's bad enough you take advantage of my injury, and usurp my place, but now you come to gloat about it and disturb my rest? Away with you!

Toran squealed in pain and backed away, shaking his silver forelock and blinking. He had meant no harm. Gryffa and Faladinn, who had come to know Réalta well, were taken aback by this uncharacteristic display.

Faladinn snorted. *This is worse than I thought!*

Gryffa nodded once in agreement. *Yes…that young fellow had best keep his distance. He means well, but he does not understand that Réalta is not to be trifled with right now. There will be a reckoning between them one of these days if nothing intervenes. That will be most unpleasant…though it should be interesting.*

Well, Sir High-and-Mighty Elf-mount had best concentrate on healing his accursed bruised foot, said Faladinn, *or he might find out that there are far more unpleasant things than younger, prettier rivals in this world.*

Ha! Everyone is prettier than you are, so you'd never need worry about it, said Gryffa, chortling at Faladinn.

I don't know…I've always considered myself rather handsome, said Faladinn. *But you're right; being the most beautiful is a thing I have never given much effort or thought to. I have more important matters to occupy me, fortunately.* So saying, he wandered into the shade, circled once, and sank down upon the sand. Though he did not stretch out flat on his side, for to do so risked sand in his ear or his eye, he was soon fast asleep. Resting and sleeping were very important matters to a practical animal like Faladinn.

Gaelen spent time currying Toran and Réalta before going up to the watch. She removed the wrap from Réalta's foot, pressing down upon the heel with her strong hands, noting his reaction with dismay. He was even more sensitive than yesterday. She sighed and shook her head, brushing the hair from her eyes. After wrapping the foot again, she stood up tall, shaking the sand from her hands before turning to regard Galador's sad eyes upon her. He knew the truth. Unless something miraculous happened, and soon, Galador would face the choice he had hoped never to make.

The dromadan and the horses lay together in the shade, all except Réalta, who stood off by himself. "He is even on three legs now," said Nelwyn with dismay. She sat beside Gaelen, who was brooding over what to do about Réalta, though she was supposed to be keeping the watch. "Did you hear me, Gaelen? He won't even place his one foot down."

"Yes, I heard you. And I cannot fathom why he is getting so much worse. He is not healing, not at all. The sand should have made the going easier for his bruised foot, yet he is worse. I don't understand."

"Sand is actually not soft, as most believe," said Nelwyn. "It's quite hard, in fact."

Gaelen sighed. "I know that, but because it shifts it makes for equal pressure in all parts of the foot. Hence it should not aggravate a bruise the way rocky going will."

"If only we had a larger water supply, we could afford to wait," said Nelwyn. "As it is, I fear we must move on very soon, and Réalta will not be able to keep up. You know what that will mean."

"Yes, I know," said Gaelen, who was frustrated with herself for failing to heal Réalta. "And where would you suggest we find a larger water supply?"

"Well…it rained once, in the dry desert, when we all sang together in grief for Elraen," said Nelwyn in a quiet voice. "Do you suppose, if we tried again, it might…rain upon us again?"

"That suggestion has as much merit as any I can come up with," said Gaelen, her voice bitter and disillusioned. "I'm willing to try."

The three Elves stood in a circle upon the stones, casting their voices aloft in plaintive harmony. The song they sang would have brought tears to anyone hearing it, save perhaps for Gorgon Elfhunter. If a song could make the heavens weep, this one most certainly would have. Yet it appeared that the clouds were not listening this time, for they did not appear.

"It's no use," said Galador at last. "It was a fine idea, beloved, and well worth the effort in trying. Alas, it has failed. I must face the fact that Réalta will not be able to continue with us, and I must now see to his ending. I held faith that he would heal, but it seems my hopes will be denied this time. I will do what I must do." He turned and went down to where his beautiful, trusting horse awaited him.

Gaelen was desperate. There had to be something she could do! She sat dry-eyed, her face flushed, her eyes almost feverishly bright, trying to think of any way to give Galador hope and delay him from his terrible duty.

"Gaelen, are you certain his foot is just bruised? Could it be that there is something else wrong that you have not noticed?" asked Nelwyn, who was in a similar state of brain-wracking desperation.

"Did you not see the huge stone that was wedged in his heel? We practically needed a mallet to remove it," said Gaelen.

"Yet the obvious difficulty is not always the only one," said Nelwyn. "You taught me that…remember?"

Gaelen did, indeed. Could it be that Nelwyn was right… that they had overlooked something? Réalta's foot should be healing if it was only bruised. Perhaps something was preventing it. She leaped to her feet and vaulted down to where Galador was standing with Réalta, a gleaming blade in his hand. He set the blade to the side of Réalta's jaw as Gaelen cried, "*No*, Galador! Do not take him yet! Let me look again…just one more time, I beg you!"

Galador needed no urging to stay his hand. Taking Réalta's life was one of the last deeds he wanted to perform. He didn't understand the reason for Gaelen's request, yet he saw no harm in it. She rushed to his side, startling Réalta, who tried to take a step back from her. "Hold him!" she said to Galador, who took Réalta's headcollar and stroked his neck, calming him. Gaelen unwrapped the injured foot, taking notice of the pain as she pressed down once more upon the tough, rubbery heel. "Give me your blade, Galador," she said. "I must make certain that all is as it seems. Your blade, if you please."

Galador was puzzled, but he knew better than to argue with her. She took the sharp blade and gave a quick slash to the cleft in Réalta's heel. The horse squealed and pulled back. "Hold him," she said, pressing down on either side of the slash she had made. There, in the center, she saw a whitish object…it looked like a very thick hair protruding from the soft tissue. She grasped it with her blunt, hard fingernails and jerked it free.

Réalta threw his nose in the air and grunted as she took hold of it, but after she removed it, he lowered his head and breathed a sigh of relief. It was a cactus spine, nearly two inches long, curved, and as hard as a steel needle. It had lodged in Réalta's foot not long after he had bruised it.

Small wonder he was lame! Gaelen placed Réalta's foot carefully on the sand, knowing that the dense, rubbery tissue would close up almost at once. He bore weight on it without discomfort, shaking his elegant head and nuzzling Galador, who was staring at him in amazement. Gaelen leaped to her feet, laughing as she showed Galador the cactus-spine, knowing that all would be well. Galador stared at her for a moment, and then began laughing along with her. "Does this mean that… that he will heal? I don't have to leave him behind?"

"Yes! Yes, it does! Oh, Galador, I'm so sorry. I will never stop looking beyond the obvious again! Please forgive me…if it hadn't been for Nelwyn, we would have lost him for no good cause."

"You are not at fault. That was a most unexpected coincidence," said Galador. "It is, however, refreshing to note that you can, at times, be wrong about something."

Réalta's foot improved very quickly, and though the Elves needed to travel slowly for a few days, they did not have to leave him behind. Gaelen, who believed that Aontar had sent the rain to them in the desert when they had sung together so long ago, still believed it. They had been denied this time, so that in their desperation they would find the insight needed to heal Réalta. Gaelen would give thanks for that insight for many nights to come, and so would Galador.

Azori's group reached the oasis without incident. The water source, a deep spring that flowed into a pond at the surface, was surrounded by trees, shrubs, and even a little fine, blond grass. All the plants here had very deep roots, for there was water below the ground in such places. The grass, though tough and dry, was still welcome feed for the animals, who set to work grazing on it as soon as they had drunk enough water. The Company erected their shelters and awaited the arrival of the Elves, watching and listening to the southeast. There were signs that other travelers had passed through, but not in a long time. A few broken crockery pots lay by the well, coated with a thick layer of dust.

"Where would such travelers have been going?" asked Estle. "I would describe this as the official middle of nowhere."

"They were traveling between Mumari and Fómor, most likely," said Azori. "It's the only thing that makes sense."

"How far is Mumari from here?" asked El-morah, who was anxious to return home.

"I would not go there," said Fima. "Look here, at the map. The Chupa is in a near-direct line to the east of this very oasis. And there appears to be another oasis…here. It's a long way—nearly four hundred miles by my reckoning—but the Chupa is within your grasp if you have enough water and provisions. Mumari is too far to the south."

El-morah's weary eyes took on a new light. He was going home. "I have faced greater hardships than this," he said. "By your leave, I will make my way home as soon as the Company is reunited."

"I'm not certain that is such a good idea," said Rogond, who was fond of El-morah. "So many hardships can befall a lone traveler. If you go with us to the River Dessa, and follow its course as we intend, you will intersect with the Ravani Road. Then you will no doubt find companions to accompany you, with much less chance of getting lost."

El-morah considered. "There is wisdom in your words, and I am weary. Therefore, I will rest here and reflect on them before I decide. Yet I am anxious to return and see whether my home and my family are still waiting for me. If not…if the vision I held was true, then I will cut my own throat. Perhaps I shouldn't be in such a hurry after all."

The first visitors to their encampment came not from the southeast, but from the northwest—five merchants, traveling between the lands south of Fómor and Mumari. They were weary, thirsty, and very glad to have located the oasis.

"All the wells to the north have dried up," they said in dismay as they examined Fima's map. "We made for this place with only the barest of provisions. It's a good thing we found it when we did."

The merchants actually hailed from Mumari, and were returning home after having traveled to Castalan and then to the markets at

Fómor. "There are things bought and sold in that market that you cannot imagine," they said. "It makes one wonder what other lands exist in Alterra. The Corsairs know something of them, but they may only be gained by water. And with Corsairs, it's hard to tell the truth from a tall tale."

One of the men sighed and smiled wistfully. "I know there are lands far, far from here, where many wonders abound. It makes me wish to be young again, with no obligations, so that I could discover them for myself."

"Be careful what you wish for," said El-morah. "To lose your obligations means the loss of your family. I would not want such a thing. I would give up all the wonders of the world to see my wife's face again. You say that you travel to Mumari…might I accompany you? I know I can make the Chupa from there, even alone."

"Can you pay for the privilege?" asked one of the merchants with a gleam in his eye.

"The Chupa?" said another. "I heard there was trouble there. Are you certain you want to go there?"

El-morah's face went pale and he looked away for a moment. "Yes," he said at last. "I must go there. As for payment, I have skills that will serve you well if enemies threaten, but I do not have money or precious things. What is the harm in helping a fellow traveler in need? The Powers of Heaven will reward you for your charity."

"Then you may travel to Mumari with us," said the first, eyeing the Company's healthy dromadan with interest, "so long as you bring your own sustenance with you."

That evening, El-morah sat with Rogond, Hallagond and Azori. "I do hope the Elves return before I am forced to depart," he said. "But I must return home. And I know the merchants are expecting payment."

"Are you not concerned about the rumor of trouble in the Chupa?" asked Hallagond, who was concerned about it himself.

"There is almost always trouble in the Chupa," said El-morah. "I must go there, no matter what I am likely to find. I just hope I can bid farewell to the Elves first. I owe them a great debt."

"I am concerned that you are going off into the wilderness with five men about whom we know very little," said Rogond. "What's to prevent them from doing harm to you once you are away from here?"

"Why, Rogond, you wound me to the heart!" said Azori, chuckling. "Are you implying that desert folk cannot be relied upon? Wherever would you have gained such a notion?" He drew a piece of hard, dry flatbread from his robes and began worrying it like a dog. As he chewed what small mouthful he had managed to rip free, he put their fears to rest. "Don't worry. I intend to ensure that El-morah's companions are well paid, and therefore they will guard him well."

Rogond, who sometimes managed to take worrying to the level of fine art, was still troubled. "But I ask again, what is to prevent them from abandoning El-morah—or worse—once they have their gold and are no longer under scrutiny?"

At this, El-morah's eyes darkened. "Now, my friend, you *are* being insulting," he said. "First of all, *I* would prevent them. I'll warrant they have never encountered anyone with my training. And, second, it is against their code."

"They are merchants, Rogond, not bandits," said Hallagond. "In their world it would be most dishonorable to harm anyone who has paid for their services. They would be forever cursed. You need not worry." He turned to El-morah. "Forgive my little brother. He has had a few bad experiences on his first trip through these hard lands. He is still learning."

Azori had given up trying to consume the stale flatbread, and now he laughed. "Yes, it's a good thing your little brother didn't run into our band of…ahhhh, free-spirited entrepreneurs…at the wrong time and place. His opinion might have been even more interesting."

"Indeed," said Rogond. Then he rose and bowed to El-morah. "Please forgive my ignorance. I would never suggest that desert folk are in themselves untrustworthy. I have, however, become somewhat shy of strangers wherever they dwell. I meant no insult."

El-morah smiled and nodded in acceptance of the apology. Then he rose and went to see to other business.

After he had gone, Hallagond turned to Rogond. "Was there another man here bearing a strong resemblance to Azori? I thought I heard that man offering to pay for El-morah's passage."

"Oh, be quiet," said Azori, scowling at Hallagond. "Can't a man offer aid without ruining his reputation?"

"In this case, no," said Hallagond. "Fortunately, I am a man of forbearance, and know better than to spread the tale that Azori has gone soft in his old age."

"Yes, fortunate for you *and* your future children," said Azori. "This reminds me…I need to find Estle and see if she needs anything, which is what *you* should be doing." He paused, as though considering. "You suggest that I have gone soft, but you forget that my efforts, as always, are self-serving. It never hurts to have a man like El-morah in your debt." He rose and went back to the shelter, where Estle was attempting to throw together something edible for their supper.

At the same time, many miles away, the Elves were preparing to move on. Nelwyn and Galador approached Gaelen as she stood, eyes closed, sampling the south wind. "We are ready to depart, Gaelen," said Galador, but Nelwyn held up her hand to silence him. Gaelen was very intent on the signs she was reading on the wind.

"What is it?" asked Nelwyn. "Are we being pursued? I have noticed you testing the breeze every time it blows from behind us. What sign do you read?"

Gaelen did not reply for a moment, as she was still trying to pick up the scent of her enemy, but for yet another time in many days, she could not. *Is he gone? Not likely. Has he followed Azori? More likely.* It made no sense. Always he had tracked Gaelen, and she had encouraged him in his efforts. Now, suddenly, he had followed Azori's group. To what end?

She sighed and gave up trying to detect Gorgon's scent, for there was none to detect. What was he up to? She could not worry about it now, as they were facing another long night with no food and little water. The animals were faring better, for they had not yet endured short rations, but the Elves were beginning to feel the first effects of deprivation. Yet all Gaelen needed to lift her spirits was the sight of Réalta, who was now nearly sound in the sand, though his foot would need padding on rocks for some time.

Gorgon had done what Lord Kotos had asked—he had followed his master in preference to his mortal enemy. Gelmyr's words had aided him, for it was true that the Vixen would eventually seek to reunite with her beloved, and therefore Gorgon would not lose track of her. Yet even as the Elves were beginning to feel deprived of water, so, now, was Gorgon. He had kept within distant sight of the oasis, hiding among piles of stone, for many days. He wondered what Lord Kotos would have him do.

Should he steal in by night to the tent of Fima, the dwarf, and try to reunite with Kotos? Should he bide his time and await some sign? Gorgon was reluctant to try to invade the oasis with so many eyes and ears keeping the watch. Yet now he was getting very thirsty, and when the wind blew out of the north the smell of the water tantalized him. Perhaps Orrion High-elven should go, just come striding up to the group saying, "I saw your campfires and thought I would stop in for a drink and a meal…I hope you don't mind."

The absurdity of this thought amused him, and he laughed deep in his broad, cavernous chest. His throat was so dry that he made very little sound, and that decided him. He needed water, and tonight he would take it, come what may.

As the sun made ready to set in another spectacular display of red and fuchsia, he prepared to exercise his considerable stealth to the limit of his ability. It was then that he saw a great, black bird moving on slow, deliberate wings toward the place where he was sheltering, carrying something large and apparently heavy in its talons. *It's a vulture—quite an unlovely creature*, thought Gorgon, taking note of the dull, blackish-grey feathers and hideous, naked grey head.

Lord Kotos had called it to the oasis, luring it with the promise of an entire rotting dromadan carcass for its very own. The vulture had gone into Fima's tent, approaching him as he slept, until it was close enough to lower its horrid, misshapen head down to lay a feather-light touch upon Fima's cheek. That was close enough for Lord Kotos, who flowed into the unwitting bird even as Fima's eyes snapped open and he cried out in startled horror.

"Agggh! Get away from me, you horrible, stinking nightmare! What, did you think me dead? Away with you!"

The vulture, now under the command of the most powerful dark servant of the Shadowmancer, flapped and screamed as it blundered from the tent, grabbing a full water-skin on the way. Then it took off with some difficulty, lifting its heavy body into the air and heading toward the south, turning a few lazy circles before making off in earnest.

Kotos then directed his host to search for the Elfhunter. If Gorgon had done as he had been told, he would not be far away. His reward—a fine, long drink—would undoubtedly be appreciated by now. Vultures have keen sight, and it was not long before Kotos spotted the familiar tall, massive figure preparing to go to the oasis in search of water. Soon, he thought with satisfaction, he would once again be in control of his destiny.

The vulture approached Gorgon in a slow, descending spiral, taking advantage of the heated air currents rising from the sun-baked sand. At last it alighted, perching awkwardly upon a stone, having dropped the water-skin at Gorgon's feet. It made no sound, but turned its tiny, ugly eyes toward the Elfhunter. They gleamed with bright, baleful intelligence.

Gorgon picked up the water-skin, knowing it to be a gift from Lord Kotos, and drank with thankful abandon. Though he was indeed a hardy creature and needed very little water to sustain him, Gorgon had been nearing his limit with respect to thirst.

Hear me, Elfhunter, came a voice inside Gorgon's head, startling him. Kotos had not been able to address him at a distance before, except from within the amulet or from a mirror wherein Gorgon could actually behold Kotos' face. Gorgon wondered what the face of Lord Kotos actually looked like, as it almost certainly did not resemble the wise old man he had come to expect. The thought both tantalized him and frightened him a little.

"It's about time you showed up. What have you to say?" he growled back at the vulture, which shook its head and blinked.

Where is my amulet? Show it to me.

Gorgon reached inside his dark breastplate and drew forth the golden thing, then held it aloft for Kotos to view. *Drop it, Elfhunter, and back away. I would rejoin my friend and reward his fidelity. Drop the amulet, and receive a great gift.*

The heavy amulet raised a small puff of dust as it landed in the sand. After Gorgon had backed away from it, the vulture approached, took it in its blunted grey beak, and promptly dropped it again. Kotos had left the dull-witted bird to wonder why it had placed itself so close to an enemy, holding onto a thing that could not be eaten. It gave a horrid, croaking call of alarm and blundered away from Gorgon—too late. The Elfhunter's enormous right hand closed on its neck as Gorgon dropped to one knee, pinning the body of the struggling bird to the ground. This was no mean feat, as the vulture was fighting for its life and its wingspan was as broad as Gorgon was tall. It flapped and beat at its captor without effect.

Gorgon loosened his grip on the vulture's neck in an attempt to gain a better hold. The desperate creature then opened its beak and a stream of the foulest, most horrid material issued forth from it, just missing Gorgon, who was wise to the ways of carrion-birds.

"Your attempts to disgust me into releasing you are to no avail. I must eat, and you have let yourself be caught. Now be still." He squeezed the vulture's neck hard enough to break it, yet even in death it still flapped and struggled for several seconds. Finally, it stopped moving.

Gorgon laid it down and approached the amulet, but as he bent to collect it he hesitated. He was not certain he wanted to look into the eyes of the Deceiver. Despite the knowledge that his heart's desire would not be achieved without aid, Gorgon had reveled in his independence over these past weeks. He was not certain that he wanted to share consciousness with Kotos again so soon.

Why do you hesitate, Elfhunter? Surely, you are not afraid? I have not harmed you despite uncounted opportunities, have I? Remember our bargain, proud Son of Evil. Lift the amulet now, and allow me to reward you beyond your wildest imagining. I can do many things, Gorgon, and I will not invade your consciousness without your leave. What is your will?

Gorgon knew what a promise from Kotos was worth. Still, his curiosity would once again rule him, as he now wanted to know what reward Kotos could give him that was beyond imagining. Kotos smiled as the thick, dark fingers grasped the amulet, for he had known it would be so. *Look into the stone, Elfhunter, and share a pleasant memory. I was present at the Second Battle that led to the downfall of*

Tal-elathas and the virtual extinction of the Èolar. Do you not wish that you had seen it for yourself?

"Oh....what I would not give to have stood in the forefront of that Dark Army," said Gorgon, his eyes misting over at the thought of it.

Then this you shall do, at least in your memory. Clear your mind and receive your gift. Kotos then shared the most exquisitely detailed memory of the Fall of Tal-elathas, for he had led the charge against the High King. Gorgon saw Dardis murdered by Kotos' hand, his neck snapped, an expression of horrified betrayal in his beautiful grey eyes. He watched as the Elves fell before the Bödvari, watched them writhe and scream as they were set upon, seeing the abject terror behind their wide eyes as they were engulfed in avenging flame.

Ri-Aldamar, withered in a storm of dragon-fire, fell at last with his bright sword still clutched in his hand. Gorgon could almost smell the stench of the worm's sulfurous breath. By the time the Great Realm fell at last, Gorgon was in a state of stunned ecstasy. He lay upon the sand with his eyes open, gazing toward the stars, but he did not see them. Kotos did not disturb him until sunrise, for he did not wish to interfere with Gorgon's reliving every deliciously horrific moment, running through the memories over and over. For the moment, the partnership was secure.

The Elves finally appeared at daybreak as a ragged dark line on the horizon, to the relief of everyone. Eros caught Réalta's scent on the east wind, untied himself from the picket line, and trotted out to meet his companion with his tail in the air. Rogond shook his head, swung onto Derrin's broad, red back, and cantered out to his friends, two full water-skins slung over his strong shoulders. When he arrived he first embraced Gaelen before bowing to Nelwyn and Galador. "I see that you have gotten here just in time," he said. "You are all looking careworn, my friends. Yet there is water, food, and rest aplenty at the oasis." He looked up at Gaelen, who favored him with a warm, if dusty, smile.

"Yes, Thaylon. Thank you for lighting a fire each day; the smoke made you easy to find. We have arrived in time...*all* of us!" Gaelen looked over at Réalta, who was renewing his friendship with Eros, each scratching the base of the other's neck with his teeth. She had kept the cactus-spine as a reminder that things are not always as they first appear, and to always look beyond the obvious in the future.

The dromadan bellowed at the distant oasis, for although it could not smell the water, it knew that water would be found there. "Let him go, Galador, he has earned it," said Gaelen. Galador released the dromadan, who set off immediately in a direct line to the oasis.

The Elves may have looked careworn, but it was the change in Fima that drew the most attention upon that morning. He appeared to have aged many years overnight, and though his hair and beard would not turn entirely snow white again for quite some time, his face had fallen once more into the semblance of an old dwarf. The wrinkles and lines had reappeared, as had the stiffness of movement and slump of his shoulders. Fima's eyes were bright and happy as he greeted his friends, yet if one cared to look deep enough, the pain and weariness had returned.

The Elves looked at one another in concern; it seemed that the desert truly did not agree with Fima. They did not yet realize that this change had come on him overnight. When Kotos left Fima, so did the vigor he had imparted.

Rogond spoke to his friend in a quiet voice. "Did you have a difficult night, Lore-master?"

Fima shrugged. "I did not think so at the time, yet this morning I seem to be a bit stiff. Perhaps I was engaged in energetic dreams, but do not recall them." He smiled at Rogond and winked.

"Well, if that is the explanation, I hope you eventually recall them," said Rogond. "On second thought…I might not want to know, if I were you."

Fima chuckled. "Ah, Rogond, those are the words of a man whose dreams are simple ones. Yours are embodied in the person of one Wood-elf. Go now and tend to her. I'm just fine, thank you. I will be even better after breakfast."

The Elves settled in for a few days of recovery, replenishing their bodies and their spirits. Réalta's foot was still in need of padding, but since the cactus-spine had been withdrawn he was not noticeably lame so long as he kept off the rocks. Now that water was available, Gaelen and Galador could wrap the foot each day with a poultice to draw the soreness from it.

Toran's tendency to mischief reasserted itself with rest, and soon he was wandering here and there getting into things. It seemed he had learned to untie himself by observing Eros. It was not unlikely that he would be found standing in someone's tent during the heat of the day, a fact that would not have been so upsetting had he been of a tidy nature. Since he was not, he would be driven forth, often chased by various objects that had been thrown at him. At such times, Gaelen was thankful that she did not understand more of the sutherling speech.

The merchants prepared to depart, taking El-morah with them, even as the Company made ready to continue northward. Hallagond, Estle, and Azori were particularly saddened at his going, and they hoped he was not returning to the horrible destruction and death he had remembered. "What will you do, my friend, if your memories are true?" asked Azori.

"If my home and family have been destroyed, I will first set myself to the task of seeking those responsible," said El-morah in a voice completely devoid of passion. "And then I will rejoin Mohani in the hereafter, either by an enemy hand, or by my own."

He looked over at Azori and smiled a grim and humorless smile. "I will do what I must—no more and no less. Gaelen is right…I must return and be certain. I honestly do not know what I will find, but I hold hope in my heart. Don't be concerned, but look to your own perils…they are far greater than the ones looming before me." He said his farewells, mounted his horse, and rode out with the slow-moving caravan. Each soul in the Company was saddened, for El-morah was a good man and he would be missed.

After he had gone, Gaelen finished securing her belongings and then went to ask Fima if she could have some parchment, a quill, and some ink to write with. She sat beside the small fire and recorded every coincidence, every strange happening, and every misgiving she had ever held concerning Orrion. It turned out to be a very long list. Gaelen enjoyed drawing pictures, and for a moment she considered rendering an unflattering caricature of Orrion at the bottom of the piece of parchment. In the end, she decided otherwise, for she would need to recall his image, and she had no desire to do that. In fact, it would not have displeased Gaelen if she never looked upon Orrion again.

13
The Company is Waylaid

"So, why are we traveling in a line directly north? Why do we not follow El-morah across to the Chupa, and then go back through the Sandstone to Dûn Bennas? It seems so much safer," said Carmyn.

"You do not know our history," said Rogond. "We dare not go anywhere near the Sandstone settlement. We have been marked for death by the Ballali, and they will not have forgotten so soon. Hallagond has assured me that they will have placed a heavy price on all our heads by now."

"Ballali? Aren't they a sort of faith-cult? I thought they were basically peaceful," said Carmyn.

Gaelen raised one eyebrow, and then her eyes went hard. "That has not been our experience with them. Because of their desire to control others, one of our Company was lost. If I never lay eyes on one of them again, it will be too soon."

"You will see worse things, I fear," said Azori. "There are settlements all up and down the river that feeds into the sea at Fómor. And the only wells and oases near to it are controlled by Fómorian Corsairs. We will be passing through their lands no matter what."

"Tell us, Azori…what might we expect in those lands?" asked Nelwyn, who had heard nothing good about Corsairs.

Azori then proceeded to inform the Company, telling what he would of these intriguing but dangerous folk. Corsairs were the most skilled of mariners, save perhaps for the lost northmen from whom they were descended. Originally a group of outcasts from Tuathas, they were now a blend of many cultures and races. They had one characteristic in common: greed. They lived for riches and worldly pleasures, and had a low opinion of anyone who worked for a living. In fact, such people existed that they might give up their hard-earned wealth for the enjoyment of the Corsairs, who would justify this attitude by saying that it was the right of the strong to take what they could from the weak.

They preferred to plunder coastal towns and waylay any ships they encountered. Depending on their mood at the time, they might leave the inhabitants alive and merely take their possessions, or they might take all things of value and then sink the ship with everyone aboard. They were both hated and feared by nearly everyone, yet they had made great explorations of the Alterran realms, and their courage at sea was legendary. They were said to possess the most detailed and accurate maps in existence. There was some speculation that they had discovered another land on the other side of the Great Ocean, yet there was no proof that the few who claimed to have returned from it had actually done so. Because the consumption of liquor and other intoxicating substances figured highly on their list of worldly pleasures, one could never be certain of the truth of any words issuing from a Corsair. They loved to tell tall tales.

"We must avoid be taken by them," said Azori. "If they are in a generous mood they will merely bind us and take us back to Fómor to be sold as slaves. I don't wish to think of what might befall the women-folk."

Nelwyn shivered. "I thought you were known to them…that they called you friend! Perhaps it would have been better to risk the Ballali. These folk sound as though they will be the death of us."

"Wonderful news," muttered Galador. "Another culture full of upstanding Defenders of Light will soon be made known to my curious mind. I can hardly wait."

"My brother exaggerates," said Estle, scowling at Azori. "All Corsairs are not killers; there are quite a few traders among them. We might obtain safe passage with only the loss of some valuables."

"What valuables?" asked Gaelen with a sardonic half-smile. "You mean valuables such as our horses or our weapons? We carry very little of value that we do not need."

"Stop panicking and listen," said Azori. "It is true that I have been to Fómor, and I have come out again alive. There are folk there who know of me. Yet it is unlikely that I will encounter them out here…better we should attempt to make the crossing unnoticed. If we are caught, I may be able to bargain for our release, but our goal will be to pass unseen. Once we are clear of the lands near the well or the river, we will be unopposed until we cross the Dessa. We might still find enemies there. Don't worry…in these times, men are not so numerous."

"I am most certainly in favor of passing unseen," said Gaelen. "I am just now wondering how we will do so, mounted and leading two dromadin. We will need to stop for water like everyone else."

"Well, that will be *your* job," said Azori with a wicked grin. "You're the hunter-scout, aren't you?"

"Oh, am I?" asked Gaelen with an innocent expression.

"At any rate, should we encounter a formidable group, you all had better let me do the talking," said Azori.

"Who has any intention of talking?" asked Gaelen. "I would prefer to demonstrate my skill at archery first, and then see if anyone feels like talking."

"We must not do that," said Hallagond. "The Corsairs have a code of conduct…a rather odd, twisted code to be sure, but they will not break it. They will not kill us until they learn of our intentions, and we must not do so, either. If we do, they will hunt us down and see to our deaths. Make certain your bows are idle until we know their intentions, won't you?" He looked over at Nelwyn. "If we're lucky, we will not encounter anyone beyond our ability."

Despite Hallagond's optimism, everyone in the Company slept with one eye open, even though they were still many days away from lands where they would need to worry about an encounter.

Now that Gorgon and Kotos had been reunited, there was no need to track the Company closely. Gorgon had discovered that Kotos was very adept at luring birds, preferably ravens, to pick up the shiny golden amulet. The moment they did, they were overtaken. Then Kotos could command them to fly forth, surveying the area and keeping watch over the Company while Gorgon trailed behind.

Once Gorgon gained the oasis he put the amulet on, the raven perching on his shoulder as he strode up to the water source unopposed. There was no one remaining to greet them, yet Kotos still flew in wide circles to make certain no travelers approached before he allowed Gorgon to resume his true appearance.

Rest for a while, and refresh yourself. It will be a long, dry march to the next oasis. Fill your vessels as full as you can manage. I will stay with the bird unless you will otherwise, or need is on us. Rest now, my impressive friend. Rest and remember.

Gorgon was only too happy to oblige. Food had been left behind, in the tradition of some desert folk, in case the next wanderers came to the oasis in dire need of it. It would then be their task to glean more to leave for those coming after. It was believed that if one took advantage of the hospitality of the desert, and did not return it, the desert would take her vengeance.

Gorgon did not fear any such consequences—he took all the food in the clay vessels that had been left. He made a small fire, for he had recently learned to relish hot meals on chilly nights. There was enough food to keep him for some time, as he required little sustenance.

Afterward, he lay on his back, listening to the wind stirring the leathery leaves of the fragrant spice-trees, and gazed at the incredible star-field that spread across the wide sky like a glittering, magical cloak. He could not remember such contentment since the death of Thorndil. This was, in fact, a different sort of feeling altogether. It sprang from being truly comfortable, secure in the knowledge that one's needs are being looked after. Gorgon had rarely felt it with such depth.

"Thank you for the gift, my lord," he muttered in a languid voice, referring to the memory of the fall of Tal-elathas that had been planted in his eager brain. Now he could re-live those horrific, delightful events whenever he wished to.

The raven fluffed its feathers and bowed. *You are more than welcome.*

After a while, Gorgon would set out again, but he was in no real hurry. He would not lose the Company, for their course was known to him. They, as with all travelers, were constrained to plot the most direct way between water-sources, and Kotos, looking through Fima's eyes, had become very familiar with the map. Gorgon could afford to lag behind a little.

"Will you tell me another tale?" he asked the raven, who had by now become quite tame whether Kotos was with it or not. It was intelligent enough to know a good provider when it saw one. It hopped down from the rock on which it had perched, stepping with calm dignity until it looked Gorgon directly in the eye. Then Lord Kotos flowed forth from it into his willing apprentice, that he might favor Gorgon with another wonderful story of hatred, betrayal, and death.

It was a pity that the northern wells had dried up, for if they had not, the Company might have avoided the river. As it was, they were forced to seek it as a source of water, and so they did, keeping ever alert for troublesome Fómorians. They encountered no one of consequence, and Azori almost seemed disappointed.

"Don't worry, my brother," said Estle. "Your descriptions of the Corsairs are very accurate. No one in the Company doubts them."

"That's for sure!" said Fima. "I, for one, am happy to put as much sand between myself and Fómor as possible."

Everyone breathed a sigh of relief as they headed northward from the riverbank. Carmyn had been taking as many readings as she could manage, as she was attempting to map the source of the river, which she learned was called the Salla-hin (mighty rain), though it was little more than a sluggish, narrow track of muddy water. "The name seems to be made from both sutherling and northern tongues. And not just northern, but Elven, if I'm not mistaken."

"The Tuathar used Elven-speech as the basis for their own," said Rogond. "Over the ages much has changed. Yet I studied the language of Tuathas in Mountain-home, and it was so similar to the speech of the Elàni that I had little difficulty."

"But, you are of the northern race yourself," said Carmyn. "Were you not taught the speech of your own folk?"

Rogond smiled and told Carmyn some of his history. Now that he knew more of it, the telling did not pain him as much. "I wish that I had been able to see Tuathas before it fell," he said.

Carmyn sighed. "Oh, my...wouldn't that have been something?"

"I can tell you much of what I saw in the northern realm, for I was there as emissary to Eádros," said Galador. "I enjoyed the hospitality of the Tuathar on several occasions."

Naturally, everyone was interested, even Rogond, despite the fact that he had heard these tales before. There was not a sound to be heard as Galador described the wonders he had seen in Tallasiar, the great western capital city.

"Dûn Arian was obviously designed in like fashion, yet the city of Tallasiar was larger and grander. Dûn Arian would have fit many times into Tallasiar. Yet they were much alike in design and in character. Tallasiar was one of the greatest centers of learning ever seen. The efforts of hundreds of generations of men, together with scholars of all enlightened peoples, went into her vast storehouses. It is said that only a small portion was saved in the end."

"First Eádros, then Tuathas," said Fima with a sigh. "And let us not forget the Great Library of Tal-elathas. The Elves barely escaped with their lives, and the library was razed to the ground, so I heard."

"Very few of them escaped with their lives," said Galador.

"Wrothgar is no friend of enlightenment," said Rogond. "He would have the Lamp of Knowledge extinguished, for with knowledge comes enlightenment. He cannot cover the world in Darkness while that Lamp burns."

"Yet not all knowledge brings enlightenment," Fima replied. "Alas that Lord Kotos the Asarla did not realize it."

"Lore-master Fima, the fall of Lord Kotos into Darkness is one of the greatest and most troubling of mysteries," said Carmyn. "What do you know of it? There has never been an explanation given that I could understand."

Fima settled himself into his woolen blanket, for it was a chilly night and the fire was dying down. He looked around the circle of friends to see whether there was any interest in hearing the tale, and the solemn expressions he beheld convinced him. "Would you have me tell of one of the most profound tragedies ever to befall the Powers of Light?" he asked. "For Kotos the Powerful was perhaps the greatest of all the Light-Bearers, save perhaps for Lord Shandor, his friend. If you would hear of it, I will tell what I know."

In answer, Gaelen brought an armload of dry cactus-wood and dropped it on the dying fire, which flared up in a dramatic display of sparks and flaming embers. Everyone leaned in closer as Fima stood, throwing off his blanket and assuming his position as story-teller.

"Kotos was once a powerful force in the fight against Evil. It was said that he could turn even the most benighted souls back to the Light if given the chance. He could heal afflictions of the mind, which were among the most difficult, but even more important was his power to influence the spirit. He was then named "Persuader." Yet he fell beneath the spell of Lord Wrothgar, thinking that he could escape the fate of all those who tried to learn the true nature of Evil.

"He wanted to know all things—his curiosity was greatest among all the Asari. He had decided that the way to defeat his Enemy was to know him, and so he descended into Wrothgar's very lair that he might learn what he needed to know. But Wrothgar caught him, and tempted him, promising that anything Kotos wished to learn would be revealed.

"The choice Kotos made was his undoing, for he was proud and thought he could prevail. It is said that the knowledge of the inner workings of Darkness actually drove him mad, but we will never know."

"Why not?" asked Carmyn. "Some believe that he still walks abroad in Alterra, and others claim that he is dead and gone. Do you know what became of him?"

"No one really knows the truth," said Fima. "But I do not believe Kotos is gone. The opinion of the remaining Èolar in Mountain-home is that his spirit still dwells in the Fell-ruin. It is also thought that he has been forever deprived of physical form, but can travel only if his spirit finds a willing host to convey him."

"Who would ever convey such a spirit willingly?" asked Nelwyn. "Perhaps he can overtake a person whether they are willing or not. What a terrifying thought!"

"Ah, but even Lord Wrothgar could not force Kotos into Darkness," said Fima, "he had to be persuaded. It is ironic that his great talent, the ability to perceive and see into the souls of others, should fail him in the end."

"It did not fail him," said Rogond. "I believe that Kotos knew he was playing with deadly fire, but his pride and all-consuming curiosity would not allow him to choose wisely. He walked down that path right into the snare, and he did it with both eyes open."

Fima then told of the consequences of Kotos' terrible choice—how he became the Beguiler and finally the Deceiver—and of the bringing of the deepest sorrows in Alterra at his hands. By the time the tale had finished, all in the Company hated and feared Kotos.

"If I could express one regret in all of this, it would be that such a bright Light turned to such hateful purpose, squandering the talents and gifts given, turning them and perverting them into evil deeds. I have tried to feel pity for Kotos, but I cannot," said Fima. "We can lay blame for the greatest betrayal in the history of our world at his feet. Thank the stars he is now relatively powerless, skulking in the Fell-ruin, if that was indeed his fate."

If it was, is the question, thought Gaelen, and she wasn't the only one.

Gaelen took the watch for much of the night, sitting like a solitary cat upon the stones, unmoving and silent. When dawn broke, she took the parchments on which she had recorded all her concerns regarding Orrion, that list of strange events and disturbing coincidences, and began to add to them. But now she looked at the list with different eyes, documenting all similarities between Orrion's behavior and the tale she had just heard of Lord Kotos. By the time she had finished, it was an extensive list. Could it be that Kotos had actually walked among them in the person of Orrion? Was Orrion a willing host? What Elf would ever suffer such an evil presence? Perhaps Orrion isn't really an Elf at all.

And what is the connection with Gorgon, if any? she wondered. There was still so much that remained unclear.

As soon as she could, Gaelen intended to ask more questions of Fima, for she was now on a quest of her own. She would not stop until the pieces of the puzzle that was Orrion fell into place, regardless of how ugly the finished image turned out to be. Had she known it, there were others in the Company whose thoughts had turned in the same direction. Fima, Rogond, Galador, and Azori each had their reasons for wondering now about the increasingly suspicious death of Aryiah, the presence of Orrion, and the tale of Lord Kotos. Yet the puzzle would not be completed for any of them as yet.

The two brothers were just about on their last legs when they finally approached the oasis. Neither they nor their beasts had taken any water since the night before last, because they had expected to find water in the wells to the north, but found only a thick, pasty sludge that was well on its way to becoming hardened clay. In desperation they had made their way here, praying that the oasis had not also dried up, and were rewarded with the sight of spice-trees and sweet water. Thank the Lord of Light they had found it!

They did not realize that watchful eyes were upon them as they filled their vessels, rinsed their tired feet, and drank their fill. They wondered who had left the remains of the cook-fire smoldering nearby—there was no other sign of occupants in the oasis other than a huge, black raven perched upon the dead stump of one of the spice-trees. The raven gave one harsh and ominous croak before flying off. The brothers touched their foreheads in supplication, as this was a bad omen. Yet the water was good and had not been poisoned. Why, then, did they feel such foreboding?

They had revived the cook-fire and settled down beside it as darkness fell, turning their beasts loose to wander and pick at the scattered blond grass, when they realized they were not alone. A tall, golden figure with odd, leaf-shaped ears and beautiful golden hair strode up to them in the firelight, looking like a vision from an ancient legend. The two brothers sat frozen as the tall figure bowed and spoke to them in a voice as deep as the ocean and as soft as velvet. He told them not to fear—that they were in no danger. He was only a traveler like themselves, and his name was Orrion, the Golden-haired.

They looked deep into the eyes of the stranger, lulled into a peaceful and compliant state of mind, asking that he join them by the fire. Orrion did so, sharing what little food remained, though there was none in the oasis to replenish it. At last he turned to them and smiled. The last sight they beheld was of the raven as it circled over Orrion's head, cawing and croaking what might have been a parody of laughter. Then there was a flash that might have been a blade, followed by fading sight and endless dark.

Gorgon smiled to himself as he went about his next task. He was leaving the oasis that very night, and now he would have fresh meat to sustain him. He gave a low, malicious chuckle as he stripped most of the good flesh from the bones of the two ill-fated brothers. The next travelers to approach the oasis would find that some food had been left behind for them after all, but Gorgon did not expect it would be to their liking. The raven helped itself to the leavings before flying out with the Elfhunter into the starlit desert night.

Just when Azori had assured everyone that they would not encounter anyone of consequence, he found himself in the very unpleasant position of having to take back his words. The Company had gone east as well as north from the last oasis, thinking they had left all threat of Fómor behind. But as they approached the River Dessa, they observed what appeared to be a very large encampment stretching up and down the banks, with other camps visible in the distance in both directions. The horses smelled the river, and they could hear other horses calling from the encampment.

Although Eros and Réalta knew better than to respond, Toran did not, and he gave out one loud whinny before Gaelen could stop him. She cuffed him sharply on the neck and scolded him, but it was too late—they had been heard, and therefore had most likely also been seen. There was little doubt of it when a party of armed riders launched toward them.

Nelwyn turned to Azori for guidance. "All right, what do we do now? Are they Corsairs?"

"Of *course* they're Corsairs," said Estle, her face pale. "But why are there so many along the Dessa, so far from the sea? A few scattered encampments makes sense, but why such a vast number?"

"Indeed," said Galador. "This looks like an army preparing for a campaign. See the flags and the rows of spears?"

Hallagond was watching the approaching riders, who bore flags of blue, red, and black, emblazoned with a red rose over two crossed, curved swords. "Whose device is that? I have never seen such a flag, Azori…Azori?"

But Azori did not answer. He had, in fact, gone quite pale. "You had better tell us what you know in the next half-minute!" said Hallagond. "Do we draw our weapons, or try to run? Tell us what we should do!"

"Do not try to run," said Azori. "If I am any judge, they already have us surrounded. Their scouts have probably been watching us for a while now." He slammed his right fist into thc palm of his left hand. "A curse upon my head for not expecting this! Now we're in for it. Just try not to threaten them, and maybe we can talk our way out."

"Talk our way out of *what?*" asked Gaelen, who preferred to meet a threat with a bigger threat. She had drawn her bow and now urged Toran forward, cantering toward the approaching Corsairs. She halted, loosed her bow, and sent an arrow into the sand at the feet of the foremost rider. Then she re-drew as they halted, having realized that she could have any of them, or their mounts, in the blink of an eye.

Nelwyn needed no urging either, and she rode up beside her cousin.

"Come no closer, I warn you!" said Gaelen in a voice that left little doubt as to her sincerity. "Until we know your intentions, you may not approach! Send one rider, and one rider only, that we may parley. This rider will not be harmed. Do otherwise, and see how I deal with those who would approach under threat of arms."

The Corsairs appeared to converse among themselves for a moment, and then one rode forward, leaving the remainder standing where they were. He rode past Gaelen and Nelwyn, who kept their bows ready, each nodding to the other as he passed. Nelwyn turned and escorted him, leaving Gaelen to hold the others at bay.

The emissary was a tall, brown-eyed man with dark hair and a very nasty scar across one brown, leathery cheek. He smiled, showing stained but otherwise perfect teeth as he drew near the Company, every one of whom had drawn some sort of weapon.

"Hail, wayfarers," he said. "Do not be dismayed, for we mean you no harm. However, you are hopelessly outnumbered and you stand no chance of escaping. Why not come down to the river and refresh yourselves? We will feed you, hear your tale, and then decide your fate. We make ready for war in this place, and have little need to harm or waylay strangers at present. Your only other choice is death." He looked around at the members of the Company. "Who leads you?"

Nelwyn looked over at Azori, who took the hint. "I do," he said. "My name is…Ali. I am a friend of Fómor and temporary leader of this Company. We are on our way to the north on urgent business, and we carry nothing of value."

The emissary laughed. "Of course you don't!" he said. "Strange that no one ever does. Well, don't worry—you will carry even less of it when we have finished with you, O friend of Fómor. Will you now come quietly? You cannot flee, as you do not have enough water to return to the last oasis, and must therefore avail yourselves of the river. Come with us and be welcomed."

"An interesting definition of welcome," said Galador. "Unless you do not actually intend to rob us of what few possessions we carry."

"Who said anything about robbing you?" asked the emissary with an innocent expression that was about as genuine as the good wishes of a serpent. "You will be fed and entertained, and made welcome among our folk. Yet we will exact payment for services rendered, as is our right. Now I ask again…will you be our guests, or will you force us to strip all possessions from your poor, dead selves here and now? Choose quickly, as my friends are growing impatient. If you agree, you have only to follow us."

He turned then and galloped back to rejoin his group. Estle was the first to speak. "Curse Gaelen for her thoughtlessness. Now she has forced a confrontation."

Azori shook his head. "No, do not curse her, not this time. She did exactly the right thing for once. She has shown them that we will not go down easily, and Corsairs are not known for their willingness to lay down their lives without benefit. They respect her already, and she has forced them to at least talk to us first."

"Still, she needs to learn to consult with us before taking action that puts us all in jeopardy," said Estle under her breath. "I choose to curse her anyway. She got lucky this time. Besides, it was her failure to control her stupid horse that got us into this in the first place."

"What, then, should we do? I suppose we must follow them," said Rogond.

"It seems we have no alternative," said Fima, with an uncomfortable shrug of his shoulders.

"We must survive to carry the message to Tal-sithian. That is all that matters," said Nelwyn. "Perhaps if the Corsairs learn of our errand, they will realize that it is in the best interests of all free folk to allow us to go on our way. The Corsairs surely are no friends of Wrothgar."

"Don't be so sure," said Galador, who could remember a time when Fómor had set itself against the peaceful people of Dûn Bennas. "The Corsairs are the friends of none save themselves, but they will ally with anyone of power if promised great reward. I do not believe they could resist temptation by the Shadowmancer."

"And so they must *not* learn of our errand, or of Dûn Arian," said Fima. "We must think of another reason for our journey, and quickly! And we must all agree to it."

"Well, you're the story-teller...think of something!" said Azori, who knew that the Corsairs were clever enough to see through all but the most convincing deception.

By the time the Company had gained the shores of the Dessa, Fima had indeed come up with a story, but the Company would not hear it until they were all brought before the Fómorian Commander.

They were taken into the encampment, enduring the curious stares and derisive laughter of the inhabitants. The Fómorians were noisy folk. They seemed to do everything with gusto, laughing and speaking in loud voices, swaggering about and gesturing with both hands to illustrate every point. The Elves, who almost never spoke with such animation or called attention to themselves in such a brazen manner, were put off at once. Every hair on Gaelen's neck was standing straight up as they were escorted into a huge, blue silken tent. Blue dyes are rare, and one who could afford such extravagance was undoubtedly a person of great prominence and wealth. There were red roses growing in clay pots set all about, spreading their delightful fragrance. Everywhere there was evidence of the opulence and excesses of the flesh beloved in Fómorian culture. It looked and smelled like a brothel.

"Please sit down and allow us to refresh you," said their escorts, grinning and pointing at the scattered cushions lining both sides of a long table set in the center of the cavernous tent. "The Queen will soon be joining you."

Azori and Hallagond looked at one another. "Did he say "Queen?" whispered Rogond, and Gaelen suppressed a snort, receiving an elbow in the ribs from Estle. They had been relieved of their weapons, with the very unreliable promise that they would be returned later. Everyone else in the command tent carried several blades, and therefore it seemed wise to behave as compliant and willing guests for the moment. After all had been seated, food and drink were set before them.

"I hope it would be considered impolite to refuse," said Fima. "After all, we must try not to offend them, is that not so, Azori, I mean…Ali?"

Azori winced at the use of his real name. "Yes, Fima, though I would like to see at least one other person eat the food and drink the wine before I partake of it myself."

"Do you think they might try to poison us?" whispered Carmyn, who sat at Azori's right.

"I don't think so. We are much too interesting and unusual for them to kill us as yet…they are too curious. Still, I'd like to be certain."

"When you saw their flag, you were dismayed," said Rogond in a low voice. "Is that why you refused to give your true name? What does it mean? Do you know who this Queen is?"

"My, but I hadn't realized I was so hungry," said Azori with false heartiness. "Perhaps I will partake after all."

At that moment, three very large, well-muscled guards entered the room. "Oh, dear," said Azori as the color drained from his face again. Rogond never got an answer to his questions, and a moment later the Queen swept into the room.

She was the largest, tallest woman the Company had ever beheld, clad all in leather and steel and flamboyance. Her eyes were the soft, violet-grey of evening mists over an angry sea, and she was crowned with hair dyed as blue as the silken walls of the tent. Her complexion was tawny, with high color in her cheeks. She was big, she was tough, and she was not to be trifled with. She drew herself up before her "guests," scanning over their faces with interest. It was doubtful that she had ever seen Elves or a dwarf before, and her eyes lingered on each member of the Company, her expression curious until she beheld Azori, who was trying his best to appear to be someone else. Then her eyes went cold as her painted lips drew into a knowing smile.

"Hello, Azori," she said in a musical but arresting feminine voice. "It is so good to see you. Very, *very* good!"

Azori looked up and down both sides of the table at his friends, who were staring at him in astonishment. Then he drew himself up and turned back toward the tall, impressive woman, his face and voice attempting to be ingratiating, without success. "Hello, Tansy," he said in a tone indicating that she was quite possibly the last person in the world he wanted to encounter. "It's good to see you, too."

14
Seven Temptations

Everyone in the Company sat staring at this huge, impressive woman who, apparently, was well acquainted with Azori. From the look on his face any relationship that might have existed in times past had not ended well—in fact, his expression was reminiscent of a dog who is thinking of bringing up what it has recently eaten. The large woman seemed not to notice, sweeping up to the head of the table with a flourish.

"You will all stand when the Queen enters, and remain standing until she bids otherwise," said a loud-voiced man who, apparently, was some sort of herald. The Company rose and bowed as the woman sat heavily upon a low, carved mahogany chair upholstered in rich deep blue brocade.

"You may sit," she said, fluttering a large-yet-feminine hand.

Gaelen looked over at Nelwyn. "The *Queen?* Are they serious?" she whispered in the Elven-tongue.

"You may call me Queen Tansy," said the woman, with an imperious look at Azori. "It has been awhile since I was favored with your company, my dear old friend. Much has changed since our paths last crossed, and my situation has seen…well, both ups and downs."

Azori bowed. "I would not have thought to ever see your lovely face outside of Fómor. To what do I owe this unexpected and sublime pleasure?"

"There will be time later for talk and meaningless flattery," said Tansy. "Where is your brother, Azok?" Azori did not answer.

"Never mind," said Tansy. "Let us eat and drink, and be entertained! The sun is setting, and I am anxious to learn more of you and of your journey here. I see you have brought me some interesting new friends." Her eyes swept both sides of the long table, alighting for a moment upon the Elves. "What sort of beings are these? They seem to be Elves, but I cannot imagine any Elves associating with the likes of you." This last statement amused her, and she laughed. Then she took a very large gulp of wine from her goblet, and looked directly at Galador. "Well? Are you?"

Galador did not reply immediately, raising one eyebrow as if to ask, Am I *what?*

Azori saved him the trouble. "Yes, my dear Tansy, they are…"

"*Queen* Tansy," said the herald.

"I beg your pardon," Azori continued. "*Queen* Tansy, they are Elves. And these men are northerners—one has been my companion for years. His name is Hallagond, and the other is his brother, Rogond. This woman is named Carmyn, and she hails from a small settlement to the southeast. This other woman is my sister, Estle."

Tansy looked the Company up and down for a moment, lingering for a moment upon Fima. "I didn't know that men like you had sisters. And is this actually a dwarf?"

"I am Fima, son of Khima, Lore-master to the Company," said Fima. "When the time comes for you to hear our tale, I will be the one who tells it." He bowed his head. "I am but your humble servant, and I am pleased to make your acquaintance."

"No doubt you are," said Tansy, her eyes narrowing. "But you should know that your tale had better be convincing, Lore-master Fima. I will know it if your words are untrue." She looked hard at Fima then, as if trying to decide whether her admonition had made him uncomfortable, but he did not appear to be concerned.

"I look forward to many intriguing evenings with such interesting and unique guests," said Tansy at last. "I must admit, it puzzles me…why would Elves have made their way so far south? It is said they do not venture here." She looked around at Gaelen, Nelwyn, and Galador, none of whom had spoken a word to her. "They don't talk much, do they?" she said to Azori.

"Perhaps not at first, but they tell the most wonderful stories once they loosen up. I imagine my friends are hungry and thirsty at the moment, and are less inclined to be talkative."

Azori knew what he was doing. There were several things that Corsairs loved, including food, drink, and other pleasures of the flesh. Rather high on their list was the love of a good story, especially stories about faraway lands and strange folk. The Elves and Fima would provide a nearly endless supply of entertainment—it was one of the things that would keep them all alive. As long as Tansy and her people were intrigued, the Company would survive. If Tansy grew bored, well…

"Let's all eat and drink as much as we can hold, then!" the Queen proclaimed, helping herself to food and to more drink. She looked around the table at her guests, who were still unsure of what to do. "You heard me. Eat!" Those words, combined with menacing looks from several of the guardsmen standing by, convinced everyone to eat and drink their fill. It was a wonderful meal. Fima apparently thought it might be his last, if his enthusiasm was any indication. The excess and abandon of the Corsairs was infectious, and no one would leave the table hungry.

Afterward, Tansy called for entertainment to begin. She clapped her hands twice, and several fine, well-muscled dancers appeared, along with musicians. The dancers were young men, very fit and pleasing to look upon, their limbs oiled and graceful. They performed several most remarkable feats of tumbling and gymnastics, interspersed with movements and gyrations that might best be described as provocative. Tansy had gotten to her feet several times and moved to join them, swaying seductively in rhythm, obviously enjoying herself. At last they finished their performance and left the tent as Tansy and her men clapped and whistled in approval. Then she turned abruptly toward Fima, her cheeks still flushed and her eyes bright.

"Tell me your tale now, Lore-master, and spare no detail!"

Fima now wished that he had not partaken of quite so much wine, for he needed his wits about him. He was about to tell a long and elaborate lie to this very perceptive woman, and he could ask for no help from his friends, for they had no idea of what he was about to say. "If it please you, Your Highness, may I not just give you the bare essentials of the tale at this time? I am weary, and the wine has left me a little dizzy. I will do a much better job of entertaining you tomorrow…perhaps tonight I should merely inform?" He punctuated this statement with a deep, sonorous belch that reeked of stale wine.

Tansy considered. "Very well," she said. "You are all weary, no doubt, and if your tale will be better tomorrow, you may provide only the essentials this night." She sighed as if disappointed, but then Galador spoke up.

"If Your Highness desires an elaborate tale this night, I will be happy to oblige. Elves do not grow weary as men do, and I will favor you and your people with stories of times long past. I have walked in this world for many an age, and I have seen many things. I will oblige you, if you wish it."

"How wonderful!" said Tansy, turning back to Fima. "Tell us the basics of your tale, then, Lore-master. Your skills will be shown tomorrow."

Fima told his version of the Company's quest. "We have been traveling north from lands to the south and east of the city of Mumari, having gone there in search of Hallagond. We are returning to Dûn Bennas—there is a pestilence spreading from those lands, and the people to the north need to be informed so they may guard themselves from another potential outbreak of Plague. The pestilence is to the east, in the Stone Desert, at present, but Dûn Bennas must be warned. We came by this road because, well…we got ourselves into trouble in the lands near to the Sandstone. There are roads which we may no longer travel. We now intend to continue north to the Ambros, and follow its course upriver to the City."

He looked hard at Tansy. "It's a good thing that we are here to warn you and your folk of this pestilence…all the Children of Men must guard themselves. It's still a long way off, but it may work its way here. I hope you will allow us to complete our task, and warn King Hearndin in Dûn Bennas. The Elves are anxious to return to their homes as well."

Tansy had a rather enigmatic expression on her face as she considered all that she had heard. At last she spoke to Fima. "Why have I not heard of this until now? Usually, word of pestilence spreads fast among men. Why do you know of it?"

"Because we were in lands near to those affected," said Fima looking Tansy directly in the eye. There was no wavering in his gaze, for he knew that all of their lives depended upon it.

"Are you certain that you did not carry this pestilence with you?" she said, still looking hard at him. Every man in the room unconsciously took a step back from the Company.

"We have been on the road for a long time," said Fima. "This sickness strikes hard, and it strikes fast. Our men are perfectly healthy, as you can see. There is no danger from us."

"Well, thank goodness for that," said Tansy. "You were just getting interesting. It would be a shame to kill you all now just to be safe."

She turned then to Azori, who was not certain he liked Fima's tale of pestilence one bit. "Wouldn't you agree?"

"Yes, I would agree," said Azori. "Tansy, my dear and most lovely friend, will you not enlighten me as to what you and your men are doing here, so far from Fómor? My companions would no doubt enjoy hearing your story. If I did not know better, I might think that you have fallen on hard times. Perhaps we can assist you?"

Tansy laughed again, but there was menace in her eyes. "Oh, you would no doubt be *most* helpful, until you escaped, perhaps. And don't try to beguile me, Azori! My memory is long, and I have forgotten none of the details of my last encounter with you, so save your promises. Yet you're right. I am in exile, and all because of that viper, Ludor! He took my City from me and drove me forth into the wilderness. But he had best not rest easily upon the throne, for I am preparing to reclaim it!" She swayed slightly, as she had consumed a considerable quantity of wine, and her anger had unbalanced her.

"Ludor?" said Azori. "But I thought he was your consort. He surely has not taken the Great City of the Corsairs!"

"That blustering, sniveling, back-stabbing coward!" said Tansy in disgust. "Apparently he made his way across the sea to unknown lands and brought back an army. They were impressed with him for some reason."

"There is nothing impressive about Ludor, begging your pardon" said Azori. "I can see why you are hurt and angry. At least if I had been deposed, I would like to have been deposed by someone other than my former consort. He must have commanded a mighty army."

"I am weary of this subject," said Tansy, and her eyes grew menacing again. Azori knew that she had suffered a near-fatal blow to her pride, and it was best if they did not speak of these matters again unless she brought them up herself. He looked over at Galador and nodded.

"Would you now like to hear a tale of the First Reckoning?" said Galador, taking the hint and rising to his feet.

Tansy took stock of his tall, straight frame and his beautiful, flawless features. Galador was very handsome and very masculine, and she was intrigued. She nodded, smiled, and moved to a well-upholstered dais, reclining upon it and inviting Galador to stand before her. The Company was directed to sit upon cushions at her feet and they were soon made comfortable, though they were surrounded by armed guards.

Galador told his tale, but Tansy did not hear the end of it, as she was soon fast asleep. Usually it did not bode well for the story-teller if he could not hold the Queen's interest, and Galador, it seemed, did not have Fima's gifts. Yet it did not matter, for Queen Tansy appreciated Galador's other gifts, and she had already taken a shine to him.

It was fortunate that the Corsairs were lazier than they were wary, otherwise they might have housed their new "guests" in separate quarters. That would have meant more guards, more trips to and from the larder, and so on. This way they would only need watch one space. No one envied the guards their task, as guards must remain sober.

The Company had noticed that the Corsairs always seemed to be in at least a partial state of mild to profound inebriation, either because of drink, or weed, or perhaps other lesser-known and best-avoided substances. Azori explained that this was typical of them when they were on land. Corsairs are happiest when they are on the sea.

"Do not underestimate them, as even when they appear besotted they are dangerous," he said. "They are simply more likely to lose control of their impulses, and more likely to laugh at you as they kill you. Never take them for granted." He shook his head, remembering some of what he had seen on his last trip into Fómor.

"If they are unhappy, then why do they stay upon land?" asked Gaelen.

"You are unhappy in the desert, yet you are here because you must be," said Hallagond. "Even the best mariners must make landfall, and the land is where the power is. Corsairs are ever-hungry for it. On a ship one may command the crew, but on land one might rule the world! Also, one may only hoard so much gold aboard ship. The Corsairs are legendary for their buried caches of treasure…a wise habit, so long as the caches can later be found! I have heard tales of the blackest-hearted and most terrible Scourges of the Sea, dreaded marauders who were all but invincible, who died wandering and witless because they simply could not locate the riches they had hidden, and it drove them mad. Even worse, some found their caches to discover that they had been robbed by other, more fortunate thieves! It's enough to make a Corsair weep to hear of it."

"Enough to make them cruise the seas in an endless quest for vengeance, more likely," said Azori. "Never steal *anything*, no matter how insignificant, from a Fómorian. You may expect him to pursue you until he recovers it, kills you, or dies."

"So, what can you tell us about our formidable hostess?" said Estle. "It would seem that you know her already. How deep is this hole we're in?"

Azori sighed. "Let me put it this way," he said. "There are others into whose clutches I would rather have fallen. Tansy may be convinced to release some of us. However, I very much doubt that we will all leave these lands alive. It would be most unusual." He looked at the wide-eyed faces of his friends. "Don't worry…I'll be the first to go. She already bears a grudge."

"For what, might I ask?" said Estle, who was now worried for him.

"I once denied her something she wanted," said Azori. "I will say no more."

"Do they understand Elven-speech?" asked Gaelen.

"Unlikely," said Azori. "However, remember that they are descended of the northern folk. Tuathan dialects have much in common with Elvish. I would be careful if I were you."

"We must escape from this place at our earliest opportunity," said Gaelen, whispering in Elvish. Azori and Estle glowered at her as Rogond translated.

"I cannot tell you how hopeless that notion is at this moment," said Azori in a low voice. "We must remain here, at least for now, and try to ingratiate ourselves. Tansy won't kill us so long as she finds us interesting. If I am any judge, she has already shown interest in Galador."

"I beg your pardon?" said Galador.

"I do not need to understand Elvish, and you do not need an explanation for the look you saw in her eyes, my tall friend. If you didn't notice, you must have been asleep. I have seen that look in her eyes before. She is taken with you, and worse, she is curious. You have just been assigned the exalted status of 'cat-toy,' O High Elf. One thing is certain—you had better be willing to play her game, or you are dead."

"You obviously refused to play it, Azori, and yet you are not dead," said Gaelen.

Galador had turned quite pale, and his hands shook slightly as he spoke his next words. "You cannot mean this. Are you saying that…that she would have me as a *consort*? That cannot happen. It is not within my power. Elves do not consort as a matter of convenience. My heart is given to one, and one alone."

"I wish you luck in explaining that to her," said Azori with a sigh. "Perhaps I am wrong, and she simply wishes to admire you. But that has not been my experience, alas. I'll warrant she has now set her sights on tasting immortal fruit, and she won't rest until she gets it. She's not interested in your heart, anyway."

"That horrible woman thinks to set her sights on Galador!" said Nelwyn, obviously outraged.

"All right, all right," said Fima. "We are all agreed that she is horrible. Yet for now, it seems, we must play her game."

"Easily said by you, Fima, yet not so easily agreed to by me," muttered Galador. "And I'm not so sure you should have frightened them with talk of pestilence."

"Well, if you are not content with my recounting of events, feel free to elaborate in your own way," said Fima. "I did not ask for the task of coming up with that story, yet it was given to me. Next time, you may have the job."

"It would seem that the only way we may escape from this place is to make the Queen happy, and then lull her into relaxing her vigilance," said Nelwyn. "How may we do that, Azori?"

"We give her what she wants, whenever she wants it," Azori replied.

"And what do we have that she is likely to want? I mean, apart from Galador?" said Gaelen.

"She will want to be entertained. Gaelen, you can amuse her by singing and telling stories. Nelwyn...your dancing is extraordinary. Rogond, Hallagond, and I can wrestle, or spar with one another in mock combat. Fima, it's obvious that your story-telling talents will be useful. I'm certain that Carmyn has talents as well, and Estle, you can tell a great story when you are so inclined, as long as you can keep your sardonic wit to yourself."

"Oh, *that* will happen," said Gaelen with a slight smile. Then she thought for a moment. "Tansy wants to re-take Fómor... perhaps we can convince her that our assistance would be valuable? I mean, most of us are warriors in some fashion. We have skills that would be useful—my stealth, Nelwyn's marksmanship, Rogond's cleverness and strength. We should convince her that we are not expendable, and that all will be useful. She benefits from all, or from none. Do you think that can be done?"

"I don't know," said Azori, "but it's a good thought. It's the only one that will keep me alive for long, I fear. If we agree that all serve the Queen, or none do, she might buy into the notion. We have some time for consideration, as she is far too curious to kill any of us as yet."

"Where are our belongings?" asked Fima, who thankfully was still wearing his leather jerkin with Gorgon's mirror safe inside.

"I don't know," Azori replied. "But I do not expect to see them again. We are in a den of thieves, after all."

Fima's question was answered upon being summoned to luncheon on the following day. When they next saw Queen Tansy, she was wearing the fire-cloak.

"I bring news, Elfhunter," said Lord Kotos, leaving the raven's willing form to occupy the amulet once more. He gazed out at

Gorgon's pale grey eyes and shook his head. "The Company has been waylaid by Fómorian Corsairs. I have flown over their encampment and have discovered where the prisoners are being kept. Up to now, at least, they appear to have been kept well. Yet we cannot allow this to continue—nothing must interfere with Lord Wrothgar's plan."

"And how would you suggest we prevent it?" growled Gorgon, who knew nothing of Corsairs. "Is the enemy few enough that I might slay them by stealth? I cannot reveal myself, or even Orrion, to the Company. I'm certain you will agree!"

"They are far too many for you to take by stealth," said Kotos. "Yet you need not fear, for I will accomplish our ends with a little aid from you, my most marvelous and worthy friend."

"And how, precisely, will you arrange to do that? Not even you could beguile an army, I'm thinking."

"One need only beguile the one who leads the army," said Kotos. "I will need to fly into the encampment and spend some time there. Once I am certain of the lay of things, I will return and explain our plan."

"Well, don't take too long," said Gorgon. "I shall be forced to hide here until you do. There are scouts, and I must not risk being seen."

"You will blend into your surroundings as never before," said Kotos. "I will bring water and food over the next few days. In fact, this may not take long at all. Now, open the pouch containing the valuables we took from the merchants at the oasis, will you? I need something from it." Gorgon did so, as Kotos once again summoned the raven and used it as host. The raven approached the bag, reached inside, and drew out one of the few things of value—a golden coin. Then it took flight, circling once over Gorgon's head in farewell before disappearing over the sand-hills to the north. Kotos knew that the way to ingratiate the raven, and therefore himself, was to bring Tansy something of value. If he could convince her that the raven would always arrive with a gift whenever it appeared, she would most likely welcome it.

Corsairs were like spoiled, intelligent children. They were very susceptible to temptation, especially to those seven temptations that were most powerful and deadly. Kotos had used them time and again to lure men, even Elves on occasion, into his service. Now he would appeal to Tansy's greed.

The sun was rising by the time the raven arrived in Tansy's private bedchamber. She had not yet stirred, as early mornings were not to her liking. The raven alighted on one intricately carved post at the foot of the bed and gave one loud croak, but Tansy was fast asleep and did not awaken. The raven gave a figurative sigh, ruffled its feathers, and waited for her to rouse herself. At first she rubbed her eyes when she saw the raven in her bedchamber. Yet the bird seemed tame, bowing when she spoke to it.

"Well, aren't you the pretty thing?" she said. "What's that in your beak, then? Did you bring a fine gift for me?" The raven bobbed its head up and down, causing her to smile again. "You did, eh? Well, let's have it!" The raven fluttered to her outstretched hand, being careful not to sink its claws in. Then it dropped the golden coin into her lap.

"Aren't you just the clever bird?" she said, examining the coin. "Such a fine, handsome lad you are. Here's a little tidbit by way of thanks." She took a sugared almond from a tray beside the bed and offered it to the raven.

After gobbling down the treat, the raven bowed again. "Thank you," it said in its harsh raven's voice. It is well known that ravens can mimic human speech, but Tansy was startled nonetheless.

"Where did you come from?" she asked. The raven did not answer, but took flight, leaving her to wonder. It sat up high upon the tallest tent-brace, preening itself.

"Fine, then, suit yourself," said the Queen. "How did you get past my guards? There is no harm in your being here, I suppose. After all, you cannot understand what you overhear. Perhaps you will stay and help keep the watch." The raven pretended to ignore her.

"Well, fine…then I suppose you aren't really interested in sugared almonds?" She held a silver bowl full of sweets toward the raven, who ruffled its feathers, shook itself, and peered at the bowl with one bright, black eye.

Over the next few days, the raven became a regular visitor in the encampment, always bringing gifts for the Queen. Sometimes they were of value, such as a coin or a small piece of jewelry. Sometimes they were not; it was just as likely to bring a bit of colored glass. But Kotos wanted the raven to keep at least a semblance of typical behavior, and thus it would not be able to discriminate a shiny, worthless object from a shiny, valuable one. The Queen was amused no matter the gift. She wore the fire-cloak always, despite the fact that she was much too large to wear it well. It looked more like a "fire-cape" on her broad shoulders and tall frame. No matter—it was shiny, gaudy, and very, very valuable. Tansy adored it, though she did not as yet recognize its properties.

The Company entertained her each evening with songs, dancing, and tales—there was a deep enough well in Fima alone to sustain her for a long time to come. In the meantime, Hallagond and Rogond made themselves useful fitting and finishing weapons for the upcoming assault. They had skills the Corsairs valued, as did Nelwyn, who saw to the re-shaping and tillering of bows so that they would send their arrows on a truer course. Gaelen, who could not stand the sight of Tansy wearing the fire-cloak, limited herself to singing.

One evening, after partaking of a particularly fine meal and an especially large amount of wine, Tansy lay in her chamber in a half-stupor, speaking her inmost thoughts to the raven, of which she had become quite fond.

"Ah, my pretty one, perhaps you can advise me. My life has been good of late, and yet I am unhappy. There is something I want, and for the first time in my life I have been afraid to take it." The raven hopped down from its perch and approached her, cocking its head to the side as though listening intently. Tansy laughed. "If I did not know better, I would think that you truly understood my concern. Yet I know I may speak to you, and no other will ever hear. It doesn't matter that you do not understand."

Tansy had never been more wrong. The raven cocked its head again as though entreating her to continue. She rewarded it with another sugared almond, which disappeared down the bird's throat with lightning speed.

"Have you ever desired something just because you are curious about what it's like? Of course you have…you're a raven! Well, I wish to know the embrace of an Elf. Only a handful of my race has ever known it, and I wish to be among them. It is my greatest desire to be with Galador, despite his cold and proud demeanor. Maybe my desire is even greater because of it! I don't know. He isn't the sort that I usually find appealing, but somehow I cannot help myself. I want to march into his chamber, drag him out by his hair, and not release him until he agrees to be my consort. Can you understand that feeling?"

Kotos could indeed, for he had witnessed and even encouraged such behavior countless times in the past. Yet now the prospect was alarming.

If Tansy tries to take Galador by force, all will be interrupted. He would almost certainly reject her advances, or even scorn her openly…some in the Company might not survive, notably Galador. Of all in the Company, Nelwyn must not fall! Our plan rests on her, yet she might try to defend Galador, at her peril. This would undoubtedly enrage Tansy, and she might just kill them all to save face. The time has come to act.

He waited until Tansy had fallen asleep, lying with her mouth half-open, snoring softly. One hand grasped the hilt of a blade, as if preparing for a sudden defense upon being awakened by an enemy. Tansy was never without a weapon, and the Company had learned that she was very accomplished with her two curved swords. Tansy was strong, clever, and surprisingly agile for her size.

She was not prepared, however, for the invasion of her mind by Lord Kotos, and she offered no resistance. The raven gave one half-hearted squawk as the evil presence left it, and then moved to the dressing-table, helping itself to the rest of the sugared almonds. If any guard had entered the room, he would have seen the Queen and the raven, just as he had left them.

Kotos knew he would encounter no difficulty, as Tansy was very susceptible to temptation, like most Fómorians. She held the same values as an intelligent, spoiled child. Kotos knew now which of his favorite temptations would bring about his desired end: not greed, nor gluttony, nor wrath; not sloth, nor envy, nor even vanity. No, this time lust would serve best.

Kotos loved all the temptations in his arsenal. Vanity, or pride, was his favorite, for he had even managed to lure Elves beneath the edge of Darkness with that one. Kotos reminisced for just a moment about Aincor Fire-heart, whose pride had served to bring about the downfall of so many servants of Light.

Tansy was no Fire-heart, but Kotos would use the fire of lust that had been kindled in her heart. He spoke to her inner mind, the one that dreams, and told her of how her great desire could be realized. He sent to her images of a High-elf so magnificent that Galador could not even compare. This Elf was golden, with golden armor. His name was Orrion, and he would come to her each night, but only in her dreams.

If she would release the Company, and return their possessions, Orrion would come to her in the flesh. Then she would receive more pleasure than even a Corsair would ever have known. It would be a night so sublime that no other experienced by a mortal woman would rival it. Kotos soothed and promised and tantalized Tansy. He beguiled her as easily as a child with the promise of sweet things.

The image of Orrion's cold, handsome face would not leave her, even upon awakening. All of her other concerns had been supplanted by deep, irrepressible longing. She went to her bed early for the next few nights, anxious to see him again, to feel the caress of his large, skilled hands, and to wander freely in the realm of dreams, where all desires were met. Lord Kotos was only too happy to oblige. Yet Tansy longed for the true possession of Orrion, not just in dreams.

Finally, Kotos grew weary of toying with her. He asserted his will, calling a council and ordering the Company to be set free, despite all expectation to the contrary. *You have not really known what you would do with them anyway,* he told her. *They are far too upstanding to deceive you into believing that they would ever really act in your favor. Now, you must not have them killed, as that will not please Orrion—your golden lover.* Tansy put forth no resistance to the idea. She would have done nearly anything to please Orrion…and the creature who controlled him.

Most of the Company's possessions were returned to them by the disgruntled Fómorians, who did not even pretend to understand their Queen's command. Azori, in particular, was stunned. "What in the world could have gotten into her? I'm not sure I want to leave the encampment…they'll probably impale me for trying to escape. I tell you, they're going to kill us all. They must have decided that we are of no use, and they would never, ever give back anything of value. They have returned our weapons, our horses, and all our valuables. This is a trick!"

"Not quite *all* of our valuables," muttered Gaelen, who was still incensed at the sight of Tansy wearing the fire-cloak. "It appears that Her Majesty has come to see us off. How very thoughtful."

Gaelen vaulted onto Toran, who had not been ridden in a fortnight and was now acting his usual childish self, prancing and dancing and annoying her. She took a deep breath, mastered her frustration, and stroked Toran's neck to calm him. As she did so, she wondered, looking upon the garish sight of Tansy in full regalia, what was different about her. *Ah! Where is the raven?* Gaelen had not seen the Queen without her black-feathered escort in recent memory. *It does not matter. Perhaps Tansy has eaten it.*

She turned to Azori. "We can't just stand here. We should cross the river before they change their minds. If it *is* a trick, they'll kill us whether we stand or go. I do not think Tansy would have come to see us off if they were trying to claim that we were escaping. Whatever she asks, they do. I'm just not sure why she would set us free."

She looked over at Nelwyn, who stood beside her. "You lead, and I will follow."

Nelwyn nodded. She had been very anxious to escape the Corsairs for some time, as the delay in reaching Tal-sithian wore heavily on her.

Without another word, the Company departed, following Nelwyn's lead. Only Azori, Estle, and Hallagond kept their eyes turned over their shoulders, expecting spears and arrows at their backs. Yet none came.

As soon as they were out of range, Gaelen approached Rogond, such that Toran and Eros trotted side-by-side. "As soon as we have gained enough distance from them and camped for the night, I'm going back," she said. "That absurd woman has something of mine, and I intend to reclaim it. We will have need of it, Thaylon, and there is no other to be found. If the Company stays far enough to the north, they will never catch us. I have observed them—they do not ride well."

Rogond knew better than to dismiss her out of hand. "You would go alone into such a dangerous place, and risk all that lies ahead? The fire-cloak has served its purpose to the Company, Gaelen. It has saved Fima's life, and yours, and Hallagond's. It aided in the defeat of Lokai. It has passed on."

"Its part in our quest is not yet fully played," said Gaelen in a deadly serious tone. "We need the fire-cloak. *I* need it. I will not leave it behind unless no choice is given me." She looked hard at him. "Please do not put me in the position where I must choose between doing what is right and doing what you and the others would have me do. Trust me, instead." She smiled at him. "You know I can do this. They are far less wary than many, and are not familiar with the stealth of Wood-elves. They will never know that I have been among them."

Rogond sighed. "You should not go alone," he said. "Someone should go with you and watch the horses while you accomplish your task. Take Nelwyn, or take Estle. And…perhaps you should ride someone other than Toran. He might make the same mistake as before and betray you unwittingly."

Needless to say, Gaelen chose Nelwyn to accompany her, as Estle would not have seen the sense in it. Gaelen asked Galador if she could ride Réalta, who was seasoned and knew to keep quiet at all times.

"Of course you may ride him. He owes you his life," said Galador, who for once did not argue, though he was unhappy with the idea of Nelwyn's returning to the enemy encampment. "At least if you are seen, you will both escape. Gryffa and Réalta are swifter than anything the Corsairs can set against them."

He shook his head. "Just try not to get caught. We cannot risk the fate of Alterra in coming after you. If you are captured, you will have to find your own way out."

Galador made certain that Nelwyn heard his rather unsettling admonition before embracing her and seeing them both on their way. Réalta lifted his proud head and taunted Toran. *Now* who was deemed most worthy? He then needed to avoid a swipe from Eros, who, though he loved Réalta, sometimes found his prideful nature irritating.

After they had gone, the remaining members of the Company sat around their small fire, knowing that none would sleep this night. It would not take long for Gaelen and Nelwyn to accomplish their task if all went as planned. If they had not returned by sunrise, there was reason to worry. Rogond looked over at Galador, who stirred the fire first one way, then the other.

"Would you really leave them behind?"

"I would not leave Nelwyn behind," Galador replied. "She has been instructed that, if Gaelen's plan fails, she is to return with the horses. She knows the importance of gaining Tal-sithian. Remember, it is her vision that drives us. She will do what is necessary." He looked into the eyes of his dearest friend, and saw consternation in them. "You know I'm right. I love Gaelen, but we cannot risk the fate of the Light because she cannot abandon the fire-cloak. That was her choice to make. Besides, she of all of our number is probably best able to escape the Corsairs. Even if they detect her, they will never catch her."

"Still, I am surprised that you would sacrifice her," whispered Rogond.

"She knows what she is doing. Have you not yet realized it?" said Galador with a smile. "I am only willing to sacrifice her because I know it will not come to that. Trust her, as you once told me to trust Nelwyn. They are both still here, you will notice."

Kotos flew on urgent wings back to Gorgon's hiding place. He encountered no resistance as he entered Gorgon's unguarded mind.

"Did you bring water?" asked Gorgon. "I'm getting tired of sneaking all the way down to the river by dark of night."

There is water in the encampment, and wine also. Now, don't argue. This night your task is important, and I have been many days in arranging it, so stop complaining. Surely the mighty Elfhunter is still strong enough to walk a few miles?

"What task?" asked Gorgon with a suspicious curl of his lip.

I will explain as we travel. Now, let me in, won't you? My strength and vitality will aid and restore you. Put on the amulet and let us go into the encampment together.

"That bird looks nice and juicy," said Gorgon, who was hungry as well as thirsty. The raven wisely took flight.

Do not even consider it. The bird has served well, and it will continue to serve. It is also our herald, and will announce our presence to the Queen.

"The Queen? What Queen? The Queen of what?" asked Gorgon, who did not like the sound of any of it. He liked it even less when Kotos finished explaining the plan, and Orrion's impending part in it. He stopped dead in his tracks and would not move forward.

"You do not understand! You want me to…to go to this woman and *consort* with her? I cannot do that! I do not have the knowledge, let alone the experience, in such things. Do not ask it of me!"

Calm yourself, Elfhunter. With luck, it will not come to that, soothed Kotos. He had expected Gorgon to be difficult.

"Yet I must at least appear to be interested!" said Gorgon in a panic. "I will not be able to do that—I don't know how. You cannot ask it of me."

Do you not know by now that I will never ask you to do anything beyond your ability? said Kotos, speaking to Gorgon as he might to a child. *You still do not trust in me, even after all we have seen together? I took you into the heart of Dûn Arian, and you stood before your enemies without detection. You can do this…Tansy does not even know you. I will speak to her through you, as I always have. I know exactly what to say to her.*

Gorgon took one tentative step forward. He wanted to trust Kotos, but trust was not in his nature. In the end, thirst drove him forward as much as anything. *Afterward I will reward you, my most mighty and valued companion,* said Kotos.

Gorgon was not taken in. He knew that by "companion" Kotos really meant "servant." But the rewards Kotos could give were oh, so sweet, and Gorgon would continue to bear his Dark Guardian for the time being.

Gaelen and Nelwyn stopped at a prudent distance from the encampment, far enough that no scouts would detect them. It was dark, and they both knew that the Fómorians would be distracted with merrymaking. Still, Nelwyn was unhappy about the prospect of being separated from Gaelen.

"Do not linger. Do what you must. If things go ill, escape with your life—don't risk it for the fire-cloak. I will wait here until I know that I must leave you. Please do not ask that of me."

Gaelen then gave a half-smirk that reminded Nelwyn of the days before they ever heard of Gorgon Elfhunter. She had always enjoyed tests of stealth. "Don't worry—this will be easy. They are half-besotted already, if I am any judge, and they aren't all that wary even when sober."

"Only remember what Azori told you…they are dangerous no matter their level of sobriety," said Nelwyn. "This is no time for testing your prowess without need. Now go and do what you must do, and then return as quickly as you may." The two cousins embraced, and then Gaelen was gone without another sound. Nelwyn patted Gryffa and Réalta, and settled herself for the waiting to come.

Gaelen forded the river easily, as it was shallow, but the Corsairs' few watchmen would have their eyes upon it and she was very careful. *The moon has risen—a pity—but moonlight also gives dark shadows, and those may be put to use.*

She had no trouble reaching the tent where the Queen's private chambers were kept. There were guards, but they did not see her, nor did they hear her. In fact, they appeared to be asleep, slumped over their weapons. Gaelen shook her head and crept beneath the wall, observing the raven perched upon the bedpost.

Tansy was standing with her back to Gaelen, the most fabulous bejeweled raiment ever to grace a mortal woman draped across her statuesque frame. In front of the Queen, to Gaelen's astonishment, stood one well known to the Company—one whom Gaelen had hoped never to see again.

Gaelen stared in revulsion as Orrion fixed Tansy with his deceiver's eyes, draining her of her will. He spoke words that even Gaelen could not hear.

Her enemies were occupied with one another, and Gaelen took advantage of the moment, slinking in the shadows until she could reach out with her long fingers to snag the fire-cloak from the pile of cushions where Tansy had tossed it. It glittered in the firelight, and Gaelen was fearful that Orrion would notice, but he did not, as he was far too intent upon his victim. His eyes held no love—they gleamed with vicious, malignant lust. He loomed over Tansy and pushed her to the floor. Then he grasped her with hands like talons, and forced his body down. Gaelen was horrified, but she could not look away. *Oh, Lord of Light…are those fangs in his mouth?*

Tansy gave an almost inhuman cry, though few would hear it through Orrion's large hand now clamped over her face. The raven responded by taking wing and calling in alarm. That brought Gaelen back to the moment, and provided all the distraction she needed. She snatched the cloak, tucking it beneath her tunic, and rolled underneath the tent wall without first checking for watchful eyes. Thankfully, there were none.

Her heart pounding, tears of terror welling in her eyes, Gaelen made her way as carefully as she could manage back to the riverbank. The horror of what she had just witnessed had unbalanced her—the unbridled essence of Evil that inhabited Orrion had been revealed to her perceptive Wood-elf's eyes. Even more unsettling, but not altogether unexpected, was the scent that pervaded the chamber. Gaelen knew the scent of Gorgon Elfhunter better than any other. Now there was no longer any doubt in her mind, but there were many, many questions. She almost felt sorry for Tansy, who had most certainly more than met her match this time.

15
Revelations and Regrets

Gaelen returned to Nelwyn on feet that were swifter than a deer in full flight—even Réalta was startled by her sudden appearance. As usual, she had made no sound. She pulled the fire-cloak from beneath her tunic and showed it briefly to Nelwyn before stowing it in her pack, wrinkling her nose as she did so, for it still reeked of Tansy's perfume.

"What happened?" said Nelwyn. "I see you were successful..." She mounted Gryffa, who had sensed Gaelen's urgency and was now unsettled.

Gaelen practically leaped aboard Réalta, even though she was out of breath and he was quite tall. She smiled in the darkness. She had become rather more accomplished at mounting taller horses lately.

She turned to Nelwyn. "*Now is not the time for explanation. The Corsairs are not pursuing us, and I don't expect them to*—my urgency is grounded elsewhere. For now, let's return to our companions with all speed. I'll explain later." She sent Réalta forward, reveling in the now-perfect symmetry of his footfalls.

Nelwyn shook her head and muttered her displeasure at hearing the words "I'll explain later" from Gaelen. This was rarely a good thing.

They were soon reunited with their relieved companions. Toran heralded their approach as Eros snorted and raised his head. *When are you going to learn that it's unwise to do that? You got cuffed for it the last time, do you not remember?*

But it's Réalta and Gryffa, and they bear our friends, said Toran, pawing and shaking his head with impatience. *I know the difference between a friend and a stranger, and I will not call to strangers again. Give me due credit, won't you? I am not addle-brained.*

"*Aiyah!* Stop that racket at once!" said Galador. Toran stopped pawing, and Eros blew though his large, soft nostrils with satisfaction.

Gaelen and Nelwyn appeared a few moments later, having made good time under the moonlight. The moon was now setting, but the sun would be rising in only a few hours. Time enough to rest, water the horses, and allow them a bit of grass. There was grass north of the Dessa; though it was dry and sparse, it was still welcomed. The Company clustered around their friends, wanting a report of the night's events.

"All is well," said Gaelen, drawing the fire-cloak forth as proof of her success, though she seemed strangely distant, even taciturn. She kept her eyes downcast, which was most unusual.

"Well, it won't be when Tansy discovers that her favorite garment has gone missing," said Azori. "She will most likely send riders out to reclaim it." He caught the scent wafting from the fire-cloak. "I see she still enjoys Passionflower Musk."

"She will not stir until the sun is up," said Carmyn. "We observed her long enough to know that."

"Gaelen, your horse betrayed your arrival by opening his mouth again," said Estle. "It would seem he has not learned his lesson, and remains a liability."

"He knows the difference between a friend and a stranger," said Gaelen. "Give him credit! He is not addle-brained."

Toran snorted and shook his head. Eros would not look at him.

Gaelen brushed the dust from her breeches. "We need to get moving and make our way to Dûn Bennas without delay," she said. "How far is it to the Ambros?"

"Only about a hundred miles, if we head straight north," said Fima. "Can't we wait until morning, say, after breakfast?"

"Indeed," said Rogond. "It's better that we travel in daylight. I doubt the Queen will notice her fire-cloak is missing until morning."

"Assuming she rouses herself before noon…" said Fima.

"Have you ever seen Corsairs when their blood is up?" asked Azori. "We had best be ready to ride at first light."

"I don't think so," said Gaelen. "Not if Tansy must order them. I sense that she is the force that unites and motivates them—without her, they may well disband. If that is so, then you needn't worry. We have plenty of time."

"What are you telling us? Did something happen to the Queen? Did you *do* anything to her?" asked Azori. "I sincerely hope not!"

"Ah, yes," said Gaelen in a sarcastic tone. "Forgive me…I had forgotten to mention that earlier this evening, when I went to retrieve my fire-cloak, I marched into the Queen's tent and slapped her until she awakened from her drunken slumber. Then I spat in her eye, and in typical blood-thirsty fashion I cut her throat. It serves her right for stinking up my fire-cloak with her foul perfume." She folded her arms and stood before Azori, defying him to comment on the matter.

"It *is* a fair question, Gaelen," said Estle. "What happened earlier that you are not telling us about?"

"I will tell you what I know, but not at this moment," said Gaelen, dropping her gaze again. "For now, you must trust me. Let me just tell you this much—I did nothing to her, but I do not believe that Tansy will be in a state to mount an attack on anyone for a while. Now, ask me no more questions. I will reveal more at a better time." She shuddered, and a strange mixture of emotions played across her face. Everyone who looked upon her was unsettled, especially Rogond, Fima, and Nelwyn, who had seen such expressions in Gaelen before.

Gorgon had removed the amulet before leaving the Queen's chamber, for he wished to go forth as himself. Kotos agreed, as it would have been unwise to cast any suspicions upon Orrion. It was best if no one in the encampment saw him, except, of course, for the Queen, who was in no condition to do anything about it. Neither were her personal guards—Gorgon had broken their necks before they had the chance to raise any alarm. He had spent a lifetime lurking in shadow, and he had little difficulty escaping unobserved.

Kotos stayed with Gorgon until they had crossed the river, the raven flying above them. When it realized that Gorgon was continuing north, it hesitated. Why would it wish to leave the Realm of Sugared Almonds?

Call to it, Elfhunter, said Kotos. *It seems I must convince our very useful friend to remain with us.* Gorgon tempted the raven with bits of meat until it came close enough, and then Kotos took it over. Soon their alliance of three was secure again.

They had plenty of provisions, and Gorgon would soon be in familiar territory. He imagined that he could almost smell the Elves as he drew nearer to their lands. He was comforted as he strode along in the dark, and when dawn came they would rest, as Kotos had informed Gorgon that they should not follow the Company too closely.

Neither of them had been aware of Gaelen as she hid in the Queen's chamber. Kotos had been entirely too focused on overtaking Tansy, who was possessed of a strong spirit and required all of his foul attention. He had appeared to Gaelen's terror-stricken eyes with no cloak of beguiling upon him, as he believed there was no need.

Gorgon had also felt the full malevolence of the dreaded spirit that dwelled within him, although it was not a new experience. When he truly allowed Kotos to take him over, his own senses were blunted, much like his experience with the mirror. Now all of his senses were in play, and he settled in to the task of following the Company with ease.

Kotos had become quite impressed with his difficult, complicated host. Gorgon was swift, he was light-footed, and his stamina was remarkable. He survived on very little and did not complain of physical discomfort. He would, in fact, outlast the raven and would cover greater distances in a day. His primary liability was his intolerance of sunlight, yet when he was wearing his armor he could deal with that, though he still did not enjoy going abroad in daylight. Gorgon traveled by night, the raven perched on one of the many thorny spikes on the top of his helmet.

By day, Lord Kotos scouted the area on dark wings while Gorgon rested in the shadows. Both Gorgon and Kotos knew that the Company would not elude them. Despite their swift horses, they would need to stop and replenish themselves in Dûn Bennas, whereas Gorgon did not suffer from the need to surround himself with social amenities.

Gaelen, who alone among the Company was aware of Gorgon, knew that he would track her despite all effort to prevent it, and so she relied instead upon the speed of her mount to outdistance him.

She spent her days and nights trying to assemble the complicated and confusing puzzle of Orrion and his role in their present course, which was now truly unclear. *Who is he? What is he, really? Gorgon is involved, I have no doubt...but there's someone else.*

They reached the Ambros without incident, turning east to follow its course to the White Fortress. One evening, Fima approached Gaelen after supper as she stood by the turbulent waters. It was early spring now, and the snow-melt had swelled the river and turned it wild. There would be no need to cross it, which was fortunate, as they could not have done so until they reached Dûn Bennas. Gaelen heard her friend approach, even over the rushing river.

"Hello, Fima," she said. "I was just reveling in the sound of so much water, after such a long time without it. And the green smells in the air are nearly overwhelming to my Wood-elf's heart. Won't you join me?"

She sat upon a stone, wrapping herself in her cloak against the chilly air. Here the cold was not like that of the desert. Air that is laden with moisture will chill to the bone, particularly when it moves as wind. Fima already wondered whether he could lure Gaelen back to the fire.

"I would speak with you, my friend," he said, moving to sit beside her. "Will you not enlighten me as to what happened in the Queen's lands, and why you have not shared it? I saw fear in your eyes when you spoke of it."

Gaelen did not answer immediately, but stared at the river for a few moments. "Fima, may I ask you something?"

"Of course," he replied in his gruff but gentle voice. "I will always aid you if I can."

"Then answer me this—do we know whether Lord Kotos is yet alive? I mean, has he fallen, or does he still dwell in this world?"

Fima was taken aback. "Kotos? I don't believe that question can be answered by anyone of good will, Gaelen, but I will speculate. Dark souls are, in my experience, much more reluctant to leave this world than enlightened ones. Some of the Asari have passed from the world—Duinar, Cuimir, Baelta, Léiras—they have all gone. Yet they were a part of the Light of Creation, and they have rejoined it.

Dark beings, like Kotos, are ever uncertain as to what awaits them in the hereafter. I believe that since worldly pleasures and powers are what sustain them, they would fight very hard to remain here. Therefore, I will not place any wager upon the likelihood that Kotos is no more. Does that make sense to you?"

"It does," said Gaelen in a very quiet voice. She was still mulling things over in her mind. Finally she turned to her patient friend, one whom she trusted more than almost any other. "What I saw in the Queen's tent that night will haunt me until the end of my days. And if I'm right, we have all been deceived. I don't know how to tell Nelwyn…that she may have been overtaken and misled by the very essence of Evil."

Fima's eyes grew very wide and he drew in a sharp breath, followed by a fit of coughing that lasted nearly a minute. Gaelen drew her cloak tighter and waited for him to calm himself. He simply sat staring at her, as though trying to make sense of what he had just heard.

"I will give you something now, Fima, and just look it over when you are so inclined." She drew forth the parchment containing her list of misgivings about Orrion. She knew he would not be able to read the words in the dark, so she folded the parchment and tucked it beneath his jerkin. "When you have considered the words on that parchment, come to me again and I shall enlighten you. Until then, you will have to trust me. I will not risk revealing my suspicions to Nelwyn until we are safe and she is under watch. I know how upsetting such revelations can be, remember?"

Fima did. When Gaelen had learned of Gorgon's mirror, and of her unwitting part in the deaths of so many Elves and men, she had attempted to take her own life rather than allow her enemy to take one more life with her assistance. His invasion of her senses had unbalanced her—Fima remembered how it had torn her apart.

"Apart from the death of my beloved, that was the most terrible disclosure my spirit has ever endured," she said. "As to the present situation, I believe I have put some of the pieces together, but until I have them all, I will not wish to upset Nelwyn. There is no harm in continuing our present course…in fact, we must not alert our enemies by diverting from it. I also believe that the Powers of Darkness may have given us a key that will bring about their undoing. Until I am certain, I must keep my thoughts to myself. I trust you will agree?"

"You ask much of me, Gaelen," said Fima, blowing softly through his fine, white mustache. "Yet I understand. When I have considered what is on this parchment, I will counsel with you again. Of course, you realize that I will not be able to wait until the sun is up, but will be reading this immediately by firelight?"

Gaelen stole a furtive glance at Estle, Galador, and Nelwyn, who sat by the fire. "Not *now*, you won't! We must not draw attention to the parchment or risk anyone's looking over your shoulder. You will need to wait until you can examine it in private." She sighed. "I hope we can get to Dûn Bennas soon. There is one there who can aid us. Astor will surely know where to look for enlightenment." She smiled then at Fima. "Between the two of you, we will be armed with all the learning we need. And when we finally gain Tal-sithian, perhaps we can look to Arialde and...and maybe Lord Shandor. Surely he is no friend of Lord Kotos!"

Fima did not sleep at all that night. The notion that Lord Kotos was somehow involved with dealings in Dûn Arian, and with the affairs of the Company, seemed quite absurd. When Fima had last seen depictions of Kotos, they had been so horrible and terrifying that he could not imagine good-hearted folk coming anywhere near without fainting. And yet, Gaelen was obviously convinced. The parchment crackled in his jerkin, mocking him. "Oh...I can't bear the suspense," he whispered to no one in particular, throwing off his blankets and heading back to the riverbank, gathering deadwood as he did so, that he might make a small fire of his own.

The Company finally drew within sight of the great bridges and towers of Dûn Bennas, which sparkled through the grey, depressing rain like beacons of welcome. They were met by advance guards, who knew them at once. There was little fanfare, for they had not been expected, but that was just fine. King Hearndin was informed of their arrival., and the horses were taken to the stables while the Company was shown to their familiar guest quarters.

The first and most important request made of the people of Dûn Bennas was for hot water, and plenty of it. There is nothing like a good soaking in steaming hot water after days and days of hard riding in the rain.

Next, it was a hot meal and a flagon of good wine, together with wonderful, warm clothing made of velvet, wool, and soft leather. The Company had been asked whether they bore urgent tidings or whether they would just as soon stand before Hearndin after a good night's rest.

"A good rest will not hurt, if it please the King," said Rogond, to the relief of Fima and Hallagond, who had both been partaking of quite a good measure of wine. Soon they were sleeping in comfort for the first time in a long while.

The rain had cleared and the stars sparkled in the night sky as Gaelen and Nelwyn made their way to one of the tall, flat-topped observation towers. The watch was being kept, but not on this tower; it was the perfect place for star-gazing. There was even a stand where a very large version of Thorndil's glass could be mounted, and objects in the heavens could be enlarged and seen with greater clarity.

"Is this a private gathering, or may anyone join it?" asked Carmyn, who had come up behind the Elves.

"You are welcome, of course," said Nelwyn. "We do not sleep, but we often enjoy lying about gazing at the heavens. It is one of my favorite times to think and wonder about the nature of things."

"Mine, too," said Carmyn, spreading a blanket upon the stones. "My father was a map maker, but he also charted the stars. He taught me many things about what is seen in the night sky."

Just then, a falling star blazed a bright golden trail in the dark, flared up, and went out forever. "What a pity," said Carmyn, and there truly was deep sorrow in her voice.

The Elves were concerned. "Why is it a pity?" asked Gaelen. "Falling stars are beautiful—sent by Aontar to delight us. It is said that all thoughts held beneath a falling star are true."

"Do you not understand that stars are not just pretty lights? They are other worlds," said Carmyn. "Even as our sun gives life to Alterra, so each bright star gives life to a far distant world. Someone has just lost their sun, and therefore their world. I'd call that a pity."

"You believe that…that stars are other worlds? That they are like the *sun*?" said Nelwyn, incredulous.

"That is what the people of Dûn Arian believe," said Carmyn. "At least some of them. Sutherling astronomers, especially those from the great desert realms, were very knowledgeable. My father knew it. He always told me that there were many worlds in creation, and that Aontar rules them all. Light is the one thing they all have in common."

"Wait a moment," said Nelwyn, who was still trying to wrap her mind around the concept that the stars were really suns. "Are those tiny lights suns to tiny worlds? They look so small and cold…their light is not the same as sunlight. I do not understand."

"They are very far away," said Carmyn. "That's why they are small and do not look the same as our sun does. Do you truly believe that all those lights, and all that blackness, were put here just to amuse us?"

"Well…they also aid mariners in steering their proper course," said Nelwyn, who had never been on a ship in her life.

"And what do you think lies beyond the dome of stars?" asked Carmyn.

"I don't know," said Nelwyn. "Perhaps…the Spirit Realm?"

"As good an answer as any I have heard," said Carmyn.

"I don't think there's an answer to that question," said Gaelen. "Might we speak of something else?"

"A good idea," said Nelwyn. "My head is hurting from such deep thoughts. But I must admit that I will not look at the stars in quite the same way again. I always thought they were lights put forth by the ancestors of the High-elves, arranged in the heavens to delight us and guide us. I never thought of them in any other way before."

"What a pretty notion that is!" said Carmyn. "Perhaps I will not look at them in quite the same way, either."

"It's cold here," said Nelwyn with a shiver.

"If you will both excuse me, I'm going now to find Rogond," said Gaelen. "All these lofty thoughts have reminded me of my clever Aridan. I'll warrant that he knows about all those other worlds." So saying, she went from the tower to the chamber where her Thaylon was sleeping. She lay beside him, sharing warmth and smiling at the odd sounds he made, knowing that he only made them when he was contented, and remained with him until dawn.

The Company had gone before Hearndin the previous day. The King expressed deep sorrow upon hearing of the death of Thorndil. "How tragic—that he should make that difficult journey, alone and at his age, only to come to such a terrible end! Our hearts are torn by it. He was a worthy and kind-hearted man. We will honor him here, for he was of our race. From now on, the southern watch-tower shall be named 'Thorndil's Tower.'"

This was a great honor, but some in the Company did not feel any better for it, Gaelen in particular.

Rogond told of their desire to reach Tal-sithian as soon as they had rested and replenished their supplies. "We will not need much," said Galador. "The way between here and the Lake is both moderate and fruitful at this time of year. There will be plenty to sustain us. We are so accustomed to carrying a large water supply… this will be an easy path!" The Company agreed that it would be most welcome to have plenty of water and grass available along the next step in the journey.

"One thing troubles me," said Nelwyn. "There will be new grass all along the way through the Srath Miadan, and the horses are not accustomed to such rich feed."

Everyone understood Nelwyn's concern. Horses did not fare well on rich, early spring grass when they were not used to it.

"Don't worry, Nelwyn," said Hearndin. "Our folk have ways of preventing your animals from over-eating. We will share them with you ere you depart."

He turned to Gaelen. "Please, will you sing for us? We have missed the sound of your powerful, soft voice swelling and echoing through the stone columns and vaulted ceilings of our halls."

Although the reminder of Thorndil had saddened her, Gaelen could not refuse. The sorrow in her voice was so deep and so poignant that even the eyes of the King were filled with unshed tears. When she had finished, he rose and bowed to her, removed a pretty golden ring from the last finger of his right hand, and held it out before her.

"With this gift I name you Most Favored Singer of the White Fortress," he said. "You must agree to sing each day until you leave us. That will be another very sad day for me."

Gaelen stood frozen until Fima, who stood beside her, spoke softly under his breath. "Take his gift, Gaelen. Take it with grace and humility, as I know you can. What he gives you is of great worth—and I am not referring to the ring."

Gaelen approached the King, bowed low, and reached out to take the ring. It would just fit on her largest finger, the middle one, and she smiled. It was very beautiful.

"The generosity and wisdom of the Tuathar are unrivaled among men," she said. "You have the deepest thanks from a humble singer, and the promise that I shall sing each day." Then she stepped back, lifting her eyes to meet his. Should an enemy threaten Dûn Bennas, she would die to protect it.

It was not usual for Gaelen to be late for anything. She was often early, in fact. Elves were courteous folk, and it was thus unacceptable to keep anyone waiting without very good cause. In the case of Gaelen, this tendency to be early often degenerated into impatience, as she might think that everyone else could be expected to be early as well. She sometimes became exasperated with Rogond, who was quite often late. He was not as adept at diverting his energies into many different tasks at once, and would get distracted by one of them. Gaelen did not see that as an excuse and, depending on her mood, might treat him with a sort of offended disdain for several minutes. This was not typical of her kind—Gaelen was an impatient Elf. Now she was the offending party, and she was not happy about it.

She ran though the stone corridors as fast as she could, for she was already late for a meeting that she herself had called. When she finally reached the Halls of Learning and Lore, making far more clamor than usual, she was stopped in her tracks by the sound of a deep, booming voice filled with reprimand.

"*Who disturbs my learned realm?*" it said, startling Gaelen, who turned to behold a tall, shadowy figure barely visible in a darkened doorway.

"Ummm…I do?"

Astor the Chief Lore-master, emerged from the doorway so that Gaelen could see him. "You're *late*, my noisy friend."

"I'm sorry…" Her ears turned red; she had never been called "noisy" before in her life.

Astor smiled his familiar chilly smile. "It's very good to see you, despite your tardiness. Come then, and join us. Fima and I have been waiting."

Astor, Gaelen, and Fima spent the rest of the afternoon examining Gaelen's parchment, and speculating as to the nature of Orrion and his connection with Gorgon Elfhunter. Astor would leave from time to time, returning with books and manuscripts as he deemed appropriate. Yet there was little to be found within that would truly confirm any of their suspicions.

At last, Astor closed one old and mighty volume, looking Gaelen hard in the eye. "You must describe Orrion to me in every detail. There may be something of significance that you have not told us. Please, little apprentice, think hard now. Close your eyes and recall him down to the last hair on his arm."

Gaelen did as she was asked, closing her eyes and taking a deep breath. She was a very observant and discerning person under normal circumstances, but in this case she had nearly been overcome, and it was difficult for her to recall anything but the evil in Orrion's eyes and the stench of Gorgon. "All right," she said at last. "I see him in my mind's eye. What now?"

"Just start describing everything you see. Ramble as much as you like. Leave out nothing that comes into your mind."

"I'm trying…but I cannot get past the eyes…and the terrible power I saw in them."

"Do not look at them," said Astor. "Blank them out if you can. The eyes are taking your mind from your task. Look instead at the rest of him now. You can do it."

Gaelen drew a deep, sighing breath. "He was beautiful, I know that," she said in a soft, drifting voice. "If not for the eyes, the rest is quite beautiful. He is tall…very, very tall. Golden armor…it has seen battle. He has golden hair, long and silken, like Nelwyn's…only with just a hint of curl.

"Gorgon also has golden hair," said Fima.

"No…his hair is paler…this was like Nelwyn's."

"The armor, Gaelen, was there any device upon it?" asked Fima.

"No…wait! There is no device upon the armor, but there is something there. It hangs around his neck, and is golden…it is some sort of amulet. It's golden, like the rest of him."

Astor had galvanized in his seat and was now leaning toward her, his entire body tense as he asked the next question. "Was there a bright stone in the center?"

"Not bright…it is deep, and golden. Yet it flashes in the fire-light." Gaelen's brow furrowed as she concentrated for a long moment. Suddenly she went pale, and all the strength left her body. "Oh…my…" she said, just before collapsing in a dead faint, sagging sideways and sliding to the floor.

"Gaelen…? *Gaelen*!" cried Fima, leaping up to aid her. He rounded on Astor. "What have you done to her?"

"I have done nothing, Lore-master. Calm yourself. She has been so intent on remembering that she has forgotten to breathe, nothing more. And I think what she has just revealed will silence any doubt I have held up to this moment." He turned to one of his reference books and began to thumb through it with great care, his white-gloved fingers caressing the pages like old friends.

Fima went to aid Gaelen, who was beginning to stir. Astor was right; she had been holding her breath. But that was not the only source of her distress. When she focused upon the amulet, she sensed the power within it, and that power could now only be used in Darkness. That Darkness had taken the light from her eyes. She moaned in pain and confusion; she had bruised herself upon the stone floor, and she did not remember where she was for a moment.

"There, there," said Fima as he patted her shoulder. He was not comfortable touching her without leave.

The color came back into Gaelen's cheeks and she roused herself, recovering her wits as she and Fima rejoined Astor at the table.

"Did you learn anything of value?" she asked Astor, who was still studying the pages of the book. He turned it so that she could see an old engraving of what appeared to be an exact copy of Orrion's amulet, inscribed in a tongue she did not know. She started to reach out to it, but drew her hand back, looking up at Astor and nodding. At last he closed the book.

"You were right, Gaelen," he said. "Lord Kotos the Deceiver has walked upon your path." Both Gaelen and Fima went pale.

"The *amulet?* Of course! I saw it, peeking out from his tunic. We all saw it! Why did I not remember it until now?" said Fima, bringing his stout fist down upon the table in frustration.

"It carries a power that allows it to be noticed…or not," said Astor. "If Lord Kotos wills it, the amulet can be so noticeable that it overcomes the beholder with desire for it, or, as in this case, it can appear to be nothing of consequence." He shook his head. "Léiras and Dardis knew what they were doing when they crafted it, but they never considered that their work could be turned to such dark purposes. How regrettably short-sighted of them."

He reached out to Gaelen and turned her left hand, observing the ring Hearndin had given her. A beautiful red ruby in the shape of a cat's eye glowed from a setting of woven gold. "That is a fire-stone. How very appropriate. Well done, and well-remembered, Gaelen Taldin. Lord Kotos has been unmasked."

"So…we can trust nothing we have seen or heard while he was near," said Gaelen. "And Nelwyn's vision, I believe, was planted by the Deceiver to manipulate the Company. The question is…in what manner, and to what end?"

"We must ask Nelwyn to describe her vision again, and to leave out no detail," said Astor.

"But we must not tell her why," said Gaelen. "The knowledge will unbalance her! I want to wait until we are in Tal-sithian. Lady Arialde will be able to aid Nelwyn when the truth becomes known.

"I will simply tell her that I wish to record every detail of her premonition for historical value," said Astor. "It is true, after all."

"The important thing is that we will not be the agents of deceit that bring about the downfall of the Lake-realm, or whatever other dark purpose Kotos had in mind," said Gaelen. "From this moment,

I must guard my thoughts. I do not wish to alert Gorgon that I have seen through his disguise."

"Indeed not," said Fima. "Gaelen, how do you know that Nelwyn's vision came from Orrion? Did she tell you he was there?"

"No, but she did not need to," Gaelen replied. "She smelled of oranges."

Although this last comment made no sense to Astor, it was not confusing at all to Fima, who smiled and nodded back at her.

It took Gaelen several days to adjust to the impact of the knowledge she had gained. She replayed her entire association with Orrion over and over, shuddering at the thought of his walking among the good people of Dûn Arian without suspicion, cursing herself for not seeing through her enemy's veil of lies. It didn't matter that the most powerful Light-bearers had been deceived by Lord Kotos—she was a hunter-scout, and she had failed to recognize an enemy. Everything made sense…and nothing made sense.

The turmoil never left her mind, except during her daily performances for the King. She did not allow any unsettling thoughts to invade the clear, rich perfection of her voice. Citizens, soldiers, and guards alike paused in their labors and turned their attention to the song that swelled forth from the Great Hall. Gaelen's voice was arguably the greatest of all her gifts. It would be awhile before any of the local minstrels would dare perform again.

On one dark night, she stood again upon the flat-topped observation tower, as the wind rose about her and the lightning flashed in the eastern sky. She did not like storms that blew from the east, as they were often violent and destructive. The east wind was wild, the eastern blizzards fierce, and the eastern rains lashed cold and hard. Even Gaelen did not understand what had compelled her to stand upon this wild and dangerous vantage point.

She saw Rogond making his way through the streets below, no doubt trying to find her, for the storm would be a bad one and he would want her to shelter with him. Just as she turned to go, a jagged bolt of lightning struck so near to where she was standing that it knocked her from her feet. She fell back, senseless, striking her head on the stone floor, blinded and deafened by the blast.

The voice and face of Orrion appeared in her mind's eye, but the voice did not sound the same as it had before. It was deeper and more malicious, and it terrified her. It did not growl like Gorgon… it was horrible! This was the voice of Kotos as she had heard it in the Queen's tent, when he held no concerns about concealing his true nature.

You think to defeat me? I am more powerful than your mind can even imagine! You are by far the most foolish soul I have ever met, you pathetic Sylvan weakling. Your people have no power over me—I ruined the Èolar long ago. I killed Ri-Aldamar, and Dardis, and by my hand the greatest realm of Alterra was destroyed. Do not think to set yourself against me. You will not survive!

Gaelen was nearly overcome with terror, but she swallowed hard. She would not—*could* not—back down.

You rule only through deceit! I have unmasked you. Whatever plan you held will not work now. Go back to wherever it is you came from, only leave Gorgon behind. I have not yet finished with him!

Kotos' laughter rang in her mind—the most horrible laughter she had ever heard. As she looked for the last time upon his face, it changed and twisted into the apparition of Gelmyr, long dead as she had seen him before. The apparition laughed, too.

I were you, I would not keep this knowledge to myself, it said. *Something bad might happen. It's a long way to Tal-sithian!*

Gaelen awoke with Gelmyr's laughter ringing in her ears, such that she could not hear the anxious voice of Rogond, who had found her at last.

She would not speak of her vision, as she did not wish to frighten Fima, who would no doubt wonder if Kotos had actually appeared in it. If that had been true, the plan already forming in Gaelen's mind would have to change. But when she looked deep within herself, she knew that the image and voice had come from her own imagining of Kotos, and not from any actual visitation by him. As for the image of Gelmyr, she knew where that had originated as well. It was the voice of her own fears, warning her. She decided to take the warning, asking that Rogond and Galador come to counsel with her that very afternoon.

She explained the entire situation to them after first exacting the promise of strict confidence. After hearing of it, both were distressed—Galador feared for Nelwyn, and Rogond for Gaelen. They also feared for the future of the Light.

Gaelen reassured them. "As with Gorgon's mirror, we now have knowledge of our enemies, and they do not realize it. With this knowledge, I believe we may defeat them both. Kotos can only prevail if we are deceived."

"What must now be done?" asked Galador. "It would seem that Kotos was trying to lead us into some action, so that Wrothgar would profit from it. What action, and to what end?"

"I have some thoughts on that," said Gaelen, "and so does Fima. Yet I believe I will put that question before Arialde when we get to Tal-sithian. One thing is certain—the end concerns the Stone of Léir."

"I don't even want to imagine what Wrothgar could do with the Stone at his command," said Rogond.

"We do not need to imagine it...Nelwyn has seen it," said Galador, shuddering with indignation at this dreadful invasion of his beloved.

"Do you both see now why we must not reveal our insights?" said Gaelen. "We must continue as we have been, as though we still believe everything Nelwyn foretold. This will be hardest for her to bear once the truth becomes known. When we arrive in Tal-sithian, all will be set right, and a wise plan can be made. Lord Kotos must not know of our insight until the time is right, nor must his servant, Gorgon Elfhunter."

She frowned and shook her head. "I must say, it surprises me to learn of Gorgon's complicity with Kotos. I had not thought him willing to be led by anyone. Kotos must have ensnared him with dark promises such that he cannot escape."

"Perhaps he has simply been overtaken, or threatened with death," said Rogond. "There may have been no complicity."

Gaelen shook her head. "No...he is a willing part of the plan. Don't ask me how I know it, but he has been convinced to go along with it somehow."

"Proof, if any were needed, that everything has its price," said Galador. "I'll warrant Kotos convinced Gorgon that this is the only way to defeat his mortal enemy, the very perceptive and admirably ferocious Gaelen of the Greatwood."

"Do not jest about it," said Gaelen.

"I was not jesting," said Galador. "I am quite serious."

"Probably the most serious person I've ever met," said Gaelen, and her somber expression was broken for the first time that day by the hint of a smile. "At least now there are four of us to carry the knowledge to Tal-sithian. It's less likely that four will fall than two."

"I am not expecting *any* of us to fall!" said Rogond.

"Nor am I," said Gaelen. "Wrothgar has no doubt ordered his minions to stay away from our path. After all, if we are taken, his delicate plan will collapse. A lot of effort for nothing…that would not sound pleasing to the Dark Powers. Yet there are perils other than Ulcas and Trolls. I still feel safer sharing these revelations."

"That's true," said Galador. "Your clumsy horse could trip and fall on you. And if he is passing too near to Eros, he might knock Fima from the saddle and trample him in confusion. Rogond might also be lost if Eros cannot keep his feet. Therefore, I believe I shall keep my distance from all of you."

Gaelen turned to Rogond. "He's just so appealing when he tries to be humorous, isn't he?" She was weary; it showed in her face as she sank back down upon the soft cushions that had been laid before the fire.

Rogond looked over at Galador, who, realizing that his presence was no longer required, bowed and took his leave. Rogond sat beside Gaelen, taking her into his arms, enfolding her in warmth and comforting strength. Then he told her the tale of a famous battle between the mariners of Tallasiar and the Corsairs of Fómor, delighting her beyond measure.

Gorgon had discovered a comfortable hole in which he could shelter from the rains and the wind while he waited for the Company to depart from Dûn Bennas. The raven, bearing Lord Kotos, went forth every few days, flying straight to the stables. As long as the horses remained, so did the Company. The bird managed to steal an occasional treat for Gorgon, be it a loaf of bread, a small sack of sweets, or even a nice bit of roasted meat. On this occasion it brought him a savory, herb-stuffed roasted pigeon that disappeared in three bites, bones and all.

"I see you have chosen to forego your newly-acquired table manners," said Kotos, frowning at Gorgon from within the amulet. "How easy it is to slip back into old habits. Just try not to forget them completely, will you? It's just possible that Orrion may need to make another convincing appearance."

"Oh, be quiet!" snarled Gorgon. "If you're unhappy with my table manners, then perhaps you should turn your attention elsewhere. That would not disappoint me."

"Or perhaps I should forego the courtesy of delivering food to your waiting mouth," said Kotos with a sneer. "That would not disappoint me."

"That would suit me just fine," said Gorgon, and he meant it. "Save your offerings for the raven. It appreciates them more than I do. I would rather eat raw, cold flesh, or nothing at all, than put up with your all-consuming arrogance."

"I thought I made it clear that you were to maintain respect in my presence?" said Kotos with a menacing look at Gorgon.

"You know, I was just thinking," said Gorgon as if to no one in particular. "My desire is a simple one…to take down Gaelen Taldin, together with as many of the Elves as I can manage. I know where she is, and I know where she is going. I could get to her with no difficulty. Some Dark Asarla believes he can control my actions through threats of force, pain, whatever…but if he could hear me now, I would tell him that he's wrong about that. The only way to ensure my cooperation is with promise of reward. Perhaps he would do better to remind me of the reward he has already promised, as I might *forget.* That would be so much more effective than threats."

Kotos could no longer be seen in the amulet, except as an inky cloud of annoyance. Finally, a voice came forth from it. "Speaking of all-consuming arrogance, it is an amazing coincidence that I happen to be thinking very similar thoughts, except that *my* thoughts have run a slightly different course. I was thinking that a certain mighty and intelligent Elfhunter, whose all-encompassing desire is to slay Elves, would not allow his woeful lack of respect to jeopardize the realization of that desire. It would seem a small price to pay. Such a pity that foolish pride, the hallmark of the Elves, will allow them to live on."

Gorgon did not answer, but growled and rumbled deep down in his cavernous chest. Kotos knew his point had been taken, but begrudgingly. *I hope we don't spend too long in waiting, as it allows Gorgon far too much time to consider things. It won't do for him to get too deep into his own thoughts.* Kotos gave a figurative sigh. Gorgon was without doubt the most difficult host he had ever encountered.

Despite mild protest from Nelwyn, the Company lingered for a few more weeks until the worst of the spring storms had passed. There was sense in waiting, as very stormy weather would slow their progress. They would make better time under the sun. They took their leave, having said their farewells to the King, to Astor, and to others in the City whom they had befriended. The Captain of the Guard, a tall, barrel-chested man named Cronar, expressed special regret at their departure, for Azori had regaled the guardsmen each night with tales of his own nefarious exploits in the south.

Of particular note was a very bawdy and now-infamous incident in a tavern known as *The Skulking Raven*, which had resulted in Azori's band being driven out of Castalan. Azori imagined that the Shade of his lost brother Azok sat at his right hand, laughing along with him, whenever he told that story. Azok had played a prominent role in it.

Gaelen very much regretted leaving Astor, for she admired him almost as much as she admired Fima. She would also miss King Hearndin, for he was just and wise, and she had grown fond of him. But her deepest and most painful regret was that Thorndil had ever left the City.

If only he had stayed here...he could have met us as we returned to share friendship and tales. She remembered him raising his arm in farewell as he stood upon the south tower that now bore his name. It was her last sight of him as a living man. Judging by the somber faces of her friends as they rode beside her, Gaelen knew that her thoughts of Thorndil were shared.

They headed north and east along the riverbank just after sunrise. The horses settled to their task, all except Toran, who played about, pretending to shy at nothing as an excuse to snort and leap forward. Gaelen was accustomed to his antics by now, and did not allow him to bait her. When they stopped to rest, she took away his good humor by allowing him only a small amount of the new grass. She fastened a leather muzzle to his head-collar that only allowed him to pick a few blades here and there. Each of the horses had been fitted with one.

"Stop your complaining," said Rogond, taking note of Eros' particularly disgusted expression. "Would you rather I allow you to give yourself a belly-ache? In a few days you will be used to this forage, and you will not need to wear the muzzle…at least, not all the time."

Eros glared at Rogond's back. He loved spring grass—sweet, tender, and green. He did not see the sense in anyone's preventing him from eating it. After carefully placing his foot on the very edge of the leather muzzle, Eros set his strong neck and threw his head in the air. The leather gave just enough that Eros' nose and upper jaw slipped around it. The edge of the muzzle was now wedged against his lower lip, producing a permanent "smile." Eros did not care how silly he looked—he had accomplished his primary objective, and was now free to eat the grass. The irritating muzzle rubbed his lip, but that was a small price to pay for victory.

Three days after they had gone, the raven noticed that the horses were no longer in the stable. It flew back to Gorgon's shelter with the news that the Company had departed. "Now we should make our way to the lands north of the Linnefionn," said Kotos. "We have plenty of time, as our enemies will linger for a while in deciding their course. Elves never decide anything without endless debate and discussion."

"We dare not come too close," said Gorgon. "I am known to them. I slew a large number of the Elves of Tal-sithian the last time

I encountered them, and they will not have forgotten it. The Vixen told me that the Elf-realms have been warned of me, and I believe her."

"Do not fear," said Kotos, "although I face the same constraints. I cannot venture too near the Island of Tal-sithian, even carried on wings. Arialde will recognize her beloved brother, no matter the disguise. Yet we will prevail, for the raven will fly through the lands north of the Lake. If our plan works, the Elves will try to move the Stone. When they do, Lord Wrothgar will have them. Once He gains possession of the Stone, all will be well for us."

"But how do you know where they will take it?" asked Gorgon. "The Linnefionn is a large lake. They could slip away from us."

"I have a fair notion ," said Kotos. "I know how Arialde's mind works. We should also expect to see some of the Elves making their way to Mountain-home. They will want to verify the massing of forces in the Fell-ruin, and they will want to alert Ordath."

"*What* massing of forces in the Fell-ruin?" said Gorgon. "Any massing would be done in the Darkmere, I expect. The Lord Wrothgar calls from Tûr Dorcha, not from the Fell-ruin."

"I assure you that the Stone will not go anywhere near Tûr Dorcha. You cannot understand, as you were not privy to the vision I implanted in Nelwyn's mind," said Kotos. "Again, you must trust me."

The journey to Tal-sithian was not eventful, except for one fine afternoon when it seemed that the question of who was the swifter of the grey stallions would finally be settled. The Company had been averaging between twenty and thirty miles a day, which is a sensible pace if one wishes to undertake a journey of nearly six hundred miles with no significant interruptions. This pace allowed them to rest between twilight and dawn, and to stop and rest during the day as required. The turf was fine and springy, but there were also long stretches of lowland that had been turned to mud by the rains, and these made for slower going.

Réalta and Toran found that they were once again trotting stride-for-stride, and this time the challenge could not be denied.

Keep to your place behind me, said Réalta, lifting his nose into the air.

I will not, said Toran, extending his stride. *Who says it is your place to lead?*

I have always done so, and the High-elf says it, said Réalta.

And who is the High-elf to say it? The Soft-singer commands me, and she does not mind if I lead. I will not back off just because you say so. Toran had grown weary of Réalta's insecurities.

Soft-singer chose me, *and not you, when it mattered, you foolish animal. You think to outrun me? You had just better think again*, said Réalta, snorting and shaking his head, his ears laid back.

We have been here before, I believe, and we were never given the chance to prove who is right, said Toran. *Well, now let us just settle this question, shall we?*

I see there are no stones to trip you up this time, said Réalta. *Yet I must not go against the will of the High-elf. I may only run if he commands it.* Both horses had been increasing their speed a little at a time, and they were already cantering.

I have an answer for that, said Toran. *Oh…my! Is that a shrubbery? It looks rather like a crouching beast! Oh dear, oh dear!* He leaped forward in mock terror as Gaelen grabbed his mane. In another heartbeat, both horses were away. Despite the soft turf, their feet thundered in an all-out effort to prevail. Toran was not as motivated as Réalta, for he was younger and less prideful, but having taken the challenge he would give it his best. Réalta had far more to lose. The older horse had always been swiftest and most beautiful, in his opinion, and he would not lose his place to this young, ridiculous upstart! Only the swiftest horse was fit to bear Galador.

They ran headlong, nose to nose, as their riders gave up trying to rein them in. "It would seem that we are in the midst of a horse race," called Galador.

"I'm ready if you are," Gaelen yelled back. It was hard to hear through the wind in her ears and the pounding of Toran's feet. She crouched low over his neck and pulled her knees up, balancing upon her lower thighs and lifting her seat from Toran's back so that she was nearly flattened. This streamlining was helpful, and Toran inched ahead. Réalta answered him at once. He would run himself to death rather than allow Toran to best him, and his speed was nearly unrivaled. It was the very reason Galador had chosen him, apart from his looks. Réalta was taller, and his legs were longer and more slender. Toran did not stand quite as tall, but he had more power and thrust in his hindquarters. This power made for a stride that matched his taller adversary.

In the end, there was no clear winner. Galador and Gaelen had set a finish to the race between two small trees, and the horses crossed it in nearly the same exact moment. Gaelen found that Toran was easy to rein in then, as he was glad for the contest to end. Réalta was not so easily convinced, for he wanted to best Toran, not match him. At last Galador cantered back to Gaelen, who had already dismounted and was checking Toran's feet in case he had picked up a small stone.

"I suppose now the question is settled," she said. "They crossed the finish together. Toran is just as swift as Réalta! I suppose he has to have some attribute that makes up for the foolishness of youth." She was proud of her horse.

"I don't think so," said Galador, patting Réalta. "Remember, Gaelen, Réalta carried twice the weight. He is still the swiftest horse in the Company. Aren't you, my beauty?"

"Never mind, Toran," said Gaelen. "Galador is right. And being almost as swift as Réalta is still impressive."

"He does have an attribute that makes up for his foolishness, Gaelen," said Galador, who would not look at her. "He has the better rider." He left her to stare at his back before she could reply, knowing that it was probably the first time he had ever given her such a heartfelt compliment. It took a few minutes for the red to fade from her ears, and from his.

16
The Secret Council

The Company finally approached the Lake-realm with mixed emotions—anticipation, apprehension, uncertainty, dread, relief…

Nelwyn hoped for healing, though she dreaded speaking of her visions to Lady Arialde, as she would need to recall them in detail. They still tormented her, especially when the moon was full. But she was most thankful to find the Lake and its environs peaceful and calm—no Darkness had yet come there.

As they made camp on the cloud-shrouded shores, Carmyn and Estle approached Nelwyn, who stood lost in thought, wrapped in her cloak against the chilly morning air.

"Forgive us for disturbing you," said Carmyn, "but we are wondering…how will the Lady know we are here? Do we need to light a signal fire, or something?"

Nelwyn shook her head. "She is aware of us…she has told me so." She drew a long, deep sigh. "A great weight has been lifted from my spirit…I was so afraid that we would arrive too late."

At that moment, Gaelen appeared from out of the mist. "Here's something to lift your spirits even more! I have just seen the most amazing sight…I have seen these folk only twice before, as they do not dwell in the northern Greatwood. It has been long since I heard any rumor or news of them. You must come with me and meet them! The rest of the Company is there already." She mouthed a single word to Nelwyn, whose eyes grew wide with surprise and delight.

Gaelen took her friends north to a point on the rocky shoreline where the Company had assembled, and called out to the misty waters:

"Heralds and Messengers of the Lady, our Company has now gathered. Please come forth that we may welcome whatever news you bring."

The steel-grey waters rippled and roiled as several large, dark, otter-like shapes glided and turned beneath the surface, occasionally flashing bright white undersides. They swam with no effort, swift and graceful, completely at home.

"What *are* they?" whispered Estle, who had spent very little time around any water-dwellers. She edged a little closer to Hallagond as about a dozen bright-eyed faces popped up above the surface at once. They were the color of ivory, with pale blue eyes and gleaming white smiles. All at once, they began to laugh.

"They're Currgas," said Gaelen. "They are among the most secretive people in all of Alterra. Yet they are peaceful, and never mean any harm to anyone. Nelwyn and I have seen them before, but not in the Lake. Usually they are river-folk. I hope they have not been driven forth from the southern Dominglas. That would mean the river has been darkened." Her eyebrows knitted together for a moment...this thought was just too close to home.

The Currgas emerged reluctantly from the water, for they spent nearly all of their time there. They dwelled in expertly-concealed burrows along the banks of the Dominglas River in the south of the Greatwood. Never many in number, their lives were inclined to be short and hazardous. Yet they were stubborn in their good humor, refusing to see anything but the best in almost any situation.

"What in heaven's name are they?" whispered Azori.

"It is said that they are Children of Men," replied Fima. "They took to the water long, long ago—during the Time of Mystery—and their choice has shaped them ever after."

Indeed, the River had shaped the Currgas. Small in stature, only a hair taller than Fima, they carried a nice layer of fat to keep them from cold and aid them in gliding smoothly through the water with little effort. Hence their contours were soft and rounded. Their short, powerful arms and legs were streamlined, with large, webbed hands and feet, yet their thumbs and index fingers were separated enough to allow them to manipulate things with clever dexterity. The palms of their hands were studded with tiny growths—hard, sharp, and directed backwards—designed to aid them in grasping and holding fish and other water creatures.

Their coloring was perhaps the most striking and remarkable aspect. They had taken the example of most water-dwellers, becoming quite pale on their undersides while their backs were very dark. Their hair , cropped shorter than Gaelen's, was snowy-white as it framed their faces, turning abruptly dark behind as though someone had painted them. Their entire bodies were covered with very thick, soft hair which they could raise and lower at will. Now that they were out on the bank they shook off the water, raising their hair for warmth. This included the hair on their heads, which stood up in damp spikes such that they rather resembled hedgehogs.

They were beautiful, gentle people, and it showed in their faces. They did occasionally get into mischief. More than one fisherman's boat had been overturned by groups of young, playful Currgas, yet no harm would ever come to the fisherman. They wore very little clothing, wrapping their loins with black and white cloth that did nothing to break their unique coloring. Males were distinguishable from females by long white mustaches, the lack of very small breasts, and slightly deeper voices.

"Why are they colored like that?" asked Estle, whose experience with water creatures was understandably limited.

"If you look down upon the water from above, all is dark," said Nelwyn, "yet from below, the surface is very bright. The Currgas cannot be easily observed, either from above or from beneath. They must be able to remain unseen by the fishes they prey upon."

"Hail, Wayfarers," said one of the larger males. "The Lady sent us to welcome you and allay your fears. A boat is being brought up even now to conduct you." He bowed low before them, eliciting quiet laughter from his companions. "My name is Collyn, and this is my mate, Gin-gin." He indicated a pretty female at his right, who smiled and bowed. Again, all the Currgas smiled and chuckled to no one in particular.

Galador bowed in return. "We are honored by your presence," he said.

This elicited outright laughter from the Currgas, who thought it uproarious that anyone would be honored to be in their presence. Galador's ears reddened, though he smiled in spite of himself.

Gaelen stepped forward and did not bow. Instead, she smiled a very warm smile and extended both of her hands, palms upward. "I'm Gaelen, of the northern forest realm, and I thank you for your message. Will you share our fire…and our food…while we wait?

This invitation was irresistible to the Currgas, who shook more water from their bodies and approached Gaelen as though inviting her to lead them. It was surprising how ungainly they were on land, displaying a peculiar, waddling gait made even odder by the large, webbed hands swinging to and fro as though for balance.

They stayed always within sight of the water's edge. Should enemies threaten, they would move with incredible quickness, disappearing below the surface in the blink of an eye.

Gaelen built up the fire so that the new, larger group could warm themselves. Then Nelwyn and Rogond broke into the last of the stores brought from Dûn Bennas. The Currgas had been enjoying the hospitality of Tal-sithian, but they preferred the food of men to that of Elves. They relished the heavy molasses bread and the wonderful spiced dried meat. They loved salty things, and spicy things, and sweets above all. Such delicacies were rare along the riverbank.

Currgas sometimes stole into the encampments of men, taking what food they desired, but they always left fresh fish and shellfish in place of what they had taken. Sometimes, their kind hearts would cause them to leave fish even when the travelers had nothing they wanted, if said travelers were low on provisions. No folk of good will would starve to death on their watch.

Rogond made a permanent friend of them when he offered a small phial of strong lemon juice. He had brought it from Dûn Bennas to prevent the ailments that come to men when they do not eat properly—it kept nearly forever so long as it did not get too warm. While there were fruits in Tal-sithian, this juice was aged, and it was stronger and more flavorful. Collyn took it with reverence. It would taste so much better than the dried rose-fruits he was accustomed to eating.

The horses snorted and backed away from the Currgas at first, for horses do not care for anything unfamiliar until it is proven harmless. The Currgas, likewise, were somewhat fearful of the horses and their hard, trampling feet. Yet trust and inherent friendliness won out on both sides.

Ever-curious, Toran actually approached Gin-gin as she sat by the fire. He snorted and blew her hair forward, startling them both, then ran backward in an awkward manner. He was so comical that everyone chuckled at him, including Gin-gin.

"Forgive my impertinence," said Gaelen after everyone had finished eating. "How came you to the Lake? My heart is filled with some dread, as I have not known you to venture from the southern riverbank. I hope...I hope all is well there." The Currgas became very quiet then, and for the first time the light of their good humor was dimmed. "I'm sorry," said Gaelen. "I did not mean to bring up bad memories."

"We don't blame you, Dweller of the Northern Forest," said Collyn. "The Evil of the Laban Fuath has spread to the River...the power of the Elves can no longer contain it."

Gaelen knew what Collyn referred to. The Laban Fuath, a most horrible bog that surrounded Tûr Dorcha, had been growing in size for over five hundred years. It had invaded the southern regions of the cold stream known as the Brunner Ia, but it had stopped short of the River Dominglas until now. Gaelen and Nelwyn hung their heads in sorrow. This did not bode well for the realm of Ri-Aruin—the Dominglas ran right through the King's fortress to the north.

"A curse on Lord Wrothgar and all who serve him," muttered Gaelen. This sentiment was shared by all. The Currgas told their tale, though it pained them. When the bog spread to the river, evil creatures came with it. The fish became unwholesome and unfit to eat, and the terrible Úlfar were everywhere.

"We had to leave, or face starvation and death," said Collyn. "The Lady called to us and we came here, though it was no easy task for us to journey so far. Yet there are those of our race who made their way to other lands farther away than this. Whether they were successful, none here can say."

"The boats are approaching," said Galador, as three long, grey boats appeared in the mist just before putting to shore.

Each boat contained at least three of the Elves of Tal-sithian. After the pleasant, cheerful Currgas, they looked rather grim. They disembarked, approaching the Company and bowing.

"We are here to conduct you to the Lady," said one. "Please make ready, for she is waiting." They were obviously in no mood for pleasantries as they gathered the horses and began packing the Company's belongings into the boats. One of the Elves grabbed the pack containing the fire-cloak. Gaelen took exception, throwing one of her leaf-shaped blades into the soil a hair's breadth from his right foot.

"Now that I have your attention, I would ask you to put my pack down," she said. "No one handles that pack without my leave, begging your pardon." The Elves of Tal-sithian paused in their labors to stare curiously at her, wondering whether she should be taken seriously.

"If I were you," said Fima with a smile, "I would remove any doubt from my mind, bow respectfully, and replace that pack where I had found it."

"Would you do me harm, Gaelen Taldin?" said the Elf who held the pack.

"Of course not," said Gaelen. "I'm sure the Lady didn't mean for you to invade our encampment and lay hold of our belongings without leave or explanation. I'm sure you simply forgot yourselves for a moment." She drew herself up, lifting her chin as though challenging the offender to disagree. The word that came at once to everyone's mind was "regal." It was enough to chagrin the Elves of Tal-sithian, who allowed the Company to gather and stow their own things thenceforward.

"By your leave, we will take your animals around to the western grasslands, the Falad Capell, where they may keep company with our own horses. They will be safer that way," said a very tall, golden-haired Elf named Aldor. "You should proceed to Tal-sithan at once. We will conduct you, and your new friends the Currgas may escort us, if they are willing."

But Collyn shook his head. "That is a long, hard swim," he said. "We will rejoin you, but we intend to take our time about doing it. We do not travel across so much open water in haste. Farewell for now!"

He signaled to the others, who rose to their feet and made straight for the water. They slipped in, hardly disturbing the glass-like surface, and disappeared. In a few moments Nelwyn spotted them, floating on their backs, looking like so many long, bright dots in the distant mist. She could hear their merry voices and their laughter. She wished for just a moment that Collyn had climbed into the boat, instead of the grim-faced Elf who now sat at the tiller.

It took several hours to reach the island, but once they made their way through the clouds and mist the journey was sunny and pleasant. Gaelen amused herself with staring into the deep blue water. It fascinated her, though she was a little fearful of it. She had no knowledge of the creatures that dwelled below. The Great Seas were even worse—Gaelen had no desire to ever explore them.

In Dûn Arian, she had been told enough stories of deadly sea creatures to preclude her ever becoming a mariner. It was best to stay with things that were at least a little familiar. Yet she had enjoyed late nights on one of the long fishing-piers that extended out into the harbor, climbing down to the braces between the huge pilings and hanging a lamp over the water. This brought a most intriguing array of living things to her curious eyes. Their variation in form, color, and size was astonishing, and she learned to bait them even closer by dropping bits of food. Some of the small fishes would even leap from the water to grab them! She stopped this practice when, one very dark night, a great fish appeared out of nowhere, leaped from the water, passing inches from her face, took one of the smaller fishes in mid-air, and came down again with a great "splash." It could easily have taken Gaelen herself, at least in her mind. She had seen the size of its teeth!

Lake-water creatures are not as colorful, and they do not occur in such variety, but at least there are very few that are threatening, thought Gaelen as she watched the little silvery fishes play beneath the boat.

"Don't lean over too far," said Aldor with a good-natured smile, "or the Guardians might decide to make a tiny meal of you."

"The Guardians?" said Gaelen, sitting quite respectfully upright again.

"Huge creatures, kept by the Lady," said Aldor. They will attack and devour any evil creatures that sully these waters. They have existed since the dawn of time, and were once found in far greater numbers, but only a few remain. They are very large, and are said to be intelligent, but they're very secretive—even I have rarely encountered one, and I patrol these waters nearly every day.

I've heard them, though, especially at night. Impressive beasts, they are. Most impressive."

"Well, since I'm not an evil creature, I need not fear," said Gaelen, who immediately returned to searching beneath the waters, hoping for a glimpse of one of the Guardians.

At last the boat gained the shores of the Green Isle. In late spring it was spectacular—the heady fragrance of a thousand flowers greeted the Company as they approached. A welcoming party awaited their arrival, escorting them without delay to the dwelling-place of the Lady. Yet they did not stand before her immediately—they were allowed to rest and wash away the dust of the journey. Later they would be treated to a very fine meal.

"We will return and conduct you to the Lady when she requests it," said their escorts. "In the meantime, our home is yours. Please avail yourselves of any hospitality we may provide."

Carmyn, Estle, and Azori had not spoken a word since they had put ashore. The new-green beauty of Tal-sithian had mesmerized them. Estle, in particular, had done very little traveling in her life—the forests of Dûn Arian were the first she had ever seen—and the lush growth of the Island nearly overcame her senses. As much as she loved her beautiful desert, she could understand why a person would never leave such a magical place. She went in search of Nelwyn and found her lying in the grass by the veranda.

"Might I join you?"

"Of course," said Nelwyn. "I'm always glad of your company, yet you seem troubled. Surely you are not uneasy in this place. We are well protected here, at least for now."

"Actually, I was about to ask you the same thing," said Estle. "I sense disquiet in you."

Nelwyn looked up at the pale blue sky. "I must soon recount the tale of horror that was revealed to me, and I don't know what our course will be afterward. I don't even like to *remember* the vision, much less reveal it in detail. Yet I will do what I must…that's why we're here."

"I'm surprised your cousin is not here to comfort you," said Estle. "I haven't seen her since the departure of our escorts."

"Where is Rogond? She is most likely with him," said Nelwyn, unaware that her cousin was engaged in a far more serious pursuit.

Gaelen had gone to the glade where the Stone of Léir was kept, telling herself that she wanted to make certain it was still there. In truth, she had gone there for reasons that not even she could understand. She was no longer so foolish as to gaze into the Stone without leave—her last experience had taught her that terrible lesson—but she crouched down upon the cold stone of the courtyard, blending at once into the fragrant cedars surrounding it. There she sat in long reflection, silent and mysterious as the Stone itself, trying to arrange her thoughts and feelings into some sort of sensible order.

"What is the meaning of all of this?" she whispered, knowing that Lord Shandor would not hear. "I hope you can aid us in telling what is true, and what is untrue. Kotos cannot prevail, not ever again. I pray that the Lady will hear me." Her eyes grew grim and sad. "I pray that Nelwyn will understand."

She sat in the glade for a long time, long enough that the Lady had dispatched messengers to locate her. At last she rose to her feet, knowing that she would gain no enlightenment in this place, and bowed to Lord Shandor before taking her leave. But she turned back toward the Stone, saying, "Such a pity that you have gone so deep within yourself. Your power could provide all the enlightenment we would need, if only you could find it again. Your enemy, Lord Kotos, still wields his power on the side of Darkness, yet you have turned to your own purposes, and you no longer defend what is good and true. The joy you find within the Stone is a lie—a shadow of the past—yet you place your own happiness above all else." She shook her head. "I never thought I would find a common ground between the mightiest of the Asari and Gorgon Elfhunter, yet love has made you both bitter…you because of love lost, and Gorgon because of love he was never given. In this moment, though I despise him, I hold Gorgon less to blame for his own fate than I hold you."

Shandor, of course, did not hear her, and would not have cared if he had.

Gaelen made her way back to the elegant marble dwelling upon the green hill. "There you are, at last!" said Rogond. "We have been waiting for you…we've been summoned. Where have you been?"

Before Gaelen could reply, Lady Arialde appeared in the doorway. "Please, come inside, all of you," she said. "Come in and be welcome!"

The Lady's well-appointed council-chambers were much larger than they appeared to be from without. Azori shook his head. No doubt he would see many unexplainable things in this strange place.

"Please be seated," said Arialde, indicating the beautifully carved chairs that had been set for the council. They were elegant and ornate, but Fima, for one, found them uncomfortable. He tried not to growl about it.

Arialde lit several tall candles of creamy-white wax, and their glow cast warm light upon the marble walls. "This is a secret council," she said. "Only the Company, Lord Airan, and I may remain."

As her attendants bowed and took their leave, Galador whispered to Rogond. "There will be many concerned voices speculating about this council in various parts of the Lake-realm tonight…"

"First, allow me to extend the warmest welcome, and to express my delight at seeing you again," said Arialde. "You have brought new friends with you, all stalwart and true, at least when they need to be."

She lifted her eyebrows at Azori, the only career criminal in the group, and he gave a small shrug of his shoulders, appearing to stare with mild interest at one of the veins in the marble wall. He was having some difficulty meeting her gaze. He had never been in the presence of such a powerful being, and he had never cared for persons of authority. Here was a person of authority whom he could not disrespect, and he was unsure of how to react.

"I see some changes have been made since last we met, Rogond Thaylon," Arialde continued. "It would seem that you have gained your heart's desire. And I rejoice that Lore-master Fima is still with you, as I'm sure he has been most useful in your quest. Galador's happiness and good humor have grown, and will continue to grow. I am also pleased to renew my acquaintance with our two hunter-scouts. Yet where is your friend Thorndil?"

Rogond rose to his feet. "I will tell our tale, but first allow me to introduce our new friends." Carmyn, Azori, Estle, and Hallagond each rose and bowed in turn.

Arialde smiled at Hallagond. "So, more than one desire has been gained, Rogond," she said. "Your brother cannot deny you. You have almost the same eyes...though his have seen sorrows you have not yet faced. Welcome, all of you. Now, gentle Thaylon, I would hear your tale."

Rogond told of the Company's adventures since they were last in Tal-sithian. Both Arialde and Lord Airan were intrigued, as were those in the Company who had not yet heard of the battle in the Barrens, or the quest for Hallagond. At last, Rogond spoke of the Scourge, of the dragon, and of the safeguarding of Dûn Arian.

When he told of the finding of Thorndil, Gaelen suddenly felt cold. She drew her knees up before her and placed her booted feet on the chair, wrapping both arms about her knees.

"So...the Elfhunter is still at large," said Arialde in a soft and solemn voice. "That is ill news, but not unexpected. My condolences go out to you for the fate of your friend. Thorndil was a fine man, and he did not deserve such a terrible ending."

"No one deserves it," said Gaelen in a quiet voice. There was silence in the chamber as she looked up and noticed all eyes turned toward her. She had not meant to be heard.

She looked up at Arialde. "Thorndil should have been defending Dûn Bennas, drinking hot mead with the King's guards and spending winter nights beside a warm fire. Yet he undertook a nearly impossible journey to follow his friends. I summoned Gorgon to follow me, and Thorndil walked right into his grasp. I have had some difficulty living with the result."

Arialde nodded, for she understood Gaelen's feeling. "Yet you should know that, had your friend Thorndil not made such a sacrifice, another would have been chosen. I should imagine that Gorgon might have crept into the City, taken one of your other friends, and done the same to him, or to her. Would you have felt any comfort in that? Gorgon is entirely to blame for his misdeeds, and your friend Thorndil was simply very, very unlucky. Remember, little fire-spirit, no one believes that Gorgon will be easily defeated. Your task has only begun, and more will die before it's finished."

By the time Rogond finished the tale, the shadows in the chamber had grown long with the onset of twilight.

Arialde rose to her feet again. "So…you are here to share a great vision, and you believe the fate of the Light hangs in the balance? Such revelations should be made when wits are sharp and all senses are in play. We should partake of a light meal first—a few of my guests are weary, I see."

She looked over at Fima, who was nearly paralyzed from sitting in the hard, ill-proportioned chair. "Let me see what I can do to aid you," she said. "Not all folk are made alike." She summoned her attendants, dismissing the Company so that they could stretch their legs, while her folk added extra cushions for the seat and the back of Fima's chair, setting a tall footstool before it. Now it would be quite comfortable.

Food had been set out, and soon most in the Company had refreshed themselves, yet none of the Elves would eat or drink. They were anticipating the recounting of Nelwyn's vision, and they were ill-at-ease.

"I will never get through this," said Nelwyn to Gaelen as they stood together in the doorway.

"You will," Gaelen replied, "because you know you must." She drew forth a small tin of dark honey from her vest and dipped two chunks of hard-crusted bread into it. "Here…eat this. It will lift your spirits," she said.

"I cannot eat anything just now," said Nelwyn.

"I insist! Trust me."

At last Nelwyn gave in, and as the dark, sweet honey flowed through her with comforting familiarity, she did relax a little. Yet when the council reconvened, she doubted that any amount of honey could quell her fears.

The telling of the vision to the Lady was one of the hardest tasks Nelwyn had yet faced. She was afraid that her words would be discounted, or that she would be thought foolish and delusional. Yet this vision had been different from any other in her experience—more vivid, more terrifying, and seemingly more real than any in the past. There were no mists or uncertainties surrounding it. Nelwyn believed that everything she had seen would happen if nothing prevented it, and she bared the innermost regions of her mind and heart.

She got through her task, setting her jaw and squaring her shoulders, leaving out no detail. By the time she had finished, she was flushed and exhausted. Her face then grew pale and she swayed as though she might sink down upon the marble floor. Galador leaped to her aid, guiding her back to sit beside him.

"Well done, beloved. Well done," he said. "Your part in this has now been fulfilled. Rest now, and let the Lady consider all she has heard." He looked up at Arialde's shocked, troubled face. "By your leave, I will take Nelwyn from this place so that she might rest. This has been a difficult task for her."

"No!" cried Nelwyn. "I won't leave until the Lady tells me her thoughts. I have just revealed foreknowledge that predicts the utter downfall of the Light! These images were so horrible and real that I have been afraid to recall them, and they torment me. I have been chosen to receive this warning, and I want to know the meaning of it, and what will be done." She looked into the wise, fathomless eyes of Arialde. "I…I want to know…everything you can tell me."

She turned to Galador. "I cannot leave others to debate my visions. The Lady's thoughts are more important to me than to anyone."

But in this, Nelwyn was incorrect. Gaelen, Rogond, and Fima were also most anxious to hear Arialde's response, for they, along with Galador, were reasonably certain of the sinister origin of Nelwyn's "vision."

"Regrettably, I shall need time to consider what I have heard," said Arialde.

"Well, don't consider for too long," muttered Estle. "We made our way here so that this horror could be prevented, and we have taken quite enough time already. It may be that the Dark Armies are preparing even now. I do hope they will not launch their first attack on Mountain-home while you Elves sit here and consider things."

"Surely you must know that such important matters cannot be decided immediately," said Arialde. "Now, let me attend to Nelwyn's request, won't you?" Estle's face flushed; she had not intended Arialde to hear her.

"It is clear from Nelwyn's vision that Lord Wrothgar intends to take the Stone of Léir," said the Lady. "Yet I have long known of his desire for it. We had not thought him strong enough to mount such an offensive. Why, now, should he choose to act?"

"He has deceived everyone into thinking he resides in the Fell-ruin," said Nelwyn. "Yet we believe he dwells in a terrible place known as Tûr Dorcha, in the south of the Darkmere. He would have you expect that he attacks from the north, and he knows you will send forces to aid Mountain-home. The Stone will reveal it—yet Lord Shandor will not uncover the most important part of Wrothgar's plan until too late. You will be overtaken, and the Stone will fall into his hands."

"Our course would seem obvious, then," said Lord Airan. "We must move the Stone to another place, where Lord Wrothgar will not discover it. It is lamentable that he knows of its whereabouts. How did he come by such knowledge, I wonder?"

"I believe he learned many things from Gorgon Elfhunter," said Gaelen. "Because I know of the Stone, so also does Gorgon, and now, regrettably, so does Wrothgar. I'm sorry to have been his vessel, more than any of you will ever comprehend."

Her voice was clear and strong, and there was no quaver of sorrow, no trepidation to be heard. "Despite Nelwyn's wishes, I must now urge you, Lady, to consider all things carefully before you decide your course. I believe it may not be as clear as might first be thought." Her bright eyes met those of the Lady, who perceived the difference in them.

You are stronger than when last we met, Gaelen Taldin. Your spirit is whole at last. A good thing, for I fear you will have great need of it. We shall counsel together, you and I.

Arialde stood tall upon her dais, a shining beacon of silver in the ever-darkening room, and spread both hands. Her expression was contemplative, eyes downcast. The candles flickered, sputtered, and went out, yet a divine glow emanated from her, bathing the room in soft, grey light. When at last she lifted her gaze, her inner light flared bright white for a moment so that she was difficult to look upon. The candles re-kindled and their warm golden light returned.

"Nelwyn has given us many things to consider, and this we shall do. I will consult the Stone and see what enlightenment it might provide—at a time of my own choosing. In the meantime, do not fear. No armies will be sent to Mountain-home as yet. The plan that was revealed in your vision will not succeed."

"But what if Wrothgar still tries to take the Stone? Can the Elves of Tal-sithian repel a full-scale attack?" asked Hallagond.

"I will not debate these matters now," said Arialde. "There are things that I must learn. Go now and replenish yourselves. We will meet again very soon. In the meantime, please avail yourselves of all hospitality. Rest well."

Her light faded as the candles went out once more. By the time Rogond had lit them again, the Lord and Lady were gone. Yet one more message had been revealed to Gaelen's inner sight: the Lady would meet her in the Courtyard of the Stone long before the sun rose in the morning.

Nelwyn confronted Gaelen as soon as they were out of sight of the Arialde's dwelling-place. "I saw you lock eyes with the Lady just before she left, and I saw you react to her. She spoke to you—I know it! What did she say?"

Gaelen looked away; she was not yet ready to deal with Nelwyn, and she could not lie to her. This only served to agitate Nelwyn further. "It's not enough that you called the clarity of my foresight into question, but now you conspire with Arialde to keep things from me? Why, in the name of heaven?"

Nelwyn's words stung Gaelen's ears, and she did not know how to respond to them. She would not lie to Nelwyn, yet she could not yet reveal the truth.

"You will need to trust me," was all that she could say at first. She looked up at Nelwyn, whose expression was torn, as she was both hurt and angry. "Remember that we have always protected each other, and that I love you, and trust that my motives are true. I cannot tell you what troubles me, only that the Lady sensed it. She has revealed nothing to me as yet. Please, Nelwyn, you must trust in me. I swear that I will reveal everything as soon as I can. For the moment, I cannot."

Nelwyn's eyes now held confusion as well as hurt. "I don't understand," she said. "If you held doubts, why have you kept them from me? You have never kept anything of importance from me before."

Gaelen sighed. "Do you love me, Nelwyn?"

"Such a question need never be asked, and you know it."

"Then trust me."

After a moment's pause, Nelwyn spoke again. "Very well, I will trust you. But I pray that you will enlighten me…I'm afraid." Then she turned and went in search of Galador.

Lord of Light help us all if I'm wrong, thought Gaelen, as she made her way to the Courtyard of the Stone.

No fire-flies hovered about the Stone of Léir that night. Lady Ariade stood alone before the crystal, which she had covered with a cloth of dark indigo. The moment Gaelen entered the Courtyard, a thick mist surrounded it that would allow no one else to intrude.

"We are alone, Gaelen, and none can see us or hear us," said Arialde. "Therefore, you may say whatever you will. Rest assured that I will carry no tales from this place." Gaelen nodded as she drew nearer to the Stone and to the Lady. Arialde looked deep into her bright eyes. "I see the lost King in your gaze," she said with a warm and gentle smile. "That is the source of your strength. You carry a part of him, and that part is strong here. He has mended your spirit. How did that come to pass, if I may ask?"

Gaelen did not answer at once, as the details of that happening were both terrifying and intimate. "We did not come here to speak of my spirit, Lady," she said at last.

"True enough," said Arialde. "Please forgive my indiscretion—I did not intend to invade your privacy. I know that you are filled with doubt concerning Nelwyn's most recent insight. Please enlighten me, for I would hear your words ere I consult with Lord Shandor."

Gaelen wrestled with herself, as she had done a hundred times already. *What if my beliefs are wrong, and Arialde acts on them? Perhaps I should not interfere with the opinions of those whose thoughts are deeper and wiser, and hope that the truth can be made known. I don't wish to set myself against Nelwyn…but it was Lord Kotos, not Nelwyn, who set this deception into place—I know it! I discovered the amulet. I alone looked into the eyes of Lord Kotos unguarded.*

"My Lady, I will tell you my concerns, for they are grave. If I'm right, everything that Nelwyn has foreseen is a lie, and we are all in the grip of a dark deception. If I'm wrong, then I hope you can set me back on the right path. All is not as it seems."

"Enlighten me so that I may consider wisely, Gaelen Taldin," said Arialde. They did not emerge from the Courtyard until the breaking of dawn.

17
The Darkening of the Stone

Mountain-home was a wondrous place in the springtime. The surrounding peaks were still covered with snow, and storms raged upon their summits and in the lands outside, but within the realm all was gentle and moderate. There were rains, yes, and even the occasional chilly wind that blew down from the western slopes, but the sun shone for part of every day. The sky was as blue as in late autumn. Green, growing things abounded, and in this time of flowering the air was heavy with scent. The melting snows had swelled the Amari streams and the River Artan—the sound of crashing waters stirred the heart of Lord Shandor as he stood upon a pinnacle of rock in the early morning. He loved the sound of rushing waters almost as much as he loved the wild winds.

Shandor, perhaps the mightiest Asarla ever to grace the lands of Alterra, was both wild and wise. His long hair was of spun silver, and his eyes—a clear, icy blue that could pierce the heart of any who looked into their depths—belied an innate compassion. He had ruled Mountain-home for many a year. All good-hearted folk loved him, though he was such an awe-inspiring presence that they could not help but be afraid of him at the same time. Therefore, Shandor was often alone.

He did not wish to be alone upon this day, so he sent forth his thoughts in a gentle call to his beloved. Liathwyn of the Èolar, one of the most beautiful maidens to ever hold the Light of Aontar in her dark blue eyes, had walked in Alterra for years uncountable. Her hair was as dark as the midnight sky. She cared not for weapons or warfare, but delighted most in growing things, seeking always to surround herself with them. An unrivaled singer and accomplished artisan in her own right, she fashioned the silken banner that would be carried first by her brother, Ri-Aldamar, and later by his son, Ri-Elathan. The battle-torn remnant would finally come to rest upon the breast of Rogond Thaylon.

Now she answered from the green glade that was her favorite resting place, calling out to Shandor and inviting him to come and join her there. She knew he preferred high places, for he was at heart as untamed as they, as rugged and beautiful as the dark grey mountain-peaks and as formidable as the foaming, crashing waters of the Artan. Yet gentle Liathwyn was more content in quiet, shady places where she could hear the singing of the birds. She loved warmth and soft, green light. Therefore, to please her, Shandor descended from his stony perch and made his way down to the glade, for the reward of her company was his greatest desire. He was never contented without her. In Mountain-home there were endless happy days and uncounted peaceful and passionate nights with his beloved.

He found her sitting upon a carpet of thick, deep green moss surrounded by white birch, her bright face illuminated by a shaft of sunlight filtering down through the new green canopy. His passions rose at once, as they always did when he had been separated from her, and he moved to her side without a word, taking her in his powerful arms and holding her slender body to his breast. She responded in kind, whispering gentle, musical words in his ear, grasping his well-muscled back with both hands.

Shandor rejoiced, for it had been many days since they had shared their love. He kissed her as gently as he could, though there was an urgency about him that could not be denied, as he prepared to lay her down upon the green floor of the glade. Yet, even as he did so, the voice of Arialde, his sister, came unbidden to his mind. It called to him—*summoned* him.

"No," he whispered, "I will not listen." Yet he had heard, and having heard, he could not linger.

Liathwyn would not hear the voice of Arialde, yet she grew pale and misty in Shandor's embrace, causing him to cry out in frustration as she faded from his awareness, so that all that remained to him were the lonely, shadowed corridors within the Stone of Léir.

Arialde stood alone in the Courtyard. Dawn brought the return of the sun and the singing of birds, but Arialde did not take notice of them as she lifted the indigo cloth that both shielded and quieted the Stone, revealing the beautiful crystal to her expectant eyes. She sent her thoughts deep within it, for she knew that the spirit of Lord Shandor dwelt there. *Shandor…beloved brother, I seek enlightenment that only you can give. I beseech you, my brother, come to me now so that truth may be revealed.*

At first there was no flicker of light within the Stone, no indication that Shandor had heard her summons. She tried again, knowing that sometimes her brother was reluctant to show himself. She hoped that she would find him in a cooperative frame of mind, as he sometimes became sullen, even wrathful, when disturbed. Arialde drew a deep breath and shook her head, her own silvery hair waving in a nonexistent breeze. She drew from her own power, flaring gently golden, enfolding the stone in her own warm light. Shandor had never been able to resist her for long, and in a few more moments she was rewarded.

I am here, Sister Asarla. What do you want of me? Shandor's voice could be heard inside Arialde's mind, and she felt a pang of longing as she did every time she spoke with him, for she loved her brother and grieved for him.

"Some most disturbing news has been brought to my ears, she replied. I seek enlightenment and insight that is only given to you. The doom I fear concerns *your* fate, and that of the Seeing Stone. Tell me of your own future, so that I may know what course should be taken. Do this, my brother, for the sake of the Light."

Arialde longed to tell Shandor of Nelwyn's vision, and of Gaelen's belief in the involvement of Lord Kotos, but she did not lest she prejudice her brother's insights. Shandor appeared within the Stone then, as a glowing being inside a swirling cloud of mist. To her dismay, she saw reluctance, even fear, in his eyes.

And why should I consult my own future? Never have you asked this of me, and never have I done so—it is probably the thing I least desire to see. What has moved you to consider my fate? The Stone is quite safe under your protection, is it not?

"Ask me not for enlightenment when it is your task to provide it," said Arialde. "Only know that this insight is of the greatest importance to the future of all beings of Light, and give the task your full attention. I cannot enlighten you further, my brother. I can only ask again…consult the Stone and reveal your future fate."

I do not wish to look into my own future, was the reply. *Enlighten me first, that I may decide the wisdom of it.*

"There is no time for debate," said Arialde, who was losing patience. "These matters are far too important to allow doubt and dread to interfere. With insight, I can protect you. Without it, I will not know what path to take. Aid me now, that I may safeguard you."

Very well, then, said Shandor, his eyes darkening. *But on your own head be the consequences. It is bad enough that you would disturb my reverie, but now you will not even enlighten me ere I set upon this path…a path that is no doubt fearsome, or you would not be asking!"*

Arialde reflected for a moment, knowing that she was asking much of him. *If I had the power to command insight into the future, would I wish to learn of my own fate? Almost certainly not. Still, I must convince him.*

"It was once said that the courage of Lord Shandor would never falter. Is that no longer true? Has thy grief stolen the strength of thy heart?"

There will be no grief for me…not ever again, said Shandor, though Arialde knew he was less than convinced. When Liathwyn had left him forever, he had been so disheartened that his bereavement had nearly destroyed him. He would not easily bear the thought of such dark despair.

"Then aid me in preserving the Stone," she said. 'Without your aid, it may fall into Darkness. Lord Wrothgar will enslave you, and all will be lost. Is that what you desire? Would you become an instrument of destruction…a tool of evil? I would imagine even the memory of Liathwyn would not long remain if that should come to pass. You will see only what the Shadowmancer wants you to see." She realized, in a fleeting, sorrowful moment, that she could no longer trust him as she once had. Liathwyn was safe in Elysia, and Shandor knew it. There was little else in Alterra that he cared about.

He was silent for a moment, and then the mists swirled about him as he vanished from her sight. *I will consider it,* he said, and the Stone went silent.

A thousand silvery planes revealed an infinite number of images to Shandor's awareness. He had only to consult them. He stood now before the mirror-like wall concealing the insight he most dreaded…that of his own eventual doom. He feared this insight more than any other, as would anyone, and yet he knew that Arialde was right. If there was any doubt as to the continuation of things as they were, he needed to be made aware of it, as his only happiness was found within the Stone. He hesitated for only a moment longer, reached out with a tentative hand, and touched the silver surface, causing a ripple in the silken fabric of time. The images of two fates, both no doubt dire and grim, began to form, and Shandor's heart filled with fear.

Unlike those who gain insight from me, I cannot act to prevent my own downfall, and I cannot be assured that others would choose the path I would ordain. I can advise, and plead, and implore, and even demand, but I cannot act…

He watched helplessly as two courses of fate began to unfold before him. He could not live with the knowledge of either of them, and he turned aside, crying aloud with frustration and grief for his failing heart. He told himself that if he did not know of these things, they would not happen. Nothing must ever come between him and his beloved.

As Arialde waited patiently for Shandor to reappear, she suddenly gasped and placed her right hand over her breast. Her vision clouded for a moment, and she swayed on her feet, yet she did not fall. As her vision cleared, she heard Shandor's cry, just before the Stone went utterly dark. She had never seen it look as it did then, lifeless and dull as a piece of glass. There was no light within—no spirit in evidence. Shandor had gone deep, and Arialde knew that not only would she receive no insight from him, but she might never behold his face again. *I have asked too much of him.* She sank down upon the stone floor of the Courtyard, swallowing hard and staring into the empty air, forlorn and hopeless. This was not the ending she had foreseen.

"My lady…?"

The deep, soft voice of Lord Airan came to Arialde as she sat alone, lost in contemplation. She had only just become aware of him, though he had been calling to her for some time.

"My lady, please take away the veil from your heart, that I may join and comfort you. The people are disquieted…Arialde? Beloved?"

Arialde realized that the Courtyard was still surrounded by impenetrable mist. It was as if Airan spoke to her through a locked door. She would have to admit him, for she could not brood alone upon matters of such importance. Airan, a very perceptive soul, would no doubt aid her in deciding what must be done. She lifted her hands to the sky, and the mists cleared, allowing her to view the myriad of worried faces peering into the Courtyard.

The Elves of Tal-sithian were very sensitive to disturbances involving the Lady. By now, rumor and speculation had spread throughout the realm. As with any rumors, the amount of truth varied according to the speaker, but even the Guardians had felt Arialde's disquiet. They clustered now in the waters closest to the Lady; huge, dark masses cruising quietly beneath the surface, awaiting orders.

Arialde emerged as Airan entered, and they embraced for a moment. Airan felt the tension and dismay that pervaded Arialde as he held her. He looked over at the Stone in dismay. "What happened? The Stone is dark and…and without life! Small wonder you are disquieted. Beloved?"

Arialde closed her eyes and collected herself, then pulled back so that she could meet his gaze. "I will not explain here, not now. Forgive me…I must master my own thoughts first. We must counsel at once with the Company, for although I hoped the Stone would bring insight, it has not aided me in deciding what is to be done. Please summon the Company. I will join you when I am ready."

Airan embraced her again, glancing apprehensively at the cold, dark Stone. "I will do as you ask. I will also speak with the people and try to quell their fears."

Arialde smiled gratefully at him, this very charming, sincere, helpful presence in her life. They had founded Tal-sithian together, and it had drawn many of the lost people of Eádros to its shores, as well as a few of the remaining Èolar. Airan had aided her greatly in safeguarding not only the realm, but her own heart.

After he had gone, her thoughts turned somber. "How will I feel when I am sundered from him for Eternity?" she whispered. "I suppose that one day I will find out, and then, like Shandor, I will face the consequences of having given my heart to an Elf."

The Company was summoned and assembled, all save Gaelen and Nelwyn, neither of whom could be found. Rogond and Galador offered to look for them, and discovered them at last—not an easy task, as they had gone into seclusion. Gaelen was disquieted, for Nelwyn still would not look her in the eye. Both were fearful of the revelations to come.

The council-chamber grew dark as tall, grey clouds formed over the island, reflecting Arialde's mood as she entered and stood before the Company. She lit no lamps or candles, but asked that her guests sit themselves down, as they would remain until matters were decided.

"This darkened chamber reflects the darkness of our business this day. We must consider all that has been put before us. Nelwyn's vision, Gaelen's insight, and the despair of Lord Shandor...all must be considered and the truth revealed. We must decide our future course, and no one must ever know what is said here. There will be no intrusion." She raised both hands, and a brilliant light flared forth from her as a mighty thunderclap startled everyone present. Outside, the people felt Arialde's warning, and they backed away from the green hill, shielding their eyes as a cold, hard rain began to fall. The Guardians broke the surface, booming with voices so deep that they were felt rather than heard. No Elf of Tal-sithian would approach the hill until summoned.

"Everyone here has been privy to Nelwyn's terrible foresight," said Arialde. "Yet Gaelen has shared thoughts with me that cast a great deal of doubt. She believes that the vision held by Nelwyn was placed there by none other than Trachair, the Deceiver, who was once called Kotos the Powerful." She looked over at Nelwyn, who wore an expression of shock and disbelief on her pale face. "I'm sorry, Nelwyn, but I believe that Gaelen is right. There have been too many inexplicable events to think otherwise. Gaelen also believes that Lord Kotos travels within the person of your enemy, Gorgon Elfhunter. Are there any among you who have already been privy to this insight?"

"I have," said Fima rising to his feet. "I became aware of it as we were traveling. When we arrived in Dûn Bennas, we learned enough to confirm Gaelen's fears." He looked over at Nelwyn, and there was regret in his blue eyes. "Both Gaelen and I thought it best to wait and reveal the truth here, in Tal-sithian, where your heart could be safeguarded and healed. Please understand that it was very difficult to keep this from you."

Nelwyn's hand flew to her throat, and she appeared to be having some difficulty breathing. The impact of what had just been uncovered was only now beginning to be made real. *The Right Hand of Wrothgar…the most powerful servant of Darkness…he who brought down Tal-elathas and killed Dardis and Baelta and Léiras…this being has beguiled and deceived me? He invaded my very thoughts and manipulated them? How could I have allowed it? I would not have!*

"You are wrong!" she shouted in a voice utterly bereft of hope. Though she denied it, she knew that it was so…yet it could *not* be so! "No, no, *no!*"

She began to wail—horrified, devastated—but nothing could undo what had been done. If this terrible thing was true, she had been chosen to be the instrument of Evil, and the Light would be quenched because of it. How could she not have known?

Galador leaped to her aid and was now holding her in his arms, though she tried to push him away at first. "How could she not tell me? How could she betray me so?" Nelwyn moaned, referring to Gaelen, who felt as though a blade had been thrust into her own heart.

"Hush, beloved," whispered Galador. "Gaelen could not tell you until she was certain. She only became certain in Dûn Bennas. It was sensible of her to wait for the protection of the Lady. In Tal-sithian the knowledge is safe, and *you* are safe. This is not Gaelen's fault, nor is it yours. Kotos has deceived the most powerful spirits in Alterra, and you were easy prey." He looked up at Arialde, his face grey with worry. "Is that not so, my lady?"

"It is so," said Arialde. "Of all in the Company, Nelwyn and Rogond are most pure of heart. Men are not given to premonition, therefore Rogond would not have been chosen. Kotos beguiled Nelwyn because she had no darkness in her heart to warn of him. Now that the truth has been revealed, we can avert the disaster Lord Wrothgar is hoping for."

"We will not just avert disaster…we can use this opportunity to *destroy* the Elfhunter, and perhaps even bring about the fall of the Deceiver," said Gaelen. "So long as Gorgon and Kotos believe that we have been deceived, they will play right into our hands." She turned to Nelwyn. "I know what you are feeling now," she said, "for I have felt it myself. We have both been used as means to evil ends, and I you are only now beginning to realize the depth of this violation. You can take heart in the fact that no Elf has died with your assistance—I cannot say the same. The deceit has been unmasked before the evil end could be achieved. Take heart."

Gaelen's eyes filled with tears. "Do you think this has been easy?" she said. "I would rather die than hurt you, yet I did what I had to do. I did what I thought was best for all, and I will not apologize for it. When you have considered these matters further, I pray you will understand. I regret hurting you more than you can know, but if I had voiced my doubts when first I held them, you would not have believed me. And if Lord Kotos had gotten wind of it, we would not now have the chance to defeat him. Who knows what he might have done to ensure the success of his plan?"

"The chance to defeat Gorgon is what you truly refer to, Gaelen. Try to deny it! Once again, you have placed your own desires in the forefront," said Nelwyn, who was not in a charitable state of mind.

At this, Fima could no longer keep silent. "It should be the desire of every Elf, nay, every true-hearted *soul*, to rid the world of the Elfhunter. Gaelen is not to blame for what has happened."

"Do not chide her!" said Gaelen. "She is hurt and angry, and I don't blame her. Yet now we cannot dwell on it, as we must re-group and decide upon a plan." She turned to Nelwyn who, to her relief, looked directly into her eyes. "I hope you will forgive me, but if not, at least you can lend the benefit of your thoughts to our debate. After all, you have a most insightful and perceptive spirit."

"Apparently not as perceptive as might have been," said Nelwyn ruefully. "If I were all that perceptive, Evil would not have chosen me."

Arialde had approached Nelwyn, and now placed a gentle hand on her shoulder. "Would you argue that the High King, Ri-Aldamar, was perceptive? That Léiras the Far-sighted and Baelta the Bright were perceptive? Would you deny their wisdom? They were deceived by Kotos as surely as you were. You are in good company."

"Small consolation, I'm sure," said Estle.

"Yet it is some consolation," said Nelwyn, and Gaelen's heart was lightened. Nelwyn's despair would not long rule her; she would be all right. She was already beginning to look on the brighter side of this very dark matter.

"And what is to be expected now, O Great Deceiver?" asked Gorgon. He had finally arrived in the lands surrounding the Lake-realm, and was now hunkered down in the marsh-meadows to the north of the Linnefionn. After the warmth of the desert southlands, the marshes felt especially chilly and damp, yet Gorgon didn't seem to mind. He gazed into the amulet as the familiar illusion of Lord Kotos appeared.

"Ah. It's probably just as well you ask," said Kotos, "for you were not privy to the images I placed in Nelwyn's mind. She has by now made them known to the Lady, and they are deciding their next course. If all has gone according to plan, they will send only about half their number to Mountain-home, and the rest will remain on the island so that they can meet the anticipated attack by Lord Wrothgar. The Stone of Léir will be moved, and they will most likely send a small party with it so as not to attract attention. I expect it to be relatively unprotected—the Elves will rely on stealth and secrecy rather than strength of arms. Yet we will not attack the party until we have surmised where they are taking the Stone, as we cannot risk matters going awry. They will either try to take it to another of the Elven-realms, or they will try to conceal it in some dark place where no one will think to look for it. Then they will post guardians, just in case. The only other Elven-realm that they will believe to be safe is Tal-ailean, in the Verdant Mountains. If they go there, we will take the Stone ere they arrive. If not, we will follow them until we have learned their destination."

Kotos shook his head, his long, grey hair and beard waving to and fro. "I do not believe they will go to Tal-ailean, for they know the Elves there are scattered and are not well armed. They would never repel an attack by Lord Wrothgar, and it is doubtful that they could defend the Stone."

"Where will they take it, then, to some dark hole in the ground? How perfect for me!" said Gorgon, who would have rubbed his hands together if he had been able. "You believe that they will rely on stealth to accomplish their end? Again, how very perfect that will be, as none can match the Wood-elves for stealth, which means that the Vixen will travel with the Stone. I shall have her when the time is right."

"When it is right, and not before," Kotos admonished Gorgon, lowering his eyebrows. "You shall have your reward, but only if you are patient. You must agree to wait until I direct you. Is that clear?"

"Abundantly," said Gorgon. "So, what do we do now? How long before you are certain that all has gone as planned?"

"I will send forth the raven in the morning," Kotos replied. Then he laughed in a very sinister and menacing manner. "I cannot pierce the veil of Arialde's thoughts, but Shandor and I have always shared a bond. He was my close friend upon a time, until he met Liathwyn and founded Mountain-home. Since his spirit became trapped within the Stone of Léir, he has not been very conscientious about guarding himself, and I have now sensed a dread in him that I thought never to sense again. It is my guess that Arialde has asked for guidance regarding Nelwyn's vision, and he cannot bear the thought of it."

"But what if Shandor reveals that the vision is false?" asked Gorgon, who was suddenly alarmed. "The Stone will surely see through your deception, won't it? If so, then our plan is undone!"

"Calm yourself, Elfhunter," said Kotos. "Shandor never could see through my deceit, whether within the Stone of Léir or outside of it. He has now become absorbed in his own pathetic concerns. In a way, he has already come to Darkness. I do not expect him to provide enlightenment regarding the fate of the Stone, for he will be too afraid to know of it. His courage has failed: it has not been tested in five thousand years."

"Yet the Vixen doubted Orrion…I know it," said Gorgon.

"And who will believe her doubts?" laughed Kotos. "After all, Nelwyn saw Orrion's doom in Mountain-home, valiant warrior that he is—horribly crushed beneath a troll's feet. Alas, poor Orrion! What a brave and noble Defender of the Light." He then favored Gorgon with a smile that was intended to be reassuring, but came off as disturbing. "And, speaking of noble, who would ever gainsay the insights of innocent, true-hearted Nelwyn, who could never be an instrument of Darkness? Remember, my very large and fearsome friend, no one in the Company will *ever* think of Lord Kotos. For all they know, I am dead and gone, or else skulking in the Fell-ruin. In fact, I'll wager they are now assuming I will lead the Dark forces in the Fell-ruin to attack Mountain-home, since Nelwyn's 'vision' has told them that Wrothgar is in the Darkmere."

"But, Wrothgar *is* in the Darkmere," said Gorgon. "And I thought He did not want the Elves to know it. Will He not be displeased?"

Kotos sighed. "Must I remind you that this entire design was put forth by Lord Wrothgar? I am only doing His bidding, as are you. Yet we both will be rewarded when all is ended. Now, enough of this discussion. Go and find yourself some sustenance, so that you may rest. I will not disturb you."

At this, the amulet went dark. The sun was setting, and Gorgon could hear the first mating calls of the marsh-frogs. There would be no rest for him this night—he would soon find himself in the midst of a deafening horde that would be croaking, peeping, and trilling until nearly dawn. *Ah, well*, he thought, *at least they don't taste bad...*

The raven went forth shortly after sunrise, taking Lord Kotos with it. It flew around the perimeter of the Linnefionn, taking notice of any Elves on shore, but there were not many. Kotos expected that the mist that surrounded the Lake could be pierced from the air, and he directed the raven to fly through it that he might gain a better look as to what was going on in Tal-sithian. Yet it was like flying through a cloud bank, and the raven was disquieted.

It broke through the mist as it approached the banks of the Green Isle, yet that was as close as it came, for a dark, serpent-like neck erupted from below in a sudden explosion of water. The Guardian's teeth barely missed closing on the raven, and it was nearly knocked from the air. Kotos caught a glimpse of at least three of the huge beasts circling below, realizing that he had nearly fallen prey to one of them. They were all booming in their deep, sonorous voices, and Kotos dared not linger. Rumor had it that water-dragons were very sensitive to the presence of evil. Better to fly from the island as fast as the raven could manage.

The assault by the great beast had unnerved Kotos, who was only just realizing the difficulty he would have found himself in had it succeeded. It was fortunate, thought Kotos as he flew back through the thick mist, that the Guardians could not speak of what they had seen. There was one other matter that had unnerved and puzzled Kotos—he had not been able to detect any trace of Lord Shandor.

In the council chamber, the debating continued. All were agreed that, if Gaelen and Fima were right, Kotos had been trying to motivate the Elves to move the Stone of Léir. It seemed to be the entire point of Nelwyn's vision. So, *was* there an army in the Fell-ruin? Would Wrothgar attack Mountain-home? Should Arialde send an army? What should be done?

"We must do exactly as Lord Wrothgar expects," said Arialde. "He must believe that we have been taken in."

Estle turned to Nelwyn. "And what does that mean, exactly? If we believed your vision was true, and I am not yet certain that we should not, what course would be taken?"

"We would send a defense force to Mountain-home, but we would keep a fair number of defenders here in the Lake-realm," said Nelwyn. "And we would, of course, move the Stone."

"Then that is precisely what we must appear to do," said Gaelen. "Yet the Stone must remain here, and be guarded as never before. It may be that some parts of Nelwyn's vision are true, and it is not impossible to imagine Lord Wrothgar sending forth a force from the Darkmere. We have long suspected that the Dark Power has dwelt there. Nelwyn and I are, in fact, certain of it."

"And how, may I ask, can you be so certain?" asked Galador, who clearly did not believe that Gaelen could know.

"Because we both ventured there on a time," said Gaelen. "And if it were not for my cousin, I would have died there. Nothing will convince me that the Shadowmancer does not rule that terrible realm."

"Will you tell me the tale?" asked Fima who was already reaching for his parchments, his lore-master's eyes alight with interest.

"We must return to the matter at hand," said Rogond. Both he and Galador had been staring at her in astonishment; they could not imagine anyone's doing anything so foolhardy.

"You *are* living on borrowed time, as if I didn't already know it," muttered Galador.

"I was younger then," said Gaelen.

"I'm afraid I must bring up another possibility," said Hallagond. "What if Nelwyn's vision really *does* outline Wrothgar's intent, and he is counting on Kotos to do exactly what he did, tipping off Gaelen so that we would do exactly what we are now doing? What if we are falling into his hands by…by *not* falling into his hands?"

"He has not had his kaffa yet this morning," said Estle. She turned to Hallagond with a familiar sardonic expression. "Have you seen Gaelen's list? Orrion is Kotos, and he is also Gorgon Elfhunter. Of that we are certain."

"But…are you suggesting that Wrothgar would not anticipate Gaelen's perceptive nature? That he would discount her? If so, then he is not as clever as I thought."

"Wrothgar and Kotos would discount Gaelen, for they do not know her," said Arialde. "To them, she is neither wise nor learned—only a Sylvan Elf. The Woodland folk have always been dismissed by the Dark Powers."

"Yet I cannot imagine that they would not take Gorgon into account," said Rogond, who was not disagreeing entirely with Hallagond's opinion, as he had thought it himself in an indecisive moment. "Wrothgar must know that Gorgon shares a bond with Gaelen."

Gaelen considered for a moment. "I have wondered whether Gorgon's connection with me will allow him to figure out what we have been planning, though I have become adept at keeping things hidden from him. My sense of Gorgon tells me that he has fallen into a mire that he cannot extricate himself from. Always he has acted alone…pridefully so. His desperation at the outcome of our battle in the Spirit Realm has forced him into submission. I would imagine that Kotos' arrogance outweighs Gorgon's caution, and Wrothgar might not know much of Gorgon at all. They may yet come to grief by underestimating both of us."

"If Wrothgar could hear you now, he would never underestimate you again," said Arialde. "How fortunate that he cannot, for I believe your instincts are the best guide we have. Wrothgar has always valued the wrong kind of strength."

"Has anyone considered a possibility that, to me, is fairly obvious?" asked Azori, who had not yet spoken.

"Enlighten us, my brother," said Estle. "Though I believe I know what you are going to say, for I have wondered the same thing myself."

"You say that the Stone of Léir must not fall into the wrong hands, or the Light will perish. You also have said that the Stone has gone dark, and that this Shandor will provide no enlightenment. Why do we not simply destroy it? It cannot threaten the Light if it does not exist." Azori looked around the circle, taking note of the variety of expressions on the faces of his companions. "It would seem to be the most sensible course to me," he said, spreading his hands. "Destroy the Stone, and none may use it for good or ill. It doesn't seem to me to be all that useful anyway. The Spirit within it is…unbalanced, even demented. Would any of you trust it to advise you now?"

Arialde was conflicted between indignation on Shandor's behalf and resignation—she had not expected her brother to abandon courage the way he had. "I do not know whether he is demented, but I do understand Azori's feeling," she said at last. "Yet it is not known what the outcome will be if we release Shandor from the Stone. Without his body to return to, he may leave Alterra forever, or he may set himself to dark mischief. He will be most aggrieved and angry, that is certain. I am not sure of what he would be capable of then."

"Are you saying that he would turn to dark pursuits out of mere vindictiveness? I had not thought him to be so easily turned," said Galador.

"Yet grief is a terrible waster of hearts and talents," said Gaelen. "You would know something about that."

"As would you."

Gaelen turned back to Arialde. "I do understand your reluctance, my lady, but…what if Shandor's body could be brought here, to Tal-sithian? Could we not then release Shandor, and restore him? Could you not heal his pain? He is trapped within a deep well of despair, thinking that the shadows of the past can heal him, but they have not. They cannot."

"Shandor was the mightiest of all of us," said Arialde, "and once his honor was beyond question. He was the strongest defender of Light that has ever been, yet now he is lost. I do not know what sort of being we will deal with if he is released."

"I would like to think that the spirit with which he was originally endowed will prevail," said Fima. "After all, he has striven to defend the good and to overcome Darkness since the Time of Mystery. That surely cannot be overcome by a few thousand years of imprisonment."

"If you had seen the vision that he sent to me, you would understand the Lady's reluctance," said Gaelen. "He afflicted my soul upon that day with a sight so terrible that it could have taken my sanity, only because I disturbed him without permission. I will admit to being impulsive, but I meant no discourtesy. To send forth such cruel retribution is not the action of one who defends the Light. Both Galador and I have lived with grief, yet we have not allowed it to take away our consideration for others. Shandor has fallen into a place of torment…a cage where there is only the illusion of joy." She paused and cast her eyes downward. "Despite my fears, I would see him set free."

"And why is Shandor a prisoner of grief? Estle and I do not know the tale, though it seems well-known to the rest of you," said Azori. "What grief could possibly be so great as to turn such a lordly being into a reclusive, self-pitying potential menace?"

"I will tolerate no disrespect of Lord Shandor," said Arialde, as distant thunder rumbled, punctuating her displeasure. "You might as well ask yourself what circumstances could turn a young man, who was born innocent and full of potential, into a self-serving, untrustworthy *confirmed* menace. Yet I will not ask you to reveal your own history. My guess is that you and Shandor have something in common, and that is either love denied or love lost. Shandor, who was so very passionate and loved Liathwyn so deeply, could not bear her loss. His spirit was torn, and he could find no healing anywhere but in the Stone of Léir."

"Yet it did not heal him, did it?" said Azori who was not displeased at being named a menace.

"It is not Shandor who puzzles me, but Liathwyn," said Nelwyn. "I have never understood her. How could she condemn her only love to die a slow death from despair? How could she bear to part from him forever? I would fight to my last breath to remain with Galador—did she not love Shandor enough to fight for him?"

"She had little choice," said Arialde. "The Fall of Tal-elathas was perhaps the greatest disaster in the history of our world. Liathwyn lost nearly every member of her family, including her beloved brother. She made the mistake of following behind Lord Shandor, and she witnessed the terrible aftermath of the Battle. Words cannot tell how grim that vision would have been, especially to a gentle soul like Liathwyn. It literally took her spirit. She lingered as long as she could, several years as I recall, but she wasted with sorrow, growing weaker day by day. Her light had been quenched, and Shandor could not revive it. Neither he nor their daughter Ordath could make any difference. Liathwyn had to be carried to the Twilight Shores, for otherwise she would have wasted unto death, and she wanted to spare Lord Shandor some of that terrible ordeal. His heart was torn asunder long before she left the shores of Alterra…he sank further into despair each day that he looked upon her decline."

"And so he chose then to enter the Stone? To what end?" asked Estle.

"He did not *choose* to enter the Stone. It drew him within," said Arialde. "He would spend days on end gazing at it, trying to recapture lost memories and assuage his terrible grief, but the power of the Stone was not enough. At last he gazed so long, and reached out to the Stone with so much longing, that his spirit was drawn there. He has dwelt there ever since. It is the spirit of Shandor that gives the Stone its power to show the future."

Azori stretched and yawned. "This has been a most interesting story," he said, "yet I would leave this matter for further debate. I am weary, and I have not eaten. Elves may do without, but men need both food and rest. Yet I would ask all of you to consider my plan—destroy the Stone, and take it from the grasp of Wrothgar. Then we can worry about Shandor. Despite your warnings, I believe we stand a better chance of dealing with him."

"I am not so certain," said Rogond, looking into the eyes of the Lady. He had not heard of the horrific, torturous images sent to Gaelen until now.

"We shall suspend the council until all have rested and refreshed themselves," said Arialde. "Do not share these matters with anyone outside this chamber in the meantime. I will recall you in a few hours." Arialde knew that food, drink, and rest would lift everyone's spirits, and she hoped it would aid them in recognizing a clear path. She wanted time to reflect upon what she had heard.

18
Raven-bait

Arialde would not reconvene the council until sunset. She had spent much of the intervening time alone, having asked Lord Airan—a very accomplished and convincing orator who could put any outlandish rumors to rest—to call the people together and allay their fears.

He came to her as she sat brooding in her private chamber. "I have done as you asked, and the people are satisfied for the time being. However, there has been a request for an audience…a message of interest."

Despite her desire not to be disturbed further, Arialde was intrigued. "Who bears the message?"

"A friend. I'll show him in." He turned and left the chamber, returning in a few moments. Arialde could hear him speaking from outside the chamber door. "Come on then…it's all right. The Lady will not harm you…she is anxious to hear your message. No, it's not at all foolish of you. Come on…that's it. Come on."

Airan reappeared with the messenger, who was none other than Collyn of the Currgas. He was not actually their chief, but he was usually appointed as spokesman and messenger. His skin was still damp, the downy fur erect against the twilight chill. He was not comfortable being so far inland, and he shivered as much with fear as with cold. Currgas were nearly helpless on land, although it was not wise to corner one.

Arialde smiled the moment she beheld him. She loved Collyn's folk, and they were always welcome. He approached her, turning his bright, ivory-colored face and sparkling blue eyes upward to meet her gaze. Then he bowed, flexing his very remarkable spine such that his hair actually brushed his toes. If Arialde found this comical, she did not show it.

"Hail, Collyn of the River-folk. You are welcome, as always. What news do you bring?" She reached over onto a small table and offered him a plump, sugared confection made from fruits and nectar.

Collyn took the offering, but did not eat it. He looked all around the chamber as if evil creatures might be listening from the shadows. When he saw none, he cleared his throat and bowed again. "Thank you, my lady. We have received a message from the Guardians that should be made known to you at once." He looked around the room again, glancing furtively left and right, and then lowered his voice to a whisper. "They said there was an evil presence over the Lake this morning. It was…a black-winged bird. From their description it sounded like a raven. One of the Guardians tried to bring it down, but failed. They were unsettled…apparently they sensed great evil within the bird. They asked me to bring you the news." He waited for a moment, uncertain of how the Lady would react. At last, she smiled.

"Well done, Collyn. The Guardians are correct—this is important news. Please be certain your people do not speak of it, won't you?"

"That is not a concern," said Collyn. "Riffle and I are the only persons who know of it. We will keep your confidence." He relaxed then, as his task was completed and he had suffered nothing dire. Now he consumed the treat she had given him with relish, his mouth widening into a bright smile. He began eyeing the remaining sweets on the tray, and she lifted it from the table, presenting it to him.

"My thanks for your good service. It was a glad day when your people arrived at these shores."

Collyn took the heavy silver tray and bowed, his eyes alight with anticipation. He would save one confection, perhaps two, to share with Gin-gin.

After he had gone, Arialde turned to Lord Airan. "This news is not unexpected." she said. "Lord Kotos is near to our shores, and he travels in the guise of a raven even as Gaelen suspected. He has come to make certain all goes as planned." She shook her head. "It would have been interesting had one of the Guardians managed to take him…I doubt a water-dragon would make a suitable or accommodating host. Yet all will unfold as intended now." Then she smiled. "Kotos could not know that the Currgas could understand the Guardians, for he has always left such 'insignificant people' out of his calculations. I believe that will be his undoing one day."

"You know that tray you gave to Collyn was of pure silver? It was quite valuable," said Airan.

Arialde laughed. "And who appointed you guardian of my treasures, beloved Light-elf? Don't be concerned…the tray is heavy. Collyn will discard it the moment he finishes the last of the sweets. We will recover it. No Currga ever cared for such things. They prefer that all their household items be made of wood."

"Why is that?" asked Airan.

"Because it floats!" said Arialde with a light and cheerful smile. She really was glad for the Currgas. Things always looked brighter in their presence.

The council reassembled at sunset. Rogond and Galador noted with some dismay that Nelwyn still chose to sit as far from Gaelen as she could manage; usually the two cousins sat together so that they could share thoughts.

The clouds still hung over the land, dark and brooding, and every now and then a brief, hard rain would fall. Arialde would not quell the weather until various matters had been decided. The grey-clad scouts ranging up and down the lake shore shivered in the wet cold.

"My friends, I hope you are fed and rested, so that we may decide what course must now be taken," said Arialde. "I have considered your views, and have formed my own opinion, yet I would hear any plan you would propose or concern you would share. First, know this: if you held any doubts as to the truth or falsehood of Gaelen's concerns, hold them no longer. Lord Kotos has been seen flying near the island, in the guise of a raven. He would only be here to ensure that his carefully orchestrated plan came to pass. If Nelwyn's visions were true, that would not be the case. She made no mention of Kotos, and Orrion most certainly would not have been seen defending Mountain-home." Arialde was silent then, awaiting any response.

Rogond spoke first. "Gaelen and I have been in conference with Fima, and we have agreed on one thing. The Stone must remain here where it may be protected, or it must be destroyed as Azori suggests. Yet although we understand Azori's reasoning, I believe that such a drastic measure is ill advised. We should not trade our present difficulties for bigger ones." So saying, he sat back down between Gaelen and Azori.

"You say 'we' and then you say 'I,' Rogond. How do Gaelen and Fima feel about destroying the Stone?" said Arialde.

"I agree with Rogond," said Fima. "Gaelen is conflicted in that she does not want to destroy the Stone, but she does wish that Shandor could be free of it. She, as with many of us, is afraid of the consequences."

"It's not just that I am afraid of the consequences," said Gaelen, and her eyes flashed as she rose to her feet. "There is a way that we might use the Stone to lure Gorgon Elfhunter to his doom. I, for one, would regret missing that chance."

"Now I *know* you have gone mad," muttered Estle. "You would risk the Stone just to kill Gorgon? It would seem that Nelwyn was right."

Gaelen bristled, and her ears flushed red. "Right about *what*? If this all it takes for you to lose faith in me, how shallow your friendship is. I am not dim-witted. Yes, the taking of Gorgon Elfhunter is often in the forefront of my thoughts. If that makes me self-centered, then so be it. He is a weight around my neck… he is a suffocating darkness upon my spirit. The fact that he is still breathing brings me constant vexation. I have endured more than any of you in all of this, and I have the right to my priorities! You do not have to agree to them. What I am proposing is to allow Lord Kotos to *believe* that we are moving the Stone. I want his plan to fail. I want to avenge the wrongs he has done to my friends, most especially Nelwyn. And I am willing to risk my own life to ensure that he takes the bait."

"Calm yourself, Gaelen," said Azori. "My sister meant no insult. You obviously have not rested, and you are far too sensitive."

"Sounded like an insult to me," said Fima, his eyes darkening.

Nelwyn rose to her feet and moved to stand before Gaelen. "I was hurt and humiliated, and I am still humiliated. I know you did what you believed was right, and I know that you tried to safeguard me. I had forgotten that you have first-hand knowledge of what I was feeling. Let us forgive each other and make our plans. I will follow you, as I have always done." They embraced, and the tension visibly disappeared from both of them.

"What's this plan you would put forth, Gaelen?" asked Hallagond. "I'm intrigued."

"It's not really a complete plan," said Gaelen, "but I thought that perhaps we could have artisans construct a…a replica of the Stone? And then I will take it to some faraway place, presumably to hide it from Lord Wrothgar. Gorgon will surely follow after, bringing Lord Kotos with him."

"And *then* what?" asked Nelwyn in alarm. "You say you will take it…do you mean alone? How will you bring down Gorgon when you are alone in some wild land? He will kill you as soon as he secures the Stone, and most assuredly when he finds that it is false!"

"He will not know that I am luring him, and I have ways of making sure that he knows what I will have him know," said Gaelen. "Kotos will go along because Gorgon will advise him. When he realizes that Gorgon was wrong, and they were both misled, I will be the least of Gorgon's troubles." A cunning smile crossed her face, unsettling all who beheld it.

"This would be a very dangerous task," said Arialde. "The idea has merit, though you cannot go alone. And we must make certain that every action that we take makes sense to Lord Kotos, or we will be unmasked."

"He will expect us to rely on stealth and secrecy in moving the Stone," said Gaelen. "I am the undisputed master of stealth, as my name, Taldin, would imply. None of your folk can rival my abilities, and I say it with some pride. Gorgon is well aware of my talent, and Kotos will be, too. Besides, I will not be going alone. Fima, at least, must go with me."

"Why Fima?" asked Hallagond, who was not surprised to see the smile on the old dwarf's face.

"Because Fima bears the mirror," said Rogond.

"Yes," said Gaelen. "Through it, I can 'show' Gorgon things I would have him know, yet keep from him what I will." She smiled another rather dark smile. "Lord Wrothgar will regret the day he bestowed that token upon the Elfhunter, if he hasn't already." She shook her head. "I will certainly need to keep my wits about me."

"Who else would accompany you?" asked Nelwyn. "You are surely not going without Galador and me!

"There must be only a few who travel this road," said Arialde, "as we would not attract attention, and the fewer thoughts for Lord Kotos to read, the better for all. You will need to guard yourselves... in fact, it would be best if you could all be convinced that the Stone is real. Kotos will pull Gorgon off the trail at the first hint that it is not."

"Ah, but you are forgetting something," said Gaelen. "Gorgon will do Kotos' bidding, but he prefers directing his own destiny. Once Gorgon is hard on my trail, he will not stop until he has taken me. One of us will surely not return, and the depth of Gorgon's hatred for me will prevail over any command given by Lord Kotos. As I said before, it does not do to underestimate either Gorgon or me." She looked around the circle of friends.

"Gorgon will not like the notion that he has been deceived any more than Kotos will…he will not allow me to manipulate him and get away with it. I saw the blood-lust on the face of Orrion when I encountered him alone on a dark night. The memory still haunts my thoughts. He will not suffer me to remain alive much longer."

She cast her eyes downward. "So long as Gorgon walks, my spirit is darkened," she said. Then she looked up at Nelwyn. "Do you perceive why I would never have been chosen by Kotos, as you were? This is my task, and my destiny. I will do what I must do."

In that moment, Azori, whose knack for breaking a tense moment was unexcelled, spoke to no one in particular. "Once again, I am very glad that I am not an Elf."

"At last, we have found some common ground," said Galador.

Arialde was not convinced. "Do not take Lord Kotos lightly, Gaelen. The Elfhunter is no match for him—make no mistake."

"I do not take him lightly," said Gaelen. "And I know that, for a time, Gorgon's every move will be directed. Yet you must not underestimate Gorgon's strength of will. If I can lure him long enough, he will not be turned back, no matter what. Besides," she said with a familiar, lopsided smile, "even if he breaks off the pursuit, what is the harm? Kotos and Wrothgar are foiled in either case. What is the harm?" At this, Rogond nodded. These were comforting words.

"And what plan would you put forward to bring down your enemy once you confront him?" said Azori. "You don't *have* a plan, do you? I thought not. If I were you, I would start planning, and not wait until you have no choice but to face him. From what you have told me, you will need to have at least a rough idea of your course of action."

Gaelen smiled again. "It will come to me, Azori," she said. "And I will not be alone, remember? I have loyal and formidable friends. Gorgon has the spirit of Kotos as his ally, but he fights his battles alone."

"You cannot count on that," said Galador. "Have you forgotten that evil beings attract evil to themselves? I expect Lord Kotos could summon an army of Ulcas if he were so inclined. They will no doubt be commanded to see to your deaths."

"They'll have to catch us first," said Gaelen. "I won't be concerning myself with Ulcas. I plan to not release my last breath until I can look upon Gorgon's carcass. Do you not understand that this opportunity may not come again for a long while? If all goes right, Gorgon will be dead. Kotos and Wrothgar will have been foiled, and perhaps even damaged. It would not surprise me if Wrothgar staged an attack on Mountain-home just to be convincing. If so, then the Elves will have an opportunity to eliminate a large number of enemies. There is much to be gained, if all goes right."

"If, if, if! You have not the slightest idea of how you will accomplish any of it," said Azori. He looked over at his half-sister, Estle. "Please tell me you aren't thinking of going along on this foolhardy quest."

"As if you have ever planned anything in your life, Azori," said Estle. "You're well known for pouncing when opportunity calls, but you and your men have lived by the skin of your teeth most of the time. Gaelen doesn't even know where she is going as yet. It would be difficult to formulate a plan."

"Well, if Gaelen succeeds in killing Gorgon…" Fima began.

"*When* I succeed in killing him," Gaelen interrupted.

"All right, *when* you succeed in killing him, what will happen to Lord Kotos? I don't expect he will be destroyed," said Fima.

"That is difficult to say, as his ways and abilities are not fully known to me," said Arialde. "Yet this much is certain—he will be seeking a new host, so you must all guard yourselves. And *do not* touch the amulet under any circumstances!"

"He will still have his raven friend," said Hallagond.

"Why would you assume that?" asked Gaelen, smiling and making a gesture with both hands as though drawing and aiming a bow into the air. "I like raven feathers as fletching. Perhaps I will collect some."

Arialde shook her head. "Our plan has begun to take form, but we must decide what else is to be done. A contingent will be sent to Mountain-home, and we must decide how many will go and what they will be told. It is my belief that they should not be aware of our deception, only that they are going to the realm of Ordath to aid her in quelling a potential invasion from the North. We should send enough of our folk to be convincing, but maintain an effective defense force here in Tal-sithian."

"And that means also that the route taken by Gaelen and her companions must be separate from the road to Mountain-home," said Fima. "I know we had discussed several possible destinations. One was the ruin of Eádros, one was the realm of Grundin, and one was the ruin of Tuathas. Which of these has the most merit?"

That was a very good question. The Company spent much of the night laying careful plans, each lending his or her thoughts, as they prepared to deceive the Deceiver. Gaelen sat back down beside Rogond, and he could literally feel waves of heat emanating from her small frame. *In the past, Gorgon's presence has chilled her, but now she thinks she holds the upper hand. This is the heat of the battle to come.* This plan could go awry so easily, and Rogond sighed, knowing that once Gaelen grabbed on to an idea there was no dissuading her. *Well, I suppose it really doesn't matter. I love her, and I'll be going with her—no matter what.*

Gaelen was not the only presence in Alterra that was sending forth the heat of impending battle upon that night. Lord Kotos had been summoned to parley with Lord Wrothgar, and this he had done. Gorgon sat nearby, as did the raven. It had learned to not fear Gorgon when Kotos was watching him.

Kotos wasn't watching now, however, and the raven decided that it didn't care for the expression on Gorgon's face. It flew to a nearby dead tree, perching high on one twisted, forlorn limb. It had been a while since Gorgon had eaten.

Kotos met Wrothgar within the confines of the amulet, where he appeared to stand before the dark throne of his Master. The voice of the Shadowmancer came to him, and there was a hint of impatience in it.

What news, Persuader? It has been long since thou hast sent word. How goes the plan?

My apologies, My Lord, said Kotos. *I have been occupied with ensuring our success, and my efforts are bearing fruit. The Elves were taken in, and even now they make plans in the Lake-realm, as we expected. I regret keeping Thee so long without news.* In truth, Kotos was unhappy with Wrothgar's timing, for he was uncertain as to whether the plans being made by the Elves were the plans he had intended, and he would not know the truth of it until they emerged from the Lake-realm. He would not dare fly near it again.

Art thou quite certain they were taken in? said Wrothgar. *I sense reluctance in thee. Is there any cause for uncertainty?*

Not that I am aware of, My Lord, said Kotos. *Until the Elves emerge, I cannot be certain what plan they have made, and what course I must take… nothing more. I can relate that I have seen several encouraging signs—the massing of the Guardians, for example, and the disquiet I have sensed from Arialde and Lord Shandor. Shandor has gone within himself. I can no longer sense him. But all these signs indicate that the Elves are preparing for war.*

I stand ready to aid thee, said Wrothgar. *I have arranged a most convincing display of force in the Fell-ruin. If the Elves of Mountain-home seek to confirm the rumor that I will soon rise up, they will not be disappointed.*

I believe that they will move the Stone in any event, said Kotos. *They have no doubt realized just how disastrous it would be for them to fail in protecting it. And they are aware that Lord Wrothgar knows where the Stone may be found.*

Yes, I have Gorgon Elfhunter to thank for that insight, said Wrothgar. *Be certain to remind him that, if this plan succeeds, he will stand very high in My favor. Stress also the dire consequences of failure, though he is already well aware of them."*

He is looking forward to the downfall of the Elves, Master. There can be no greater reward for him, said Kotos.

Carry on, then, My loyal and most valuable servant," said Wrothgar. *Only be advised that I will want news of thy progress upon the rising of each full moon. Carry on now, and do not disappoint Me.*

That is indeed the farthest thing from my mind, Great Lord, said Kotos.

"*Yes, I am sure it is,"* said Wrothgar. "*Remember to call upon Me at need, and also know that the taking of the Stone must be done with delicacy. The Elves will destroy it rather than allow it to fall into My hands. Thou must act in secret, spiriting the Stone away. Do not attempt to take it by force. The Elves may destroy it, and that would not please Me, not at all. Use thy guile, and the stealth of the Elfhunter. Until our next meeting then… Farewell.*

Kotos was now alone within the amulet. His spirit was unsettled, as it usually was when confronted by Lord Wrothgar in the midst of a plan. Now he would summon Gorgon and convey the Shadowmancer's message. He hoped the Elves would not take too long in plotting and planning, as Kotos disliked uncertainty, particularly when the good graces of Wrothgar depended upon his success. He was not prepared to live outside those good graces.

It wouldn't matter how impatient either Kotos or Gaelen might have been—the implementation of the Elves' plan would take some time to achieve.The artisans of Tal-sithian would be tested in creating a crystal to match the great Stone. Yet, as Arialde pointed out, this replica would not need to bear close scrutiny, therefore a perfect match was not required. The artisans were sworn to secrecy, and they worked in seclusion.

A messenger would be dispatched to Mountain-home, for if the Elves had believed Nelwyn's vision, they would have sought to warn Ordath at once. Therefore, a small party mounted on swift horses rode forth a few days later, expecting that the raven might take notice of them. Nothing must interfere with the illusion that Lord Kotos' plan was succeeding.

The Company kept to itself much of the time, as all had been instructed not to discuss the plan with the people. Yet there were happy times in that wondrous place. Azori, Estle, Carmyn, and Hallagond, who had yet to experience High-elven hospitality, were enchanted. The Company would not leave for several weeks, which would allow all in the group to gain a thorough acquaintance with the food, drink, and beautiful vistas of the Island.

One evening, as the owls called in the trees and the stars brightened overhead, Gaelen and Nelwyn called down to Estle, asking that she climb a tall tree so that she might experience star-gazing in true Wood-elven fashion. "Come, Estle, and watch the skies with us. The breezes are warm, and the leaves are fragrant. Come up and join us!"

Estle was reluctant, but she did not wish to refuse the invitation, as she did not wish to admit that she was afraid. "I have no experience in tree-climbing," she said. "Will you not come down that we might lie upon the soft grass and view the sky?"

"The stars will be obscured by the canopy from the ground, Estle," said Nelwyn. "You cannot appreciate this fine view until you have shared it. Do not fear…we will not let you fall."

"Is there honey involved?" asked Estle with suspicion. She did not trust any Wood-elf who was under the influence of sweet things. In answer, Gaelen suddenly appeared to her immediate left, with barely a rustling leaf. She was quite sober.

"I am going to join Rogond and Fima, who have asked for my presence in a matter of debate this evening," she said. "Nelwyn would much prefer to share this fine night with a friend, and we do not know where Galador is. You would not wish for Nelwyn to be lonely, would you?"

"Of course not," said Estle. "But I do not enjoy tree-climbing, as I have no experience in it."

"Then how do you know that you do not enjoy it?" asked Gaelen.

"Because I don't like high places," said Estle. "There. I have admitted it. Now taunt me if you will, Gaelen. I know you will appreciate the opportunity."

Gaelen just stared at her. "Taunting by invitation is not all that rewarding. And, begging your pardon, you have already given me plenty of opportunity, and I have used utmost restraint in taunting you. You expect such behavior because you cannot resist doing it yourself. Am I right?"

"You're Gaelen, aren't you? That means you're always right," said Estle.

"You see? You have just proved my point," said Gaelen, smiling at her. "Will you not at least try to climb up? I assure you that the end will be worth the effort."

"It's the 'end' I'm worried about," Estle muttered, having already imagined falling to her death several times.

"Just follow my lead," said Gaelen, and a moment later she had vaulted into the lower branches, scrambling up like a very limber squirrel. Estle shook her head. What a ridiculous notion!

"I'm sorry, but as I claim no squirrels or fruit-bats among my ancestors, I will just keep my feet on the ground, thank you very much!" A moment later both Elves dropped down beside her as she turned to leave.

"If you would truly enjoy lying upon the soft grass, then that is what we will do," said Nelwyn. "It is worth it to have your company. I would never intend to make you uncomfortable." Estle smiled, unable to imagine that anyone could dislike Nelwyn.

"Farewell then, both of you," said Gaelen. "Until we meet again!" She gave a short, musical laugh and walked away, turning back at the last minute. "You really don't know what you're missing, Estle," she said and winked.

"On the contrary, I believe I do," Estle replied. "I also know what *you* appear to be missing!" She twirled an index finger beside her right ear.

Gaelen laughed again, but did not reply. Then she was gone.

Nelwyn and Estle made their way to the shoreline, where the trees were kept back by high water during the rains. The water level had fallen enough since the snow-melt and early spring weather that there was a nice grassy area to lie upon, and they did so. "Tell me a tale, won't you?" asked Nelwyn.

"I will, if you will in return," said Estle. "Let me see…would you like to hear a story of how El-morah met his bride?"

"Oh, yes!" said Nelwyn. "And in return, would you like to hear a story of the Greatwood, in which Gaelen made a complete fool of herself with one of our friends, named Cúingael?"

"A complete fool, eh! *How* complete?" asked Estle.

"Let me put it this way...she was nearly thrown into prison for a week. There is something not so wise about digging a pit-trap for game and ensnaring the King instead!" At this, Nelwyn began to giggle. "And then there was the weasel..."

"Oh...I can't think of anything that would please me more than that," said Estle, her eyes gleaming in the ever-brightening starlight. She knew that she would soon have more grist for the mill of Gaelen's future taunting.

Gaelen was unaware of the inevitability of future taunts from Estle as she made her way to the library. In Tal-sithian, as in many Elven-realms, it was below ground to keep it from fierce winds and extremes of heat and cold. When she arrived, she found Fima and Rogond sitting on either side of a low stone table on which was spread a very large map. Of the three proposed destinations, it had been decided that Tuathas was the most sensible. No one wanted to bring enemies among Grundin's folk, and the ruin of Eádros was too close to Tûr Dorcha.

It was rumored that the northern realm had begun the slow process of recovery from near-total destruction. The fire-mountains had deposited so much poisonous ash and molten rock that all living things had perished. Only now, after hundreds of years, were things beginning to grow again.

"Ah, Gaelen, there you are!" said Fima. "Rogond and I were just trying to decide our future course. We would like your opinion, if you don't mind."

Gaelen nodded and sat down beside Rogond, who pointed to the map. "We have three possible ways in mind, but each has its difficulties. The first is to go north from here, cross the Artan, and then follow the Ambros north to the Eros. It takes us nearly all the way to the northern realm. The second way goes straight west, to the verdant mountains, and then north. The third crosses the mountains and goes north along the sea."

"And how long will the journey take?" asked Gaelen. "We will not be able to travel swiftly, as we will be burdened with the replica of the Stone."

"By my reckoning, this journey will extend for at least a thousand miles no matter what," said Fima, "although the way along the Ambros is a little shorter."

"I doubt we can make more than twenty miles a day, particularly since we are expected to travel *only* by day," said Gaelen. "After all, we certainly would not risk an encounter with Ulcas or bandits by traveling in darkness, would we?"

"Even if we can make twenty miles a day, it will mean a journey of nearly two months," said Rogond. "And we will not be able to travel without a few days of rest now and then. Depending on weather and unforeseen events, we may be delayed even further."

"Summer will be coming on," said Gaelen. "I would say our timing is excellent."

"Our timing is vital," said Fima, "for the northern lands may suffer violent weather, even in autumn. We must arrive before the onset of winter in any event. I know that I cannot ride twenty miles a day for two months without rest."

"Even if we slow our progress down by half, we still will have one hundred days," said Gaelen. "That will put us in the northland at harvest, and we will not be lingering long."

"Yet in Tuathas there is still danger," said Rogond. "Since the eruption of the fire-mountain, it is said that freakish blizzards assail the land as early as late summer. We had best carry warm clothing and be prepared for the worst."

"I have not heard tell of those blizzards in many a year," said Fima. "And I am not certain the accounts were reliable in any event. The fire-mountains continue to throw ash into the air whenever it pleases them, and ash looks very much like snow."

"We will all find out the truth of it soon enough," said Gaelen. "Meanwhile, we still have not agreed upon which path to take. I suggest that, of the three you have mentioned, the only acceptable way is the first one. The others pass near to Tal-ailean and the Twilight Shores. You forget that Gorgon will be following behind."

"Yet he will be directed by Lord Kotos," said Fima. "I doubt that the Deceiver will allow the Elfhunter to stray from the pursuit just to hunt Elves, as they might risk losing track of us."

"Still, I cannot take the chance," said Gaelen. "I have sworn that I will lead Gorgon away from the Elves, not bring him to their doorstep. Most certainly I would not direct him anywhere near to the Twilight Shores, as that is hallowed ground."

"Fair enough," said Rogond. "I also like this way, as it avoids the mountains. We will be in river valley for much of the time."

"Crossing the Brocca should be interesting," muttered Fima, who did not like swift water any more than he liked a swift horse. He most certainly was not looking forward to crossing swift water while trying to remain seated upon a swift horse.

"I would suggest that we not cross the Brocca," said Rogond. "We should cross the Ambros instead, as it will be calmer and shallower in summer. The Brocca is too fierce at any time of year. There is no reason we cannot travel the southern bank of the Eros, as it is far enough from the Greatwood."

"One thing is unfortunate," said Fima. "A very large number of ravens dwell in the north. We may not be able to tell a harmless bird from a deadly foe."

"That's a cheery thought," said Rogond. To his surprise, Gaelen began to laugh.

"What could you find amusing right now?" asked Fima.

"Oh, it's just that I was remembering Sajid the Spider and his words to me in the Ravi-shan. He was doing his ridiculous rhyming speech, warning me to take his advice. He said, 'I fear your fate will be Raven-bait.'" She laughed again. "And now, that is *exactly* what I will be."

"Perhaps," said Fima who did not care for the idea. "But I will tell you both something—if I ever get my hands on *that* raven, we'll be eating it with a light sage dressing and fried apples."

"Let us just hope it takes the bait," said Gaelen, and she did not smile.

19
Difficult Decisions

Fima gathered the Company together with Arialde the following day. He stood before his friends, old and new, and laid before them the plan to lure Gorgon and Lord Kotos to Tuathas. "A small contingent will take the replica of the Stone northward, ensuring that Lord Kotos and Gorgon will follow. The membership of this contingent is as yet undecided, although it will include Gaelen and myself. We are both necessary to ensure Gorgon's willing participation."

"Tuathas!" said Hallagond. "Have you lost your minds? There must be another way."

"Would the Shadowmancer expect Arialde to charge Gaelen with such an important task?" said Estle. "Would she not send her own people, those she knows are especially capable and trustworthy?"

Everyone looked at Arialde, and then at Gaelen, who did not take offense. "Lady Arialde knows that I'm capable as well as trustworthy," she said. "But more important—Gorgon knows these things, too. Lord Kotos may dismiss me, but Gorgon will not, I assure you. This will make perfect sense to him. And if you believe that the Elfhunter is only the thrall of Lord Kotos, allow me to enlighten you. Gorgon is cooperating, and it is true that he has been persuaded, but he will not be subjugated. He serves his own ends, as he has always done. And what he wants more than anything in the world is to see to my death, followed by the deaths of every other Elf in Alterra." She shuddered. "I would rather not try to imagine what Lord Kotos has promised him."

Arialde looked around the circle of companions. "Gaelen has spoken well, and I agree. But only a few may go with her. You must decide who will go, and who will aid in some other fashion. I will also send forces to Mountain-home, and I believe in my heart that Kotos will be expecting Nelwyn to go there, so that the full impact of her 'vision' may be shared."

At this, Nelwyn rose to her feet, her cheeks and ears flushed. "And what is to prevent Lord Wrothgar from sending an army of Ulcas and Trolls down upon Gaelen the minute she is out of your influence? After all, that is what he wants…to seize the Stone. What is to prevent him from doing exactly that? And then, not only will he be aware that we have not been deceived, but he will have killed Gaelen and all who travel with her. I doubt very much that anyone will get anywhere near Tuathas. This plan is suicidal!"

"This sounds like one of Rogond's ideas," said Hallagond. "Have any of you been near the ruin of Tuathas? Well, I have. Long ago, while my brother was being wet-nursed by Elves, I dared to draw near to the fire-mountains of Monadh-ainnas, and I actually set foot in Tuathan lands. I was younger and more inquisitive then, and I thought myself invincible. I learned otherwise in that terrible place."

"You must enlighten me, Hallagond," said Fima. "Yet in Mountain-home the word is that things have improved."

"And what fool brought *that* news?" growled Hallagond.

"That would be Lord Magra, who once ventured even as far as the eastern city of Tallanor," said Fima. "I'm not certain I would classify him as a fool. He described a desolate and terrible place, as you suggest, yet it is not lethal to go there."

"What interest would Lord Magra have in Tuathas?" asked Rogond.

"There were tales of men who still lived there," said Fima. "We all wanted to know whether they were true. If any had survived the cataclysm, Magra wanted to find them and aid them. Surely no one would settle there by choice, and therefore it was thought that any men living there would be descended of the original stock…the followers of Duinar."

"I'm guessing that he did not find anyone," said Hallagond.

'No, he didn't," said Fima. "Nor did he discover any recent evidence of them. However, I did learn many things of interest from him. Magra has the heart and soul of a warrior, but he has the mind of a lore-master." This thought made Fima smile. "At any rate, what he described to me will be daunting, but not impassable. And Wrothgar would realize that it's an excellent place to hide something, as few have ventured there. It's not such a bad idea, Hallagond."

"To get to Tuathas, you must pass near the Northern Mountains," said Carmyn, who had studied the map. "Are they not perilous and full of enemies?"

"We will follow the River Eros," said Gaelen. "We might draw within fifty miles of the foothills of the Northern Mountains, but even that does not concern me."

"How could it not?" asked Estle. "You believe you are formidable, but there are enemies in the North that are beyond you."

"None of it will make any *difference*," said Nelwyn, whose blood was still up. "They will be taken long before they gain the lands near the Northern Mountains." She shook her head. "This is a fool's errand."

"My cousin has forgotten something, as have the rest of you, apparently," said Gaelen. "I do not fear attack from Wrothgar. He will wait until we have hidden the Stone to take it."

"And you know this…how?" asked Hallagond, who thought Nelwyn's assessment apt.

"Because I will let it be known to Gorgon Elfhunter that should I catch a whiff of an army or any sort of attempt to take the Stone, I will destroy it at once. A well-placed hammer-blow is all it would take. Wrothgar would regret the loss of the Stone more than anything, as he believes it will bring about his eventual return to power. Kotos would be cutting his own throat to risk having it destroyed. Gorgon will assure him that I mean what I say, because I *do* mean it. Any sort of attack, any sense whatsoever of enemies threatening, and I will shatter the 'Stone.' It would not be a bad thing for Wrothgar to believe it has been destroyed. He will not allow any of his minions to come near me in the meantime."

"He will know it has not been destroyed," said Arialde. "I should imagine that shattering the real Stone would be felt by every being of insight in Alterra. And Shandor's spirit is most powerful… Wrothgar would know that his ancient enemy still dwells in this world." She looked hard at Gaelen then. "Are you certain you can convey this message, little fire-spirit? Nelwyn's concern is well-founded if you cannot."

"Gorgon will hear me if the mirror is near," said Gaelen. "That's why Fima must go with us, for he carries the mirror, and Gorgon knows it. Even if the creature loses our trail, he will follow the mirror, for he can sense its presence, as can I. And so long as it exists, our thoughts may be shared, unless we guard them. We have both become very adept at guarding our thoughts, yet I can also make certain that Gorgon hears them, if I desire it."

This seemed to satisfy Arialde, who turned back to the circle. "Who, then, shall go with Gaelen, and who shall go to Mountain-home? You must decide," she said. "I will leave you to your circle, where all may speak their minds. Please inform me of your decisions once they have been made." So saying, she swept from the clean, white chamber, leaving the Company to stare at one another in silence.

"I do not ask any of you save Fima to go with me," said Gaelen after a long, awkward moment. "Once the 'Stone' has found its new resting place, I will be in peril. Gorgon is a wily adversary, and he will have laid his plans well. Kotos will not deny him his heart's desire. They will take any who stand with me, as well."

She stood before them, slight of stature but full of resolve and courage, a soul worthy of the ancient line of Kings. "Who wishes to witness the death of Gorgon Elfhunter?" she said.

"I wish that very much indeed," said Rogond, rising to his feet. "Gorgon will expect me to accompany you. Besides, I want to visit the land of my forefathers. Despite my brother's warning, I want to know what lies beneath the city of Tallasiar, where Duinar tried to stand against the Mountain."

Hallagond shook his head, his light brown hair waving in a silken tangle.

"I know this will come as a great shock to everyone," said Azori, who had not yet spoken, "but I do *not* wish to witness the death of anyone, particularly me."

"Oh, yes, that *is* a shock," said Estle. "You would allow me to walk into peril without you, then?" She smiled wickedly at him.

"You wouldn't do that to me, would you?" said Azori with a horrified expression.

"That depends on Hallagond," Estle replied. Azori threw his head back, closed his eyes, and gave a deep, heart-felt groan.

"I still believe this course is ill-advised," said Hallagond. "There will be nothing wholesome to eat or drink, and the air is full of ash and choking dust. The mountains are forever belching and spewing and rumbling. I tell you, this is a mistake."

"Sounds a lot like the southern desert," said Fima, who would not be dissuaded despite the prospect of choking dust.

"You have no idea," said Hallagond. "At least in the desert there is beauty, and water may be found that is fit to drink. Imagine the worst hell you encountered in the desert, and then treble it!" He folded his arms and stood in defiance before Fima and Rogond, as though daring them to disagree.

"We do not have to make our choice now, at this moment," said Gaelen. "As it stands, Rogond, Fima, and I will take the 'Stone.' If Estle, Hallagond, and Azori choose to go to Mountain-home with Nelwyn and Galador, then I will not blame them." She turned to Nelwyn, who was on the verge of tears. "I know you don't like having your course chosen for you by Arialde, yet she is right. We must do as Wrothgar expects."

Nelwyn struggled to keep her voice calm. "Do you remember how you felt when you realized that Gorgon had used you to aid him in killing Elves? You wanted more than anything to exact vengeance upon his accursed black heart. You were only content because you were allowed to be instrumental in bringing about his downfall in the Barrens. There is more to this than my love for you. You honestly expect me to run to the safety of Mountain-home while you accomplish my vengeance for me?"

She looked around at her friends, who had not expected such words from her. "I am not naïve!" she nearly shouted. "Whatever imagined innocence made me the target of Lord Kotos' invasion has been forever lost! If Orrion stood before me now, I would attempt to kill him with my bare hands. No one directs my fate. I make my own choices!" Her willowy frame was trembling, her elegant fingers clenched into fists. There was no doubt of her sincerity. She looked desperately at Gaelen, imploring her to see that Arialde's declaration was wrong and unfair.

Instead, Gaelen spoke calm, clear words that could not be denied. "This is why we cannot take you with us. If Kotos catches any hint that you even know he exists, we are undone. If he is diverted from you, he will never know. If you go with me, he will not understand why, and he will question it. After all, my errand is a secret one, and Wrothgar would not know of it. There would be no reason for you to be compelled to accompany me, for as long as I keep to secret paths I should be safe. Kotos will expect you to go to Mountain-home where, according to your 'vision,' the *real* danger lies. Therefore, for the sake of your vengeance, you and Galador must go to Mountain-home."

"Then I am without hope," said Nelwyn. "I would never prevent you from doing what you think is right, even if I thought it ill-advised. Do you realize how many times such a choice has been placed before me? Always, I have followed your wishes. The worst part is that I *know* you're right this time, but that doesn't make it any easier to bear." She looked away from her friends. "This errand will mean your death, Gaelen. Gorgon is too great an enemy, and he will thrive in the poisoned darkness of Tuathas. I fear never to see you, or Fima, or Rogond again...and there is, apparently, nothing I can do about it." She left the chamber then, her pain and frustration evident.

Galador looked at Gaelen and shook his head. "I wish there had been some other way," he said, getting to his feet and following after his beloved. After he had gone, there was silence. Everyone was sorry for Nelwyn's plight, for she had done nothing to earn it.

Not long after the departure of Nelwyn and Galador, Gaelen also left the council. She knew there would be many discussions and debates shared among her friends, especially Estle, Hallagond, and Azori. Gaelen's thoughts were confused and conflicted as she sat alone among the cedars in the Courtyard of the Stone.

Despite Arialde's having covered the Stone with the indigo cloth, Gaelen could still sense the sullen darkness within. Saying such words to Nelwyn had been one of the most difficult tasks she had ever faced, and now she was filled with regret. She could not deny that it would have been unwise to allow Nelwyn to accompany her. Yet now she had broken the heart of her dearest friend. Was there not a way to make things right?

Rogond found her soon after. She was startled, having been so deep in thought that she had not heard him approach. "Is that it?" he asked in a quiet voice full of reverence and awe. He had not been in the Courtyard before. "Is that the Stone?"

Gaelen nodded. "Yes, Thaylon, that is the Stone. Though it has gone dark, and I do not sense any spirit moving within it."

Rogond shook his head and then sat beside Gaelen. It was a chilly night, and she drew against his side to warm herself. He knew that she was troubled, and he knew why, yet he would not ask her about it. She would get around to speaking of it on her own.

"This business with Nelwyn cannot stand," she said at last. "I will not hurt my friend so. There must be another way, as Galador has suggested."

"He has not suggested any other way," said Rogond. "He only wished that it could be so. What other way could there be?"

"I was hoping you would think of something," said Gaelen.

Rogond drew back from her just a little. "Why would you expect such a thing of me?" he asked. "You are the one with all the insight, remember?"

"Ah, but you are the clever, mortal one," said Gaelen. "Your kind do not have ages to get over your disappointments, therefore you must be more adept at avoiding them."

"If only that were true, but alas, our lives are fraught with disappointment," said Rogond. "And if I were you, I would not go against the advice of the Lady. I have heard this tone from you before, Gaelen, and it worries me."

"Stop worrying. I have no inspiration or plan to go against the Lady," said Gaelen. "For now, you should sleep. All this worrying has worn you out. I will keep the watch, as always."

"There is nothing to fear here in Tal-sithian," said Rogond. "Yet you're right…I am weary. My head is heavy and my eyes don't want to stay open."

He fell asleep a few moments later, resting his head on Gaelen's shoulder. She took comfort in the deep, regular sound of his breathing, and it relaxed her. Her thoughts, which had been so muddled and confused, became clear. There was a way to aid Nelwyn, and it made a great deal of sense! Why had she not thought of it before? No matter. She would seek out her cousin as soon as was practical, and hope that Nelwyn would hear her plan.

Lore-master Fima sat alone in a dimly-lighted alcove of the underground library and wondered what his fate would be. He reflected upon the course his life had taken since his good friend Rogond had appeared in Mountain-home, and then he smiled. *I have seen wonders that none of my race has ever beheld, and now I am about to embark on a journey that, while dangerous and difficult, will take me to a long-forgotten realm full of unknowns. The only problem is that I most likely won't live to share the knowledge.* He sighed and stroked his full, white beard with a thoughtful hand. *While the idea of death doesn't frighten me, it does imply a serious interruption of my work…* For perhaps the second time in his long life, Fima realized that he would not be able to learn all that there was to know.

Carmyn appeared in the warm glow of the candle-light, a sheaf of parchments in her hand and a worried look upon her face. "Lore-master, I have come to counsel with you. Please forgive my intrusion but…there are things I must say."

Fima gestured toward the chair opposite his, and Carmyn sat down, placing the parchments on the table. Fima saw that her eyes were red. Either she had been crying, or trying not to.

"Please, my friend, tell me what troubles you," he said. "It's plain to see that you're unhappy. How can I aid you?"

Carmyn wrestled with her own thoughts for several moments, sitting silent and tense. At last she blurted out: "I intend to go with you to Tuathas. Yet I am afraid, and I'm ashamed of my fear." She had declared her intention at last, and it seemed to aid her, for she visibly relaxed.

"Why would you choose such a course, Carmyn?" said Fima. "This journey will be dangerous, and you have very little stake in it…why would you walk into such peril?"

"I have followed you from Dûn Arian because you are the most fascinating and learned person I have ever met," she replied. "Did you not know it? I wanted to be your apprentice and learn all you would teach me. Now I want to protect you, for you will need aid." She paused again, allowing Fima to absorb all that he had heard. "I'm not adventurous by nature," she said at last, "and I truly wanted to produce an accurate map of the Linnefionn. But I have already decided that I will go wherever you go, unless you forbid me."

Fima had rarely been so touched. Carmyn's genuine admiration and affection for him was moving, and he placed a gnarled, strong hand upon her arm. "I am honored," he said. "Yet I fear that there is another destiny awaiting you. You are a scholar that few in the North can rival, and I have a very, very important task. I will entrust it to no other."

Carmyn was on the verge of tears. "What…what task?" she asked in a halting voice.

In answer, Fima reached beneath the table and drew forth a scorched, battered leather case. Inside were his journals and parchments: everything he had recorded since his journey began. "This is very precious to me..."

He placed it on the table and then, with a small sigh of regret, he pushed it toward her. "You must take it to Mountain-home, and then you must tell Lady Ordath of Dûn Arian. You must provide as much history as you can. Alas, I did not have as much time to record it as I needed. And you must tell her that it was I who discovered these wonders and brought them back."

"You must take them yourself," said Carmyn, who was now weeping, for she understood his motivation. "You should not entrust them to me…what if I fail in my task and lose them? Why not take them after you return?"

Fima shook his head. "I do not expect to return. I am old, and my vigor is much diminished. You know, I used to think that I would live forever. Perhaps the influence of so much time among the Elves." He smiled at her. "I have now finally realized that I am mortal and my life must end. This journey is important; it must be undertaken for the sake of all people of Light."

"But, *why?* I still do not understand why," said Carmyn. "Lord Kotos' dark deception did not work. We have seen through it. Wrothgar's plan is foiled. Why do we care about luring him to Tuathas? Why can we not stay here, or go to Mountain-home together? Think of all you could teach me! I would serve you until the end of your days, many years hence."

"Will you agree to do as I asked, and take my journals to Mountain-home?" said Fima, as though he had not heard. Carmyn rubbed her eyes with one hand and nodded. Fima patted her arm and squeezed it. "I would love to do as you suggest, and live out my days in comfort, but it's too late for that. I have sworn to see to the death of Gorgon, and I cannot abandon Gaelen now. She needs me to play my part." He looked hard at Carmyn. "I am not afraid. You should feel no shame in your own fear, for you have nearly a lifetime ahead of you. Mine is ending. I will go to a new beginning and learn the answers to some mysteries that have puzzled me for many a year. Take heart, my friend, and *do* make certain I am credited with my discoveries, won't you? Through them I will be immortal, in a way."

"My heart is broken," said Carmyn, "and I will mourn if you do not return. Yet there is another way in which I may aid you. I notice that no one here possesses a detailed map of Tuathas. There is not even a good one in the library…I have searched it. I once copied such a map in Dûn Arian, and…and my memory is excellent, nearly unrivaled among the scholars."

"Is it, indeed?" asked Fima, his blue eyes wide and sparkling again.

"I thought perhaps I could re-create the map from memory," said Carmyn. "A map will be needed. And it would be better than nothing."

"I think that's the most hopeful idea I have heard since we arrived here," said Fima. "Apart from Gaelen's fletching arrows with Lord Kotos' raven, that is. And you never know, my dear apprentice, perhaps I will return. I will do what I can to avoid disaster. It never pays to leave a Dwarf out of your calculations." He patted her arm again and she smiled, though fresh tears threatened to come forth. "Now, my remarkable cartographer, let us set to work. I have never observed anyone with a perfect memory before."

They drew out a piece of thin leather and spread it upon the table, as Carmyn set to work with a sharpened piece of charcoal. Later, she would use ink. When she finally finished, the map was incredibly detailed, and had taken three days and nights to complete.

Gaelen knew that she would find Nelwyn among the trees. The forests of the island were like gardens, with many varieties of trees, shrubs, and flowers, some that were said to be found nowhere else in Alterra.

Gaelen sensed Nelwyn's presence long before encountering her, for the heat of betrayal and despair could be clearly felt. She knew that, since establishing the unwanted connection with Gorgon, she had become more intuitive than ever. Soon her inner senses would rival those of any who had come before her, if that connection continued.

If it continued.

If *she* continued.

Her abilities were growing, overwhelming her uncomplicated nature. Gaelen was a small vessel for so much power—she could only contain and control it for so long. She had to see to the end of it, and soon, or be forever altered by it. She had not shared her fears with anyone, not even Nelwyn or Rogond, but Gaelen *was* afraid. The spiritual bond with Gorgon, though unwanted and unbidden, was deep. At times, when she held a thought or an emotion, she wondered whether it was truly her own. She had to be free of him.

Her heart sank as she drew near Nelwyn's refuge, feeling all connection with her cousin go dark. Nelwyn had sensed her presence and had veiled herself, but Gaelen would not be put off. She drew closer, calling in her clear, soft bird-voice, asking to be allowed to approach. There was no response from Nelwyn. Then Galador appeared, startling Gaelen, whose senses were trained elsewhere. His dark silhouette stood in stark contrast to the graceful, silvery tree-trunks and feathery shrubs that surrounded him. His eyes were cold.

"What do you want?" he asked. "I doubt very much that you have anything to say that Nelwyn will want to hear."

"Well, then I must convince her otherwise, for I do have things to say that she will wish to hear," Gaelen replied. Galador had come a long way in recent months, but there was still no question that his trust of Gaelen turned on Nelwyn's fortunes. She set her jaw and drew a deep breath. "You must allow me to spend some time with Nelwyn alone," she said, to which Galador raised both of his eyebrows.

"Why should I allow that, precisely?" he asked. "Do you have any notion of how distraught she is at this moment? Although I understand your motivation, as does Nelwyn, she feels betrayed. You would feel the same. If I were you, I would stay away from her for a while and allow her to come to grips with it. You will not comfort her now."

Gaelen moved to stand within arm's length of Galador so that he could look into her eyes. "You don't know what I will say to her, Galador. You must trust in me despite your natural inclination. I will comfort her, I assure you. But only if you will stand aside and allow me to do so!"

Galador stood for a moment as though frozen in thought, debating Gaelen's words. Then the tension flowed out of his shoulders and he nodded. "All right, I will trust you once more," he said. "But if you upset her further…" He tensed up again as he said this.

"I won't," said Gaelen. "At least, I will try my best not to." He stood aside then, so that she could continue with her plan.

Nelwyn was easy to find, as all Gaelen had to do was track Galador's path. She sat alone, surrounded by fragrant spice-bushes and vines of jasmine and silver-leaf that encircled her like a cocoon. They seemed a part of her. Her eyes widened when she saw Gaelen, and then narrowed as she drew back into the shadows. "So, have you come to pat my head and tell me that all will be well? You can save your effort, because it won't be. And if you are wanting to assuage your own guilt by repeating that you had no choice but to betray me, then save it. I don't wish to hear any words from you just now."

"I would never pat your head, Nelwyn," said Gaelen, who had cringed inwardly at Nelwyn's choice of metaphor. Gaelen hated being patted on the head, having her hair ruffled, or otherwise being patronized by persons taller than herself. When she was young, this had been done to her often by her elders and peers, until one day she drew a blade on one of them, a very tall male who was being particularly annoying. Gaelen's body language was enough to dissuade anyone from placing a hand near her head—not even Rogond could do so without striking a brief spark in her eyes. "I was wrong, and short-sighted. I am not coming to assuage my guilt, but to suggest an alternative plan. Will you hear it?"

"Does it involve my going to Mountain-home, and parting from you and Rogond?" said Nelwyn.

"Yes, it still involves your going to Mountain-home," said Gaelen. "Wrothgar has eyes everywhere, so that we dare not stray from the path he expects us to take. Yet beyond that, the path is quite different. I have realized that I cannot succeed without your aid. Will you give it?"

Nelwyn brightened at once, seeming to visibly grow larger as she no longer sought to shrink back into the shrubbery. "What do you propose?" she asked.

Gaelen smiled. "Proper planning must be done in tree-tops, where none but hunter-scouts can hear," was her reply.

"Then let us away at once," said Nelwyn, "for proper plans take time to make and refine. I know just the tree-top for the task."

They made their way under the moonlight to the tallest, most venerable oak on the island, climbed into its welcoming branches, and laid their plans far into the night. By morning, when Galador next beheld her, Nelwyn was of cheerful demeanor once again and seemed at peace with the plan to go to Mountain-home, though she would not tell him why.

The news came as the sun rose high on the following day. Soon the entire island was astir with anticipation: the riders had returned with emissaries from Mountain-home. Apparently, they carried important tidings, as their mounts had been ridden nearly to the limit of their endurance. The Company assembled, together with the most trusted and valiant Elves of Tal-sithian, to hear the report from the realm of Ordath.

The faces of the Elves of Mountain-home were drawn with worry, for Lady Ordath had much ill news to impart. She was greatly concerned, for when Shandor had withdrawn into the Stone, Ordath had been aware of it, and it had alarmed her. She had already been receiving reports of large numbers of Ulcas, Trolls and brigands making their way north from the Darkmere, massing in the east of the Greatwood. Brave scouts had been sent northward to the dreaded lands of the Fell-ruin, and the few who returned brought grave news. Wrothgar was preparing an assault.

Arialde was not surprised by any of this news. She had not enlightened Ordath, for the riders of Tal-sithian had not been privy to all insights known to the Company, and they had not carried any message that could have fallen into the wrong hands. Therefore, as far as the Elves of Mountain-home knew, their realm was under imminent threat of attack.

They were not aware of Wrothgar's deception, or of his collusion with Lord Kotos. They had already sent for aid from the Greatwood, and Ri-Aruin had promised to send as many as he could muster. Now they asked for help from Tal-sithian.

Nelwyn was mesmerized as she sat beside Gaelen in the Hall of Council. Her 'vision' was playing itself out before her eyes! Both Wood-elves felt a deep pang of sorrow at the mention of Ri-Aruin. How they longed to join their friends and kin, and march beneath his banner! Nelwyn looked over at Gaelen, whose face bore no expression as she heard what the emissaries revealed. None of this made any difference to her plan.

Arialde stood before the assembly, tall and silver-white, her power comforting all who perceived it. She did not enlighten them, or assuage their fears, for they must be led to believe that Nelwyn's 'vision' was true. She asked that everyone present disperse and retire to consider what they had heard, take rest and refreshment, and meet again when plans were agreed upon. At the last, she called Nelwyn aside.

"Do you now perceive your importance?" she said. "You will carry the message of Wrothgar's deception to Lady Ordath. I cannot enlighten my people, as there will be too many unguarded hearts and minds for Lord Kotos to invade and perceive. He must not know that we are aware of him in any way. I intend to send my army with the news that the Stone of Léir is being moved, but you will carry the reality to Ordath's realm. Once you are there, I expect Kotos' attention will have been diverted into following Gaelen and her Company. Yet the spies of the Enemy move through the lands between here and Mountain-home, if I am any judge. All must appear as if we have been taken in."

She looked deep into Nelwyn's eyes. "If we are successful, Wrothgar will not threaten the Light for a long time to come. We will quell his 'uprising' and foil him utterly. His forces will be decimated, and we will all breathe more easily. If Gaelen fulfills her destiny, Gorgon Elfhunter will be removed from the face of the world. I suspect that she also has plans to exact revenge upon Lord Kotos, though I would not wager against my life in such a venture."

Arialde smiled again, and it filled Nelwyn with hope and comfort. "The outcome of this conflict turns on the fortunes of two Wood-elves," she said. "I, for one, am confident."

Preparations for the departure of the army of Tal-sithian were made in haste. Arialde did not send all her forces, however. She held back a loyal and dedicated company of warriors, in case the island needed protection. Arialde knew in her heart that Wrothgar did not have the strength to overcome her defenses. Never had he done so, even at the height of his power. Lord Kotos would not dare bring his twisted spirit near the island again, that was certain. He could not see into the hearts that dwelt there. Yet Arialde needed to behave as though she believed in the truth of Nelwyn's false vision, for her people needed to believe in it, too. Therefore, she held back her defense force.

All were told that the Stone of Léir would be moved to a new, hidden location until the Uprising of Wrothgar was quelled. This would be done in secret, and only the Lady herself would know when and where the Stone would be taken. Though this prospect filled the people with apprehension, they understood the need. Should a spy overhear any whisper or thought, Wrothgar would be told that all was according to plan.

The Company met in council with Arialde, and each was asked to declare intentions. All eyes turned to Hallagond, for his decision would set not only his own course, but those of Estle and Azori. He had spent many sleepless nights in consideration and debate with himself, with Estle and with Azori, but in the end the decision had come to him alone.

"I am conflicted," he said, "for I don't wish to leave my brother to an uncertain fate. I have already tried to influence him to choose another destination, but he has refused, and I won't lead Estle into such a dangerous place. The Elves of Mountain-home will need warriors like me to aid them. Therefore, I will go to Mountain-home to aid the Lady Ordath."

He looked over at Rogond, two nearly identical pairs of grey eyes meeting in acknowledgment. Rogond nodded and bowed, but Hallagond lowered his gaze, for he was disheartened. It would almost have been easier had Rogond been even a little indignant, rather than being so confounded understanding.

Estle then rose and declared her intention to accompany Hallagond, followed immediately by Azori, who had rarely looked so pleased about anything.

Carmyn did not know whether she could declare herself in front of the Company without weeping, and she sat staring down at the floor until Fima saved her the trouble.

"I have been in consultation with Carmyn, and though she had wanted to go with me, I convinced her otherwise. I have charged her with a task in Mountain-home, and she will be going there," he said.

"Then only Gaelen, Rogond, and Fima are set upon this northward path?" said Arialde, looking with some concern upon Gaelen. "It seems so few to face so great an enemy. Yet there are stalwart representatives of three worthy races—Northmen, the Deep-caverns, and the Elves of the Wood. I can also send my most trusted guardians to aid you, if you deem it wise."

"Thank you, my lady," said Rogond. "We shall consider it."

At last the day of departure came, and the boats were laden and made ready to carry the warriors of Tal-sithian forth to Mountain-home. They were resplendent in their armor of grey and silver, their banners floating on a gentle southwesterly breeze.

Instead of following the Brunner Aigred they would travel north, through the marsh-meadows, and then turn eastward, negotiating the tricky path through the mountains between the two turbulent Amari streams. They did not concern themselves with stealth—they wanted Wrothgar to notice them.

Nelwyn stood upon the shores of the Lake, scanning the waters, looking for signs of Collyn and his folk, yet they were nowhere to be seen.

"The Currgas are not comfortable with the sight of so many weapons," said Lord Airan, smiling at her. "Collyn did say that he wished you well. He and his people have provided a supply of salted, dried fish, as they knew that you would need sustenance. I did include some of it among your stores." He shook his head. "It is an acquired taste."

The Company had not rested, having spent what might prove to be their last night together in fellowship. They had shared tales, songs, food, wine, and ale, and generally had reveled in their companionship. They did not mention that any one of them might not return to see the others again, though all were thinking of it. At one point, Hallagond drew Rogond aside.

"There is something I must share with you, my brother," he said. "It is more than just my love for Estle that prevents my going into the heart of darkness with you."

"That is reason enough," said Rogond. "If Gaelen were not the primary reason for going to Tuathas, I would not wish to take her there, either."

"You do not understand," said Hallagond. "Estle is...well, she might be...she believes that she is..."

"Is what?" asked Rogond, who thought he knew the answer already.

"She is not certain," said Hallagond.

"She is with child?" said Rogond, smiling.

"Maybe," said Hallagond.

"That is wonderful news," said Rogond. "At least, it may be." He smiled again. "It must be the water in Tal-sithian."

"Or the wine," said Hallagond, shaking his head and smiling back at Rogond. "At any rate, I trust that the reason for my choice has become clear to you. And, I would ask that you not share it. I could not talk her out of going with me despite everything. She is as stubborn as Gaelen."

"Is Gaelen stubborn?" asked Rogond, his eyes wide and innocent.

"Not in the least," said Hallagond. "Now, let us return to our friends. There's an excellent cask of ale that I discovered in the cellar, and I would share it with you."

The sharing of the ale might have been a mistake, if the expression on Hallagond's face the following morning was any indication. Neither he nor Azori were in any mood for bright light or loud conversation as they awaited the departure of the boats. Both were unshaven and disheveled, though Hallagond had at least made an effort to be clean. Estle shook her head. She would not drink liquor of any sort until she was certain of her condition, one way or the other. That would not dismay her, but she would also forego marwani and her much-loved kaffa. Her temper was likely to be a bit testy for a while.

When Rogond arrived he was a little rumpled, though he had shaved. His eyes did not seem to be quite focused, and he squinted painfully into the rising sun. Once the boats were laden and made ready, it was time to say farewell. Arialde went to each member of the Company in turn, presenting them with various useful tokens to aid them in their journey. Nelwyn was last to receive her gift, and Arialde sent an unspoken message into her thoughts. *Nelwyn, your task is of great importance. You must carry your message to Lady Ordath, and I am certain that you will not fail. You will see Gaelen again, if all goes right.* She presented Nelwyn with a beautiful silver flute. "For your dancing," she said. *There is a message inside the flute. Make certain the Lady Ordath receives it, won't you? It is of grave importance.* Nelwyn nodded, and tucked the lovely flute away inside her pack.

It was time for the boats to disembark. Estle, Hallagond, Azori, Carmyn, and Nelwyn stood by, preparing to take their leave. Rogond strode up to Hallagond, and took his hand in a firm grip. "You had just better not do anything foolhardy, my brother, after all the trouble I went through to find you. Keep safe, and may we meet again at journey's end."

"You're the one who needs that admonition, little brother," said Hallagond. "Remember, I have Azori to use as an example. You have only Gaelen."

"In that case, I will begin writing his epitaph right now," muttered Azori. No one laughed.

Rogond approached Galador, and placed a hand upon the shoulder of his dearest friend. "Keep safe," was all that he said. In answer, Galador did a most uncharacteristic thing and embraced Rogond. It was a brief embrace, and somewhat awkward, but it was undeniably an embrace. Then he turned from Rogond without a word, getting into the boat to sit opposite Nelwyn.

Gaelen, to the surprise of everyone, also got into the boat with Nelwyn, settling down beside her. "And what do you think you're doing?" asked Galador.

"I am riding with my cousin for a while once we make landfall," said Gaelen. "I am not yet ready to say farewell, and I need a good ride to lift my spirits. I will turn back after an hour or two. Besides, Toran needs the exercise. I must make certain he hasn't forgotten all I have taught him."

"Very well then, Gaelen, but do not stray too far," said Arialde. "Remember that your task begins here, in Tal-sithian. You cannot delay your farewell forever." Gaelen did not answer, but edged closer to Nelwyn. They both knew the truth of it. Yet it may have been that the person who sorrowed most deeply upon the departure from the Lake-realm that morning was Carmyn, the map-maker.

The trip across the Lake was a somber one. It was the desire of every heart to remain in that twice-blessed realm, for there was only war, pain, and death ahead of them. There was separation, and worry, and fear for beloved friends. Yet there was hope, also, for a more enlightened and peaceful world.

The Elves of Tal-sithian, who did not know of the deception, held less hope. In their minds, Lord Wrothgar stood a good chance of overtaking the Light. They would fight to the last to prevent it, but there was no certainty of victory.

The boat fetched up onto the sandy shore, emerging from the ever-present mist to behold a wonderful sight. Hundreds of helms, spear-points, and bright banners flashed and glinted in the sunlight. Horses whinnied and fretted and paced to and fro. Arialde fielded only a small cavalry; most of the Elves of the Lake went forth upon their own feet. Yet they were enduring and fleet-footed, and none would hinder the progress of the column.

Gaelen whistled for Toran, and he appeared, calling to her as he trotted forward. The Elves of Tal-sithian were also glad to see Gaelen, as Toran had apparently been making quite a nuisance of himself, investigating everything and everyone he encountered, trying to make trouble with the other horses, and in general just being himself. He squealed when Gaelen swung onto his back; she was out of practice and had to claw her way aboard.

Eros also approached Gaelen, for he liked her. He wondered why Rogond was not with her, and called out in his very deep voice, looking back toward the boats.

"Rogond is not here, Eros," said Gaelen. "Do not fear…he will come for you soon enough. You must stay here in the meantime, together with Faladinn." She turned to the boatmen. "Will you stay and make certain the horses do not follow?"

"One of us must stay, at least, to ferry you back," answered one. "And that means two will stay. You needn't worry about the horses."

The column of foot-soldiers had already begun to make its way northward, stretching for nearly a mile. Gaelen joined the rest of her mounted friends, and they put their backs to the Lake-realm. Only Gaelen would be returning.

They rode together for several hours, until the afternoon waned. Galador rode up beside Gaelen as Réalta briefly pinned his ears and wrinkled his nose at Toran. "You had best be turning back," he said. "Otherwise you will not arrive before sunset, and we will all be concerned for your safety. You know that you must leave us…there's no reason for further delay."

"Yes, you're right, I suppose," said Gaelen, looking at Nelwyn with a resigned yet forlorn expression. "I have been delaying what must be." She asked Toran to halt, Nelwyn followed her example.

They dismounted so that they could embrace one another properly, as Galador moved on. This was a private farewell.

"I nearly forgot this," said Gaelen reaching into her pack and drawing out a small parcel wrapped in linen. "I thought you might encounter Wellyn in your travels, and if you do, will you give him this token from me? Tell him, also, that I still have faith that his premonition will prove false."

"What premonition?" asked Nelwyn, tucking the parcel away.

"It is of no importance…he will know the meaning of the message," said Gaelen. "Now, my dear friend, my soul-sister, we must be parted. Remember your task, and do not fail me. I am relying on you!"

"I will not fail," said Nelwyn. "But you must guard yourself in the meantime…it is you who will face the fire, not I."

"In that case, it's a good thing I recovered the fire-cloak," said Gaelen.

"Do not jest about it," said Nelwyn, her voice breaking a little.

"I'm not jesting," said Gaelen. "Safe journey, and regards to Lady Ordath. Oh…and to Lord Magra. Tell him that his gift has seen very productive use!" She made a gesture as though drawing the longbow that Magra had given her. Then she grew somber. "I hope to look upon you again." Her face brightened. "What a tale this will make some day for those long, cold nights in the Greatwood. If only the King could see us now!"

"True—we haven't made such a bad accounting of ourselves for a pair of lowly hunter-scouts," said Nelwyn.

"Yet the greatest test still lies ahead," said Gaelen. "And now, I must get back to it. My destiny calls me to a different path."

"May those paths soon converge and bring us together again," said Nelwyn, just before she vaulted onto Gryffa's back. Gaelen, however, merely turned and began walking back to the south, leading Toran. "Why are you not riding?" called Nelwyn.

"I need to find a large rock to stand on," was the reply. Nelwyn turned from her cousin then, and did not speak another word to anyone for a long while.

20
Secret Tasks

Kotos had observed the departure of the Elves of Tal-sithian, flying near enough to see them while still maintaining a prudent distance. None save the Company would pay any heed to what appeared to be an ordinary raven, yet Kotos could not risk the chance that one of the Elves would use it for target practice. His raven host had been sorely tested these past weeks, and it was becoming exhausted with so much flying and spying. Kotos, however, was unaware of this for the most part. He had no empathy for any living creature, as he was not truly alive himself. For now, he had only to await the departure of the Stone of Léir and to follow behind it. Then the raven's flights would be shorter and less frequent.

Wrothgar had sent almost all of his servants to the Fell-ruin; there were few remaining in the Darkmere other than his personal guard. These were highly skilled and experienced trackers and fighters, and they were formidable. Kotos knew that Wrothgar would dispatch them as soon as the word was given that the Stone had left the protection of the Lady. Kotos also expected that they would have no trouble, as the retinue of Elves guarding the Stone would be small and secretive. They would be overcome with little difficulty. All Lord Kotos had to do was watch and wait.

"Come in, Gaelen, and see what my people have made." Arialde had summoned Gaelen to show her the replica of the Stone, which had just been completed. It rested in a wooden casket, wrapped in dark blue velvet to cushion it from the stress of the journey. Gaelen approached and peered inside.

For a moment, she could not find words. "That is remarkable!" she said at last. "May I touch it?"

"Certainly you may," said Arialde even as Gaelen reached out with curious fingers, tracing and caressing the cold, clear surface of the finely-wrought crystal. The resemblance to the real Stone was outstanding, but even though it would bear close visual scrutiny, it was apparent that no power dwelt within. The replica had no life of its own. Arialde closed the lid of the wooden casket, handing Gaelen an ornate brass key on a cord of silk. "Do not lose it," she said with a smile. Gaelen placed the cord around her neck and tucked the key inside her tunic.

"The real Stone has been removed to an underground vault," said Arialde. "Only a few of my most trusted people know of it. The rest believe that you are taking the Stone to Tuathas. If Kotos observes them, he will not learn of our deception. I will send very capable guards, who will form a perimeter around your Company. You will not see them, but know that they are there. Their purpose is to keep you safe from unpleasant encounters. I know that Wrothgar will be expecting this…I would never send you forth without protection. Your guards all believe that your errand is true."

Gaelen felt the hair on the back of her neck raise, and she shuddered. "Just be certain that they are aware that the Elfhunter will be following behind," she said. "I doubt that the restraint he has shown recently will continue. He has worn only a thin coating of civilization over his savagery, and he will not be able to resist picking off your people one by one. Make certain that they are warned!"

Arialde nodded. "I will warn them only to be very wary, for they must not be aware that we know of Gorgon's presence," she said. "Yet they are skilled and experienced."

"There's no way for an Elf to gain experience with this enemy and live to tell about it," said Gaelen. "If you do not warn them, they will be taken. If you had seen what remained of Gelmyr, and of our friend Thorndil, you would reconsider."

"Yet you have gained such experience, Gaelen, and you still live," said Arialde. "I cannot control your actions, therefore you may give warning if you so choose. But on your head be it if our deception is unmasked."

Gaelen shrugged. "We won't be unmasked. I choose to warn them, for the warning may or may not save their lives. It's quite possible they would know of Gorgon anyway. After all, your folk have encountered him before, or at least what he has left behind.

They might recognize his scent, or his sign." She was silent for a moment. "I would rather risk the very small likelihood of being unmasked than the near certainty of more deaths that I might have prevented."

"The death that I would most have you prevent is your own, Gaelen," said Arialde. "If the Elfhunter overtakes you, your fate will be unimaginable. And this place where you are going will task you to the limit of your skills and endurance." She looked away for a moment. "I do hope you have some notion of a plan," she said. "You will have need of one."

"I do have a notion," said Gaelen. "It's my plan to lure Gorgon and Kotos into the wasteland, and then to deal with both of them."

"We have already established the luring part of that plan" said Arialde, "but what about the part where you deal with Gorgon and Kotos? Have you thought that part of the plan through?"

"Rogond will think of something," said Gaelen. "He always does."

Arialde smiled at her then, though she shook her head. It was refreshing to see such an honest expression of faith in another, even if it was naïve.

It was decided that Gaelen and company would leave at the next new moon. This would be a dark night—a night for secret tasks. Rogond, Fima, and Gaelen kept to themselves, for they did not desire the company of the curious Elves of Tal-sithian. Fima, in preparation for the journey, had given up wine and ale—even beer—and he climbed up and down the stone stairways of the library many times each day to build his strength. Rogond practiced with sword and spear, wishing that he had his brother to spar with. Gaelen went forth each night while Rogond slept, sitting alone in a tall tree beneath the stars, and she did not sing.

The new moon would come in three days. A deep melancholy had come over Gaelen, and she had gone out to sit beside a deep-running spring that fed into the lake. It broadened into a channel that could not easily be crossed, flowing toward the vast waters of the Linnefionn, making a very pleasant sound as it did so. Gaelen was surprised to see dark shapes making their way against the current just before two bright heads popped up above the surface, drew breath, and ducked back under. When they reached the bank where Gaelen was sitting, they emerged. Collyn and Gin-gin smiled as they approached, waddling in their ungainly fashion. Gaelen held up a hand in greeting, as her melancholy vanished like water in a well full of sand.

"Hail, Collyn of the River-people. What brings you to me on this fine evening?"

Collyn looked over at Gin-gin, and they both laughed, amused at Gaelen's formality. They shook the water from their bodies, being careful to direct it away from Gaelen, who then invited them to sit with her awhile. They shook their black-and-white heads to and fro.

"We do not care for sitting," said Collyn. Gaelen imagined that would be true, for their bodies were long and sinuous, and their arms and legs were short. Sitting was probably not a comfortable posture for them. Yet now they rested in a sort of half-reclining position, eventually rolling onto their backs.

"The stars are bright tonight," said Gin-gin.

"Yes," said Gaelen. "The moon is waning. Do your folk also love the stars?"

"We do," Gin-gin replied in a dreamy voice. "Yet we are often sleeping when the stars are high, unless called forth to some other purpose."

"And what is your purpose this night?" asked Gaelen. "I'm glad of your company, for soon I will be leaving this realm, and you have cheered me. I'm glad your folk are thriving here."

"It is our purpose to cheer you," said Collyn. "The Guardians have seen you sitting alone each night. They have told us that your heart is sorrowful."

"Then your task is done, for I am no longer sorrowful," said Gaelen with a warm smile. The Currgas seemed pleased. Then Collyn's eyebrows drew together, and sadness touched his face.

"Will you do a thing for us?" he asked Gaelen. "Will you return and tell us how our people are faring in the North, if they still dwell there?" He was quite solemn. "If you accomplish your task, it may be that Darkness will be driven back, even in the Darkmere. The

Forest River may be made wholesome again, and we can return to our homes."

"That would be my hope," said Gaelen. "I may not return here once my task is done, but I will find a way to send word of your people should I learn of them."

"Our thanks," said Collyn, and they spoke no more of such matters. The Currgas remained with Gaelen until the sky began to warm in the east, and then they left her, having shared many a tale to gladden her heart.

On the morning before their departure, Rogond, Fima, and Gaelen met in Rogond's chamber to make certain all was in readiness. They were well provisioned with food and warm clothing, their weapons had been looked to, and there were few farewells still to be said. Yet Gaelen had one more task to perform, and that was the meeting with the Elves who would be sent out to guard her. They had been instructed to establish a perimeter, fanning out and surrounding Gaelen as she and her friends went forth by dark of night. Gaelen did not expect to see any of them again, except by accident, for they had been ordered to remain in concealment.

They were assembled in the council-chamber of the Lady in late afternoon so that she could address them. They stood before her, clad in grey and brown clothing that would conceal them well, as she reminded them of the importance of their task: to safeguard the Stone of Léir. They were to dissuade anyone from continuing on a path that would cross with Gaelen's, on pain of death.

"Be certain that you are not seen without need," said Arialde at last. "You have been chosen for your prowess as guards and scouts. You are the pride of this realm, and my blessings go with you." She extended both hands toward them, and her power flared forth. Every Elf in the group felt it—Gaelen saw their eyes fill with determination and fortitude. As the light faded, the determination remained.

"Forgive me," said Gaelen, who was awed by what she had just seen. "I must speak to you. I know that all here are capable, and I know that we will be much safer because of your efforts, but I must warn you of one who follows me—always he shadows my footsteps—and he will not be dissuaded. His name is Gorgon Elfhunter. I believe most of you know of him already. I will not be able to aid you once we set forth, for he will make certain that I do not see him. Therefore, he will not draw close to our Company, but he will take you unaware, one by one. Do not have any doubt of it!"

"And how do you know this?" asked a tall, well-made Elf with dark hair and blue-grey eyes. "How do you know that Gorgon follows you? Perhaps he will be the one taken unaware."

"Yes, and if he has followed you for so long, then why are you not dead?" said another. "If he is so formidable, why has he not killed you already?"

"I know what I know," said Gaelen. "Don't ask me how. And don't ask why he has not killed me. Just be more wary than you have ever been in your lives! If you smell a strange foulness on the wind, do not linger…although I very much doubt that Gorgon will allow such a warning. He is the wiliest of foes."

The Elves bowed in acknowledgment and then turned to depart, but Gaelen called them back. "Wait!" she cried. "I have forgotten…" The guards all looked at her in anticipation. She wanted to warn them of Orrion, that if they should behold a High Elf in golden armor they should not allow him to approach, no matter what he told them. She wanted to warn them that this seeming friend was a dreadful enemy! But she knew that she could not. No one else could know that Orrion had been unmasked, even to save their lives. Gaelen had to be satisfied with a veiled warning. "Trust none whom you do not know, no matter how they appear," she said. "Not all beauty is well-intentioned. Again, you must not ask questions, and you must not doubt me. Believe my words. They will save your lives."

Satisfied that she had done all that she could to protect her protectors, Gaelen bowed her head. The guards had looked into her eyes, seeing neither deceit, nor arrogance, nor foolishness. Her warning had been taken to every heart.

"You were wise to withhold knowledge of Orrion," said Arialde after they had gone. "We will hope that our scouts will be wary enough to avoid being taken. After all…would you have trusted him, even on first glance?" Gaelen thought for a moment. She did not really know the answer to that question.

"The boats are laden and they await your departure," Arialde continued. "It is time for you to leave us. Yet there is one last audience that must be given." She turned to a doorway at her left. "Come in, and speak your piece," she said, as two golden-haired Elves entered. One of them bore a bundle in her arms, but it was the other, a male, who spoke.

"My name is Gwaryn, and this is my sister, Eryn," he said. "We are the children of Amandir and Brinneal. We have a gift to aid you in your journey, for we have been told of the Elfhunter and your desire to fell him. May our gift aid you in accomplishing what others could not."

Gaelen knew that they were thinking of their father, Amandir, who had died while trying to defeat Gorgon. "I knew your father, and I fought beside him. He was courageous, and true of heart. One day I will accomplish his vengeance. I thank you for the gift." She bowed, took the bundle from Eryn, and carefully unwrapped it.

It was a warm winter cloak of beautiful, thick wool of a soft blue-grey color, the hood trimmed in cream-colored fur that Gaelen recognized as the winter coat of a northern fox. It was very old, but had been carefully looked after.

"This was our mother's favorite cloak," said Gwaryn. "She said that she was never cold while wearing it, and the color reminded her of mists upon the Lake. She would want you to have it now."

Tears came to Eryn's eyes. "This creature, Gorgon, has brought nothing but suffering to my mother's people and shame to her memory. He killed her, there is no doubt of it, yet it was not his doing. He is only what fate has made him. Please, when you take him, do not cause him any more suffering than you must, no matter what vengeful desires you might hold. Our mother would not have it so."

"You must desire his death, surely," said Gaelen, who had not expected such an expression of mercy.

"We do," said Gwaryn. "Yet he is, after all, our half-brother. It nearly sickens me to say it, but it is no less true. By all means, take him from the world, but do not visit pain upon him on our account."

"I doubt very much that I will be given that opportunity," said Gaelen. "I would not toy with such a fearsome foe. When the chance comes to strike, I will strike. Yet, though I will not cause him pain on behalf of Brinneal, neither will I withhold it! Do not hold hope that Gorgon will go easily into death."

"Wear this, then, and think of the tenderness of our mother's heart," said Eryn. "May it warm you and comfort you when the nights are cold and the lonely winds chill your spirit."

"I will think of Brinneal's tender heart," said Gaelen, "lest my own heart grow too cold and hard. My thanks for your gift…it is fitting." Gwaryn and Eryn bowed, and then left Arialde alone with Gaelen, Fima, and Rogond.

"I must say my farewells to you now," said Arialde, "for there will be others attending your departure. My estimation of the Woodland folk has grown since knowing you, Gaelen, though I have always held them in esteem. Farahin made a wise choice. Rogond, take care as you travel to the land of your ancestors. You may not find welcome there now, yet Gaelen trusts in your clever mind to rule the day, and hence I will not worry so much. Fima…your heart is as true as that of any dwarf who ever walked in this world. Guard it well." She bowed then, and spoke to them one final time. "Receive now your gift, and farewell. I hope that we might meet again."

She reached out toward them with both hands, as she had to the scouts, and they felt her power surge forth, filling them with resolve and hope. They would take comfort in that power in times to come. Arialde grew bright with inner light, then slowly faded, and was gone. Yet her voice was heard within every heart.

Be blessed…

Gaelen, Rogond, and Fima set out just after midnight, having ferried across the lake to the grassy meadows where their horses waited. Toran, Eros, and Faladinn stood by, laden and ready. The boatmen and the horse-handlers were the only ones to see them off, but no one minded. After all, this was a secret quest. Toran stood, quiet and meek, knowing that the task before him was an important one and he must not play about.

Faladinn was resigned to bearing the wooden casket containing the Stone, along with their other gear, but he bore the load with no complaint. This was nothing new to him. Rogond marveled once more at the fortitude of their little brown Kazhi-horse, who had not once been lame, had maintained his condition on practically no feed, and who had never complained about his lot in life. He was a stoic little spirit, and he absolutely loved Gaelen, who groomed him and gave him apples. In her opinion, they had much in common.

They set out in darkness, Fima riding with Rogond while Gaelen led Faladinn at an easy, ground-covering trot. It was a good thing that Eros ran as gently as the river he had been named for, or else Fima would have been most uncomfortable. As it was, he said nothing about it, though he gripped Rogond's midsection tightly, knowing that there were many, many miles to go. They made their way northward through the marsh-meadows, unaware that, at the same time, their friends would soon draw within range of Mountain-home.

Gaelen rode in silence. Both she and Rogond trained their senses outward, as wary as they had ever been, though they knew the greater peril was north of the river. She intended to make certain that Lord Wrothgar paid for his violation of her spirit, and her thoughts were dark and violent—exactly the kind that would be difficult to keep from Gorgon Elfhunter. She mastered herself… such thoughts would not do! She left them behind in Tal-sithian, where they belonged.

Far to the northeast, Nelwyn was also keeping her thoughts to herself. She had been riding behind the column of warriors dispatched by the Lady to aid the Elves of Mountain-home during the anticipated upcoming attack; they had been on the march now for over a fortnight. They had crossed the treacherous waters of the southern Amar Dess, and that task alone had taken nearly two days.

They had since been met by grey-clad scouts who conducted them toward a plateau surrounded by tall, snow-capped peaks—the hidden realm of Mountain-home. The way in from the southwest was difficult and treacherous, as were all ways into Mountain-home, but it was the most direct.

Nelwyn tossed her golden head with impatience. She was tired of riding so slowly, though it would have been increasingly difficult to go at a faster pace as the terrain worsened. Considering that most of them were on foot, the Elves had made very good time, yet Nelwyn was still impatient.

Galador wondered about it, for impatience usually was not in her nature. "Be at ease," he said. "We'll get there soon enough. Why are you in such a hurry?"

"Because I have much to do," she replied. "I want to speak to Ordath and deliver all messages to her. It seems as though we are moving at a snail's pace."

"We're not," said Galador. "We are making good time. Don't be in such a hurry to get to Mountain-home…we don't know what we will find when we get there."

"Precisely why we should make even *better* time," said Nelwyn. "You heard the reports of the scouts earlier—word is that Wrothgar's northern armies are gathering for an attack. There will be battle soon, and there are things I must do first."

"What things?" asked Galador, his voice deep and gentle. He reached across the gap between them and took her hand. "What things, Nelwyn?"

"I will share them when the time is right," she said. "For now, I would prefer to keep them to myself."

Galador scowled. "What have you and Gaelen been planning? Both Rogond and I noticed that you brightened up immediately upon spending time with her. I know you have formed some sort of plan. What is it?"

"I'll tell you later," she said. "For now, I must keep my own counsel." She looked up at the column of Elves in front of her. "*Now* what? Why are they slowing down…*again*?" Galador sighed and shook his head. There would be no cure for her impatience that he could think of.

At last, Nelwyn's prayers were answered as one of the scouts rode back to speak with her. "Please," he said, "who leads your Company?"

All eyes turned toward Nelwyn. "It would seem that I do," she said. "I am Nelwyn of the Greatwood Realm. I bear a message for Lady Ordath from Lady Arialde."

"So we have been told," said the scout. "Please, move to the front of the column. We will conduct you with all speed."

"At last!" said Nelwyn under her breath.

Galador shook his head. "You're acting like Gaelen," he muttered.

Nelwyn sighed. "If that is true, then I don't know how she has managed to not explode into a thousand pieces. I have not experienced this sort of impatience often, and it wears me down."

Galador shook his head again, but he did not reply. Nelwyn would feel better once they got into Mountain-home. He wondered about the nature of the message Nelwyn was to bring to Lady Ordath, but even if he had asked her about it, he suspected she would not have known what to tell him.

Gaelen and company had been on the northward road for three days and had just crossed the southern river Artan. This had proved to be something of a trick, and it was fortunate that the spring rains had already come and gone. Gaelen and Rogond had tracked up and down its banks for several hours until they finally found a suitable crossing point. They were most concerned about Faladinn, who supposedly bore the most precious object in the world on his back. "Don't worry," said Gaelen. "This is the only river crossing we'll need to make if we keep to our plan."

"The casket is heavy," said Fima. "I can't help but worry. Why did we need to put it on such a short horse?"

"Would you rather Toran bear it, or Eros?" laughed Rogond. "Then you could ride Faladinn."

Fima grumbled and blustered at the thought. They all knew that Faladinn could not be ridden by anyone except Gaelen.

"Don't worry, Fima," Gaelen repeated. "Faladinn may be short, but he's capable. This is not the first stream he has crossed." She turned Faladinn loose so that he could find his own way across the river. "Besides, if the casket falls off, we'll just...retrieve it."

"Oh, won't *that* be a pleasure then?" said Fima. "I can just imagine chasing it all the way down the Ambros into Wrothgar's waiting arms."

"Not likely, my good dwarf, as it will not float," said Rogond.

"Hmmph. I suppose not," said Fima. "But you will be the ones dredging it up from the bottom if it falls in!"

"I trust Faladinn," said Gaelen simply, and that was that.

As soon as the crossing was made, they camped for the night. It was a sobering time, as they had truly left Arialde's influence. From now on, they were vulnerable.

"Have you seen any ravens?" asked Fima, who knew that both Gaelen and Rogond would see things that he could not. They looked at him and nodded. They had each seen several ravens, often two at a time. It was, after all, their nesting season, when raven parents would be out foraging on behalf of their young chicks. "I wonder if any of them has taken notice of *us,*" Fima whispered, though it was on all of their minds.

Kotos had, indeed, taken notice of the Company, flying high and fast. It was important that his raven should appear to be engaged in business of its own, therefore it would not do to fly too low, or to circle over the heads of the Company. That would amount to posting a banner saying "Lord Kotos is here!"

His partnership with Gorgon was working well at present. During daylight, as the Company moved on, Gorgon would rest while Kotos took wing. After dark, the Elfhunter would emerge and track his quarry while the raven roosted with Kotos. Gorgon was always easy for Kotos to find, as he carried the amulet and it called to its master. As a result, Kotos and Gorgon spent very little time together, which pleased them both. Kotos knew that it was unwise to wear out his welcome, and the relief he saw on Gorgon's face each time they were reunited reassured him. Gorgon knew that, should he defy Kotos and go his own way, the raven would catch him quickly. He suspected that he was no match for the power an enraged Lord Kotos could wield against him. Besides that, he had been directed to follow Gaelen, which was just what he wanted to do anyway. All was well for the moment.

Kotos had returned, having observed the river crossing, and had gone back into the amulet to report to Lord Wrothgar. Gaelen and company had ventured outside Arialde's influence—from that point on, no power of Light would assist them. Kotos described the casket borne by the pack horse. Though it was covered with a canvas drape, he had caught a glimpse of it on one of his many flights.

Wrothgar praised Kotos and Gorgon, promising to reward them both, and then he sent forth his personal guard—one hundred fierce, wily Ulcas and five evil men—all professional killers. The Stone would be taken with little resistance. Arialde's Elven guards ranged in a wide circle around the Company and they could not reassemble quickly enough to defend against an attack. The poor fools did not expect one.

Deep within the bright fires of Tûr Dorcha, Wrothgar laughed. The Elves had played right into His hands, and the Stone of Léir would soon be under His control. He reveled in the thought of Shandor, once His greatest foe, forced to submit to His directives. He would use Shandor's grief, promising that Liathwyn might again be his, luring Shandor into a snare from which there would be no escape. Then Wrothgar would know whatever He desired, and they would all fall before Him. Lord Kotos would receive great reward... but what of Gorgon Elfhunter?

Wrothgar had always been dismayed by Gorgon's inherent disobedience, and some of the behaviors reported by Lord Kotos were disturbing. The Shadowmancer did not tolerate defiance, and once the Elves were defeated, who could know where Gorgon's thoughts would turn? Wrothgar resolved to promise reward, but once victory was certain, He would kill Gorgon at the earliest opportunity. The Elfhunter was, after all, half Elven.

Gaelen waited until Fima and Rogond were both sleeping to accomplish her task, for it was delicate, and she could bear no distraction. She sat in the branches of a lonely pine overlooking the grasslands north of the Artan, which they had crossed two days before. She had seen no sign of the raven since yesterday.

Gaelen had become very, very adept at controlling her thoughts and emotions in recent months. Her mind, once undisciplined, was now very well ordered. It had to be. This was taxing to her nature—not all the silver in Gaelen's hair had come from her direct encounter with Gorgon—yet this was their last journey "together," and Gaelen knew it. *Either he falls this time, or I do…*

Therefore, she set herself to her purpose, clearing her mind of all other thoughts, and opened herself to the Elfhunter.

She imagined herself within a waking dream, as she and her friends moved northward, carrying the Stone. All seemed well, but then the servants of Wrothgar converged on the Company. Gaelen acted the moment they appeared, grasping a large rock, uncovering the casket and jerking it open. There lay the precious Stone, the one thing Wrothgar desired above all else, the thing that he knew would bring him back to power. Gaelen did not hesitate, but raised the rock high and, with a cry, brought it down upon the crystal, shattering it beyond repair. She imagined Shandor's cry of anguish, visualizing the release of his spirit into nothingness, and focused on the fragments of the Stone, which had all gone dark. The Ulcas reeled back, knowing that their mission had failed and the wrath of Lord Wrothgar would now fall upon their heads. Gaelen then repeated the same thought over and over.

I must do this…I must destroy the Stone…I will destroy it…it will not be taken!

She then imagined waking from the dream and crying out to Rogond, who came to aid her. In her mind she told him that she had held a most dreadful vision, and that whatever else happened, she would destroy the Stone if any servant of Wrothgar appeared, just in case. "If I fall to an enemy, you must do the same," she told Rogond. "It is better to remove the Stone from this world than to allow it to fall into Darkness. It is under our control now, and I will do what I must do." She sent that thought out as well, repeating it several times. *I will do what I must…I will do what I must…I will…*

Gorgon was in that moment making his way toward her, at about ten miles distant. He had not as yet encountered Arialde's scouts, yet that would not dismay him. They thought they were skilled? Ha! Gorgon had already worked his way past them twice… none in the world save the Vixen could match him for stealth. Now he stopped in his tracks, sensing some strong thoughts…very strong.

Apparently, the Vixen was lost in some sort of waking dream, and she could not guard herself. He took in her thoughts as though they were his own, seeing and hearing as though he held the mirror again. What he saw both fascinated and terrified him. By the time her thoughts finally faded from his awareness, he was utterly convinced that she would make good on her word.

He had to warn Lord Kotos at once! He knew that Wrothgar had sent forces to take the Stone. At least some of them would no doubt rendezvous with Gorgon and Kotos, but what about the others? *Even if they do not attack, if the Vixen became aware of them she might destroy the Stone just to be safe.* He looked into the amulet, calling to Lord Kotos.

When Kotos heard Gorgon's urgent call, he roused the raven, which had been standing on one foot with its head tucked under its wing. Ravens do not like to fly in darkness, as they are not made for it, and this one gave several loud, harsh calls of protest before Kotos could convince it.

Gaelen heard the distant calls of the raven and smiled in the dark. The seeds had been planted. "Now let's see what will be done about it," she whispered, shifting her position in the tall tree so that she faced the south.

Lord Kotos heard the news with dismay. Gorgon allowed him to enter his thoughts, and when he searched them, Kotos knew that Gorgon had not imagined them, nor was he trying to deceive.

"The Vixen will smash the Stone at the slightest excuse," said Gorgon. "I do hope Lord Wrothgar has not sent anyone out to intercept her."

Never mind about that, thought Kotos. *Are you certain this vision is true? If you are, I must take action at once.*

"She cannot guard her thoughts from me," said Gorgon. "In dreams, all thoughts are known. She has told me of her plan, though she does not realize it. These thoughts were as clear to me as if I looked through her eyes." He drew a deep breath. "I would most certainly take action if I were you."

His pale eyes narrowed. "As I said before, I do hope Wrothgar has not sent out forces as yet. And if he has, I trust they have been instructed to do no harm to the Vixen. She is mine, remember? No matter what else befalls, the Vixen is mine!"

Of course, Kotos soothed, even as he knew the absurdity of it. Wrothgar's Ulcas would not spare Gaelen. *We would never rob you of your vengeance, for you have served well. Have no fear.*

"Well, you had just better make certain of it," growled Gorgon. "I'm not sure I believe a word you have just said, but if you have any sense, you will make certain my desires are met."

They will be, I assure you, said Kotos, just before flowing back into the amulet. This would no doubt be a dreadful conversation with Lord Wrothgar, who would not take at all well to the notion of reining in His forces for the time being. This would be more difficult than it sounded. Kotos would just have to convince the Shadowmancer, who was not exactly renowned for patience, that it would be prudent to wait until the Stone arrived at its new destination. When the Elves thought it safely hidden, Gaelen would not be guarding it anymore, and it could be taken without risk of destruction. Gorgon was exactly the creature to slip in and accomplish that task, if Kotos could convince him.

Once Kotos had gone from his awareness, Gorgon hunkered down to await further instructions. He noticed the rather woebegone raven perched on a nearby stone. In the dark, without Kotos, it could not see well enough to fly, and it felt vulnerable in the open. Gorgon, unlike Kotos, could and did feel empathy with it. He shook his head and spoke to it in a harsh whisper, knowing that Kotos was preoccupied and would not hear him. "Go on…now's your chance! I would fly from this place, if I were you. Return to what is left of your life. Go *on*, now!" Gorgon shook his head again. *It's a pity that I cannot take that advice myself.*

The raven ruffled its bedraggled feathers and shivered in the cold. It would not take wing…not in the dark. "Well, I tried to warn you," said Gorgon. "You will not keep this up much longer." He felt a momentary pang of fear as he realized that the raven could not have left even if it had wanted to. *I wonder…could I have made such a choice, if it presented itself? Of course I could…*

He resolved then to take a lesson from the bird; he would not allow himself to be used up. He would appear to go along with Kotos for as long as it suited him, but there were thoughts that he would keep to himself. Gorgon, like Gaelen, had become very adept at doing that.

Kotos finally emerged from the amulet at the breaking of dawn. Wrothgar had taken the news gracefully, considering. Yet now their task was formidable; they had to ensure that no man or Ulca interfered with Gaelen and the Stone. Wrothgar could possibly reach out to some of them, the Ulcas in particular, but there might be those who did not receive the message. They would need to be intercepted and waved off by Kotos and Gorgon; there was no other to do it.

Kotos informed Gorgon of the change in plans just before sending the raven aloft. He had already decided that he would need to secure a new host—his bird was getting too weak to be of use for much longer. This would not be difficult in an area where ravens abounded, and they would get even more numerous farther to the north. Ravens were inquisitive birds, and they would be drawn to the sight of one dead or dying. Therefore, Kotos intended to push his current host to the limit of its endurance. It would need to fly on swift wings to encounter Wrothgar's forces, who were still over a hundred miles away.

Gorgon would continue to follow the Stone, but he was instructed that, should any servant of Darkness appear, he was to slay it at once. He smiled at the irony, as he was now in the rather strange position of protecting the Company.

The raven flew as fast as it could manage back toward the southwest, toward Tûr Dorcha. Kotos knew that Wrothgar's small but potentially deadly force would be under cover during the day, as it was comprised mostly of creatures that disliked the sun. They would have been told to make swift progress, but they would not have been driven without rest.

Kotos sent his thoughts out in a wide net, questing for them, as he had a very wide path to search. The raven endured this assault of malevolent energy for three, perhaps four minutes, and then it fell from the sky to land hard upon the earth with a forlorn squawk. It rolled several times, appearing as a disorganized lump of dusty black feathers, and then was still.

This turn of events had not been in Lord Kotos' plan at all. He had underestimated the draining effect the broadcasting of such powerful dark thoughts would have on his unassuming host. Now he was trapped within the personage of a dying bird, and he did not have his amulet. Meanwhile, Wrothgar's forces had not been found, and Kotos would need to assume that they were still making their way toward the Company. Kotos gave a proverbial sigh of frustration. He knew that the sight of dead and dying things attracted new hosts, such as ravens, crows, and (ugh!) vultures. It was also possible that a non-winged scavenger such as a fox, a wolf, or a cat might come to investigate. That would not do...Kotos required wings to accomplish his tasks.

He had always preferred the company of ravens. They were intelligent enough to serve him for a long time, as this one had. And they could be beguiled, oh yes! Ravens were subject to at least three of the seven temptations: vanity, gluttony, and greed. Yet a few of them were wise, particularly those that dwelled in the southern Monadh-hin. They were great friends of the dwarves who ruled the underground caverns, flying forth and gathering news in exchange for food and warm lodging. Yet the ravens of the North had been divided. Some were very wise, but others were little better than common crows.

To have his dying raven assailed by crows would be a bad turn of events for Lord Kotos, but that was exactly what happened. Kotos looked through the bird's failing eyes to behold several dark shapes wheeling and cawing overhead. *Move on, you vermin,* thought Kotos, to no avail. Ravens and crows are bitter enemies; they will not tolerate one another for long. Now, here was a helpless enemy, and the crows swooped down upon it, pecking and worrying the raven, who was too weak to defend itself.

All right, you lot, thought Kotos, *taste of my power!* He sent a blast of pain out through the raven's brain that killed it instantly, but it also stunned and confused the crows. They made an immediate and hasty retreat. Kotos gave another proverbial sigh as he felt the raven's flesh turn from living into non-living. He could have inhabited one of the crows, he supposed, but they never had served as well as ravens, and as long as he was trapped within a crow he might never get near enough to another healthy raven.

He could no longer see through the raven's eyes, yet he could sense his surroundings. Night was falling, and that was a pity. He hoped he would not be picked up by some night-hunting creature before dawn came, when he might lure a fresh raven into his service. His arrogance would not allow him to truly appreciate the predicament he was in.

Wrothgar's forces had separated into two contingents, for the men did not like traveling with the Ulcas, and the Ulcas could see little benefit in tolerating the presence of men. These Ulcas were larger, fiercer, and cleverer than most, and all had seen battle. They had been kept in Tûr Dorcha to safeguard it, honing their battle-skills with constant training and sparring. Now they were to retrieve the Stone and take it back to the Shadowmancer, killing all who stood in the way. They were not heavily armored, for armor favors neither speed nor stealth. They were clad more like assassins, with heavy robes and hoods to help block the sun. Wrothgar knew that the Company numbered but three, and that the Elves who guarded them were few and scattered. His victory was nearly assured. Still, he sent five men out with his Ulcas, for they could travel by day, and they were all highly trained experts in the art of murder.

Wrothgar had ensnared these men, as he always did, with promise of power. Men always desired control over other men, and since the Plague this had become even more important to some. The sons of rulers who found their kingdoms ravaged, such that they had little to inherit, were quite vulnerable to the suggestion that their prominence could be restored. Wrothgar had found three such men—the son of the King of an eastern realm from beyond the Stone Desert, the son of the leader of a mighty clan of northern mountain-folk, and the second son of the ruler of the realm that had once been home to Talishani Ali. In that case, the firstborn son had refused temptation, and Wrothgar had convinced the younger son to slay him. All three of these men, who felt that they were entitled to rule a great realm, had been promised that when the Stone was in the possession of Wrothgar, their desires would be met.

The men were skilled and motivated, but they did not work well together. It's difficult to throw three dogs in a pen with a single scrap of meat and have all emerge unscathed. Their pride and arrogance amused Lord Wrothgar, who saw them only as the means to achieve his ends. He would probably slay them all eventually if they did not behave.

The other two men were mere brigands—a sutherling and a Corsair—simple greed had ensnared them. Wrothgar favored them, for they were easy to please, as neither held any desire to be responsible for anything. They actually worked in partnership, for they were not particularly courageous and knew that they stood a better chance of survival together.

They had resolved to allow the other three men to range ahead. The arrogant fools would flush out any defenders, and would be the first to fall. The two brigands would come in from behind if the situation allowed. Both were accomplished and deadly assassins, and Wrothgar had no way of calling them back without Kotos' assistance. The Company was in grave peril.

The five men had drawn far ahead of the Ulcas, for they spent less time hiding from the sun and were now mounted on stolen horses, appearing as ordinary travelers. They had not kept to the same course as the Ulcas, for their horses could cross the Ambros, whereas the Ulcas would be forced to use the abandoned ferry that lay about fifty miles to the north of the junction with the Artan. The horses would make a silent approach difficult. They would be turned loose as soon as the men drew near enough to their quarry.

The dead raven lay about five miles from the ferry, but not for long. Kotos would soon be rescued, but it was not the outcome he had hoped for. A vixen fox had picked up the faint scent of carrion. She approached, her brushy tail low behind her, looking all around for enemies. She did not sense any danger, and she moved in to take the dead raven, for she had a litter to feed. Birds were not her favorite food, as she found the feathers annoying and there was not much meat underneath them, yet she could not afford to be choosy with five mouths to feed. A robust, healthy vixen, she had no difficulty dragging the carcass back to her den.

Kotos knew he would have to use her as host, and he entered her small but well-ordered mind with ease. None of the so-called "lower creatures" could resist him; they did not know of such things.

He explored the thoughts of his new carrier with dismay. He knew that foxes were very intelligent when compared with vultures; in fact, they were as intelligent as some ravens. The females, however, were difficult for Kotos to control, particularly when they had litters to raise. They were not easily distracted, were not susceptible to temptations, and were unlikely to listen to any suggestion that would take them from their all-important task. This one was no exception. When Kotos tried to influence her to take him near the abandoned ferry, she blinked her amber eyes and shook her head as though trying to dislodge a fly from her ear. She would not be dissuaded from taking the dead raven back to her den, and Lord Kotos had no choice but to accompany her.

Gorgon kept to his northward course, following the Company as instructed, but now he turned his senses back to the south as well. So far, there was no sign of any pursuit. Gorgon decided to spend less effort in concealing his tracks so that the Ulcas would be drawn to follow him and he could intercept them. It was also likely that Lord Kotos had found them by now and warned them off. Yet until Gorgon knew the facts he would not relax his vigilance.

This pursuit was wearisome. Perhaps it was time for a little diversion? Gorgon had shadowed the Elvish scouts upon several occasions now…it might be a good time to take one for amusement. He liked to stalk the Elves by night, as he could see as well as they in the dark, and the shadows helped conceal him. He sighted one of the sentinels as the moon was just becoming visible through shrouds of grey and white cloud above the trees. This one was sitting on the bare limb of a large oak, gazing at the sky as usual. Elves were so predictable!

Gorgon crept closer, reaching for his marvelous weapon of oak and sinew and leather, inserting it into a socket in the armor of his left arm and fitting a steel projectile into the pouch. It took inhuman strength to draw this weapon, but it was very accurate and effective.

He planned his attack carefully. The Elf would be hit between the eyes with the steel projectile and knocked to the ground, then Gorgon would approach. If the Elf was not yet dead, Gorgon would toy with him for a while before killing him. First, however, he would prevent his victim from screaming—he knew just how that could be done.

He drew the weapon in the dark, straining his powerful shoulders and arms, preparing to release. The Elf in the tree tensed and sat upright. *He thinks he's heard something*, thought Gorgon, *but he soon won't be thinking anything at all!*

Then, to Gorgon's profound disappointment, the Elf gave a soft, hooting call to the west. He was communicating with another of the accursed scouts; apparently they were not as widely scattered as first believed. Gorgon knew that he dared not take his victim now, as there might be a way of arousing and summoning the others. The last thing Gorgon needed was to be forced to deal with forty of the Elves of Tal-sithian (or thirty-nine, as would be the case). That would not please Lord Kotos. He sighed and lowered his weapon. He would just have to content himself with re-living the downfall of Tal-elathas this night.

The four little fox kits in the den made short work of the dead raven, scattering black feathers all about. They would derive far more pleasure in playing with it than from eating it. Their teeth were not yet fully grown, though they were sharp, and their mother aided them by stripping most of the tough, stringy flesh from the bird herself, swallowing it so that it would soften a bit, and then bringing it back up for them. Once they had eaten and played their games, they fell asleep. Though foxes are often abroad at night, this one would not leave the den until morning, lest any night-hunters come to take her kits. She watched over them, curling around their soft, warm bodies and covering them with her tail until the rising sun brightened the entrance.

The vixen gave her kits a milk feeding before she left to go out hunting, wincing as their sharp little teeth assailed her, and then went forth into the chilly morning. *At last,* thought Lord Kotos. Today he would see about finding another host. A bird, any bird, would be better than this! He suffered through several anxious hours while the vixen hunted mice and crayfish, until at last he spotted a group of ravens circling over a distant meadow. He tried to influence the vixen to investigate. *Look there. The ravens are gathering...they must have found a splendid feast. You could gorge yourself, and take a fine meal back for your kits to thrive on. We must go and see!* Kotos was a very patient being when he wished to be, but the thought of missing the Ulcas and incurring the wrath of the Shadowmancer caused whatever patience he had to evaporate. *Go on, now! You don't want to miss the feast! Do you want the ravens to take it all, and leave none for your family?*

The vixen sat down on her haunches and scratched behind one ear with her hind foot. She appeared to be thinking things over. Foxes often hunted together with ravens, following the birds, which would spot prey for them, and then sharing the result. These ravens were far away, farther that she normally traveled when she had kits in the den, but if she could find a fabulous meal at the end of it...Kotos would have screamed by now had he been able. At last the vixen got to her feet, shook herself, and trotted off toward the ravens. As far as she was concerned, this was her own idea.

When the vixen arrived in the meadow, she found that the ravens had discovered the carcass of a half-grown lamb and were feasting upon it. They were not inclined to allow the fox to approach at first, but she whined and cringed, creeping forward and waving her brush of a tail to show that she was not a threat. After chasing her a few times the birds grew weary of it and allowed her to approach. Now, how to ensnare one of them? Kotos knew that the fox and the raven would need to be touching one another for the exchange to be made. He prepared to react the instant this contact occurred, as he urged the vixen to attempt to take the same piece of flesh being tugged at by the largest raven in the group. *That is the best, the most tender and the most nourishing. You must take it!*

Well, why not, thought the vixen, grabbing at the meat. The large raven croaked at her and flared its wings, but it did not let go. The moment the vixen's muzzle touched the raven's beak, Kotos made his escape into his new host. And a fine host it was—a strong male. It would not object to the directives of Lord Kotos for more than a few moments. *Why waste your time with this paltry meal? I will take you to a place where you can feast all day long, where you will want for nothing. Let us go there together now!* The raven dropped the meat, to the satisfaction of the vixen; she then proceeded to gorge on the slightly-ripe mutton. Kotos could hardly wait to see the back of her.

His fine, new raven lifted into the air, to the puzzlement of the others, and flew back toward the abandoned ferry. Another raven followed behind, most likely its mate. Kotos reveled in the freedom provided by his new host—he had grown weary of the drudgery of going about with his feet on the ground all the time. Flight was a wondrous endowment in his opinion, though he supposed most birds took it for granted. Now he would locate Wrothgar's Ulcas, and then return to Gorgon on swift, welcome wings.

21
Three Messages

It was raining in Mountain-home, and the somber grey clouds reflected the mood of the people. The travelers had been welcomed, fed, and rested, and now they awaited an audience with Lady Ordath. Nelwyn paced to and fro on the veranda, reminding Galador again of her cousin Gaelen. A knock at the door startled them both, and they called out in unison.

"Who's there?"

"It's Hallagond. May I come in?"

"Of course," said Galador. "Please do. Perhaps you can convince Nelwyn to stop her incessant pacing."

"Oh. Is this a bad time?"

"Not at all," said Nelwyn. "You are always welcome. I just wish you were the escort sent to conduct us to the Lady…I will be much less restive once I have delivered my message."

"There's still plenty of time for that," said Galador. "Scouts have indicated that Wrothgar's armies have not even gained the Eastern Hills as yet. We have plenty of time to prepare."

"This is a different message," said Nelwyn. "It was given to me by Arialde, and she said it was of utmost importance."

"What is it?" asked Hallagond.

"I don't know," said Nelwyn. She had not read the message, nor even laid eyes on it. "I wish I could get in to see Lady Ordath at once. Arialde was most insistent." They all heard the rumble of distant thunder, as the rain came down harder.

"Where is Estle?" asked Nelwyn.

"She is resting," said Hallagond. "The journey has worn her out."

"Truly?" said Galador. "She seemed hardier than that to me. Are you certain she is not ill?"

"No, I am never certain of anything where Estle is concerned," said Hallagond. "But I expect there are, umm, other elements at work." The Elves just stared at him as though awaiting an explanation, therefore he changed the subject. "Azori has been having quite a time here already," he said. "It seems he has decided that Elven-realms are most impressive places, and he is looking forward to exploring this one."

"No doubt," said Galador. "I am certainly gratified to hear that our realms are to the liking of a man with such superb, cultured tastes and talents. What a relief!" He looked over at Hallagond. "Was there something you wanted?"

Hallagond smiled and shook his head. Galador was a stalwart friend, he was even likeable, but at times he seemed to personify the word "haughty."

"No, thank you. I just wanted to check on my friends…and to mention that, if your weapons need looking after, the smiths are hard at work forging and sharpening." He pulled out his curved sutherling blade. "I thought I might let them have a go at this. Well, I will leave you both to your pacing and waiting." He bowed and took his leave, but as he walked down the corridor he encountered the very escort Nelwyn was hoping for.

The entire Company had been summoned to take early supper with Ordath. Soon they had assembled beneath the round roof of one of the garden-houses, so that they might all enjoy the air while keeping from the rain. The fire-pit in the center of the large, circular structure was most welcome, and the tables had been laden with the finest Mountain-home could offer, to the enjoyment of everyone. Yet they could not help but think of their friends, laboring toward the north with only wild fare and dried provisions.

"I would imagine that Fima would trade places with me right now," said Hallagond as he reached for another sweet fig stuffed full of honey and nuts. "At least, he would trade for the duration of this meal, if he could then be whisked back to rejoin Gaelen and Rogond."

"Don't worry about Fima or Rogond," said Azori. "They have Gaelen to look after them. She will make certain her hunting skills are well used, I'm sure. They'll be having fresh-roasted meat every night."

"Rogond is no dullard, either," said Hallagond. "I notice that, despite his having been raised by Elves, he is fairly adept at making his way in the wild."

"Rogond was raised by Elves?" said Azori, who apparently was unaware of it. "That explains so much…his unhealthy and unreasonable addiction to bathing, for instance."

"And the fact that he smells so much better than you do?" said Estle.

"Yes, that too," said Azori. "You know, Hallagond, I wish I had known of this earlier. I could have taken advantage of it in our last card game."

"What are you talking about? You nearly cleaned him out as it was," said Hallagond. "I feared I was going to have to intervene on his behalf."

"Be silent, both of you, and show respect to Lady Ordath's table," said Galador. "There will be no talk of wagering and taking advantage here."

"You see?" said Azori. "That just proves my point. It's small wonder Rogond is the way he is." He turned to Galador. "Lady Ordath is not here to take offense."

"But I *am* here, Azori," said Ordath, who suddenly appeared from out of the rain, gliding up behind him. "I trust you have all eaten your fill? Splendid. Now let us counsel together. I understand that you have serious matters to impart, and I have asked Lord Magra to join us."

She indicated Magra, who was now standing just inside the doorway, leaning against one of the carved pillars supporting the roof. He had just come in from the march. His hair and clothing were soaked with rain, yet he seemed not to mind.

"My lord, please come and sit by the fire," said Nelwyn, rising to her feet and offering him a seat. Magra bowed, and then sat between Galador and Hallagond.

"Good *heavens*," whispered Estle, who had not yet beheld Magra. He was the first Elf of the Èolar that she had seen, apart from Orrion. In fact, they bore a strong resemblance until you looked into their eyes. Orrion was almost perfectly beautiful, but his glance was cold. Magra was weathered and battle-scarred, but there was warmth, kindness, and good humor in his gaze. Where Orrion was intimidating, Magra invited trust. When he sat upon the long bench at the table, it groaned.

"This message is mine to convey," said Nelwyn. "For in it lies the essence of the Shadowmancer's plan. And I have another message to give to you, my lady." She drew forth the silver flute from her jerkin and handed it to Lady Ordath. "The message is inside," she said. Then, she looked shyly up at Ordath. "When you have extricated it, may I please have the flute back? I have always wanted to learn to play one."

Ordath favored her with a smile so warm that everyone who beheld it felt safe— as if no evil could possibly assail them. "Of course you may! I look forward to hearing you play in the future. There are those here who can instruct you." Ordath tucked the flute inside the sleeve of her dark blue robes, and her face assumed its former serious expression. Everyone turned their attention to Nelwyn, who did her best to recount the events concerning Orrion, Lord Kotos, and the Stone of Léir.

When she had finished, Nelwyn sat back down beside Galador. All eyes turned then to Ordath, who had been listening with a pensive, rather melancholy expression. She sat quietly, lost in her own thoughts for a few moments. Then she rose and addressed the Company.

"So, Lord Wrothgar has planned this deception, and he now expects that the Stone of Léir is being moved to a new resting-place. Yet he sends forces from the Fell-ruin and from the Darkmere, planning to attack us anyway? I expect he means to convince us further that Nelwyn's insight was true. And Arialde has done nothing to disillusion him, sending forth a replica of the Stone that is meant to be taken the moment it is hidden. I would not want to be anywhere near Tûr Dorcha when Wrothgar learns that the Stone is false, and the Deceiver has been deceived."

"How may we turn this to our advantage?" asked Magra. "The reports from our scouts to the north indicate that the forces amassing there are formidable, perhaps even formidable enough to succeed. Yet they have seen no sign of any Bödvari or other creatures of fire. How can we use this failed deception to crush our Enemy?"

"I would suggest that we do exactly as expected," said Nelwyn. "We should rout Wrothgar's forces utterly. After all, according to his plan, we should not know that he has followed the replica of the Stone and taken it. We should believe that our primary purpose is simply to defend Mountain-home. Arialde has held back forces in Tal-sithian, as Wrothgar would have expected, for according to the deception she would now anticipate an attack from Wrothgar himself. Yet that attack will not come, for Wrothgar now believes that the Stone has been moved."

"He is not strong enough to attack Tal-sithian, much less prevail there, unless we have profoundly underestimated him," said Magra.

"Precisely why he orchestrated this attempt to convince us to move the Stone," said Ordath. "He did not count on the perceptive nature of this Company."

"One of them in particular, I expect," said Magra, thinking of Gaelen.

"What he did not count on," said Ordath, "is the unique situation that exists between Gorgon and Gaelen. Had Lord Kotos chosen a different host, this might not have gone as well for us."

"I hope Gorgon eventually becomes aware of the irony of it," muttered Nelwyn. "He deserves to kick himself a thousand times."

"All is not ended as yet," said Ordath. "We might be the ones kicking ourselves. We must take this coming attack very seriously. But if we succeed in crushing our attackers, I sense we will have done far more damage to Wrothgar than he might ever recover from. He has no other forces. His entire plan rests on acquiring the Stone."

"He will attack, and then retreat before we can do much damage," said Hallagond. "He is saving the real assault in anticipation of gaining possession of Lord Shandor."

"Then when he retreats, we must pursue him," said Magra. "We should surprise him by driving back north and decimating his army. Then he will not be able to mount another assault, Stone or no Stone."

"All this sounds too easy," said Estle. "What if, like the Scourge, he has a weapon of which you are unaware?" Ordath looked puzzled.

"The Scourge was an army of villains in the southern desert," Galador explained. "They had a dragon with them, but we did not know until the last minute. It was…a bit of a challenge." He smiled over at Hallagond, and they both raised their glasses to the memory.

"Our scouts have seen no dragons," said Magra, "nor have I heard rumor of any. They are not exactly easy to conceal. Yet that does not mean you are wrong, Estle. It is not like Wrothgar to hinge his entire plan on one event. We will need every strong hand, true heart, and keen eye to defeat him."

"My thoughts keep turning back to Gaelen, Rogond, and Fima," said Ordath. "Their part in this is most perilous. They will face Lord Kotos and Gorgon together…a more formidable foe I cannot imagine!"

"Now would be a good time, then, to reveal my plan of action," said Nelwyn rising to her feet. "Gaelen and I agreed that, as soon as my messages were delivered to you, I should leave Mountain-home and travel westward, stopping in the Greatwood Realm for reinforcements. I will then lead them to Tuathas, that we might all aid our friends in defeating Gorgon and Lord Kotos. And of course they will agree, for they despise Gorgon Elfhunter."

Galador looked unhappy at this news, but he was not surprised. "So *now* you reveal the scheme you and your cousin hatched in Tal-sithian," he muttered under his breath.

"You should know that I have already requested aid from the Greatwood, and Ri-Aruin has granted it. There will be a contingent already on its way here," said Ordath.

"Ri-Aruin would rush to the aid of our friends in Mountain-home," said Nelwyn, "but he will not have left the Woodland without protection. There will be plenty of help still to be had there, I'm sure."

"Naturally, I must go with Nelwyn to assist her," said Galador.

"And I am grateful for your assistance," said Nelwyn. "I am also grateful for your forbearance. I know it was not easy for you to hear this plan for the first time."

"Oh…I expected nothing less, after all," he said. "There are two Wood-elves whom I have come to know very well indeed. And when they conspire together, schemes like this invariably result." He shook his head. "I have to admit, it's not exactly a bad plan."

"I agree," said Ordath. "Yet we shall miss your strengths on the battlefield."

"The rest of the Company should remain here to aid you, if they are willing," said Nelwyn. "Galador and I can accomplish the necessary task. We will be riding on swift horses through familiar lands. Yet we must leave soon, before Lord Wrothgar's armies surround Mountain-home and make our escape difficult."

"I have taken a look around," said Azori. "I cannot imagine the difficulty of mounting an assault here."

"The mountains have served us well," said Ordath, "but Wrothgar's forces are skilled in mountain combat. Do not underestimate them."

"It's just that my brother has rarely even seen a mountain in his life," said Estle. "Not like these, at least."

"Will you all agree to remain here, and aid in our defense?" said Ordath. "If you wish to return home, there will be no shame in it."

"If I had to undertake another journey right now, I believe it would be the death of me," said Estle. "I have never traveled so much in all my life! I am staying right here, maybe forever! Besides, thanks to certain members whose names shall be withheld, my home is no longer safe to return to." She fixed Hallagond with a baleful stare.

"I took care of that, remember?" said Azori. He bared his teeth and growled to punctuate his remark, though he was smiling.

The council disbanded at sunset, each member leaving to see to his or her own affairs. Lady Ordath moved to her private chamber, extracted the flute from within her robes, and handed it to Lord Magra, who examined it. There was a parchment rolled neatly and inserted into the silver barrel, and Magra attempted to remove it, but his fingers were too large for the task. "Here," said Ordath, "allow me." She reached inside and deftly removed the parchment, being careful not to tear it. Magra lit several candles and they sat down together. Ordath's brow furrowed as she read Arialde's message, and then she handed it to Magra, who spread it out upon the table.

My Dear Lady Ordath:

It has occurred to some that the Stone has outlived its usefulness, and is too great a liability.
They have suggested destroying it to keep it from hands that must never hold it.
If you would consider this, have Lord Shandor brought to Tal-sithian at once.
Do this, My Little Sister, before Wrothgar's army arrives.
If you would not, I will understand, for not even I can see into my brother's heart.
I do not know what may be unleashed if he is set free.
May victory be ours, and may Darkness flee before the Light.

As ever,
Arialde.

Magra looked up to see that Ordath had gone quite pale. There was pain and doubt in her eyes, for she had felt Shandor's madness herself upon a time, and she had not wanted to face it. She loved her father, and longed for a reunion with him, but she did not know whether it was wise to release him. So long as he was trapped within the Stone, at least he was safe. And she understood Arialde's veiled admonition—no one, possibly not even Shandor himself, knew what would be unleashed if he was set free.

"I will assume that you wish to ponder this for a while," said Magra, placing a gentle hand upon her arm.

"Yet I must not ponder too long," said Ordath. "For if Lord Shandor's body is to be moved, then we must do so before the vanguard of Wrothgar's army arrives. And that might be sooner than expected."

"I expect a month at the most," said Magra. Then he looked deep into her eyes. "If you will permit me, I would offer an opinion," he said. Ordath looked at him with gratitude—she would always hear him. "I have fought beside Lord Shandor on many occasions. His character and his valor were second to none. I cannot believe that, even if madness has afflicted him, he could not overcome it. He has never backed down from a challenge that I am aware of, and he has surmounted every obstacle in his path."

"Not *every* obstacle," said Ordath, her voice full of sorrow. "He could not overcome the loss of Liathwyn. That obstacle is what trapped him in the Stone."

"I know," said Magra, "yet the imprisonment of such a great spirit offends my soul. He cannot deal with his pain so long as he is a prisoner of it. I would see him set free."

"Even if he has turned to Darkness?"

"He would not turn," said Magra. "Search your heart, my lady, and you will know it." He rose and bowed to her. "I will leave you now to your debate. Yet know that I am yours to command, no matter your decision." He turned then, and left her alone. She took a great deal of comfort in the knowledge that Magra would remain faithful until he breathed his last.

Kotos had finally located Wrothgar's Ulcas, the raven flying in circles over their heads and calling to them. It landed on the outstretched arm of one of the Ulcan lieutenants, allowing Kotos to share consciousness with a being who could speak.

"We must interrupt our plan for now," said Kotos through the Ulca. "You should track the bearers of the Stone, but at a distance. They must not know that you follow behind."

"Why not?" growled the Ulcan commander, who was disinclined to trust Kotos' words over those of Lord Wrothgar. "We have our orders, and they say that we should kill our enemies and bring the Stone to our Master as soon as possible. Why should we believe you?"

"Allow me to explain," said Kotos, approaching the commander and placing a hand on his shoulder. Kotos invaded him easily, and then he shared an image of Gaelen shattering the Stone of Léir. "That is what will happen if your presence becomes known," said Kotos. "And here, my good commander, is what will happen after that." Kotos then sent an image of the commander, together with his regiment, writhing in the Black Flame of Wrothgar's wrath. "There will be nowhere to hide," said Kotos. "You *will* convince your comrades now, won't you?"

Kotos then returned to the raven as it perched upon the bald, scaly head of one of the Ulcas, who knew better than to do anything about it. The raven took flight, retracing its path back toward the north. Kotos hoped that Gorgon had not done anything foolish, but at least the Ulcas had been waylaid, and that was a relief. Now he would try to find Wrothgar's five assassins before they could do too much damage.

"I would like to make a few more miles before dusk, Fima," said Gaelen. "Will you not ride?"

Fima had been walking on his own feet for the last several miles. The pace of the Company had been slow and deliberate. Fima had not slowed their progress…not yet…but he was getting weary at last.

"If I did not ache so from sitting atop those enormous animals, my legs could carry me all the day and night," he grumbled. Yet despite his wish to deny it, he knew that his weariness was only due in part to soreness from riding.

"Well, then, let's try to solve the problem," said Rogond, who knew that Fima was sensitive about the fact that age was catching up with him. "If it is your legs and seat that ache from straddling my broad-backed horse, perhaps we should try another method." He reined Eros to a halt and dismounted. "Where sitting is painful, standing might do."

He lifted Fima onto Eros' back, placing him behind the saddle. Then he remounted with some difficulty. "All right, Fima, now place your hands on my shoulders and try to stand up."

"What?" said Fima.

"Try to stand up! Place your feet behind the back of the saddle, and stand up. Use my shoulders to balance, and brace your feet between my saddle-packs."

Fima struggled to follow Rogond's directive, grumbling and growling as he pulled himself into a standing position. Finally, he stood upon the back of the saddle-skirt, looking over Rogond's head.

"Now, you see? You are the perfect lookout in that position," said Rogond. "As long as Eros only walks, you should have no trouble."

Fima discovered that this was more comfortable than sitting. It was, in fact, a lot like walking with no effort, as his feet rose and fell alternately with Eros' hindquarters. Yet he grew dizzy if he looked down at the ground. He focused on the horizon ahead of him, and took a deep breath. "All right," he said. "Let's move on."

At last they decided to camp for the night. Gaelen tended the horses and soon had a fire going, while Rogond went out foraging. He came back with two plump squirrels in his hand, as well as some fine wild greens. Though the meal wasn't quite a match for the cuisine of Mountain-home, it was much appreciated. Gaelen settled down by the fire, listening to the barely discernable but comforting sound of the scouts of Tal-sithian calling to one another from the distant tree-tops.

The Elves were watching for ordinary travelers, and were not anticipating three black-clad assassins. Wrothgar's men stole in toward the Company's encampment from the southwest, against the night wind. They knew of the Elven guards, and they knew how to avoid them. Their instructions had been very clear. They were to kill everyone in the Company, and then take the Stone back past the guards. If they did their work well, there would be no sound and the Elves would not be aware of anything until dawn. By then it would be too late. Wrothgar's Ulcas should be approaching from the south by this time. The men could have waited for reinforcements, but they had no desire to share the glory—or the reward—with Ulcas.

Three dark shapes crouched in silent concealment, near enough to cast their blades. Gaelen lifted her head, listening. She sensed something amiss, and they knew that it was time to act, lest she warn the others. Each man focused his attention on a different member of the Company, as all had agreed. They drew their dark blades forth without a sound. The first man nodded and raised his arm to strike, yet the blade flew wide of its target. There were two reasons for this: one was that Gaelen had heard the sound of the blade slicing through the air and had moved out of the way, and the other was that the man now had a black dagger buried in his throat. The second man raised his own blade to cast it at Rogond, but a second black dart took him and he fell, crying out in surprise. The third looked around in panic as a lone, black shadow came from nowhere, breaking his neck with a single blow. He fell in a disorganized heap.

By this time, all three members of the Company had drawn their weapons, preparing to face their unknown assailant. Who had managed to get past the Elves?

"Lay down your weapons, and do not fear!" said a voice. "I am a friend. I have just killed three men who were trying to do harm to you. Please allow a friend to approach you, Gaelen, Rogond, and Fima Lore-master, for there is a message I would bring."

"Show yourself!" said Gaelen, who was not in a good humor, for she had just been caught with her guard down. "I will not shoot you until I have seen you, but if I see you holding a weapon, I will shoot you just to make certain. Show yourself!"

A dark shape emerged slowly into the fire light, hands held before it with palms upward. There was no weapon in evidence.

"Who are you?" asked Fima. "Your voice is oddly familiar. If you are a friend, tell us your name, as you appear to know ours already."

The dark figure removed the grey cloth from his face.

"Carefully…" Gaelen warned, tightening on her bow string.

Then, his face uncovered, the stranger stepped forward. It was quite possibly the last person they expected to see.

"El-morah?" said Gaelen in wonder.

"*El-morah!* My friend…how? Why?" said Rogond.

El-morah smiled at them. "Yes, it is I. And a fine, long journey you have set me on. I believe you can rest easily now, as I saw no others. Those three are dead."

"Who are they?" asked Fima. "They must have been skilled to make their way past the Elves."

"I made my way past them," said El-morah. "It's not so difficult for a man of my background. These men were trained killers, I would guess. I expect their intent was to rob you of your valuables."

"No doubt," muttered Rogond.

"You saved our lives," said Gaelen, who had always liked and respected El-morah, and was now very glad to see him. "Yet I would never have expected to see you again. How is it that you have come so far north? And how in the world did you find us?"

"You're not as hard to track as you believe…not for a Shadow-man like me. There's no mistaking Faladinn's hind foot-prints. I followed you from the Chupa to bring a message." El-morah's eyes grew even darker than usual. "Let's sit by the fire and I will tell my tale."

"Have some roasted squirrel!" said Fima, for Gaelen had not eaten her full share.

"When I have finished, I would enjoy that very much," said El-morah. "But now I must convey the message. As you know, I made my way back home to the Chupa, hoping that I would not find disaster waiting for me. What I found was my wife and my four children coping as best they could. They had no notion of why I had left them. All the memories that I held were false, as Gaelen thought. She suspected Orrion, but I feared that she might relent as time passed. The more I considered, the more I began to fear that you would all side with Nelwyn's vision, which I knew then was also false. I now believe that Orrion has been manipulating all of us for some dark purpose. Therefore, I had to do my part, or take responsibility for aiding him. Mohani understands, and I am here with her blessing. Knowing what I know, I had to find you, Gaelen, and tell you that you were right about Orrion. If your friends were not convinced of it, I came prepared to convince them."

"You are a noble and a kind man, El-morah," said Gaelen. "Your sacrifice is much appreciated, though my friends require no convincing. You needn't have left your home, yet I am very glad you did. It would seem that fate sent you here, just when you were most needed."

"Indeed. Perhaps I am your Guardian Spirit," said El-morah as Gaelen handed him the rest of the roasted meat, together with a vessel of sweet water. He ate and drank before settling in for the night.

"What was the rumor we heard at the oasis about trouble in the Chupa?" asked Rogond.

"Ah. There is always trouble of some sort in the Chupa," said El-morah. "I expect it was nothing of real consequence. Oh, and speaking of no consequence, I have brought you a gift from my wife. Though it is of little consequence, it is from the heart." He drew forth a package from his robes, and they could all smell the scent of kaffa on the night breeze. "Is that what I think it is?" asked Rogond.

Gaelen looked back and forth between Rogond and Fima; for a moment she thought they were going to weep. She did not understand this devotion to the dancing goats, and she shook her head until El-morah brought out another small package of dark, sweet koka and handed it to her. Now *there* was something she could understand.

She took the package with thanks, bowing to El-morah, and then turned and made her way up to the watch. Gaelen nearly always chose some high place, climbing a tree or a tall stone, where she could survey in all directions. The wind was in the west, and that pleased her, as she could smell the distant river. It was a good, brown smell like freshly-turned earth, full of life and energy. She settled herself to her task for the night, alert to every sign.

Rogond sighed, drawing his cloak about him. Fima was asleep already, as the day had been long and they had traveled many miles. El-morah looked over at his friend, and their eyes met in the fire-light. "She has done this every night since you began the journey?" he asked.

"She knows that Fima and I must sleep, and therefore she keeps the watch," said Rogond. "I have tried to stay awake with her, but I always end up falling asleep eventually. She is not very talkative when she is on guard."

"That must be frustrating," said El-morah. "I know I enjoy my wife's company each night when I am at home. You have been traveling for so long, and yet you stay apart?"

"This journey is different from most we have taken together," said Rogond. "There is no lightness in any of us. We know what waits at the end of it."

"It's a shame that I must leave you," said El-morah. "But tomorrow I will be returning to my family. I promised them nothing less, and I always keep my word. Yet tonight I will keep the watch, so that you and Gaelen might share some time together. It's a small gift, but one I am happy to give." He flashed a grin in the dark. "Don't worry, I will not sleep. I can sleep all day tomorrow if I wish, whereas you cannot." He rose to his feet, striding out to meet Gaelen, who was perched upon an outcropping of rock. After a few moments, she came back into the fire-light to find Rogond waiting for her.

On that same evening in Mountain-home, Nelwyn and Galador also shared warmth and love, wrapped in their cloaks against the chill of the night air. Hallagond and Estle had gone back to the garden-house and had built up the fire, sitting close together in the bright circle of warmth, talking and laughing until they fell asleep in each other's arms. It was a night for sharing love among many in the Company. Perhaps, as Rogond had suggested, it was something in the water.

22
Many Miles to Go

Nelwyn and Galador spent several days in preparation for leaving Mountain-home. They had been advised that Wrothgar was mounting forces not only in the Fell-ruin, but also in the Darkmere. There was said to be a gathering point set in the forested area that lay to the east of the river, nearly due west of Mountain-home, and that area must be avoided at any cost.

"So it will be the High Pass again," said Nelwyn. "But this time there will be no snow or ice to contend with. I would expect the way will be clear to the west of the mountains. Ri-Aruin's people will most likely choose that way as well. We should encounter them at some point, and that will be reassuring. They can tell us whether there is danger on our path to the Elven-hold."

On the evening before her departure, Nelwyn sought counsel with Lady Ordath, standing beside her on a high ledge overlooking the Amar Tuath. Nelwyn had chosen this place because the sound of the wild water would prevent anyone from overhearing.

"My lady," she said, "will you reveal the nature of the message I carried? I would truly like to know."

Ordath drew a long breath. "Perhaps it would be prudent to share that message with you, Nelwyn, as you could then offer your advice as to what should be done," she said.

"Oh, my lady…I would not presume!" said Nelwyn, lowering her gaze and blushing slightly. "I'm sure that any matters of concern between you and Lady Arialde are far too great for me."

"Then give me your thoughts anyway, because you are true-hearted. I want to hear them. Lady Arialde believes that the body of Lord Shandor should be moved to Tal-sithian so that we may then decide whether to destroy the Stone and set him free. What say you to that notion?"

Nelwyn considered for a long moment. "I do not know what to say," she said.

"That is wise, as there is no clear choice," said Ordath. "One thing is certain. If the Stone is destroyed, Lord Wrothgar cannot use it against us."

"But neither can you use it in defense against him," said Nelwyn. "Should Lord Shandor be set free?"

"Does he desire to be free?" asked Nelwyn.

"I would say not, yet I cannot say for certain," said Ordath. "I suspect that he does not truly know his own heart's desire."

"I would do what I thought best for Lord Shandor," said Nelwyn at last. "After all, we are dealing with his very life. As long as he is trapped in the Stone, he really hasn't much hope. Without his presence, the Stone is but a Stone."

"Thank you, Nelwyn...your words have aided me," said Ordath. "Here is your flute. I look forward to hearing you play as you dance. May Aontar speed you on your journey tomorrow, the sooner you may return."

When Nelwyn next looked in her direction, the Lady had gone.

Ordath made her way to the underground vault that was her father's resting-place, and wrestled with her decision. She was reluctant to subject Shandor's body to a journey of so many miles where so much could go awry. Yet she sensed that the way between Mountain-home and Tal-sithian was devoid of enemies for the time being—Wrothgar would be focusing his energies on Mountain-home, and on the "Stone." If she acted quickly, she could spirit Shandor away long before the battle was joined. Tal-sithian would be the safest place for him.

She knelt beside the clear glass casket, looking into her father's lifeless eyes. "Forgive me," she said in a voice tinged with regret. "I will miss looking upon your face and sitting by your side when I need counsel. Though I know you cannot give it, it always aids me to be here. Yet Wrothgar mounts an attack against us, and I am uncertain of the outcome. You will be safer in Tal-sithian." She left him then and summoned Lord Magra. He would be the one to select the elite guard that would transport the body of Lord Shandor to the Lake-realm.

Nelwyn and Galador said their farewells to Hallagond, Estle, Azori, and Carmyn, who had come to see them ride forth in the early morning. Naturally, Ordath and Magra were there as well, but they had said all that was needed the night before. They stood in silence, right hands raised in farewell, as Azori called after Galador:

"Remember, my most principled friend, there are no rules of war where you're going! Don't waste your time with formalities. Make certain you strike first, whether the enemy is ready or not!"

Galador looked back over his shoulder and favored Azori with a withering glance that rapidly degenerated into a smile. "All right, Azori…I surrender. You have turned me to the dark side at last. You will be certain to make yourself useful to the Lady, won't you?"

"Ah, my friend, you have never truly seen me in full battle-cry," said Azori. "Those creatures won't be able to find their own heads with both hands!"

"Take care of Hallagond, Estle," said Nelwyn. "After all the trouble we went through to find him, it would be more agreeable if he was still alive to greet his brother when we return."

"I will," said Estle, but she did not speak further. She knew how unlikely that reunion would be.

Réalta and Gryffa trotted through the gates, disappearing into the mist almost at once. Hallagond put his arm around Estle's shoulders, for he shared the profound sadness that had overtaken her, quenching the light of her good humor.

"Well, no sense in standing around here forever," said Azori in a voice that was perhaps just a little too loud. "We should all go and have some breakfast. After all, we've a battle to prepare for." Estle closed her eyes and tightened her lips, quelling any tears that threatened. It was clear that her half-brother was showing a rare streak of sentiment.

Rogond had not spent such a pleasant night in a long time. He awoke to find El-morah already gathering his few belongings, preparing to depart. Fima was still sleeping and Gaelen was nowhere to be seen, though Rogond thought he heard her singing for the first time in many weeks.

"Gaelen is tending the horses, taking them to water," said El-morah. "I promised I would not leave you until she returns."

"It's unsettling when she goes off alone like that," said Rogond with a slight grimace of pain. Apparently there had been a rather large rock beneath his bedroll. He rolled up his blankets and found a small stone. *Why do they always feel bigger than they look?*

"Here she is at last," said El-morah upon hearing the sound of the horses approaching.

"Yes, here I am," came a cheery voice, "and not empty-handed! There is a veritable bounty of crayfish in the pond yonder. We'll have a fine breakfast before we start our travels this morning."

She drew forth a makeshift basket of woven reeds, which was now filled with wet, shiny carapaces, snapping claws, entangled legs, and black, beady eyes waving about on stalks. She looked plaintively up at Rogond. "Please tell me we have time to boil water and share them with El-morah..."

Fima had awakened by now; he was trying to rise to his feet without betraying the stiffness in his limbs. "We will make time, Gaelen," he said. "I would appreciate a hot breakfast this morning." He was looking forward to the first of the kaffa.

"What, exactly, *are* those things?" asked El-morah with an expression of barely concealed distaste. He did not favor eating any creature with more than four legs.

"Delicious is what they are," said Gaelen. "And we can also dine on sweet cattails. I found heaps of those as well." She produced a healthy pile of cleaned, white roots. They were sweet, crunchy, and full of moisture. Gaelen liked to eat them raw.

Fima had already gone for his cook-pot and had set some water on to boil. Gaelen then took charge of cooking the crayfish, popping their heads off just before tossing them into the boiling water. Soon a little pile of black-eyed heads stared at all of them in accusation.

Gaelen poured off the water, leaving the crayfish to steam in the pot. They had turned bright red, to the wonder of El-morah. "And how, exactly, do you eat them?" he asked.

Gaelen demonstrated by laying several crayfish upon the grass to cool. She then peeled the slick, hard shell from the tail of one and offered it to El-morah. He just stared at her.

"Just eat the tail, like this," said Rogond, peeling a crayfish of his own. He bit off the meat and chewed slowly with an expression of sublime pleasure.

El-morah then took the crayfish from Gaelen and followed Rogond's example. His eyes lit up when he tasted the sweet, tender meat. "These are…good!" he said, as though surprised.

Gaelen, meanwhile, had separated out the females, noting that several were full of roe—an unparalleled delicacy among pond-fare. She pulled off the tough carapaces and extracted the bright orange roe with care. Soon, all four travelers were quite satisfied.

"That was a fine meal," said El-morah. "My compliments to your cuisine, though I am still not certain that it rivals Mohani's cakes."

"Well, Gaelen may not bake cakes, but she certainly knows how to feed herself in the wild," said Fima. "I'm glad to have a Wood-elf as a traveling companion, especially a hunter-scout. I haven't been hungry since I left Tal-sithian."

"Yes, you have," said Gaelen. "Still, I thank you for your kind words. El-morah, I bow to Mohani's cakes. Yet my crayfish were tasty enough in a pinch…so to speak."

At last, El-morah said farewell to his friends. "I do not expect that we shall see each other again," he said, his voice somber. "I wish you well in your quest. Make certain that you strike at least one blow to Orrion from me, won't you?"

He bowed low, touching his forehead with a flourish, and spoke to them in Elvish. When translated, the phrase said: "May the big tree intentionally confuse you."

All three of his friends, who spoke fluent Elvish, stared at him for a moment. "What's that?" asked Gaelen.

"I…I don't know, I have always had difficulty with Elven-tongues," said El-morah. "I meant to say, "May the Way of the Woodland guide you."

"Ah. Well, that's pretty much what I heard," said Gaelen.

"Farewell," said Rogond. "May your journey homeward be swift and sure. Please give our best to your family. Be certain you tell your children that your actions saved all three of our lives. We are forever in your debt."

"If it were not for Gaelen, I might never have returned home," said El-morah. "There is no debt between us. Farewell."

He turned from them and made his way back toward the southland and his beloved, wayward oasis.

Kotos caught up with Gorgon at last, having instructed his Ulcas to keep their distance. "About time you got back here," Gorgon grumbled. "You leave me alone, following a group of witless Elves, and expect me to do nothing about it? I don't know how much longer I could have resisted temptation."

The raven sat placidly upon a stone and preened, seeming unconcerned. His mate had fallen behind and had since gone back to her familiar range, as he was obviously not behaving in normal fashion and she no longer claimed him. That was just as well. The summer brought storms in late afternoon that sometimes blew up out of nothing and, as the raven looked skyward, it appeared that the weather was about to turn nasty. The air was still, the sky was an ugly, dark grey with a sort of greenish tint, and approaching thunder could be heard.

Gorgon wanted to converse with Kotos, so he drew forth the amulet and laid it at the raven's feet. At the directive of its master, the bird picked up the golden thing and held it in its dagger-like beak. Gorgon then beheld the familiar visage of Lord Kotos, appearing as the old man, reflected in the crystal.

"So, you thought of giving in to temptation, did you? How fortunate for both of us that you did not. I regretted having to leave you, Elfhunter, knowing that you could not hunt Elves for the time being. Take comfort in the notion that you will have more than you can dream of when we are victorious."

"What did you learn on your flight?" said Gorgon.

"In a few moments we will be assailed if we do not find shelter. First I'll find a place to wait out the storm, and I will tell my tale to you then. Follow the raven."

The dark bird lifted from its perch and flew north for a short distance, still carrying the amulet. Kotos spotted a small alcove cut into the side of a knoll that would make a fine shelter, and he ordered the raven down. Gorgon was right behind him.

They shared the alcove just in time—the wind picked up to a frightening intensity, roaring through the trees, whipping them to and fro. The sky darkened further and the lightning snaked down, punctuated by loud cracks of thunder. The rain came, and then the hail. Gorgon chuckled as he sat in his sanctuary. He was thinking of the Elves, who were most likely not weathering the storm in such comfortable surroundings. The Vixen was mounted, and therefore almost certainly out in the open.

"Enjoy the hail on your proud head," he said, settling back into the comforting shadows.

Gaelen, Rogond, and Fima had not escaped the storm, but they had taken advantage of the rolling terrain, finding the lee of an outcropping of rock and huddling there with the horses. When the rain and hail came down, the animals dropped their heads low and flattened their ears, relying on their thick manes and tough backs to resist the weather. The two-legged members of the Company sheltered beneath the horses, and would have emerged nearly dry had the wind not blown so hard. As it was, Gaelen felt no hail on her proud head. Faladinn, for once, was glad of his burden, as his packs shielded him from the worst of it. They did make him less streamlined, however. Had he been in the open, the wind might have blown him off his feet.

Rogond sighed. This would become a familiar pattern throughout the summer in the northlands, and they would have to get used to it.

Gaelen seemed to share his thoughts. "It would be worse if we were in the forest…the trees that cannot withstand the wind become deadly, falling in unpredictable ways upon the heads of travelers. No hunter-scout of the Greatwood rests easily during such storms. Here, in more open country, the chief peril is lightning, but so long as we keep close to the earth, away from trees and high places, a strike is unlikely."

She wondered about her distant guardians, the Elves of Tal-sithian, who had lived for so long under the protection of the Lady. Their experience with northern summer weather might therefore be limited.

"Look on the bright side—at least it's rain, and not sand!" Fima declared. He, among all in the Company, held the lowest opinion of the desert. The farther north they traveled, the more at home he would be.

The storm passed quickly, as was typical. No damage had been done to any of the travelers, but the same could not be said for some of the trees. They were in summer leaf already, and those that were tall with large crowns had caught a lot of wind. They had lost limbs, or even been blown over. Fima shook his head. "An example of the maxim that bigger is not always better," he said.

Gaelen thought of Gorgon at once. "If he is an evil tree, then I shall be grass," she whispered. "A storm is coming to us both, but I will weather, whereas he will fall." That said, she settled back into the journey, knowing that the real storm would come at the end of it.

Gorgon, Kotos, and the Elves of Tal-sithian did the same, contending only with the ordinary trials of the journey. As with Gaelen, they knew that the true fulfillment of purpose would come at journey's end.

As Gaelen and company made their way north along the river, Nelwyn and Galador were making steady progress toward the High Pass, the way over the Monadh-hin.

"This certainly looks different from the last time I saw it," said Galador. "Of course, that was in the dead of winter."

"Have you ever seen it, I wonder?" asked Nelwyn. "We did not manage to cross it the last time. We were trapped by a snow-slide and were forced to go beneath the mountains, remember?"

Galador did, though the memory seemed to belong to someone else, in another time and place. It was so long ago, before Nelwyn's love had flowered—he had been reborn on that day. Yet now, he sat tall upon his mount, lifting his head and scanning the path ahead. "Nelwyn, look…the horses are alerted to something. We had better conceal ourselves until we have learned the nature of it."

Nelwyn agreed, as both Gryffa and Réalta were lifting their feet high, ears pricked, obviously at attention. Then the sound of horses drifted to them on the west wind. "Evil creatures do not ride horses," said Nelwyn.

"Evil men do," said Galador. "Given the present situation, considering Wrothgar's intention to surround and attack Mountain-home, I still believe we should hide ourselves until we know the lay of things."

Nelwyn saw the sense in this, and so they hid among the rocks. The sound of feet upon stony ground drew nearer, until the first banners were seen, followed by the most welcome sight of all—Elves of the Greatwood Realm. Friends and kin to Gaelen and Nelwyn, they were led by Wellyn, son of Ri-Aruin.

Wellyn sat tall and proud upon his fine, grey mare, looking every inch the future king. He raised his hand and called the column to a halt. The only dust came from the feet of the horses, and Galador marveled at his woodland cousins, who were the most light-footed of all Elves. It was a large column, only a part of which could be seen at present, yet he had heard only the sound of the horses approaching. In fact, there were nearly a thousand Wood-elves marching to Mountain-home.

Nelwyn knew how to properly announce herself, and she did so, calling out in a hunter-scout code that Wellyn recognized at once. Though he did not answer, he spoke to his standard-bearer, who dipped his banner down twice, giving Nelwyn permission to approach.

"Come on," she said to Galador. Then they trotted out to meet the Elves of the Greatwood.

The Wood-elves made camp in the mountains that night. Wellyn was overjoyed to see Nelwyn again, but he sorrowed that Gaelen was not with her.

"She thought that perhaps you and I might be meeting, and she sent a gift," said Nelwyn. "She also asked me to remind you that she does not believe in premonitions, and that she fully expects to see you again one day." She looked around at the impressive collection of well-armed Wood-elves. "I do not see Ri-Aruin…has he remained in the Greatwood?"

"Yes. He placed me in command of this venture," said Wellyn. "Apparently, he sees it as a test of his son's ability to replace him as Ruler of the Realm. He thinks it will make a king of me." He sighed. "I have never been interested in ruling the Greatwood, but this is an important task—I suppose I should feel pride that my father would have sufficient faith to charge me with it."

Nelwyn had always liked Wellyn, and he looked very young in that moment. Then the moment passed, and the future King returned.

"Now you must finish your tale," he said. "You intend to rendezvous with Gaelen after you acquire reinforcements in the Greatwood?"

"Yes, that was our plan," said Nelwyn, "though it looks as if most of the fighters are marching to Mountain-home. Will there be aid still to be had in the Elven-hold?"

Wellyn laughed. "How many will you need? There will be at least a hundred who will go with you. And you will no doubt be pleased to learn that the sons of Talrodin march with me, and I will release them to accompany you. They will no doubt want to help with the downfall of Gorgon Elfhunter, that their father might be avenged."

Nelwyn was pleased to hear that news. "Have they seen battle?" she asked. "They are still young."

"War has not come yet to the Greatwood, though darkness spreads up the river from the Darkmere," said Wellyn.

Nelwyn then told him of the Currgas, who had been driven from the river into Tal-sithian.

"Yes, we knew they had been set upon," said Wellyn. "We found several dead along the riverbank." His eyes grew sad at the memory; few things are more disheartening than the sight of a dead Currga. "Please, Nelwyn, tell me all of your adventures. I will provision you and send you forth tomorrow or perhaps the day after, together with the sons of Talrodin. There is no darkness at our backs that I am aware of; you should have a clear journey home."

Home!

What a wonderful, wonderful word. Nelwyn's heart yearned for it, and she did not want to waste any time in getting there. Yet Wellyn was most insistent that she tell her tale, and when she looked into his winsome blue-grey eyes, so eager for news, she knew that she could not disappoint him. No matter. They would make up the time later. At least now Nelwyn knew that she would not encounter opposition, at least not on this side of the Elven-hold.

Two days later, Nelwyn said farewell to the Woodland Elves and set off once again on her westward journey with Galador and the sons of Talrodin. She had given Gaelen's gift to Wellyn, but he had tucked it away without opening it. Nelwyn did not know what it was, nor would she ever learn.

As promised, Kotos made his report to Lord Wrothgar on the night of each full moon. This was the third such report. Both good and bad tidings would be shared, for although there had been no serious disruption of the plan as yet, three of Wrothgar's most valuable assassins had been found slain, and Kotos could not account for the other two. El-morah had concealed the bodies, but they had not been missed by Gorgon, whose keen senses had picked up their scent.

"I smell…death nearby, the death of men," he said, pausing and scenting the breeze. He looked into the amulet. Though it was dark, he could still hear the voice of Kotos in his mind. "Do you think we should investigate?"

Yes, of course, said Kotos. *I want to know of anyone you detect, whether living, dying, or dead.*

Gorgon located the three assassins where El-morah had hidden them. After a very thorough investigation, Gorgon gave his assessment of them. "There is no Elf-stench on or about them," he said. "And there are tracks leading here…man-tracks. It would seem that a single man killed all three of them, and from the signs, that man was not of the Company. They did welcome him into their encampment, however. They feasted on crayfish and cattails." Gorgon favored Kotos with a superior smile, for he was proud of his tracking abilities.

Kotos dismissed him. *Yes, yes…very good. So this man was a friend. That explains why the Company was not alarmed into breaking the Stone. They must have thought Wrothgar's three assassins were ordinary brigands who somehow managed to slip past the Elven guards.*

"That is not so difficult," said Gorgon, who had learned that he could slip past them himself.

So you keep saying, said Kotos, *yet these men were as skilled as any Elf, and so are you. Most would not be so adept.* He was puzzled as to the identity of the strange man, this unknown friend to the Company. Kotos did not like to include many "unknowns" in any report to Lord Wrothgar.

That report was made a little easier by the upcoming attack on Mountain-home, as the Shadowmancer's energies were divided in at least two different directions. His displeasure at the loss of his assassins was expected, yet it was tempered by the news that the Company was still keeping their northward course. Nothing had disrupted the plan.

When they have hidden the Stone, we will secure it for Thee, my Lord, said Kotos. *Though I do not know where they are taking it as yet.*

Keep to thy path then, most faithful Deceiver, and bring Me what I desire, said Wrothgar. *Find also My two remaining men, and keep them from assailing the Company until the time is right. They will be able to aid thee, for they are skilled. Farewell.*

The cold, dark image of the Shadowmancer faded from Kotos' awareness. By directive of the Highest Dark Power, he was now saddled with locating and controlling the two brigands, and that displeased him, though it could have been worse. Men, though sometimes unpredictable, were easy to control.

In the end, it would not be necessary for Kotos to deal with Wrothgar's men, for they had underestimated the skills of the Elves of Tal-sithian. After hearing nothing from their three associates, curiosity had gotten the better of them, and they had crept toward the Company by night. The Corsair called the sutherling to a halt, whispering to him in the dark. "There is an Elf in yonder tree…do you see it?"

At first the sutherling did not perceive, but at last he, too, saw the Elf keeping watch in a tall tree not far from where the men now lay in concealment.

"I don't reckon he has seen us," said the Corsair. "We should move on."

"Not so fast, my friend," said the sutherling with a wicked look. "I cannot pass up this chance, and we dare not risk being seen. I will fell him easily." He drew his curved bow on the watcher and took careful aim, holding his breath. Yet he never had the chance to draw another, as his arms flew forward, the arrow flying wild. He stiffened, eyes bulging in surprise, and fell with a feathered shaft protruding from between his shoulder blades.

A second shaft—grey-feathered, Elven-made—drove into the soil at the other man's elbow, its implied message clear: *Leave at once and never return!*

The Corsair got slowly to his feet, backing away from his dead companion, holding both hands in the air to show that he held no weapon. He now assumed that the three other assassins had faced the same fate, and he decided without further debate to abandon his task and return to Fómor by any means required. No reward would be enough to convince him, and he was not sufficiently afraid of the Shadowmancer's wrath.

Gorgon Elfhunter sat alone during the exchange between Kotos and Wrothgar, brooding over his own situation. For the first time since he had set upon the northward path from Tal-sithian, he wondered whether all was as it seemed. Gorgon was a most circumspect and suspicious creature, and these qualities had aided him greatly in remaining alive. Something about the present situation worried him, though he did not know why.

The worrisome thoughts had come to him after Lord Kotos had flown off to find the Ulcas. Something was being overlooked... Gorgon just knew it. *Kotos tends to dismiss "lesser" beings as unimportant... is he dismissing something or someone that he should not? This plan is working too well. Would the Elves really take their most precious possession and allow it to play right into the hands of their greatest enemy? Would they stake so much on a premonition?*

Gorgon brooded by himself in the dark, hiding from the moon.

There was someone he knew well, one whom he had warned Lord Kotos never to dismiss, and that was the Vixen. She had allowed herself to dream, and had not guarded her thoughts, and therefore had warned Gorgon of her intentions regarding the destruction of the Stone. What if that had been intentional, to prevent Wrothgar from attacking the Company? It had certainly succeeded. No...she was not that clever, and he was not that gullible.

Are you not? said a familiar voice inside Gorgon's head, causing him to tense his entire body with loathing. *You seem fairly gullible to me!*

Gorgon knew better than to tell Gelmyr to go away, for he would not. He would leave only in his own good time. *Let us recall a few events, then, shall we?* said the hideous, decomposing Elf who now appeared to be sitting at Gorgon's right hand. *Let me see...you were gullible in the Barrens. You were gullible in the desert. You have been spectacularly gullible with respect to Lord Kotos. A few pretty visions were required to win you over, but look! You are now completely under his control. I'd say that just about defines "gullible," wouldn't you?* Gelmyr laughed then, a remarkable act considering that much of his neck had fallen away from the bone by now.

"Well, if you are so all-knowing, tell me the truth of things!" said Gorgon. "Why can I not believe that all is as it seems? There are doubts that assail me...the Vixen is luring us, I just *know* it." He shook his head and grimaced. "I cannot believe I'm actually asking *you* for guidance."

Yes, you should no doubt slap yourself for entertaining such a thought, said Gelmyr. *Go ahead and do it…pay me no mind! Yet you are right. I am your enemy, for I am you, Elfhunter, and therefore I cannot be all-knowing—I only know what you know. Yet the fact that I'm here at all should prove that your doubts are real, and that they have foundation. I can assure you that they do, O Baleful Bungler. It is your task to figure out why. In the meantime, I shall enjoy visiting you when "You-know-who" is away again. Of course, you know to whom I refer…that would be your master, the all-knowing, all-seeing Lord Kotos, who is even more gullible than you are? The Lord Kotos who thinks that Gaelen is only a lowly Wood-elf? You remember, the Lord Kotos who has promised you such great reward for your service, and who now forces you to walk unseen within striking distance of Elves, yet leave them untouched?* That *Lord Kotos?*

"Yes, I remember. You've made your point," Gorgon muttered.

I have made your *point, Gorgon,"* said Gelmyr, as he faded from view. *Do not forget it!*

Even though his doubts had receded for the moment, Gorgon still brooded over what to do about them. 'Should I express them to Lord Kotos?" He emitted a low, sardonic chuckle at the very thought. "Kotos would most likely not believe me. Either that, or he will become disagreeably insecure about it until matters are made clear. And what would I tell him, anyway? I don't really have specifics. One thing is certain—he would somehow manage to blame me for anything that displeased him. Why should I hasten the inevitable rebuke and retribution?"

His worst fear, after all, was that Kotos would become convinced that their current pursuit was vain and would pull him back before he could see to the demise of the Vixen. He decided to keep his thoughts to himself, at least until they became more substantial. Then he would need to decide whether to act upon them. After all, he would accomplish his objectives whether or not Kotos acquired the Stone of Léir.

While Gaelen and company continued on toward Tuathas, Nelwyn and company traveled in a straight line from the High Pass to the Greatwood, passing to the north of Wrothgar's western army. Both Gaelen and Nelwyn crossed the river Ambros, not an easy task for either of them. Then Nelwyn continued straight west through the Greatwood, while Gaelen followed the southern bank of the Eros. Nelwyn's path had eventually crossed Gaelen's. Nelwyn had noted with dismay that Wrothgar's Ulcas followed behind her cousin, although, from the signs, they appeared to be keeping their distance.

"It would seem that Gaelen's ruse has succeeded," said Galador. "They follow behind, but they do not attack."

"Yet they will attack one day," said Nelwyn. "Therefore, we must not delay." She was unaware that Gaelen, Rogond, and Fima were guarded and defended by Elves of the Lake-realm, but it would have made little difference. Nelwyn had resolved to stand with Gaelen, and that was the end of it.

"Did you find any trace of the Elfhunter?" asked Galador.

"No…he has left no sign of his passing, but this is nothing new."

The only difficulty Nelwyn encountered on her way to the Elven-hold was the crossing of the Brunner Ia, which was by now thoroughly infested with Úlfar. She dealt with the problem by crossing at night, after luring the Úlfar upstream by placing a torch near the water. Úlfar can detect light, though they are eyeless, and a torch at night often means prey. Nelwyn also placed into the water a cloth bag containing garments that had been worn, and thus carried the scent of the wearer. The Úlfar were drawn to it at once. The horses then leaped across as quickly as they could manage. Nelwyn's eyes were hard, her jaw clenched, as she rode on. She had loved the Brunner Ia.

She gained the Elven-hold two days later, having made good time through the familiar lands. In a matter of hours, she and Galador were in counsel with Ri-Aruin, and that night they feasted at the King's table. Nelwyn's heart nearly burst with joy and relief, for she was home at last. She might have reveled in it but for the small voice saying, *You cannot stay...you know it. Do not become too well entrenched, for you cannot stay.*

Nelwyn had no difficulty in finding aid. Ri-Aruin marveled at the tale of her adventures. "So, our two hunter-scouts now find themselves at the center of things," he said. "Our people are proud that your actions have shaped, and will continue to shape, this opportunity to sway the balance of Light and Dark. Even I, who have lived long and seen much, am having difficulty imagining the ways you have traveled. Please make every effort to return to us. When you do, both you and Gaelen will be accorded exalted status in our kingdom." Ri-Aruin rose and bowed low before Nelwyn and Galador. This was an act that Nelwyn had seen him perform only once before.

Gaelen and company encountered little resistance on their way along the Eros. The real troll country was farther north, though they did pick up the sign of hill-trolls ranging near the riverbank, and thus were ever alert after nightfall. Yet good fortune was with them, and they did not encounter any trolls. Fima had been correct in his prediction of the number of ravens, however. Because they are inquisitive birds, they were always flying near the Company. Gaelen could not rely on the sound of raven-cries to alert her to the presence of Lord Kotos in these lands.

"I have noticed that the farther to the north and west we travel, the less brightly the sun shines," said Rogond. "I have heard that clouds of ash can hang in the air for years after being spewed forth by fire-mountains, depending on the movement of wind. Is that true?" He turned to Fima, who walked beside him.

"It is," said Fima. "And I have noticed that the sunsets in these lands are distressing in their spectacular brilliance. We learned what that means when we were crossing the desert. I would guess that the Monadh-ainnas have not been idle recently." He blew a sigh through his mustache. "I'm so looking forward to choking on inhospitable air again."

"To know for certain, all we need do is look at the river," said Gaelen. She stooped upon the bank and drew a handful of sediment forth from the shallows. "This is full of ash. I would say that you are both right concerning the fire-mountains. Now, are you surprised by it, I wonder? You heard what Hallagond said. This journey has been easy up to now. The trials have not even begun."

"Ah. Well, thank you for stating that obvious jewel of optimism," said Fima. As though to punctuate his remark, a chilly, dull rain began to fall.

Nelwyn and Galador left the Elven-hold with their new escort—about one hundred of the Greatwood's finest. Wood-elves do not care to leave the forest, but they are curious folk, and these had been more than intrigued upon hearing the tales Nelwyn had told. The sons of Talrodin, named Arlan and Fynn, rode at their head. The rest were not mounted, as Nelwyn had reasoned that horses might be at a disadvantage in the rugged, ruined northern lands. She hoped she would not need to bid farewell to Gryffa.

The elder brother, Arlan, was tall for a Wood-elf, and he was strong of limb. His eyes were most compelling, as they were nearly identical to those of his father's brother, Halrodin. Had his uncle still been living, it would have been difficult to tell Arlan apart from him. Fynn, the younger brother, had been named for his fair coloring. He had very light blond hair and pale blue eyes—even his eyelashes and eyebrows were a light golden color. Neither Fynn's father nor his mother had such coloring, as it is very rare among Sylvan folk. It was said to have come from his great-grandmother, who had passed on long before he was born.

In temperament Arlan resembled his father—gentle and introspective. Fynn, on the other hand, was wild.

Fynn had decided that he would become a warrior; it was his ambition to become captain of the King's Guard. He practiced with his weapon of choice—a heavy broadsword—at every opportunity. He was therefore possessed of great, strong shoulders and arms, and in that respect he reminded Nelwyn of her own beloved uncle Tarmagil. Because of his strange coloring, Fynn had often felt that he was not accepted among his people, and he was sensitive about it. In truth, any separation between Fynn and his friends was of his own making, but he covered his insecurities with a veil of bravado. He seemed to be good-humored, but was quick to take offense.

Nelwyn, an excellent judge of character, sized him up at once. She won him over on first meeting. "My word…is this really young

Fynn? I can't believe it. How impressive and golden you are. You remind me of Lord Magra himself!"

Fynn, who was still very young, believed every word.

The brothers would prove to be amiable traveling companions, and they were both quite keen to see to the death of Gorgon. Nelwyn and Galador were glad of their company. Fynn, in particular, would tackle any hard chore just to show that he could do it. Nelwyn worried about him…she hoped he would be able to restrain his bravado when the time came, as it would not mix well with Gorgon Elfhunter.

Nelwyn knew where she was going, but she had not been there before. She carried a map of the lands between the Elven-hold and the source of the river Eros, which was their destination. They would meet up with Gaelen and company there, if luck was with them.

Gaelen was only a few days' march away from the meeting-place, and she would arrive nearly a week ahead of Nelwyn and company. Yet the journey had taken longer than expected already. It was still summer, and the two hundred mile change in latitude had little effect, but the fire-mountains of the Monadh-ainnas had darkened the climate of the these lands due to the ash-clouds veiling the sun. Though they were very high, and therefore did not affect the quality of the air near the ground, one could feel their effects in other ways. The lands to the east and north were most affected, as the high air currents moved in that direction. Sometimes the rains that fell over the Northern Mountains were unclean, being tinged grey with ash, and the sunlight was always dim. Gaelen and company had noticed it as they moved farther west along the Eros. No wonder trolls and other sun-hating creatures found the area to their liking.

"I believe we should make camp here for a while," said Gaelen. "Faladinn seems off to me, and I don't want him to go lame."

"Music to my ears," said Fima, who was weary and sore. He walked over to Faladinn and actually patted him. "Well done," he whispered. "Do you suppose you could manage to be 'off' for a few days, then? There's a good fellow."

Gaelen did not want to tell Rogond and Fima about her arrangement with Nelwyn—not until the discovery was imminent. She knew that she could not justify waiting too long in one place, but an extra day here and there would not arouse suspicion. Then something happened that changed her mind at once.

She was keeping the watch on one dark night when she suddenly felt a chill in her blood. Gaelen found the night sky disappointing in these lands, for the brilliance of stars and moon was always hidden, but Gorgon appreciated the oppressive darkness, and he was on the hunt.

Gaelen sat bolt upright, crying out in dismay: "No, no…be vigilant! Do not let your mind wander. He will take you! Do not let your spirit fall…hear me, please, *hear me!*" Then she felt the triumph of the Elfhunter, and the despair of his victim. She could do nothing but sit and weep, and try to shield herself from both the hapless Elf's agony and from Gorgon's twisted, bizarre gratification. It would seem that Lord Kotos had deemed it acceptable to allow the Elfhunter to hunt Elves once again.

Gorgon had not felt such fulfillment in what seemed like years. Lord Kotos had advised him that this body must not be found, and so, after a rather prolonged death, the Elf had been dismembered and his body scattered among the rocks over a wide area. Gorgon actually sang and hummed as he roamed here and there, dragging the dead Elf by the hair, occasionally pausing to remove a large piece of flesh or a limb and then toss it aside.

Kotos had insisted on coming along, and he spoke now to his apprentice. *You remind me of a gardener planting seed. I wonder if fresh Elves will sprout up here?*

"That is not amusing," said Gorgon, though he was in too good a humor to care.

Later, as the sun began to brighten the eastern sky, both Gaelen and Gorgon were sitting alone in contemplation. Gaelen had realized that she could not linger in one place for long, or Gorgon would find the time and opportunity to prey on the Elves of Tal-sithian.

Gorgon's thoughts were more convoluted. He had felt Gaelen's dismay at the taking of last night's prey. He knew she was aware that he followed her. She had done nothing to the Stone of Léir, even though her guardians had been attacked. She had done nothing in response to the three assassins converging on her, either. She had not even been thinking of the Stone as far as he could tell.

He thought he knew Gaelen very well by now…well enough to know that if safeguarding the Stone of Léir was really her primary task, she would not have failed to show concern for it. Gaelen usually showed fierce devotion to a task once it was given her.

Did he know for a fact that the Stone was there at all?

Lord Kotos has gone forth with the raven to spy on Gaelen and company many times, and he did not appear to be distressed or in doubt. He described the heavy oaken casket; supposedly he had even caught a glimpse of the Stone within. Surely, my concern is unfounded. Still, I should ask him…though I will need to be very cautious. I don't want him to know of my suspicion that our errand is false. If he did, he might not allow me to complete it, but will instead run back to Mountain-home in an attempt to waylay the attack before too much damage is done to Wrothgar's armies. And somehow he would manage to make it all my fault!

Gorgon was unlikely to survive if that happened. He would accomplish two ends by keeping his suspicions from Lord Kotos—Gaelen would be dead, and the Elves of Mountain-home would hopefully be diminished. And, of course, Gorgon would have no constraints against taking Nelwyn and Galador, or any of the Elves of Tal-sithian that he could manage. At least it was something. By the time the raven had returned from its morning foray, Gorgon had resolved to keep his suspicions entirely to himself.

Gaelen had suffered through several more deaths by the time she gained the source of the Eros. It did not seem to matter, then, whether the Company moved on each day or stayed in one place. She had shared the news with Rogond and Fima, and though they were dismayed, they were not surprised.

"You knew this was likely, Gaelen," said Fima. "We all knew it. You tried to warn them in Tal-sithian. This is not your fault."

"I have learned that I am not responsible for Gorgon's actions," said Gaelen, "but I would save lives if I can. May we not call our guardians here, that we might all camp together and protect one another? Gorgon would not dare steal so close. He only preys on those who are alone and unwary."

"And how do we justify calling so much attention to ourselves?" asked Fima. "Remember...we are not to invite curiosity. We are supposed to be traveling in secret!"

"A group of forty Elves will most certainly attract attention," said Rogond. Gaelen looked away, wondering what he would think when Nelwyn and her reinforcements appeared. She still had not informed him of that part of the plan.

"There are far fewer than forty Elves now," she said. "There will be even fewer if we do not act! At least allow me to speak with them and advise them to move in closer around us. If they tighten the circle, they will be able to assist one another. They will also be more effective in guarding us." This seemed a sensible compromise, and Gaelen wasted no time in doing it. Even so, by the time Nelwyn's contingent gained the rendezvous point, ten of the Elves of the Lake-realm had fallen.

The journey had not been an easy one for Wrothgar's group of Ulcas. They had run afoul of a pair of hill-trolls, and as a result there were five fewer Ulcas in pursuit. The ones who remained were restive and unhappy; they did not like being asked to remain vulnerable for so many weeks, to no apparent end. They had left Tûr Dorcha, having been called to a great mission by Lord Wrothgar, and they were still on the trail with their thirst for blood and violence unsatisfied. At least they were not weary, for the pace had been slower than expected. And they were comfortable in the knowledge that they still greatly outnumbered the Elves.

Toran and Eros gave the call at almost precisely the same time, looking out toward the horizon. They had both been alert for several minutes when they announced the arrival of friends. Gaelen could not have imagined many sights that were more welcome than the one that now appeared from the south. Four mounted riders and what looked like a hundred foot-soldiers bearing the banner of the Greatwood Realm were making their way northward. Eros called again, and Réalta answered.

Rogond and Fima got to their feet in surprise as Gaelen whistled for Toran. She vaulted onto his back—in her excited state she needed no stone to stand on—and cantered out to meet Nelwyn and company, who had found her at last!

Rogond called for her to wait, but she pretended to not hear him. *So much for not calling attention to ourselves,* he thought, whistling for Eros.

"Rogond, do not pursue her as yet," said Fima. "You must allow her time to make up some excuse as to why she has not told us what she has been planning all along."

"You think this is amusing?" said Rogond, who was surprised and dismayed that Gaelen had not told him of her plans. "I didn't think we held back secrets from each other—this shows a lack of trust, and it hurts my soul. It makes me angry, in fact! It's…it's like a betrayal."

"Calm yourself. There are other reasons," said Fima. "Gaelen trusts you utterly. I will place a wager right now that she will have a reason other than lack of trust. Now you must trust *me.* Stay here and wait for Gaelen. She will explain herself." He settled back against his pack in total nonchalance. Rogond muttered something about the dwarf's maddening lack of insecurity, while clenching both hands in suppressed outrage.

"There is Gaelen!" said Nelwyn. "Let's ride forth and meet her." Without waiting for a reply from Galador, she urged Gryffa into a canter, and the two cousins soon were reunited. They slid down from their horses and stood facing one another.

"Well, I'm glad to see you finally made it," said Gaelen, pretending that she was not at all excited about it.

"Well, you know," said Nelwyn, "it wasn't such an important task that I felt the urge to hurry, after all."

Gaelen yawned. "Yes, well, since you're here, I suppose I am glad to see you. Though I was doing just fine with my escort of

Elves…you needn't have brought so many from the Greatwood. I suppose now we'll need to slow our progress just to take the time to feed them."

"What escort?" asked Nelwyn, pretending that she had not seen signs of them. "Well fine, then, since you are already well protected, I suppose I might as well go home." The thought of it brought tears to her eyes. "Oh…Gaelen, things are happening at home…bad things. The Brunner Ia is overtaken now and is not safe. Terrible creatures are migrating up the river as well. I'm so glad to have found you alive and whole. This thing we are doing…we must make certain it is done!"

Gaelen nodded, tears welling in her eyes also. The two Elves then embraced, all feigning of indifference discarded. "It will be done, Nelwyn," said Gaelen in a soft voice that left no doubt in either of their minds. They broke their embrace and wiped the tears from their faces. "The greatest task I face at present is explaining this meeting to Rogond," said Gaelen.

"What…he did not *know* of it?" asked Nelwyn in disbelief.

"If he knew of it, then I would not need to explain it to him *now*, would I?" said Gaelen.

"Well, why ever did you not tell him earlier?" asked Nelwyn, who knew that Gaelen did not usually keep things from Rogond.

"Because he would have done nothing but worry about the wisdom of it," said Gaelen. "The plan was already set into motion; there was nothing to be done about it. Still, he would have fretted and mulled over and thought about and worried. I wanted to save him some grey hairs."

"His hair will start falling *out* if he thinks you do not trust him," said Galador, who had ridden up behind them and had overheard. "If I were you, I would be crafting a mighty apology about now."

"Rogond will understand…he always does."

"Well, let's not delay in easing his mind then," said Galador.

"I did not tell you of my plan to rejoin Gaelen until the time came to leave, remember?" said Nelwyn to Galador as they rode together toward the encampment.

"Yes, and I was not happy about it, remember?" said Galador.

"Yes, but you got over it. Rogond will, too."

As it happened, Nelwyn's assessment of Rogond's response was perhaps a little optimistic. He listened to Gaelen's shaky explanation and to her mighty apology, and then barely spoke to her for three days. By the end of the third day she was so miserable that he took pity on her.

"Do you see now how much it hurts when you keep things from me?" he said.

Gaelen did. Yet she could not resist one final comment.

"Plans were made in Tal-sithian by some, and they were changed in Tal-sithian by others. As a result, you and I are much more likely to survive the trials to come. I promise that I will not change plans again without consulting you unless I have no other choice. But I'm afraid you will have to live with things as they are, beloved, and I most humbly beg your pardon."

"Can't you just say, 'I'm sorry, Rogond,' and *mean* it?"

"I'm sorry, Rogond. And I *do* mean it."

"All right, then. I forgive you," said Rogond. "But I will hold you to that promise!"

There were no more hunting forays for Gorgon, as the Elves of Tal-sithian had combined with the Elves of the Greatwood, and all now traveled together. The Elves of Tal-sithian, who had journeyed long and suffered great loss, were given the choice to return home. Yet none took it. They were more determined than ever to assist in the death of Gorgon, and were not about to be overshadowed by Wood-elves.

Rogond understood the real motive for the reunion with Nelwyn; Gaelen had made this plan to save her friend's heart from despair and humiliation. Yet now there was no hope whatsoever of not calling attention to themselves, a fact that Rogond pointed out in the next council-meeting with Fima, Gaelen, Galador, and Nelwyn.

"Our tactics have changed," said Nelwyn. "We are now going forth as a force formidable enough to protect the Stone, having gotten all the way to the borders of Tuathas. The lands beyond are said to be uninhabited. We don't need to worry about unwanted attention there."

"Kotos won't buy it," said Fima. "He might even realize that we're on to him. Hopefully he has not realized it already!"

"If he has, he has not informed Gorgon," said Gaelen, "for he is still following close behind, and there are Ulcas not too far behind him. They are still keeping their distance."

"How do you know about them?" asked Galador.

"Well…the wind is not always out of the west, is it?" said Gaelen.

"We have made our way to the borders of Tuathas," said Rogond, pointing to their position on Carmyn's map. "Now we should decide whether to try to take our large contingent of guardians with us, or to leave them behind. Our task here, presumably, is to find a new hiding place for the Stone of Léir. That would be the most secret of tasks!"

"It would," said Fima. "But we would not leave the Stone there without guardians. Kotos must think that we intend to establish a permanent, if small, garrison. Therefore, several of our associates should come with us, leaving the others behind to battle the Ulcas. Then we won't need to worry about any pursuit."

"Only pursuit by Gorgon and Lord Kotos, Lord of Light willing," growled Gaelen under her breath.

The Company, now reunited, surveyed the scene before them. The borderlands of Tuathas looked innocent enough, yet they could still see tall plumes of steam from the Monadh-ainnas, and a few in the distant south of the forgotten lands they were about to enter. "Well, let's go on then," said Fima. "After all, it's all uphill from here!" He started forward, striding confidently and with purpose, knowing that he would face the test of his life in the time to come.

23
Things Unexpected

The stage was set. Gaelen and company would proceed deep into the heart of Tuathas, luring Gorgon and Kotos behind them. Lady Ordath and Lord Magra made ready the defenses of Mountain-home, as Wrothgar's forces converged from the north and west. Lady Arialde prepared to safeguard the body of Lord Shandor, which had been removed from Mountain-home to Tal-sithian. She also prepared to defend the real Stone of Léir, if necessary.

Lord Wrothgar had a few tricks that he had not revealed through Nelwyn's false vision. He had shown Bödvari invading Tal-sithian, but there were none of these remaining in the western lands. Yet Wrothgar held other weapons that the Elves would not expect, and he was stronger than they realized. He had virtually emptied the Fell-ruin, calling forth a swarming mass of Ulcas, trolls, foul beasts, and evil men. It was these evil men who posed the most deadly threat to the Elves of Mountain-home, for they would command the Dark Army.

When the next report from Lord Kotos came to Tûr Dorcha, the news was not quite as cheerful as anticipated. It seemed that the Elves transporting the Stone had called for reinforcements, and now they outnumbered his Ulcan forces. Wrothgar knew that his Ulcas were outmatched. They may have been fierce fighters, but they would not prevail against superior numbers. Yet he was not concerned. *Keep to thy course,* he told Kotos.

We are placing much faith in the Elfhunter, my Lord, said Kotos.

All will be clear to thee, said Wrothgar. *There are things in Tuathas which will thwart them. The Elfhunter will not suffer the Elves to prevail. Our faith is well placed.*

Thy Will be done, my Lord, said Kotos, his dark spirit both encouraged and in doubt.

The Company had plunged into Tuathan lands, taking their vanguard of Elves with them. They had agreed to continue until the way became too difficult, and then only a few Elves would go on with Gaelen and company. The rest would keep Wrothgar's Ulcas at bay, but they were not to interfere in any way with Gorgon Elfhunter.

It would soon be autumn in the northlands, and the Company began to feel the chill. "It doesn't make sense," said Fima on one miserably damp, cold night. "We are moving south, yet it is getting colder."

"It will start snowing soon," said Galador, who was highly attuned to such things. Soon after the last words left his lips the first tiny specks of white could be seen on his cloak. This was sleet, and not snow, but it was close enough.

There were other signs that the realm into which they now walked was not a happy one. The ground grew very stony, with peculiar patches of barren, pitted black rock that resembled the hardened flow of some liquid. "We have encountered the first of the lava-flow," said Fima. "This was molten rock vomited up by one of these mountains...I would guess that large one there."

Nothing grew on those sprawling, black drifts except tiny grey lichens and some struggling moss. And though there were plants growing elsewhere, they were diminishing in size and vigor. The air now smelled of sulfur, reminding the Company of their encounter with the Mountains of Dread in the southern desert. One of the more ominous signs was the first appearance of twisted, grey-green brambles with long, wicked thorns. These soon became the predominant form of life, as they could grow where nothing else would.

Finally the day came when the terrain became too difficult for the horses. The horrible thorn-bushes had increased both in size and in number, and a blade was necessary to make any progress through them. Rogond, Galador, and Fynn had been especially helpful in clearing the way, but the horses could not cope with such narrow quarters. Besides, they could not eat the brambles. They would need to make their way back north, to where there was forage. Thus it was that the Company said farewell to their beloved mounts and to their Elven protectors. The Elves were to take the horses back to a suitable encampment and wait there for the return of the Company.

"You must move on before the onset of winter," said Rogond. "Do not wait until the land freezes or you will be hard put to survive. We will make our own way back." He steeled himself for his next words. "If I do not return, please take good care of Eros. Watch that he does not escape you...he will not understand why I haven't returned for him. Take him to safety and convince him to stay there!"

He walked over to his wonderful horse and patted the now-furry neck. Eros would not suffer in the cold—that was certain. Rogond looked his old friend over carefully, noting the tiny white hairs flecking the darkness around his eyes and muzzle. "Well, Eros, it seems that we both have gotten older on this journey. You must stay here and mind the Elves for me." He patted Eros again, and then turned from him.

Gaelen, Nelwyn, and Galador were also quite grieved to leave their mounts behind. "Toran will make a fine mount for someone in the Greatwood," said Gaelen, "though it should be someone taller than I, such as Wellyn. Take good care of him. He has proved his worth."

"Everyone in the Greatwood is taller than you are," whispered Nelwyn, who had just said goodbye to Gryffa.

"Yes, I know," said Gaelen with a sigh. "Now let us move on, before I start weeping over that ridiculous, huge animal."

"Who would weep over a horse?" said Galador. Everyone in the Company knew the answer to that question, as Galador's eyes were red.

It was slow going from that moment on. Fynn and Rogond walked in front, hewing the brambles with their blades, while Galador and Arlan carried the casket containing the replica of the Stone on two stout poles. It did not overburden them, for though it was heavy, they were both strong and tireless. Gaelen, Nelwyn, and Fima bore the rest of the provisions.

"I hope there is water here that isn't full of poisonous ash," said Nelwyn. "We only have enough for about three days' march."

"There's snow on the brambles," said Gaelen. "Snow may be melted."

"Yes, but, this close to the Fire-mountains, will it be fit to drink?" said Nelwyn.

"I suppose we'll find out in about three days," said Gaelen, and they spoke no more of it.

Gorgon managed to circumvent the Elves' encampment, following the Company. Tracking was easy…all one had to do was follow the only path cut through the brambles. They had taken the Stone with them. "What do they intend to do once they have hidden it?" asked Gorgon. "Surely they won't just drop it in some hole and leave it unguarded."

"*It is obvious,*" said Kotos as he peered out at Gorgon from the amulet. "*Have you not noticed the tracks of two Elves who travel with them? They are obviously the appointed guardians. They will be left in charge of the Stone, and every so often new guardians will be sent from the garrison to relieve them. They probably intend to take the Stone back to Tal-sithian when the war has ended and they believe their lands are safe again.*"

"Hmmmm…" growled Gorgon, but he was not convinced. What would they eat? What would they drink? How would they survive? And surely the garrison of Elves left behind did not intend to spend the winter in Tuathas! That would probably kill them all… they must have thought of it. Was it possible that Kotos had not? He no longer ate, or drank, or shivered in the cold. He expended no energy in survival. But then, Gorgon reconsidered.

Kotos had not dwelled within a body of his own in five thousand years, but his spirit had lived in the world for time out of mind, and he was shrewd. If Gorgon had held these doubts, Kotos had, too. Yet a force drove him on despite all doubt—Kotos could not fail in his task, and he knew it. Again, Gorgon kept his thoughts to himself.

As he followed the well-hewn path before him, Gorgon reflected on the Company's choice of hiding places. *I wonder who has chosen it. Certainly, the ruin of Tuathas would be a good place to hide the Stone, as it is at least believed to be uninhabited. It was not likely that anyone would wander into such a fierce and unforgiving place. Yet the Elves could not leave the Stone unguarded. Why, then, would they choose to subject their chosen guardians to such hardship? Perhaps there is something about this lost realm that I did not know.* He was looking forward to finding out. Gorgon was an inquisitive creature, a trait inherited from his mother. The world had yet to witness the birth of an inquisitive Ulca.

In Mountain-home, the preparation for the upcoming battle continued. Everyone in the Company had been pressed into service, even Estle. Her condition was no longer in doubt; if she kept safe she would bring forth Hallagond's child in late winter. She would fight now only out of dire need. As ever, Hallagond had proven useful, and though it took a while for the Elves of Mountain-home to accept Azori, they were glad of his aid once they did.

There were said to be men of low character directing some of Wrothgar's forces, and the Elves could not anticipate their plans. Azori had lived all of his life among such men. "Who better to foil brigands than another brigand?" he said, laughing in his loud manner and clapping the Elves on the back or the shoulder. They winced, smiled, and said nothing, knowing he was right.

Lady Ordath had sent messengers to the Deep Caverns of Cósdomhain to ask for aid from the dwarves of Grundin's realm. The dwarves were divided as to their desire to aid the Elves in warfare, yet when Lord Grundin allowed each one to choose, he found a large contingent ready and willing to march into battle. Grundin would not go with them, as he would be needed to defend his own realm if all did not go as hoped.

Farin, the Smith, was appointed commander of Grundin's army, for he was a battle-hardened dwarf if ever there was one. No Ulca would stand up to him in a fight. With him also went Dwim, who was a friend to the Company. Grundin also sent the request for aid to the clans of the Northern Mountains, using ravens as messengers.

Many weeks earlier, Magra had asked Ordath if she would summon aid from Dûn Bennas, for King Hearndin was known to be courageous and loyal to his friends. Surely, he would send a regiment or two. "Will they be needed, do you think?" Ordath asked Magra. "Hearndin's people were winnowed thin by the Plague, and are only now rebuilding their numbers. If you do not believe they will be needed, I would rather not cause them hardship. Besides, we do not know whether Wrothgar plans to assail them from the south. I am told that there is much of darkness in those lands."

Magra considered. "I cannot say for certain if we will need them, my lady, and prudence would have me stand on the side of caution. Still, from the reports we have been given, I believe that we will be ready to withstand the force from the north. Of course, that is provided the Shadowmancer holds nothing unexpected."

"What we have learned from our scouts is that Wrothgar's strength is greater than anticipated, but I have heard of nothing unexpected," said Ordath. "Ulcas, trolls, and men…it is the men who give me pause. The nights will be long once battle is joined."

Far away, in Tal-sithian, Arialde had gone deep into the carved stone chambers that lay beneath the surface of her beautiful, green island. There she beheld the body of Lord Shandor, wrapped in silk, and beside him a sarcophagus of black granite containing the Stone of Léir. She smiled at the memory of how he had arrived—tied up in a sack like common cargo, borne on the back of a mule, his guardians dressed as peddlers and merchant-men—such a lowly sight would never arouse suspicion.

She drew the silken wrap back from Shandor's face and closed her eyes...the sight of him lying empty and lifeless grieved her. She touched his ivory cheek, caressing it with the back of her right hand, but there was no warmth or life in his flesh. Ordath had closed Shandor's eyes, and had bound them with a band of soft deerskin to protect them from the journey. Arialde had removed the wrap, and the ice-blue eyes opened again, but they were as dead as the rest of him.

What Arialde did next she did as much for herself as for anyone. She approached the granite casing, removed the lid, and gazed down at the dark crystal within. Shandor was there still, but he had withdrawn into the deeps. Now there was a battle to win, and Arialde greatly desired insight. She had to convince Shandor to face his fears and come to her aid.

She lifted the Stone with both hands, though it was very heavy. Then she set it upon the platform next to Shandor's body and knelt beside it. She reached out with both hands, gripping the Stone, and gathered herself for the effort to come. Arialde breathed hard and fast, as though she ran the race of her life, then took one last breath, closed her eyes, and sent her own mighty spirit within.

She had never before seen the sights that assailed her, and she was not prepared for them. She heard a thousand voices—some screaming, some laughing, some speaking gentle words—and saw a myriad of images ranging from simple and benign to terrifying. And she knew that, of the infinite number of planes that would show the fate of the world, one of them would show her own destiny. She understood why Shandor had been afraid.

She did not know where to find him, and she also knew that he would not answer her call, yet she called nonetheless. She wandered the chaotic realms of the Stone, wondering why her brother would choose to house his spirit in such a place. The farther she wandered, the more frightened she became.

Three days had come and gone, and three more, and then three more. The Company had discovered that the melted snow was indeed fit to drink, but only after they filtered it through very fine silk to remove the grey ash and yellow sulfur—no wonder the snow was not bright white. Food was a more pressing concern, as there was none to be found.

"Something lives here," said Gaelen, "because I can hear creatures scuttling and rustling in the brambles. I believe it's time I discovered them." She looked around, seeing nothing but a thorny tangle, a view that had not changed in many days. "This looks like as good a place to stop and rest as any," she said. "Nelwyn, are you up for a challenge?"

"I am," said Nelwyn, "anything that will break the tedium of this place."

"Then let's clear a place to make camp, and you and I will see what we can discover. Something is making that sound, and if that something is not fit to eat, then perhaps it can show us what is. Our provisions will not last much longer."

"You don't know what creatures lurk in these hard lands, Gaelen," said Fima. "They have fought very hard to survive here. They may be venomous, or have some other dire means of defense you are unaware of. I am not certain your idea is wise."

"And why would they be venomous?" said Nelwyn. "Venom against what? We have seen no fearsome hunters here. A few birds have crossed in the sky, but we have seen or heard little else."

"Just be careful, is all Fima is saying," said Galador. "And I'm saying it, too."

"As ever, Galador, do not worry!" said Gaelen, tossing her hair from her eyes. She hated tedium even more than Nelwyn did, and was looking forward to the diversion. She looked over at Rogond, who raised one eyebrow at her, but said nothing. Then she and Nelwyn removed their cloaks and crouched near the ground, where the stems were thick but widely spaced. In a moment, they had disappeared into the bramble-thicket.

The sun was beginning to set when they finally reappeared. The sky was not bright during the day, as it was always gloomy and clouded, but they could tell that the day was waning.

"Good Lord of Light! What happened to you?" said Galador in alarm. Gaelen and Nelwyn were in a good humor, yet their clothes were torn in several places, as was their skin. Most distressing to Galador was the patch of Nelwyn's hair that had been cut short and now hung over her forehead. "Look at your hair!" he gasped, reaching out with one hand to brush the uneven locks aside.

"Never mind that," said Nelwyn. "Look at what we found! There is more to this land than meets the eye." She opened the leather bag she carried and upended it. Out came a collection of mushrooms, a quantity of dark red berries, and what appeared to be a small pile of orange roots. "We just needed to know where to look," she said.

"Never mind that," said Galador, "what happened to your hair?"

"If you must know, it became hopelessly entangled in the briars. Gaelen very considerately cut it free." Galador just looked at her in shock. "Oh, for the love of mercy!" she said. "It's only hair. Would you rather Gaelen have left me entangled?"

Galador did not speak for a moment, almost as though he debated the question. But, of course, the answer was "no."

"How do we know that any of this may be eaten?" said Fima. "And is there any meat to go with it? We will not last long on berries and mushrooms."

"Ah! For that, you must turn to me," said Gaelen. "Behold, the huntress returns in triumph." She reached into her bag and drew forth four brown-furred creatures with short, flat tails. They resembled a cross between a squirrel, a rat, and a beaver. "The briars are thick with them. They feed on the berries and the orange roots. They smell wholesome enough, though they are a challenge to catch. Now let's see how they taste!"

The clouds had thickened, further blocking the light, as it began to snow. The brambles did not burn well, at least not until Gaelen applied a tiny drop of dragon-fire to them. She skinned the four "squirrel-rats" and roasted them. They weren't bad eating, once one adjusted to the slightly sulfurous smell of their flesh.

Gaelen saved the skins, scraping away all trace of fat. She rolled them up tight, after first applying some of the dusty soil to dry them. They would not spoil in the cold. The fur was beautiful, waterproof, and would be unbelievably warm. Fima wrinkled his nose at her. "You cannot be thinking of carrying those with you," he said.

"They who waste things will want them," was the reply.

"Wood-elves!" muttered Galador. He shared Fima's opinion that carrying uncured skins was disgusting. Yet Rogond understood Gaelen's reasoning, and praised her for it. "Well, Rangers are obviously no better than Wood-elves, after all," said Galador. He sighed and looked over at Nelwyn. *Her hair will grow back…*

The berries and the orange roots were determined to be safe to eat, in fact they were almost tasty when stewed with a small amount of water. None would try the mushrooms, however, as neither Gaelen nor Nelwyn had observed them being eaten by anything. Besides, even if they were not poisonous, mushrooms provided little sustenance. They were useful mainly as flavoring.

"Well, this will show my brother Hallagond that he was wrong about something," said Rogond. "He said there was nothing fit to eat here."

"He did not know where to look," said Nelwyn.

They kept to their course toward the south and west, skirting the mountains, until one memorable evening when the clouds cleared, allowing a rare view of the brilliant red-orange sunset. "Look at that mountain yonder!" said Fynn, who was hacking brambles at the front of the line. "It looks as though it is on fire. I have never seen such a sight."

Indeed, one mountain seemed to give off its own orange light. It stood at a distance from its fellows, alone and beautiful and terrible. It seemed to glitter, as though it were made of crystal. Then the sunset faded, and it was only a mountain again.

"That was a sight to see," said Rogond. "I don't suppose we shall ever see such a thing again."

"Yet we may," said Fima. "That is no ordinary mountain…do you see, now, how it gleams pale beside the others? In the morning, when the light returns, you will see that it is entirely covered with ice and snow. Ash does not sparkle in the sun."

They saw the raven three days later, flying over their heads. "You know…I could take care of this problem right now," said Galador, fitting an arrow to his bow and drawing on the dark shape as it flew above him. Yet, something gave him pause, and he stayed his hand. "That is without doubt the largest raven I have seen," he said.

"Don't kill it!" Fima cried, reaching out to take hold of Galador's arm. "This is not Lord Kotos. Wait, and let's see what the bird will do." Then Fima did a most unexpected thing, calling out to the raven in a harsh, croaking voice.

The raven circled, spiraling down over the Company, finally coming to rest on one of the small evergreens that had begun to appear amidst the thorn-trees. It fixed Fima with a bright black eye, which then constricted to show a rim of golden iris. Its name, when translated from raven-speech, meant "golden-eye," yet when spoken it sounded like "Krraah."

Fima spoke then in the Dwarf-tongue and to his delight the raven responded. They conversed for quite some time, as Fima's friends looked on in awe. Then Fima reached into his pocket and pulled out a bright silver coin. He handed it to the raven and bowed. The raven took the coin, returning Fima's bow, and then went aloft on its great, black wings. It had soon flown beyond their sight, back toward the north. Fima turned back to his astonished friends.

"Well, that was certainly worthwhile," he said. "It would seem that the northern ravens have not lost their gift of wisdom."

"Did it tell you anything of interest?" asked Rogond.

"Oh, without a doubt," said Fima.

"Well…are you going to tell *us*?" said Fynn, who was nearly beside himself with curiosity.

"I asked how near we are to Tallasiar, and the bird has told me that we should gain it in a day or two if we could fly, but as we are it will take closer to a fortnight. He said we should go to the Cold Mountain, for the doom of Tuathas lies there. He said it would make a grand hiding-place, if one wished to hide things.

"I am intrigued by this 'Cold Mountain,'" said Rogond. "Yet I am ill-at-ease. The farther I travel through these lands, the more convinced I am that there is nothing here for folk of good will."

"What is here even for folk of ill will?" asked Nelwyn.

"We are," said Fima. "Yet we cannot concern ourselves with such things. Look, here…on Carmyn's map. The Mountain that led to the downfall of Tuathas, the first one to erupt, was this one here. It set off the cataclysm." He pointed to a peak labeled Monad Ëthas, meaning "Mountain of Dread."

"This is the Cold Mountain that the raven referred to," said Fima. "It's the one we have been seeing that is covered all in snow and ice. Krraah said there is something there of interest to us. Tallasiar lies not far beyond it."

"Should we make for the Cold Mountain then?" asked Fynn, who was eager to see what great sight lay beneath the so-called "Doom of Tuathas."

"It's on our way to Tallasiar…why not?" said Fima.

"If the mountain is a good place to hide the Stone, then we should hide it," said Gaelen. "I'm ready to resolve this matter with the death of Gorgon, and I do not care where I do it."

"You spoke to the bird, Fima," said Nelwyn. "What would you advise?"

"I would go under the mountain," said Fima. "If there are wonders there, I would see them. And it seems as good a course as any. Besides that, I have suspicions concerning what lies at the heart of the mountain. If I am right, it is a sight that I must see."

Arlan shook his head. "I do not like the sound of a mountain named Ëthas!"

"Yet the Doom of Tuathas has long passed," said Rogond. "I'm not afraid."

The Company set off toward the Cold Mountain, not knowing what they would find when they got there…yet they were all united in the belief that it would be something they did not expect.

"Where are they going?" Gorgon mused as he followed behind. "And why is that mountain covered in white?" He rolled his eyes heavenward toward the raven, which was perched on his helmet at present. "Well? Do you know anything about this?" He reached up with his right hand so that Kotos could gain entry, flowing from the raven into his own being.

That is the mountain that brought about the chain of disasters resulting in the Doom of Tuathas, said Kotos. *A very nasty place, I'm told. Watch the Company with care—if they go underneath the mountain you might lose them in the maze of tunnels and chambers. If their intention is to hide the Stone there, we must stand ready to seize it.*

"We?" said Gorgon. "You are incapable of seizing anything, Great Lord. It is I who will do the seizing, not 'we.' I just thought I would remind you of it, in case you had forgotten."

Of course, said Kotos, *I had not forgotten. Yet we are partners in this venture, Elfhunter. That is one thing you must not forget, otherwise my raven-friend and I might just take the amulet and fly away, leaving you alone to face your fate. Would that please you?*

"You wouldn't dare," Gorgon rumbled, though he was smiling. "Wrothgar expects a result, and it is your job to ensure that He gets it. You wouldn't *dare!*" Kotos did not reply, but left Gorgon for the comforting environs of the amulet. He did not want Gorgon to know that he was absolutely right.

The Cold Mountain seemed unnatural and out of place. All the peaks around it steamed and fretted, and they were crowned with very little snow. Yet here was this tall peak that stood alone in a casing of white. Fima had said nothing concerning his mysterious hunch, despite entreaty from his friends. It was maddening to listen to him. As he walked along he would make some observation or other, punctuated by such wise declarations as "hmmm..." and "interesting..." yet he would not elaborate.

The chill of the mountain had spread even to the surrounding lands, and the Company shivered as they stood upon a tall, rocky hill. Gaelen climbed up to scout the area, and her vantage point provided an excellent view. She saw something in the distance, so she summoned the others that they might see for themselves. "Look, out there to the southwest, by the sea...is that Tallasiar?"

Rogond drew Thorndil's glass from his pack, for the sea was still quite distant. Yet he could see the ruins, or what remained of them. There had been tall towers in Tallasiar, but no longer. It was said that the city sparkled like a jewel on the harbor, but now it was as black and forlorn as the magma-flow surrounding it. Rogond felt pain slice through his heart as he beheld it—the city was gone.

"It would appear that the Cold Mountain did not do the damage," he said. "That tall, dark peak there...that was the one that rained fire upon the city."

"It was a great realm once," said Galador in a quiet voice. He alone among the Company had actually been to Tallasiar. "I cannot believe that such a center of enlightenment has been reduced to this. The sight of it fills my soul with despair."

"Then why are we going there?" asked Nelwyn, who had also been discouraged at the sight of Tallasiar lying dejected and in ruin.

It was an excellent question, yet Rogond knew that Fima's curiosity was at the heart of it. Now Fima was struggling with the notion that Tallasiar might not prove to be the intriguing exploration he had hoped for.

Krraah caught up with them as they stood at last upon the frozen mountainside, pulling their cloaks tight against the cold. He spoke briefly with Fima before taking wing again. "Follow him," said Fima, eventually coming upon a dark crack in the ice that was the entrance to a darker passageway.

"Well, now, isn't this familiar?" said Galador, remembering his last journey down unknown black passages under mountains.

He was not happy in the memory. They had brought torches in anticipation of taking the false Stone belowground, but not many of them. "The fewer who travel below, the fewer torches we will need," said Rogond. "Are there any who would just as soon remain above ground for the moment?"

"I would," said Arlan at once. "My folk do not care for underground realms, and I am no exception. I would just as soon not venture into the dark."

Fynn shook his head. "If my brother would remain here, I must stay with him. None should be in these lands alone." He pursed his lips at Arlan. "You're such a forest-dweller!" He would not have admitted that he did not like the look of the passage either, now that he had seen it.

"Well, that's fine. Give us your torches then" said Fima. "And take the extra cloaks, as you will suffer the cold more than we. It's always warmer below ground when it is cold above."

The Company left Fynn and Arlan well provisioned, but Gaelen admonished them ere she left. "Keep out of sight, light no fires, and *do not* interfere with Gorgon, no matter your desire. You must allow him to pass. He comes for me, and I will see to his ending. Believe me when I tell you that he is an enemy beyond any you have yet faced. Let him pass!"

She spoke quietly to Arlan, who bore Turantil at his side. "Honor your father's memory, and do not let yourselves be taken," she whispered. Then she turned and followed Rogond into the mountain entrance. She had given good counsel, but to the wrong brother.

The Company plunged into the darkness of Cold Mountain. Against Fima's prediction, the air grew colder the deeper they traveled. Soon Gaelen drew Brinneal's woolen cloak from her pack and put it on, marveling at how warm and light it was.

"Where did you get that? It's beautiful," said Nelwyn.

"Arialde's people gave it," Gaelen replied, offering no further history of the cloak as yet. "When we stop to rest, I will share it with you."

"Fima…are you sure of this errand?" asked Rogond, who carried the Stone with Galador. He was shivering in the cold by now.

"Reasonably sure," said Fima.

"Look!" said Gaelen, who had elected to scout the way ahead. "There is light!"

"Yes, there is," said Fima. "It is as I thought."

"You know, I have had just about enough of your mysterious pronouncements," said Rogond through chattering teeth. "Will you not share with the rest of us? We are all facing the same dangers here."

"If I'm right, there is no danger," said Fima. "It might be the last thing any of you will expect, but it's not dangerous." He was so eager, and yet so stubborn, that Rogond wanted to throttle him.

They entered the heart of the Cold Mountain at last. The light had grown brighter even as the cold had grown deeper. Fima walked into an enormous chamber hung with columns and curtains of ice, approaching what appeared to be a gigantic mass of crystal in the center. All around were walls and hillocks of black lava, but they, too, were encrusted with ice. The crystal mountain was the source of the light; Fima's eyes glittered with it as he drew closer. Then he stopped and knelt in reverence. "It is as I thought…alas!"

There, frozen at the moment of his greatest failure, was Duinar, the Asarla of Tuathas.

24
The Stone and the Mountain

"Is that…who I think it is?" whispered Galador. "And if it is, how did he come to be in such a state?"

Fima was still kneeling, his head bowed, eyes closed. When he looked back into the faces of his friends, his eyes filled with a mixture of wonder and deep sorrow. "I must take in the impact of this discovery for a few moments…please forgive me. I will enlighten you to the extent I am able, but I must collect my thoughts first." He rose to his feet, approached the wall of ice in which Duinar was imprisoned, and placed a thoughtful hand upon it.

"You were thought lost, all the tales said so," he whispered. "You were frozen here…in the midst of your attempt to quell the mountain, and you failed. Does your body still house your spirit, I wonder?"

After a few more silent moments, Fima took his hand from the ice and faced his friends again. "Here is the tale in brief, as I understand it. Duinar was one of the most unassuming of the Asari, and yet it was said that he wielded great power. He delved deep into the inner workings of nature, including the forces of wind, water, and earth. He was a great master of many things, and there was much of magic in him. He alone among his brethren chose to live among men, which is why he appears as a man. Tuathas flowered and grew wise because of his influence. It's what set the Tuathar apart from other men."

Gaelen looked closely at Duinar. He appeared as a man of great age, with a long, grey beard and thinning grey hair. On his brow was bound the silver star of a lore-master, and at his feet lay an ancient, battered text inscribed with seven stars arranged in a familiar, special pattern. His right hand was raised high, as though summoning aid, but his left had come up before his face, as though warding off. The expression in his clear, blue eyes was of desperate hope.

"I do not understand why he is encased in ice," said Nelwyn. "We are in the middle of the fire-mountains, and they are not quiet now.

Obviously, they were not quiet then. How does ice come to be in the midst of fire?"

"If I'm right, the ice came at Duinar's bidding, though it did not have the effect he had hoped for," said Fima. "The two enemies of fire are water and cold. I'm thinking Duinar summoned them, hoping to quiet the heart of this mountain, for it was in the center of the disturbance. Yet his powers were not sufficient, and they turned back upon him even as he expended his last effort to put them forth. That is why the Cold Mountain is so cold...Duinar's power still affects this place."

He shook his head. "He was stronger than ever I imagined, to have done such a thing. The sorrow is that he *did* prevent the eruption of this mountain, but not in time. Fire-mountains here are all connected, and the disturbance spread outward like ripples on a pond. Duinar felt it, and knew that he had failed. It was the other mountains that ruined the land...one in particular. You all saw it. It was once called Monad Fumar, the Mountain of Smoke. No power could have held back such a cataclysm."

"Why did the people stay? Did they not know disaster would come?" asked Gaelen.

"They stayed because they trusted their Asarla. Their faith in him was unshakable. The few who doubted were ridiculed and even despised for it."

"You mean men such as Salasin, and the founders of Dûn Bennas?" said Nelwyn. "It would seem that they were wise to doubt Duinar. It is only because of them that the Tuathan race has survived."

"You're right, yet faith is a powerful force," said Fima. "Men and Elves alike have relied on faith when doubts assail them. Sometimes it's all we have. One cannot blame the people for having faith in Duinar...the alternative was simply too horrific. They could not accept it."

"Still, I might have taken precautions just in case," said Gaelen. "Then, if my doubts were without foundation, I could be happy about it."

"Ha! You would have been down here in case Duinar needed *your* help," said Galador.

Gaelen's ears turned red with shame, for the suggestion that she would so overestimate her importance, even in jest, humiliated her. She cast her eyes downward and did not speak again.

Rogond turned to Galador. "She doesn't deserve that," he said with an edge in his voice that could be heard despite the chattering of his teeth.

"I would rather not stand here in the presence of Duinar, while Gaelen discusses her own compelling hindsight," said Galador. "It is insulting to the memory of the people of Tuathas. Rogond, do you believe that if the Greatwood were threatened, Gaelen would run away and leave it to perish, if there was one of great power whom she thought could prevent it?"

"I'm standing right here, Galador, and I will answer that question for myself," said Gaelen. "I would stay in the forest because I would rather die there than live somewhere else. It is my sworn duty to protect the Greatwood, and I would not leave it in peril if I had a choice. It would have little to do with faith in someone else."

"That is because you have so little faith in anyone save yourself," muttered Galador. They all wondered what had come over him.

"Enough of this, all of you!" said Fima. "We're cold, and we are dispirited as we stand in the presence of such great power, so terribly ineffectual. One cannot look into Duinar's eyes and not grieve. It's no reason to turn on our friends."

Galador took the point and bowed, but Gaelen would not look at him.

"We must warm ourselves," said Nelwyn. "We are all shivering and unhappy. Might we go back to warmer environs now?"

"I need to stay a while," said Fima. "There are things I must consider. You should all go on back, and have a warm fire waiting for me."

"I will not leave you alone," said Rogond. "I think you might just freeze to death in the midst of your contemplation."

"Gaelen and I will go and find something that will burn," said Nelwyn. Galador started to accompany her, but she gave him an insistent look. "Stay here," she whispered, just before leaving the chamber with Gaelen in search of anything made of wood. They took one of the torches with them.

Once outside, Nelwyn turned to her cousin and bade her stand and listen. "Galador was cruel to you because this discovery has unsettled him," she said. "He remembers the tale of Cuimir, the Asarla of Eádros, and the War of Betrayal. Galador knew Cuimir, and his faith in Cuimir's wisdom was unassailable, yet Cuimir could not save Eádros from her own people. Now he sees that Duinar could not save Tuathas, either. Galador once believed the Asari to be infallible. Your suggestion that such faith was unwise has wounded him."

"All right, I understand now," said Gaelen. "But I will not ask his pardon for believing as I do."

"That's because you're as stubborn as he is," said Nelwyn. "It's one of the endearing qualities you share." Then she grew serious. "If it is of any help, I agree with you. I would have been tempted to doubt the wisdom of blind faith, especially where these accursed fire-mountains are concerned. Can you feel them? They have been sending forth tremors for days."

"Of *course* I can feel them, and I don't like it. It's like a less intense but more widespread version of the tremor we felt near the Mountains of Dread."

"The one that came right before the eruption," said Nelwyn. "Let's hope it means something different this time."

It was colder in the chamber of Duinar than it was outside, but Fynn and Arlan were still facing a long, cold night with no fire. They had taken up positions on opposite sides of the doorway into the mountain, hiding among the rocks, wondering whether they should rejoin and share warmth.

Neither Arlan nor Fynn were hunter-scouts, but they were both quite capable of surviving winter in the Greatwood, and the weather on Cold Mountain at present was not as bad as mid-winter near the Elven-hold. Still, they shivered a little in the rising wind. They both tensed as they heard the faint cry of a raven, but they knew that such sounds were common, and they were not concerned.

Wrothgar's forces had surrounded Mountain-home, though the battle had not yet begun. Ordath and Magra knew that their own forces were as ready as could be. Their people were poised to fight, weapons were in good order, and the Elves of the Greatwood and of Tal-sithian had added their numbers to the defense force. The dwarves of Grundin's realm had also arrived as anticipated, and they had been made welcome. It would be difficult to breach the defenses of Mountain-home.

No dwarves had yet come from the north, but the journey from the northern mountains was long, probably too long for Beori's folk to undertake in any numbers.

Magra stood upon the northern battlement, his keen eyes scanning the darkness. Beside him stood his battle-commanders—Wellyn of the Greatwood, Farin of Cós-domhain, and Artemys of Tal-sithian. The sight of a thousand torches burning in the dark forests near Mountain-home was disquieting, though it was expected. Magra and Farin discussed tactics in quiet voices, awaiting some sign from the enemy.

Then a sign came.

Wellyn and Artemys perceived the enormous, dark shadow an instant before it arrived, gliding through the air on silent wings. They opened their mouths to shout a warning, but Artemys caught a glimpse of a dark crossbow and a swift, deadly bolt.

"*My lord!*" she cried, flinging herself upon Magra—even as the shaft that was meant for his great heart pierced her own. It drove her forward with such force that Magra was very nearly knocked from his feet. The dark shape soared over the heads of the defenders, and a sudden blast of flame came forth from it. Many of the dwellings of Mountain-home were made of carved stone, but some were made of wood, and one of them burst into flames like so much dry tinder.

In the light of the fires, the horrified onlookers beheld a large and fearsome black dragon, wings fringed like an owl's for silent flight, scales dull and dark to remain unseen by night. This was no Lokai, no dim-witted desert worm. This beast was sly and cunning.

A dragon-rider commanded it, perched just behind the massive head on the end of a long, serpent-like neck. That rider had aimed a lethal dart at Magra, for he knew that the way to throw the Elves' defenses into disarray was to kill their supreme commander. The sacrifice of Artemys was all that had prevented it. The dragon circled once over Mountain-home, as the Elves rushed to quench the flames it had created.

"Take cover!" yelled Magra, even as he leaped down from the battlement with Artemys in his arms. The Elves of Tal-sithian looked on in dismay, for Artemys was their most capable tactician, and they moved at her direction. Magra set her down, as Ordath ran forward to aid her.

One glance told them both that there was no need, and Magra removed his cloak, covering Artemys, for she was dead. "I will avenge thee, proud lady of the Lake-realm," he said. Then he turned to Ordath. "That bolt was meant for me. The rider knows what he's doing." He cast his eyes upward in search of the beast, but it had flown off, disappearing as quietly as it had come before the archers of Mountain-home could threaten it.

"Where did they ever find such a beast as that?" exclaimed Farin. "I have not heard tell of a winged dragon in many a year."

"Nor have I," said Magra. "And why did we not know of this one? The presence of a worm like that would be difficult to keep from our scouts."

"With all due respect, not difficult enough, apparently," said Farin. The sight of the dragon had unnerved him, as dwarves and dragons have ever been at odds. A dragon threatening a dwarf-realm meant a pitched battle, and sometimes the dragon would prevail.

"We should not spend time in wondering where it came from," said Wellyn. "We must deal with it. We were not expecting such a fearful menace, and we have no defense against it."

"There's no time to worry about that dragon," yelled Hallagond, who had been looking out over the north wall. "The battle is on! Guard yourselves, for they have archers!" No sooner had he said the words than the first volley of arrows flew over the walls. The defenders crouched beneath their shields, as the archers of Mountain-home prepared to take some blood of their own.

Gaelen and Nelwyn had explored a new passage beneath the Cold Mountain and had found the remains of an old wooden hand-cart. Though it was hundreds of years old, the cold had preserved it. They upended it and wheeled it back to the chamber where their friends waited. Fima's axe made short work of it, and soon, with the aid of another few drops of dragon-fire, there was warmth to be shared. After dealing with the hand-cart, Fima took his axe to the ice-wall near Duinar's feet, chipping away carefully at the clear surface.

"What are you doing?" asked Rogond.

"I would very much like to get my hands on that manuscript," said Fima. "It might contain some recorded history that is as yet unknown concerning the fall of Tuathas." He kept on chipping away at the ice with diligent concentration.

"Has anyone remembered why we are here, and what our primary objective is?" asked Gaelen.

"We have not forgotten," said Rogond. "Yet you must allow Fima to practice his craft. After all, he is a lore-master."

"Practice my obsession, you mean?" said Fima with a chuckle.

"Yes, that too."

"At least I'm warm now," said Nelwyn. "Gaelen did not need to share her cloak with me after all."

"This cloak is very special, though I would have been happy to share it," said Gaelen. "It belonged to Gorgon's mother, Brinneal. I'm sure she would approve of my wearing it, if it will warm my limbs and steady my aim as I take Gorgon from this world. I'm certain that her spirit hopes for such an outcome." Gaelen thought for a moment. "It is ironic…I saw neither Brinneal nor Amandir when I called upon the Spirits of the Vanquished. Perhaps they could not bear the sight of Brinneal's misbegotten child. For my part, I do not blame them." She shuddered at the memory of Gorgon's chaotic, tormented soul.

At this, everyone stayed silent for a time, thinking of Gorgon and his upcoming reckoning with the Company.

In the briar-forest just to the north of Cold Mountain, Gorgon perceived. He was drawing ever nearer to that reckoning, and the thought recharged his spirit and gave lightness to his feet. He tracked the Company to the dark opening of the passageway.

Kotos spoke to him from within the amulet. "*Be cautious, Elfhunter. From now on you should watch for your enemies, as they may try to take you unaware. The raven cannot help you here, as there is no way to send it forth belowground without suspicion. Be very cautious.*"

"Right you are, my lord," said Gorgon. He had caught the scent of Elves; it drifted from either side of the doorway. "We are being watched even now," he said.

"*Retreat, then, and take no chances!*" said Kotos. "*You must not risk being taken, or we will not be able to get Wrothgar's prize.*"

"No, we won't," said Gorgon. "But then, if I am taken, I'll be dead, and I won't care, will I?" He chuckled silently, knowing his words would upset Lord Kotos. As an afterthought, he spoke again. "Just allow me to practice my skills without interference, and all will be well." He then made a deep thrumming sound in his chest that was reminiscent of a huge, evil cat purring on some hellish hearth—the sound of a hunter who has sighted his quarry after a long and difficult pursuit.

Arlan had decided that he and Fynn would be more effective keeping the watch together, and he moved to join his brother on the other side of the doorway. They caught Gorgon's foul scent on the north wind, having been warned that such an unexplainable odor heralded the approach of their enemy. They had never seen Gorgon before, and therefore they did not fully appreciate the danger they were in, but they had been told to allow him to pass unchallenged. Arlan heard the sound of a blade being drawn slowly from the sheath, and turned to behold Fynn with his sword at the ready.

"Put your blade away. We are not to engage this enemy," Arlan whispered.

"And who says so? I thought that killing the Elfhunter was the main objective in this whole elaborate ruse," said Fynn, gripping his sword tighter. "There are two of us, and we know our enemy is there. We are fierce fighters! If we can take down the creature and avenge our father, I say why not?"

"We have been told to let him pass!" said Arlan. "This creature killed our father and his brother Halrodin, and they were more experienced than we. You should cool your temper and listen to Gaelen's words. She has seen what this enemy can do, whereas we have not."

"I saw our father's body," said Fynn in a grim voice. "You saw it, too. How can you have looked upon what was done to him and let this creature pass?"

"Because I trust those who have been charged with the task of killing him," said Arlan. "You must listen to the voice of good sense that I know you possess. Please, my brother, listen to it just this once."

Fynn would not be dissuaded, though it would not have mattered if he had. Gorgon leapt upon them like a cat upon two rabbits, and though Fynn and Arlan fought with ferocity, they were no match for the tiger. Gorgon was armored, and they were not. Gorgon was ruthless in his attack, and he was larger, heavier, and stronger than they. Their last moments were terrifying, though they fought with valor, Arlan in particular. Fynn had been more reckless, but he was no match for the Elfhunter, and like his father he had been first to fall. Sadly, the line of Talrodin ended upon that dark, cold night.

Gaelen's screams of grief and outrage echoed in Gorgon's mind—she knew what had happened—and he laughed aloud at the thought of it.

Afterward, he dragged the bodies off and hid them among the rocks. They would soon be covered with snow; there was a fair blizzard blowing by then. "Well," he growled after he had finished, "that's two less to worry about."

He had recovered Talrodin's sword, Turantil, from Arlan's hand, and now held it up before his dark, ugly face, admiring it again. "Hello, my beauty. You will cleave more Elves before the dawn comes." He drew the glittering blade along the gap in his armor, grimacing as it bit into the flesh of his arm. "As sharp as ever."

Kotos knew of Gorgon's tendency to inflict pain upon himself, and he was not disquieted, yet he would bring Gorgon back to the moment. *Now that you have practiced your skills, might we return to our course? You have a much more important job to do. At least now these erstwhile door-wardens will not be able to warn the others of your approach.*

Gorgon laughed aloud. "Oh, but they *have* been warned," he said. "Did you not hear the Vixen screaming? She knows what has happened, and could do nothing about it. The irony of this is just delectable. It would seem that these two were the sons of the first Elf I slew in the Greatwood."

What Elf in the Greatwood? I do not understand, said Kotos.

"It's a long, long story," said Gorgon, who was still smiling. "One day, when this is ended, perhaps I will enlighten you."

Yes, perhaps..." said Kotos, who could imagine few fates worse than enduring an endless telling of Gorgon's adventures in Elf-slaying. *I shall look forward to it. However, it is unfortunate that the She-elf knows you have come. Now we cannot take the Stone by stealth, but must take it by force! And in doing so, we risk its destruction. If I had known this would alert our enemies, I would not have allowed you to take the guards.*

"It would not matter. The Vixen always knows that I follow her," said Gorgon. "But what she does not know is that I intend to take the Stone. She does not know that you travel with me. She believes that my only task is to pursue her."

Are you certain? said Kotos, who had detected some hesitance in Gorgon's voice.

"Of course...they have not destroyed the Stone yet, have they?" Gorgon growled. His nose had been in the wind for a long time now.

Gaelen had sensed Gorgon's stalking of Fynn and Arlan, and she began to cry, shivering and clenching both hands into fists. "They will be taken...they have allowed Gorgon to find them...Fynn means to attack, but, but they are taken unaware! Oh...no, *no!*"

She leaped to her feet and drew her blade, slashing at anything non-living out of grief and frustration. As she did so, she fairly screamed. "You have ended Talrodin's line, you foul, horrible... *thing!* You are dead, do you hear me? *Dead!* Come on, you monster! Come on and get some of me then!"

She punctuated her words with repeated clashes of her bright blade with the icy walls of the chamber. No one dared approach her until she had spent herself, though they were all horrified. At last she stood, panting and trembling, trying to regain her breath. She drew the blade of her short-sword across the flesh just above her left elbow, bringing blood, before re-sheathing it. "Gorgon has killed two more of our friends," she said, her voice disturbingly calm.

"Yes, I know," said Rogond as he approached her. "Gaelen, are you all right?"

"Of course," she said in the same calm, stony voice. "Why would I not be?"

Shocked and horrified at what he had just witnessed, Fima shook his head. "So much for the element of surprise..."

Arialde made her way deeper into the Stone of Léir, searching for Shandor and trying not to look into the infinite planes of past and future flickering before her. It was Shandor who had infused this power into the Stone. Its creator, Dardis of the Èolar, would never even have imagined it. Now, as Arialde wandered past the images of fates dreadful and glorious, she resolved that such a thing could not continue. The Stone, while useful at times, was simply too great a liability. It had taken the spirit of Shandor and held him captive. She would try to persuade him to leave it of his own volition...if she ever found him.

If not, she would destroy the Stone and hope that her brother's spirit would find its former house...that he would be restored. She hoped also that he had not been twisted into someone, or something, that she would not recognize. She shuddered as she considered enduring imprisonment in this chaotic, terrifying place for so many ages. Who wouldn't go insane?

She kept calling to Shandor, telling him that she was afraid, asking for his aid. In truth, she merely wanted to coax him into the light, but he did not respond. He crouched in a dark corner of the Stone, bitter and withdrawn, wishing that she would leave him in peace. He knew what she wanted. She had asked him to look into his own dark future, and he had not had the courage to do so. The ability to foretell the fate of others had come at a terrible price.

Perhaps, if he made no move toward her, she would leave him. He knew that her cries for aid were exaggerated, that she was trying to appeal to his protective nature. Arialde was a strong and courageous spirit—the Stone would not thwart her.

Shandor whispered the name of Liathwyn, hoping she would comfort him, but she did not come. Liathwyn had not been a part of his present for a long time. She was only a part of his past. He wished himself back into her domain, back into the past, where he had once been happy. Yet so long as Arialde called his name, he could not escape there.

Go away! he said at last. *Can you not leave me in peace? Go away, and fight your battles. They are mine no longer.*

Arialde heard him. *Shandor, come to me. I summon you, my brother, and I will not be denied. Come now to me!*

She demanded his presence, and he could not refuse her. His image wavered before her, surrounded by an aura of white and pale, silvery grey. Shandor was a spirit of air. Arialde, like Nelwyn, was a water-spirit, her aura a cool blue shot with violet and pale green, like the waters of the Lake.

They regarded one another for a long while. Shandor spoke first. *I did not expect to see your face here. What would you ask of me?*

My brother, you have aided me countless times when I have asked for insight. You have shown me images of dire things to come, that I may prevent them. Now I ask you to aid me once more.

Do not ask me to look into my own fate, said Shandor, *for I cannot. My heart will not allow such a fearful sight to be seen. Do not ask it of me.*

I know, said Arialde. *I understand your fear, and I do not ask such a thing of you now. The aid I would seek is of a much different nature.*

She collected herself and then put forth her request. *I would have you leave this place forever, and be restored to us. I would see the Stone forever darkened.*

Shandor did not move, nor did he speak at first. He simply stood before her, absorbing what she had said. Then his aura changed from silvery white to the dark, angry grey of clouds heavy with rain. His eyes darkened with it. His hair, that had seemed to be lifted by a gentle breeze, was now blown back as though by fierce winds.

He spoke to Arialde in a cold, menacing tone. *I cannot leave this place. You know it! The Stone is the only realm in which Liathwyn still shares her warmth with me...I cannot leave it, or grief will consume my soul. I will not be persuaded otherwise.* His face had now gone quite pale at the very thought of facing an eternity without his beloved.

Liathwyn is not here, said Arialde. *She never has been. She is but a memory, my brother. Liathwyn dwells in Elysia. You love a shadow only.*

She is real enough to me, said Shandor. *I have been content with shadows for five thousand years. I will not give up my dreams, for I have nothing else.*

*But, you do…*she said. *Shandor, who was once mighty…your friends need you now. The Light calls upon you for aid, yet you hide from it. You once battled with Wrothgar himself, and you prevailed. Your eyes beheld the downfall of the Èolar, and you swore then that darkness would never threaten the Light in such a way again, yet here you are. Your only child is beset, and you do not aid her? She is the child of Liathwyn, too. Liathwyn lives on in Ordath, my brother, yet if you do not aid her she may be lost. You cannot aid her from within the Stone. Come out, Shandor, come out and fight for the world you once loved!*

He did not answer her, but the wind in his hair calmed as he considered. Arialde spoke to him again—she had to convince him. *Love is a power that cannot be denied nor overcome. It is the strongest power in both this world and the next, when it is given freely. Yet now your love for Liathwyn has turned into an instrument of darkness. It is not love any more, but is only the desire to turn aside the grief and pain of your loss. This perversion of love has corrupted you. Somehow, you must prevail over it.*

His eyes filled with tears then, as Arialde had seen them do only twice before. *I cannot. I have tried…don't you think I've tried?"* he said. *"There is no cure for my affliction, no balm to soothe my spirit other than my memories. Now you would take them from me?*

You will still have your memories, my brother, said Arialde.

But I will not be able to live them. In the Stone it is as though Liathwyn is alive again. If I leave it, she will die.

He grew darker again, and the unseen winds surrounding him became wild. He appeared to grow more massive and more threatening as he spoke. *I showed the fate of Ri-Elathan ere he went into battle, and I showed him what would happen if he did not. He perished in flames to protect the Light, knowing full well that he would endure that terrible fate. He was sundered from the one he loved, and yet he went to his death knowing that one day he would be reunited with her. I would burn a thousand times to trade places with him.*

Arialde knew that Shandor would debate with her to no end unless she could convince him otherwise. She also sensed the urgency that was building in Mountain-home. She was running out of time.

Would you leave your only daughter to die?"

Shandor fixed her with his ice-blue eyes, and considered.

"We must prepare to make our stand against Lord Kotos," said Fima. "And I believe we must make it here. We dare not leave Duinar for Kotos to find."

"Why not?" asked Nelwyn. "You already have your manuscript, and Duinar is dead."

"Is he?" asked Fima. "We don't know for certain."

"He has been frozen in a block of ice for five hundred years," said Nelwyn. "To me, that would be likely to mean that one is dead."

"Ice is a tricky thing," said Fima. "It can kill, or it can preserve. We do not yet know Duinar's fate."

"Besides that, he is an Asarla," said Rogond. "As we have seen, to our regret, their spirits may live on even when they have no body of their own. I know that I sensed something of vitality when I entered this room."

"Duinar is not dead." Galador left no room for doubt.

"If he's not dead, why do we not release him?" asked Nelwyn.

"And what would you suggest?" said Fima. "We can't just go and smash the ice and drag him out of there in haphazard fashion. If he is to be revived, it must be done with delicacy; otherwise we might kill his body with good intentions. It would take time and care to release him properly!"

"We have no time now. We must make ready, for Gorgon is drawing near," said Gaelen. She threw the remaining wood on the fire, and it blazed up in flames of bright, pale gold. The ice beneath it had melted away, the water draining beneath the surrounding ice to reveal a floor of porous, black lava.

Rogond did not like the look of it, as he did not know what lay beneath it, and a heavy being like Gorgon might well break through.

The layer of ice had strengthened it. As though to confirm his insecurities, Rogond now felt the mountain shudder. *Had that crack in the black, hardened magma been there before?*

Gaelen and Nelwyn carried the casket containing the replica of the Stone into the center of the room, not far from the fire, and set it down. "Rogond and I will stand in plain view," said Gaelen. "The rest of you should hide yourselves. The moment Gorgon comes for us, attack him, but do not come within arm's length. If he takes one of you hostage, I will not give you any consideration, for he will not allow you to live no matter what else happens. He will not allow any of us to live."

"If he tries to take *me* hostage, please shoot me," said Fima. "I have no desire to be kept alive for his amusement later." He then took his axe and retired to a hiding place near Duinar.

"I would rather shoot *him*," muttered Galador, who alone among them had a bow powerful enough to pierce Gorgon's armor. He had three arrows that had been made for him in Mountain-home. They were fitted with heavy shafts and points made from steel that had been tempered and folded like a sword-blade. They would pierce nearly anything.

He turned to Gaelen. "I'm sorry for the discourtesy I showed you earlier," he said, and then took up a position of concealment before she could reply.

Nelwyn stood before her cousin and dearest friend. "May luck be with us," she said. "And…take no foolish chances. Remember that you are not alone in this fight. We have all lost things we loved to the Elfhunter."

Gaelen's face was stony as she replied. "Then I will make certain that you all get a piece of him. There will be plenty of him, I'm sure." She embraced Nelwyn and took up her own position with the casket before her. Nelwyn concealed herself on the opposite side of the chamber from Galador, and readied her own stout bow.

All was in readiness. Gaelen stood with her sword in one hand and her long knife in the other, one of Fima's small throwing-axes thrust into her belt. She had removed Brinneal's blue-grey cloak, replacing it with her precious fire-cloak. It glittered and flashed in the eerie light, looking more alive than ever. The casket containing the replica was open. Gaelen tried to remain calm, but her face and ears were flushed with battle-lust, and her breaths came faster than usual. Every muscle in her body was tense, like a whip that is bent back upon itself.

Rogond stood in plain view, but he was not near to her. His intent was to engage Gorgon from behind, thereby distracting him from Gaelen.

There was no sound to be heard in the chamber. Rogond saw Gaelen lift her head, scenting the air, her eyes narrowing, grip tightening on her blades. They all heard it then…the sound of an enormous, evil cat purring upon some hellish hearth.

25
Facing the Fire

Dawn had finally broken over Mountain-home, giving the defenders a much-needed respite. Magra and Wellyn had managed to survive, as had Farin, but there had been great loss on both sides of the battle. Now was the time to re-group.

The dragon had made three more forays over the realm, and each time it seemed to focus its attention upon Magra, who had barely escaped with his life. At last Ordath ordered him to retire with Farin and Wellyn into the Great Hall.

"You must not fall," she said. "The hearts of the people will fail if you are lost. Go now, and we will deal with this together when the situation allows." Ordath knew, as did Magra, that Wrothgar's intention was not to besiege Mountain-home, but to attack it with every means available. This conflict would be over quickly, one way or another.

"There has been no sign of the dragon since daybreak," said Farin.

Indeed, there had not, for this dragon was different from any the defenders had seen before. It, and its twin sibling that now rested with it belowground, had been reared in darkness. Bred for night flying, they were as dark as doom, as cunning as cats, as graceful and silent as serpents, and twice as lethal. They were Drach and Garthor, the Night-fliers. Hatched in far eastern realms, they had been reared in the Fell-ruin under the directive of Lord Kotos.

The men who rode them were members of the dragon-cult of the Anori, lured into service with promises made by the Beguiler. Their bows were nearly as powerful as Galador's, and their aim was deadly. They had been ordered to kill those in command, throwing the enemy into chaos

The defenders of Mountain-home had little recourse against such beasts, and they had beheld only one of them up to now. Archers had sent forth a storm of arrows against it, but it was a rare bow that would pierce dragon-scales. The leathery wings were another matter, and the archers soon discovered that they could discourage the dragon by taking aim at them. Drach had sustained many small holes in his wings, but he was not unduly dismayed. The archers who had caused them had not been so fortunate. Drach learned to turn his fiery breath upon any bowman he beheld.

Estle had been ordered to remain in the Great Hall, away from the fighting, as she had some skill in tending to the wounded. "Fetch Hallagond," she said to Lady Ordath. "He killed the dragon in Dûn Arian, and he may have some knowledge of how to deal with this one." Hallagond was brought to sit with Magra and the others in council. Azori had insisted on coming with him.

"We may not have much time," said Magra. "The dragon has gone to ground with the arrival of the sun, but the attack is likely to continue. They will try to wear us down further before nightfall, and then we will face the beast again." He shook his head. "I have never seen the like of it. I heard nothing of its approach." He turned to Hallagond. "Well, Worm-slayer, have you any thoughts?"

Hallagond's eyes grew wide. "My thoughts at the moment are limited. They center upon one question—why are you asking me?" He shot a black look at Estle as he said so.

"Has anyone else here ever slain a dragon?" asked Farin, glowering beneath his peppered brows.

"All right, so I killed a dragon. It was nothing like the one that flew over our heads last night."

"That's true, but you must tell us how you killed it," said Ordath. "You have slain at least one dragon more than we have."

"Yes, tell them, for all the good it will do," said Azori. "Unless something changes, we will not withstand another night like the last one." Although everyone sitting at council found Azori's pessimism exasperating, they knew he was right.

The next hour was spent in discussion, as Hallagond recalled the slaying of Lokai. When he had finished, Magra sat with his fingers interlaced, resting his chin upon them. "So…you aimed for the roof of the dragon's mouth, yet this dragon could not fly, and was standing right before you with its mouth wide open?"

"That's about right," said Hallagond. "I told you it would be of little benefit to consult me. This night-flying dragon has smoother, thinner scales, and its mouth is much smaller. It also has a long neck, unlike the desert beast, which could not even turn its head without moving its torso. I don't believe we should count on a clear shot straight to the vulnerable spot in its mouth."

"What then should we do?" asked Wellyn. "There are many fine archers here, but our bows will not penetrate the beast's hide.

"Mmmm…" said Magra, lowering his eyebrows.

"Some are powerful enough," said Azori. "We are using them to defend the battlements, and they could skewer the dragon if the chance came." He referred to the small, elegant ballistae that the defenders had used to hurl stones upon the enemy. They could also be used to launch a great spear.

"The dragon-rider has seen them, and he is clever enough to avoid them," said Magra. "They are powerful, but not precise enough to take such an agile beast. Unless…."

"Unless what, my lord?" asked Hallagond.

"Unless we deceive the rider and lure him right into them. I have an idea that might work. In the meantime, we must press our enemies during the daylight hours. Let us lay our plans and then go forth to command our comrades. We'll take some of our own back before nightfall."

The forces of Mountain-home fought throughout the day, raining stones down from the battlements, using fire and oil and any other means at their disposal. The archers were busy sending arrows down upon the foul assembly.

The Ulcas did not enjoy the light, and many had retreated. The trolls, who could not bear it at all, had gone belowground. Yet they would all return when darkness came.

"There are underground ways into Mountain-home, but the enemy does not know them," said Farin to his folk. "Let's take advantage of the opportunity. The trolls have gone below to rest from the sun, yet we know these paths better than they do. I'll wager we could do some damage before they emerge again at dusk—who will march with me?"

It was an unnecessary question. Soon every dwarf in Mountain-home had left to go troll-hunting, and a number of the Elves of Mountain-home had gone with them.

By the time they returned, some things had changed, but not for the better. The Ulcas had taken pitch and black oil, and had now set the lands around Mountain-home ablaze. The trees were burning, but it was the choking black oil-smoke that was most distressing—it confounded the aim of the archers atop the walls and dimmed the sunlight beneath it.

Magra, who had made a friend of Farin, was very pleased to see that he had survived the expedition. "How fared you against the trolls?" he asked. "It appears that most of you have rejoined us."

"We lost a few, but we definitely won the day," said Farin with some pride. "The trolls were weary from last night's battle. They have not the stamina of the Children of Fior!" He lowered his voice and winked. "You now have seven fewer trolls to contend with, my lord. I'm just sorry it isn't twenty."

Magra was impressed. "Seven is a very satisfactory number, my friend," he said. "I just hope you have not spent your strength before the battle tonight."

"That I should live to hear such an obscenity from the mouth of a friend! Don't worry about the folk of the Deep-caverns. Troll-hunting is fine exercise, and we needed it."

Despite Farin's bravado, the dwarves were weary—one could see it. Troll-hunting might have been fine exercise, but it was taxing and difficult, in addition to being potentially lethal.

Wellyn appeared at Magra's right hand, his young face distressed. "The sun is setting," he said. "We must make ready."

"Indeed, we must," said Magra. "If you will forgive me, Farin, I have an important role to play in tonight's conflict. It seems that I am to be dragon-bait."

Magra then drew Lady Ordath aside. "You must safeguard yourself…it is my task to lead the people in battle, and it is your task to make certain you do not fall. Please, my lady, remain beneath the realm tonight and secure yourself within the safety of walls. Take guards with you. When all is safe, I will summon you."

Ordath started to protest, but she did not, for Magra was right. If Ordath fell, Mountain-home would fall with her. She looked into his scarred, earnest face, knowing that she would never have a more devoted and faithful protector.

As he left the Great Hall, Magra was met by Hallagond, who carried the shield of dragon-scale he had been given in Dûn Arian and the dragon-hide gloves Gaelen had made for him. "It seems I might have something you need, my lord," he said, bowing and handing the items to Magra. "Gaelen made the gauntlets, but apparently she believes me to be bigger than I am, as they are too large for me."

Magra took the items with thanks. The gauntlets would prove to be a perfect fit. He then retrieved his own mighty shield, which was of blued steel emblazoned with the white flame and seven silver stars. He offered it to Hallagond, saying, "Take this in exchange for your thoughtful gift, for you may have need of it. I know it has seen me safely through many battles."

Hallagond bowed and accepted Magra's shield, though it was far too large and heavy for his liking. Yet the spirit behind the exchange had moved them both.

The sun set over the mountains, and long shadows fell. Magra now stood, clad in full armor, bearing Hallagond's dragon-shield, clearly visible despite the dark smoke carried on the west wind. He stood upon one of the vaulted rooftops, presumably to better order his warriors.

He carried the most powerful bow ever made in his left hand, and at his feet were tempered steel barbs that would almost certainly penetrate the dragon's hide. Two of the ballistae had been concealed; they were aimed into the air above Magra's head. When the worm came to take him, it would be first to fall. "Come on, then," Magra muttered, scanning the dark sky in all directions.

The Elves of the Greatwood caught the first flickering glimpse of Drach in the orange light of the burning trees. "Look to yourselves!" they cried. "The dragon comes!"

Magra steadied himself, still shouting orders to his archers, trying to keep up appearances. This was not difficult, as the Ulcas were storming the walls, yet because of the terrain there were relatively few places that their efforts would be effective. The defenders concentrated on making things as difficult as possible, now looking nervously into the air, watching for the dragon. Without further warning, it appeared.

Magra's prediction that Drach would come for him was well founded. The huge, dark triangular shape made straight for the rooftop as Magra stood ready. At the direction of its rider, the beast opened its mouth and sent forth flames to engulf the Elven commander, but Magra crouched beneath his marvelous shield. Though singed, he was not damaged. The dragon passed over him, wheeled about, and came back for another try, its black-clad rider preparing to aim a killing shot. Magra's bow and quiver lay at his feet, and he dropped the shield the moment the flames faded, fitting the bow and drawing it before the creature could get another good breath. He sent forth a shot straight toward the dragon, which swerved, but not in time to avoid being hit hard at the base of its right wing. The rider's shot went wild.

"Now!" yelled Magra, for the beast was directly over his head. Azori and Hallagond manned the two ballistae, and they loosed the weapons, hurling two great spears straight toward the dragon.

Despite Magra's arrow, Drach avoided one of the spears, but not the other. It tore through the dragon's breast, sending it wheeling in the air to sail headlong into the south wall, nearly demolishing it. It crashed down onto one of the rocky mountainsides, taking a number of unfortunate Ulcas with it. Its rider did not survive his great beast's fall.

The dragon, wounded but not yet dead, turned on Wrothgar's army as it thrashed about in agony, sending flames forth in several directions. It struggled to its feet, trying to lift from the ground to no avail, stumbling and flopping like a wounded eagle, crushing all in its path. Finally its struggles diminished, and it was still.

There was no time for celebration, for the walls on the south march had been breached, and the defenders fought hand-to-hand. Archers were useless here, as their arrows would just as likely take one of their own. Bows were laid aside and blades were drawn. Wellyn led about half of his folk into the fray, leaving the others to defend the north and west walls.

Farin and his dwarves were pleased that the battle had come to blades, for their axes and hammers would now be quite busy. They concentrated on several hill-trolls that had made their way through the breach.

Hallagond and Azori fought side-by-side, in the manner of sutherling swordsmen, with a short blade in each hand. They were more than a match for any Ulcan invader. Yet Ulcas came, and more after them, and still more after them. Azori and Hallagond grew weary, and their blades had lost both speed and accuracy.

"At least you were not required to slay a dragon by yourself this time," said Azori, grinning at Hallagond, though he was panting hard.

"No, and I'm glad of it," said Hallagond. "But if these creatures keep coming I fear it will be the death of us both. I'm winded, and I cannot gain my breath."

"That will not do," said Azori as he ran his blade through the neck of another Ulca. The horrid, hairless creature flopped at his feet like a dying fish. "I told Estle I would see to your safety, and I would rather not face her wrath if I fail. Let's retreat for the moment." His face was red with exertion, sweat running in rivulets through the grime that had stained it. He finished off two more attackers, and then turned and made for cover. Hallagond followed his example. They had to catch their breath and recover, if only for a brief while.

Magra leapt down from the rooftop, drew his own great sword, and plunged into the heart of the fighting. His people rallied to him and drove the Ulcas back—it would have been a dire blow to the defenders had Magra been taken from them. The night would be long, dark, and red with blood. And it had only begun.

Gorgon had finally arrived at the chamber of Duinar, but he had not yet entered. He hesitated, smiling as he beheld his mortal enemy, Gaelen Taldin, who was guarding the Stone of Léir with her blades drawn.

"Come on, then," said Gaelen. "Show yourself! The blood of the sons of Talrodin still stains your remaining hand. Show yourself! I'm waiting." Gorgon took notice of the blood on her left sleeve and wondered.

Kotos had been somewhat taken aback at the sight of Duinar, though he relaxed when he realized that Duinar could do no harm. He spoke to Gorgon from the amulet.

Be cautious! Remember your task—to secure the Stone. Slay the She-elf before she has the chance to destroy it! You have the means to shoot her unaware. Kill her now, for the casket is open and she may attempt to destroy the Stone if you rush into the chamber and attack. Remember your task.

"That is *your* task, Great Lord. Mine is somewhat different," said Gorgon. "Do not interfere with this encounter now, for I will not brook it. Calm yourself. The Stone of Léir is not in peril."

Why say you so? growled Kotos. *I have sensed a change in your attitude toward the Stone for some time now. What do you know about it?*

"You'll see," said Gorgon as he stepped forward into the chamber. He had donned the amulet and now appeared as Orrion High-elven, bearing an ugly sneer on his otherwise handsome face. Galador and Nelwyn prepared to draw their bows on him from the shadows.

"At last we come to reckoning, Gaelen Taldin," said Orrion. "It has been long since I laid eyes upon you. These journeys have not been kind to you, have they? You have aged, and you are weaker than when last we met."

"I routed you when last we met," said Gaelen with a cold smile. "Or, have you forgotten? Of course, I'm not counting all the times I met you when you were pretending to be someone else. The last time I met you as Gorgon, you were vanquished. Don't speak to me of weakness, Elfhunter. I see you brought your master along—you haven't the courage to face me alone! A good thing, as you will have need of him."

She looked into the amulet that hung from Orrion's neck. "We have known of Lord Kotos for quite a long while. He is not nearly as adept at deception as he believes himself to be. It will come as no surprise, then, when I destroy the Stone?"

"It will not," said Orrion, to the horror of Lord Kotos, who realized that he, the Great Deceiver, had been deceived…and Gorgon had known of it! Kotos attempted then to enter Gorgon's mind, to take control of him, but Gorgon had expected this and would not let him in.

Gaelen set her long knife down, and took up the small axe, placing it upon the Stone. "This truly was a fine replica," she said. "It's a pity to break it. Yet I'm sure we've all realized by now that Lord

Kotos' errand has been in vain. If not, we will in a moment." She struck the crystal with the hardened steel, and it shattered. There was no effect whatsoever other than a few flying shards. Gaelen smiled a dark, sardonic smile. "Now, that wasn't quite the catastrophe we all expected, was it?"

Kotos was dumbfounded, then enraged. He railed within the amulet, cursing Gaelen, Gorgon, and everyone else involved. Yet he had to calm himself, for he could not yet afford to sever ties with Gorgon, lest he find himself abandoned in this frozen place. It would be a long time indeed before he would be visited by a friendly raven in this deep hole. There would be time later for punishment.

Gaelen had laid the axe aside and now picked up her long knife again. "Well, aren't you going to attack me now?" she said. "I have laid the axe down…you no doubt have bad memories of Wood-elves with axes in their hands, don't you? We don't smell of oranges any more, do we? Try to take me if you dare, you half-rotten, freakish pile of filth! Of course, I forgot—you move now only at the bidding of your master."

"It will be my pleasure," said Orrion, who lowered his visor, brandished Turantil in his right hand, and rushed at her.

At this, Rogond leaped forward. He swung his broadsword at Orrion, placing a rather large dent in the golden armor. Gaelen cast her long knife at her foe, but he moved too quickly and it did not find its intended mark. She met his blade with her own, snarling at the sight of Turantil. Nelwyn took aim, but Rogond's movements were unpredictable and she was afraid of wounding him. Galador, however, had a clear shot, and he took it.

Alas, the heavy arrows were unfamiliar, and the first shot veered off to the right. Galador cursed himself for his failure to compensate. He had only two arrows left, and he drew the second, but his opportunity had passed. Gaelen and Rogond fought hard, but even together they were outmatched.

Fima rushed into the fray, bearing his battle-axe. He swung at Gorgon twice, further denting the heavy armor. Then he hauled back and swung with all his strength, giving a loud cry of effort.

Such a blow might have cleaved Orrion's armor had it found its mark. Regrettably, it found only empty air until it struck the block of ice in which Duinar was imprisoned, causing a great crack that spread rapidly throughout.

"Oh, dear..." said Fima, even as the three combatants separated for a moment, staring at the ice. The sound of it was alarming. All at once it began to fall apart. Large, heavy pieces tumbled at random, and everyone had to move out of the way. Duinar remained standing for a moment, freed of the ice, before collapsing in a forlorn heap.

"So much for delicacy," said Fima, who most sincerely hoped that he had not brought about the death of Duinar all by himself.

Orrion was distracted by the liberation of Duinar, as were they all. Kotos took advantage of the opportunity to invade Gorgon's unguarded mind. *You must make certain Duinar is dead*, he said. *No matter what else you do this day, we must not leave him alive.*

Gorgon did not know of Duinar, he only knew that none in the Company would leave the struggle alive.

"Do not invade my thoughts while I am at war," he growled, just before a blinding pain struck his left arm above the elbow. Galador had taken his second shot, aiming for Orrion's heart, but it had gone to the right of his intention again. The third shot would be true. "Do you see what you've done?" Orrion gasped through clenched teeth. "Do not distract me again!"

The cracks in the floor of the chamber had widened, and with the release of Duinar the air grew warm, melting the ice. The destruction seemed to have set off more tremors within the mountain, alarming Rogond, who had not trusted the security of the floor from the beginning.

"Get back, Gaelen!" he cried, as several additional cracks in the black magma appeared, venting hot, foul-smelling steam. An orange light could be seen beneath them. Orrion had attempted to tear the arrow free of his arm, but it would not budge. He roared and ripped the amulet from around his neck, thrusting it into his belt. Now the dark armor of Gorgon appeared, with Gorgon inside it. He roared again and leaped at Gaelen, even as the mountain trembled beneath her feet.

Gorgon weighed nearly as much as the rest of the Company put together, and he was not concerned with being light-footed. When he came down upon Gaelen, the fragile, cracked floor gave way, spilling Gorgon, Gaelen, and Rogond into an unknown fate below. The cries of Fima, Nelwyn, and Galador were lost in the rumbling of the collapsing floor. When it had calmed, there was a nearly perfect hole in the center of the chamber, glowing with red-orange light. Fima knew that light well…it was like the forges of Cós-domhain. Yet there were no forges beneath Cold Mountain. Apparently, it was cold no longer.

Fima approached the edge of the hole with Nelwyn and Galador, but they could not yet determine the fate of their friends. Nelwyn cried out in grief and terror, grasping Galador's arm. "Oh, Lord of Light…they are lost! They are in that horrible, dreadful place, trapped with the Elfhunter. We must go after them…and pray that they have not burned alive." Her hands twisted upon Galador's arm. "It cannot end this way!"

Galador's face was grim, and he could not console her. "Even if they have survived, they must now deal with Gorgon alone," he said. "I would imagine that sulfurous abyss is more to his liking than to theirs."

"Indeed," said Fima in a horrified whisper. "I would guess that they are in some corner of Hell."

The report that came back to the commander of Wrothgar's northern army was not up to his expectations. The loss of Drach was no surprise, as everyone either saw, heard, or felt the dragon's fall. But now the commander learned that his trolls and Ulcas he were being decimated. The commander was concerned, but not yet dismayed. He knew there was another dragon waiting to be sent aloft, and he had other forces that he could deploy now that there was a way through the south wall. He had to act quickly, before the Elves sealed the breach.

"Send in the cavalry," he ordered the lieutenant who had brought the news. "Send them through the wall. Let's see how the Elves enjoy dealing with them, and with their mounts."

Then he summoned his second dragon-rider. "They do not as yet know of you," he said. "And my guess is that they no longer fear attack from the air. Therefore, you must wait a short while and let them deal with the cavalry. When that damage has been done, and they are weary, you will strike. Take Magra, and Ordath if you can."

"My lord," said the dragon-rider, bowing and backing out of the command tent. He would not turn his back to anyone of importance in Wrothgar's legions.

Hallagond and Azori aided Farin's dwarves in sealing the breach, assisted by the Elves. Farin watched as Magra lifted a stone of about twice his own weight and hurled it deftly into place.

"Hmmmph! They're stronger than they look," said the dwarf.

The Ulcas had retreated for the moment, which disturbed Magra—he did not understand why they would allow the defenders time to seal the wall again. The beautiful granite slabs of Mountain-home were covered with dead Ulcas, making footing treacherous. They had fallen faster than they could be dragged away.

Why have they retreated? Surely their captains would drive them until they were completely spent, or face the wrath of those above. They fought like typical Ulcas, relying on overwhelming numbers rather than on skill or courage. Magra could attest to this, as he had slain thousands of them in his life. *There is something else afoot…*

Had Gaelen been present, she would have detected the cavalry on the west wind. Nearly a hundred fierce riders on savage mounts converged on the south wall, and their scent was not a subtle one. Yet it mingled with the stench of a thousand dead Ulcas, and therefore went unnoticed.

Magra was first to hear the cries of dismay coming from outside the walls. Since the retreat, a few of Farin's folk had gone to work on the breach from outside, but now they ran back through as fast as their sturdy legs would carry them. "Riders!" they cried. "They have sent forth their black cavalry!"

"They must not gain entrance," cried Magra in a booming voice. "Wellyn! Field your archers!"

The archers of the Greatwood were more skilled than any in Alterra, especially in darkness. They seemed to have an innate sense of their enemies, and they rarely missed a shot once given. However, they were most adept with light hunting bows, not heavy war bows. At this distance, light bows would not do. They had been pulling war bows for hours now, and they were weary. It took away some of their power and spoiled their aim. The targets they faced required precision to bring down—enormous, thick-skinned, bristle-backed boars—arrows would slay them only through the eye, the mouth, or just behind the shoulder.

Many arrows found the riders and their mounts, but whereas the riders were killed, the boars were only made more savage. Now that they were on the attack, they no longer needed to be silent. Their horrible, squealing roars froze the blood of the defenders.

Bred in the Fell-ruin, they were shorter and broader than a horse but weighed the same. Swift over short distances, they could rush an enemy with lightning speed. They would kill by trampling, tearing with sharp, curved tusks, or savaging like dogs. And, of course, many still had armed riders aboard when they leaped over the stones of the breach. The boars were agile and sure-footed, trampling the bodies of the fallen with neither difficulty nor regard. Though intelligent, they had first and foremost been bred to kill, and when they were excited they did not always discriminate between one army and the next. This explained the retreat of Wrothgar's Ulcas, for they were just as likely to be taken. For the riders, a fall often meant death.

The boars overwhelmed the breach, killing all who stood in their way. Archers had taken a few, and many were now riderless, but they were a fearsome sight. The beasts would charge through the Elven-realm, running headlong through the winding paths and stairs. They would not bother with bolted doors as long as there were victims in plain sight, otherwise they would batter down all but the heaviest barriers. In fact, many of the dwellings of Mountain-home had no doors at all.

Magra, one of the few remaining Èolar in Alterra, was an unparalleled warrior. He was also an ancient and powerful being, and he had not yet called upon his inner light, for to spend it would exhaust him. Now, however, it seemed he had little choice. He stood before the onslaught of beasts and riders, raised his sword high over his head, and uttered words that he had not spoken since the Third Battle. His blade flared a bright blue-white, like a bolt of lightning, and his tall, broad form became the center of a glowing mass of light.

Elves and men averted their eyes, as the riders and their fearsome mounts reeled back, the riders shrieking in agony. The great boars, blinking and snorting, appeared stunned and confused for the moment.

The defenders took immediate advantage and rushed forward. The dwarves swung their bright axes and heavy hammers, cleaving the throats and crushing the skulls of the animals. This proved to be a very effective way of killing them, though they would still stand for several seconds, looking around in bewilderment before they fell. The Elves attacked with blades and bows, for at such close range hunting bows would serve, and many a yellow-tusked veteran fell with an arrow of the Greatwood in its eye. The Elves of Talsithian and Mountain-home stood upon the battlements, for they were deadly with their heavy war-bows, and they repelled the ranks of Ulcas that now came in from behind the cavalry.

Hallagond and Azori found themselves in the thick of things. They tried to do as much damage with their curved blades as they could without being trampled, but it was the most difficult few minutes of hand-to-hand fighting that Hallagond could recall. The stench was overwhelming. The footing, slick with the blood of Ulcas, Elves, and wild boars alike, had become treacherous.

Hallagond caught his left foot as he lunged forward to drive his blade behind the shoulder of one of the wild pigs. The leg twisted, and it broke as he fell upon it. He gave a strangled cry of pain and frustration as the animal turned its vicious, tiny red eyes upon him. It had not long to live, but it would exact pain and death upon its attacker ere it fell.

"I'm sorry, Estle," Hallagond whispered, as he prepared his last defense.

Azori saw Hallagond's fall from the edge of his vision, and he heard his friend's cry of anguish. Although leaping to the defense of anyone except himself or his own family was not in Azori's nature, he rushed to aid Hallagond without thinking, brandishing his two blades as the mortally-wounded boar lowered its head to charge. It took every scrap of courage Azori possessed to keep from leaping aside, but he stood firm. He drove both blades into the beast's brain, killing it at once, but not before it had driven its dagger-like tushes into his midsection. The wild pig fell hard, taking Azori with it, barely missing Hallagond, whose cry was so loud and full of loss that even Lady Ordath might have heard it in her sanctuary.

Hallagond's face twisted with pain as he jerked his shattered leg free of its entanglement. The boar was dead, but Azori was not. His bearded face was sweat-soaked and pale, his strong teeth bared in a grimace of agony. He closed his eyes, and when he opened them again Hallagond was at his side, assessing the wounds with despair.

"So now I go to join my brother Azok," said Azori, managing a weak smile. "This is what comes of trying to be respectable." His body shuddered, and he gave a heart-wrenching moan. His belly had been laid open...there was no hope. Hallagond tried to lift him, but Azori was pinned beneath the boar's head.

Hallagond could not free him. He shook his head, refusing to leave his dying friend, and covered Azori with his own body, hoping that someone would come to aid them.

Magra's light had faded, and though he was now drained of power, he stood forth against the dwindling cavalry, swinging his bright sword with his remaining strength. He had not seen the fall of Hallagond, nor the sacrifice of Azori. He was engaged in rallying his defenders and dispatching the few riders that still threatened them. He did not see or hear the approach of the night-flier until the beast's shadow fell upon him.

Rogond gasped as the acrid, poisonous air stung his eyes and filled his lungs with burning. He coughed, wiping his streaming eyes on his sleeve, looking around in confusion. The fall from Duinar's chamber had stunned him, but now he remembered it, and began looking for Gaelen. He tried to call to her, struggling to his feet and staggering away from the red, steaming volcanic vent that he had fallen near. He was fortunate not to have landed a few feet to his right, or he would have perished.

He found one of the rock walls, and leaned against it. The air here was better, but not good. Still, he breathed as deeply as he could manage, coughing and clearing his lungs and his throat.

He regained his breath and looked around, though he could not see clearly for more than a few yards. This was at once the strangest and most terrible place he had ever beheld. It appeared to be a labyrinth of honeycombed walls filled with chambers and pillars and corridors, pervaded everywhere by deep clefts of bright, red-orange molten rock. It was difficult to see, and even more difficult to breathe.

He tried again to call to Gaelen, but he was overcome by a fit of coughing. He shook his head. It would be all but impossible to hear Gaelen calling back to him over the echoing roar of steam and the rumbling of the mountain. They had fallen together…she could not be far away. And where was Gorgon Elfhunter?

In fact, Gaelen was not far away. She had thankfully not fallen into one of the vents, but she did not see Rogond, having landed upon a pillar of black rock almost immediately above him. Her lungs and her voice were less vulnerable, and she called to him, but he didn't answer. She leaped from the pillar of stone onto a ledge that led into a twisted passage, intending to make her way downward in search of him.

Gorgon had also fallen into the abyss, and although he was uncomfortable, he was not dismayed. *Now you've done it! You must find your way back to the chamber above*, said Kotos. *Duinar is alive, and he is now free. You must return and finish him, do you understand?*

"All in good time," said Gorgon as he looked all around for members of the Company. He knew that Gaelen, at least, had fallen with him. But where was she? He rose to his full height, brushing the ash and bits of black lava from his armor, grimacing as Galador's arrow drove itself a little deeper into the flesh of his arm.

There's no time for the killing of that She-elf, said Kotos. *We must salvage something from this useless endeavor. The death of Duinar might just pacify Lord Wrothgar…ever has He wondered as to Duinar's fate. If we do not see to his death, we are doomed.*

"If we cannot escape this place, we are doomed anyway," said Gorgon.

We will escape, and we can still prevail, said Kotos. *Don't lose your courage now—we can still achieve victory. The She-elf still lives…I know that you want to make an end of her. It should be easy in this place. Let us do it, and be done. Then you must deal with Duinar.*

"I will do it without any help or interference from you, thank you very much," said Gorgon.

Get on with it then. Every minute that we delay the death of my long-lost brother unsettles me. Now, do something about that arrow.

Gorgon winced at the thought of his next act, but Kotos was right—the arrow would hinder him. He grasped it with his right hand, pulled the shaft through the plate armor to the extent that it would come, and then opened his fearsome mouth and bit through it as close to the steel as he could manage. The remainder of the arrow withdrew into the flesh of his arm. Gorgon gripped the hilt of Turantil and smiled at his reflection in the blade. Then he crouched like a night-hunting beast and went in search of Gaelen.

In the chamber above, Galador, Nelwyn, and Fima made ready to aid their friends. Fima sat beside Duinar, trying to revive him. He had opened his eyes, to Fima's relief, but there was nothing but emptiness and confusion within them. "We must go at once and aid Rogond and Gaelen," said Galador. "We do not have time to tend to Duinar—our friends are in dire need."

"And where will you look for them? How will you aid them?" asked Fima. "If I can revive Duinar, it is likely that he knows the mountain. He should be able to guide us. Have patience!"

"If Gorgon attacks in that place, they will not survive for more than a few minutes!" cried Nelwyn, wringing her hands. She knelt beside Fima and looked into Duinar's blank gaze. "Duinar, come back to us, please!" she said in a plaintive tone, and then she took his face in both hands. "Duinar…you must help me. Please, for the sake of the Light, you must hear me!"

Duinar's eyes flickered like a spark that brings forth a flame. He blinked twice, and then focused his eyes on Nelwyn, who began to weep. "An Elf?" he said. "Yes…you are an Elf. And you are weeping. This cannot be a good thing. Why are you weeping?"

His voice was so gentle and full of wisdom that Nelwyn and Fima both looked upon him in awe. They were in the presence of one of the ancient Light-bearers. Nelwyn had dared touch him! She bowed in reverence, quelling her tears.

"Please, Master, we have freed you from the ice," said Fima. "Now we need your aid, for two of our most valiant friends are lost, and we must find them before a great evil takes them. Will you help?"

"What evil? Where? What place is this?" asked Duinar in confusion.

"We are deep under the mountain…the one that set off the fall of Tuathas," said Fima. "You tried to quell it, remember?"

"Tuathas…fell?"

"I'm sorry, Master. You put forth all the effort you could muster, but it was not enough," said Fima, his eyes full of grief for Duinar and the people he had failed to save.

All at once, awareness flooded back into Duinar's eyes. He gasped and wrapped his arms about himself in horror. "Oh…the memory!" he cried. "My people were lost. I could not save them… the memory of it drowns my spirit." He turned to Fima. "How much time has passed?"

"Tuathas was lost in the year 6740. It's now autumn of 7269," said Fima.

"Second Reckoning?" asked Duinar, his eyes wide.

Fima raised both eyebrows. It had not occurred to him that the passage of ten thousand years might not seem all that strange to an Asarla. "Yes, Second Reckoning."

Galador started toward the chamber doorway. "I have no time for history lessons and the ramblings of a confused old man," he said. "I must act now if I am to save Rogond. You two stay here and enlighten Duinar if you will…I am going now."

"If you do, it will mean your death," said Duinar. "The mountains are no place for a stranger. I will guide you, if you will only give me a moment's rest."

"Galador, if you're not careful you will turn into Gaelen," said Fima. "That's the sort of thing she would have said. I had thought the Eádram were wiser."

At this, Duinar whispered to Fima aside. "You obviously have not met many of the Eádram." Then he looked up at Galador's determined face and rose to his feet. "All right," he said. "That's enough rest. Let's go and look for your friends. I hope I can remember the inner paths of the mountain…it has been a long time." He made his way to the edge of the hole and looked down into it. "They fell in *there*?"

Fima nodded. "I have faith that they are alive, Master, but we haven't much time. They face a terrible enemy, and Lord Kotos guides him!"

"*Kotos!* That black-hearted demon of darkness! Wouldn't I love to see to his end!" When Duinar looked at Galador again, his eyes were fierce. "I will be able to find Lord Kotos, don't you worry about that," he said.

"Much may have changed, Master," said Fima. "Still, you fill me with hope. Guide us, and we will follow."

The next sight Rogond beheld was of Gorgon emerging from the rubble and swirling ash to stand before him. They had fallen on opposite sides of the same chamber, but had not realized it. Now they faced each other with blades drawn, ready for the attack. "You are searching for the Vixen, aren't you, Aridan?" said Gorgon in a voice that was almost cheerful. "Well, you can give up now—she is dead already. I came upon her, and I threw her into a pit of fire. A fitting end, don't you think?"

Rogond gripped his sword-hilt tightly and favored Gorgon with a cold smile. "You're a liar," he said, mimicking Gorgon's light-hearted tone. "If you killed her, where is the proof? You would have kept some token of hers, I'm certain. Prove to me now that she is dead."

Gorgon chuckled and nodded. "Very good, Tuathan. It seems you know me well. Alas that you will not ever get to know me better, as this is your final moment." Without warning, he leaped at Rogond, who barely managed to raise his blade in time.

Though he fought to the limit of his considerable strength, Rogond was no match for Gorgon. The poisoned air had affected him, and he gasped for breath even as Gorgon swung at him again and again.

Fortunately, Gaelen heard the sound of blades despite the echoing rumbles and hissing, bubbling vents. She traced the source of the sound to discover Rogond and Gorgon engaged in combat. Rogond appeared to be failing, and as Gorgon pressed his advantage, Gaelen knew that she must act at once or lose her beloved Thaylon. She leaped down from her vantage point and rushed at Gorgon before he could turn.

She launched her agile, whip-like form onto his broad back, a gleaming dagger in her hand, and drove it into the junction of his neck and shoulder, for there was enough of a gap in his armor to allow it. He threw his head back and roared, as much with rage as with pain.

Gaelen gripped his helmet with a strong left hand and tried to jerk it free so that she could cut his throat, but it was so heavy that she could not lift it high enough. She did effectively block his vision for a moment, and Rogond, who had regained his feet, now made for his enemy again. Gorgon now fought two enemies, and his lack of a left hand was a liability.

Rogond was out of breath, and his head swam with exertion and lack of air. Gorgon disarmed him with an unfortunate thrust to his right shoulder, causing him to cry out and drop his sword. Then Gorgon reached back over his head with his armored right arm, grabbed Gaelen by whatever part of her he encountered, and ripped her from his back, flinging her as hard as he could into the wall of the cavern.

"You see, Kotos? You didn't need to worry," said Gorgon. "Did you actually believe they would prevail?"

Rogond was barely conscious, but he rallied and struggled to his feet, standing before Gorgon with his sword clutched in a shaky left hand.

Gaelen had hit hard, and it took her a moment to come to herself. As Gorgon raised a killing blow over Rogond's head, she threw her one remaining blade with all the skill she possessed. It found its mark beneath Gorgon's right arm, and he bellowed with pain and surprise, dropping Turantil as he had done before, so long ago.

Gaelen darted toward him and grabbed the sword, then took a stance in front of Rogond, who was nearly spent with effort and blood loss. She had pulled the neck of the fire-cloak over her nose and mouth, and she breathed more freely than either Rogond or Gorgon. Her eyes narrowed and she snarled at her aggressor.

"I have recovered the sword, Turantil, yet again. It seems you cannot hold it long! Were you not armored, you would have fallen already, Ravenshade! I have already wounded you twice. It's only a matter of time."

"Whom are you trying to convince?" said Gorgon with a pained smile. His wounds hurt him, especially the one at his neck. "The truth is that I *am* armored, and the Aridan is of no use…they are such weaklings! As for you, my clever little Vixen, your time is near. That cloak will not save you when I cast you into the fire. Prepare yourself! I only regret not having more time to toy with you."

You are the one who should prepare, thought Gaelen. She thought she knew a way to even out the battlefield. She drew forth the phial of dragon-fire, removed the stopper from it, and readied herself for another attack. She raised Turantil over her head. "You favor this blade, don't you? Well, go and get it, then!" She hurled it into a pile of jagged rocks against the opposite wall.

At first, Gorgon just stood there. He had seen no other blade in Gaelen's hands. Had she truly just disarmed herself? If so, then he would retrieve Turantil, and she would be helpless to defeat him. He chuckled at her. Surely the heat and the fumes were affecting her reason! He moved to retrieve the sword, delighted that she had given him the opportunity. In doing so, he turned his back to her.

She was on him before he could blink twice, clinging to his neck with her left arm around his throat. He gave a sort of startled bark, and then gripped her left arm with his strong right hand.

"You will regret wearing that armor," she said, pouring the dragon-fire beneath his iron collar, sending it down his back, setting his flesh aflame instantly.

Gorgon's skin was thick, but it was not without feeling, and his back was relatively free of scars. At first, he did not seem to react to the fire in his flesh, concentrating instead on crushing Gaelen's left arm in his iron grip. She cried in pain, then gritted her teeth and hung on. Yet she could not withstand the force with which he jerked her free of him. If she had not let go, she would have lost her arm.

As it was, he whipped her over his head, even as the fire took him, and he screamed.

He could not stand the flames beneath his armor, and he ripped it off piece by piece. He cast it from him, hurling it into one of the vents. The dragon-fire clinging to the armor reacted with the molten rock, sending up a wall of fire from the vent that was frightening to see. Gorgon rolled upon the rough, stony floor in an attempt to extinguish himself, to little avail. Rogond, meanwhile, had gotten to his feet. Gorgon was no longer armored, and he was on fire! Now the odds were more even.

"Please, Master, try to remember," said Fima as the remainder of the Company moved through the mountain, following Duinar. They had made several wrong turns already. Duinar seemed confused, and they were all growing impatient. "You said you would be able to find Lord Kotos, Master, can you not get a sense of where he might be?"

"I *know* where he is, I just cannot determine how to get there," said Duinar. "It's not that I don't remember…these paths have changed."

"Someone had better figure it out," said Galador. "Nelwyn, do you have any sense of your cousin?"

"I know that she is not yet dead, but little else," said Nelwyn.

"You will just have to rely on me, my friends," said Duinar. "I will see us there as soon as I can manage it."

Galador was nearly trembling with frustration, but it was reassuring to know that Gaelen was still alive. At least it was something.

Gorgon screamed with pain as the flames worked through the thick, leathery skin of his back. He was armored now only to the waist. Much of his hair had been singed away, and the back of his head was blackened and blistered, the skin destroyed. He was in great distress.

Rogond had rallied again and stood before him with a long blade, ready to run him through, and Gorgon had no sword. He saw

Gaelen struggle to her feet, her face twisted with pain. At least he had done some damage.

Run, you fool! RUN! said Kotos, and for once Gorgon did not ask questions. He turned and ran toward the only apparent way out, but Rogond blocked his path. *The wall of fire…it is not that wide*, said Kotos. *Leap through it! Your enemies will not follow.*

Gorgon turned back toward the leaping flames, but he hesitated, until he heard Rogond's footfalls behind him. *You must trust me,* said Kotos, *or you will end here!*

Rogond raised his broadsword, ignoring the pain in his shoulder and the burning in his lungs. He gave a great cry as he prepared to bring the blade down upon Gorgon, but the wretched creature sprang through the wall of fire, and Rogond saw him no more.

Gaelen screamed in frustration. "You're not getting away from me again, you *coward!*" Jerking her leather belt free, she whipped it around the right side of her neck, re-fastened it diagonally across her chest, and pulled her left arm through to stabilize it. Then she wrapped the fire-cloak around her, pulled the hood down over her face, and launched herself toward the flames, leaping through them before Rogond could stop her. She bore Turantil in her right hand.

Rogond stared at the flames, gasping and struggling to breathe. He staggered back, trying to clear his head. His vision closed around a dark tunnel as he turned back toward the passage where the air was better. Then the tunnel closed completely, his ears roared, and his legs gave way. Rogond would be of no further help to Gaelen, not this time.

At last the dragon-fire had burned itself out. Gorgon's back was like a smoldering cinder, and it was agony to move his arms, especially to raise them. He leaned against the rock wall, pressing his forehead against it, trying to quell the pounding in his brain. Then he heard his enemy's cry as she leaped after him. He turned to behold her standing with Turantil in her hand, her fire-cloak glittering in the red light.

She cast back the hood so that he could look into her eyes, and then rushed at him without further pause. Gorgon knew that she was determined to put an end to him, and he had no choice but to engage her.

His pride and hatred of her saw him through the pain as he met her attack. He was unarmed, but that did not dismay him. She was too small and too weary to prevail over him, blade or no blade. Like Gorgon, she now had only one working hand. Her arm would unbalance her; all he had to do was catch her in an awkward moment.

The Vixen was weary, she was unbalanced, and she was small. Still, she gave him more trouble than he had expected. Yet now, as she darted in to drive her blade home, she faltered, and he had her. He held her right arm, twisting it hard as she cried in pain.

"Drop the sword!" he roared at her.

"I will *not!*" she replied, her face twisting into an expression of agonized determination.

"I think you will," said Gorgon, jerking her from the floor. She struggled and writhed in his grasp, but she could not break free of him. She managed to kick him hard several times, but he only laughed at her. "After setting my back on fire, you think a few hard kicks from your very small feet will distress me? How pathetic of you. Now, drop it, or I will simply tear your arm off. The choice is yours."

Gaelen knew that she would not be able to hold the sword now, even if Gorgon released her. She had felt all sensation leave her right hand when Gorgon had wrenched her from the floor. He might as well tear her arm off, but she would not give him the satisfaction. She gathered herself, and put forth a last effort, bringing both legs up before her and thrusting as hard as she could into Gorgon's throat.

This was definitely unexpected, and he reeled back, letting go of her arm. He tasted blood in his mouth, and he could not get his breath. If that blow had been just a little more forceful, it might have killed him. He sagged back against the wall, coughing and gasping, unable to breathe. The wretched Vixen could have taken him then, had she been able, but she could no longer wield a weapon.

She has taken her last bit of you, Elfhunter, said Kotos. *Now, swat her and be done with it!* Gorgon's shoulders sagged with pain and weariness as he turned back around to face her. There was only one way out of this place, and that was back through the wall of fire. The Vixen would not be able to make that leap...not now…and she apparently knew it. With obvious regret, she kicked Turantil into the volcanic vent, where it was lost.

Despite the lack of weapons, it did not take more than a few moments for their conflict to end. Gaelen tried to avoid Gorgon, but she was weary and in pain, and without the use of either hand, she was not as adept. Gorgon battered her, but did not kill her, striking her with his right arm again and again. Still, she fought him. At last she lay before him and did not get up again, for although her spirit was willing, her body betrayed it. Now, as she resigned herself to her fate, even the light of her eyes had dimmed, and though Gorgon thought it strange that he should do so, he almost regretted her fading.

26
The Fate of the Stone

In Mountain-home, the defenders had rallied and driven back the enemy. They had all but sealed the breach in the south wall under the direction of Magra, who had used his inner light to bewilder beasts and Ulcas alike. Everyone who had borne witness was now in awe of him.

Yet Garthor, the night-flier, had not borne witness, and it glided silently over the eastern battlement, appearing like a great shadow through the smoke. It swooped down upon Magra, even as he turned to behold it. He reached for his great bow, but the creature extended its huge talons as it passed over, snatching Magra from the ground and taking him aloft.

Magra numbered among the strongest of Elves, yet he grappled with the dragon to no avail. The beast circled above the defenders, directed by its rider to climb to a dizzying height. From there, it would release Magra to his death. If all went as planned, his broken body would land upon the heads of the people, and their resistance would fail.

But Lord Magra would not give in so easily. He still bore his sword, sheathed at his side, and now he struggled to work it free. At last he was successful. The dragon circled higher and higher until Magra looked down upon Mountain-home to behold only the torches and oil fires, which had just about burned themselves out. The smoke had cleared, but he could not see the stars for the vast wings above his head. *A pity*, he thought, as he set to work.

He began hacking at the dragon's feet, which were covered with heavy, thick scales. Yet Magra could thrust the point of the blade between them and cause great pain. This had unfortunate consequences, as the beast closed its talons. Though Magra still wore his armor, it could not withstand the force behind the great claws, which were as hard as diamond. Magra writhed and gasped as the talons slid through his flesh and bone and entrails. Despite indescribable pain, He kept to his course, goading the dragon with the sword. Finally, the beast did as desired, and snaked its head around to face Magra, intending to tear him to pieces and devour him. It opened its serpent's mouth, long teeth gleaming in the starlight, and darted forward.

Magra thrust the blade of the great sword into the roof of the dragon's mouth, even as Hallagond had described. Garthor made no sound, as though too surprised to do so, and then listed to the right, its flight now ungraceful and irregular. Its eyes glazed over, for it was dead as a stone, even as its rider now sent a shot into Magra's breast. The great talons relaxed, but Magra could not gain his freedom. The dragon began to turn over in the air, allowing him a last sight of the stars.

Ordath had come up from her sanctuary, knowing that her people were in desperate need of her. She felt Magra's pain as he was taken, and she rushed into the courtyard to behold the dragon's flight high over Mountain-home. She clenched both of her hands, her blood rising in the midst of her grief, and gave a great cry of pain and loss. She flared like a blue-white torch in the courtyard, as bright as Magra had been, and brighter. No one could look at her until the light subsided.

High over the courtyard of Mountain-home, Magra the Mighty drew his last breath. He looked down upon his beloved realm and bore witness to Lady Ordath's beacon of light. "So…she is an Asarla!" he whispered, and then he died.

The dragon fell faster and faster until it burst into flame, incinerating its rider, who had wisely taken his own life already. Magra's body burned along with it, looking for all the world like a falling star.

Every enlightened being in Alterra felt Magra's passing, though only a few recognized it. To most, it would seem as a sudden, unexplained sadness…a cloud across the sun. To others, Ordath and Arialde in particular, it was like a knife through the heart.

Lady Arialde had confronted Lord Shandor within the Stone of Léir in an attempt to persuade him to leave it, so that he might add his strength to the battle. When Magra gave up his spirit, Arialde felt pain like a fire in her breast. *Magra has fallen,* she said. *Does that not convince you?*

Shandor said nothing, but Arialde could see in his eyes that he had also felt the loss of his friend and steadfast comrade-in-arms.

"*What have you to say, my brother?*"

Arialde was at a loss. She had to make Shandor realize that other concerns were more important than his own. *Do you not know that all of this…this battle, and the sacrifices that have come with it, is because of you? If Wrothgar did not desire to enslave you, we would not be here. If you had not stayed within the Stone for so long and given it the power that you have, Magra would be alive, and your daughter Ordath would not now be faced with death. Does that not convince you? You fear to look into your own destiny…is that because you know that you will not like what you see?*

Shandor had never dropped his chilly gaze from her until now. *I have looked long enough to know that I have no destiny of which I can be proud,* he said. *My only joy has come in this place. Will you see me undertake an endless life of sorrow?*

There is other happiness to be found, said Arialde. She could feel his grief, and it nearly overwhelmed her. Yet he had to overcome it now…he had to leave it behind.

If you do not come out from the Stone, you will never see your child again, and we risk your being taken and subverted into darkness. You must hear me! There is nothing for you here, and there is everything outside. Come with me, my brother, you must come with me. Trust me, as you did before.

She looked back over her shoulder as though responding to an unseen call. *I cannot linger here any longer,* she said, *for if you will not fight this battle, then I must. I will await your decision, but choose quickly, and choose wisely.* So saying, she willed her spirit to return to her body, awakening to behold the anxious face of Lord Airan.

"Were you successful, my lady?" he asked.

"I don't know. Oh, Airan…he is so hurt and he is so alone. But if he does not come out of his own accord, I shall forever lose faith in the ultimate power of love."

"It is love that holds him there," said Airan.

"No," Arialde whispered. "Grief holds him there. Love will send him back to us." With those words, she settled herself beside Shandor's body, taking his cold hand in her own, awaiting his decision.

Shandor debated with himself for only a few moments longer, then turned and retreated back into the depths of the Stone. He sought enlightenment from the one he loved, and he summoned Liathwyn, who, as always, came to him at once. She sat upon a bench of carved marble in one of the many glades of Mountain-home, water gurgling from a cold spring beside her, soft grass at her feet. Shandor went to her side and took her hand.

Liathwyn, my love, you must guide me. Long have I lived here in happiness with you, yet now I am told I must leave the Stone for the sake of the Light. I do not wish to leave you, but I cannot allow others to give their lives for my sake. Yet I would remain, if you desire it. Would you have me stay by your side? If I leave you, I will not return.

Liathwyn turned her deep blue eyes upon him, piercing his heart. Then she smiled a hopeful smile. *Shandor, my beloved, I know that you must go forth to this conflict. I also know that you will return, and I shall send forth my prayer each day until I behold you again. Be not dismayed.*

Shandor wept as he held her, for he knew the truth. This was but a memory of his farewell to Liathwyn ere he went off to the Third Battle. She could not enlighten him, for she was not really here.

He could not sacrifice the life of his only child for the sake of a memory…no matter how precious. He held Liathwyn, fierce tears of overwhelming sorrow coursing down his face, for he knew that this would be the last he would ever see of her. He rose, stroked her beautiful, gleaming hair one last time, and then turned from her.

Shandor…keep safe, and return to me. I will always be waiting.

He paused, and turned his silver head back toward her. *Oh, beloved…if only it were true.* Then he did the hardest thing he had yet done in his life—he walked away from her.

"Rogond!" cried Nelwyn, as she rushed to his side.

Duinar had led the Company there, and they had found Rogond lying where he had fallen. Nelwyn and Galador turned him over, shocked at the blood on the stone beneath him and at the pallor of his face. He was still breathing, but not well.

Duinar shook his head. "We must get him to good air, and now, or he is lost," he said. "No mortal man can live long in this place."

In fact, Fima had been left behind already; he could not withstand the poisoned air, and they would not risk his life.

"But there is another of our Company, a Wood-elf like me," said Nelwyn. "I cannot leave without her. She is my cousin and dearest friend."

"How will we find her?" asked Duinar, who could see that Nelwyn was not about to be dissuaded.

"She will be wherever Gorgon is," said Nelwyn. "She has set herself to the task of killing him. If she has left Rogond in such a state, it can only be in pursuit of Gorgon Elfhunter. And Lord Kotos will be there as well."

"Lord Kotos is quite near," said Duinar. "I can practically put my hands around his throat!"

"If only you could," said Galador.

"Well, then we must search for him," said Nelwyn. "Galador, only you are strong enough to save Rogond. He is too tall and heavy for me to carry. Take him back to Fima, so that he can be tended to. Duinar and I will search for Gaelen."

"And what if you find her?" said Galador. "Gorgon will be there...do you expect me to let you face Gorgon alone?"

"I expect you to do what you must to save the life of your friend," said Nelwyn. "I am not alone...I have Duinar to aid me. And do not count Gaelen out as yet."

"Oh, in that case, I can *surely* put my fears to rest," said Galador, who had been faced with a nearly impossible choice.

Duinar stood before Galador, forcing him to look into his eyes. "I know that your faith in me, and in my race, has been shaken," he said in a voice so gentle and caring that it nearly brought Galador to tears. "Trust me now, my proud friend. I will not disappoint you again. No harm will come to Nelwyn through any failure of mine, I promise you."

Galador swallowed hard, looking from Duinar to Nelwyn, and back to Duinar again. Then he stooped and lifted Rogond, hoisting him over one shoulder. "I will rejoin you once I have delivered Rogond into Fima's hands," he said. "Until then, I will place my faith in both of you." He looked over at Nelwyn. "Keep safe," he said, and was gone without another word.

Nelwyn looked into Duinar's aged, earnest face. "What do we do now?" she asked.

"We find Lord Kotos and see to your other friend," said Duinar. "We must be swift, yet we must be cautious, for I would sooner throw myself through that wall of flame than prove unworthy of Galador's faith in me."

Arialde first felt Shandor's return as a warming of his cold, lifeless hand. She dropped it abruptly, for she had been lost in contemplation and it had startled her. She rose to her feet, calling for Lord Airan, for she did not know whether Shandor would need aid, or whether he would be successful in his return. No Asarla had ever left his body for so long and returned to life. Yet Arialde held to her faith, and waited.

The body galvanized as though it had been struck by lightning, arching its back and lifting from the slab on which it had been laid. Shandor's eyes bulged and his jaws clenched, along with every other muscle in his body. His limbs were stiff and hard as marble, every sinew and vessel clearly visible, as he opened his mouth at last and cried out in pain. He began to thrash from side to side, his beautiful head whipping back and forth, fighting like a gaffed fish as Airan held him down. Then it was over, and he collapsed.

"Is he breathing?" asked Arialde, for she could not tell.

"He is," said Airan, panting with the effort he had made. He turned to Arialde. "Your brother, it would seem, has a strong spirit. His body resisted, but he won out in the end."

Arialde knelt beside Shandor, whose eyes were now closed. "Shandor? Shandor…my brother, will you not greet your sister, who loves you?" She caressed his face, and he opened his eyes.

"I have returned to you," he said. "I finally realized the wisdom in your words. Yet you must leave me alone…to do what I must do."

"But you are not strong," she said. "You should rest for a while. I will stay with you."

"I cannot rest, for in my next action lies the hope of the future. You must not remain here, and you must not hinder me." He smiled, which was a rare thing. Then he took her hand, flushing with humiliation as he asked the next question. "Please…will you help me to rise?"

Arialde and Airan both aided Shandor in gaining his feet, though it was difficult. His body had lain for so long with no spirit to guide it that it did not answer his commands at first. Yet he stood, naked and trembling, but upon his own feet at last. He closed his eyes, took four very deep breaths, and drew himself up tall and proud. When he next turned his gaze to them, it was piercing, valiant, determined, and just slightly imperious. Shandor had returned.

"Now leave me," he said. "Leave me to my task, and ask no questions. I will summon thee when I have finished."

Arialde and Airan left Shandor alone, as he had asked. "Will he be all right, do you think?" asked Airan. "What task does he mean to do? Are you certain we may trust him?"

"I am certain that I have never been as glad to see anyone before in my life," said Arialde. "He will be all right."

Shandor composed himself, preparing his next act with care. He stood before the Stone of Léir, gazing down at its surface with longing. It looked small and harmless without his mighty spirit within. It would be so easy to return to his life with Liathwyn...

He lifted the Stone in graceful, sinewy hands like carved alabaster and held it before him. It was beautiful, and it was harmless now, but Shandor could take no chances.

You did a fine job, Dardis, my friend. Perhaps you were too good at your craft. Forgive me."

He raised the Stone high over his head. He hesitated for only a moment longer, knowing that he would never see her again—not in this life, and not in the next.

Farewell…

He brought the Stone down hard upon the polished marble floor, where it shattered in an explosion of light and sound and imagery. Shandor wailed as he saw his beloved reflected in each and every fragment: Liathwyn laughing, Liathwyn smiling, Liathwyn weeping. He lunged forward and fell to his knees, reaching out to her, gripping the crystal shards in desperate hands. But the images of Liathwyn had faded, and she was gone.

Arialde rushed in to aid him, finding him on his knees, his head bent down to the floor, crying in grief and loss. His hands were bleeding, as he had clenched the sharp fragments of the Stone. Arialde did not dare approach him for a moment. She had not ever in her life heard Shandor truly weep until now.

Airan had come in behind her, alarmed. "He has…destroyed it?"

Arialde held up her hand to silence him.

"Leave us alone," she said. "Do not speak of what you have seen. He has done a great thing…the only *right* thing. I will comfort him, do not fear. Make certain we are not disturbed."

Airan bowed and did as she asked, but his heart was troubled. It was discomfiting to see a mighty soul such as Shandor in the grip of such terrible, unrelenting woe.

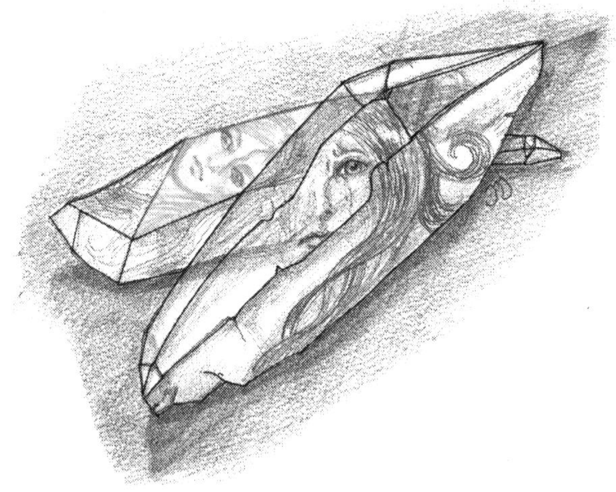

Unlike the death of Magra, the destruction of the Stone of Léir was felt by relatively few beings in Alterra, but it profoundly affected those who did, no matter which side of the Light they stood upon.

It set off a reaction in Tûr Dorcha that reached all the way to the Greatwood, to Tal-ailean in the Verdant Mountains, and to the Lake. Every Elf in those realms instinctively placed a hand upon his weapon, and every eye was turned with vigilance toward the Darkmere. Lord Wrothgar was, as his name implied, quite wrathful indeed. This had not been at all the outcome he had anticipated. *If the Stone is still in Tal-sithian, where is that fool, Kotos? What is he doing chasing shadows in Tuathas?*

Every Ulca within a half mile of the Tower fell dead, as Wrothgar exuded a suffocating tidal wave of malevolent energy. The Ulcas were creatures of evil, but they could only withstand so much.

In Mountain-home, Lady Ordath felt the death of the Stone and the return of Shandor to the world of the living. She rejoiced, for he was free, but she wondered whether he would be whole, or whether his grief had damaged him beyond hope. She could not concern herself with such things now, as she had a battle to win. She hoped that, with the destruction of the Stone, the enemies of Mountain-home would realize that they could not prevail.

The commanders of Wrothgar's forces sensed their Lord's dismay, and they knew that the war they had waged could not be won. They had lost their dragons, and they had lost most of their fearsome black cavalry. Many trolls had fallen, and thousands of Ulcas. But the greatest concern was the loss of support from Tûr Dorcha.

Without Wrothgar to drive them, without a plan of action that they thought could succeed, the dark forces were disheartened, even as they had hoped to take the heart of Mountain-home with the death of Magra. They had been abandoned, and without the fear of Wrothgar to keep things in order, chaos crept into the ranks.

The Elves took heart, and pursued their enemies, who now found themselves engaged in hasty and dishonorable retreat. The battle was over, and Mountain-home would live on in glory. Yet the losses had not been counted.

Hallagond had been found and brought into the Great Hall, where he told Estle of the death of her brother. Estle sorrowed not only for Azori's death, but also for Hallagond's misery. He blamed himself for the loss of his friend. He did not tell Estle the final words Azori had uttered as they lay together on the battlefield in the midst of the fighting.

"I must leave you now, Hallagond," he had said, his eyes bright but unfocused. "Do not be concerned, for the pain and thirst have left me, and I am at peace. Lift a tankard to Azok and me the next time you find yourself in the Skulking Raven."

"*Why*, Azori? Why did you do this?" asked Hallagond, though he tried not to weep.

"If my sister had lost her only love, she would have been unhappy," said Azori, his breath hitching in his chest, color leaving his cold face. "I could not allow that, as you well know." His back arched, and his eyes lost their light. Then he was still.

The news was not all bad. Wellyn had survived, though he had taken a knife-thrust to one forearm. Farin was in surprisingly fine fettle, and more than half of his people still lived. Yet the Elves had suffered great loss, the most profound of which was the death of Magra. There would never be another Elf of his kind in Alterra, and Mountain-home was diminished.

The destruction of the Stone of Léir was of great dismay to Lord Wrothgar, but it might have unsettled Lord Kotos even more. He dwelled in the person of Gorgon Elfhunter and, at the moment the Stone had shattered, he was deep beneath Cold Mountain, looking down upon the helpless form of Gaelen Taldin. Pain exploded in Gorgon's brain as Kotos reacted to the loss of the Stone and to Wrothgar's obvious displeasure.

No…no…NO! This cannot have happened. All of our plans are ruined…it has been for nothing. I am undone!

Gorgon did not know what had befallen Kotos, as he had no sense at all of the Stone of Léir. "What happened?" he asked.

It would have been better for Gorgon if he had not asked. *You…YOU! This is all your doing! You knew the Stone was false, and yet you deceived me just so you could kill one Wood-elf? You will face my wrath, you worthless, disobedient, intractable, irritating…*

"…Host?" said Gorgon.

Gaelen, though failing, was surprised to find that if she concentrated hard upon Gorgon, she could hear the voice of Lord Kotos as well. She listened to his railing against Gorgon, and she heard the reply. Then Kotos was silent for a moment. Gaelen smiled to herself. Gorgon was no fool.

We are still partners, Elfhunter, said Kotos. *And we have much to do. Come now, and let us work together. You should not have deceived me, and I do not approve, but you were yourself deceived, and so you are not entirely at fault. Now go on, and exact your vengeance. Your enemy is helpless! Go on then, and take her. Then we can get back to more important business.*

"That's right," said Gaelen to the surprise of both Kotos and Gorgon. "Just do it! And be sure you make a quick and painless end of me. You wouldn't want to inconvenience your master, now, would you?" She was exhausted, and she was in pain, but she had kept her wits. "Kotos thinks he owns you, after all."

Do not listen to her. She is only trying to save her own life, said Kotos. *She thinks that by distracting you with doubts, she can buy time for her friends to arrive. You know how clever she is. Do not be fooled!*

Gorgon looked down at Gaelen and rumbled deep in his throat. He was still in great pain, and his temperament was tenuous at best.

"Yes, go on and kill me," said Gaelen. "Put me out of my pain. At least I am what I am…I have not lost myself to the will of another."

Gorgon's eyes narrowed and he flexed his right hand, preparing to throttle her.

"You have not been yourself since our last battle, have you?" she said. "Your spirit has been taken, your essence overcome. You no longer move at your own direction. You dwelled among the people of Dûn Arian, and you sat at the table with your enemies, and yet you let them live! You have forgotten your mission, and you will never accomplish it now."

"On the contrary, I plan to accomplish it in only a few moments," Gorgon said in a voice that was meant to be falsely ingratiating. Yet Gaelen could hear the doubt beneath it.

Yes, yes! Kill her at once, before she can spread more lies, said Kotos. To this, both Gorgon and Gaelen laughed.

"Oh, yes," said Gaelen, "Lord Kotos certainly would not want to encourage the spreading of lies. Oh, the absurdity of it! Even through our pain, we still have our good humor, do we not, Elfhunter? We can still appreciate irony." Then she grew serious again. "He means to kill you, you know. He will not suffer you to live, and neither will the Shadowmancer. Their promises mean nothing. If you would kill me, at least do it because it is your will, not his. And you might as well enjoy it, for you are doomed. I am the last Elf you will hunt, Gorgon."

Have the Elves so corrupted you that you would listen to one of them? She is manipulating you! Do you not know it? Kotos fairly screamed.

"I suppose you would know, my lord," said Gorgon. "You have been trying to manipulate me since the day we met. There's no use in denying it. Yet I saw through your deceptions, and here we are, accomplishing my will, not yours."

"You're desperate, Ravenshade!" said Gaelen. "Your alliance with Gorgon has brought you to ruin. You underestimated him; he is not the hapless dupe you thought him to be. Now you fear him, for you are at *his* mercy. Admit it!"

I will teach you both that it is unwise to defy me! said Kotos, and sent forth pain into Gorgon's already tortured brain. The pain was unbearable, and Gorgon raised his arms to cradle his head between his right hand and the stump of his left.

Gaelen felt it, too. Her bond with Gorgon was deep, and she gasped as searing pain nearly blinded her. She blocked it by closing her thoughts, but Gorgon did not have that choice, and he groaned in agony as Kotos tormented him. At last, it was over.

Now, will you do as you are ordered? said Kotos, who was both impatient and angry.

Gaelen could no longer hear Kotos, and she did not dare open her thoughts to him again. Yet she could still speak to Gorgon. "Through me you have gained much. I showed you the stars, and I let you see into my world. This is the world of Light. What has your hatred gained for you? What dark and lowly end will you endure? No one will remember you, Gorgon. Your tales may be told for a while, but they will fade. You will be remembered only as the instrument of Lord Kotos, who aided him in his most spectacular failure. Is that what you wanted?"

Silence her! Silence her, or I WILL!

"If you do not stop trying to order me, I will walk away from her *and* from you," said Gorgon. "No one orders me! You want to see this…Duinar… dead? You want to escape from this mountain? Then you had better remember which of us has a body, and which of us does not. Try to force my actions with pain again and I will destroy your precious amulet! What say you to *that* notion?"

Gaelen tried to stand, but her broken body would not permit it. She settled for crawling back and working herself into a half-reclining position against a stone. The effort nearly took the last of her strength. The poisoned air had not been her friend, either.

"Not very beguiling now, is he?" she said. Her head swam, and her vision blurred. *It will not be long now…* "I will leave you soon. If you would kill me, you had better be quick about it."

Gorgon could not allow Gaelen to die on her own, not after pursuing her for so long. He approached her and reached down with his right hand to take her by the front of her jerkin. Then he lifted her from the floor. She did not resist him.

This was not the ending he had foreseen. He wanted Gaelen to cry, to plead for her life, to fight! It was the first time he had ever known her to give up. "You could at least put up a struggle," he said under his breath.

"Why? I know I'm dying," said Gaelen. "I will not give you the pleasure of taking my dignity. I will die knowing who and what I am, in my right mind, and in my own way." She smiled, though her voice was fading. "It's not so bad, considering."

"But...I have *beaten* you!" said Gorgon. He did not understand.

"There is much of innocence still in you," said Gaelen. "Lord Kotos has beaten us both. Yet I will lose only my life, whereas you have already lost far more than that. You cannot help who and what you are, but now you do not even have that. Farewell, Gorgon. You will not long outlive me—that is certain."

In that moment, Duinar and Nelwyn appeared on a ledge above where Gorgon stood. "Drop her, Gorgon, right now!" yelled Nelwyn, drawing her bow on him. Duinar's eyes narrowed and his face drew into an expression of loathing.

"Yes, Kotos, *drop her!*" he said.

Duinar! Now see what you have done? You will have a difficult time in killing him now, you short-sighted idiot. Stop making conversation with your enemy, and KILL her!

Gorgon looked down upon Gaelen, knowing she was right. She was an Elf, the Elf he most hated, and yet she was an honest adversary. She had not tried to take his will, nor had she beguiled him with false promises. Kotos had taken far more from Gorgon than Gaelen ever had. In that moment, the Elfhunter made his decision.

"No, I don't believe I will kill her," he said. "My enemies have brought me to bay, and I must taste defeat at last. I am weary, I am in pain, and I have not felt real freedom since you cursed me with your presence."

He turned to Gaelen, who was still dangling before him. "You say that no tales of me will be told. You may need to re-think that, if you survive. Now I will show you that I have not lost myself…that the spirit of Gorgon Elfhunter has not been taken. I hate you, as I hate all of your kind, but I know much of you, and alone among the Elves I have come to respect you. I know that what you say is true. I spare you now, only because it is not what Lord Kotos wishes. Farewell…Gaelen Taldin."

He dropped Gaelen painfully to the floor and turned toward Duinar and Nelwyn.

"No! Don't kill him!" Gaelen shouted with the last of her strength, wondering how such words could ever come from her mouth. Then she was silent.

Kotos tried with all his might to stop his wayward host. He tried pleading, he tried cajoling, and then he tried fear and the worst pain he could muster. None of it had any effect, as Gorgon almost strolled to the edge of a deep, wide vent, peering curiously over the edge. "How does it feel to be controlled?" he whispered through the blinding pain in his head. Blood ran from his nose and mouth—Gorgon was dying. "Shall we face the fire together, you and I?"

Then, at the last, he turned to Gaelen, his mortal enemy, who had come to know him better than anyone else. "Tell my tale," he said, as Kotos screamed in frustration, finally taking Gorgon into death. The Elfhunter hesitated only a moment longer, and then fell headlong into the pit, taking Lord Kotos and the amulet with him. Gorgon did not feel the pain as his body burned away, but he did feel a last surge of pride. In the end, he had shown as much courage as any of them.

27
The Fate of All Concerned

Duinar and Nelwyn had made their way down to where Gaelen lay, though it was difficult. The violence of Lord Kotos, who now dwelt in a pit full of molten rock, could not help but anger the mountains. There was no time to waste. Nelwyn wondered at the strength and agility of Duinar; he was much more vigorous than he appeared.

The tremors that had rumbled beneath their feet for many days had now increased in both number and in power. Duinar and Nelwyn knelt beside Gaelen, who appeared as little more than a small, bloody pile of rags surrounded by the fire-cloak.

"What did he *do* to you?" whispered Nelwyn, as tears started in her eyes. Duinar placed gentle hands on Gaelen, carefully examining her and straightening her limbs. She was beyond caring and did not feel the pain, yet with the death of Gorgon some of the years had fallen away from her face.

"She has been beaten almost beyond recovery," said Duinar. "I would say that Gorgon disarmed her, almost literally, and then savaged her." He glanced around the area, not seeing any weapon in evidence. "He was just too large and powerful an enemy. A sparrow trapped in a cage with a wolf will eventually be eaten, though it is quicker and more elusive."

"Yes, especially when it is wingless and cannot fly," said Nelwyn, looking in despair at Gaelen's arms.

Duinar probed Gaelen's throat, feeling for a heartbeat. To his relief, he found one, but it was rapid and shallow. "We must get her into the fresh air, and away from this place," he said. "I will take her, Nelwyn. Let us away."

"Are you certain you are strong enough to carry her and climb out of here?" said Nelwyn.

"Now that I have my bearings better, I do not believe it will be so difficult," said Duinar. He focused his attention on the fiery barrier that separated them from the other chamber and the doorway. "Get ready to leap across it," he said to Nelwyn, who just stared at him. Duinar smoothed Gaelen's hair back from her face.

"Hello, little Fire-heart," he said. "Trust in Duinar. He will not fail you." He lifted Gaelen and approached the fire. "Take hold of my arm," he said to Nelwyn, who could not imagine what he intended. He closed his eyes and summoned forth his power.

Nelwyn felt herself surrounded by a covering of blue light. "Leap across the gap with me," said Duinar. "One, two... *three!*"

Nelwyn was afraid, but she placed her faith in the wisdom of Duinar, and they leaped together across the fearsome crevice, barely feeling the heat of it. She looked around in wonder. "So, they were just on the other side of this wall of flame, and I did not know it? So much time could have been saved had I known... I could have leaped across and saved her."

"Without me or this fire-cloak, that would have been difficult," said Duinar. "And had you intervened, Gorgon might not have come to his decision to foil Lord Kotos." He shook his head. "It will be a long time indeed ere a living host comes near to the Deceiver. Besides, it was fitting that Gorgon should have regained his pride and dignity at the end. He did not ask for the fate he was given."

"You did not know him," said Nelwyn. "He was cruel, and a scourge upon the Elves. His actions sprang from his own misguided sense of self-importance. He deserves no consideration in my opinion."

Another fierce tremor ended all debate. "Come on!" cried Nelwyn, and they hurried from the horrid, stinking oven back up to where their friends were waiting.

They ran into Galador, literally, as he made his way back down to aid them. All three were out of breath, as the air had worsened since the downfall of Kotos. Duinar was weary after having called upon his power, but he was still hale. Nelwyn, who had faced too many trials in recent days, was nearly exhausted.

Galador took one look at Gaelen and his heart despaired. Somehow, though he knew it was unreasonable, he had expected her to prevail.

Soon the Company was reunited. Fima had been tending to Rogond, who remained senseless and unaware. *That's just as well*, thought Fima, as Gaelen was laid beside him, for she did not appear to be alive. Yet Fima had no time to grieve for her…not now.

"We have to get out of here at once," he said. "I'm sure you've noticed that this mountain is about to rise up."

"Let Nelwyn catch her breath first," said Galador. "I'll take Rogond, as he will be a heavy burden. One of you must carry Gaelen."

Duinar shook his head. "You are strong, Galador, but you are weary. I will take Rogond. He is one of my own, after all!" He took notice of the doubtful expression on Galador's face. "What, you think I am an old man?" he said. "I am much stronger than I appear!"

Nelwyn raised her eyebrows in affirmation. "It's true. He is."

"Well, then, be our guest," said Galador, backing away from Rogond. Duinar approached, bent down, and lifted Rogond's tall, heavy frame with some difficulty, draping him over his right shoulder before regaining his feet. Once he was balanced, Duinar bore Rogond with relative ease. Galador's eyes grew wide and he pursed his lips. He was impressed.

"I will bear Gaelen," he said, lifting her easily. He could feel how broken she was, and he grimaced in sympathy. Every movement would be agony for her. Anger and indignation swelled within him, and he turned to Nelwyn. "Where is Gorgon? I would hope that he has fallen?"

"He has indeed," said Nelwyn. Though that fact brought some comfort, it was not the jubilation she had anticipated.

Fima took in the sight of his two dear friends, Gaelen and Rogond, neither of whom was likely to see another sunrise if things did not improve. So…Gorgon was dead. "Well, at least that's something," he muttered, though as with Nelwyn it brought him little comfort.

The pain of Hallagond's shattered leg and his grief over the loss of Azori had compelled Estle to give him a sleeping-draught, for he was in desperate need of peace so that he could recover some of his strength. She sat by his side, lost in grief herself, and sorrowed for him. Like Hallagond, she had wondered at Azori's sacrifice, as he had never really shown such tendencies in the past. Perhaps in the heat of battle his true nature had surfaced and courage had prevailed over self-interest. Azok, who was (probably) Azori's brother, had died with valor, but he had been given no real choice. Azori had chosen death to save Hallagond. There was a difference.

Now Hallagond wandered in the realm of dreams. He had not gone willingly, for his mind was in turmoil and he feared that his dreams would be unpleasant. His heart reached out into whatever unknown regions it could, seeking answers.

He had failed Azori, and he had failed Magra. He had been taken from the fighting without even the loss of one more enemy, and Azori, who was one of the fiercest fighters on the day, had fallen to save him. Hallagond's honor had been restored in Dûn Arian upon the death of Lokai, yet now he feared he had lost it again. He sent forth a wave of doubt and despair, crying out a single question: *why?*

Against any real expectation, his cry was answered. *Hallagond? Why do you grieve?*

It was Gaelen's voice, clear and compelling as always. Yet, Gaelen was not with him…how could she be? "How is it that you are here?" he asked. "Are you not far away, in Tuathas?"

Never mind that. Answer my question first, as I have asked. Why do you grieve?

"I grieve for my brother, who gave his life in battle," said Hallagond. He was not yet ready to tell Gaelen why Azori had sacrificed his life.

Ah. That is ill news, said Gaelen. *I'm sorry for your loss. How goes the battle? Are you whole? What of Estle, and Wellyn, and Lady Ordath?*

"They are well, and we are victorious," said Hallagond. "But Lord Magra…"

I know of Magra, said Gaelen. *It is a great sorrow. Magra was the last of them.* She paused, deep in reverent regret, before turning her attention back to Hallagond. *There is more to this than the death of*

Azori. Now, tell me what troubles your heart, and do not tarry, as I do not know how much time has been given me.

"Are you…are you dead, Gaelen?" asked Hallagond. "Is that how you have come to me?"

What troubles your heart? she asked again, and Hallagond knew his question would remain unanswered. She listened patiently while he described Azori's heroic action in his behalf. Then he was silent.

Did you fight well, to the limit of your ability?

"Yes…I certainly gave it my best effort," said Hallagond.

And was it your intention to break your leg, so that you could not avoid being trampled?

"Of course not!"

Would you have given your own life to save Azori, had he been lying helpless before the onslaught of an enemy?

"I believe I would have. But I was not given the chance. I was not tested."

You know you would have. I know it, too. Rest well, for you need not fear the loss of your honor. Rest and rejoice that Azori found his own honor in the end. You helped him do that.

Hallagond was weeping now, for he knew Gaelen was right. Estle had been listening with fascination to his words, for he had actually spoken them aloud as he lay beside her. Now she tried to rouse him, because he wept.

"Are you dead, Gaelen?" he asked again.

I do not believe so, yet I am not exactly alive…I do not know what my fate will be.

"You must not forsake Rogond! You must fight to stay with him, to the limit of your strength."

I will stay if I can, for I would not leave Rogond. It will be my great pleasure to inform him that his valiant brother still lives, if Aontar allows it. Farewell, Hallagond the un-forsaken, and take heart. Then she was gone, and Hallagond heard the voice of Estle. When he came to himself, he had much to tell her.

The Cold Mountain was rapidly becoming the Mountain of Intolerable Heat. The Company wound back through the dark corridors, ascending toward the doorway and the world outside. Had they lingered even a short while, they would have been lost in the waves of heat and acrid vapor that rolled forth from below. As it was, they could barely see for the tears flowing from their irritated eyes. Even Galador was coughing.

Lord Kotos was certainly making matters difficult, as his rage upon being entrapped in the mountain's heart had caused disturbances that would be felt as far away as the ruins of Tallasiar and the abandoned eastern city of Tallanor.

The walls and ceilings of Cold Mountain were cracking in response to the tremors that shook them, and sometimes it was difficult for the Company to stay on their feet.

"Hold together, my petulant beauty," whispered Duinar as he paused and shifted Rogond to his opposite shoulder.

Suddenly, Fima looked back the way they had come, and when he turned back toward his friends there was panic in his eyes. "*Get down!*" he shouted, flattening himself upon the stone as a huge jet of steam shot from the darkness, passing over their prone bodies for several seconds before dying back. Everyone was fortunate to be wearing heavy clothing, yet there was some exposed skin, which was now red and blistered.

"Fine. Now I've been parboiled," Fima grumbled as he struggled to his feet again. He hurried to catch up with Duinar. "That seemed to be ordinary steam," he said. "Where would water come from to make steam in this place?"

"From melting ice, I'm afraid," said Duinar. "Yet the news is not all bad, for the steam has cleansed the air, and now I am feeling a cold draught from outside."

"There is the reason," cried Nelwyn, who scouted ahead. "The doorway is there!" She pointed to a blessed patch of greyish light. It was the dim light of early morning, and snow was still falling. Yet there was a sound that Nelwyn had not heard upon entering the mountain, and that was the sound of rushing water. "More melting ice, I expect," she said, turning to Galador.

"Who cares?" gasped Fima, whose breath had given out long ago and who could barely keep up with her. "Just get me out of this mountain, and then I can die happy." When they emerged, the landscape had changed. Much of the snow and ice had already faded from the lower elevations, though snow still fell from the sky. The inner heat of the mountain and the release of Duinar had worked together to free Mount Ëthas from its cold shell.

Duinar set his burden down so that he could take in his surroundings. He had not viewed the outside world in five hundred years. To the surprise and relief of his friends, Rogond stirred, opening his eyes as he fought to draw a decent breath, gasping and wheezing.

Fima was at his side at once. "You're alive, my friend!" he said. "Easy, now…try to clear your lungs as best you can. Breathe easy, that's it."

Rogond rolled with difficulty onto his side, grasping his shoulder in pain. Fima had staunched the bleeding, but the wound burned and throbbed. Rogond tried to groan, but no sound came forth. His throat, like his eyes and his lungs, had been burned by the poisonous vapor.

The stones rumbled beneath their feet, and Duinar was nearly bowled over. "This is going to be a bad one," he shouted. "Keep alert, and watch for stones falling upon your heads."

This proved to be wise advice, as the mountain shook chunks of stone, earth, and melting ice from itself, and the Company barely avoided some of them.

"We must get away from this mountain," yelled Galador. "The next tremors will finish us! Let's make our way down, back the way we came. At least we know there is a path there." He held Gaelen's body close to his breast to avoid jarring her as best he could, and started back down the path with his friends not far behind. Rogond could not yet stand—in fact, he could not even sit on his own—but hardy Duinar bore him without hesitation. Still, it was slow going.

Nelwyn, as usual, led the group down the mountain-path, but she called the others to halt, turning her very distressed face back toward them.

"We're trapped! We'll never make it now," she yelled over the din of crashing stones and rushing waters. They had been blocked by a veritable torrent that roared down from the mountain, bringing debris, mud, and ice with it. This path was closed to them.

"Master, what should we do?" asked Fima. Duinar set Rogond down and wrung his hands, trying to think of something. He had run out of wisdom for the moment.

"There is the answer!" cried Galador, whose voice had rarely been so hopeful and jubilant. He pointed across the torrent and the Company beheld four sets of pricked ears and four pairs of dark, intelligent eyes looking back at them.

"*Eros!*" cried Fima, causing Nelwyn to turn and smile at him. Fima never called any of the horses by name. "Umm…I mean… the horses are there!" he said, remembering that calling a horse by name was tantamount to admitting he actually cared for the beasts.

"May the heavens love him for his disobedience," muttered Galador. "Eros! Come on, my brave one, come on and aid your friends. You can do it!"

Eros rose majestically on his hind legs, snorted, and plunged across the raging watercourse. It was a difficult task, but Eros was large and strong, and he managed. Toran was right behind him. Réalta, who was more finely made, was nearly swept away. Faladinn knew better, and stood placidly where he was.

There was no time for happy reunions. The ice-melt worsened with each passing moment. If they waited too long, the horses would have an impossible task in returning, for they would carry riders, and the icy torrent would be too swift and deep.

"We must secure Gaelen and Rogond, or they will be lost. We won't be able to hold them," said Galador.

Rogond was hoisted aboard Eros, and he grasped the dark mane with feeble hands as Galador lashed him to the horse's neck. Then he instructed Duinar to ride behind. "Eros is the only one stout enough to carry both of you. Now, get on over, Eros. Don't fear…we are right behind you!" He slapped Eros on the hindquarters, sending him across.

Eros grunted and strained with the effort, nearly knocked off his legs, carefully placing each foot to avoid falling, as that would have meant the death of Rogond. He heaved himself up on the opposite bank, which was becoming increasingly steep and treacherous as the racing waters tore into the path.

Nelwyn, Fima, Galador, and Gaelen were left as their chance of escape ticked away. "All right, Toran, now show us what you're made of," said Nelwyn, fairly leaping onto his strong grey back. "Give Gaelen to me," she cried, reaching out to Galador, who placed Gaelen in front of her.

"Here…let me secure her as I did Rogond," said Galador, taking the broken length of rope from Réalta's head-collar and lashing it quickly around Toran's neck. "Réalta can only bear me. He barely made it across without a rider. Toran must carry Fima, too."

"*What*?" Fima cried. "Me, ride on that beast's hindquarters? He'll pitch me off for certain."

"No…he won't," said a voice they had thought never to hear again. Gaelen's eyes were closed, but it was she who had spoken.

"If Gaelen has such faith in him, can you not, Fima?" asked Nelwyn, who was on the edge of tears.

Fima, who had no answer for that, allowed Galador to set him behind Nelwyn. "If I can just make it across, I can die happy," he muttered.

Toran leaped into the foam, bracing his strong legs against the ever-increasing force of the waters, squealing at the impact of stray limbs and debris, using every ounce of power he possessed. Gaelen smiled through her pain, managing to stroke his neck with her nerveless right hand. Toran's ears were flattened, his nostrils wrinkled against the water, his head lowered as he strained and lunged, every muscle and sinew in his fine-sculptured form standing forth. At last he gathered himself for a mighty leap, and scrambled onto the bank with Eros.

The roar of the water had muffled the cries of alarm from Nelwyn, Galador, and Fima as the final effort broke the dwarf's hold and he slid off the back of Toran's rump. Yet now, as the great horse emerged, Fima clung with grim tenacity to his long tail. Though waterlogged and nearly frightened to death, he was unhurt.

Gaelen had fallen again into darkness, reflecting that her beloved Finan would not have been able to do what Toran had just done. Sometimes, bigger was better.

"Come on, Galador!" Nelwyn screamed as Réalta plunged into the freezing waters. Réalta was not about to fall, not when he carried the mighty Galador! Nelwyn looked up the mountainside, and her heart nearly stopped. "Galador! Hurry as fast as you can! Réalta, pull for your life!"

The flood had broken free above them, and they had perhaps ten seconds to get out of the way. "Come on, Fima," called Nelwyn, struggling to pull Fima up behind her again. Réalta grunted with effort and gained the bank just in time to run the race of his life, charging down the path out of the way, following Toran as the flood claimed the ground on which they had all been standing.

They had escaped for the moment, but the mountains would not relent. Plumes of vapor and black ash shot from the summits of several surrounding peaks, as well as from Mount Ëthas, as another tremor seemed to shake the world loose. Nelwyn saw trees falling and sagging above and below her, and she was terrified. The terrible, hot magma would come next.

"We'll never make it," muttered Fima from behind her. The horses milled about and screamed in terror.

"Oh, for heaven's sake," growled Duinar, leaping off of Eros' back. He flared with blue-white light, and there was fury in his face as he strode across the rocks to climb onto a very large stone. He had taken more than his fill of Lord Kotos. He stood facing the mountain, raised both his arms toward it, and uttered a single, deafening word.

"*ENOUGH!*"

The sound of Duinar's voice was so full of power and authority that everyone who heard it closed their eyes and winced. No one dared move for a moment. At last, Galador opened one eye. Could it be that the tremors were quieting down? They were, in fact! No more would be heard from the mountains other than a few distant rumbles and quakes. Galador looked over at Duinar, who was staring at his own hands in wonder, as if he did not believe he had succeeded. He felt Galador's gaze upon him and turned toward the Company with an expression of delight.

"Ha! That should do it," he said. Then he looked away. Galador knew that he was thinking of the cataclysm of 6740. Duinar had not borne witness to the ultimate destruction of his realm, as he had been frozen deep underground during his vain attempt to prevent it. Although some in the Company had expressed an interest in exploring

Tallasiar, Galador was now glad that they had not, as the telling of that tale would have broken Duinar's heart.

He approached Duinar and spoke to him, for there was a question that he would ask.

"Master…forgive my asking such an indelicate question, but how is it that you quelled this uprising of the fire-mountains, yet you could not prevail when you tried…when you tried to save your people?"

Duinar's eyes remained downcast for a moment and he drew a long, deep sigh. "Perhaps it is because this upheaval was due in part to the influence of a dark Asarla, and *that* I could deal with. I always suspected that I held more power than Kotos, though it is not written in the books of lore.

"Well, we can certainly remedy that," said Fima, who had overheard.

"As to the first tragedy, I failed to realize that neither man nor Elf nor Asarla can match the raw power of nature. The land we are standing on is believed to have been made during just such an upheaval, way back during the Time of Mystery. Tuathas and her beautiful mountains would not be here at all if not for such violent birth. The forces of nature do not care what cities have been built, or what people thrive, or what man believes he rules what lands. And I should have known better…I did prevent Mount Ëthas from erupting, but I failed to account for her sisters. One of them did most of the damage, as it appears."

He turned to Fima and Galador, and they were pleased to see that his good humor had returned. "One thing is certain," he said. "These experiences have just about cured me of my unnatural fascination with fire-mountains."

"They have certainly cured me of whatever small interest I might *ever* have had in them," said Nelwyn. "We have delayed long enough. We must tend to our friends and take them from this terrible place. Winter is coming, and we must make it to the Greatwood Realm before the weather sets in."

"Yes, we must do those things," said Duinar. "First allow me to see to Gaelen and Rogond. Gaelen in particular will not live long if she is pressed too hard by the journey. A little more time at rest won't hurt."

Gaelen was laid upon the ground before Duinar, and he ministered to her as best he could. "The funny thing about Elves," he said, "is that, although they can heal from nearly anything, they have the tendency to be subjected to the most shocking damage. These injuries would have killed a man thrice her size." He moved his hands over her body and limbs, speaking incantations and bathing her with light. It seemed that her pain was eased, and she opened her eyes.

"You…you are Duinar!" she whispered, managing a faint smile. "Welcome back." Then she closed her eyes and rested.

Fima was most impressed. "I had no idea you had such healing powers," he said. "It would seem that they rival those of Lady Ordath."

"I am the only Asarla who chose to live among mortals," said Duinar. "Which of us would have greater need of healing skills than I?" Then he shook his head. "The power I possess is not so much in healing, but in soothing and comforting. Sometimes, if you can just quiet a damaged body by comforting it, it will heal on its own."

Duinar moved next to Rogond, placing both hands on his broad chest, flooding his ravaged lungs with light. "This will take time, my friend," he said. "Yet you will regain your strength as your breathing improves. Your shoulder will heal, but you must not be taxed until you are stronger." He looked into Rogond's eyes and smiled. "You are Tuathan?"

Rogond nodded. "I am the son of Diomar, of the line of Allydar. My mother was Rosalin, who traced back to Syrus, the mariner," he said in a croaking voice. Duinar was delighted.

Fima told Duinar of the realms of Dûn Bennas and Dûn Arian. "Your people did not forget their enlightenment, Master," he said. "Those cities were built on learning, and the people thrive in the light of knowledge. The legacy of your teachings lives on in them."

Nelwyn had wrapped Gaelen in Brinneal's warm cloak, and was now tending the horses. They were unhurt, though they had lost some of their condition due to the very austere food supply in the region, and had suffered quite a few cuts and tears from the thorn-trees.

"However did you survive, my friends?" Nelwyn wondered, stroking Eros' shaggy neck. As if in answer, Faladinn approached one of the scraggly bramble-shrubs, worked his very adroit upper lip in between the sharp thorns, and delicately pulled the leathery leaves off one by one. They were tough, but satisfying. It was the resourceful Faladinn who had demonstrated this skill for the others. Without him, they would have starved.

It was slow going back through the bramble-forest, and without Gaelen to catch squirrel-rats it was nothing but roots and shriveled berries to eat. Yet they still had a path to follow, and Nelwyn had a little of her dragon-fire left, so they were warm, at least.

Rogond held Gaelen by the fire, both covered by the blue-grey cloak, as Duinar and Fima examined Gaelen's fire-cloak in sorrow. It had tarnished in the poisonous fumes of the mountain, and it was unlikely ever to shine with the same brilliance.

"It doesn't matter," said Nelwyn. "I do not suppose we shall need it again."

By the time they approached the encampment of the Elves of the Greatwood and Tal-sithian, Rogond's lot had improved enough to ride with Fima unassisted. Gaelen still could not ride, but Duinar carried her, striding along beside Toran, who worried about her and could not resist occasionally reaching aside to nuzzle her.

"You're quite the devoted gentleman, aren't you?" said Duinar, as he resumed the tale he had been telling Gaelen.

"Why do you tell your tales to a sleeping Elf?" asked Fima. "Why not tell the wide-awake Dwarvish lore-master instead?"

Duinar and Galador both laughed at him. "Fima, how long have you lived among Elves?" said Galador. "You should know that we may appear to be sleeping, but we hear every word you say."

"You…you *do*?" said Fima, with an expression of abject horror. Then he turned back to Nelwyn and winked.

"And have you been saying things near to sleeping Elves that should not be heard?" asked Duinar with a low chuckle.

"Look!" cried Nelwyn. "There is the encampment! And there… there is Gryffa!" She urged Toran forward and rode toward the sight of distant campfires.

The Company had left the bramble-forest behind, and soon they were surrounded by their friends and allies. Galador asked about the possibility of attack by Wrothgar's Ulcas.

"What Ulcas? Our Woodland cousins haven't caught a whiff of them in over a fortnight," said the Elves with a smile. "We expected they had given up waiting, and would not risk attacking now that there are so many of us. They have no courage in them. Besides, if you had absolutely no hair at all, would you wish to wait around through the onset of a northern winter?"

The Elves told the tale of the clandestine activities of one Eros, who had managed to free all the horses but Gryffa on one dark and rainy night. "A good thing, too," they said, "for not only did they survive, but they found you and aided you. In this case, we're glad that our attempts at detaining them were not successful."

The Elves of the Greatwood were very distressed to learn of the deaths of Arlan and Fynn, and of the loss of Turantil. Though Talrodin's line had ended, it would not be forgotten.

Everyone bowed in reverence to Duinar, who had been thought lost. A great treasure had been restored to the World that Is. Duinar, who was fundamentally a humble soul, accepted their admiration gracefully.

"My thanks for your heartfelt appreciation, but I expect we had best be moving on southward now," he said. "The cold and snows of winter are beyond my influence. For that, you would need my sisters!"

The point was taken, and the Elves made their way back toward the Woodland, eventually emerging from the dark and depressing lands near the Monadh-ainnas to the grasslands, and then back into the forest. By the time they arrived there, winter was well underway.

Ri-Aruin was astonished at the arrival of Duinar. It was the first time an Asarla had set foot in his kingdom, so far as he was aware. He bowed and offered his crown to his impressive guest, but Duinar bade him rise. "This realm is yours, O Woodland King, even as it has always been. And although it has not seen the enlightenment of the Asari, still it is enlightened. While I am here, I am at your command."

All were made welcome. Gaelen and Rogond were taken to a warm chamber where they could rest in comfort, and they healed quickly. Gaelen spent much time in reflection, for she knew that she did not need to guard her thoughts from anyone—not ever again.

Fima had come to her side on one cold, rainy afternoon and had placed the mirror in her hand. "When the Creature died, it went dark," he said. "I felt it, even through my jerkin. It can do no harm now."

Gaelen had nodded, her eyes filled with tears. Gorgon's death had affected her in ways she did not yet understand. Though she had felt joy and freedom as his dark spirit faded, she also felt, for the moment, as though a part of her had faded with him. She had grown accustomed to his presence, and she felt an inexplicable sense of loss. Gaelen's tears, though shed more in relief than from grief, were the only tears to be shed in Gorgon's memory.

Nelwyn and Galador spent nearly half the winter working with their comrades to construct a barrier to the wretched Úlfar, for in winter they migrated back downstream to the unnaturally warm sludge-fens surrounding Tûr Dorcha. The Elves made a great dam of stones, over which the waters of the Brunner Ia could flow without restriction, but the horrid Úlfar, who were not sufficiently strong swimmers, would not be able to scale it from below. Soon the waters were clean again.

By the time Nelwyn had finished with the dam, Gaelen had emerged back into the forest, where she took up her old habit of wandering for days. But this time Rogond wandered with her. At first she was at a loss, for since her enemy had been vanquished she had lost the purpose that had compelled her for the past several years. Yet there were always new challenges to be met, and Gaelen would soon find them.

Fima and Duinar were like old friends already. Fima explored the admittedly limited library of the Greatwood, finding some things of interest. He spent endless hours in debate and conversation with Duinar, for each had much to learn from the other. The winter passed quickly, and the spirits of the Company were high.

But then the arrival of spring brought with it some difficult decisions. Not everyone wanted to spend the rest of their lives in the Greatwood, yet there were some who would not leave it.

Fima wanted to return to Mountain-home, as did Rogond, for his brother was there. Duinar would go with them, for he would look upon the Lady Ordath again. Then he would decide whether to journey to Dûn Bennas, or to Dûn Arian, and make a permanent home.

Gaelen, of course, would not forsake Rogond. That meant she would leave her dearest friend behind. Nelwyn, who had never cared for long journeys, would not leave the Greatwood. Therefore, Galador's traveling days had ended.

They spent as much time as possible in fellowship as the time of departure drew near. They laughed and played, told tales, and told themselves that there would be no parting, but they knew otherwise, and the sadness they felt could not be denied.

One day, as Gaelen and Nelwyn sat together in the hollow trunk of a tall tree, Nelwyn suddenly blurted out: "You must come to the Greatwood each and every spring, Gaelen, and spend time with Galador and me."

"I cannot promise that," said Gaelen. "I do not know where my path will lead."

"Still, you must try," said Nelwyn. "You must come and see my daughter, for I would have her know her most famous and valiant relative." Gaelen looked at her cousin in wonder. "It's true," said Nelwyn. "If all goes right, Gwynnyth will come after summer's end, during the harvest."

"Then by all means, I shall try to come," said Gaelen. "After all, autumn is my favorite time of year in the Greatwood."

The day of parting came at last. Friends and loved ones had spoken very little to one another in recent days, as though they grieved already. Eros and Toran stood ready with the ever-useful Faladinn, as Galador and Nelwyn embraced Fima, Rogond, and Gaelen. There were few words to say that had not been said already. Even Duinar, who had seen much of sadness in his very long life, wept for his friends. He was a kind and sympathetic spirit, and their sorrow tore his heart.

Ri-Aruin had wanted to bestow the status of Most Honored Warrior upon Gaelen for seeing to the death of Gorgon, but she had declined. "He took his own life, my lord," she said. "In the end, his pride accomplished what I could not." Still, Ri-Aruin insisted upon giving her a token, another beautiful ring of gold and adamant. Gaelen thanked him, thinking to herself that if people did not stop bestowing rings on her, she would no longer be able to conceal herself for all the glittering and flashing of stones and gold.

The King attended the departure, wishing them safe journey. Fima was silent as he waited with the horses…he loved Nelwyn dearly, and his heart was broken.

Galador and Rogond now said their last farewells.

"We have journeyed long and seen much," said Galador. "I will not wish to live forever without hearing news of you. Will you make certain that you return once in a while, so that I may recall your face?" Rogond nodded, as words had failed him. "Take care of the Fire-heart, my friend," said Galador. "I shall miss her."

"One day, I shall send her back to you," said Rogond. Then he turned away, lest tears should come.

Gaelen and Nelwyn embraced long, and their tears were plain to see. Yet they could not remain so forever, and at last they parted, saying no words. Gaelen walked Toran over to a fallen log, and turned back toward Nelwyn with a wry smile. "Ridiculous, huge horse," she said, and swung gracefully aboard.

She turned and left her friends without another word, riding with Rogond and Fima, as Duinar walked beside her. Réalta called plaintively from the courtyard, but Eros did not answer him.

They left the Greatwood, and Gaelen's old life, behind them. Yet as they walked, and the time and miles passed, their silence gave way at last. They had not seen the last of Galador and Nelwyn. Fima reflected on the vast distances they had traveled and the many realms they had seen.

"If these experiences have taught me anything at all, it is that the world is a whole lot bigger than I ever knew it was. I suspect there are vast lands and fascinating people that even we have not yet discovered."

"Yes," said Rogond. "I believe that. Still, from what I have seen, the world is small."

Lady Ordath looked out over the south marches of Mountain-home at the ruined forest, wondering at the slight tingling in her fingertips as the west wind stirred her long, dark hair. She was not concerned for the forest, as it would renew itself, but there was something else that had aroused her this morning. The horn-calls from the watchers to the west announced the arrival of a lone traveler, and she hurried to see who might approach. Yet when she arrived on the west march, the sentinels were simply staring out in puzzlement.

Ordath trained her sharp eyes on the distant walker, and her face filled with joy at what she beheld. For there, striding toward the gates of Mountain-home with power and purpose, his grey cloak unfurled behind him, was Shandor, the Asarla of Mountain-home. His cold blue eyes beheld Ordath and filled with warmth and light, as a rare smile played across his beautiful, stern face. He was home at last, and he knew that he was loved.

Epilogue

Gorgon Elfhunter stood upon the Shores of Eternity, wondering what his fate would be. He was not a little afraid, for he had never known belonging or acceptance ever in his life. Though his mother was Elven, he knew that the realm of Elysia was closed to him. No ships came to bear him, and no voices called to him. Would he stand forever, alone and wondering?

The waters of the dark lake grew turbulent, roiling and swirling until they threatened to rise up and engulf Gorgon, who took a step backward. Yet they did not escape their banks, rising instead into the air and parting as a dark curtain drawn back from a vast stage.

Now Gorgon beheld a wondrous sight as two realms were shown to him. On his one hand was Darkness, on the other was Light. He knew then that he was being shown the Fate of Men, for although his mother was an Elf, he was a half-blood Ulca, and Ulcas claimed men as their ancestors. An unknown voice was heard within his mind. "*Choose*" was all it said.

Gorgon looked into the Light, and for once it did not pain him. This was the light of love, the Light of Aontar. Gorgon had always cursed the Light, and he knew that, to choose it, he would need to lay aside his pride and forsake his power. He could not enter the Light without recognizing that all his life had been lived in error, and that love was the real power. He could not enter the Light without renouncing the darkness of his life. Yet the soft glow invited him, and he knew that, against all he had been taught, he would be welcome.

He turned back toward the comforting, familiar Darkness. It sought to persuade him, promising both power and freedom. He would be the Mighty Elfhunter once again. He could exercise his pride to the limit; there was no need for humility. The enemies of Light would welcome him also. They would set him high in favor among them. It seemed that, for the first time in his life, he truly had a choice.

Gorgon looked from the Darkness to the Light, and then back to the Darkness. What had the light of love ever done for him? Could he surrender his pride and humble himself? Was love a choice that he could make? The Darkness had always comforted him, yet he had seen the stars, and they had filled him with wonder.

Choose.

Gorgon considered for only a moment longer, and then he made his choice.

Glossary of Names with aid to pronunciation

Aeglainor (EYE-glay-nor): Elves name for the Fell-ruin, it means "place of grief."

Agean calad (AH-gay-ahn CAH-lad): The large inlet between the lands of Tuathas and the mainland. Name means "deep harbor."

Aincor (INE-cor): Elf of the Èolar, a great scholar and warrior, known as the Fire-heart. He was among the most skilled and passionate of his people, but he was prideful and his reckless acts bore terrible consequences. It is unflattering to be compared with him in terms of willfulness. He produced two sons, Asgar and Dardis. Name means "fire-heart." (ain-fire, cor-heart)

Ainya: The substance from which dragons generate flame; it will burn through nearly anything. It is also known as dread-fire, swift-fire, or dragon-fire.

Airan (EYE-rahn): Lord Airan, Elf of the Eádram that founded the realm of Tal-sithian with Lady Arialde. From airith (noble).

Aiyah! (EYE-yah): Elvish expression, translated as "Attend me!" It is also an expression of alarm (Pay attention! Look to yourselves!).

Al-amand (AL-amand): Name taken by Hallagond for use in the southlands, it means "the forsaken one."

Alduinar (AL-dwee-nar): Ruler of Tuathas at the time of the Third Uprising. He successfully repelled Kotos, and was a good friend and ally of the High King. His name means "worthy guide."

Allydar (AL-lee-dar): Noted ancestor of Rogond's father, Diomar. Allydar was among the most reknowned of Tuathan swordsmen.

Alterra (Al-TAIR-ra): The World That Is; the Realm in which these tales take place. From terra (earth) and alta (being).

Amandir (AH-mahn-deer): Elf of Tal-Sithian, spouse of Brinneal. His name means "artful one." From aman (artful).

Amari (Ah-MAR-ee): Collective name for the Amar Tuath and the Amar Dess.

Amar Dess (AH-mar DESS): The stream that flows into the Artan from the south of Monadh-talam. Name means "south-channel." Known also as the Nachtan.

Amar Tuath (AH-mar TOO-ath): The wild stream that flows into the Artan from the north of Monadh-talam. Name means "north channel."

Ambros (AHM-bros): Great River of Western Alterra, it is formed by the Eros and the Brocca in the north. From ambra (great) and ros (river).

Anori-men (Ah-NORI-men): Men who dwell in the eastern regions of Alterra. They are fierce fighters, have golden skin and dark brown eyes, and are slight of build. From anoir (east).

Aontar (Ay-ON-tar): The One Lord of All; the Creator.
Arad (Ah-RAHD): Elf of Eádros, brother of Miradyth.

Araman (AR-ah-Mahn): False name given El-morah by Lord Kotos.

Arlan (AR-lan): Elf of the Greatwood, elder son of Talrodin.

Arialde (Ah-ree-AL-deh): Lady Arialde, the Asarla who founded Tal-sithian with Lord Airan. She is the only female Asarla, and is the keeper of the Stone of Léir. From arialdas (beautiful).

Aridani (Ah-ree-DAHN-ee), sing. Aridan (AH-ree-dahn): Men. Name means "those that fade." From aridas (fading).

Arrah!: Elvish expression of disgust, as when encountering something foul or distasteful.

Artan (AR-tan): River formed by the two streams that flow from Monadh-talam. From artan (stone).

Artemys (AR-teh-miss): Elf of Tal-sithian, master tactician sent to defend Mountain-home. Her name means "maiden of stone."

Aruinnas (Ar-WEE-nas): The Greatwood Forest. From aruinnas (forest).

Aryiah (Ah-RYE-eeyah): Dark-skinned, blind Seer of Dûn Arian.

Asari (Ah-sah-REE) sing. **Asarla**: Immortal beings endowed with great knowledge, sent to enlighten the Children of Aontar. They were generally of the Light, but could be turned. Name means "teacher."

Astor (AS-tor): Lore-master and chief of the Library of Dûn Bennas. His name means "of great worth."

Avinashi (ah-vee-NAH-shee): Ravani name for Elves, it means "immortal ones." (Sing. fem. avinasha, sing. masc. avinashan).

Azok (AH-zok): Second-in-command and brother of Azori, half-brother of Estle.

Azori (ah-ZOR-ree): Leader of Hallagond's band of thieves, half-brother of Estle.

Ballali (bah-lah-LEE): Repressive cult of the Sandstone oasis. The Ballali are dangerous to anyone who disagrees with their very restrictive set of beliefs.

Baelta (Bah-EL-tah): Asarla, friend of Kotos, whose dark influence turned him into the unwitting servant of Wrothgar. Baelta so regretted the destruction caused by his deeds that he took his own life, the only Asarla ever to do so. His name means "bright light."

Belegund (BEH-le-gund): Northman, Ranger, and friend of Rogond. His name means "noble warrior." From bele- (noble) and gunnar (warrior).

Beori (Bay-OR-ri): Dwarf of the Northern Mountains; eldest son of Belko.

Bint Raed (Bint Rah-YED): Masterful weaver-woman, originally a citizen of Dûn Arian. Her name means "daughter of Raenien."

Bödvari, sing. Bödvar (BODE-var): Dreadful servants of Wrothgar, they are the offspring of Dark Asari. They are as black demons that kill their enemies with fire after first paralyzing them with fear. They are terrible enemies in battle. From bödvar (demon).

Brinneal (BRIN-nee-al): Golden-haired Elf of the Èolar, she moved to Tal-sithian after the fall of Tal-elathas. She is the mother of Gorgon Elfhunter and the spouse of Amandir. Name means "beautiful young maid."

Brocca: The river in the north that, along with the Eros, gives rise to the Ambros. It is as wild and turbulent as the Eros is smooth and gentle. From broca (restive).

Brunner Aigred (BROO-nair AYE-gred): The cold-spring that flows from the Monadh-hin into the Linnefionn. From aigred (cold, High-elven dialect) and brunner (spring).

Brunner Ia (BROO-nair EE-ya): The cold-spring that flows through the Greatwood, eventually entering the Darkmere. From ia (cold, Wood-elven dialect) and brunner (spring).

Carmyn: Masterful map-maker of Dûn Arian, friend of Fima. Carmyn has a near-perfect memory.

Castalan (CAS-tah-LAHN): Coastal city near the mouth of the Ambros, it is known as a center of trade from the south. It is the home of Harsha, the wine-merchant.

Chupa-jul (CHOO-pa-JUL): Oasis settlement, home of Estle and the House of El-morah. The name means "hidden water."

Collyn: Spokesman of the Currgas of Tal-sithian.

Cós-domhain (Coss-Dome-Ha-EEN): Great Dwarf-realm, known as the Realm of Caverns. Ruled by Lord Grundin. From cós (cavern) and domhain (domain).

Cronar: Captain of the Guard in Dûn Bennas.

Cuimir (COO-ee-MEER): Asarla who founded Eádros, the Realm of Light, lost during the War of Betrayal. Name means "comely, handsome." From cuimas (handsome).

Cúinar (COO-ee-nar): Sylvan Elves, Wood-elves. Considered to be of lesser stature than High-elves, they did not have the benefit of Asari influence. They inhabit and defend the Forest Realm of Greatwood. Examples are Gaelen and Nelwyn. From cúin (silent).

Cúingael (COO-in-gale): Greatwood Elf, friend of Gaelen and Nelwyn. She once tried to set a snare for Wellyn, and ensnared Ri-Aruin instead. Her name means "silent valor."

Currgas (KOOR-gahs): Small, otter-like river people of western Alterra. They are secretive, but friendly and gentle. They prefer to live in the southern Dominglas River, but have recently been driven into the Lake-realm.

Dardis (DAR-dees): The second son of Aincor, a highly talented and inventive artisan and lover of learning. Unlike his father, Dardis was of gentle temperament and was revered especially by the dwarves. He was apprenticed to an Asarla named Léiras (the far-sighted), who taught him of the making of things that could be endowed with magical properties. It was Dardis who made the mirror given to Gorgon Elfhunter; he also created the Stone of Léir and the Amulet of Kotos. He was killed on the eve of the Second Uprising.

Darkmere: The name given to the Great Forest Realm (Greatwood) when Wrothgar's power began to grow there. The Elves refer only to the southern part of the Forest as the Darkmere, but others make no such distinction. See also Dominglas Forest.

Dessa (DESS-sa): River that marks the southern boundary of King Hearndin's influence.

D'hanar (Dah-NAHR): The ruin of Tal-elathas. It is now an evil place inhabited only by dark beings. The name is dwarvish for "land of darkness."

Diomar (DYOH-mar): Man of the Tuathar, sire of Rogond. His name means "the proud," from diomas (proud).

Dominglas Forest (DOME-een-glas): The vast woodland occupying approximately one-third of the northern lands of Alterra. In the north dwell the Sylvan Elves, and in the south Wrothgar has made his new, Dark Tower. From domhain (domain) and glas (deep green). See also Greatwood, Darkmere, Aruinnas.

Doniol (DON-ee-ol): Lord of Eádros during the War of Betrayal. His name means "he who possesses many gifts."

Drach: Night-flying northern dragon of the Fell-ruin. Night fliers are kept belowground during daylight, emerging only at night. They fly in near-total silence and are very difficult to see, as they are a dull black. They resemble enormous bats. Drach has a twin sibling named Garthor.

Dromadan (pl. Dromadin): Desert-dwelling beasts used by the Ravani-folk, often in place of horses. They are a type of camelid.

Duinar (DOO-ee-nar): Asarla who founded the northern realm of Tuathas. He appeared to be very old, with a long, snow-white beard and a lined, weathered face. He was thought slain during the cataclysmic rising of the Fire-mountain that destroyed Tuathas and all lands near it. Name means "guide."

Dûn Bennas (Doon-ben-NAS): City of Men founded by the Tuathar, located in the southern tip of the Monadh-ailan. Name means "white fortress." From dûn (fortress) and bennas (white).

Dûn Arian (Doon-ah-ree-AHN): Largely unknown City of Men founded by the renowned scholar Salasin, located in the far southern lands. Also known as The Citadel. Name means "fortress of silver." From dûn (fortress) and ariant (silver).

Eádram (Ay-AH-drahm): High-elves, Elves of the Light. Their realm was called Eádros. Examples are Galador and Lord Airan of Tal-ailean. From eádra (light).

Eádri (Ay-AH-dree): The Evening Star.

Eádros (Ay-AH-dross): Elven-realm, greatest of the Eádram. It was lost in the War of Betrayal, destroyed by the Dwarves of Rûmm.

Elàni (El-LAN-ee): Elves.

Elathanar (EL-ah-tha-NAR): Elvish name for Dûn Arian, it means "place of wisdom."

El-morah (El-MOR-rah): Kindly host of the kaffa-house in the Chupa-jul oasis, he and his family are friends of the Company.

Elraen (EL-ray-en): Greatwood Elf, lost and taken to Wrothgar. The name means "star-elf," from elàn (elf) and réalta (star).

Elysia (Eh-LEE-see-ah): Eternal Elven-home that has been provided to house the spirits of the Elàni after death. It is a paradise separate from the afterlife of Men. From elàn (elf).

Èolar (AY-oh-lahr): High-elves who achieved the highest level of learning and skill, but were deceived by Wrothgar and Kotos the Asarla. They were mostly lost during the second uprising. Examples are Aincor, Dardis, Magra, and Ri-Elathan. From Èolas (knowing).

Eros (EH-rohs): Sturdy, intelligent dun horse of Rogond. Also a smooth-flowing, gentle river that gives rise to the Ambros in the north. From eran (soft, easy).

Eryn (AIR-in): Daughter of Brinneal and Amandir, and half-sister to Gorgon Elfhunter.

Estle (ES-tle): Hard-bitten but endearing half-sister of Azori and Azok, the bandit brothers, Estle is forced to join the Company. Her mother was a citizen of Dûn Arian. She is beloved of Hallagond.

Falad capell (FAH-lahd ka-PELL): Horse pastures of Tal-sithian; from falad (pasture) and capella (horse).

Faladinn: Small brown Kazhi-horse given to the Company. His name means "hill-pony."

Farahin (FA-ra-heen): Given name of Ri-Elathan. Name means "welcome rain," from farath (welcome) and hin (rain).

Farath-talam! (Fa-RATH TAH-lahm): Elvish welcome, it means "you are welcome among us," or "welcome to our realm."

Farin (FAH-rin): Dwarf of Cós-domhain, eminent craftsman, and maker of Rogond's ring. Farin is also an accomplished battle-commander.

Fima (FEE-ma): Dwarvish Lore-master, originally of Cós-domhain and now serving Lady Ordath in Monadh-talam, he is a good friend of Rogond.

Finan (Fih-NAHN): Doughty bay horse, rescued by Gaelen, he becomes her favorite mount. His name means "the fair."

Fiona (Fee-YO-na): Elvish name for the constellation Orion, it is named after Fiona, the Huntress.

Fior (FYOR): The Dwarves" name for Aontar. Name means "The Maker."

Fómor (FOE-mor): Southern coastal city, ruled by the Corsairs. It is not a place for either the faint-hearted or those of upstanding character.

Fynn: Elf of the Greatwood, younger son of Talrodin.

Gaelen (GEH-lehn): Sylvan Elf of the Greatwood, daughter of Tarfion and Gloranel, cousin of Nelwyn. Name means "daughter of valor." From gael- (valor, feminine).

Galador (GAL-ah-dore): High-elf, formerly of Eádros, beloved of Gwynnyth and later of Nelwyn. Friend of Rogond. From gal- (valor, masculine).

Garthor: Night-flying northern dragon of the Fell-ruin. Night fliers are kept belowground during daylight, emerging only at night. They fly in near-total silence and are very difficult to see, as they are a dull black. They resemble enormous bats. Garthor's twin is named Drach.

Gelmyr (GEL-meer): Èolarin Warrior-elf of Monadh-talam, friend of Magra, slain by Gorgon. From gal- (valor, masculine) and mirys (graceful).

Gin-gin (jin-jin): Beloved mate of Collyn of the Currgas.

Gorgon (GORE-gun): Dark and mighty perversion brought into being by Wrothgar, he is also known as the Elfhunter. Name means "one who is dark," from gor- (dark).

Gryffa (GRIF-fa): Chestnut horse ridden by Nelwyn, his name means "the red."

Grundin (GROON-din): Dwarf-lord, ruler of Cós-domhain. Grundin was very wise and reasonably open-minded, and he could trace his lineage back directly to the Five Founders. Name means "solid-as-stone."

Gwaryn (GWAR-in): Son of Brinneal and Amandir, and half-brother of Gorgon Elfhunter.

Gwynnyth (GWIN-nith): Beloved mortal woman, lost love of Galador. Her name means "blissful."

Gwyr Farsing (Gweer FAR-sing): From gwyr (grass) and farsa (wide); wide grasslands to the west of the Ambros, also known as Lón Ailan, from lón (marsh-meadow) and ailan (green).

Haifa (HYE-fah): Unsavory tavern-keeper of the Chupa oasis.

Haji (HAH-zhee): Sturdy roan horse of Carmyn, the map-maker.

Halladin (HAL-la-deen): High-elf held captive by Wrothgar, charged with the task of educating Gorgon Elfhunter and later slain by him. Also referred to as "The Old One."

Hallagond (HAL-la-gond): Older brother of Rogond. His name means "tall stone" from halla (tall) and gondas (stone).

Halrodin (HAL-roe-din): Hunter-scout of the Greatwood, friend of Gaelen, slain by Gorgon. His name means basically "tall-tree," from halla (tall) and rodo (trunk of a tree).

Hamir (Ha-MEER): Merchant of the Ravi-shan, friend to the Company. He is the head of a large family.

Hari (HA-ree): Horse-merchant of the Sandstone settlement.

Harsha: Wine-vendor of Castalan, friend to the Company, slayer of Asaad.

Hattaras (HAH-ter-rahs): Sutherling, a member of Azori's band of outlaws.

Hearndin (HERN-deen): Present King of Dûn Bennas.

Iolar (Yo-LAHR): Also called Monadh-iolar. Two tall peaks comprising the Iolari Pass, the best way across the Monadh-hin in the region of the Linnefion. Name means "eagle."

Iomar (Yo-MAR): Elf of the Eolar, elder son and heir of Ri-Aldamar, elder brother of Farahin (Ri-Elathan). Iomar was in line to succeed Ri-Aldamar as High King, but he was slain during the Second Uprising. His name means "eagle."

Ivar (EE-var): Dwarf-lord of the City of Rumm during the War of Betrayal.

Kaffa (KAFF-fa): Sutherling drink, akin to coffee, highly prized and very costly when of fine quality.

Karatsu (Ka-RAHT-soo): Tame crow, originally the companion of Ikari the easterner. He follows the Company to Dûn Arian.

Kazhi (Kah-ZHEE): Short, stocky, good-natured people of the eastern stone-desert. They are nomads of a strong horse culture, and are generally hospitable to well-meaning strangers. They are a type of Anori-folk.

Khandor (CON-door): Master of Horse of Dûn Arian. He is at least half Khazhi.

Killim (Kil-LEEM): Door-warden of Lord Salastor.

Kino (KEE-no): Leader of one of the clans of Rûm-harnen, Kino is the sire of Noli.

Koka: Dark, bittersweet material relished by the people of the Ravani. It is most likely akin to chocolate.

Kotos (KO-tos): Dark Asarla, formerly of Tal-elathas, whose desire for power and to learn all things turned him to the service of Wrothgar. He can see into the hearts and minds of those he encounters. Since the Third Battle, Kotos no longer has a physical body and must be carried by a living host. He possesses a magical amulet that allows him to alter his host's appearance. Before the Third Battle, he served Wrothgar as his emissary, turning men to Darkness through deception and promise of reward. His name means "the powerful," but it can also mean "wrathful." He is called "the deceiver" by the Elves, and they name him Trachair, the treacherous.

Krraah: Raven of the Northern Mountains. Krraah was Dwarf-friend. His name translated means "golden-eye."

Kro-aark: Raven of the Fell-ruin, used by Lord Kotos as host to carry him to the Darkmere.

Laban-fuath (la-Ban-foo-ath): The great evil bog surrounding Tur Dorcha in the south of the Darkmere. Name means "terrible mire," from laban (bog) and fuath (terrible).

Léir (Stone of Leh-eer): Great crystal made by Dardis and presently located in Tal-sithian, in which one may behold visions of the future or of the past, and gain enlightenment. It derives much of its power from the grieved and bitter spirit of Shandor, the Asarla, who is entrapped within. Kept by Arialde, it must only be used in her presence.

Léiras (LEH-ee-ras): Asarla, friend and mentor of Dardis. He instructed Dardis in the making of objects that could be endowed with magical properties. Name means "the far-sighted."

Liathwyn (Lee-ATH-win): Elf of the Eolar, mother of Ordath, espoused to Shandor the Asarla, with whom she founded Monadh-talam. Her name means "blue-eyed maiden." She relinquished her spirit after the Second Uprising. She was kin to the High Kings Ri-Aldamar and Ri-Elathan. From liath (blue).

Linnefionn (Lin-neh-fee-YON): The very large, deep, clear lake in the center of which is located the Elven-realm of Tal-sithian. It is generally shrouded in mist and cannot be seen by unwelcome visitors. Name means "clear lake." From linne (lake) and fionn (crystal-clear).

Lokai (LO-kye): Fearsome, ugly dragon of a rare desert variety. Lokai cannot fly, but he has many fearsome weapons, including venom and fire.

Lón Artan (Lohn ARE-tan): Marsh-meadow to the south of the river Artan.

Ludor: Corsair, former consort of Queen Tansy, he betrayed her and took over lordship of Fómor.

Magra (MA-gra): Mighty Èolarin Elf-lord, second-in-command and kinsman of Ri-Elathan. Name means "mighty." Magra was very tall and strong, and has golden hair. He is related to Liathwyn, and hence to Lady Ordath.

Maidrin (MYE-drin): Name given to Gaelen by Gorgon, it means "fox."

Maji (Mah-ZHEE): Minister of Omens in Dûn Arian, she is a woman of great insight and vision.

Marwani (Mar-WAH-nee): Herb that is frequently used in the southlands for its mood-enhancing and mildly intoxicating properties when dried and smoked. It is used as a medicinal herb rather than for recreation in the North, as it is difficult to obtain there.

Mikla (MEEK-lah): Man of the Chupa oasis, known as "the Poisoner." He can provide any poison for a price.

Miradyth (MEER-a dith): Elf of Eadros, beloved of Varni, the dwarf. She admired Varni, but did not love him. Her actions, in part, brought about the War of Betrayal.

Mohani (Mo-HAH-nee): Spouse of El-morah, the proprietor of the kaffa-house in the Chupa oasis. Her name means "beautiful." She is small, comely, and capable.

Monad Ëthas (Monad EE-thas): Fire-mountain that set off the Cataclysm that destroyed Tuathas. Name means "Mountain of Dread."

Monad Fumar (Monad FOO-mar): Great Volcano that destroyed Tuathas, set off by tremors in the Monad Ëthas. Name means "Mountain of Smoke."

Monadh-ailan (Monath-EYE-lan): The Verdant Mountains; gentle, coastal peaks that run along the sea, they are inhabited by folk of many races, notably the Wood-elves of Tal-ailean. Name means "green-mountains." From monad (mountain) and ailan (green).

Monadh-hin (Monad-HEEN): The Great Mountains, largest of all mountain-ranges in Alterra, they are a daunting obstacle for travelers. Snow-covered in winter, they are shrouded by clouds year-round. Name means "peaks of rain," from hin (rain).

Monadh-talam (Monath-TAH-lahm): Elven-realm presided over by the Lady Ordath. Hidden among tall peaks of the Monadh-hin, it is also known as Mountain-home. It is perhaps the greatest remaining Elf-realm and holds great stores of written record. It is a place of healing, study, and enlightenment, and is home to folk of many races. Name means "mountain-realm." From monad (mountain) and tal- (realm).

Mumari (Moo-MAH-ree): Small desert settlement and last outpost on the way to Dûn Arian.

Nachtan (NOCH-tan): Narrow and turbulent cold river that flows to the south and west from Monadh-talam. From nachta- (wild), it is also called Amar Dess.

Nelwyn (NEL-win): Sylvan Elf of the Greatwood, daughter of Turanen and Elwyn, younger cousin of Gaelen. Name means "tree-maiden," from nellas (tree).

Olan Estelar: Apprentice star-master of Dûn Arian. Olan served briefly as host for Lord Kotos.

Ordath (OR-dath): The Lady Ordath, very powerful overseer of Monadh-talam. She is the product of a union between a powerful Asarla (Shandor) and an Elf of the Èolar (Liathwyn). She is a great healer and protector of Monadh-talam. Name means "treasure-of-the-land." From or- (golden, gentle) and dath- (of the land).

Osgar (OSZ-gar): King of the Greatwood and sire of Ri-Aruin, he was known as "the fierce." Somewhat impulsive and reckless, he was slain during the Third Uprising. From osgar (fierce).

Quarinar (KWAH-ree-nahr): People of Tuathas who did not hold sufficient faith in Duinar's ability to quell the Fire-mountain that destroyed it. They were the only people who escaped the Cataclysm. There is some question as to whether their lack of faith lessened Duinar's power, and hence the descendents of the Quarinar carry some guilt with them. From quarinas (to doubt).

Radeef (Ra-DEEF): Very unsavory horse-trader from whom Gaelen acquires Finan; he orchestrates the deception of Rogond for a price, and is later beguiled by Lord Kotos.

Ravi-shan (RAH-vee- SHAHN): The southern desert region of Alterra. Name means "sun-country." It is also known simply as the Ravi or even the Rav. The people are known as Ravani or Ravani-folk. From sutherling Rav (sun) and shan (realm, land, country).

Réalta (ray-AL-ta): Swift and beautiful grey stallion, favored mount of Galador and companion of Eros. His name means "star."

Ri-Aldamar (ree AL-da-mar): Second High King of the Eolar, brother of Liathwyn and sire of Farahin. He was killed by a dragon during the Second Uprising. His name means "most noble ruler." From ri- (ruler), aldos (high, noble) and –amar (great, majestic).

Ri-Aruin (ree-AR-oo-een): Ruler of the Sylvan Elves of the Greatwood Realm. His name means "King of the forest." From ri- (ruler) and aruinnas (forest). (Note: the prefix "ri" was not adopted by the Sylvan Elves until the death of Ri-Elathan. Prior to that time, it was reserved only for the High King.)

Ri-Elathan (ree-EL-a-than): Last High-elven King, Ri-Elathan left no one to succeed him. He was arguably the wisest of all the High Kings, and was both feared and beloved, but he lived a very lonely and arduous life. Beloved of Gaelen Taldin, he was killed during the Third Uprising during pitched battle with Wrothgar himself. His given name was Farahin, and Gaelen calls him "Rain." His name means "King of Wisdom." From ri- (ruler) and elathas (wisdom).

Riffle: Currga of Tal-sithian.

Rogond (ROE-gond): Man of the Tuathar, born during the Plague Year and fostered by the Elves of the Verdant Mountains. Name means "treasure-stone." From oro- (golden, gentle) and gondas (stone).

Rosalin (ROS-a-lin): "River-beauty." Woman descended of Tuathas, mother of Rogond. From ros (river) and –aille (beautiful).

Rûmhar (ROOM-har): Dwarves. Their speech is known as Rûmhul. From Rûm- (to delve).

Rûmm (RHUM): Ancient and Great Dwarf-realm, known as the Deep Delving, which was lost in the War with the Eádram. From Rûm- (to delve).

Rûndiam-har (Roon-dee-ahm-HAR): The Book of Mystery, an accounting of what is known of the time before the First Reckoning begins. From rûndiam (mystery).

Salasin (SAH-lah-seen): Chief Lore-master of Tuathas, he was prominent among the Quarinar. He founded the City of Dûn Arian after the Cataclysm, having been carried there by great waves, bearing much of the library of Tuathas with him.

Salastor (Lord Salastor): Present Lord of Dûn Arian, and her chief lore-master, he presides over the High Council. He is descended directly from Salasin, who founded the City.

Salla-hin: River of the northern Ravi-shan. Name means "mighty rain."

Scourge: Fearsome, savage army of the Ravi-shan; vanquished by the people of the Citadel. It was made up of fierce warriors, gleaned from Plague survivors, and was a very dark and dreadful enemy.

Shandor (SHAN-dor): Arguably the most powerful of the Asari, he loved Liathwyn, an Elf of the Èolar, and together they founded Monadh-talam. He actually challenged Wrothgar in battle and defeated him during the Second Uprising. He is the sire of Lady Ordath. When Liathwyn relinquished her spirit and went to Elysia, Shandor withdrew from the world, eventually seeking refuge in the great stone crystal of Léir, which is presently in the keeping of Lady Arialde, the Asarla of Tal-sithian. He allows visions to be seen through the crystal, but those who seek his vision outside the grace of Arialde risk madness, for Shandor may send a vision so terrifying that they cannot ever be free of it. His name essentially means "great spirit."

Siva (SEE-va): Silver-white horse ridden by Gaelen, her name simply means "grey."

Srath Miadan (Srath mee-ah-DAHN): Meadow to the east of the Ambros and west of the Linnefionn; from srath (riverbank) and miadan (meadow).

Sylvan elves: Wood-elves, or Cúinar.

Syrus the Mariner: Tuathan mariner, said to be the greatest who ever lived. Rogond's mother, Rosalin, was his descendent. He is revered especially by the Corsairs.

Tal-ailean (Tal-EYE-lee-ahn): Elven-realm located in the Monadh-ailan. It is inhabited by various small, secretive groups of Cúinar known as the Elàni-ailan (green-elves). From tal- (realm) and ailan (green).

Taldin (TAl-deen): Name given affectionately to Gaelen by Ri-Elathan, it means "walks unnoticed, stealthy."

Tal-elathas (tal-EL-a-thas): Ancient realm of the Èolar, it was the greatest center of invention and discovery that has ever been. At one time there were no less than three Asari who resided there; they were Leiras, Baelta, and, regrettably, Kotos. It was destroyed by Wrothgar's army when Kotos betrayed the Elves, aided unwittingly by Baelta. From tal- (realm) and elathas (wisdom).

Tal-fásath: The Elves" rather unflattering name for the Ravani desert, it means "realm of barren waste" or "land of terrible loneliness." From fás (lonely, barren) and tal- (realm).

Talishani Ali (TAL-ih-SHAH-nee Ah-LEE): Battle-seasoned Minister of Defense in Dûn Arian, he commands the City forces. He is a worthy and likeable man. Hallagond, in particular, admires him. He is usually called simply "Ali."

Tallanor (TAL-ah-NOR): Great Eastern City of the lost realm of Tuathas.

Tallasiar (TAL-ah-SHAR): Western Capital City of the lost realm of Tuathas, it was reputedly very beautiful. Dûn Arian is said to resemble it in design.

Talrodin (TAL-roh-deen): Hunter-scout of Greatwood, friend of Nelwyn and brother of Halrodin. He was slain by Gorgon. His name means "strength of the realm," from tal- (realm) and rodos (as the trunk of a tree).

Tal-sithian (SITH-ee-ahn): Green forested island in the Linnefionn; the Elven-realm of Lord Airan and Lady Arialde. From sithion (deer), it means "realm of deer roaming."

Tansy (TAN-zee): Corsair, flamboyant former ruler of Fómor, displaced by her former consort, Ludor. She is known as "Queen Tansy."

Tarmagil (TAR-mah-geel): Fraternal twin brother of Tarfion and favorite uncle of Gaelen and Nelwen. Known for being free-spirited and of good humor, he was slain in the Third Uprising. Name means "strong ally', from tar- (of the realm) and magra- (mighty).

Thaylon (THAY-lon): Given name of Rogond, it means "trustworthy." From thala (to trust).

Thorndil (THORN-deel): Northman, ranger and friend of Rogond, companion of Belegund. His name means "Piercing gaze, eagle-eyed." From thorn- (to pierce).

Tibo: (TEE-bo): Dwarf of Grundin's Realm who was known for his love of Elves, Tibo wore a green jacket. He was slain by Gorgon.

Toran (Toh-RAHN): Tall, strong, grey horse, given to Gaelen. His name means "gentle thunder."

Trachair (TRACH-eye-eer): "The treacherous." Asarla also known as Kotos, Trachair is the name given him by the Elves.

Tuathas (TOO-ah-thas): Greatest of all realms of men, Tuathas alone possessed an Asarla. Because of this they were more enlightened than other men, and were nearly as fair as the Elves. It was destroyed during an eruption of one of the great Fire-mountains that bounded it, and very little of the realm survived. From Tuath (north).

Tuathar (TOO-ah-thar) sing. Tuathan: men of the northern realm of Tuathas, lost in the rising of the Fire-mountains. Because of the influence of their Asarla, they are tall and comely, hardy and strong. They are more enlightened than other races of men.

Turantil (TOOR-an-TEEL): Sword of Halrodin, prized heirloom stolen by Gorgon. Name means "scourge of the north." From tuath- (north) and ranta (scourge).

Tûr Dorcha (Toor DOR-ka): Wrothgar's stronghold in the Darkmere, it is a pale stone fortress shrouded in a sickly grey mist, surrounded by a fetid bog.

Ulcas (UL-cas), sing. Ulca: Evil servants of Wrothgar. They are undoubtedly perversions of other races, as Wrothgar is incapable of true creation. They are varied, and some are quite formidable in battle, but most can prevail only through sheer numbers. All are ugly. They dislike sunlight, are hairless, and live in dark places.

Úlfar (OOL-fas): "Fen-serpents," vile, slimy eels with rasping, suckerlike mouths. Arguably the most unpleasant creatures in Alterra, they ensnare wading travelers or animals by miring them in slime and entangling them. Once the prey is brought down into the water, they attach to any hairless area and give an envenomed bite. The venom subdues the victim, whereupon the creatures enter through body orifices and consume it from the inside out. They are normally found in bogs but can travel up fresh waterways for a considerable distance. They cannot live in salt water. Their bite is so septic that a man bitten by an Úlfa is doomed to a very bad death. They are undoubtedly a perversion of normal eels, designed by Wrothgar.

Varni (VAR-nee): Son of Ivar, Lord of Rûmm. Varni was a sensitive and talented artist, and he loved the Elves of Eádros.

Visili, Haleck (Vih-SEE-lee): Criminal, imprisoned in Dûn Arian, freed by Hallagond, and later redeemed. Visili appears to be of northern descent.

Wellyn: (WEL-lin): Son and heir of Ri-Aruin of the Greatwood and very dear friend of Gaelen. His name means "courageous, one who is brave."

Wrothgar (ROTH-gar): Evil Being of Alterra. The Lord of Darkness, also known as the Shadowmancer and the Black Flame. Name means "Dark Fury." From wroth (fury, wrath) and gor (dark).

About C.S. Marks

C.S. Marks has often been described as a Renaissance woman. The daughter of academic parents, she holds a Ph.D. in Biology and has spent the past two decades teaching Biology and Equine Science. She is currently a Full Professor at Saint Mary-of-the-Woods College in west central Indiana.

She began writing shortly after the untimely death of her father, who was a Professor of American Literature at Butler University. A gifted artist, she has produced illustrations and cover art for all three books. She plays and sings Celtic music and a few examples of her songwriting may be found within the pages of Fire-heart. She enjoys archery, and makes hand-crafted longbows using primitive tools.

Horses are her passion, and she is an accomplished horsewoman, having competed in the sport of endurance racing for many years. One of only a handful of Americans to complete the prestigious Tom Quilty Australian national championship hundred-mile ride, she has described this moment as her finest hour.

Website: CSMarks.com

Facebook: Facebook.com/Alterra

CSMarksTwitter: Twitter.com/CSMarks_Alterra

Goodreads: https://www.goodreads.com/author/show/521676.C_S_Marks

C.S. Marks Mailing List Sign Up: http://eepurl.com/st8Vj

Books by C.S. Marks

Tales of Alterra (The Elfhunter Trilogy)

Elfhunter

Fire-heart

Ravenshade

Alterra Histories

The Fire King

Fallen Embers

The Shadow-man

Undiscovered Realms

Outcaste

We hope you've enjoyed reading the Elfhunter trilogy. Please consider leaving a review on Goodreads and your point of purchase.

Where to Find C.S. Marks

The Author's Website: CSMarks.com
Facebook.com/Alterra.CSMarks
Twitter.com/CSMarks_Alterra

Stay up to date with what's happening with C.S. Marks by joining the mailing list. You will receive exclusive teasers and be the first to know when a new book has been released.

Sign Up For the C.S. Marks Mailing List at

CSMarks.com

31851776R00350

Made in the USA
Charleston, SC
30 July 2014